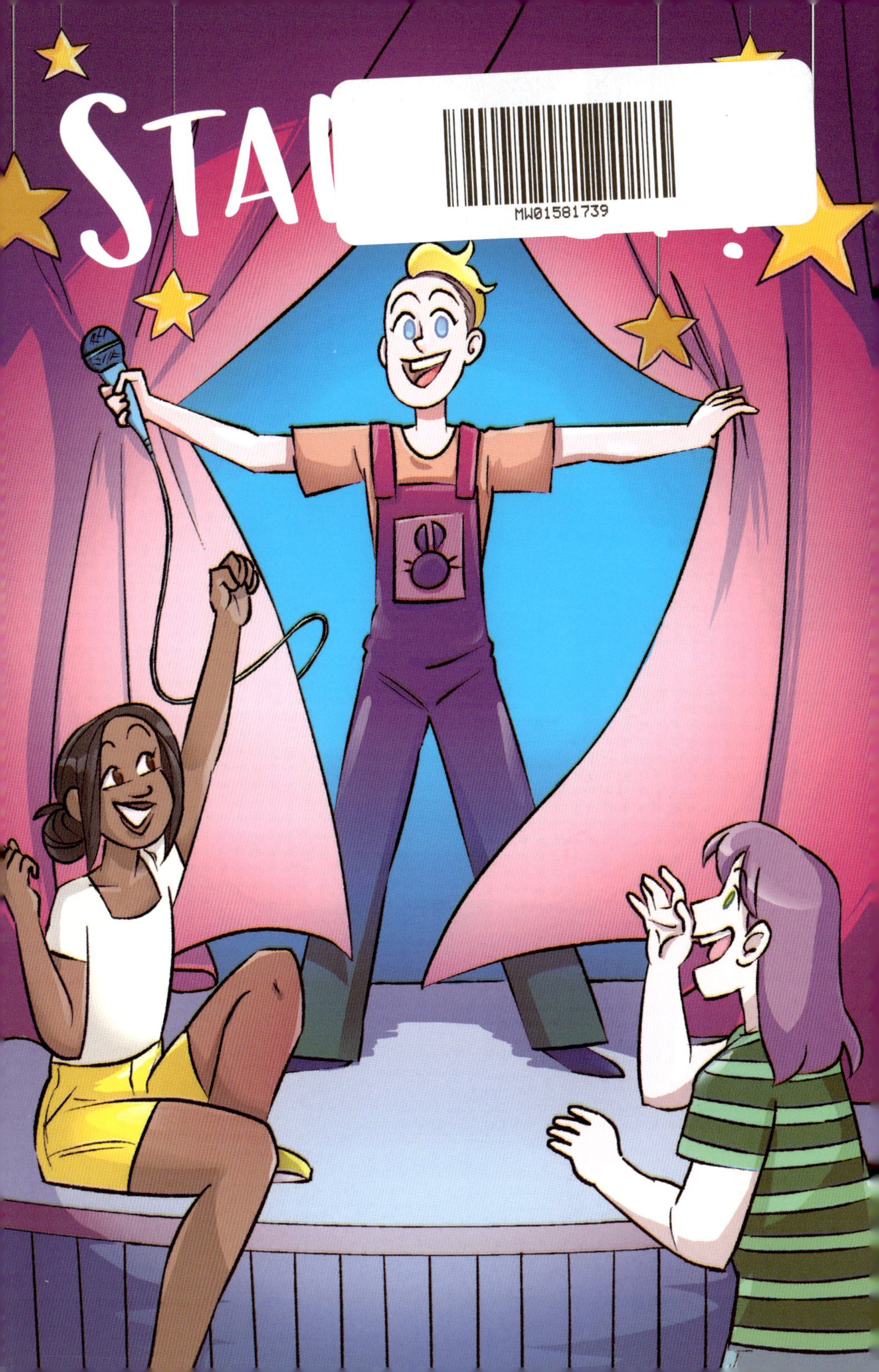

Also by Tori Sharp

JUST PRETEND

TORI SHARP

Colors by Andrea Bell

Little, Brown and Company
New York   Boston

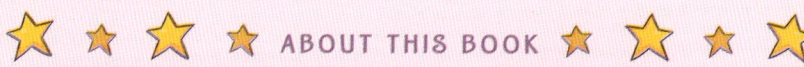

ABOUT THIS BOOK

The illustrations for this book were done in Procreate on an iPad Pro, with ink corrections in Clip Studio Paint Pro. This book was edited by Andrea Colvin and designed by Ann Dwyer. The production was supervised by Bernadette Flinn, and the production editor was Jake Regier. The text was set in Anime Ace 2.0 BB, and the display type is Chin Up Buttercup Cutecaps.

This book is a work of fiction. Names, characters, places, and incidents are the product of the author's imagination or are used fictitiously. Any resemblance to actual events, locales, or persons, living or dead, is coincidental. Copyright © 2024 by Tori Sharp ★ Colors by Andrea Bell ★ Lettering by AndWorld Design ★ Cover illustration copyright © 2024 by Tori Sharp. Cover design by Ann Dwyer. Cover copyright © 2024 by Hachette Book Group, Inc. ★ Hachette Book Group supports the right to free expression and the value of copyright. The purpose of copyright is to encourage writers and artists to produce the creative works that enrich our culture. ★ The scanning, uploading, and distribution of this book without permission is a theft of the author's intellectual property. If you would like permission to use material from the book (other than for review purposes), please contact permissions@hbgusa.com. Thank you for your support of the author's rights. ★ Little, Brown Ink Hachette Book Group ★ 1290 Avenue of the Americas, New York, NY 10104 ★ Visit us at LBYR.com First Edition: October 2024 ★ Little, Brown Ink is an imprint of Little, Brown and Company. The Little, Brown Ink name and logo are trademarks of Hachette Book Group, Inc. ★ The publisher is not responsible for websites (or their content) that are not owned by the publisher. ★ Little, Brown and Company books may be purchased in bulk for business, educational, or promotional use. For information, please contact your local bookseller or the Hachette Book Group Special Markets Department at special.markets@hbgusa.com. ★ Library of Congress Cataloging-in-Publication Data ★ Names: Sharp, Tori, author, illustrator. | Sharp, Tori, illustrator. ★ Title: Stand up! / Tori Sharp. ★ Description: First edition. | New York : Little, Brown and Company, 2024. | Audience: Ages 8–12. | Summary: "A middle-grade graphic novel about two best friends who want to be comedians and start a podcast." —Provided by publisher. ★ Identifiers: LCCN 2022056378 | ISBN 9780316538916 (hardcover) | ISBN 9780316538930 (trade paperback) | ISBN 9780316538923 (ebook) | ISBN 9780316385961 (nook edition) | ISBN 9780316386067 (kindle edition) ★ Subjects: CYAC: Graphic novels. | Best friends—Fiction. | Friendship—Fiction. | Podcasts—Fiction. | LCGFT: Graphic novels. ★ Classification: LCC PZ7.7.S4539 St 2024 | DDC 741.5/973—dc23/eng/20230406 LC record available at https://lccn.loc.gov/2022056378 ★ ISBNs: 978-0-316-53891-6 (hardcover), 978-0-316-53893-0 (pbk.), 978-0-316-53892-3 (ebook), 978-0-316-38596-1 (ebook), 978-0-316-38606-7 (ebook) PRINTED IN GUANGDONG, CHINA ★ 1010 ★ Hardcover: 10 9 8 7 6 5 4 3 2 1 ★ Paperback: 10 9 8 7 6 5 4 3 2 1

For my dad, who has the best laugh and makes the silliest faces. I love you!

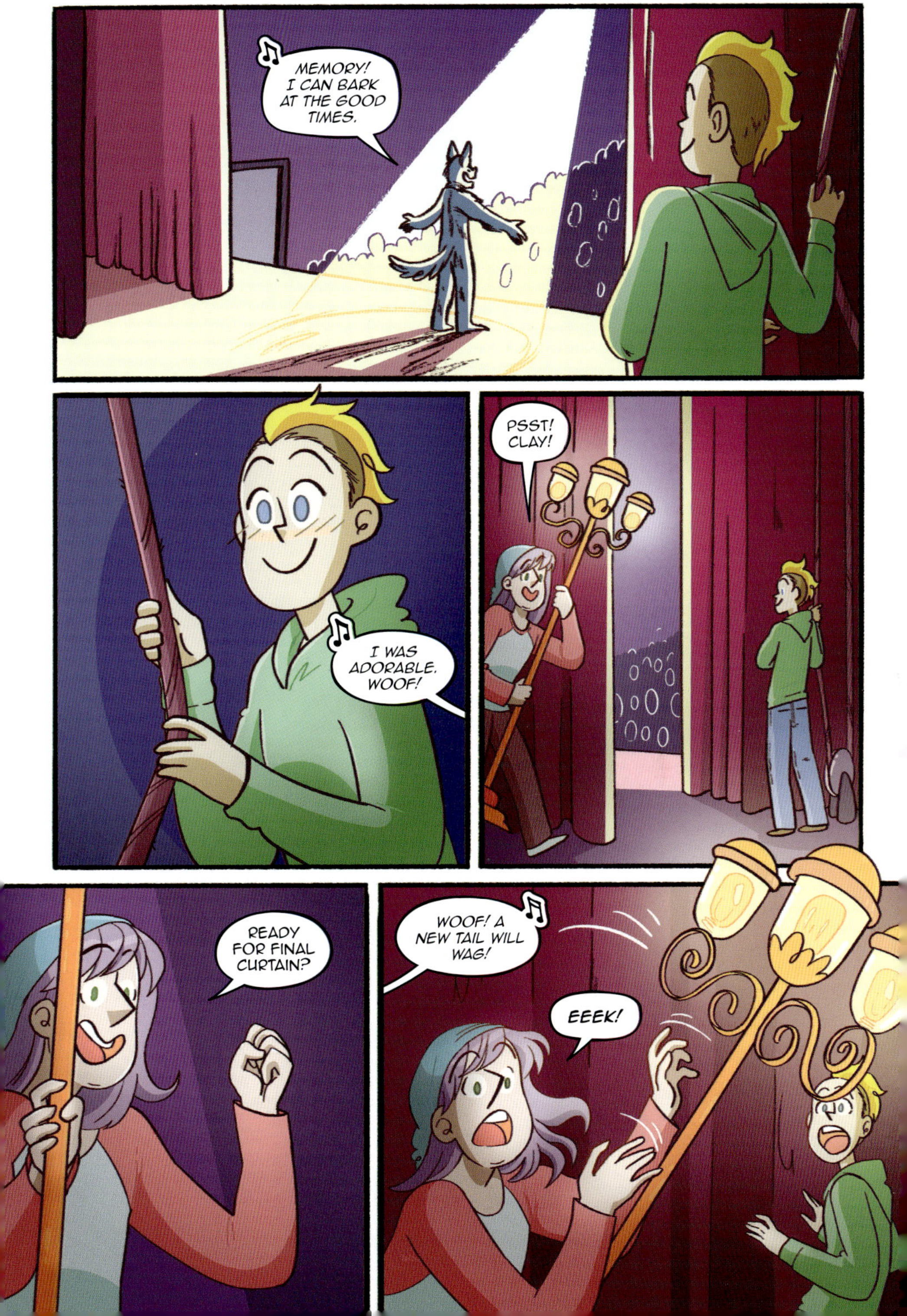
MEMORY! I CAN BARK AT THE GOOD TIMES.
I WAS ADORABLE. WOOF!
PSST! CLAY!
READY FOR FINAL CURTAIN?
WOOF! A NEW TAIL WILL WAG!
EEEK!

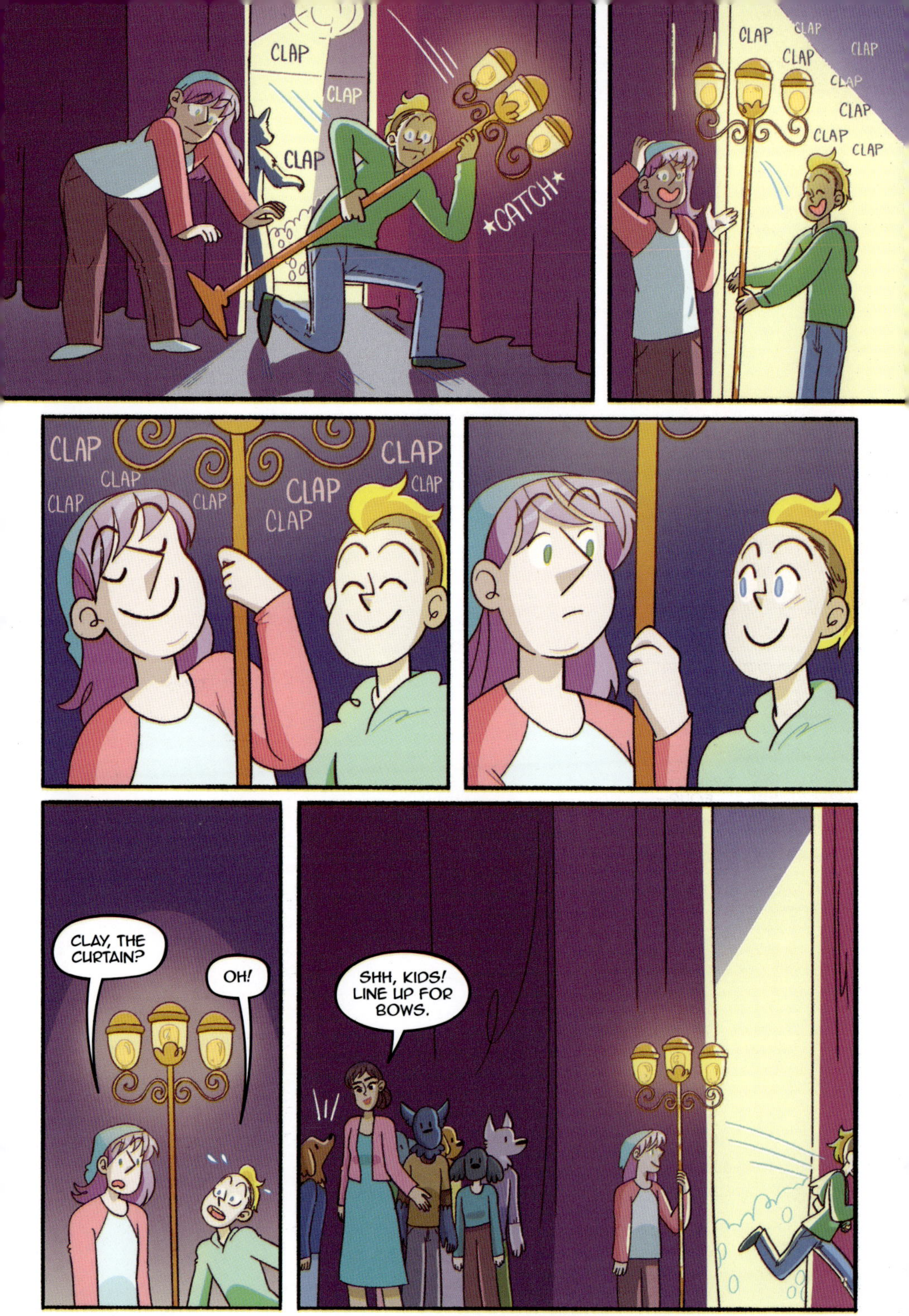
CLAP
CLAP
CLAP
★CATCH★
CLAP
CLAP
CLAP
CLAP
CLAP
CLAP
CLAP
CLAP
CLAP
CLAP
CLAP
CLAP
CLAP
CLAP
CLAY, THE CURTAIN?
OH!
SHH, KIDS! LINE UP FOR BOWS.

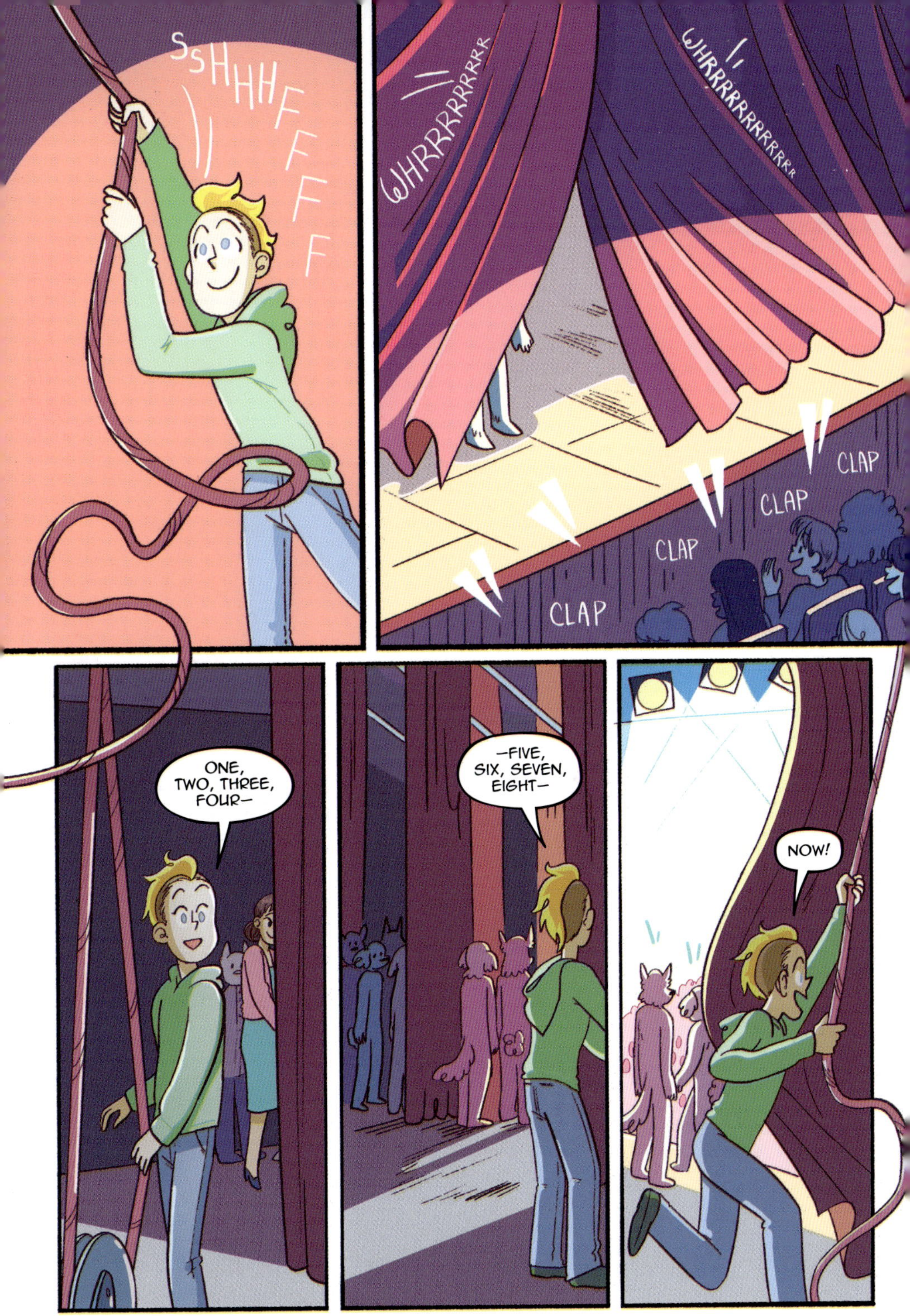
SSHHHFFFFF
WHRRRRRRRRR
WHRRRRRRRRRRRRR
CLAP
CLAP
CLAP
CLAP
ONE, TWO, THREE, FOUR—
—FIVE, SIX, SEVEN, EIGHT—
NOW!

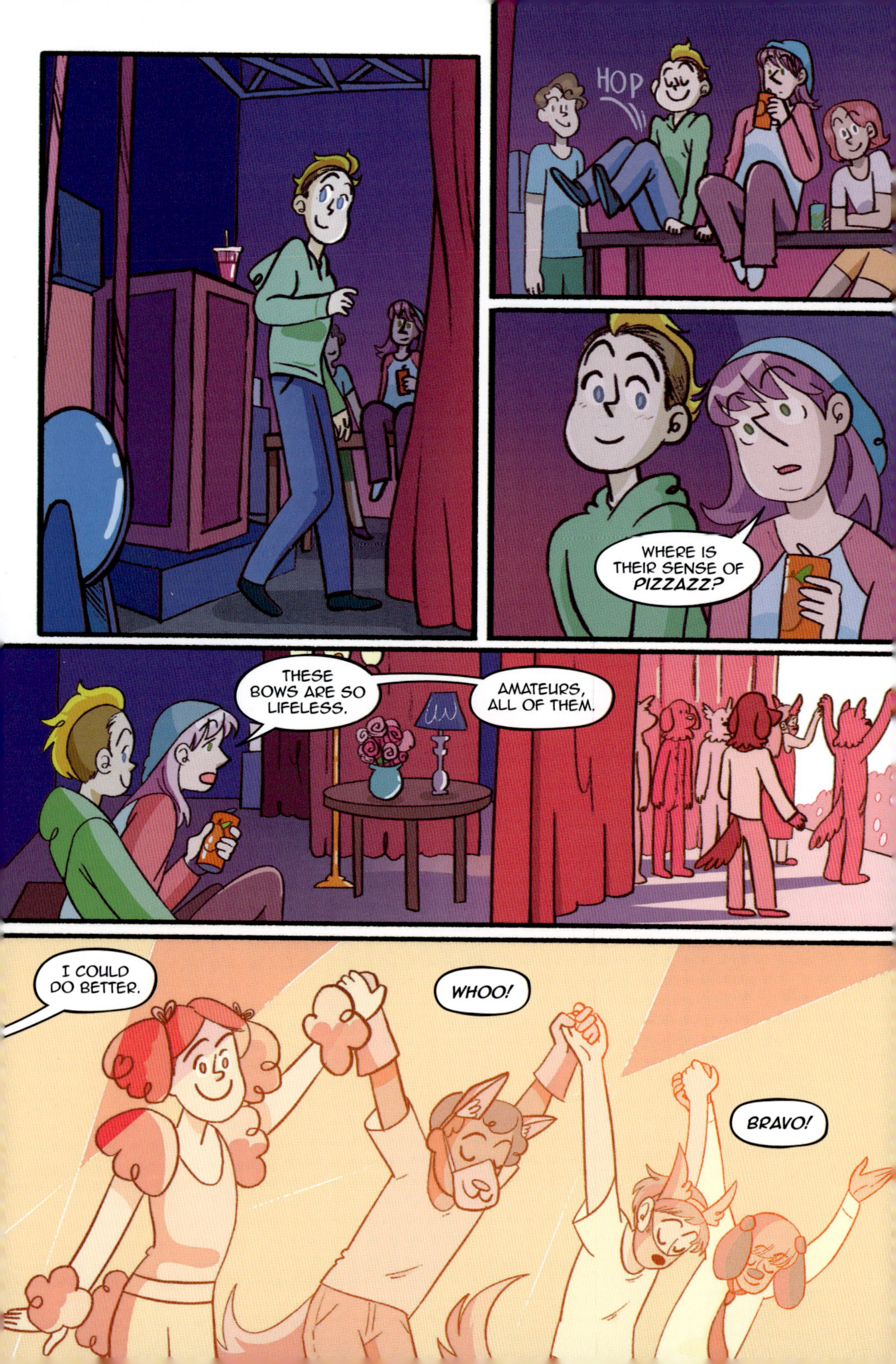
HOP
WHERE IS THEIR SENSE OF *PIZZAZZ?*
THESE BOWS ARE SO LIFELESS.
AMATEURS, ALL OF THEM.
I COULD DO BETTER.
WHOO!
BRAVO!

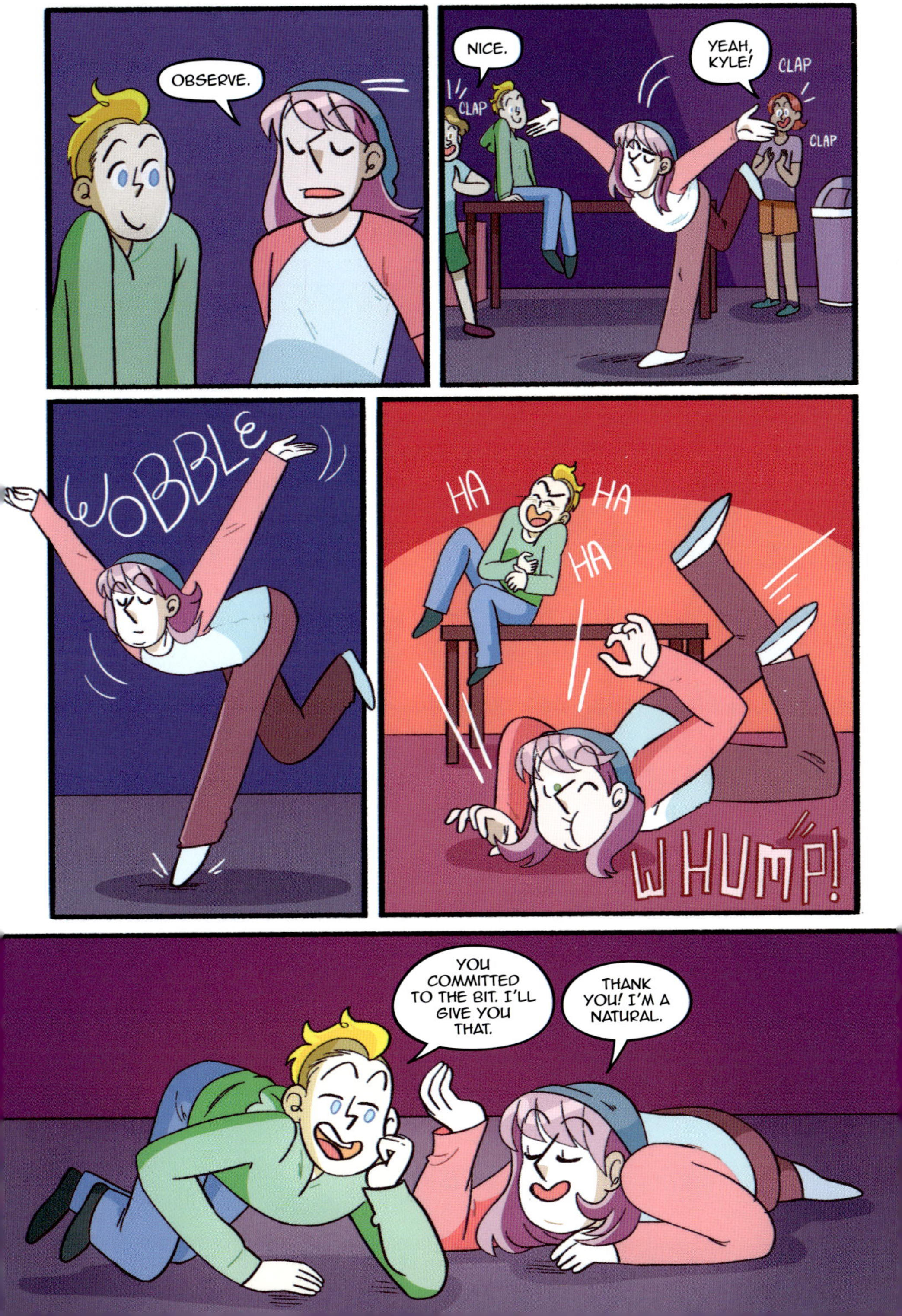
OBSERVE.
NICE.
CLAP
YEAH, KYLE!
CLAP
CLAP
WOBBLE
HA
HA
HA
WHUMP!
YOU COMMITTED TO THE BIT. I'LL GIVE YOU THAT.
THANK YOU! I'M A NATURAL.

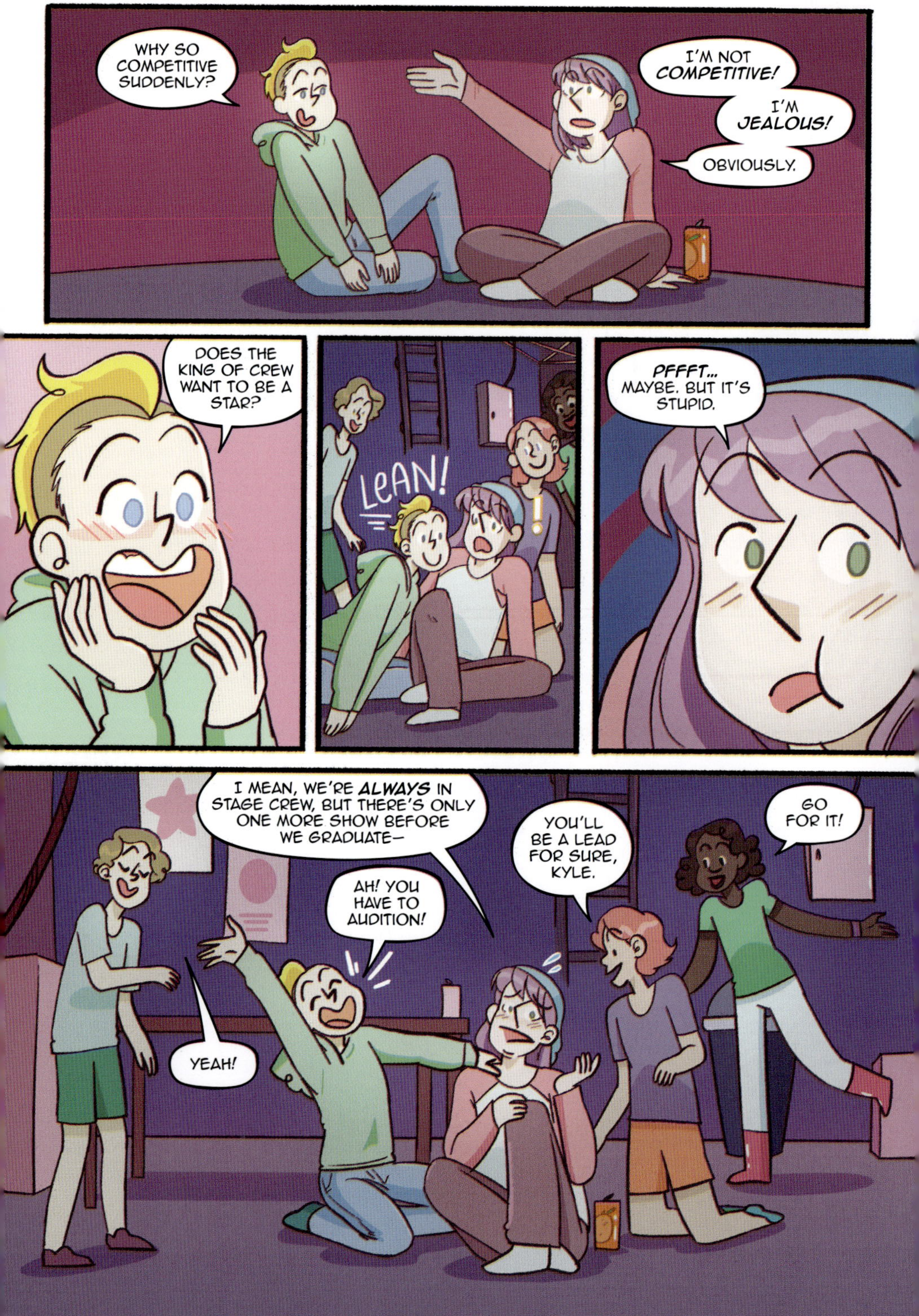
WHY SO COMPETITIVE SUDDENLY?
I'M NOT *COMPETITIVE!*
I'M *JEALOUS!*
OBVIOUSLY.
DOES THE KING OF CREW WANT TO BE A STAR?
LEAN!
!
PFFFT... MAYBE. BUT IT'S STUPID.
I MEAN, WE'RE *ALWAYS* IN STAGE CREW, BUT THERE'S ONLY ONE MORE SHOW BEFORE WE GRADUATE—
AH! YOU HAVE TO AUDITION!
YEAH!
YOU'LL BE A LEAD FOR SURE, KYLE.
GO FOR IT!

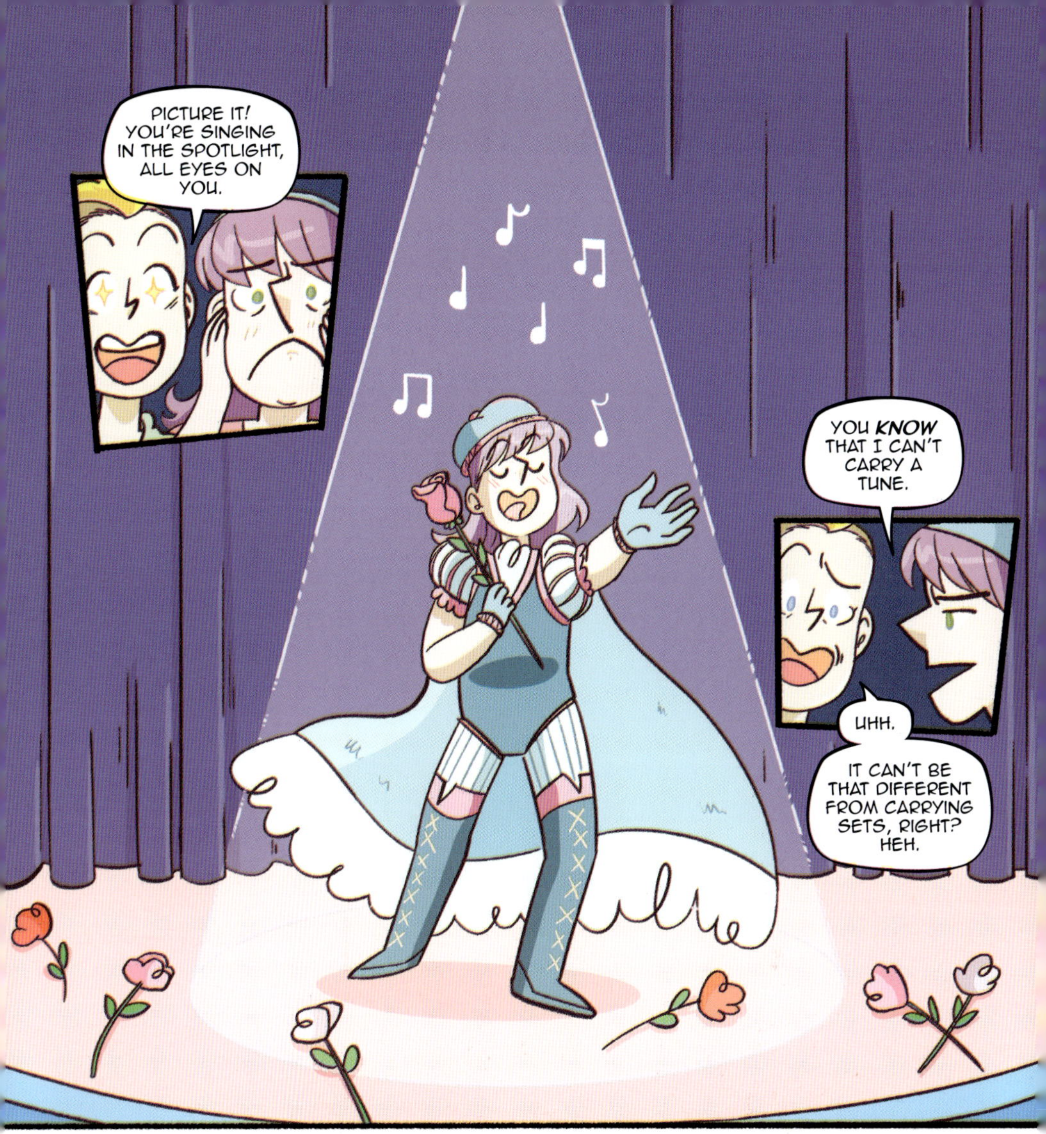
PICTURE IT! YOU'RE SINGING IN THE SPOTLIGHT, ALL EYES ON YOU.
YOU **KNOW** THAT I CAN'T CARRY A TUNE.
UHH.
IT CAN'T BE THAT DIFFERENT FROM CARRYING SETS, RIGHT? HEH.

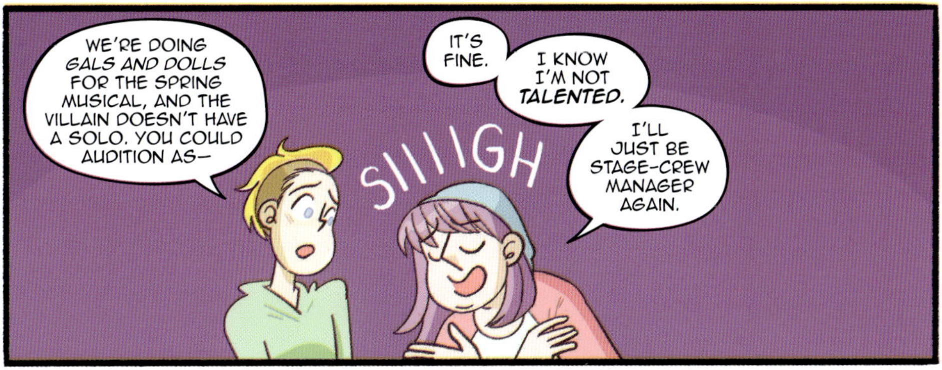
WE'RE DOING *GALS AND DOLLS* FOR THE SPRING MUSICAL, AND THE VILLAIN DOESN'T HAVE A SOLO. YOU COULD AUDITION AS—
SIIIIGH
IT'S FINE.
I KNOW I'M NOT ***TALENTED.***
I'LL JUST BE STAGE-CREW MANAGER AGAIN.

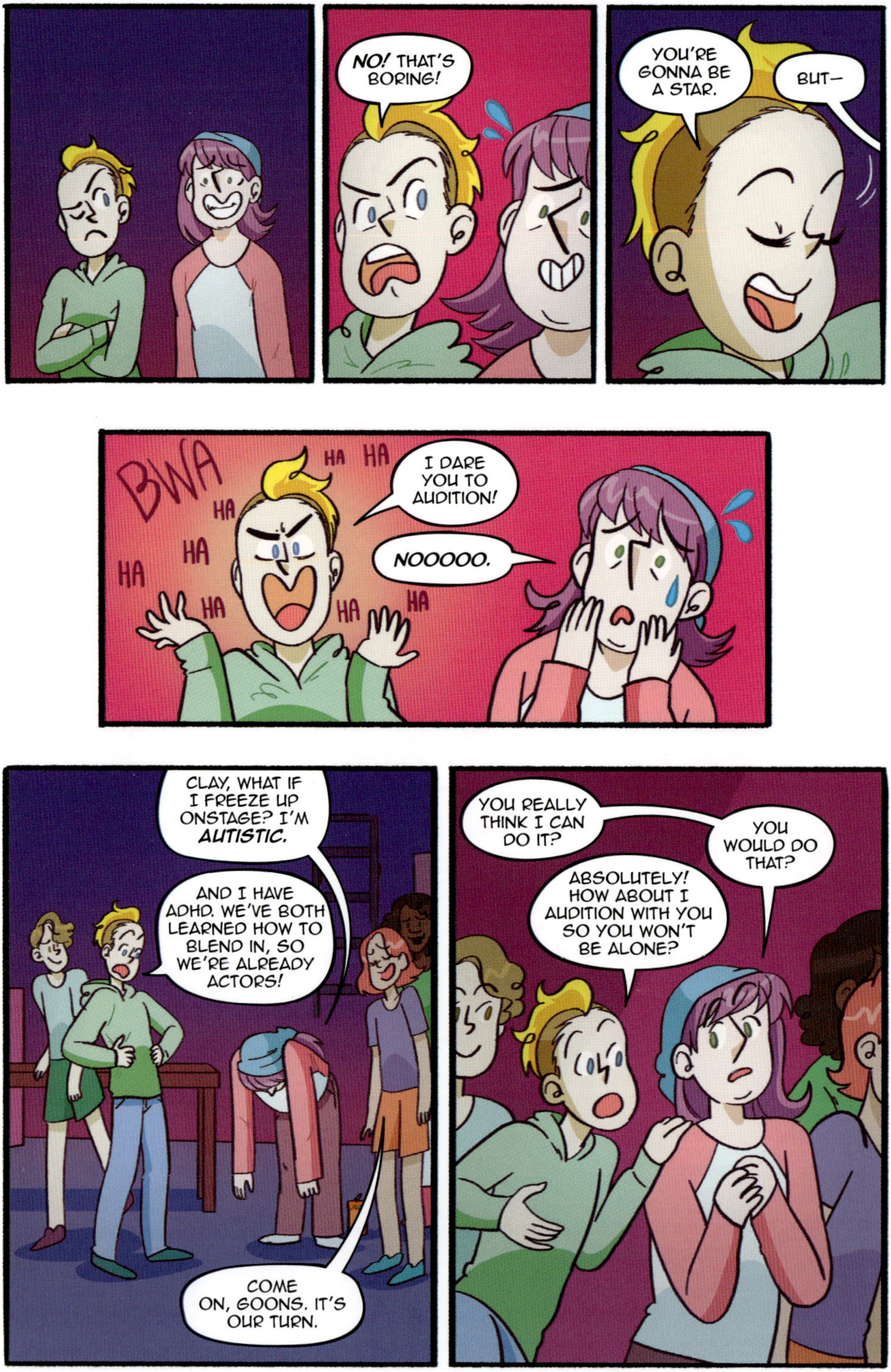
NO! THAT'S BORING!
YOU'RE GONNA BE A STAR.
BUT—
BWA HA HA HA HA HA HA HA HA HA
I DARE YOU TO AUDITION!
NOOOOO.
CLAY, WHAT IF I FREEZE UP ONSTAGE? I'M AUTISTIC.
AND I HAVE ADHD. WE'VE BOTH LEARNED HOW TO BLEND IN, SO WE'RE ALREADY ACTORS!
COME ON, GOONS. IT'S OUR TURN.
YOU REALLY THINK I CAN DO IT?
ABSOLUTELY! HOW ABOUT I AUDITION WITH YOU SO YOU WON'T BE ALONE?
YOU WOULD DO THAT?

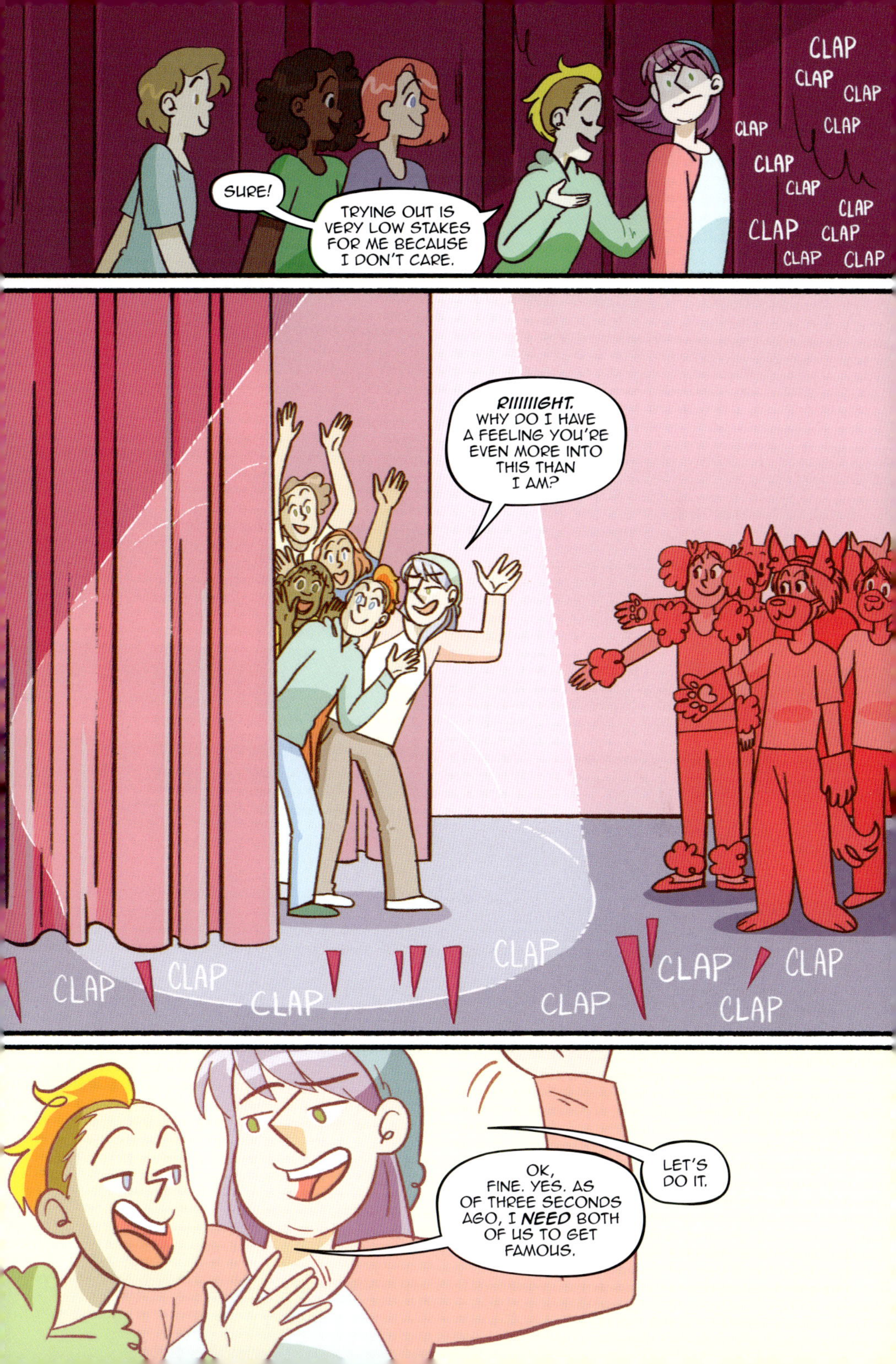
CLAP CLAP CLAP CLAP CLAP CLAP CLAP CLAP CLAP CLAP CLAP CLAP
SURE!
TRYING OUT IS VERY LOW STAKES FOR ME BECAUSE I DON'T CARE.
RIIIIIIGHT. WHY DO I HAVE A FEELING YOU'RE EVEN MORE INTO THIS THAN I AM?
CLAP CLAP CLAP CLAP CLAP CLAP CLAP CLAP
OK, FINE. YES. AS OF THREE SECONDS AGO, I NEED BOTH OF US TO GET FAMOUS.
LET'S DO IT.

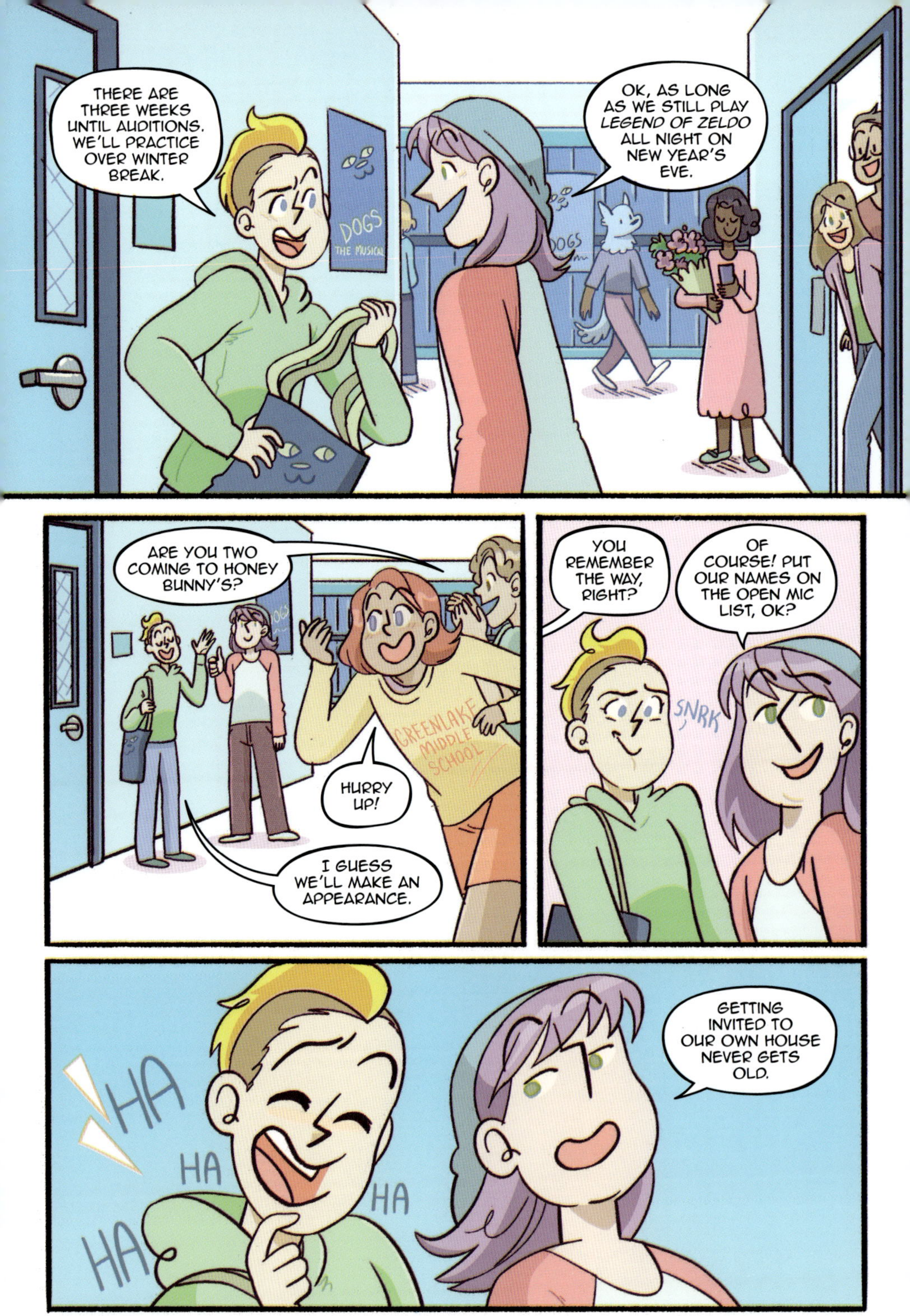
THERE ARE THREE WEEKS UNTIL AUDITIONS. WE'LL PRACTICE OVER WINTER BREAK.
DOGS THE MUSICAL
OK, AS LONG AS WE STILL PLAY *LEGEND OF ZELDO* ALL NIGHT ON NEW YEAR'S EVE.
ARE YOU TWO COMING TO HONEY BUNNY'S?
HURRY UP!
I GUESS WE'LL MAKE AN APPEARANCE.
GREENLAKE MIDDLE SCHOOL
YOU REMEMBER THE WAY, RIGHT?
OF COURSE! PUT OUR NAMES ON THE OPEN MIC LIST, OK?
SNRK
HA HA HA HA
GETTING INVITED TO OUR OWN HOUSE NEVER GETS OLD.

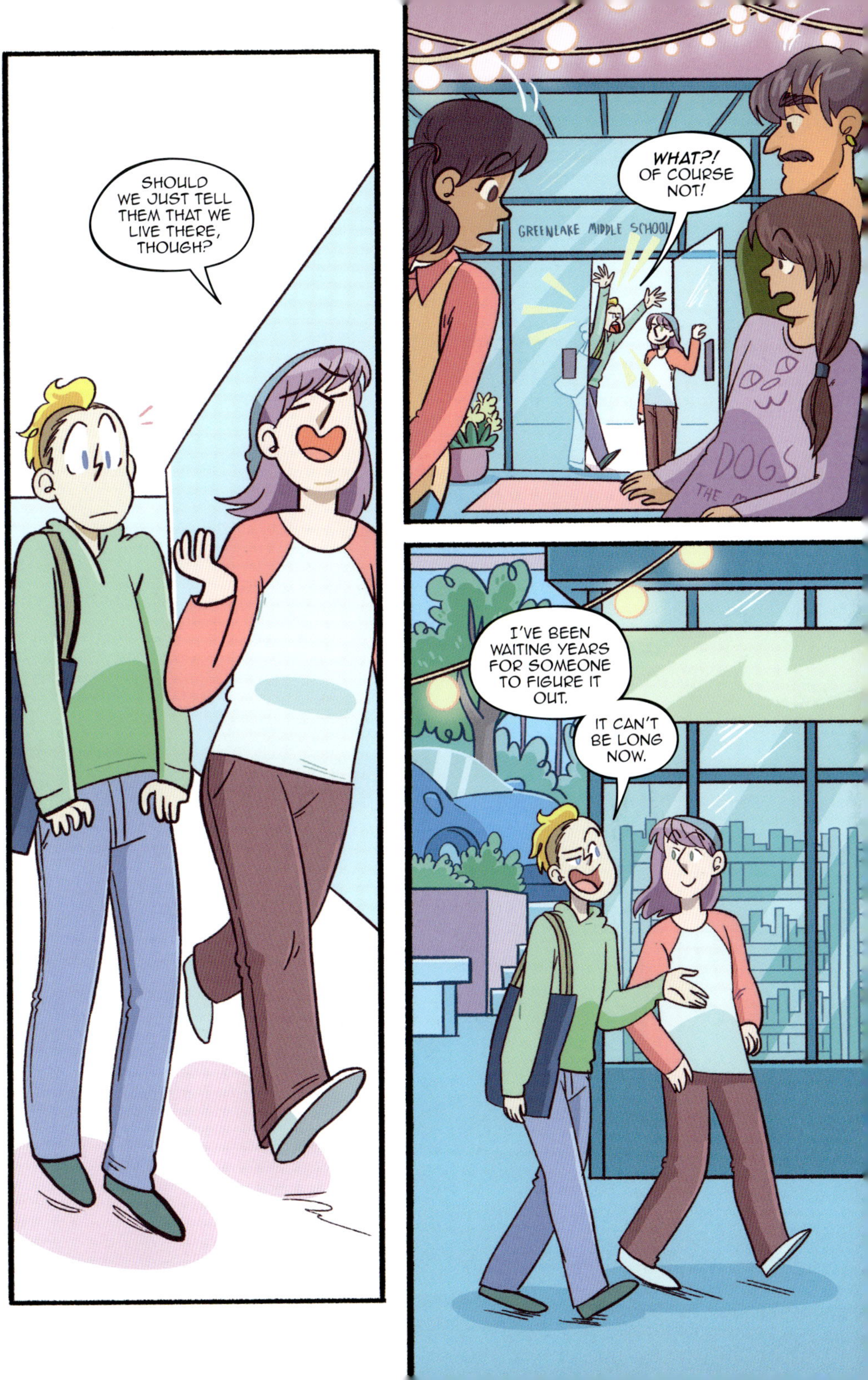
SHOULD WE JUST TELL THEM THAT WE LIVE THERE, THOUGH?
GREENLAKE MIDDLE SCHOOL
WHAT?! OF COURSE NOT!
DOGS
I'VE BEEN WAITING YEARS FOR SOMEONE TO FIGURE IT OUT.
IT CAN'T BE LONG NOW.

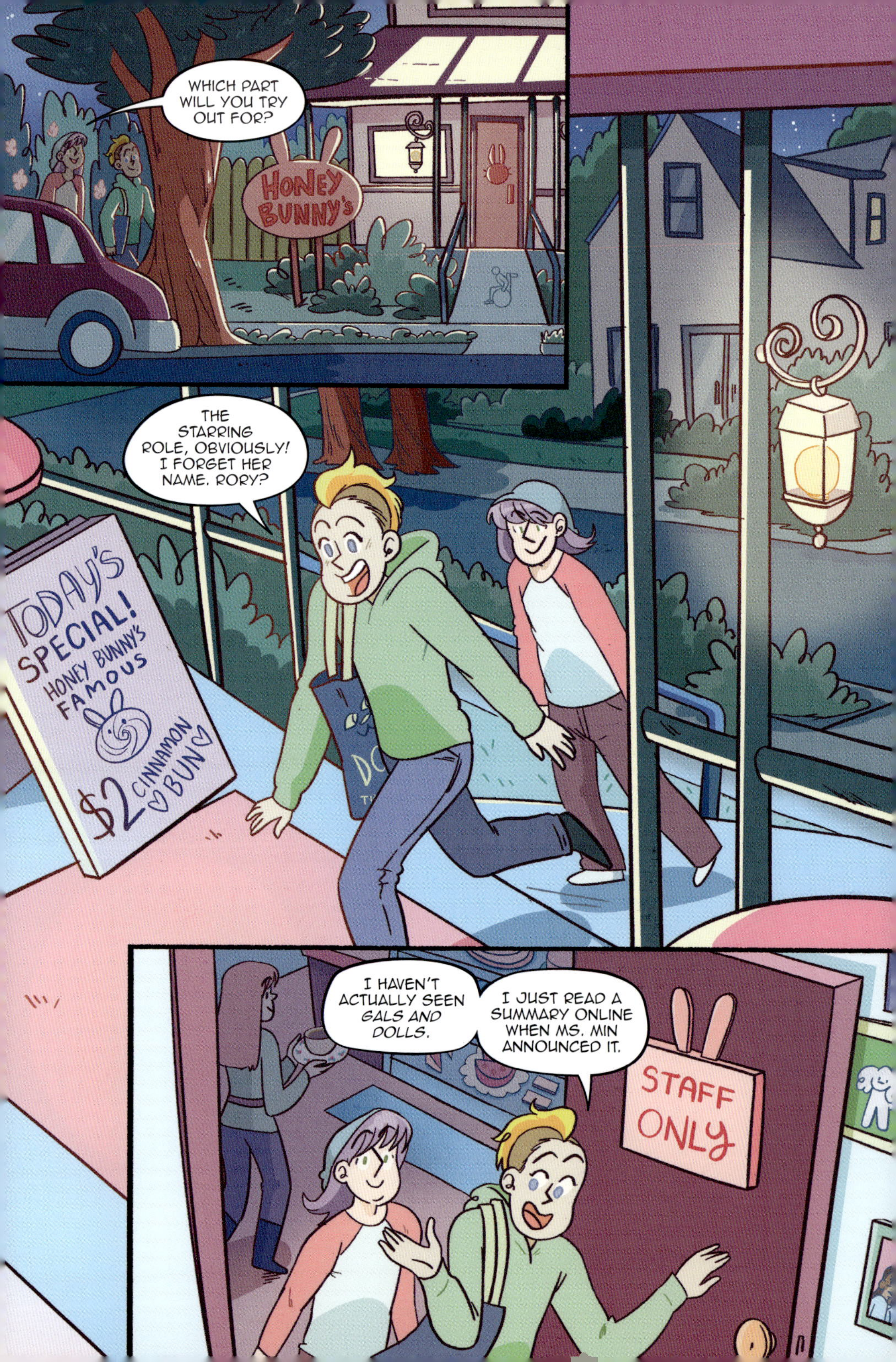
WHICH PART WILL YOU TRY OUT FOR?
HONEY BUNNY'S
THE STARRING ROLE, OBVIOUSLY! I FORGET HER NAME. RORY?
TODAY'S SPECIAL! HONEY BUNNY'S FAMOUS CINNAMON BUN $2
I HAVEN'T ACTUALLY SEEN GALS AND DOLLS.
I JUST READ A SUMMARY ONLINE WHEN MS. MIN ANNOUNCED IT.
STAFF ONLY

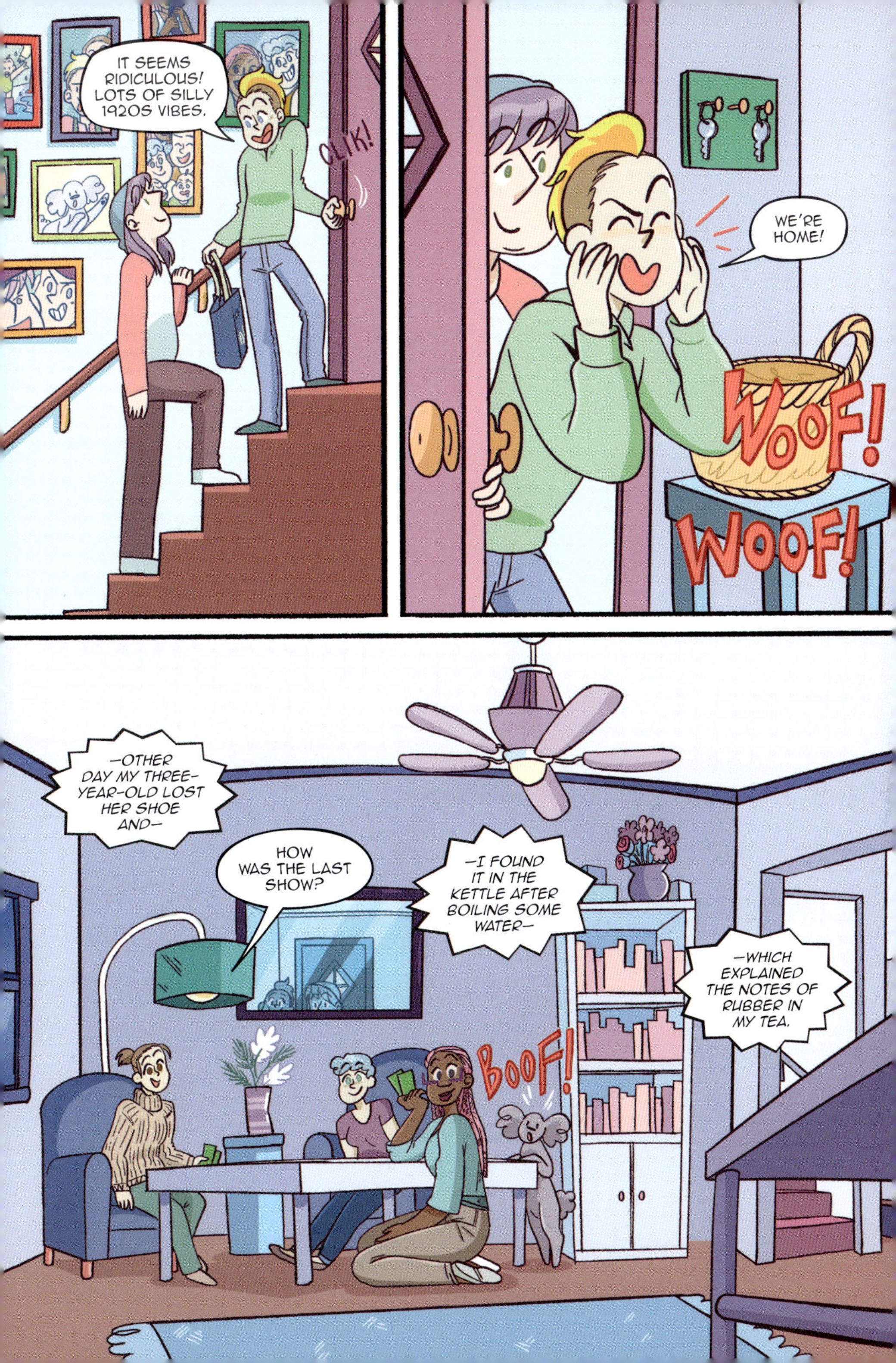

IT SEEMS RIDICULOUS! LOTS OF SILLY 1920S VIBES.
CLIK!
WE'RE HOME!
WOOF!
WOOF!
—OTHER DAY MY THREE-YEAR-OLD LOST HER SHOE AND—
HOW WAS THE LAST SHOW?
—I FOUND IT IN THE KETTLE AFTER BOILING SOME WATER—
—WHICH EXPLAINED THE NOTES OF RUBBER IN MY TEA.
BOOF!

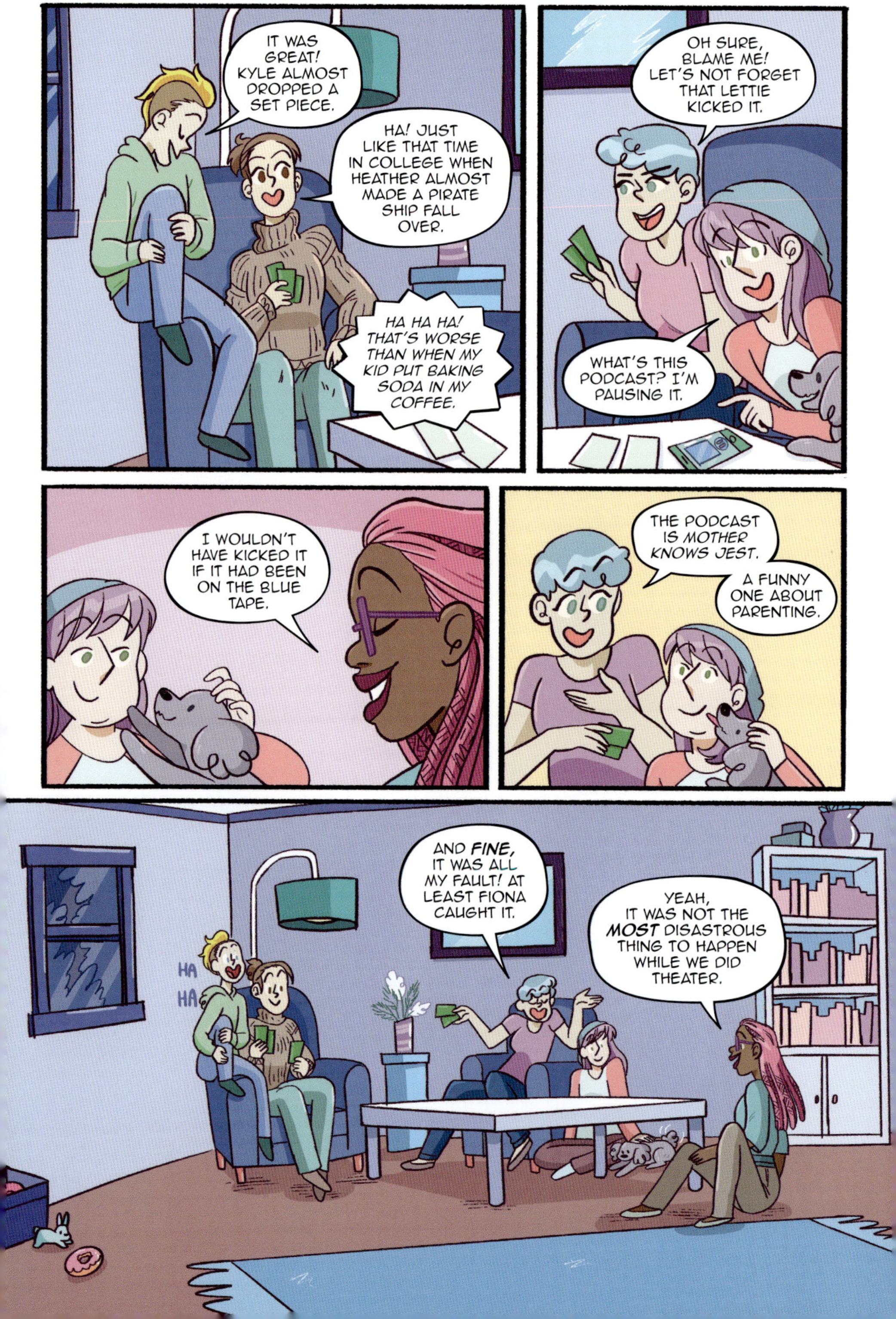
IT WAS GREAT! KYLE ALMOST DROPPED A SET PIECE.
HA! JUST LIKE THAT TIME IN COLLEGE WHEN HEATHER ALMOST MADE A PIRATE SHIP FALL OVER.
HA HA HA! THAT'S WORSE THAN WHEN MY KID PUT BAKING SODA IN MY COFFEE.
OH SURE, BLAME ME! LET'S NOT FORGET THAT LETTIE KICKED IT.
WHAT'S THIS PODCAST? I'M PAUSING IT.
I WOULDN'T HAVE KICKED IT IF IT HAD BEEN ON THE BLUE TAPE.
THE PODCAST IS MOTHER KNOWS JEST.
A FUNNY ONE ABOUT PARENTING.
HA HA
AND FINE, IT WAS ALL MY FAULT! AT LEAST FIONA CAUGHT IT.
YEAH, IT WAS NOT THE MOST DISASTROUS THING TO HAPPEN WHILE WE DID THEATER.

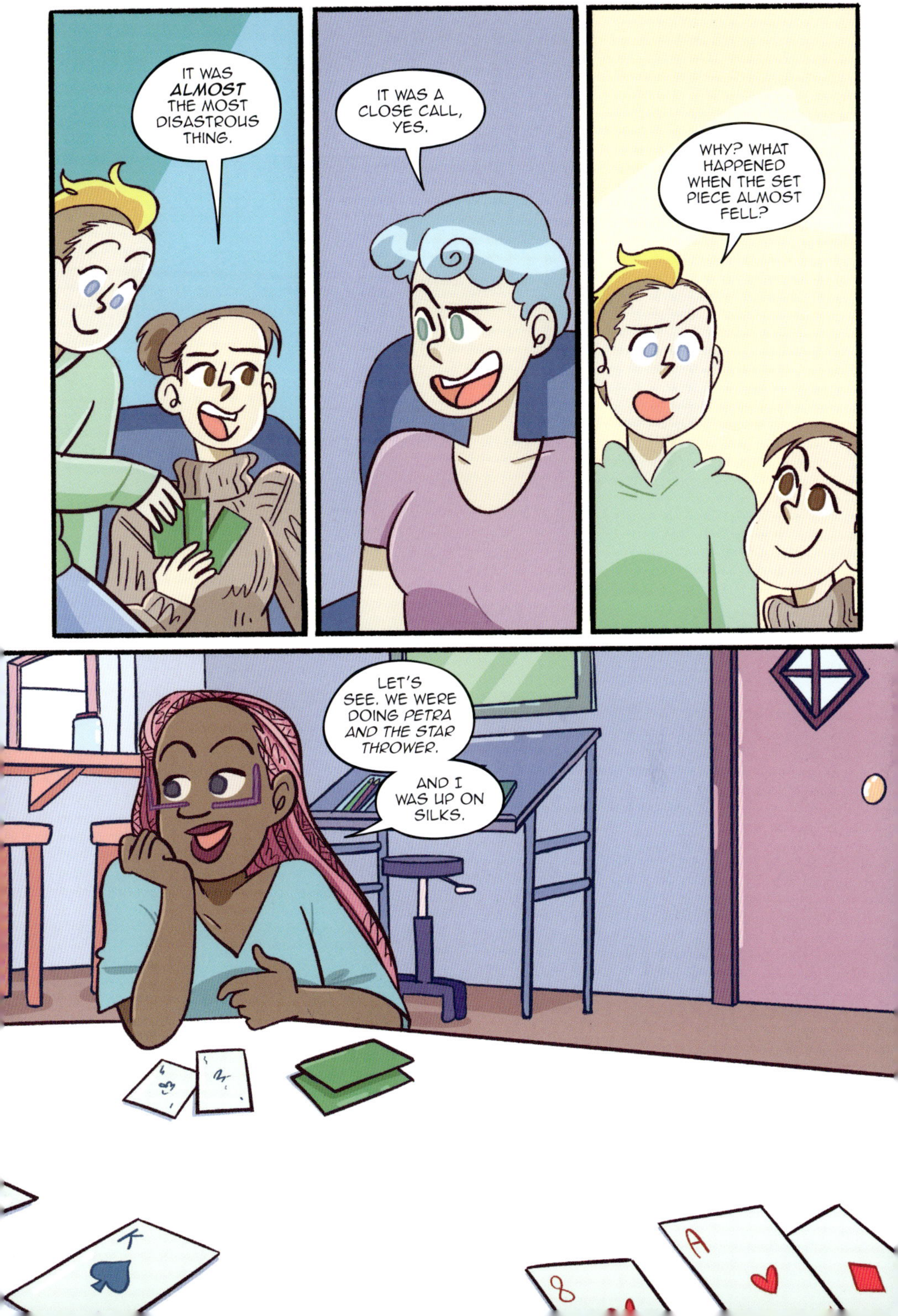
IT WAS ALMOST THE MOST DISASTROUS THING.
IT WAS A CLOSE CALL, YES.
WHY? WHAT HAPPENED WHEN THE SET PIECE ALMOST FELL?
LET'S SEE. WE WERE DOING PETRA AND THE STAR THROWER.
AND I WAS UP ON SILKS.
K
A
8

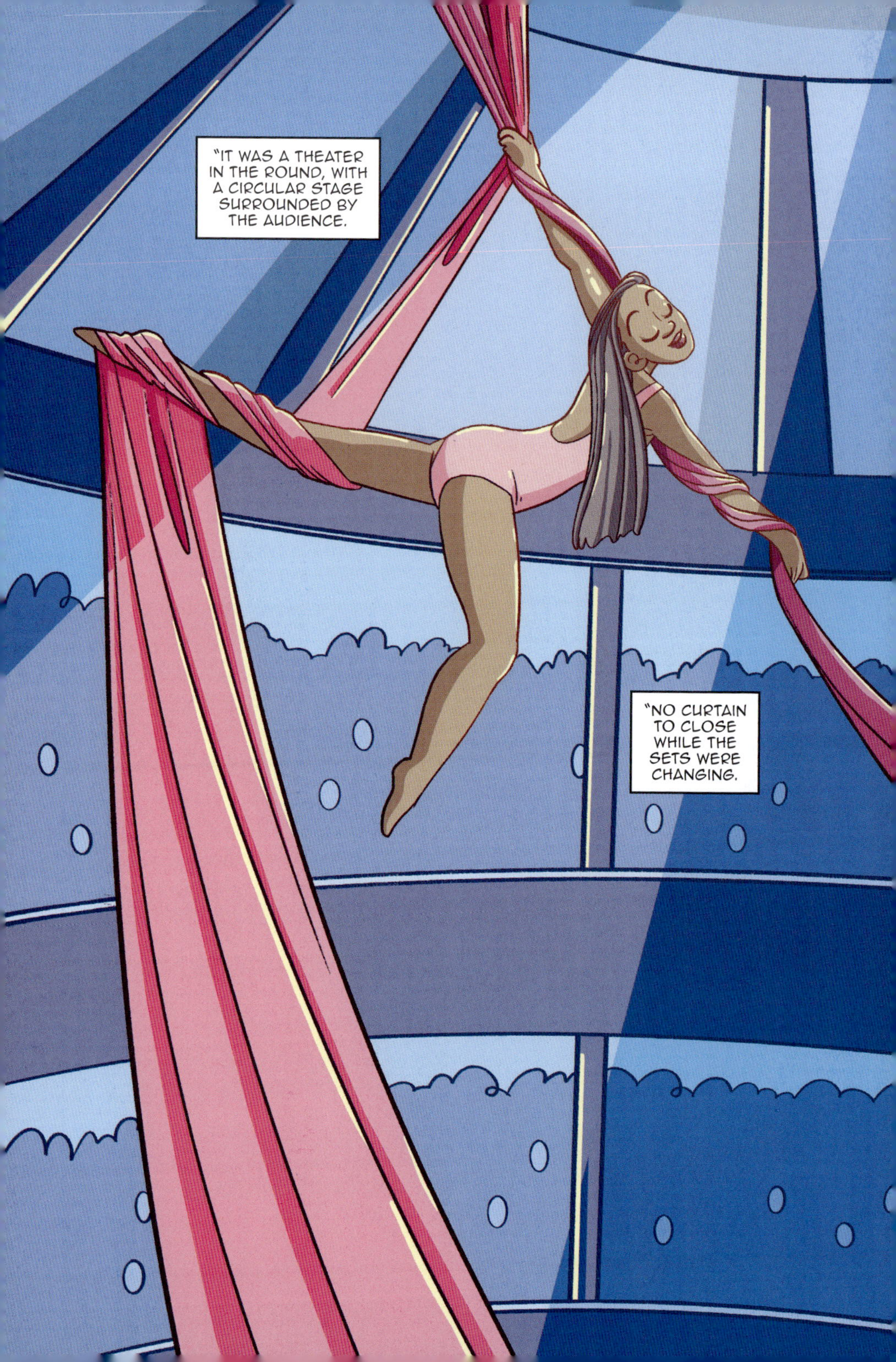
"IT WAS A THEATER IN THE ROUND, WITH A CIRCULAR STAGE SURROUNDED BY THE AUDIENCE.
"NO CURTAIN TO CLOSE WHILE THE SETS WERE CHANGING.

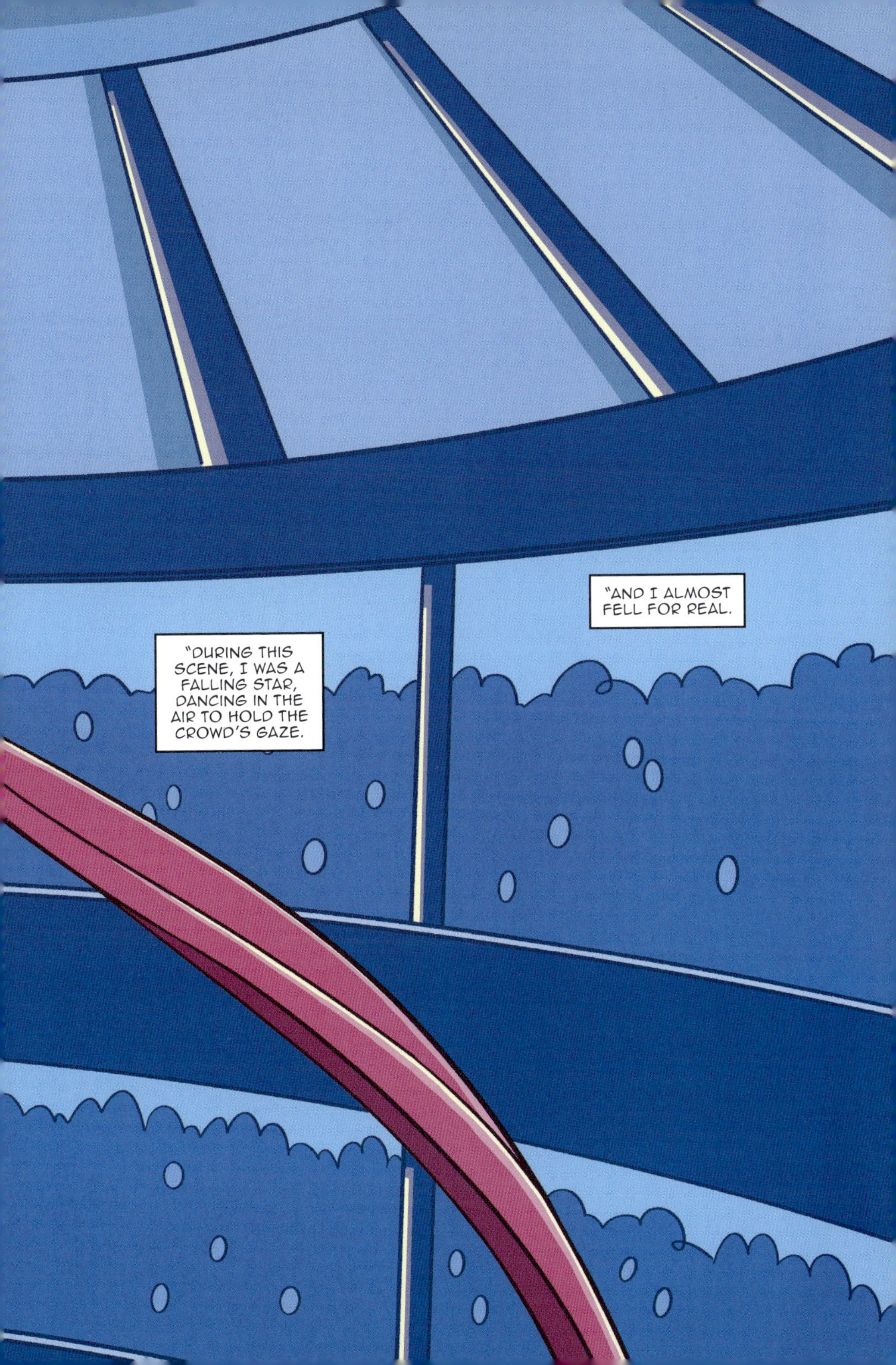
"DURING THIS SCENE, I WAS A FALLING STAR, DANCING IN THE AIR TO HOLD THE CROWD'S GAZE.
"AND I ALMOST FELL FOR REAL.

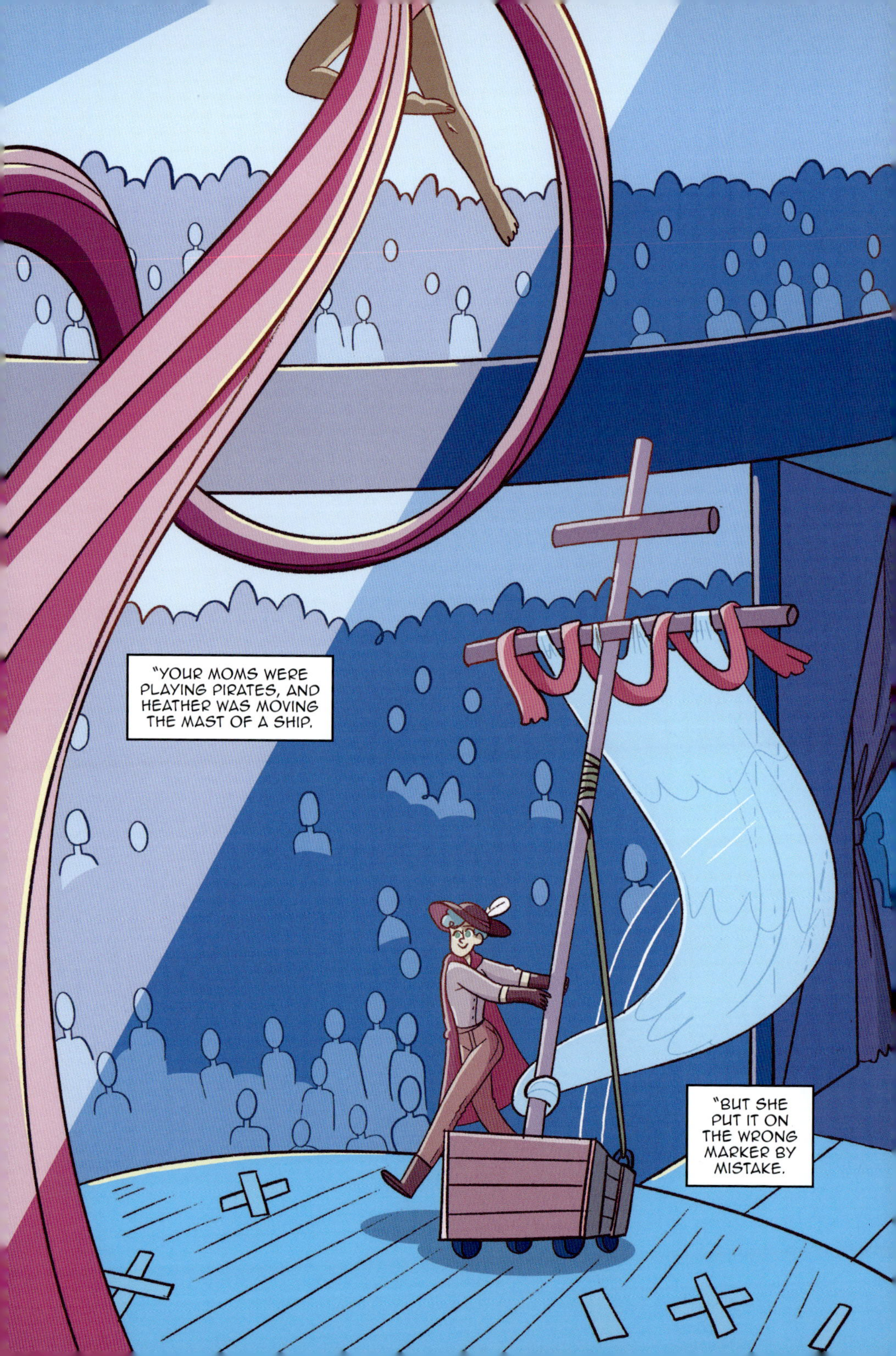
"YOUR MOMS WERE PLAYING PIRATES, AND HEATHER WAS MOVING THE MAST OF A SHIP.
"BUT SHE PUT IT ON THE WRONG MARKER BY MISTAKE.

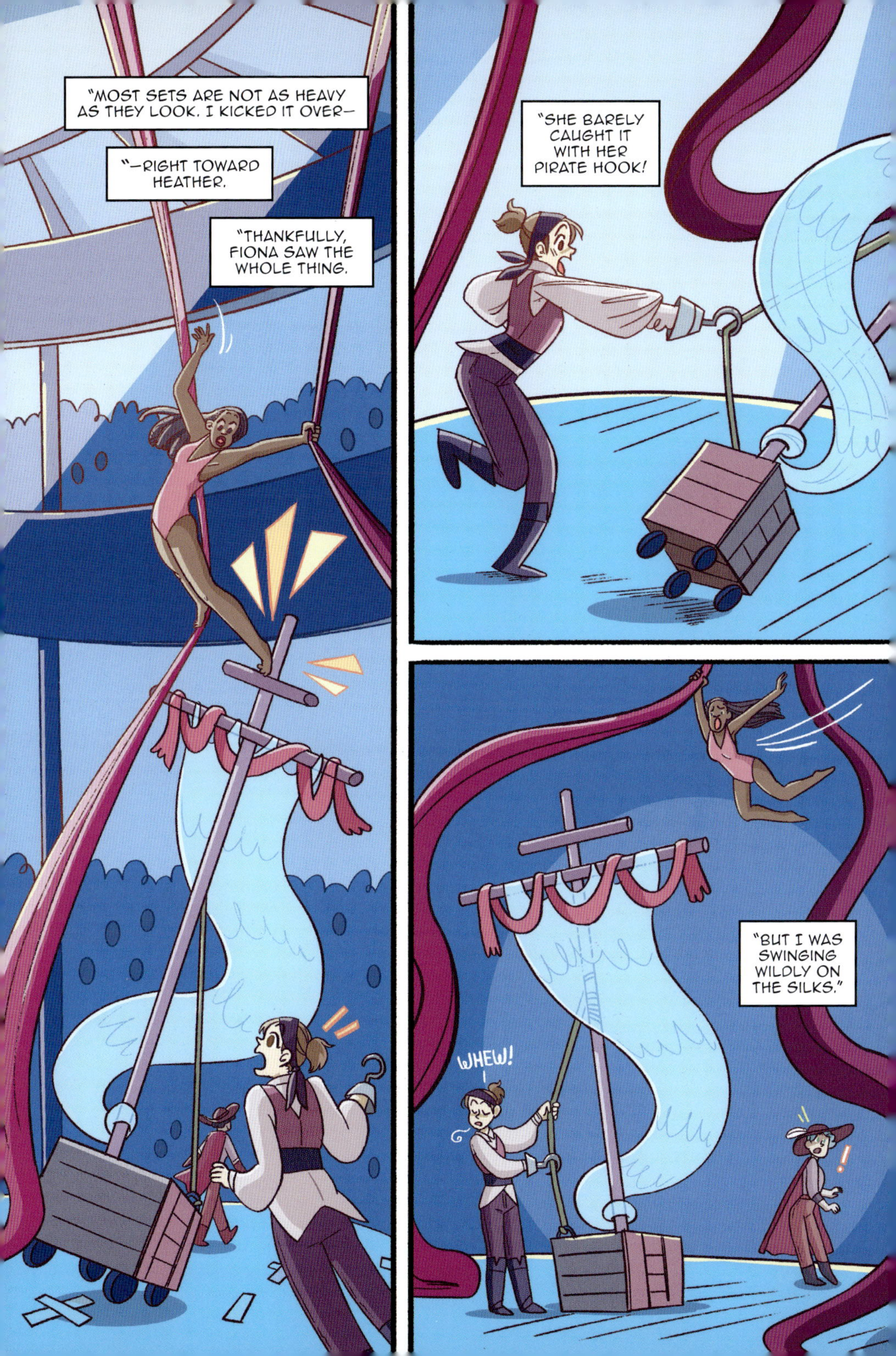
"MOST SETS ARE NOT AS HEAVY AS THEY LOOK. I KICKED IT OVER—
"—RIGHT TOWARD HEATHER.
"THANKFULLY, FIONA SAW THE WHOLE THING.
"SHE BARELY CAUGHT IT WITH HER PIRATE HOOK!
"BUT I WAS SWINGING WILDLY ON THE SILKS."
WHEW!

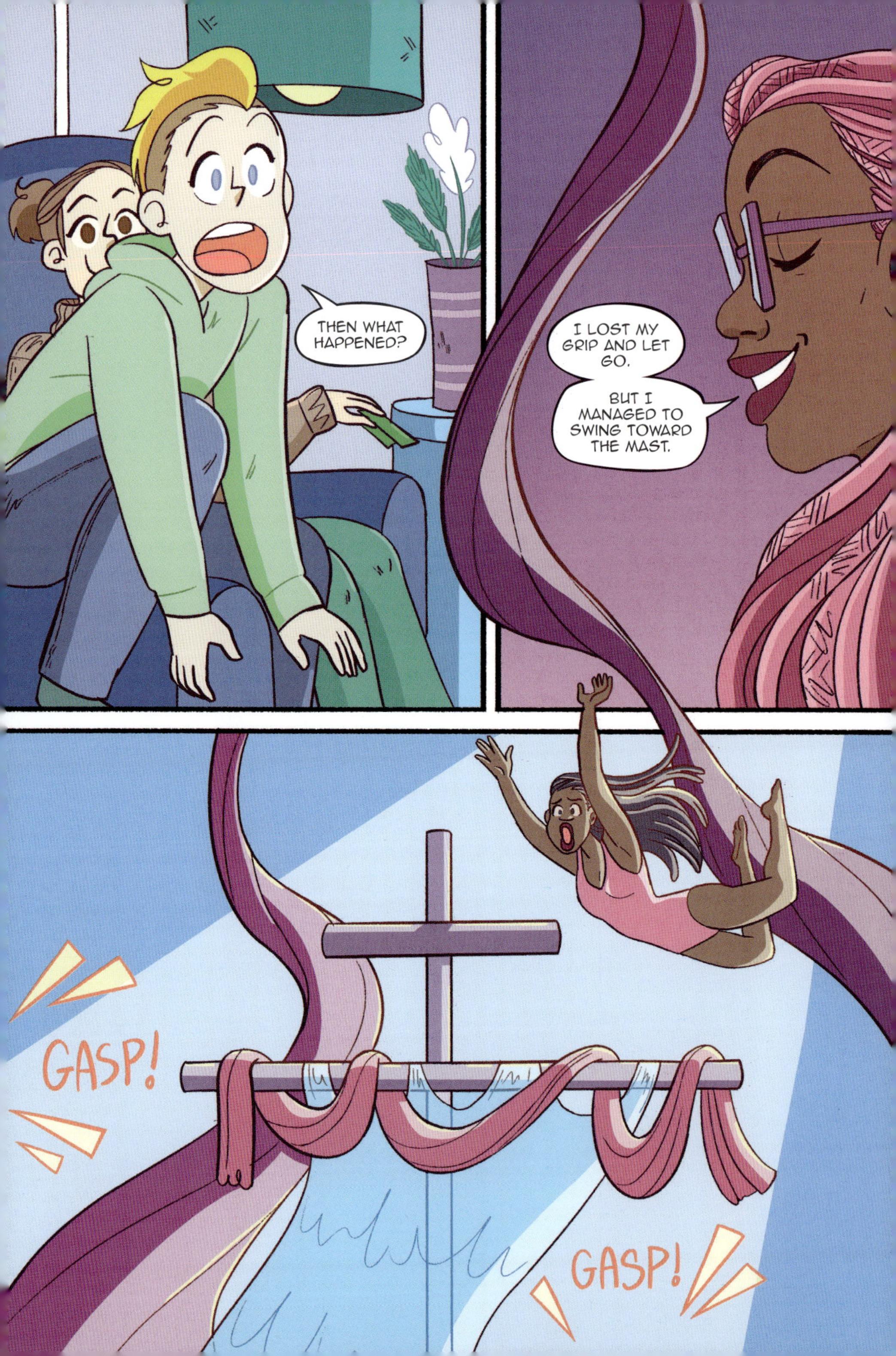
THEN WHAT HAPPENED?
I LOST MY GRIP AND LET GO.
BUT I MANAGED TO SWING TOWARD THE MAST.
GASP!
GASP!

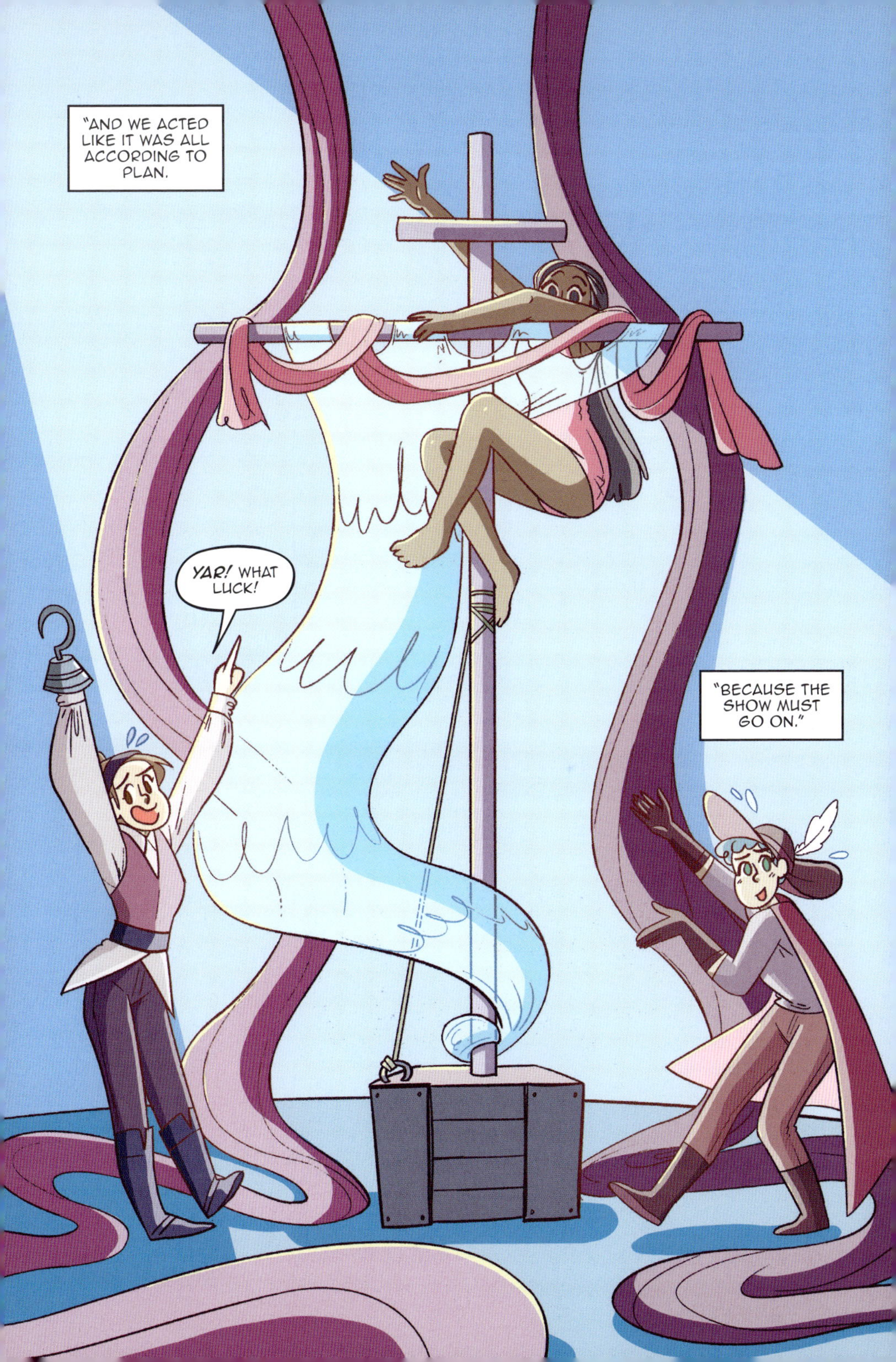
"AND WE ACTED LIKE IT WAS ALL ACCORDING TO PLAN.
YAR! WHAT LUCK!
"BECAUSE THE SHOW MUST GO ON."

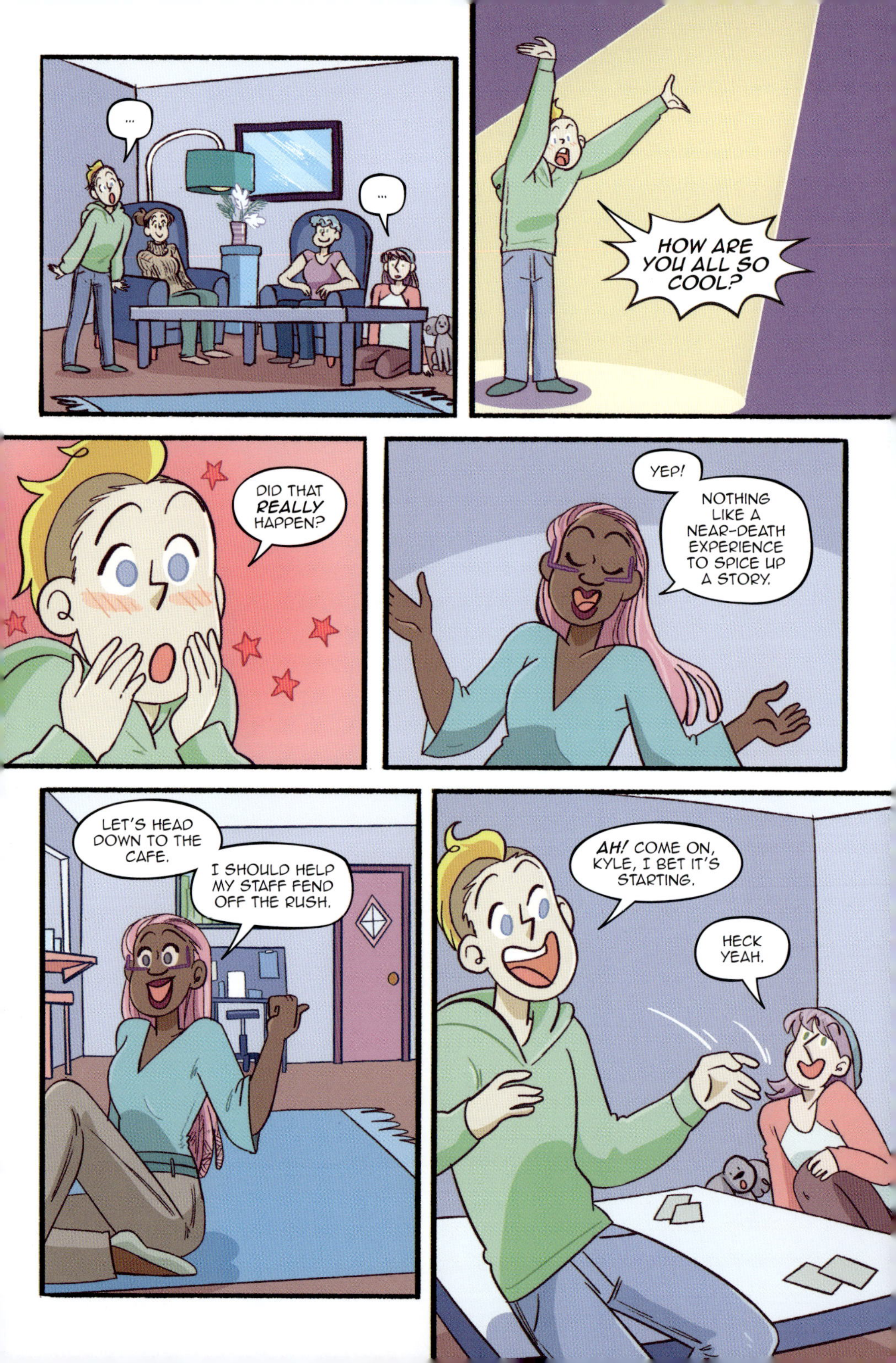
...
...
HOW ARE YOU ALL SO COOL?
DID THAT *REALLY* HAPPEN?
YEP!
NOTHING LIKE A NEAR-DEATH EXPERIENCE TO SPICE UP A STORY.
LET'S HEAD DOWN TO THE CAFE.
I SHOULD HELP MY STAFF FEND OFF THE RUSH.
AH! COME ON, KYLE, I BET IT'S STARTING.
HECK YEAH.

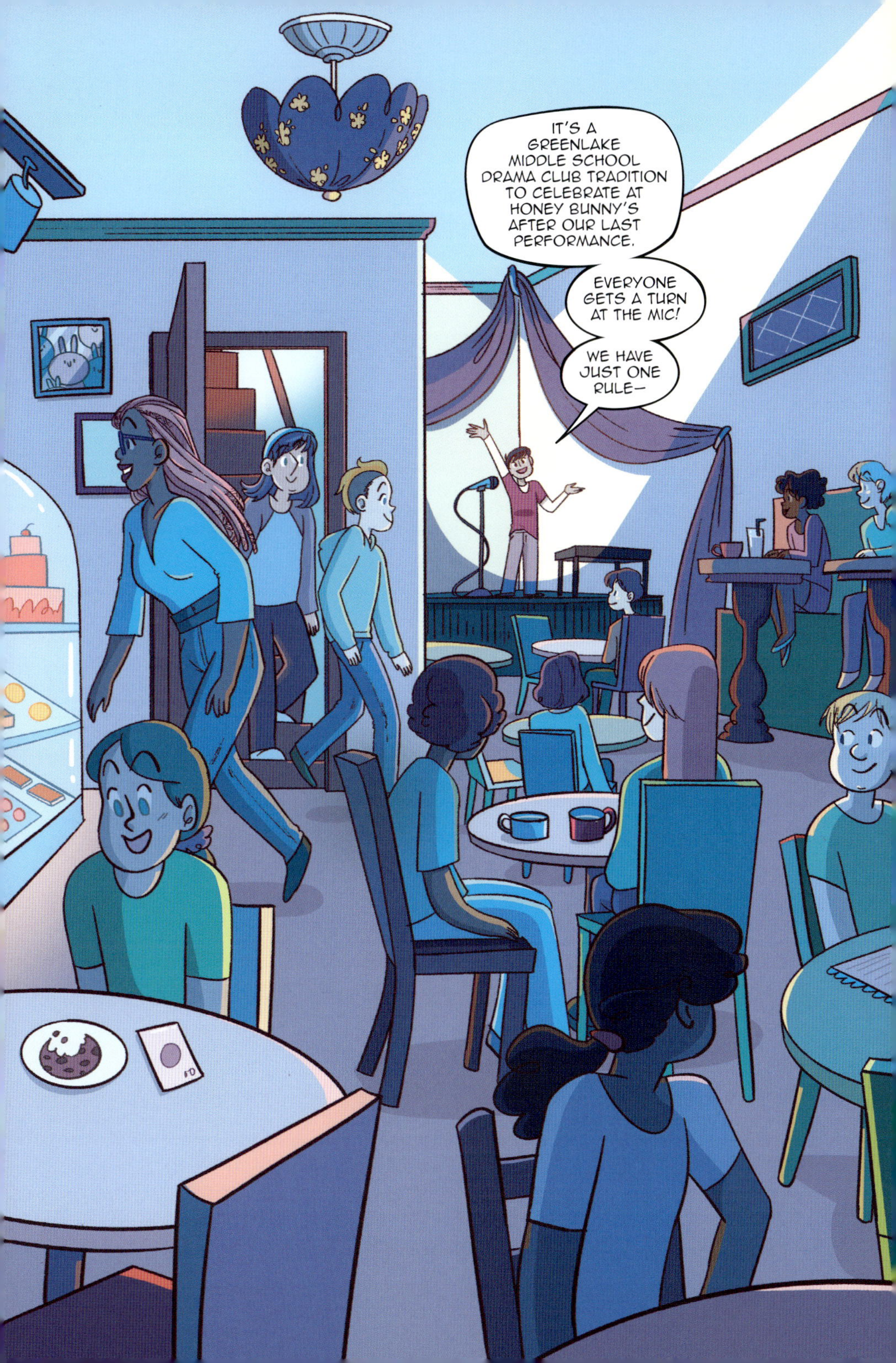
IT'S A GREENLAKE MIDDLE SCHOOL DRAMA CLUB TRADITION TO CELEBRATE AT HONEY BUNNY'S AFTER OUR LAST PERFORMANCE.
EVERYONE GETS A TURN AT THE MIC!
WE HAVE JUST ONE RULE—

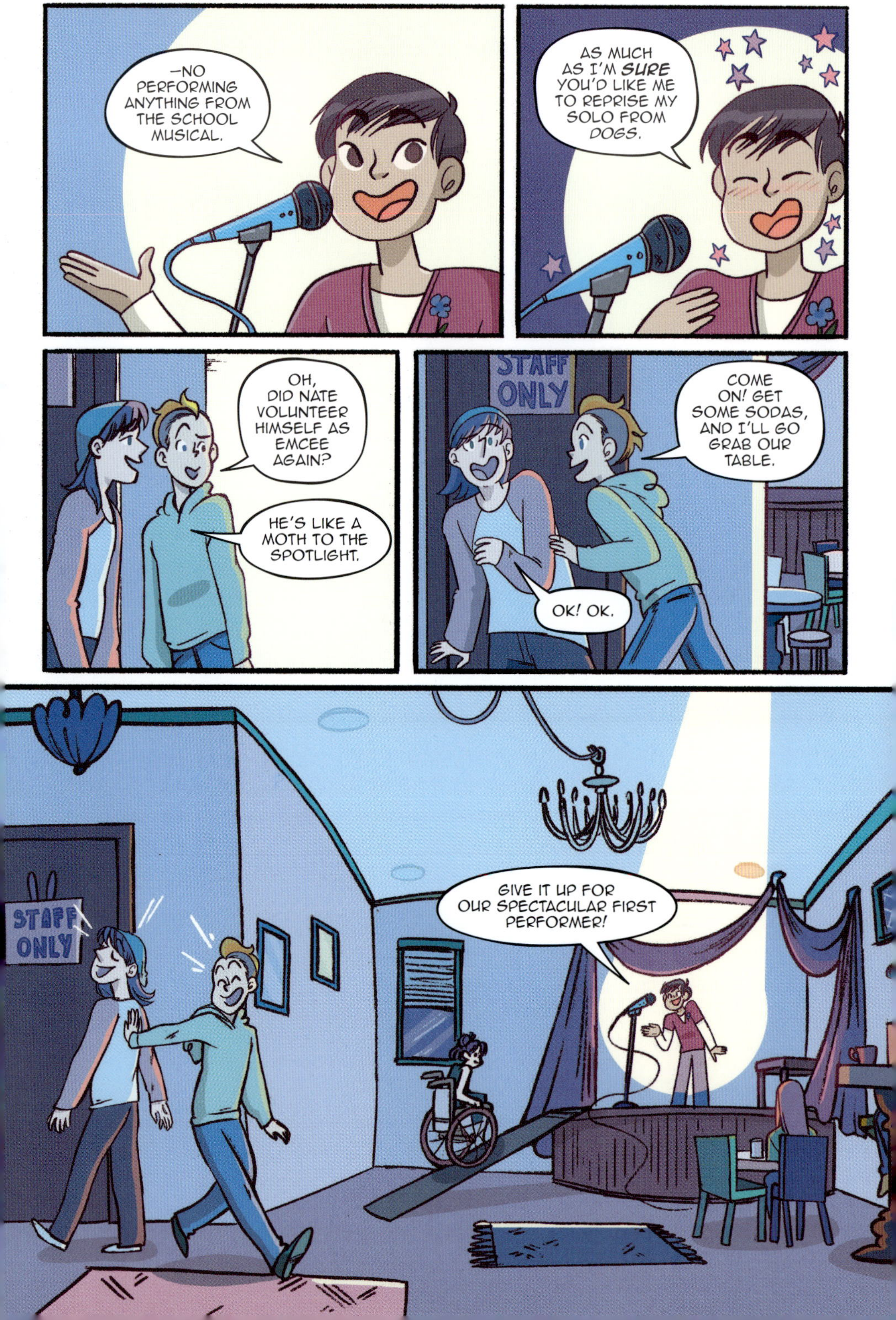
—NO PERFORMING ANYTHING FROM THE SCHOOL MUSICAL.
AS MUCH AS I'M **SURE** YOU'D LIKE ME TO REPRISE MY SOLO FROM *DOGS*.
OH, DID NATE VOLUNTEER HIMSELF AS EMCEE AGAIN?
HE'S LIKE A MOTH TO THE SPOTLIGHT.
STAFF ONLY
COME ON! GET SOME SODAS, AND I'LL GO GRAB OUR TABLE.
OK! OK.
STAFF ONLY
GIVE IT UP FOR OUR SPECTACULAR FIRST PERFORMER!

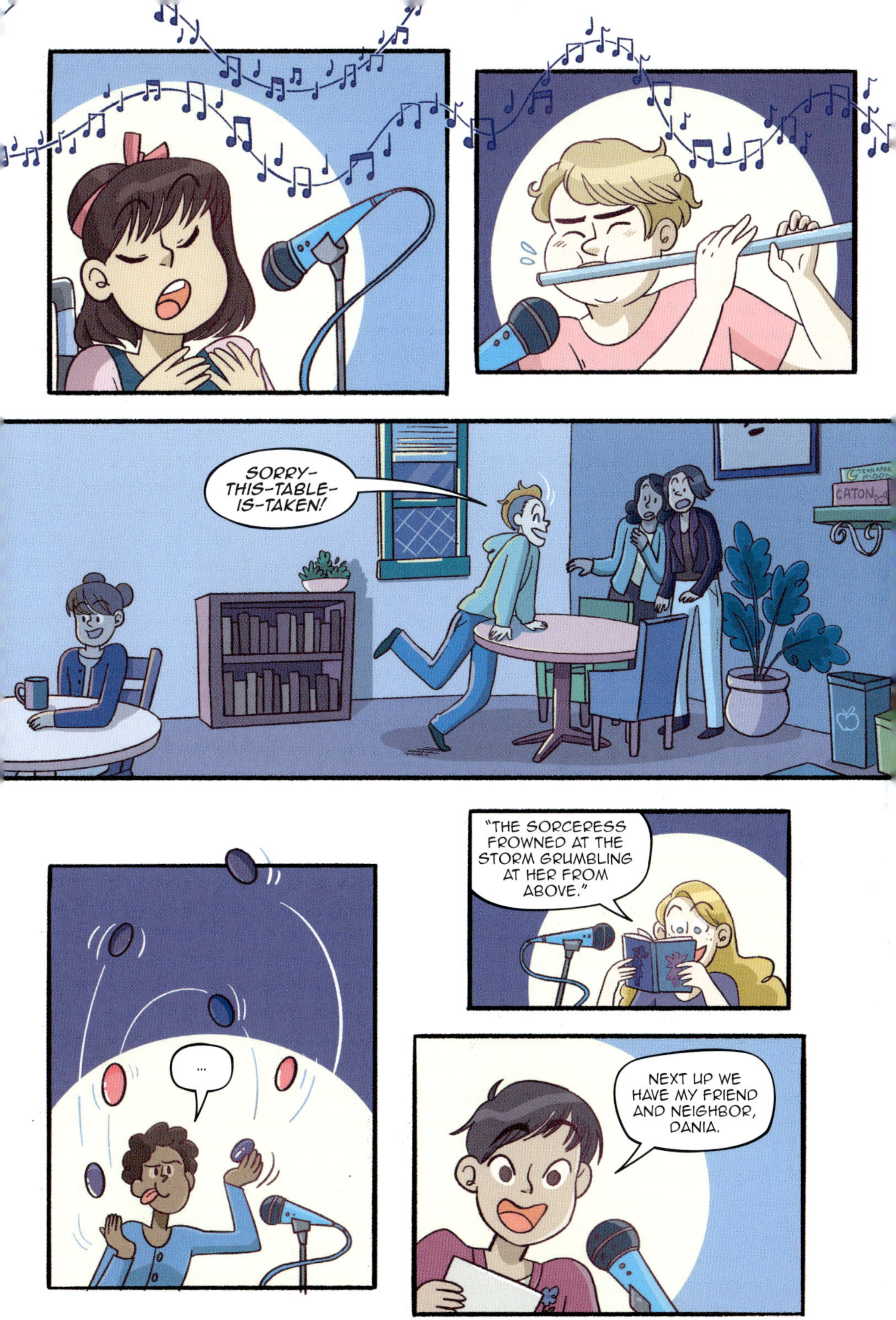
SORRY-THIS-TABLE-IS-TAKEN!
TERRAFORM MOON
CATON
"THE SORCERESS FROWNED AT THE STORM GRUMBLING AT HER FROM ABOVE."
...
NEXT UP WE HAVE MY FRIEND AND NEIGHBOR, DANIA.

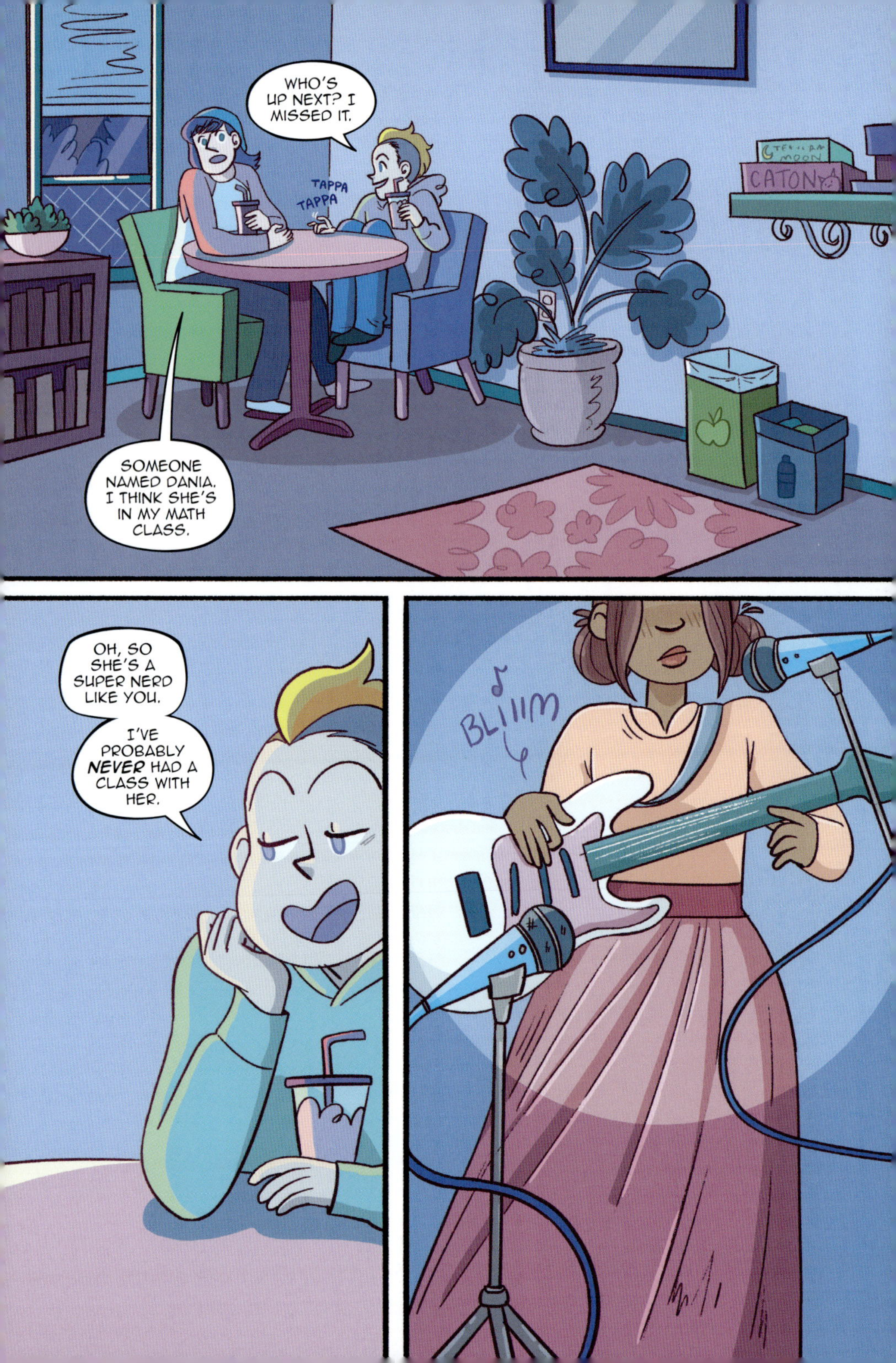
WHO'S UP NEXT? I MISSED IT.
TAPPA TAPPA
SOMEONE NAMED DANIA. I THINK SHE'S IN MY MATH CLASS.
OH, SO SHE'S A SUPER NERD LIKE YOU.
I'VE PROBABLY ***NEVER*** HAD A CLASS WITH HER.
BLIIIM

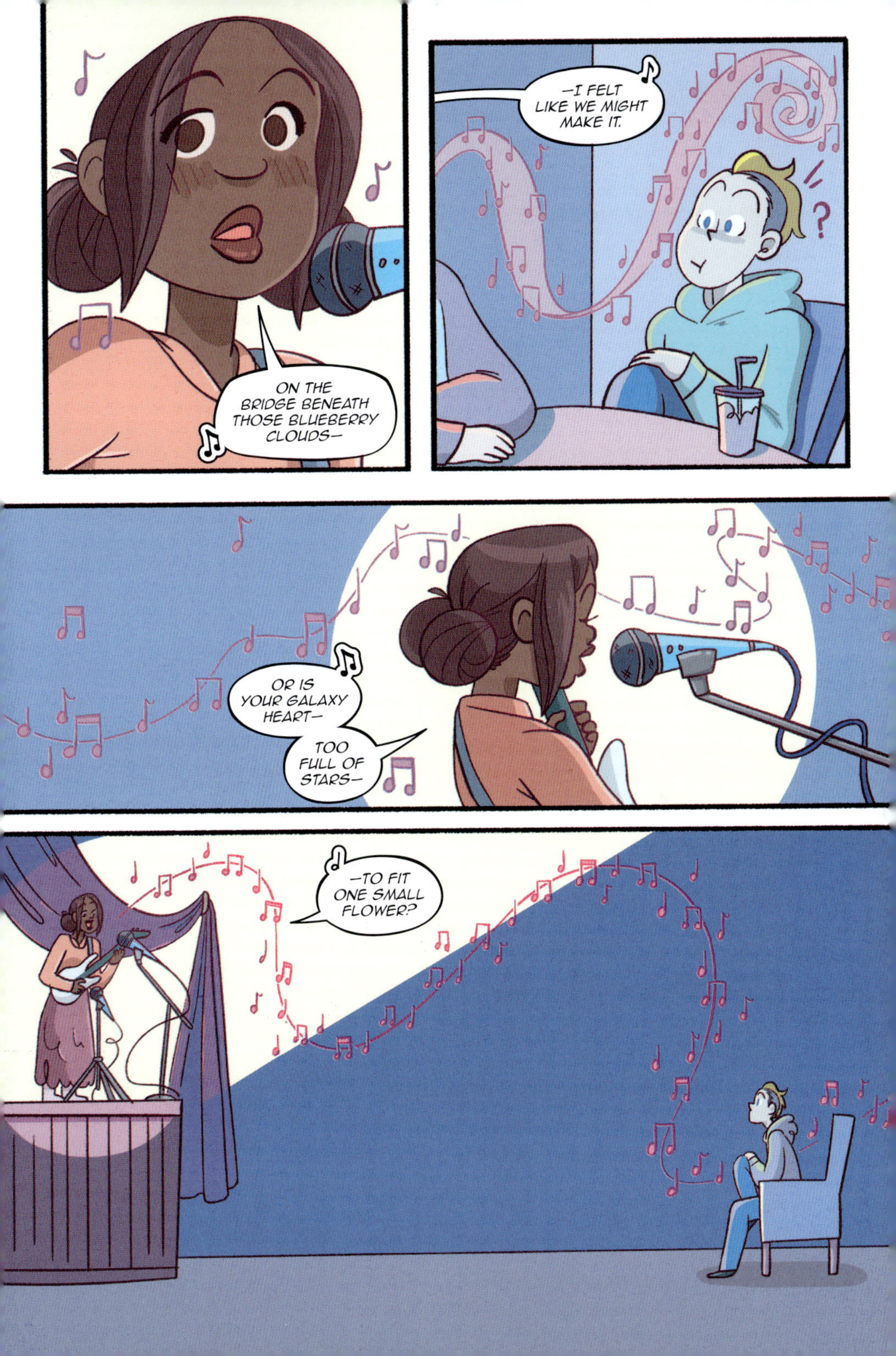
ON THE BRIDGE BENEATH THOSE BLUEBERRY CLOUDS—
—I FELT LIKE WE MIGHT MAKE IT.
?
OR IS YOUR GALAXY HEART—
TOO FULL OF STARS—
—TO FIT ONE SMALL FLOWER?

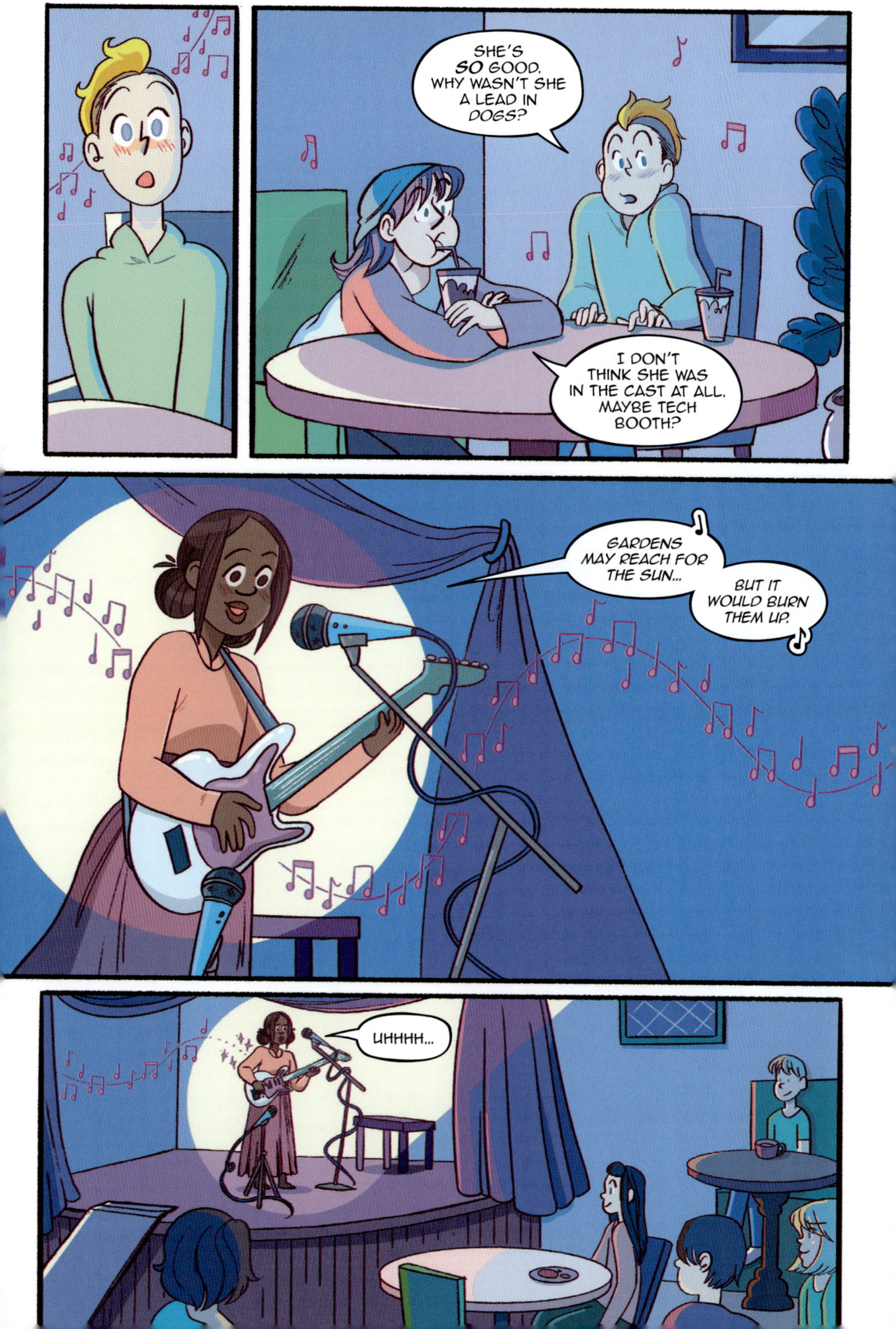
SHE'S SO GOOD. WHY WASN'T SHE A LEAD IN DOGS?
I DON'T THINK SHE WAS IN THE CAST AT ALL. MAYBE TECH BOOTH?
GARDENS MAY REACH FOR THE SUN...
BUT IT WOULD BURN THEM UP.
UHHHH...

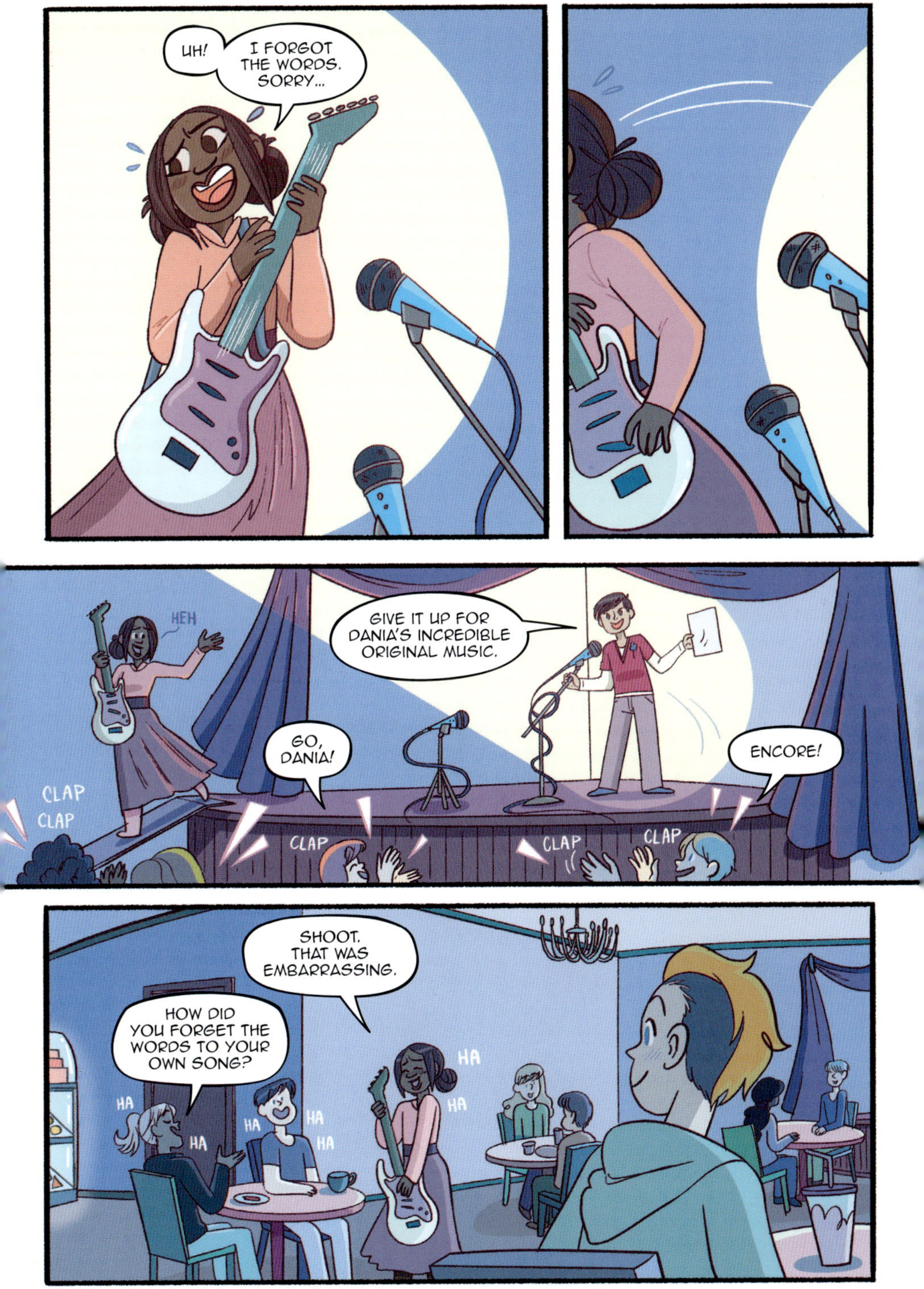
UH!
I FORGOT THE WORDS. SORRY...
HEH
GIVE IT UP FOR DANIA'S INCREDIBLE ORIGINAL MUSIC.
GO, DANIA!
ENCORE!
CLAP
CLAP
CLAP
CLAP
CLAP
SHOOT. THAT WAS EMBARRASSING.
HOW DID YOU FORGET THE WORDS TO YOUR OWN SONG?
HA
HA
HA
HA
HA
HA
HA
HA

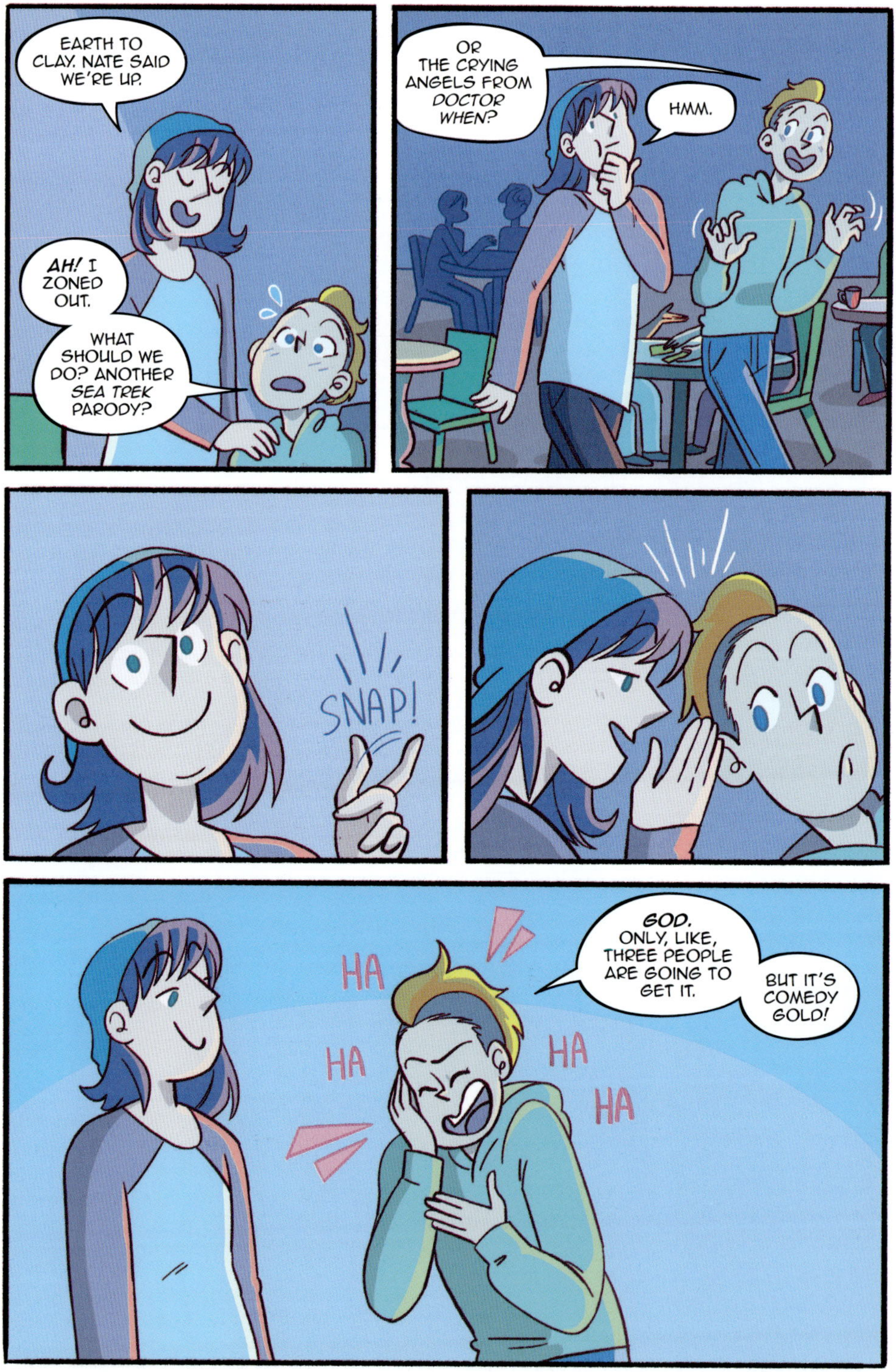
EARTH TO CLAY. NATE SAID WE'RE UP.
AH! I ZONED OUT.
WHAT SHOULD WE DO? ANOTHER SEA TREK PARODY?
OR THE CRYING ANGELS FROM DOCTOR WHEN?
HMM.
SNAP!
HA
HA
HA
HA
GOD. ONLY, LIKE, THREE PEOPLE ARE GOING TO GET IT.
BUT IT'S COMEDY GOLD!

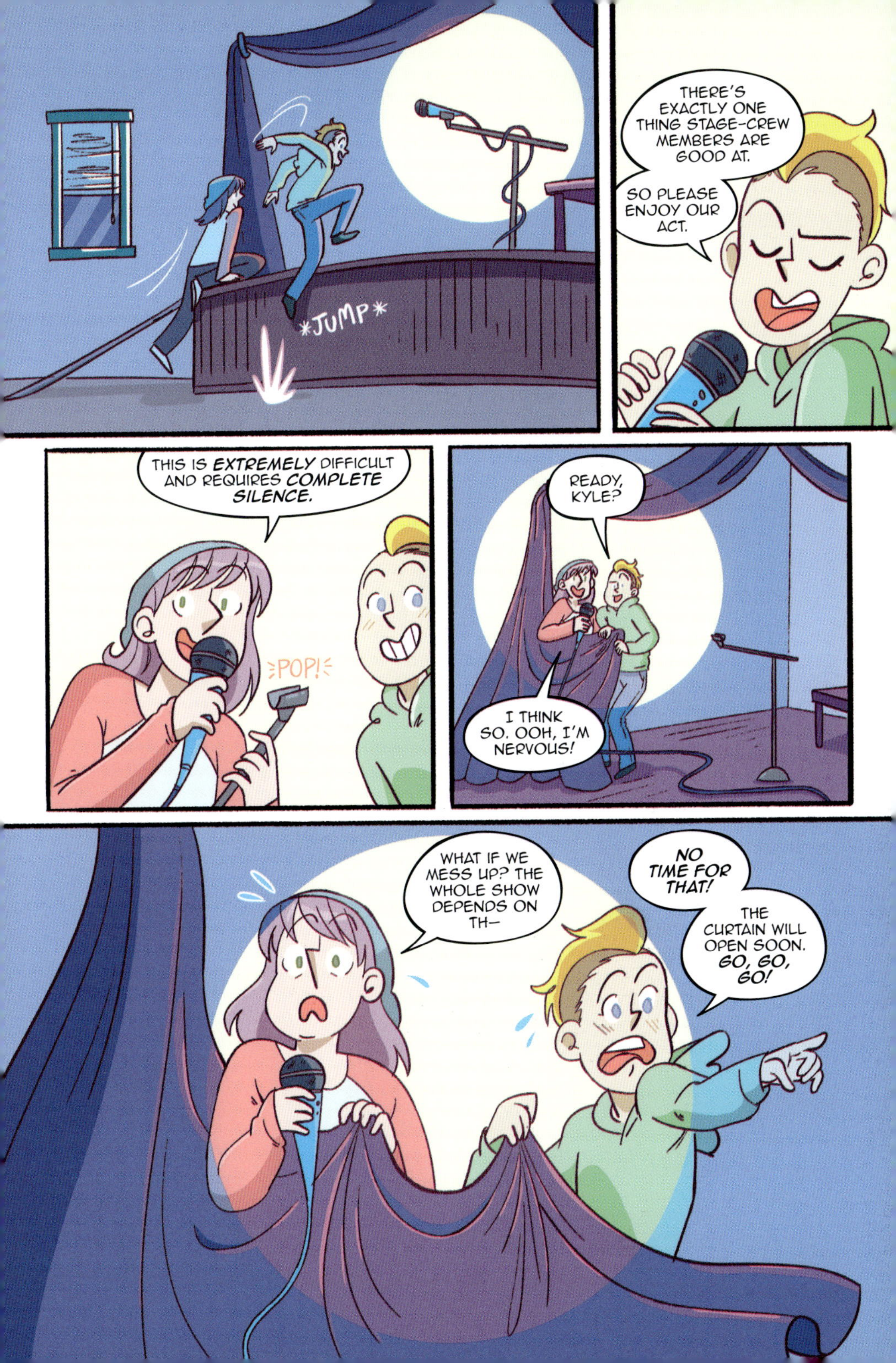
JUMP
THERE'S EXACTLY ONE THING STAGE-CREW MEMBERS ARE GOOD AT.
SO PLEASE ENJOY OUR ACT.
THIS IS EXTREMELY DIFFICULT AND REQUIRES COMPLETE SILENCE.
POP!
READY, KYLE?
I THINK SO. OOH, I'M NERVOUS!
WHAT IF WE MESS UP? THE WHOLE SHOW DEPENDS ON TH—
NO TIME FOR THAT!
THE CURTAIN WILL OPEN SOON. GO, GO, GO!

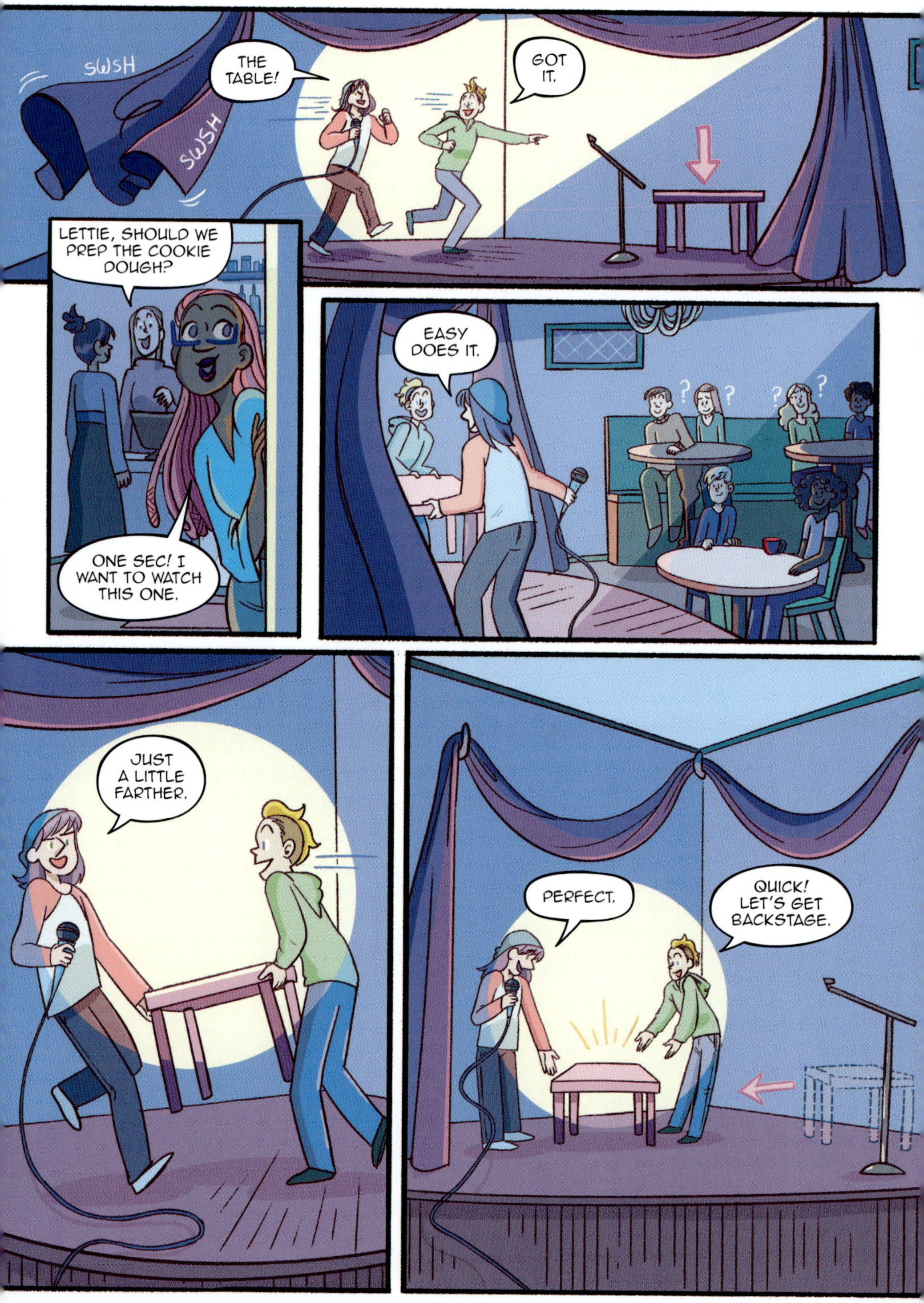
SWSH
SWSH
THE TABLE!
GOT IT.
LETTIE, SHOULD WE PREP THE COOKIE DOUGH?
ONE SEC! I WANT TO WATCH THIS ONE.
EASY DOES IT.
? ? ? ?
JUST A LITTLE FARTHER.
PERFECT.
QUICK! LET'S GET BACKSTAGE.

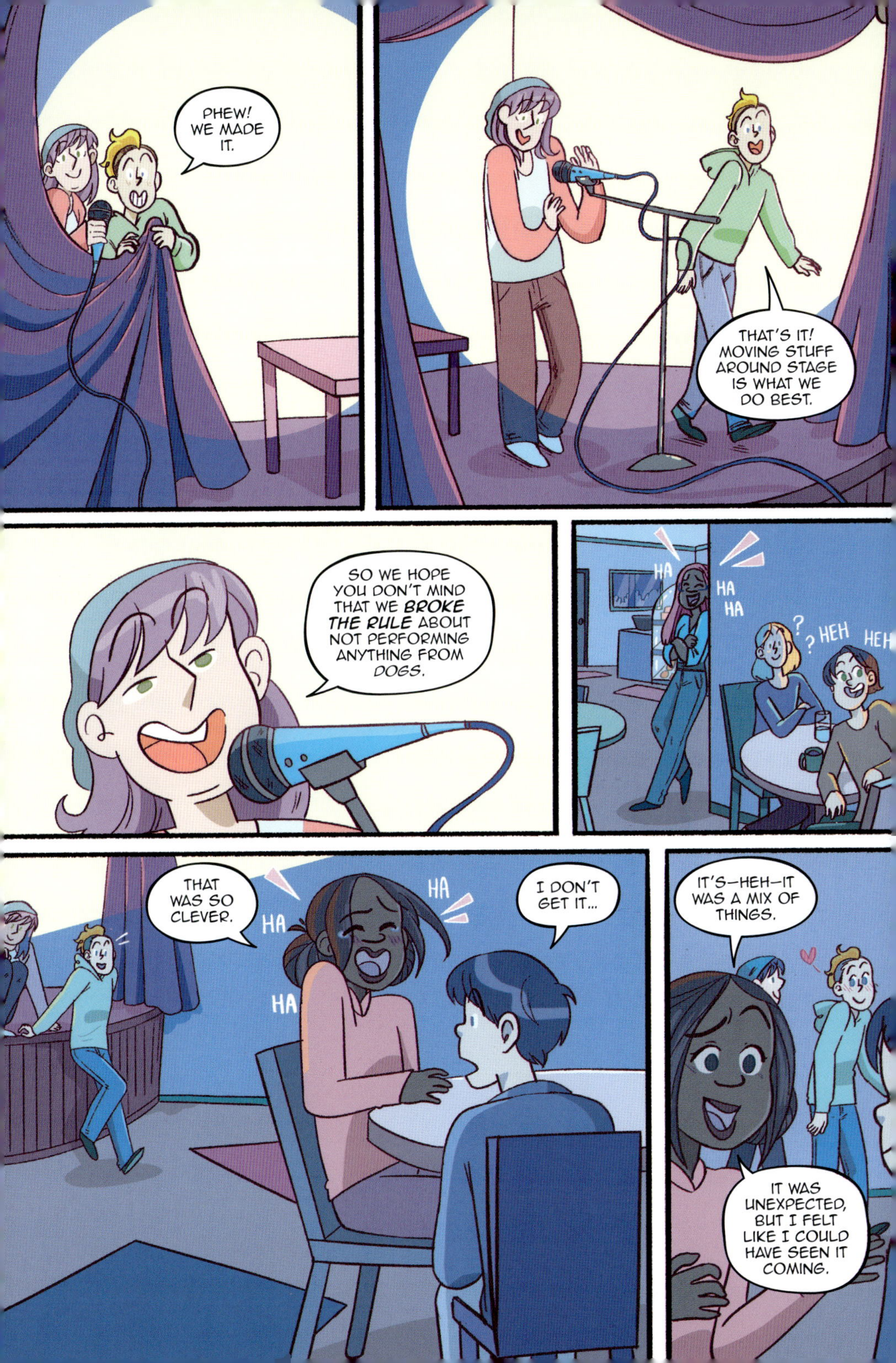
PHEW! WE MADE IT.
THAT'S IT! MOVING STUFF AROUND STAGE IS WHAT WE DO BEST.
SO WE HOPE YOU DON'T MIND THAT WE BROKE THE RULE ABOUT NOT PERFORMING ANYTHING FROM DOGS.
HA
HA HA
? ? HEH HEH
THAT WAS SO CLEVER.
HA
HA
HA
I DON'T GET IT...
IT'S—HEH—IT WAS A MIX OF THINGS.
IT WAS UNEXPECTED, BUT I FELT LIKE I COULD HAVE SEEN IT COMING.

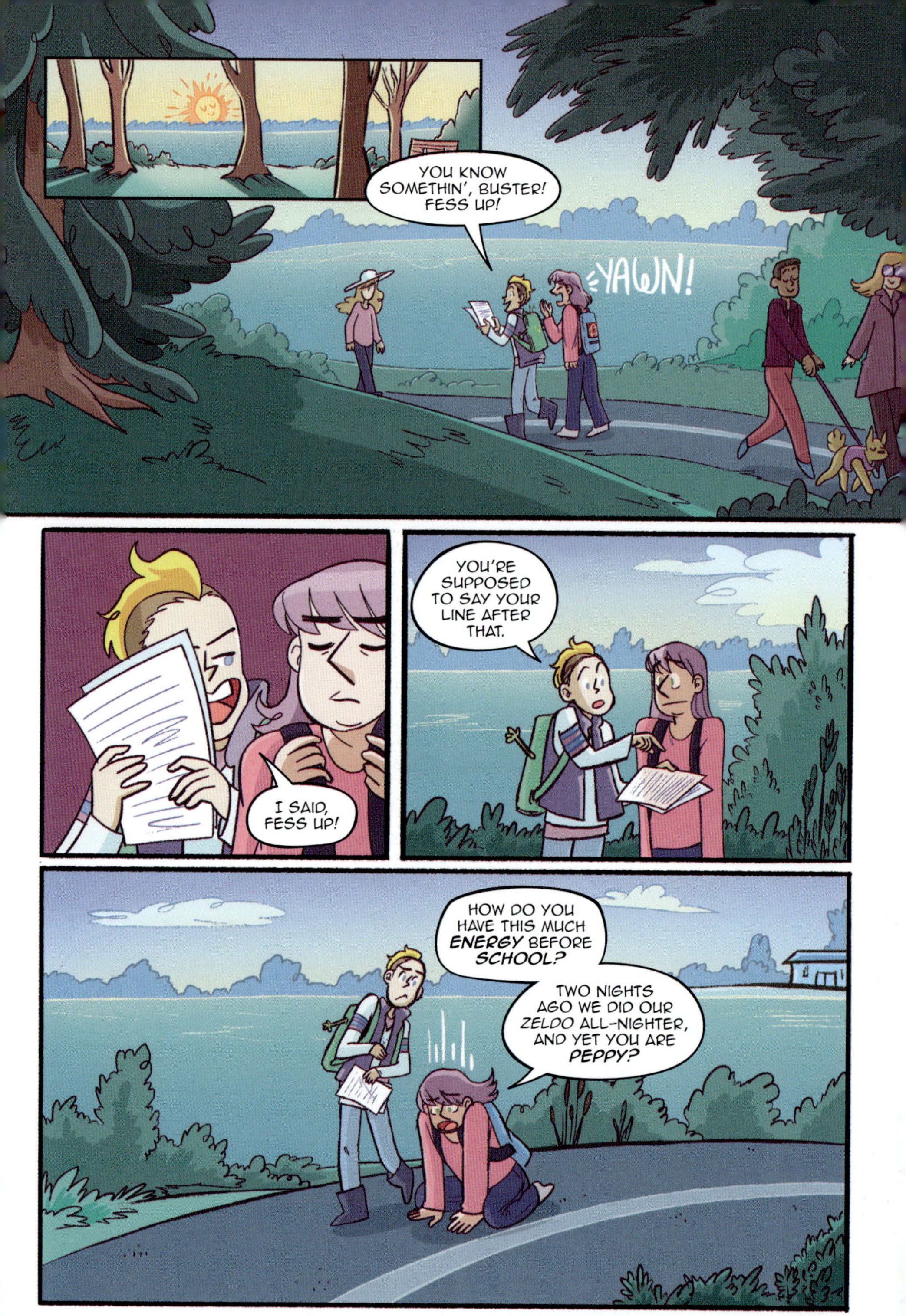
YOU KNOW SOMETHIN', BUSTER! FESS UP!
YAWN!
I SAID, FESS UP!
YOU'RE SUPPOSED TO SAY YOUR LINE AFTER THAT.
HOW DO YOU HAVE THIS MUCH ENERGY BEFORE SCHOOL?
TWO NIGHTS AGO WE DID OUR ZELDO ALL-NIGHTER, AND YET YOU ARE PEPPY?

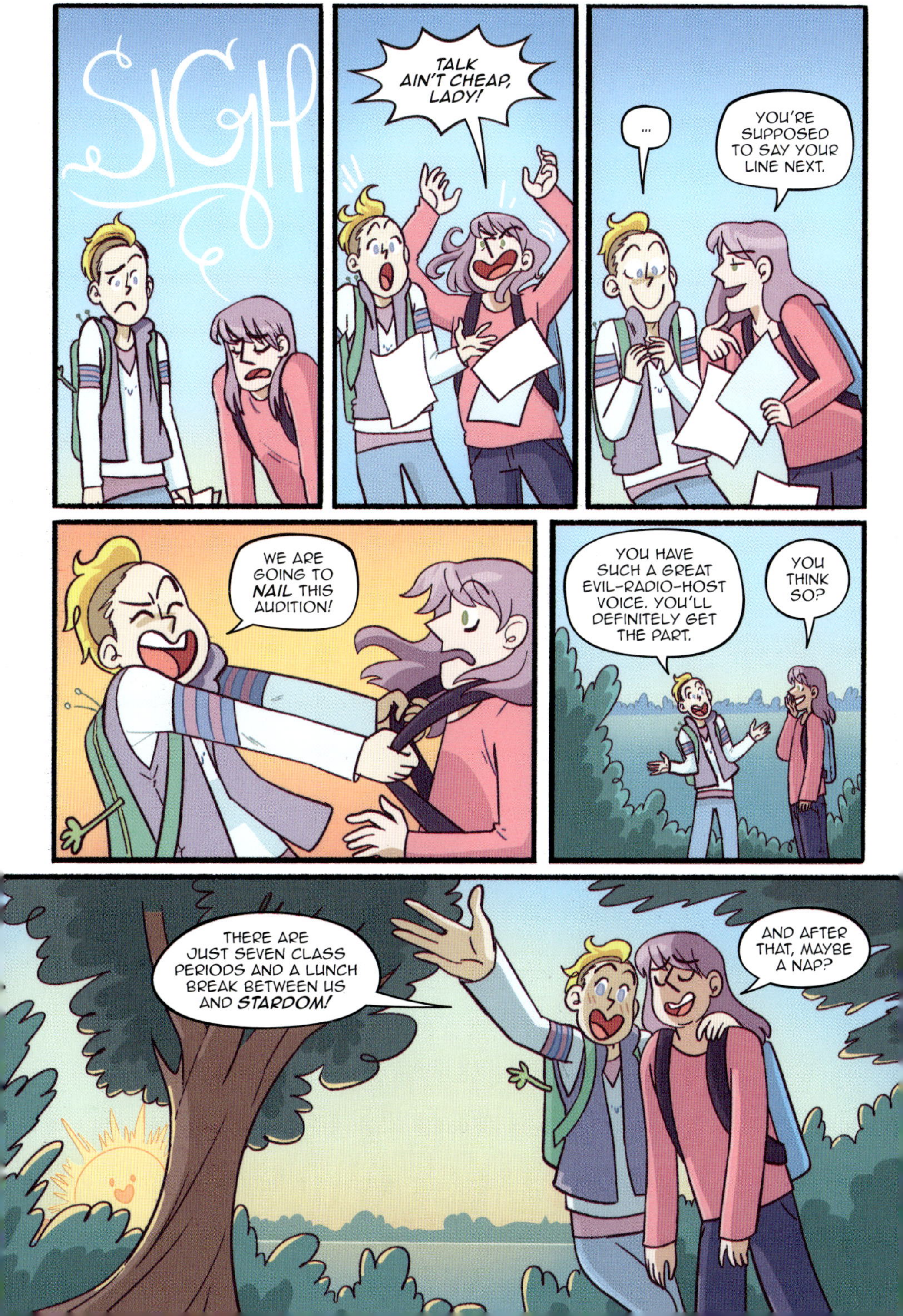
SIGH
TALK AIN'T CHEAP, LADY!
...
YOU'RE SUPPOSED TO SAY YOUR LINE NEXT.
WE ARE GOING TO NAIL THIS AUDITION!
YOU HAVE SUCH A GREAT EVIL-RADIO-HOST VOICE. YOU'LL DEFINITELY GET THE PART.
YOU THINK SO?
THERE ARE JUST SEVEN CLASS PERIODS AND A LUNCH BREAK BETWEEN US AND STARDOM!
AND AFTER THAT, MAYBE A NAP?

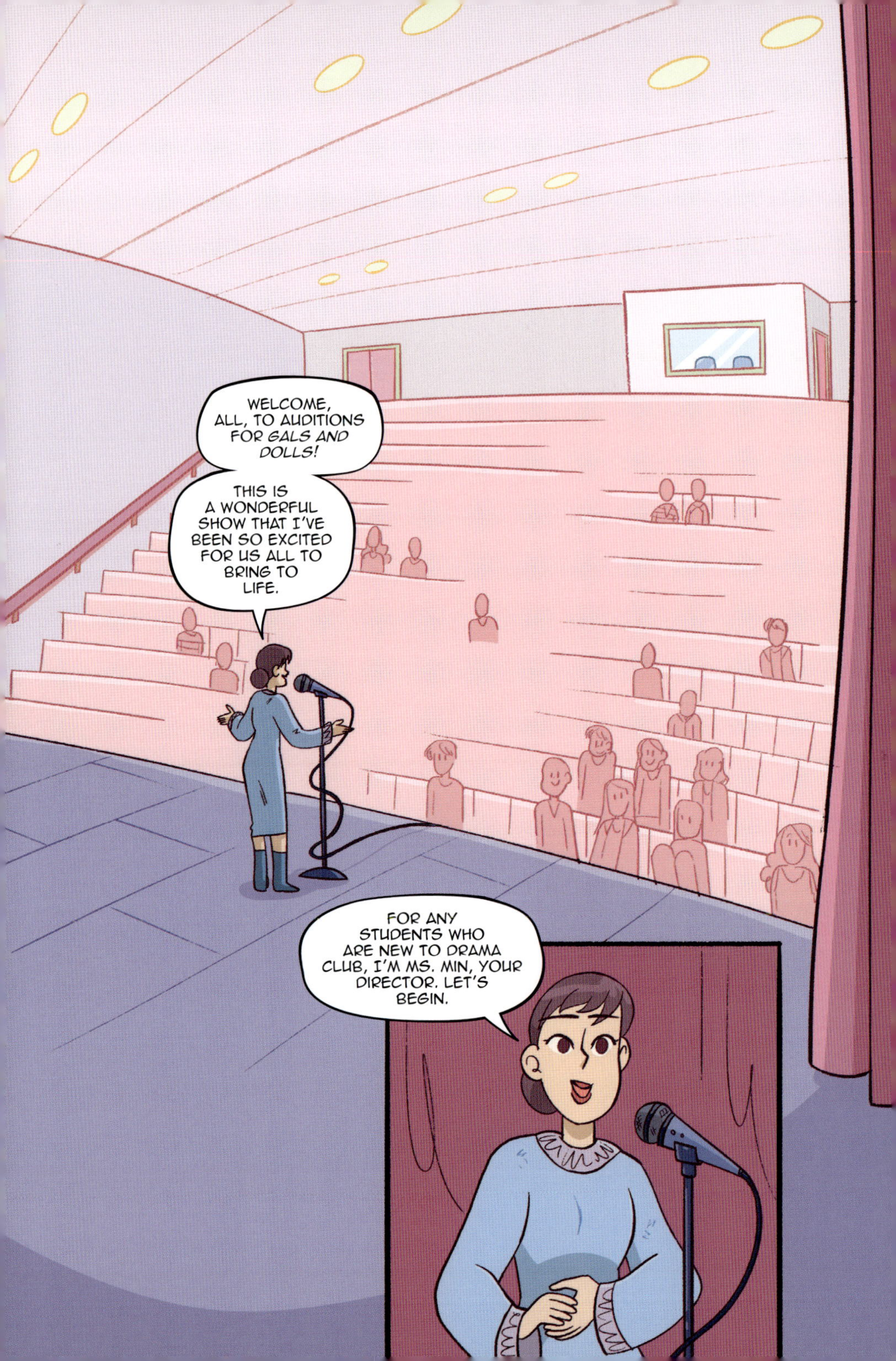
WELCOME, ALL, TO AUDITIONS FOR *GALS AND DOLLS!*
THIS IS A WONDERFUL SHOW THAT I'VE BEEN SO EXCITED FOR US ALL TO BRING TO LIFE.
FOR ANY STUDENTS WHO ARE NEW TO DRAMA CLUB, I'M MS. MIN, YOUR DIRECTOR. LET'S BEGIN.

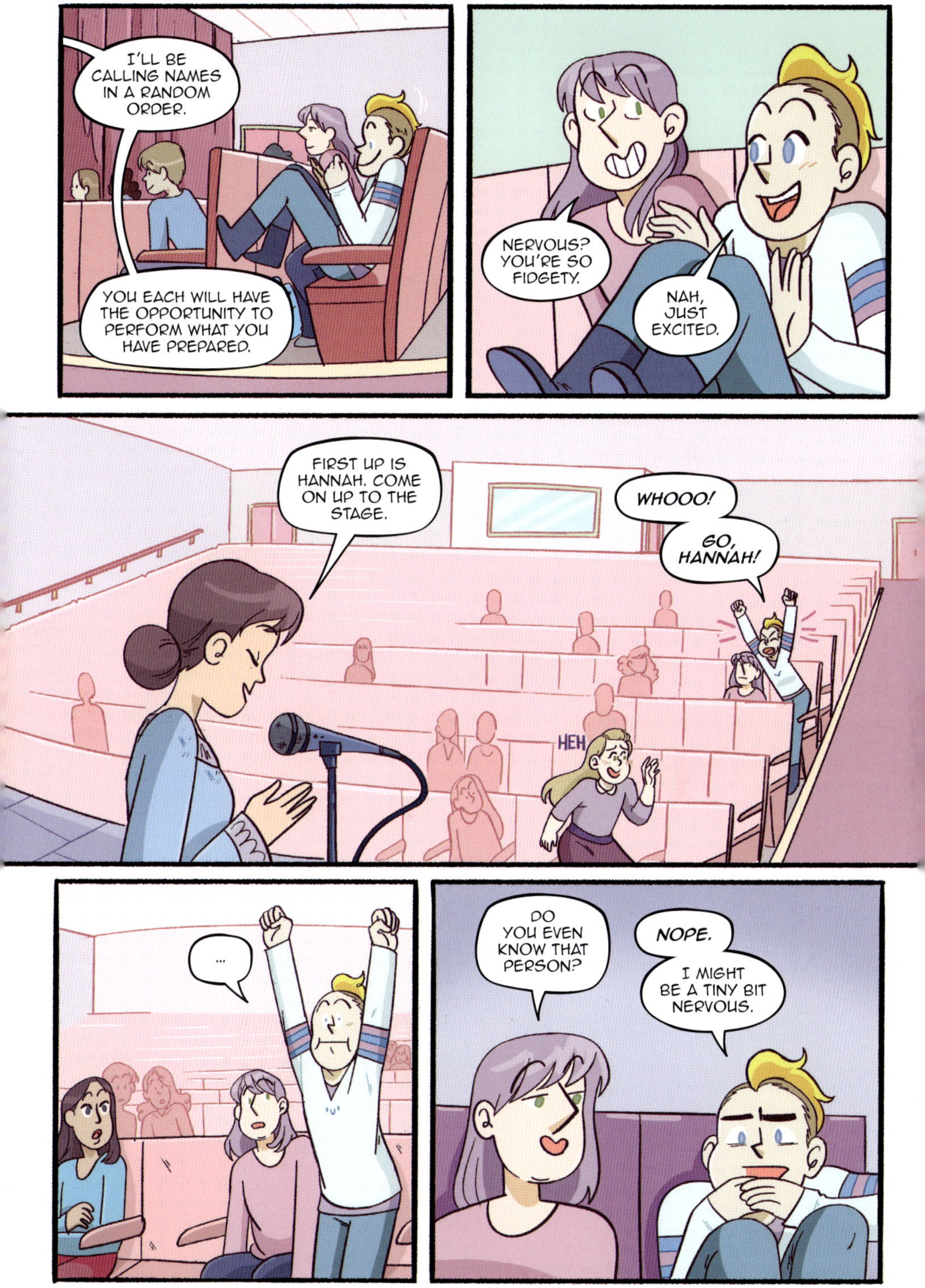
I'LL BE CALLING NAMES IN A RANDOM ORDER.
YOU EACH WILL HAVE THE OPPORTUNITY TO PERFORM WHAT YOU HAVE PREPARED.
NERVOUS? YOU'RE SO FIDGETY.
NAH, JUST EXCITED.
FIRST UP IS HANNAH. COME ON UP TO THE STAGE.
WHOOO!
GO, HANNAH!
HEH
...
DO YOU EVEN KNOW THAT PERSON?
NOPE.
I MIGHT BE A TINY BIT NERVOUS.

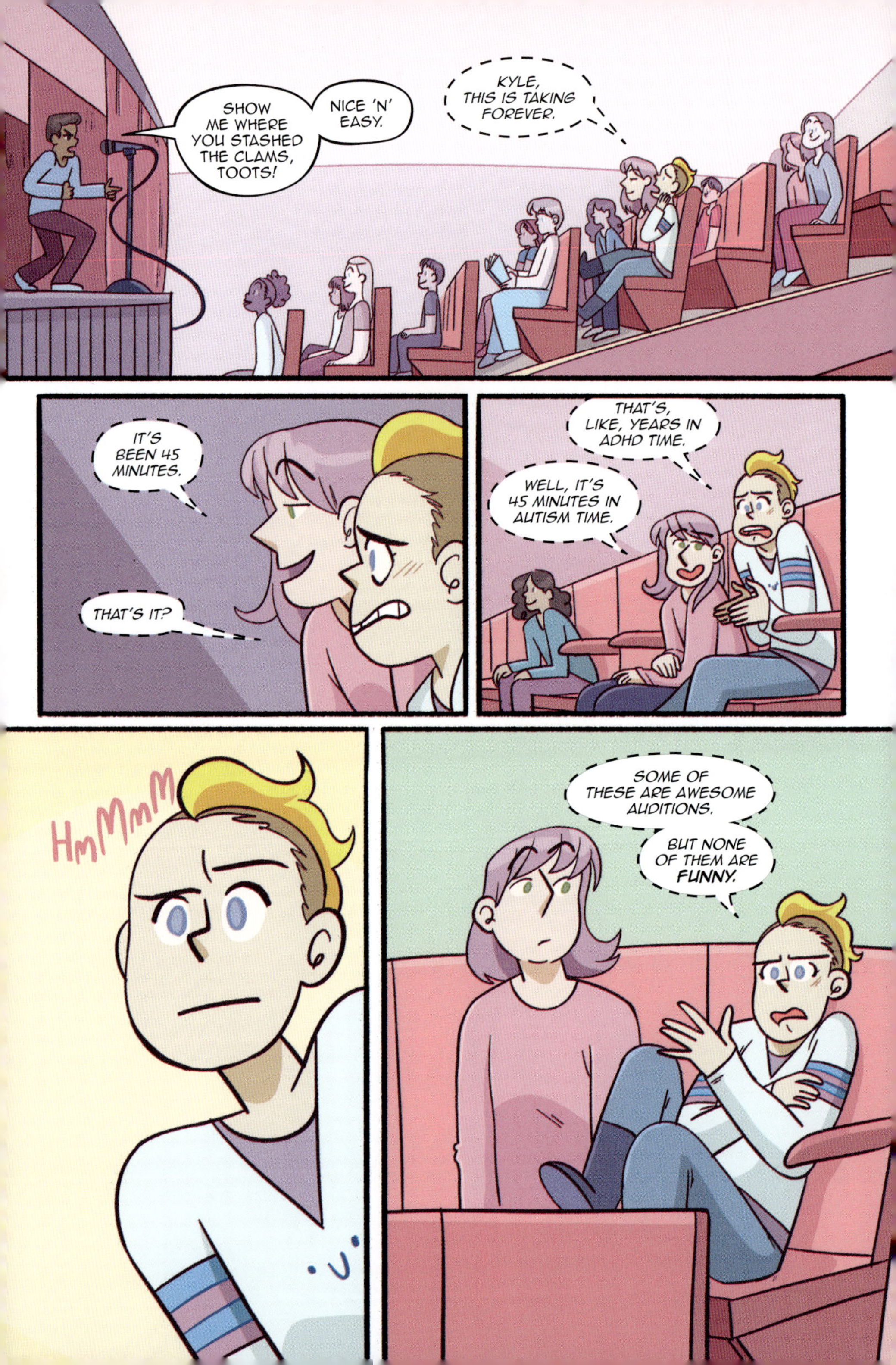
SHOW ME WHERE YOU STASHED THE CLAMS, TOOTS!
NICE 'N' EASY.
KYLE, THIS IS TAKING FOREVER.
IT'S BEEN 45 MINUTES.
THAT'S IT?
THAT'S, LIKE, YEARS IN ADHD TIME.
WELL, IT'S 45 MINUTES IN AUTISM TIME.
HmMmM
SOME OF THESE ARE AWESOME AUDITIONS.
BUT NONE OF THEM ARE **FUNNY.**

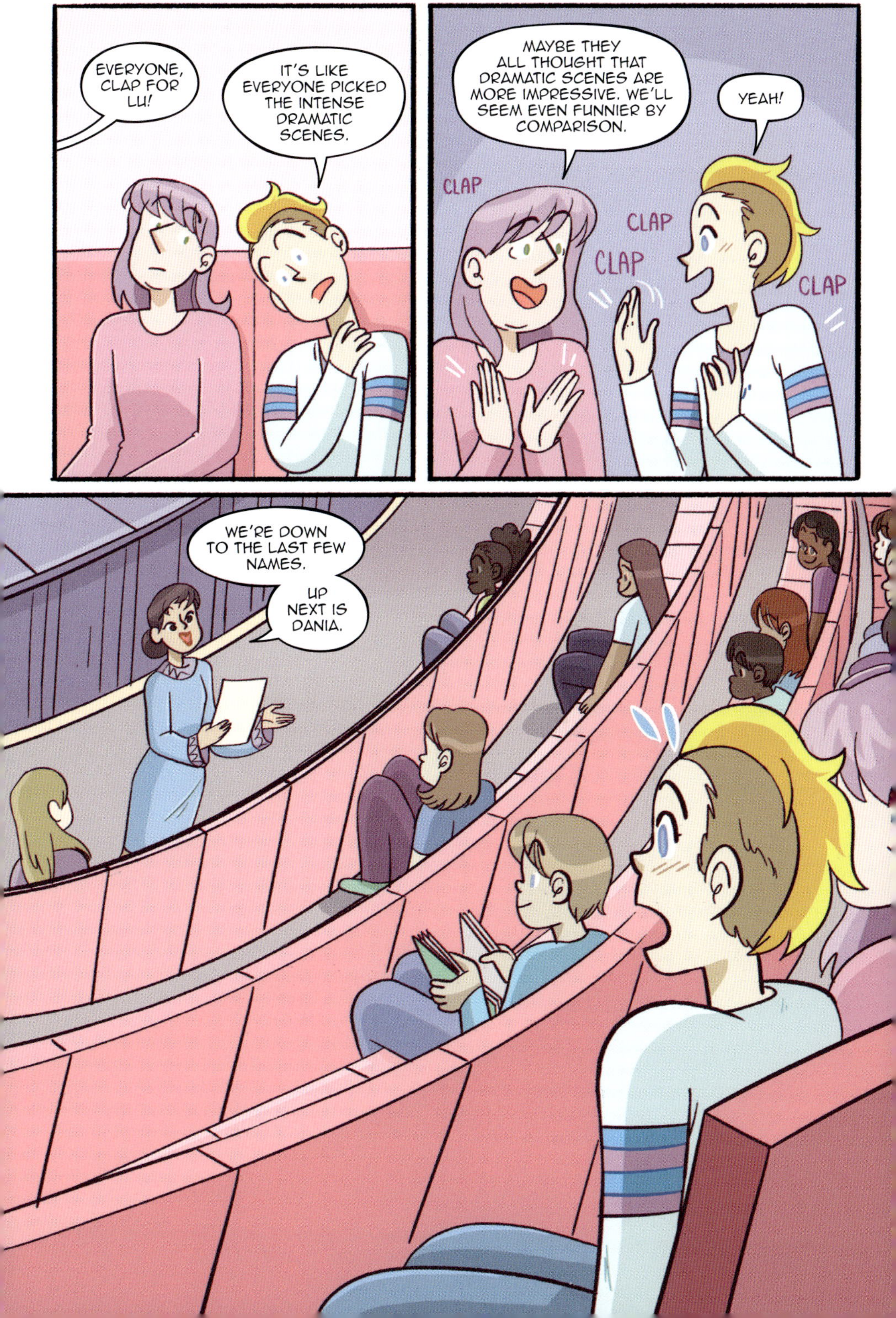
EVERYONE, CLAP FOR LU!
IT'S LIKE EVERYONE PICKED THE INTENSE DRAMATIC SCENES.
MAYBE THEY ALL THOUGHT THAT DRAMATIC SCENES ARE MORE IMPRESSIVE. WE'LL SEEM EVEN FUNNIER BY COMPARISON.
YEAH!
CLAP
CLAP
CLAP
CLAP
WE'RE DOWN TO THE LAST FEW NAMES.
UP NEXT IS DANIA.

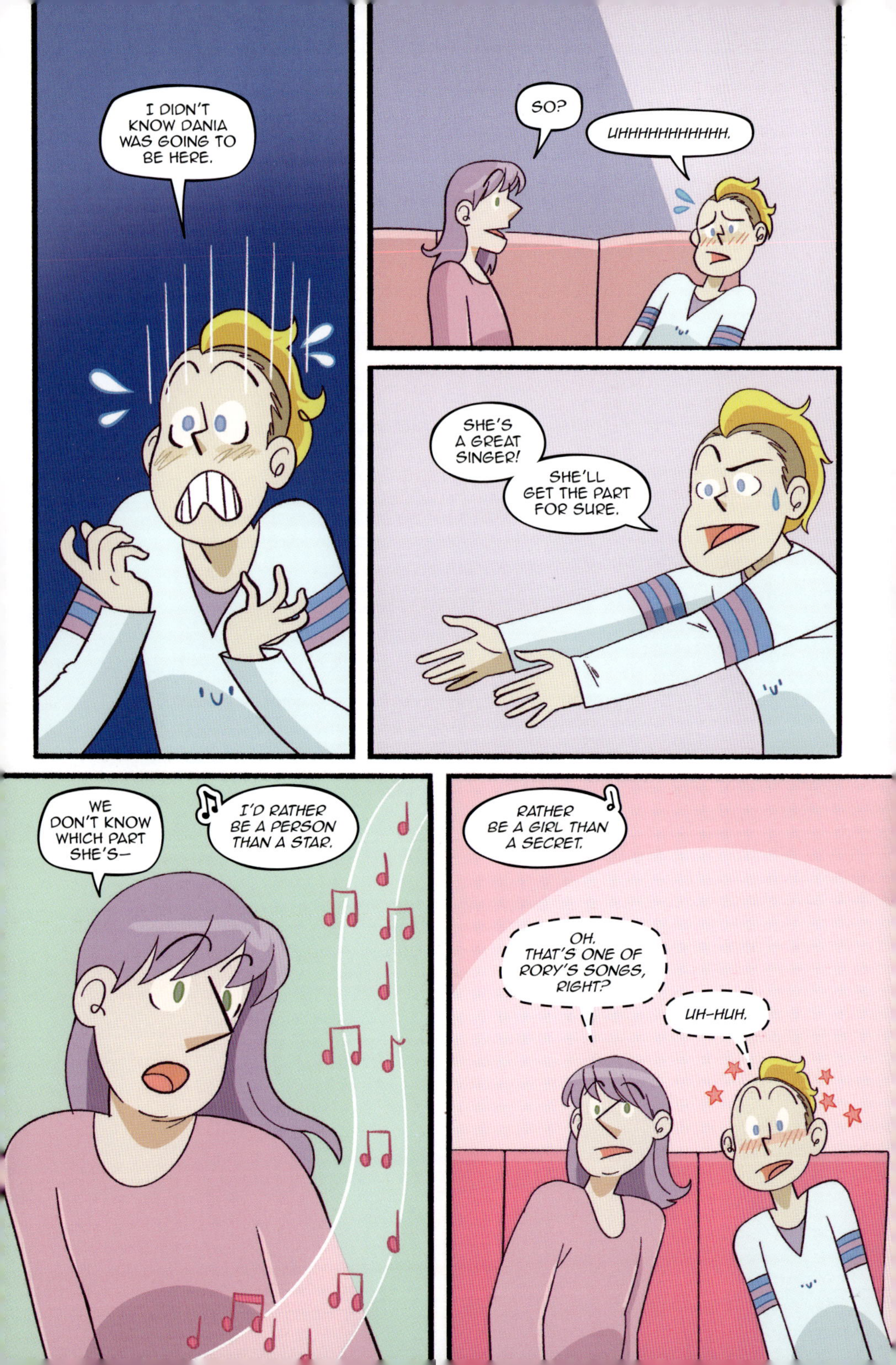

I DIDN'T KNOW DANIA WAS GOING TO BE HERE.
SO?
UHHHHHHHHHHH.
SHE'S A GREAT SINGER!
SHE'LL GET THE PART FOR SURE.
WE DON'T KNOW WHICH PART SHE'S—
I'D RATHER BE A PERSON THAN A STAR.
RATHER BE A GIRL THAN A SECRET.
OH. THAT'S ONE OF RORY'S SONGS, RIGHT?
UH-HUH.

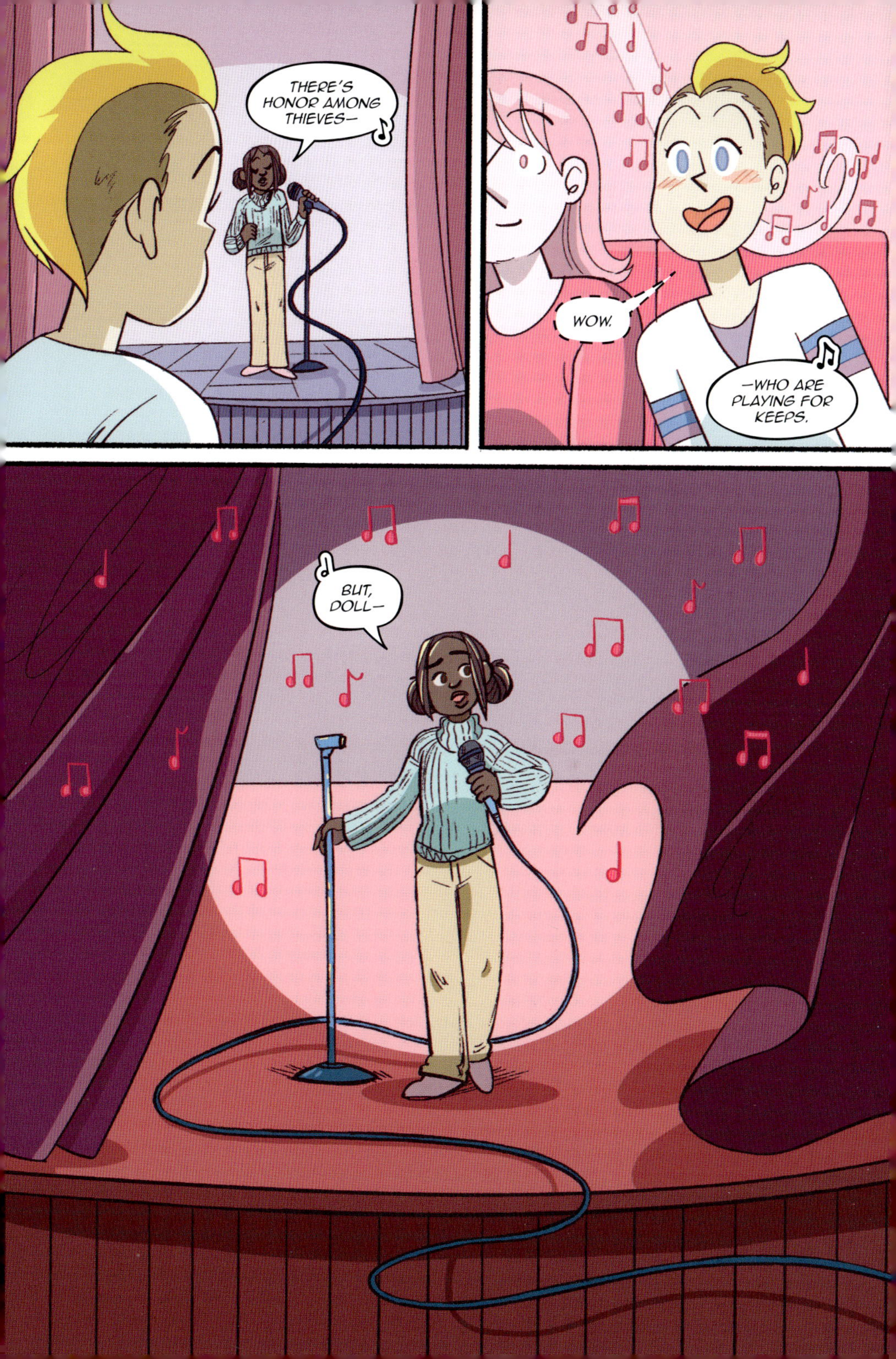
THERE'S HONOR AMONG THIEVES—
WOW.
—WHO ARE PLAYING FOR KEEPS.
BUT, DOLL—

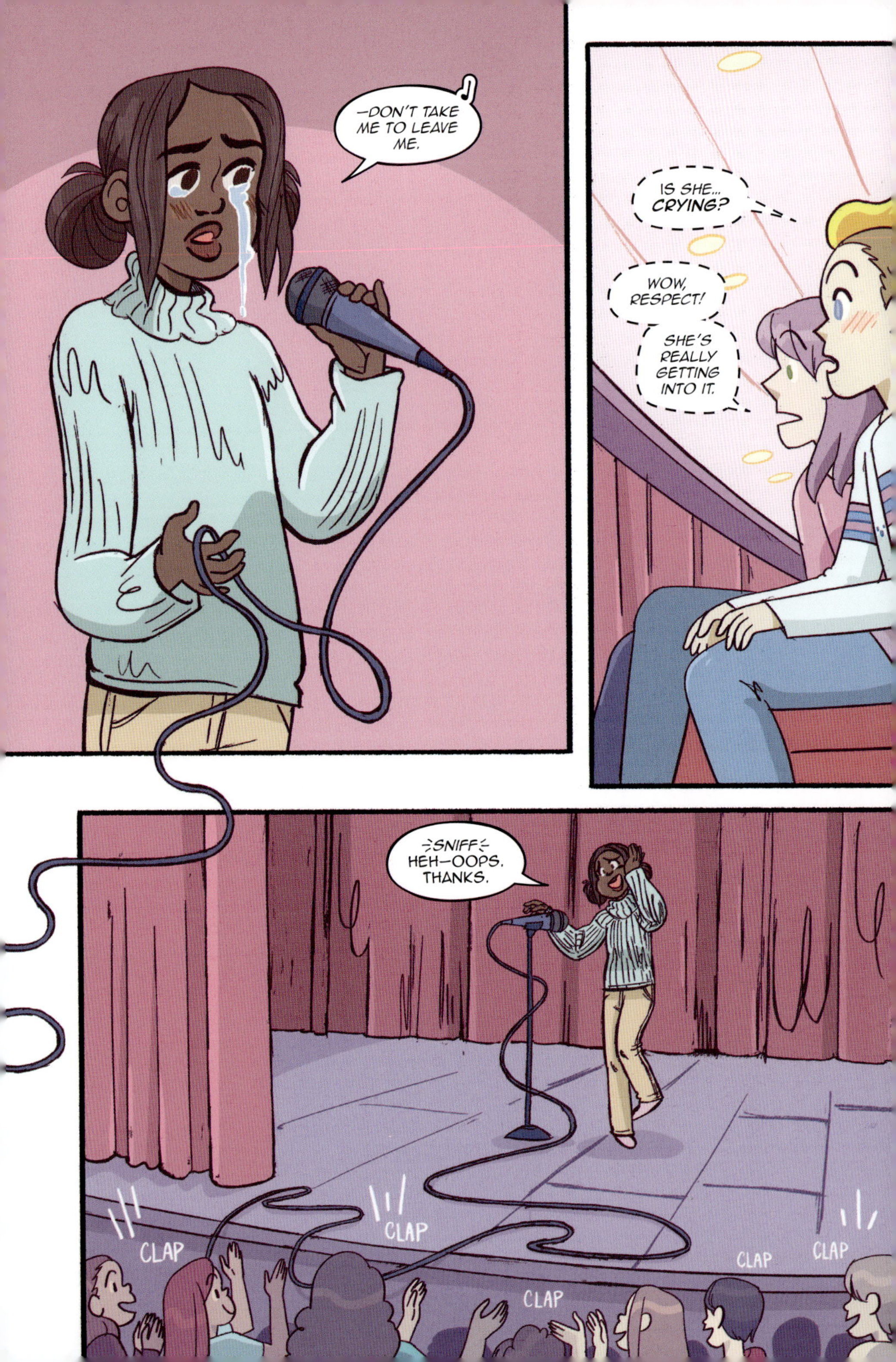
—DON'T TAKE ME TO LEAVE ME.
IS SHE... CRYING?
WOW, RESPECT!
SHE'S REALLY GETTING INTO IT.
SNIFF HEH—OOPS. THANKS.
CLAP
CLAP
CLAP
CLAP
CLAP

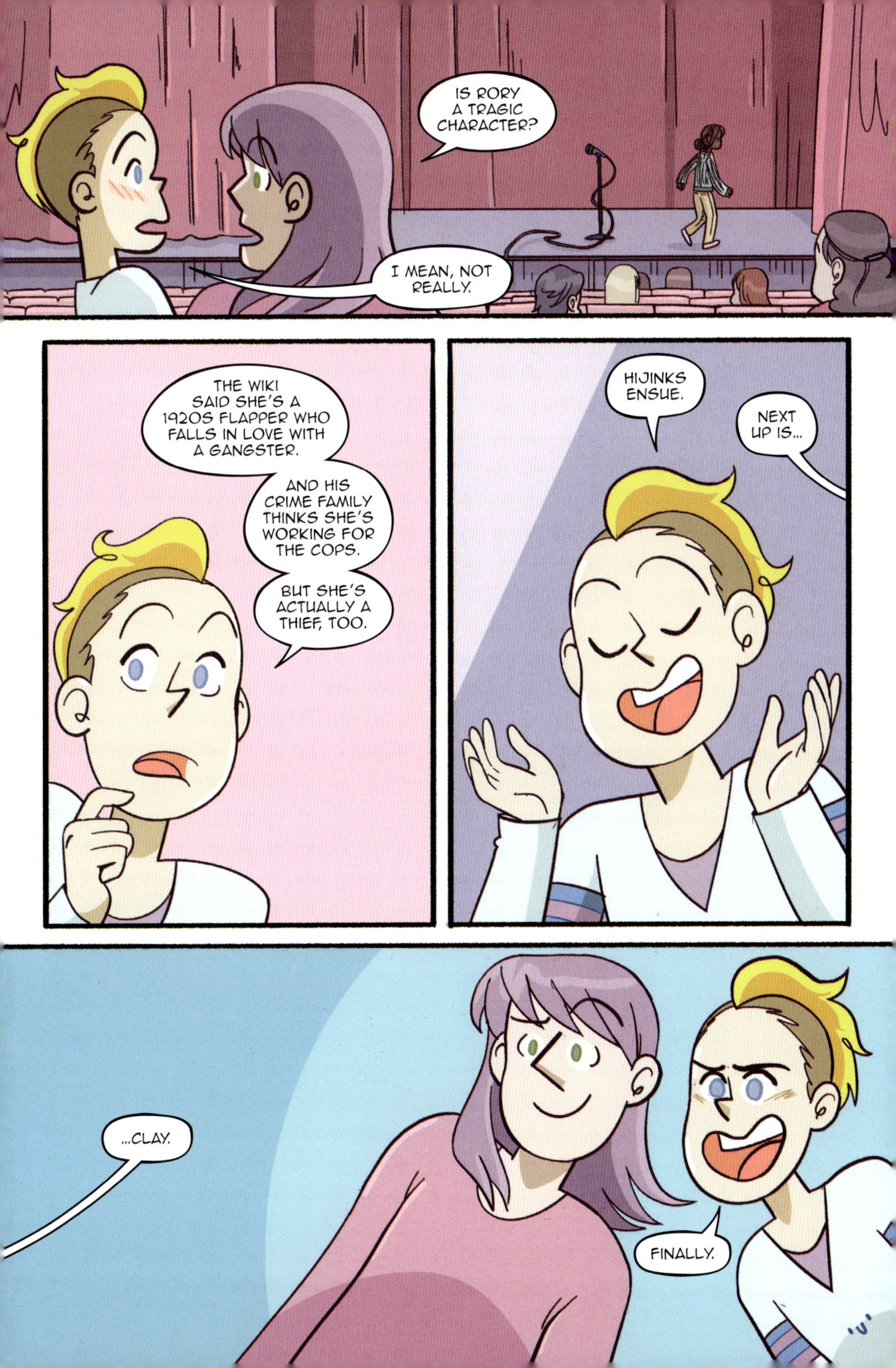
IS RORY A TRAGIC CHARACTER?
I MEAN, NOT REALLY.
THE WIKI SAID SHE'S A 1920S FLAPPER WHO FALLS IN LOVE WITH A GANGSTER.
AND HIS CRIME FAMILY THINKS SHE'S WORKING FOR THE COPS.
BUT SHE'S ACTUALLY A THIEF, TOO.
HIJINKS ENSUE.
NEXT UP IS...
...CLAY.
FINALLY.

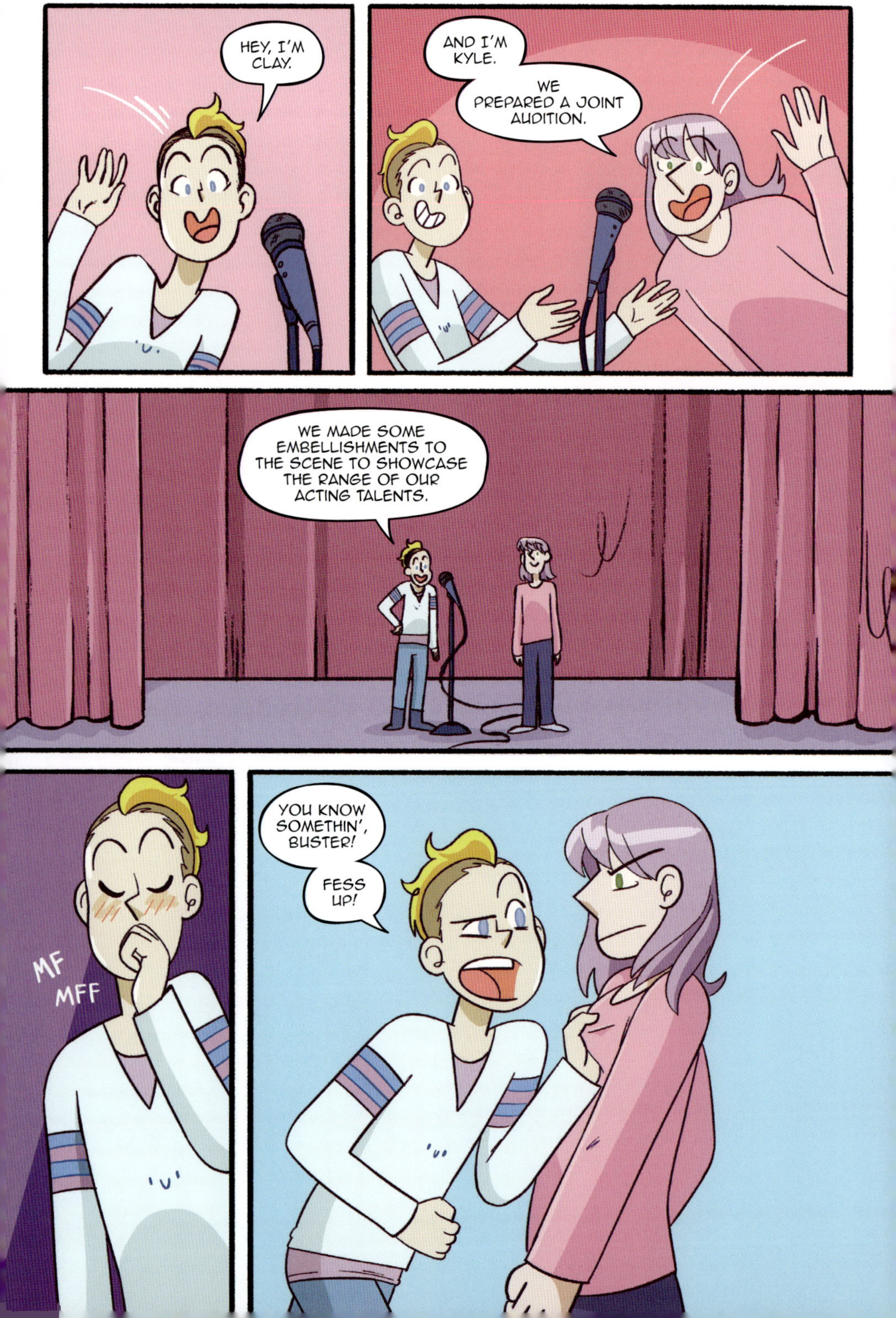
HEY, I'M CLAY.
AND I'M KYLE.
WE PREPARED A JOINT AUDITION.
WE MADE SOME EMBELLISHMENTS TO THE SCENE TO SHOWCASE THE RANGE OF OUR ACTING TALENTS.
MF MFF
YOU KNOW SOMETHIN', BUSTER!
FESS UP!

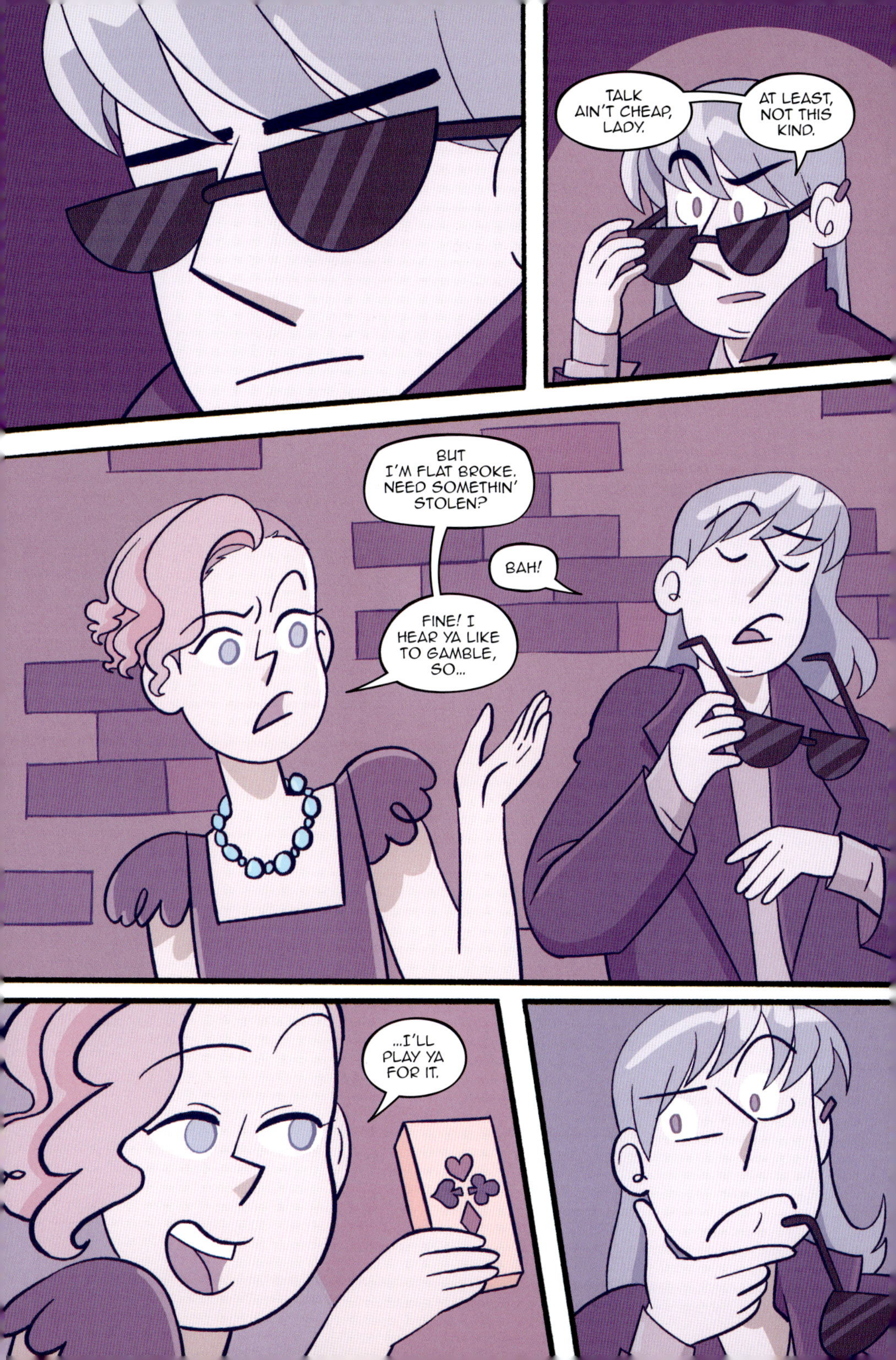
TALK AIN'T CHEAP, LADY.
AT LEAST, NOT THIS KIND.
BUT I'M FLAT BROKE. NEED SOMETHIN' STOLEN?
BAH!
FINE! I HEAR YA LIKE TO GAMBLE, SO...
...I'LL PLAY YA FOR IT.

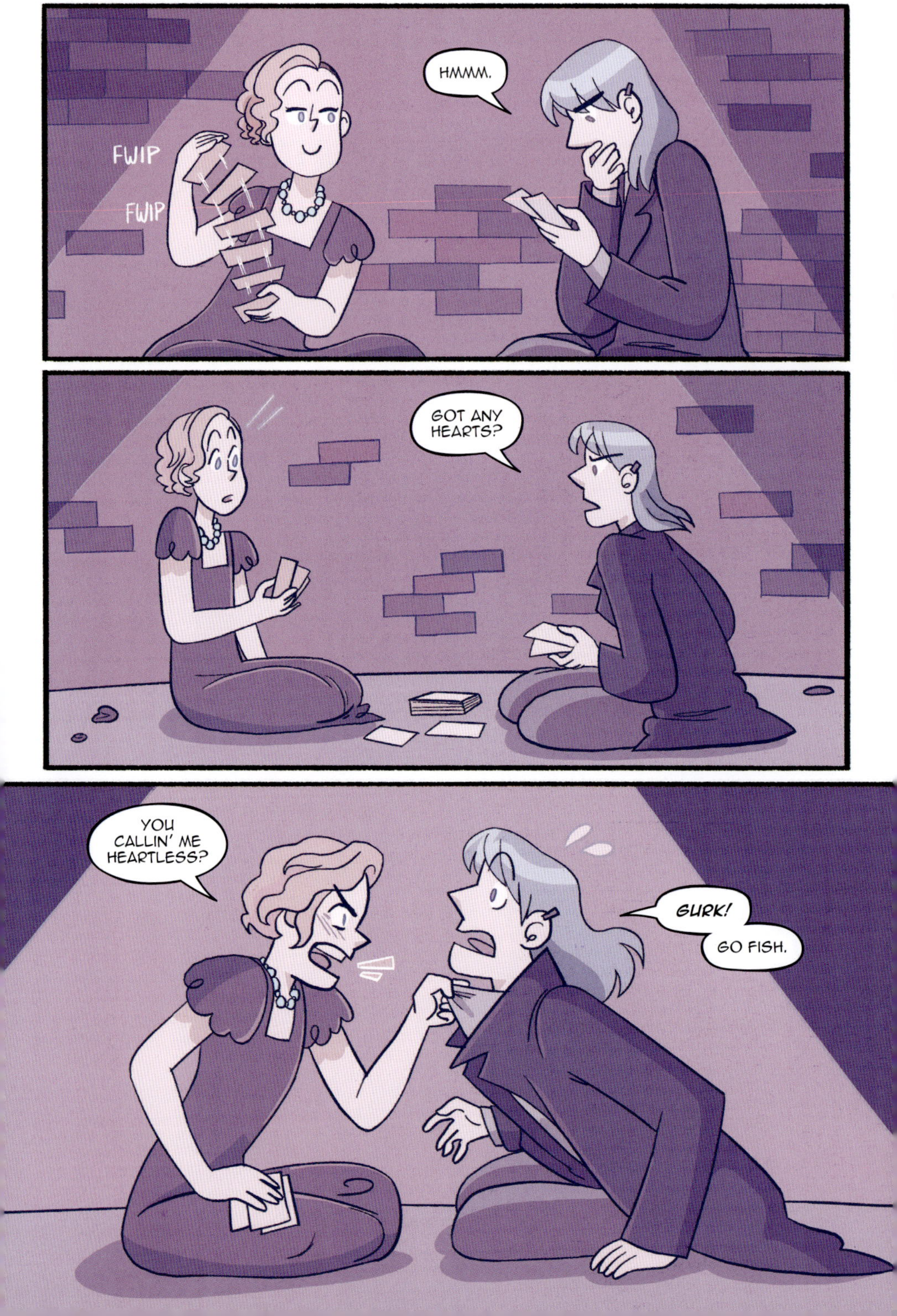
HMMM.
FWIP
FWIP
GOT ANY HEARTS?
YOU CALLIN' ME HEARTLESS?
GURK!
GO FISH.

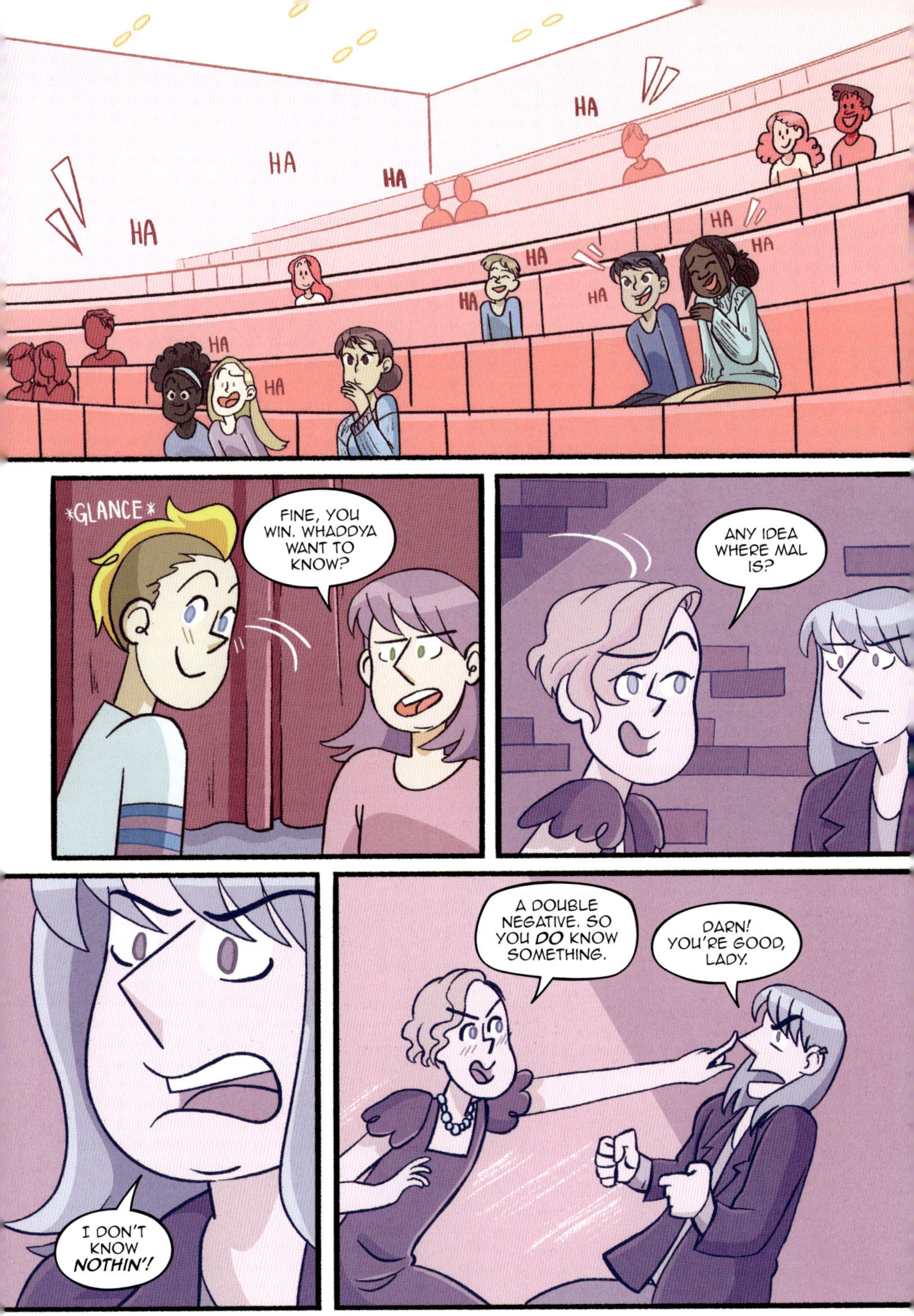
HA
HA
HA
HA
HA
HA
HA
HA
HA
HA
HA
GLANCE
FINE, YOU WIN. WHADDYA WANT TO KNOW?
ANY IDEA WHERE MAL IS?
I DON'T KNOW **NOTHIN'**!
A DOUBLE NEGATIVE. SO YOU **DO** KNOW SOMETHING.
DARN! YOU'RE GOOD, LADY.

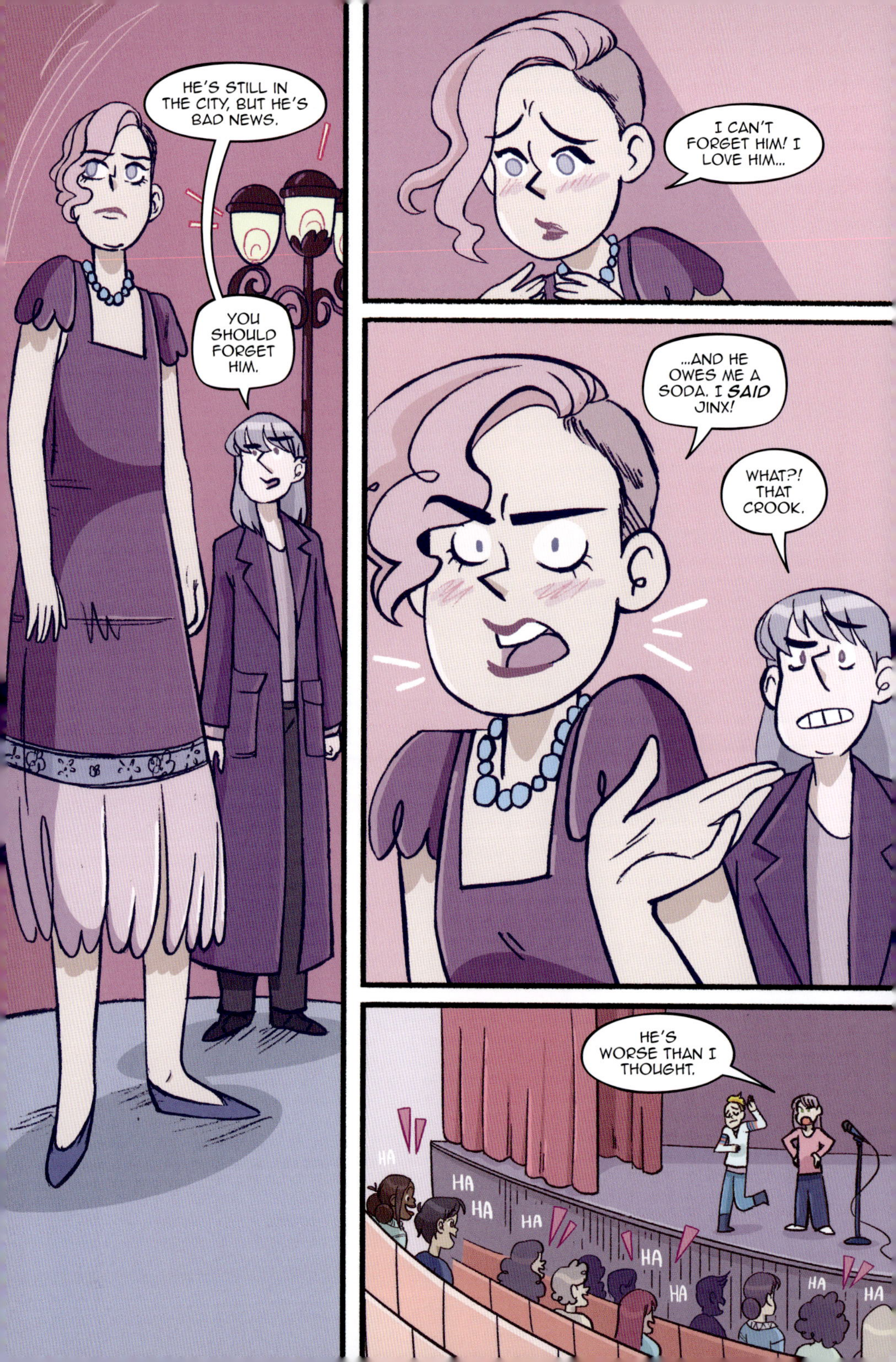
HE'S STILL IN THE CITY, BUT HE'S BAD NEWS.
YOU SHOULD FORGET HIM.
I CAN'T FORGET HIM! I LOVE HIM...
...AND HE OWES ME A SODA. I **SAID** JINX!
WHAT?! THAT CROOK.
HE'S WORSE THAN I THOUGHT.
HA
HA
HA
HA
HA
HA
HA
HA

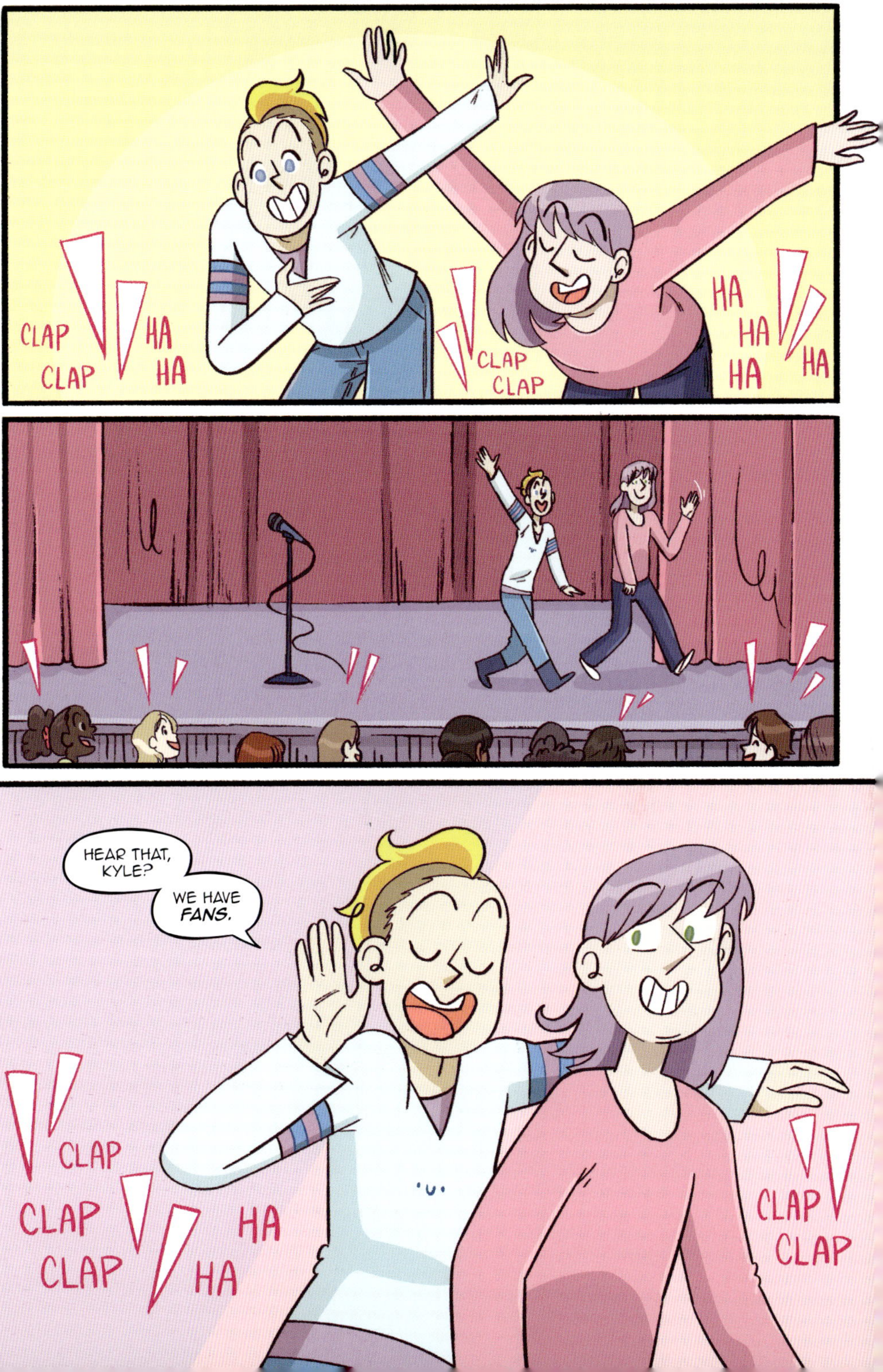
CLAP
CLAP
HA
HA
CLAP
CLAP
HA
HA
HA
HA
HEAR THAT, KYLE?
WE HAVE *FANS.*
CLAP
CLAP
CLAP
HA
HA
CLAP
CLAP

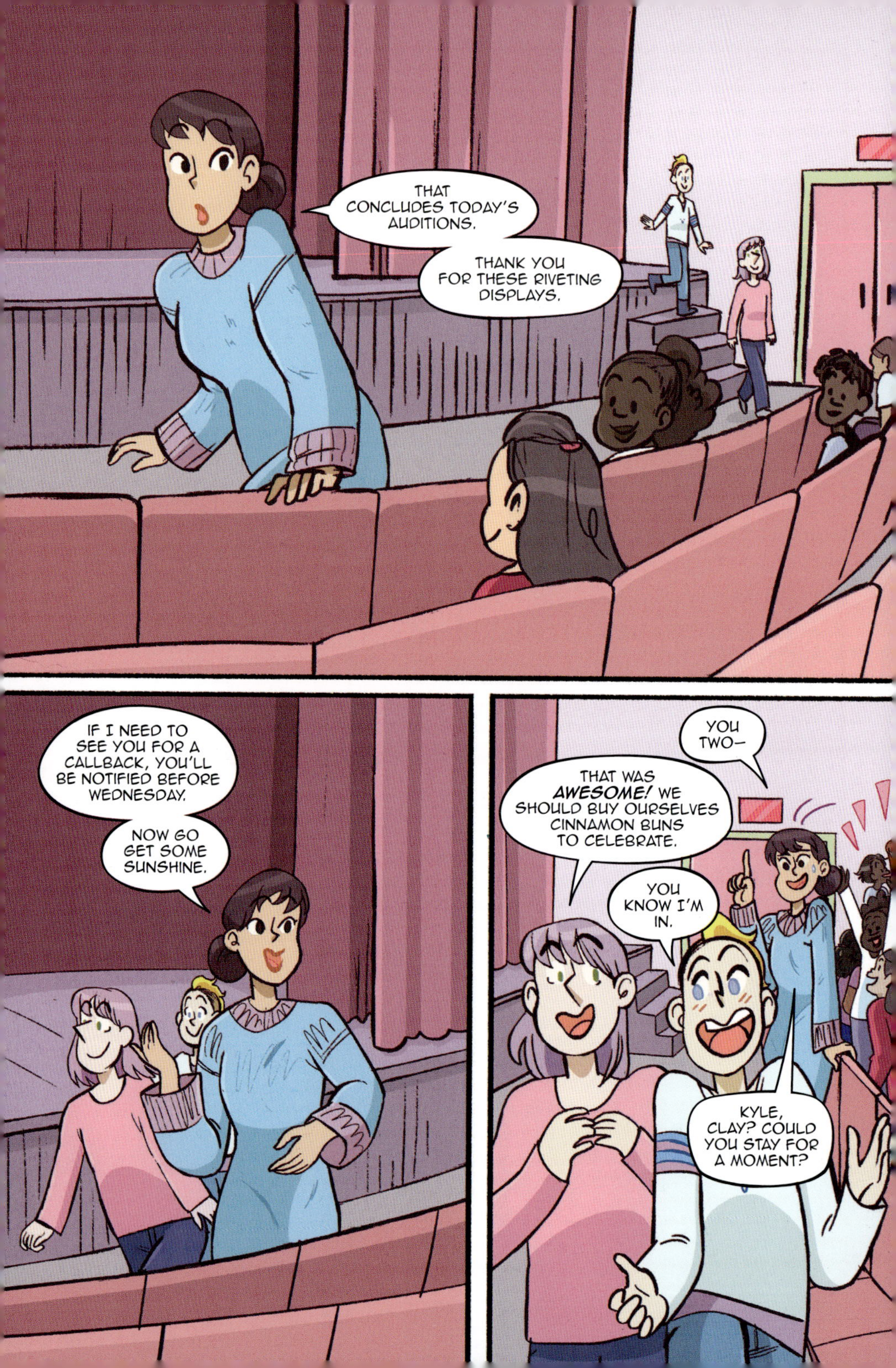
THAT CONCLUDES TODAY'S AUDITIONS.
THANK YOU FOR THESE RIVETING DISPLAYS.
IF I NEED TO SEE YOU FOR A CALLBACK, YOU'LL BE NOTIFIED BEFORE WEDNESDAY.
NOW GO GET SOME SUNSHINE.
YOU TWO—
THAT WAS *AWESOME!* WE SHOULD BUY OURSELVES CINNAMON BUNS TO CELEBRATE.
YOU KNOW I'M IN.
KYLE, CLAY? COULD YOU STAY FOR A MOMENT?

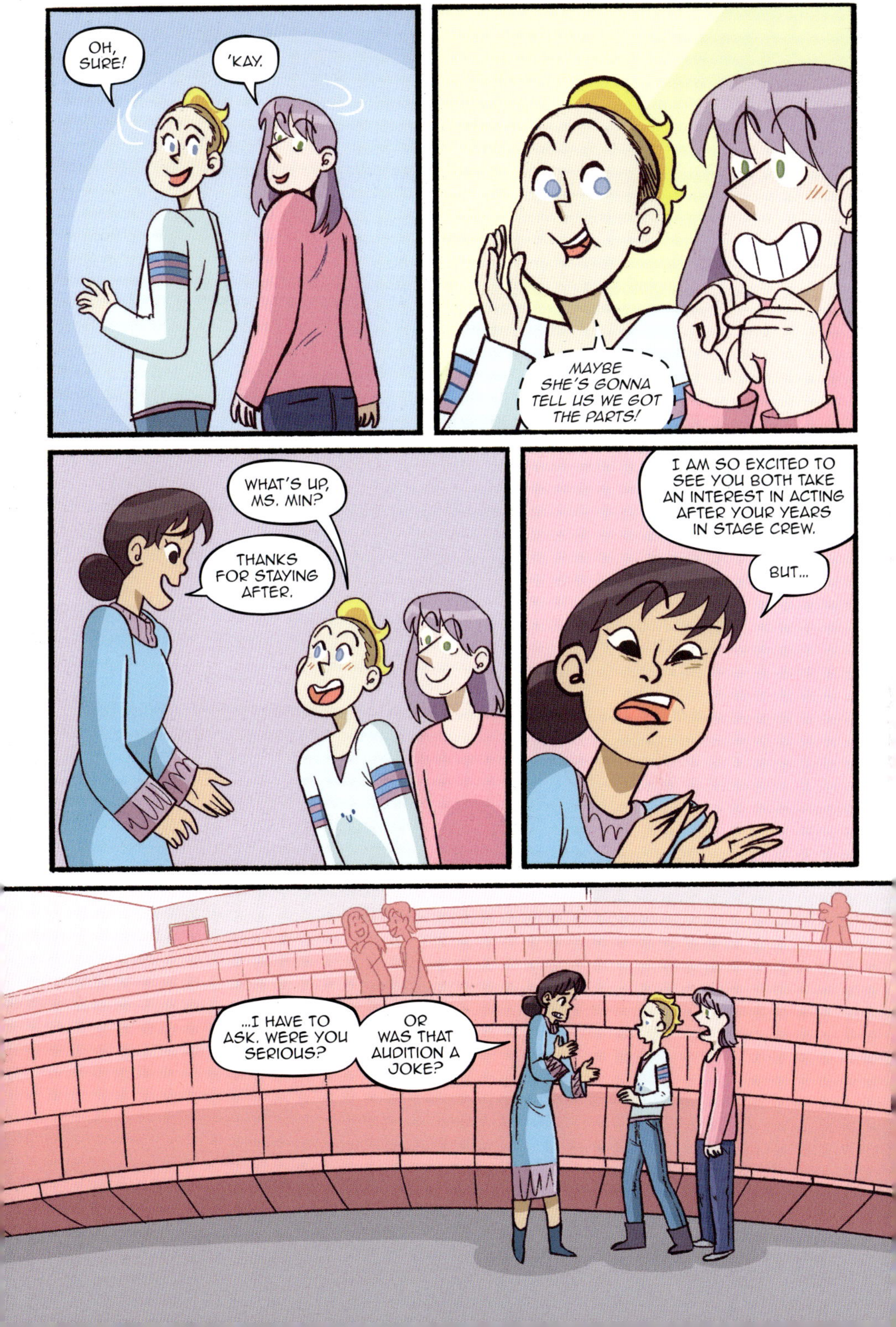
OH, SURE!
'KAY.
MAYBE SHE'S GONNA TELL US WE GOT THE PARTS!
WHAT'S UP, MS. MIN?
THANKS FOR STAYING AFTER.
I AM SO EXCITED TO SEE YOU BOTH TAKE AN INTEREST IN ACTING AFTER YOUR YEARS IN STAGE CREW.
BUT...
...I HAVE TO ASK. WERE YOU SERIOUS?
OR WAS THAT AUDITION A JOKE?

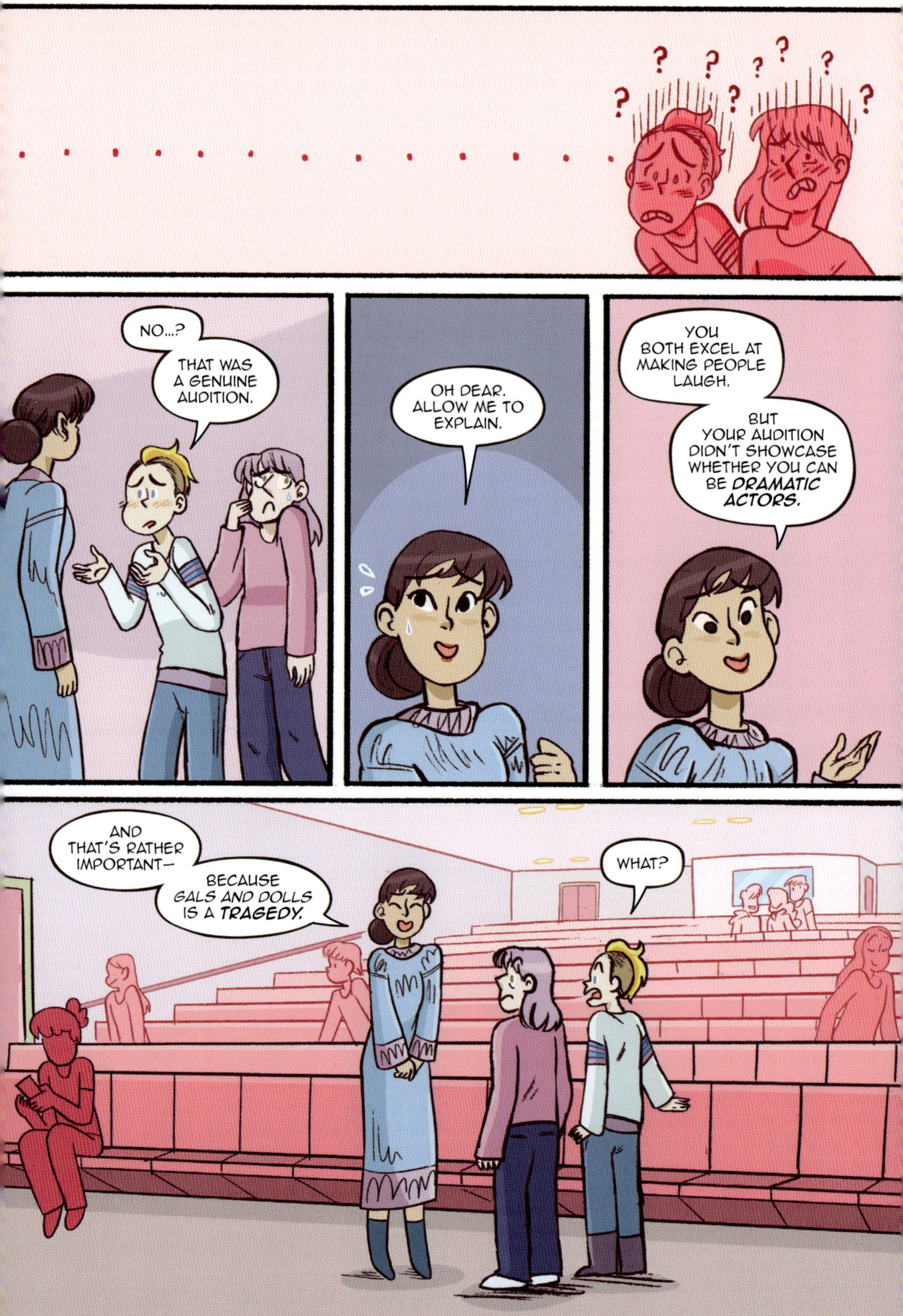

NO...?
THAT WAS A GENUINE AUDITION.
OH DEAR. ALLOW ME TO EXPLAIN.
YOU BOTH EXCEL AT MAKING PEOPLE LAUGH.
BUT YOUR AUDITION DIDN'T SHOWCASE WHETHER YOU CAN BE ***DRAMATIC ACTORS.***
AND THAT'S RATHER IMPORTANT—
BECAUSE *GALS AND DOLLS* IS A ***TRAGEDY.***
WHAT?

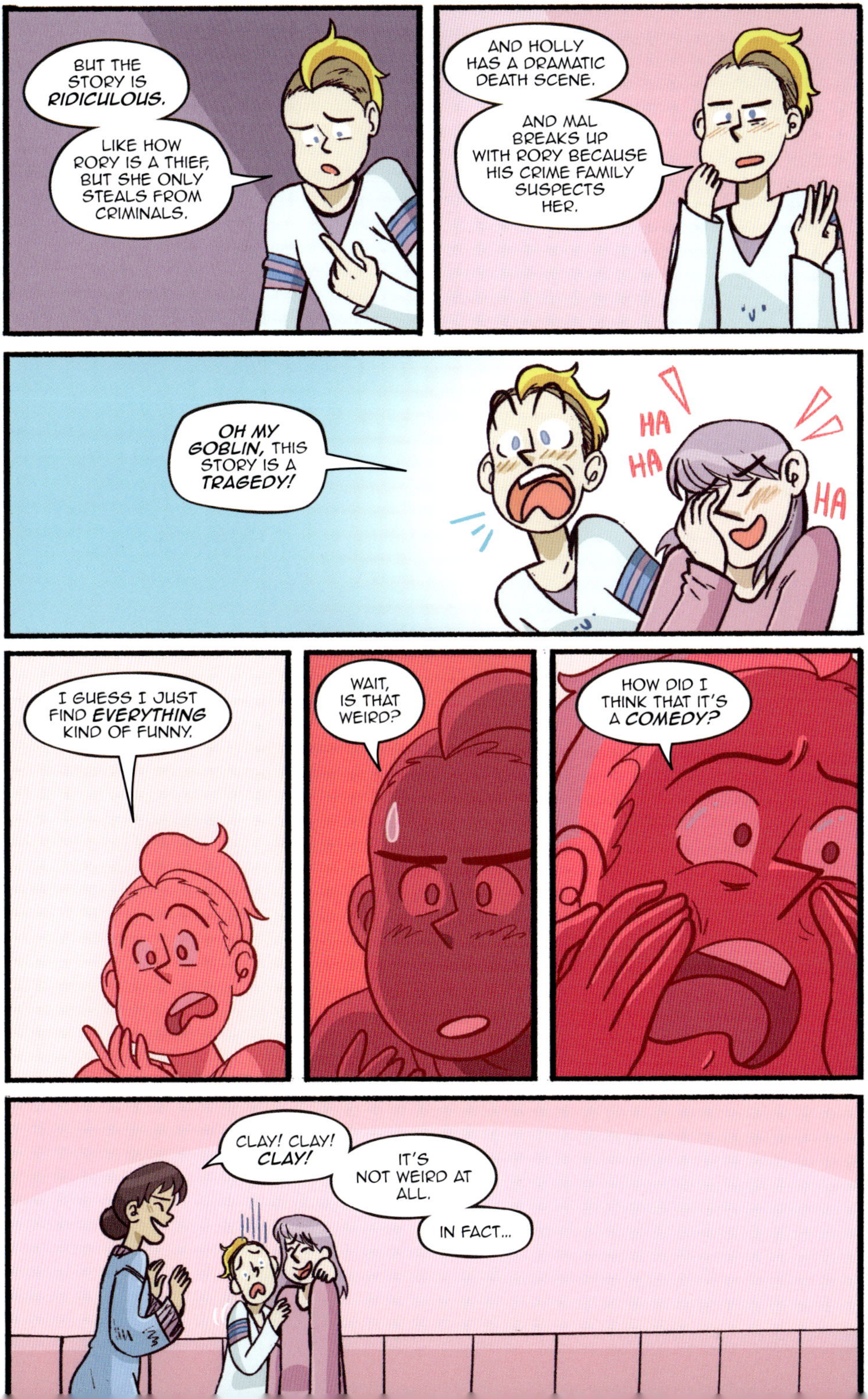
BUT THE STORY IS RIDICULOUS.
LIKE HOW RORY IS A THIEF, BUT SHE ONLY STEALS FROM CRIMINALS.
AND HOLLY HAS A DRAMATIC DEATH SCENE.
AND MAL BREAKS UP WITH RORY BECAUSE HIS CRIME FAMILY SUSPECTS HER.
OH MY GOBLIN, THIS STORY IS A TRAGEDY!
HA
HA
HA
I GUESS I JUST FIND EVERYTHING KIND OF FUNNY.
WAIT, IS THAT WEIRD?
HOW DID I THINK THAT IT'S A COMEDY?
CLAY! CLAY! CLAY!
IT'S NOT WEIRD AT ALL.
IN FACT...

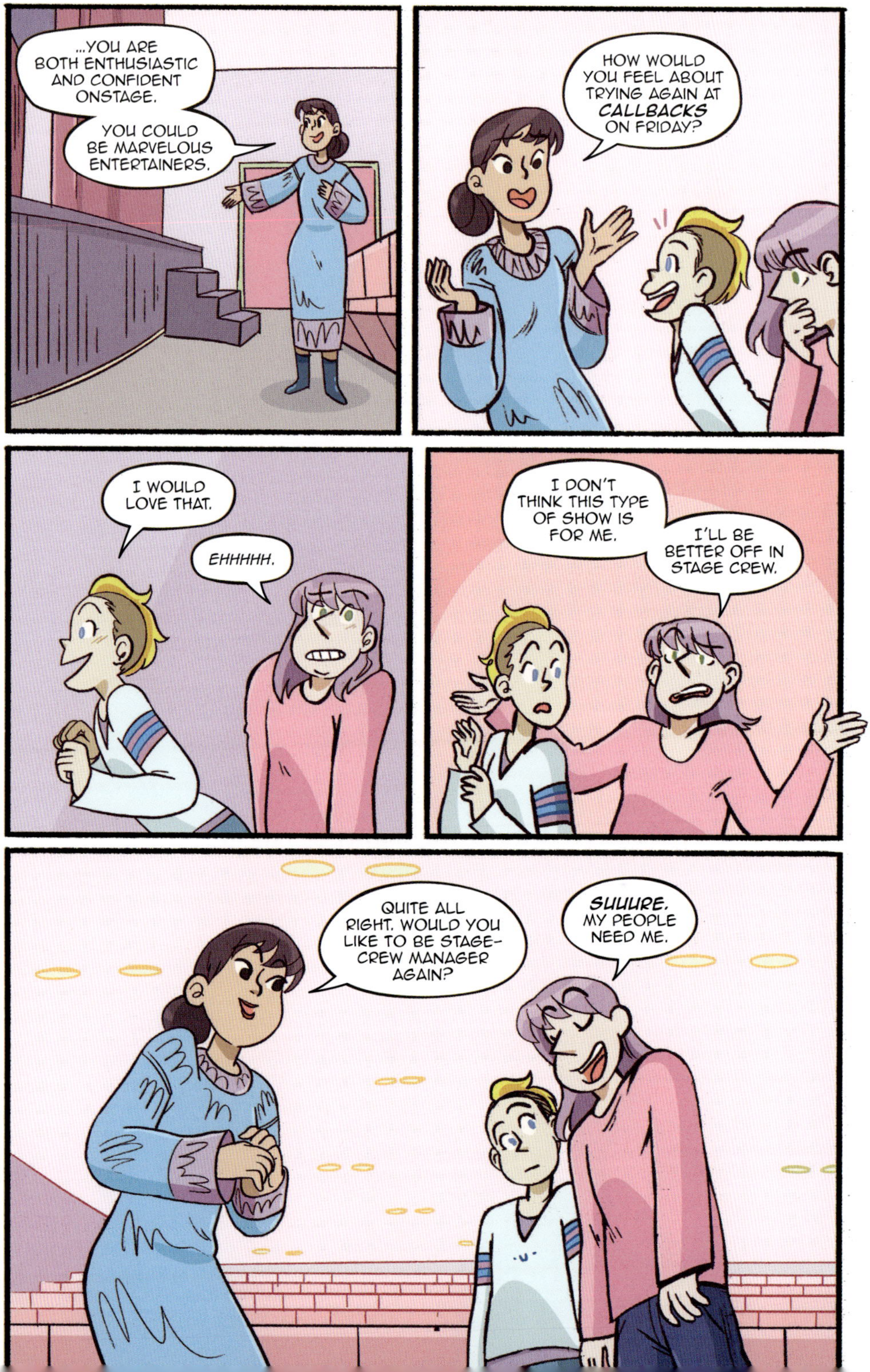

...YOU ARE BOTH ENTHUSIASTIC AND CONFIDENT ONSTAGE.
YOU COULD BE MARVELOUS ENTERTAINERS.
HOW WOULD YOU FEEL ABOUT TRYING AGAIN AT *CALLBACKS* ON FRIDAY?
I WOULD LOVE THAT.
EHHHHH.
I DON'T THINK THIS TYPE OF SHOW IS FOR ME.
I'LL BE BETTER OFF IN STAGE CREW.
QUITE ALL RIGHT. WOULD YOU LIKE TO BE STAGE-CREW MANAGER AGAIN?
SUUURE. MY PEOPLE NEED ME.

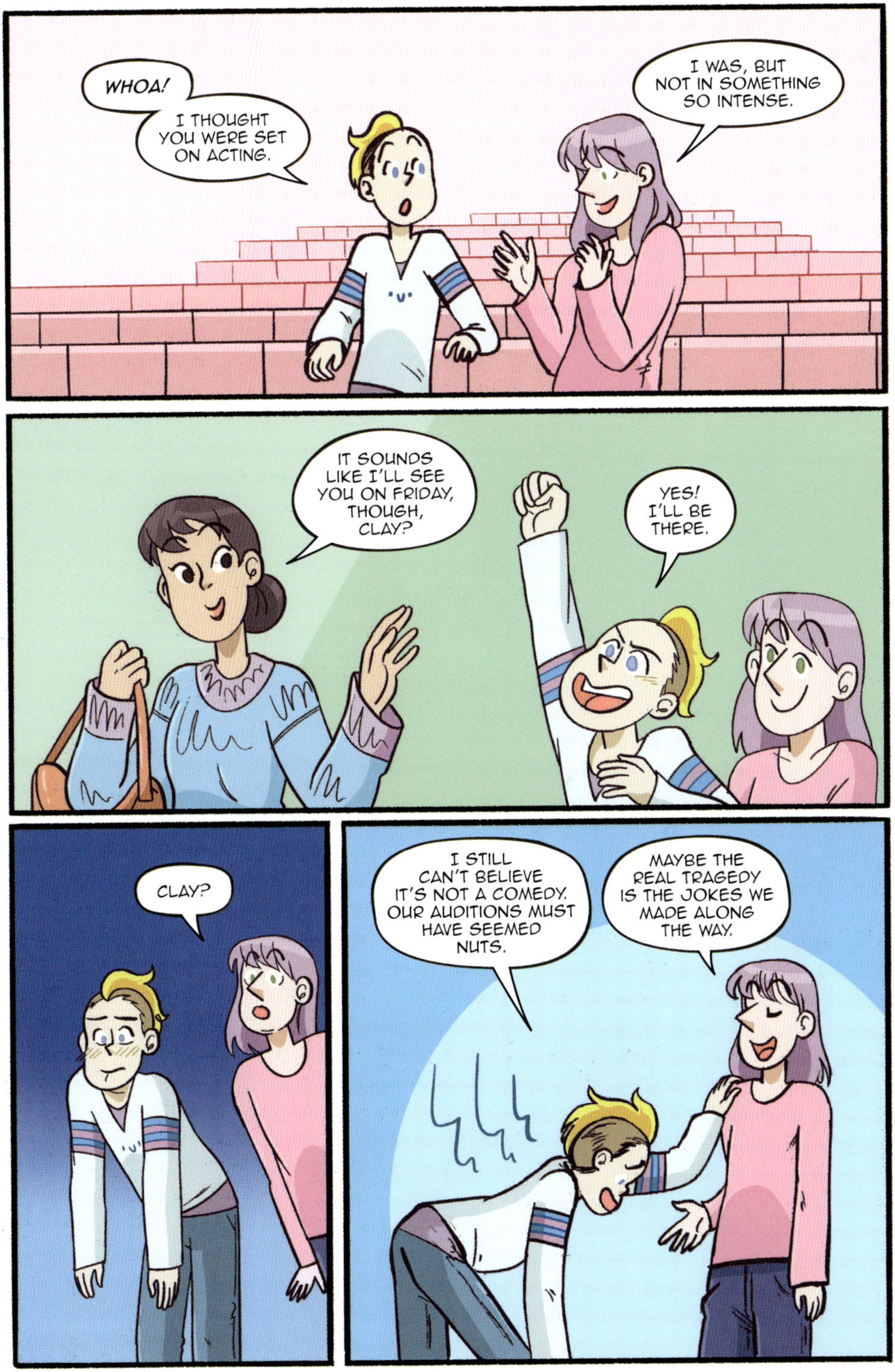
WHOA!
I THOUGHT YOU WERE SET ON ACTING.
I WAS, BUT NOT IN SOMETHING SO INTENSE.
IT SOUNDS LIKE I'LL SEE YOU ON FRIDAY, THOUGH, CLAY?
YES! I'LL BE THERE.
CLAY?
I STILL CAN'T BELIEVE IT'S NOT A COMEDY. OUR AUDITIONS MUST HAVE SEEMED NUTS.
MAYBE THE REAL TRAGEDY IS THE JOKES WE MADE ALONG THE WAY.

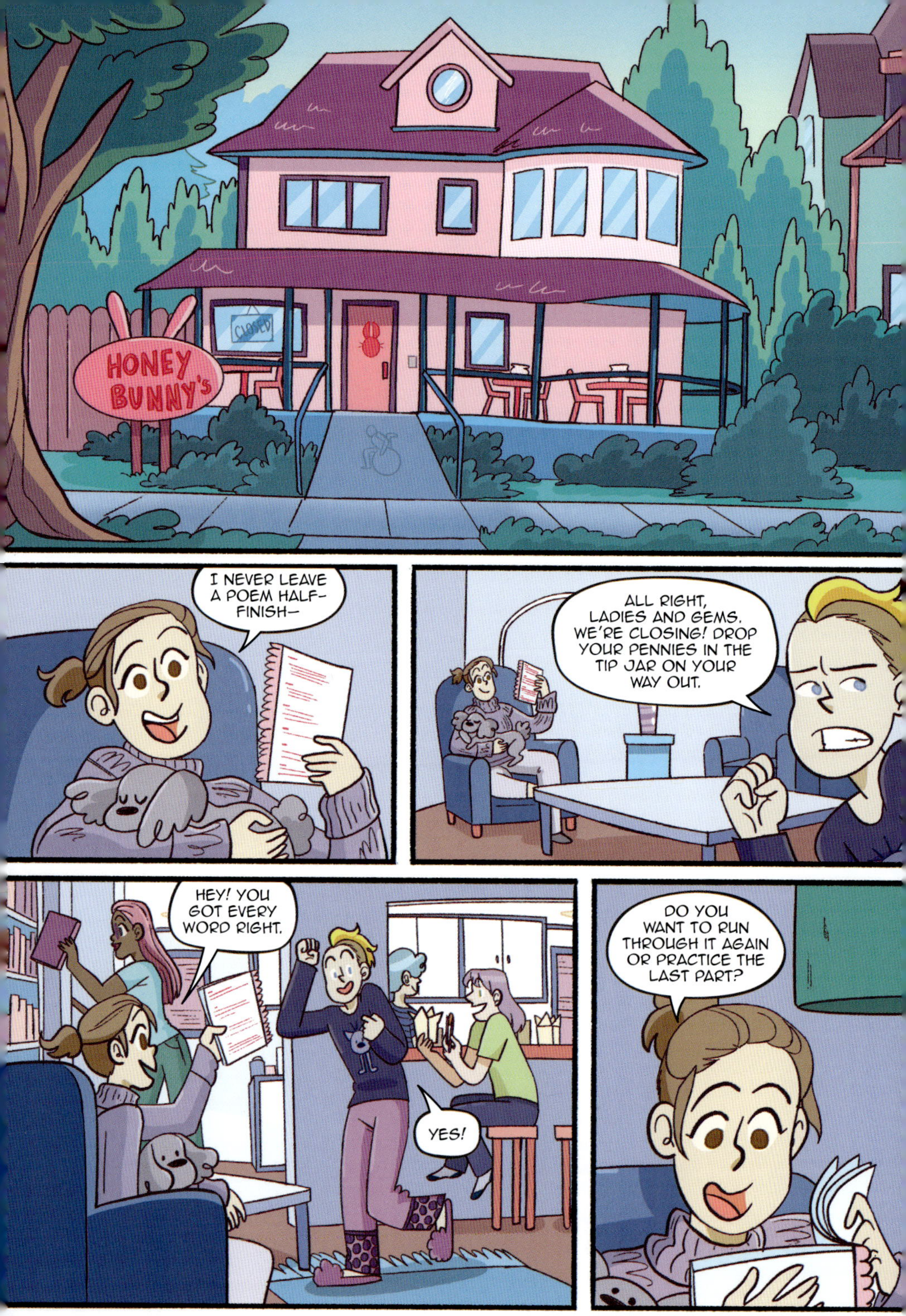
HONEY BUNNY'S
CLOSED
I NEVER LEAVE A POEM HALF-FINISH—
ALL RIGHT, LADIES AND GEMS. WE'RE CLOSING! DROP YOUR PENNIES IN THE TIP JAR ON YOUR WAY OUT.
HEY! YOU GOT EVERY WORD RIGHT.
YES!
DO YOU WANT TO RUN THROUGH IT AGAIN OR PRACTICE THE LAST PART?

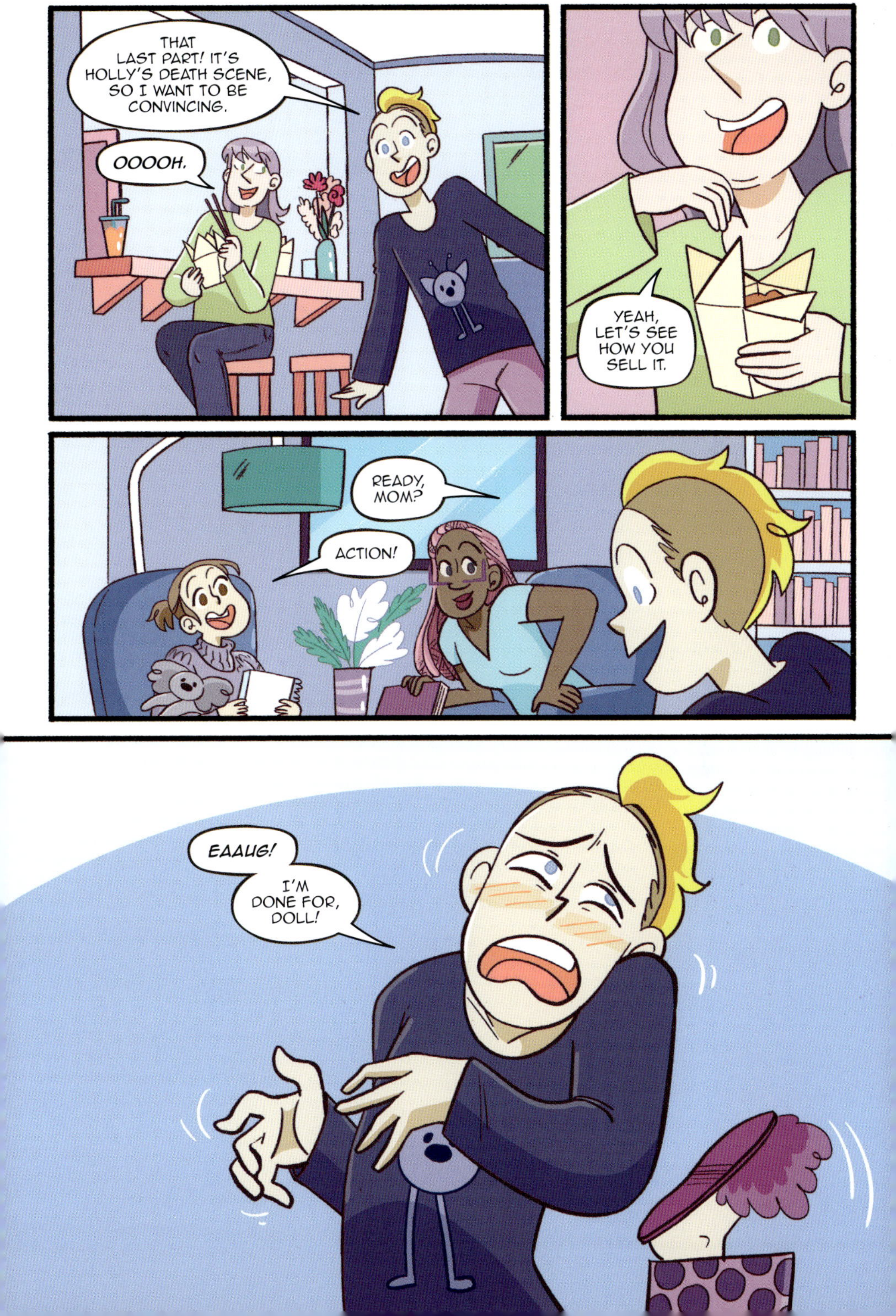
THAT LAST PART! IT'S HOLLY'S DEATH SCENE, SO I WANT TO BE CONVINCING.
OOOOH.
YEAH, LET'S SEE HOW YOU SELL IT.
READY, MOM?
ACTION!
EAAUG!
I'M DONE FOR, DOLL!

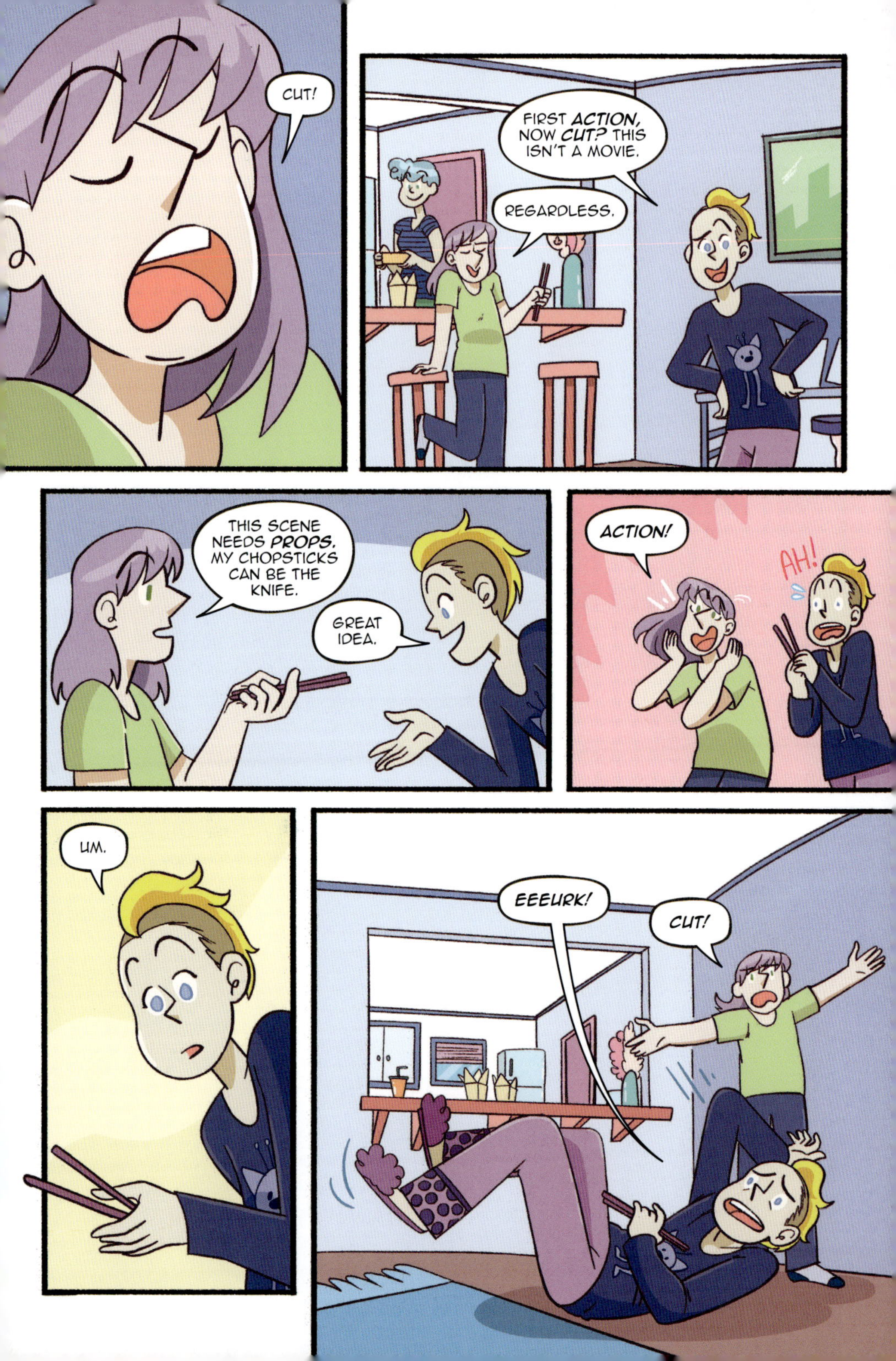
CUT!
FIRST ACTION, NOW CUT? THIS ISN'T A MOVIE.
REGARDLESS.
THIS SCENE NEEDS PROPS. MY CHOPSTICKS CAN BE THE KNIFE.
GREAT IDEA.
ACTION!
AH!
UM.
EEEURK!
CUT!

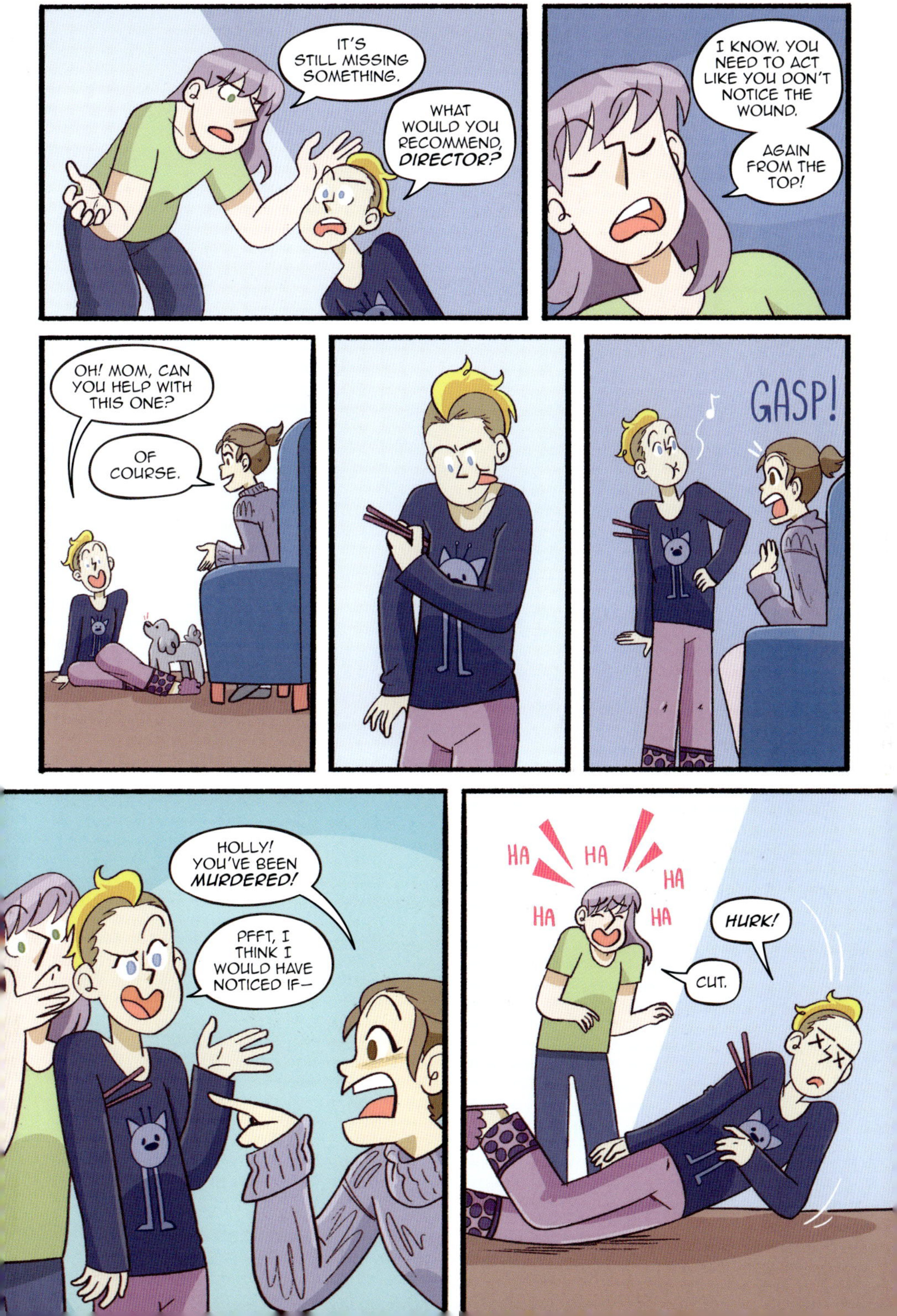
IT'S STILL MISSING SOMETHING.
WHAT WOULD YOU RECOMMEND, *DIRECTOR?*
I KNOW. YOU NEED TO ACT LIKE YOU DON'T NOTICE THE WOUND.
AGAIN FROM THE TOP!
OH! MOM, CAN YOU HELP WITH THIS ONE?
OF COURSE.
GASP!
HOLLY! YOU'VE BEEN *MURDERED!*
PFFT, I THINK I WOULD HAVE NOTICED IF—
HA HA HA HA HA
HURK!
CUT.

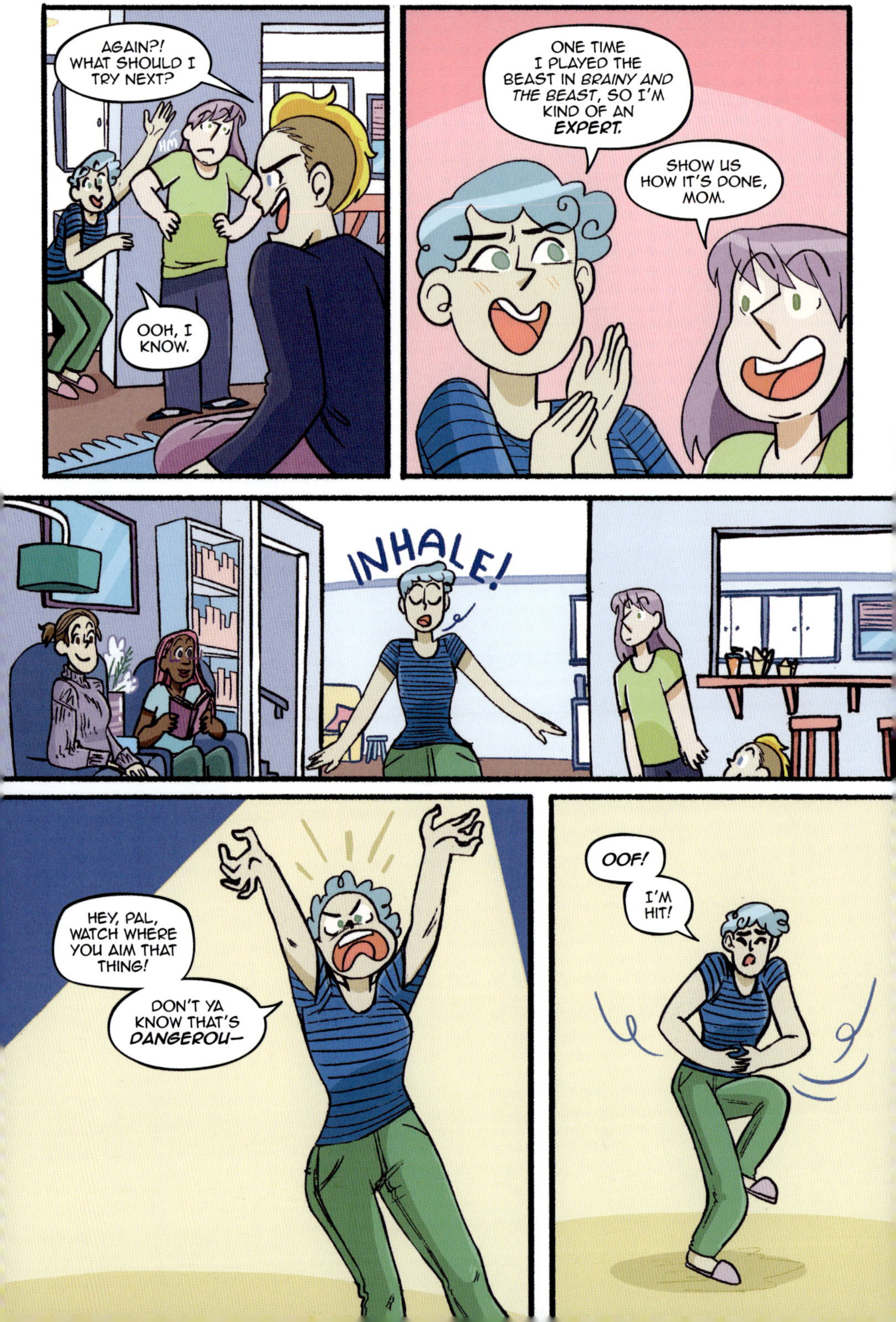
AGAIN?! WHAT SHOULD I TRY NEXT?
HM
OOH, I KNOW.
ONE TIME I PLAYED THE BEAST IN *BRAINY AND THE BEAST*, SO I'M KIND OF AN ***EXPERT.***
SHOW US HOW IT'S DONE, MOM.
INHALE!
HEY, PAL, WATCH WHERE YOU AIM THAT THING!
DON'T YA KNOW THAT'S ***DANGEROU—***
OOF!
I'M HIT!

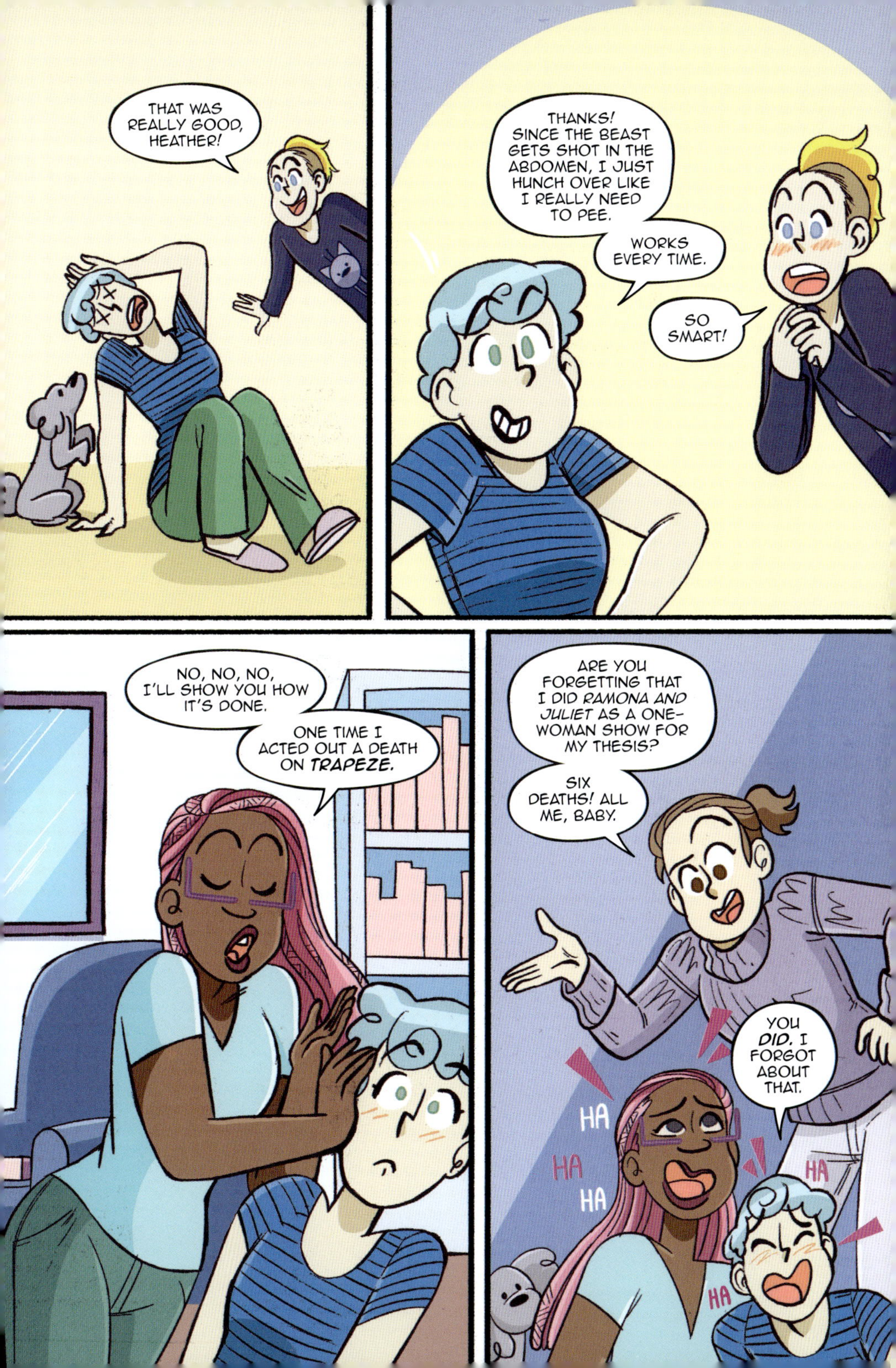
THAT WAS REALLY GOOD, HEATHER!
THANKS! SINCE THE BEAST GETS SHOT IN THE ABDOMEN, I JUST HUNCH OVER LIKE I REALLY NEED TO PEE.
WORKS EVERY TIME.
SO SMART!
NO, NO, NO, I'LL SHOW YOU HOW IT'S DONE.
ONE TIME I ACTED OUT A DEATH ON *TRAPEZE.*
ARE YOU FORGETTING THAT I DID *RAMONA AND JULIET* AS A ONE-WOMAN SHOW FOR MY THESIS?
SIX DEATHS! ALL ME, BABY.
YOU *DID.* I FORGOT ABOUT THAT.
HA
HA
HA
HA
HA

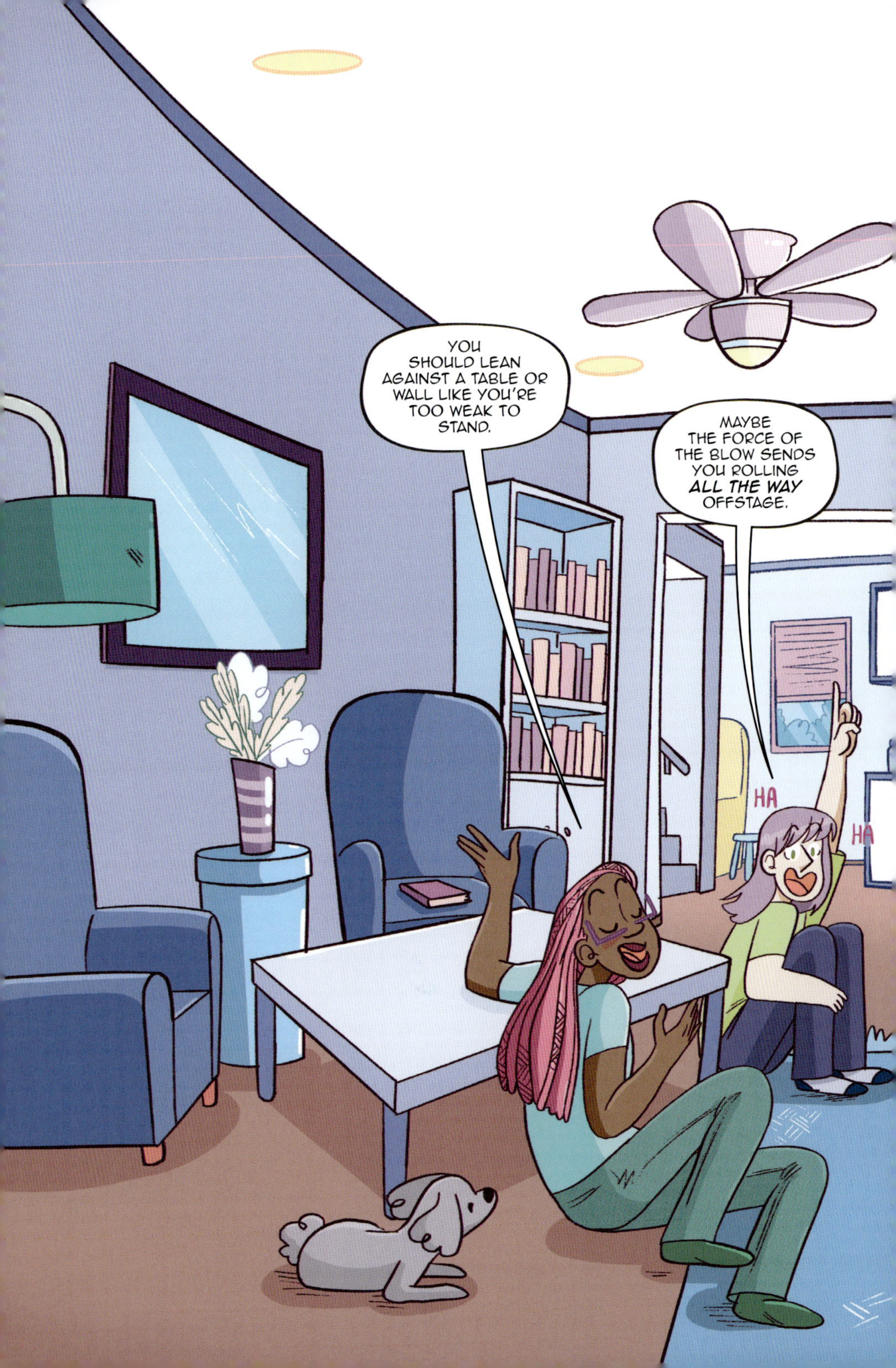
YOU SHOULD LEAN AGAINST A TABLE OR WALL LIKE YOU'RE TOO WEAK TO STAND.
MAYBE THE FORCE OF THE BLOW SENDS YOU ROLLING **ALL THE WAY** OFFSTAGE.
HA
HA

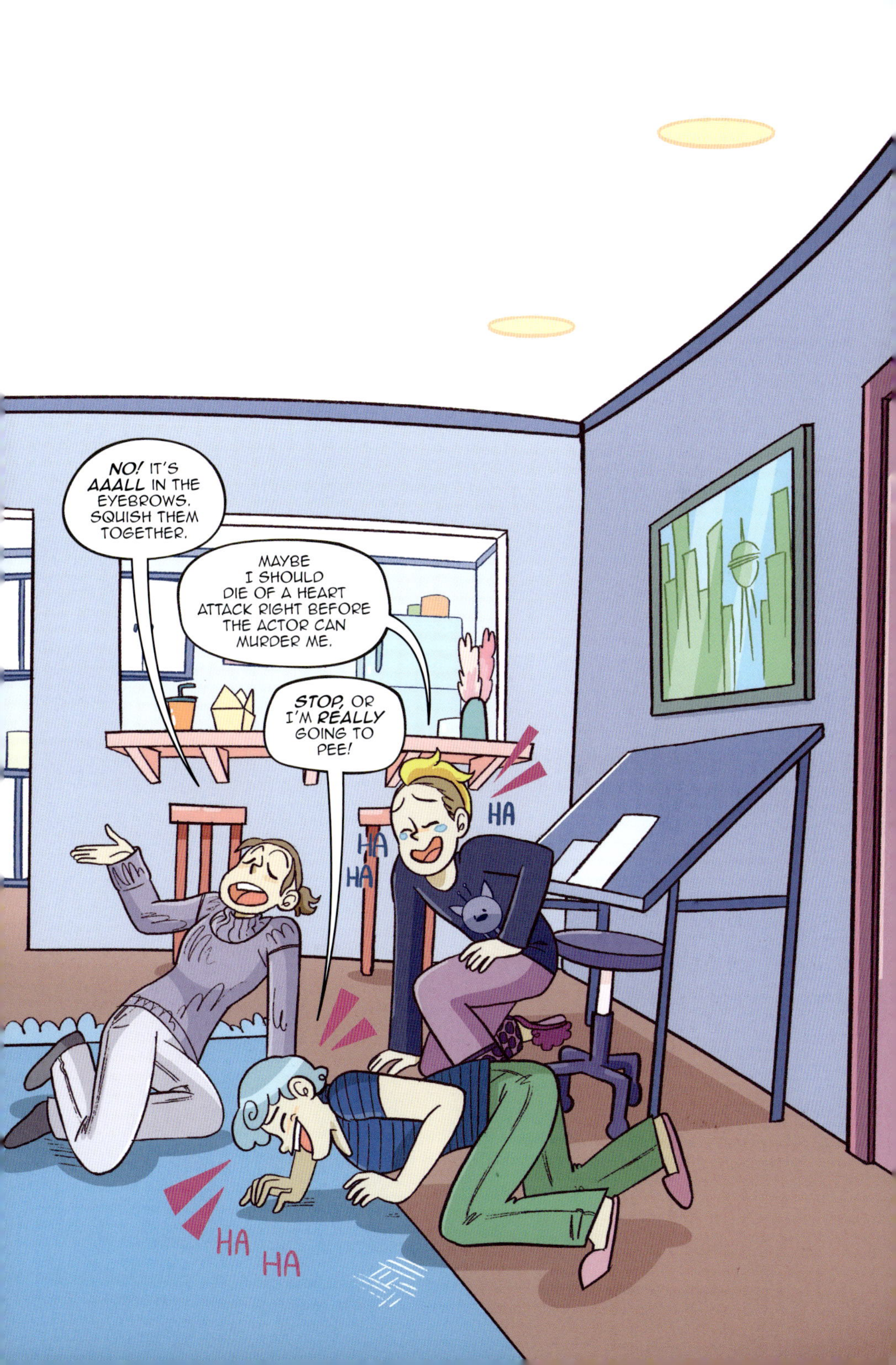

NO! IT'S AAALL IN THE EYEBROWS. SQUISH THEM TOGETHER.
MAYBE I SHOULD DIE OF A HEART ATTACK RIGHT BEFORE THE ACTOR CAN MURDER ME.
STOP, OR I'M REALLY GOING TO PEE!
HA
HA
HA
HA
HA

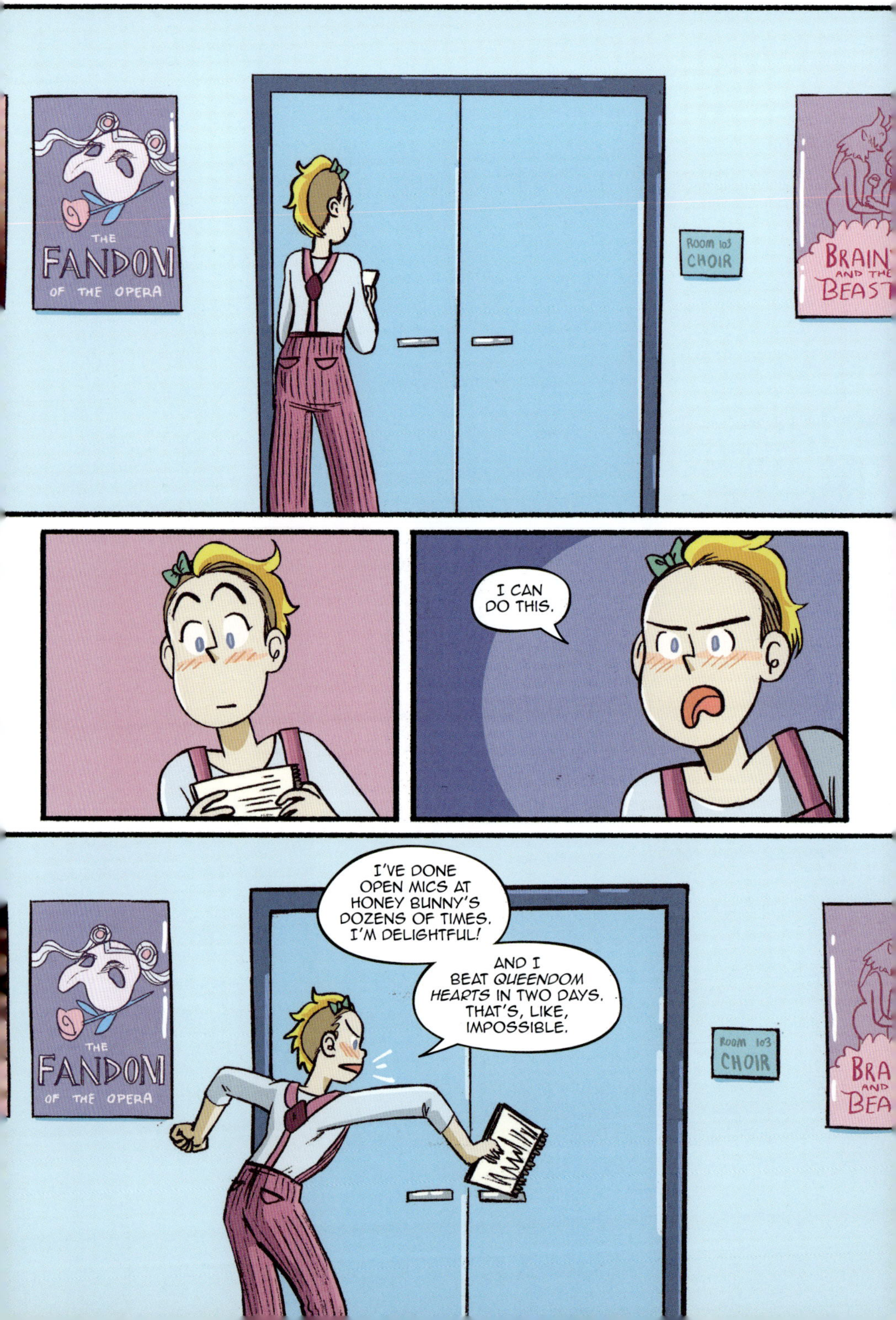
THE FANDOM OF THE OPERA
ROOM 103 CHOIR
BRAIN AND THE BEAST
I CAN DO THIS.
I'VE DONE OPEN MICS AT HONEY BUNNY'S DOZENS OF TIMES. I'M DELIGHTFUL!
AND I BEAT *QUEENDOM HEARTS* IN TWO DAYS. THAT'S, LIKE, IMPOSSIBLE.

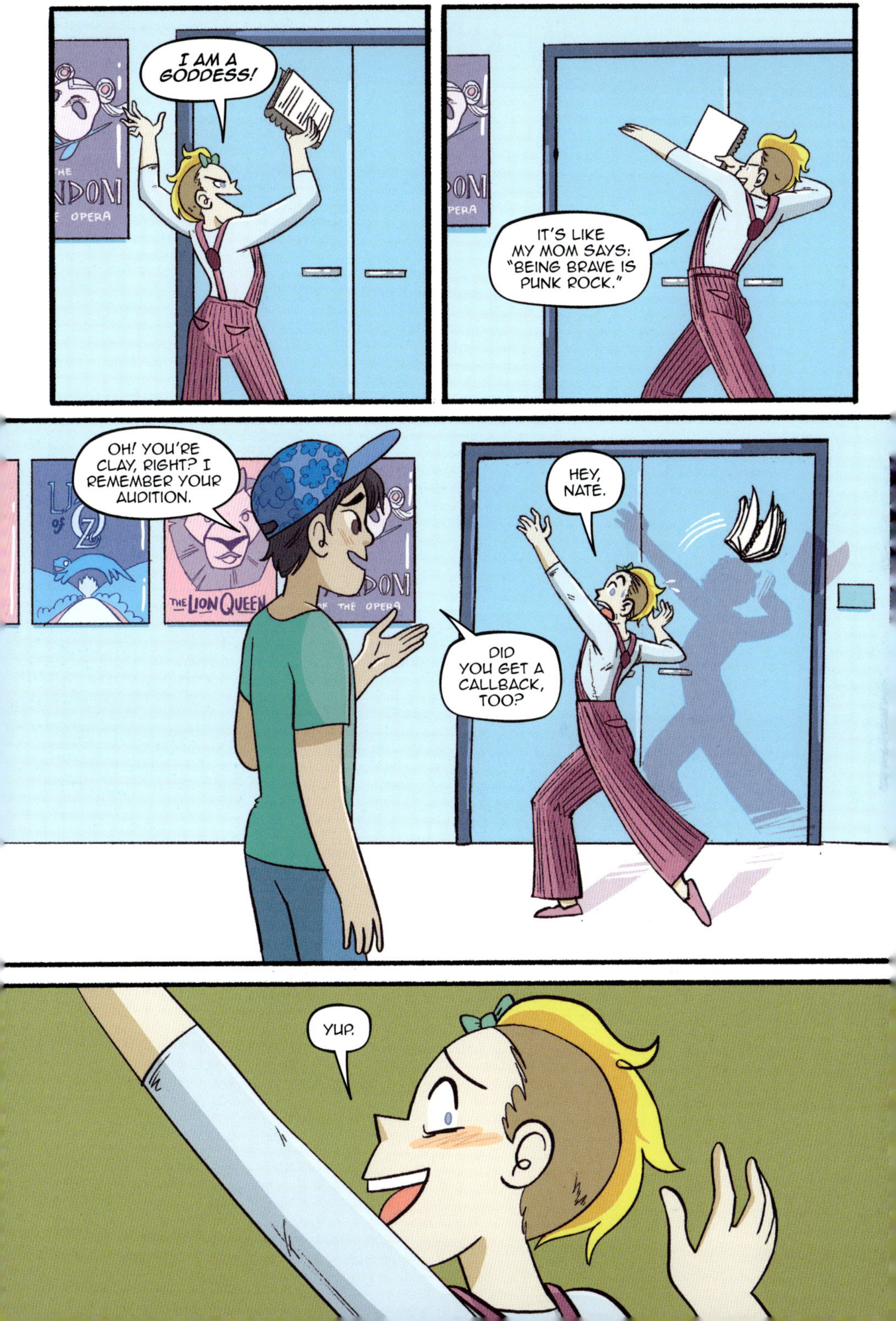
I AM A GODDESS!
IT'S LIKE MY MOM SAYS: "BEING BRAVE IS PUNK ROCK."
THE LION QUEEN
OF THE OPERA
OH! YOU'RE CLAY, RIGHT? I REMEMBER YOUR AUDITION.
HEY, NATE.
DID YOU GET A CALLBACK, TOO?
YUP.

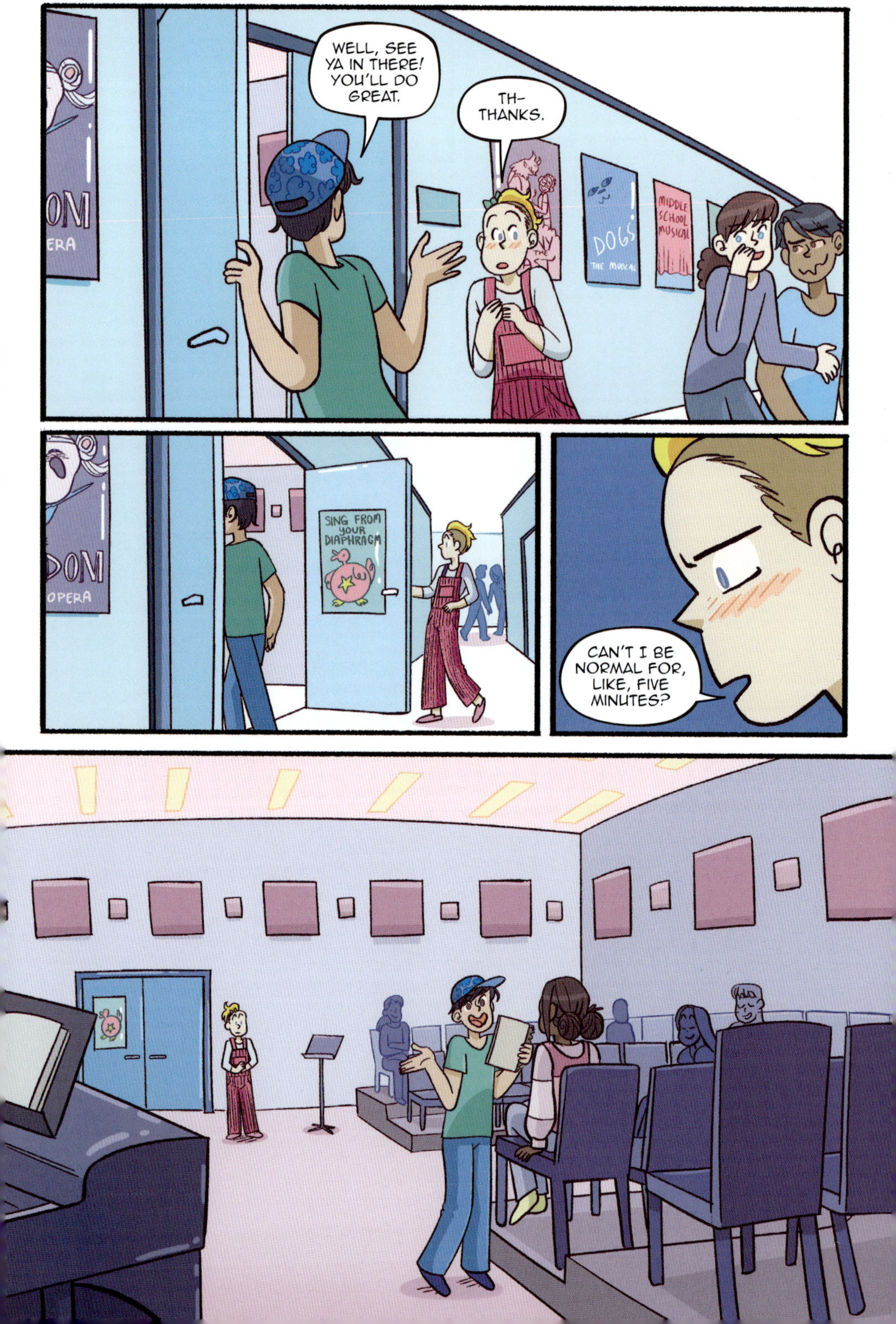
WELL, SEE YA IN THERE! YOU'LL DO GREAT.
TH- THANKS.
DOGS THE MUSICAL
MIDDLE SCHOOL MUSICAL
SING FROM YOUR DIAPHRAGM
CAN'T I BE NORMAL FOR, LIKE, FIVE MINUTES?

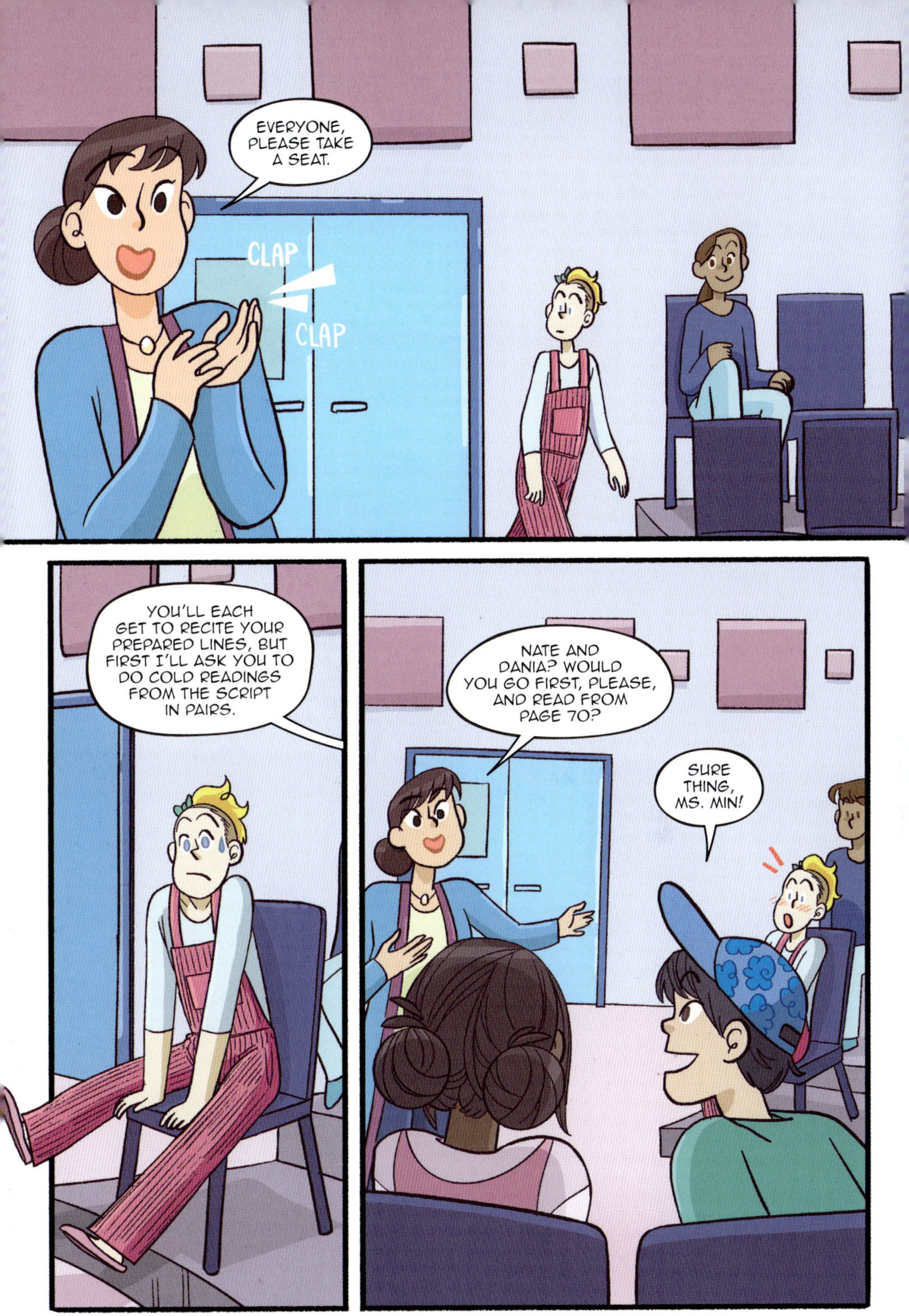
EVERYONE, PLEASE TAKE A SEAT.
CLAP
CLAP
YOU'LL EACH GET TO RECITE YOUR PREPARED LINES, BUT FIRST I'LL ASK YOU TO DO COLD READINGS FROM THE SCRIPT IN PAIRS.
NATE AND DANIA? WOULD YOU GO FIRST, PLEASE, AND READ FROM PAGE 70?
SURE THING, MS. MIN!

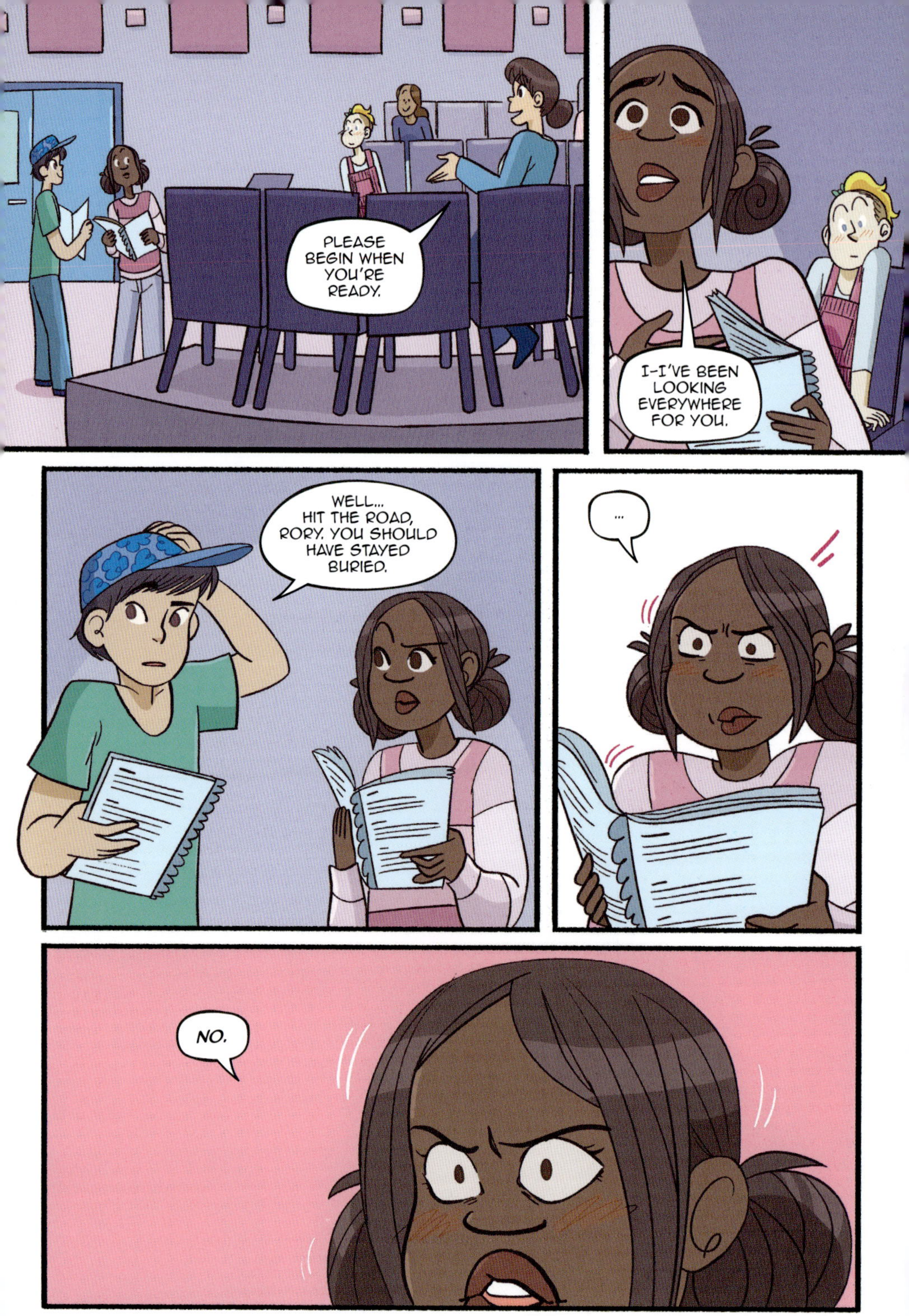
PLEASE BEGIN WHEN YOU'RE READY.
I-I'VE BEEN LOOKING EVERYWHERE FOR YOU.
WELL... HIT THE ROAD, RORY. YOU SHOULD HAVE STAYED BURIED.
...
NO.

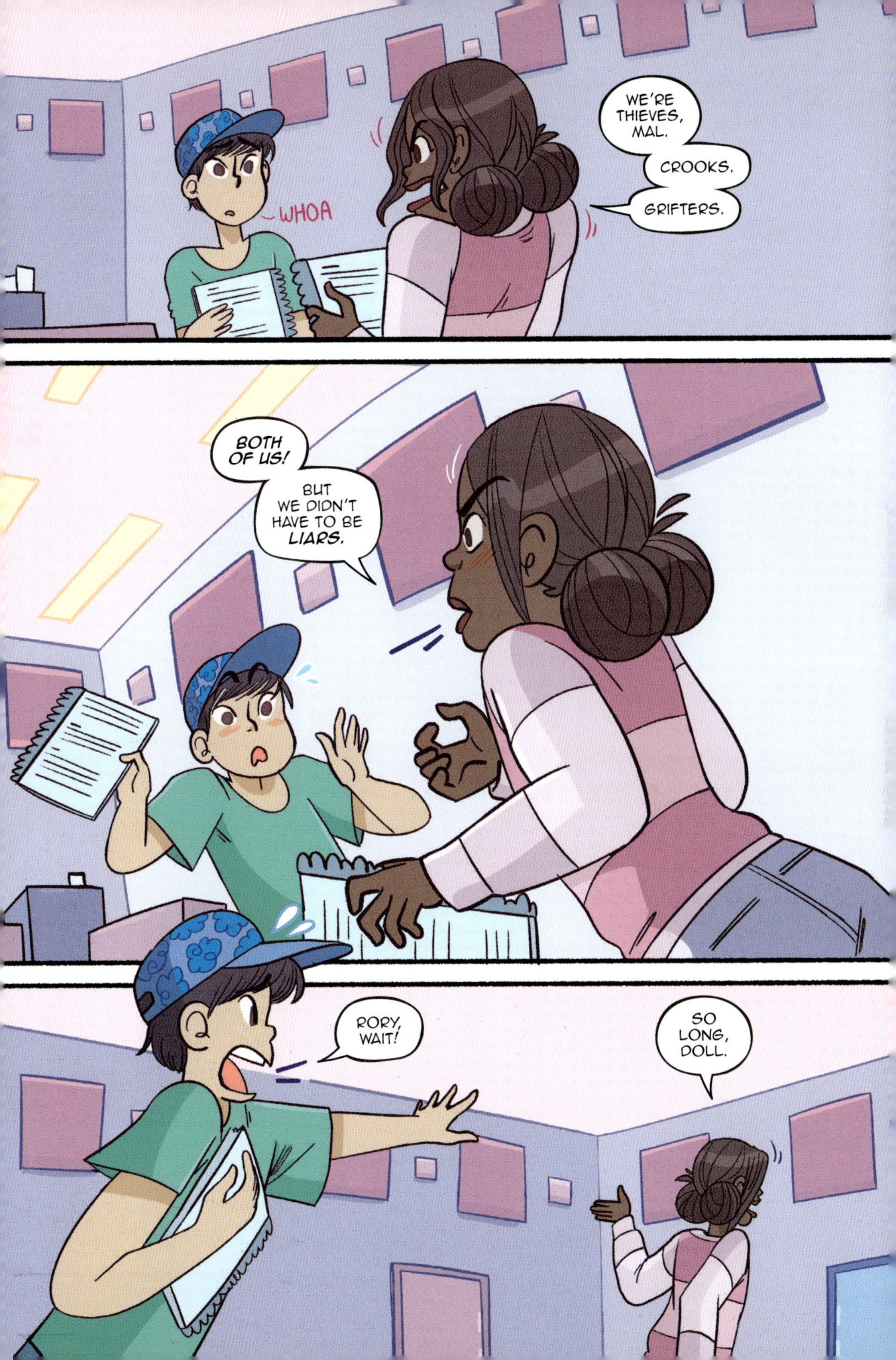

WHOA
WE'RE THIEVES, MAL.
CROOKS.
GRIFTERS.
BOTH OF US!
BUT WE DIDN'T HAVE TO BE LIARS.
RORY, WAIT!
SO LONG, DOLL.

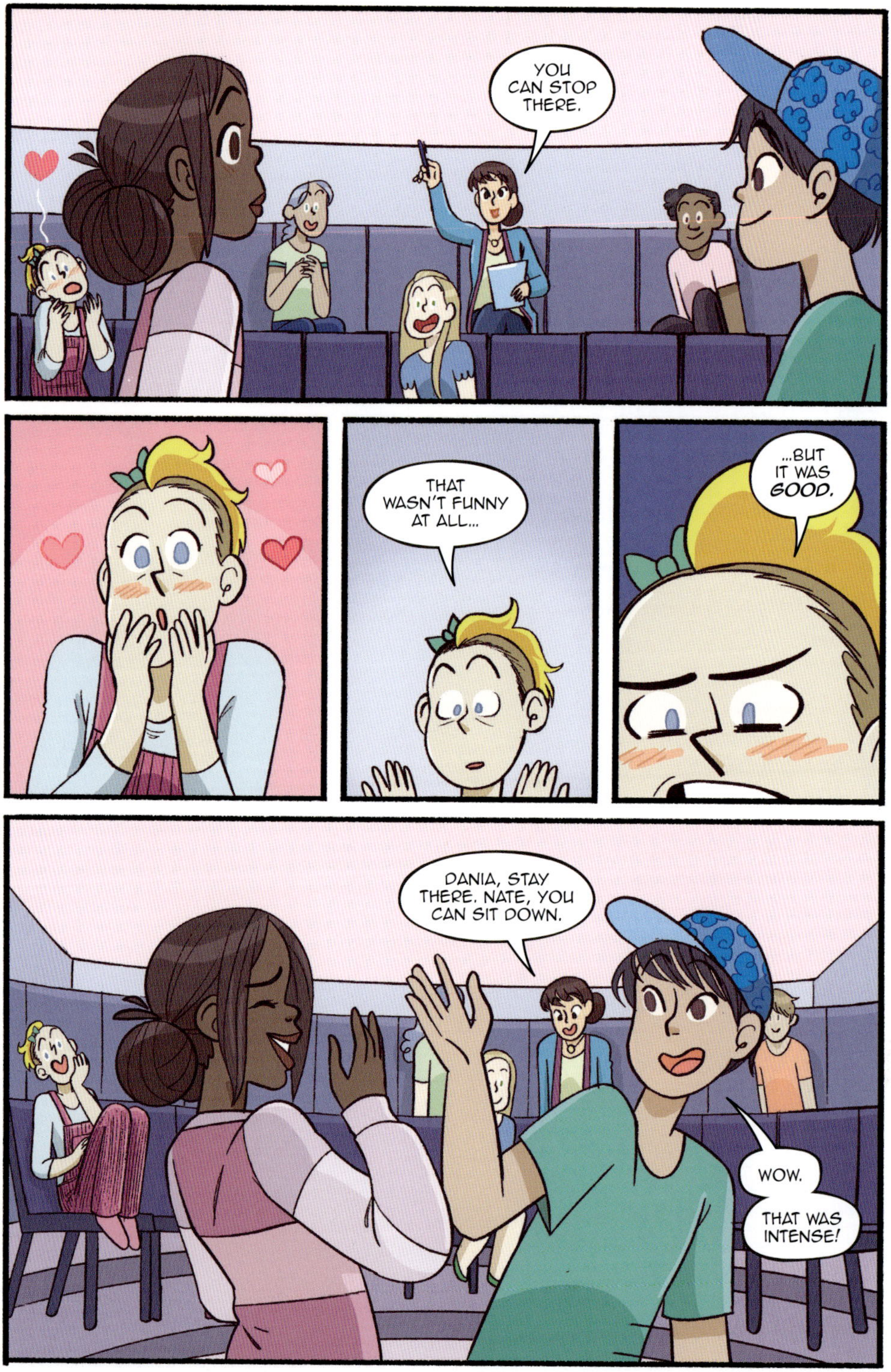
YOU CAN STOP THERE.
THAT WASN'T FUNNY AT ALL...
...BUT IT WAS GOOD.
DANIA, STAY THERE. NATE, YOU CAN SIT DOWN.
WOW.
THAT WAS INTENSE!

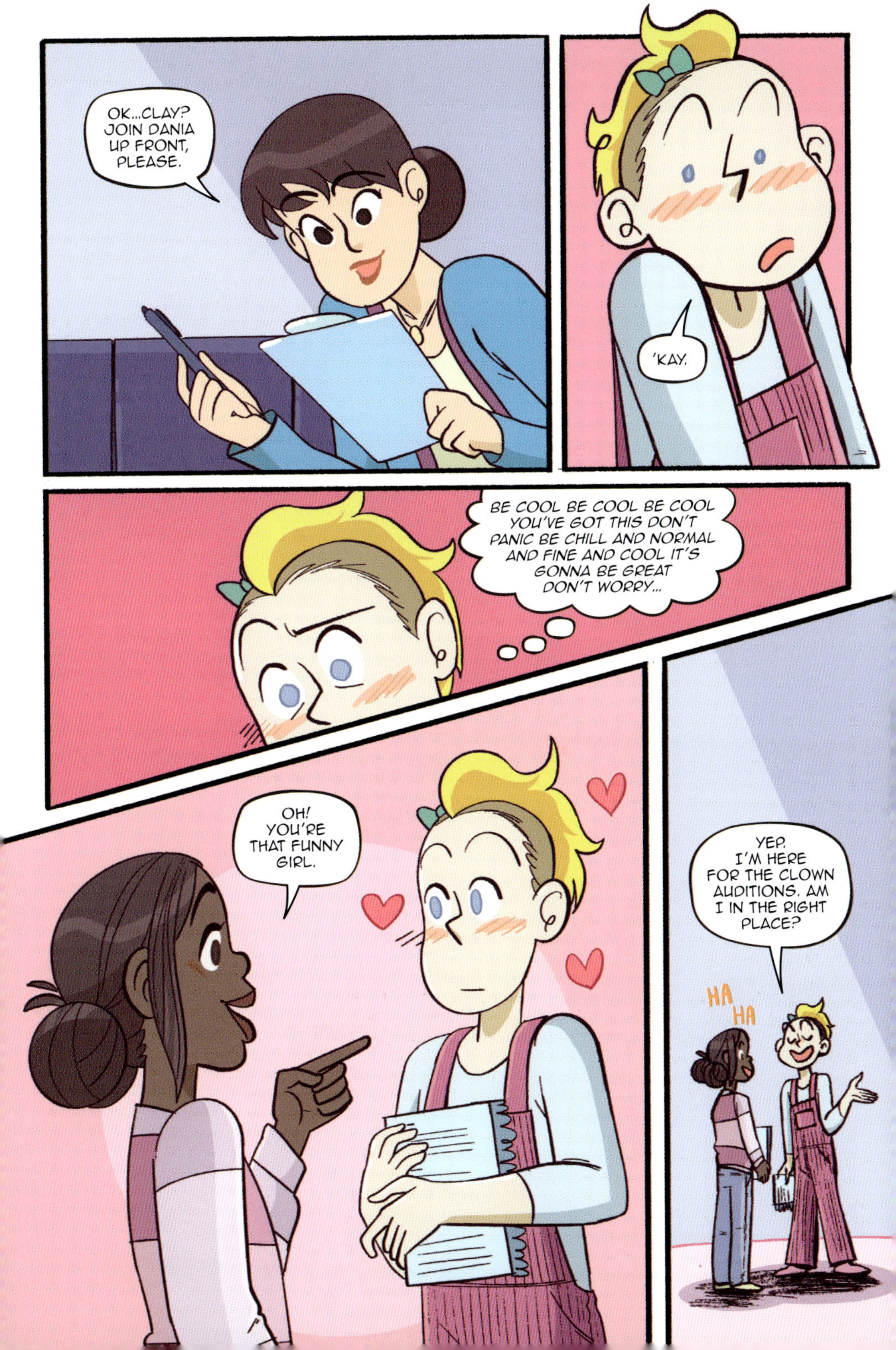
OK...CLAY? JOIN DANIA UP FRONT, PLEASE.
'KAY.
BE COOL BE COOL BE COOL YOU'VE GOT THIS DON'T PANIC BE CHILL AND NORMAL AND FINE AND COOL IT'S GONNA BE GREAT DON'T WORRY...
OH! YOU'RE THAT FUNNY GIRL.
YEP. I'M HERE FOR THE CLOWN AUDITIONS. AM I IN THE RIGHT PLACE?
HA HA

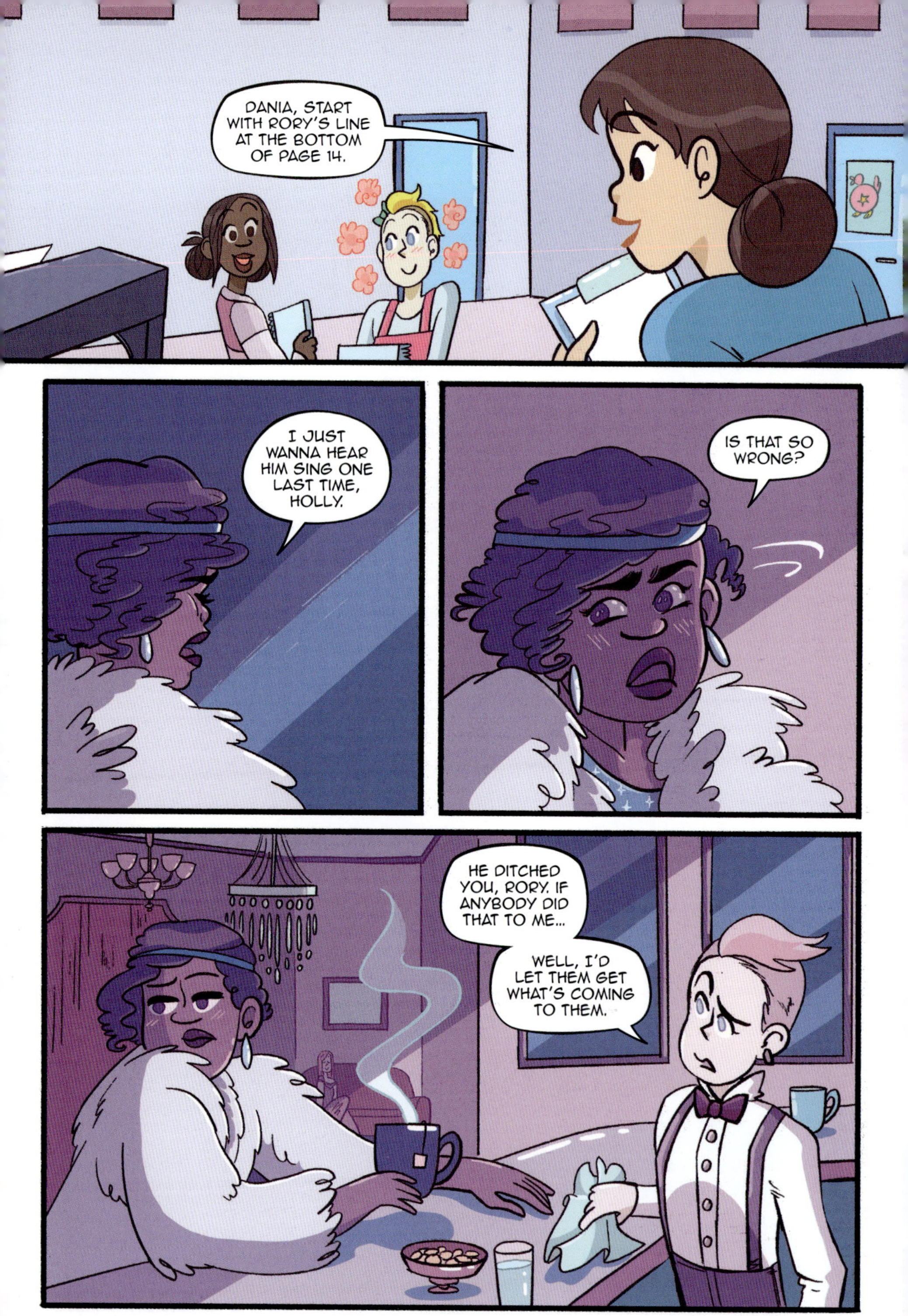
DANIA, START WITH RORY'S LINE AT THE BOTTOM OF PAGE 14.
I JUST WANNA HEAR HIM SING ONE LAST TIME, HOLLY.
IS THAT SO WRONG?
HE DITCHED YOU, RORY. IF ANYBODY DID THAT TO ME...
WELL, I'D LET THEM GET WHAT'S COMING TO THEM.

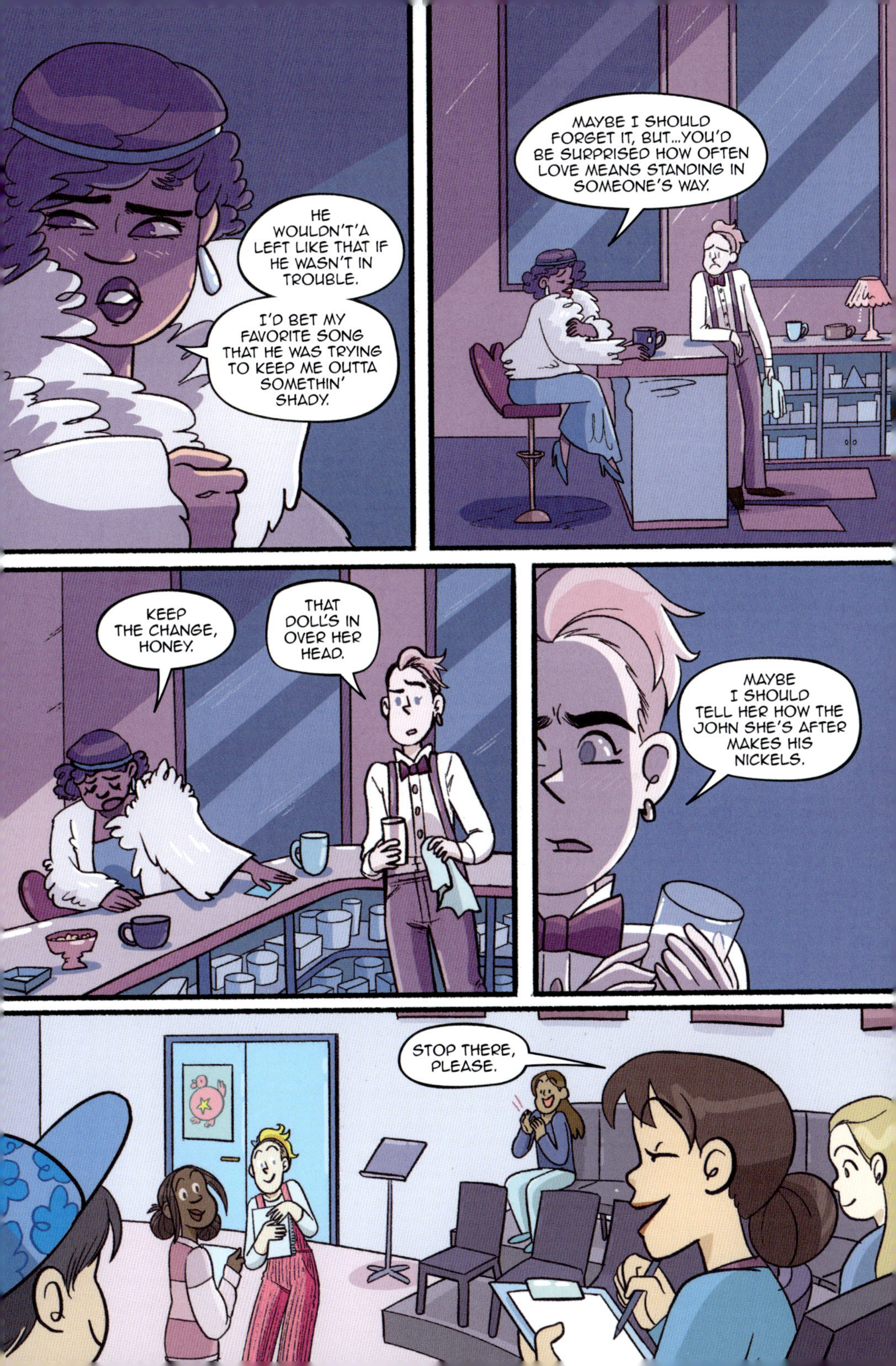
HE WOULDN'T'A LEFT LIKE THAT IF HE WASN'T IN TROUBLE.
I'D BET MY FAVORITE SONG THAT HE WAS TRYING TO KEEP ME OUTTA SOMETHIN' SHADY.
MAYBE I SHOULD FORGET IT, BUT...YOU'D BE SURPRISED HOW OFTEN LOVE MEANS STANDING IN SOMEONE'S WAY.
KEEP THE CHANGE, HONEY.
THAT DOLL'S IN OVER HER HEAD.
MAYBE I SHOULD TELL HER HOW THE JOHN SHE'S AFTER MAKES HIS NICKELS.
STOP THERE, PLEASE.

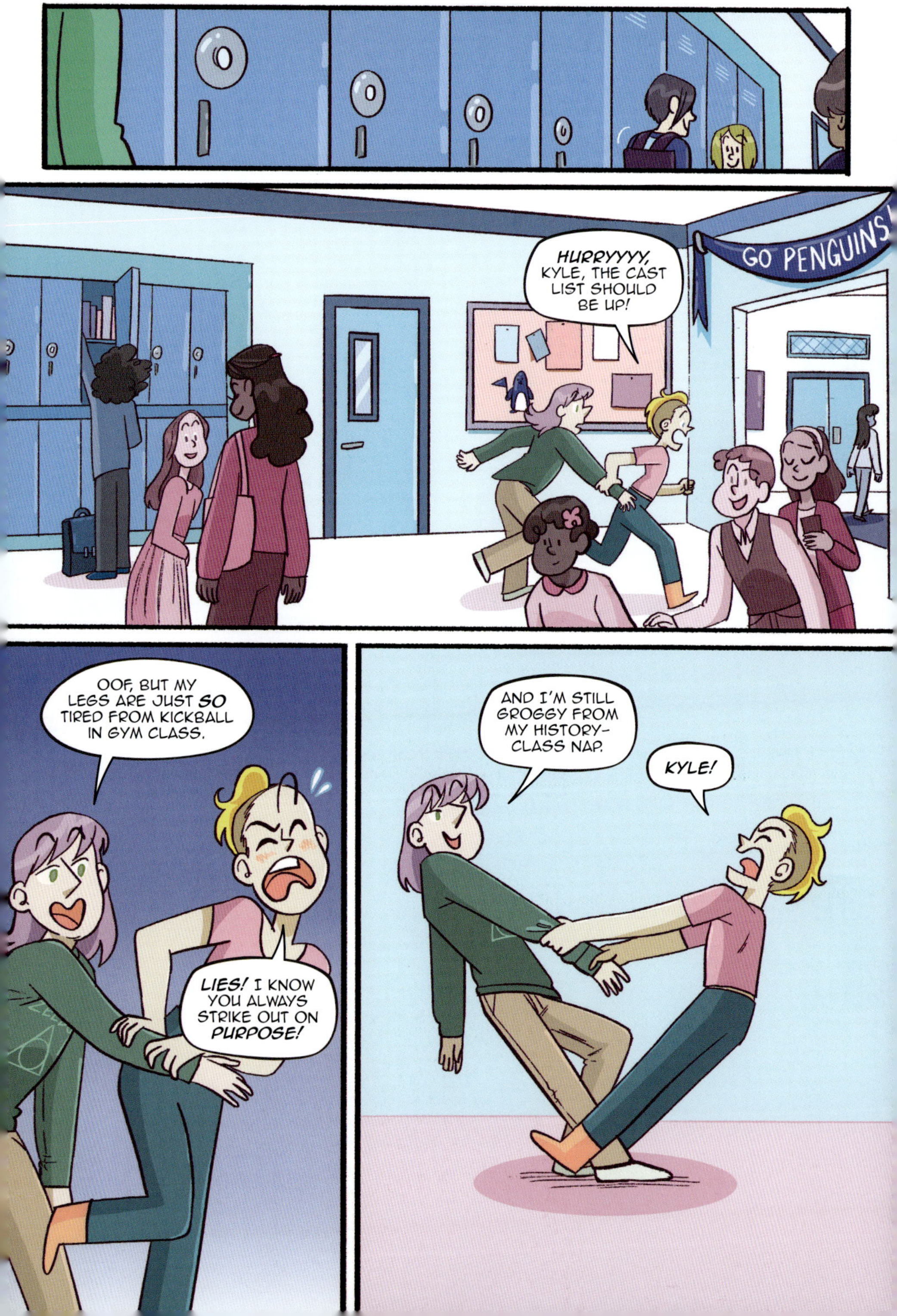
GO PENGUINS!
HURRYYYY, KYLE, THE CAST LIST SHOULD BE UP!
OOF, BUT MY LEGS ARE JUST SO TIRED FROM KICKBALL IN GYM CLASS.
LIES! I KNOW YOU ALWAYS STRIKE OUT ON PURPOSE!
AND I'M STILL GROGGY FROM MY HISTORY-CLASS NAP.
KYLE!

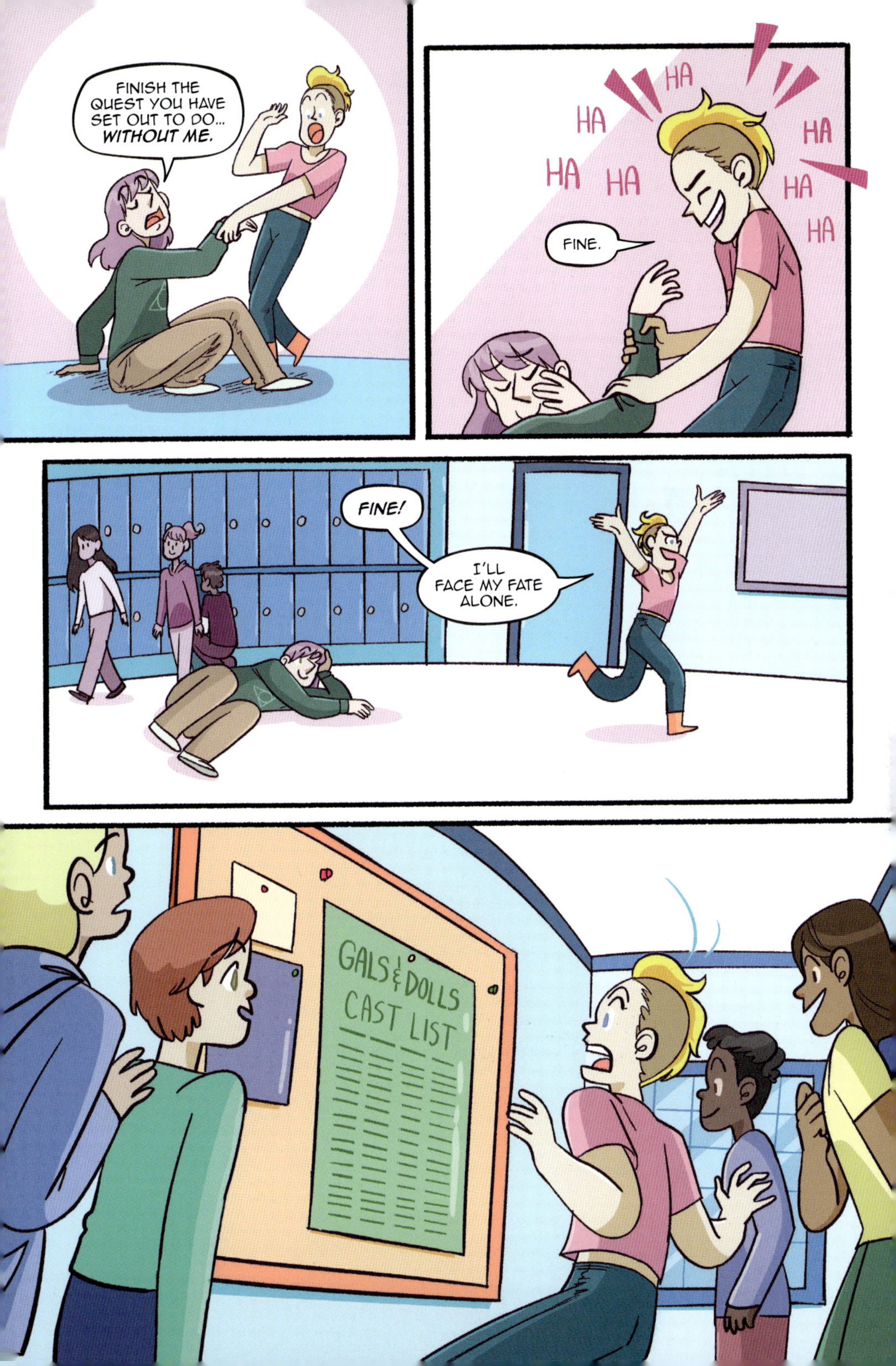
FINISH THE QUEST YOU HAVE SET OUT TO DO... *WITHOUT ME.*
HA HA HA HA HA HA HA HA
FINE.
FINE!
I'LL FACE MY FATE ALONE.
GALS & DOLLS CAST LIST

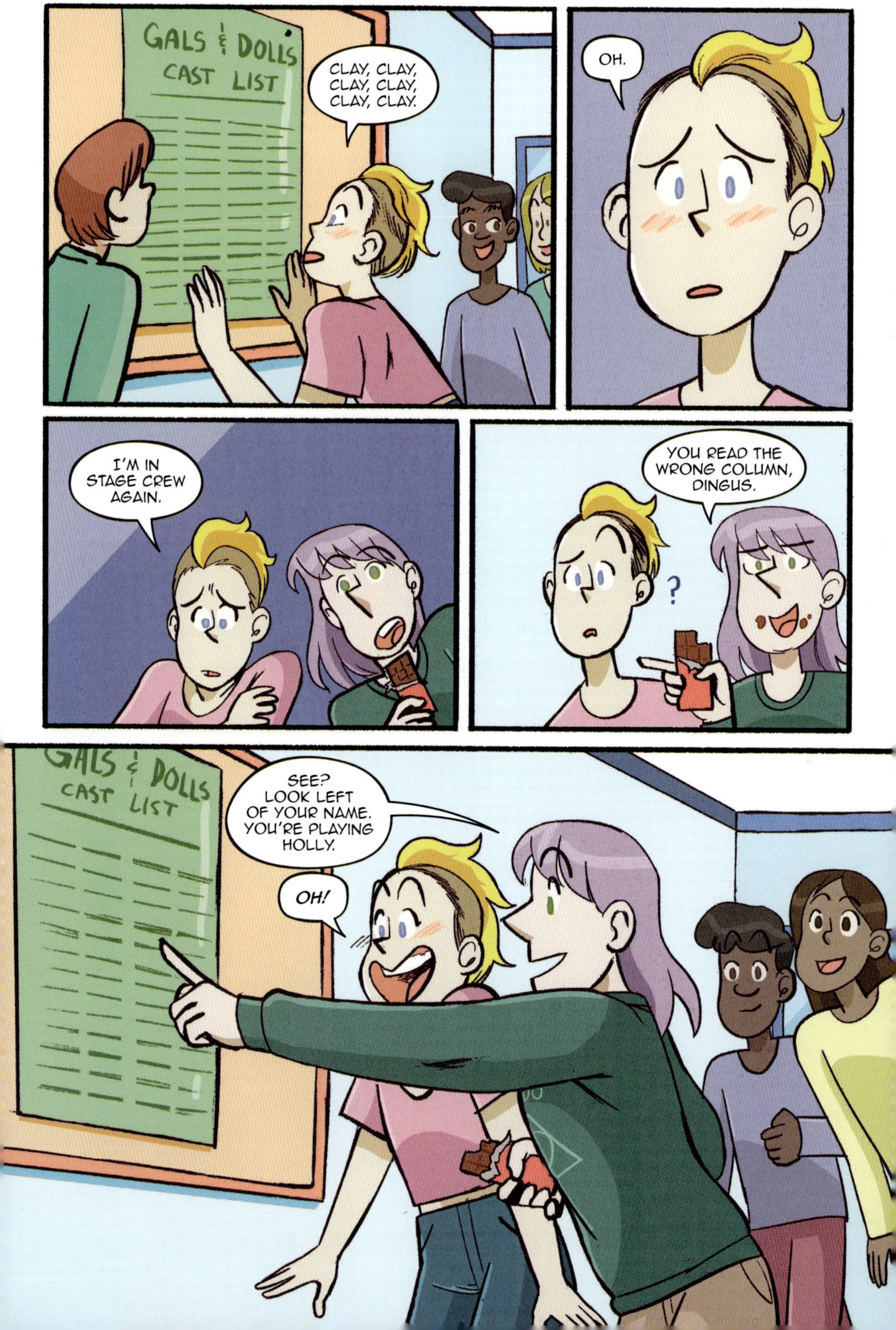
GALS & DOLLS CAST LIST
CLAY, CLAY, CLAY, CLAY, CLAY, CLAY.
OH.
I'M IN STAGE CREW AGAIN.
YOU READ THE WRONG COLUMN, DINGUS.
?
GALS & DOLLS CAST LIST
SEE? LOOK LEFT OF YOUR NAME. YOU'RE PLAYING HOLLY.
OH!

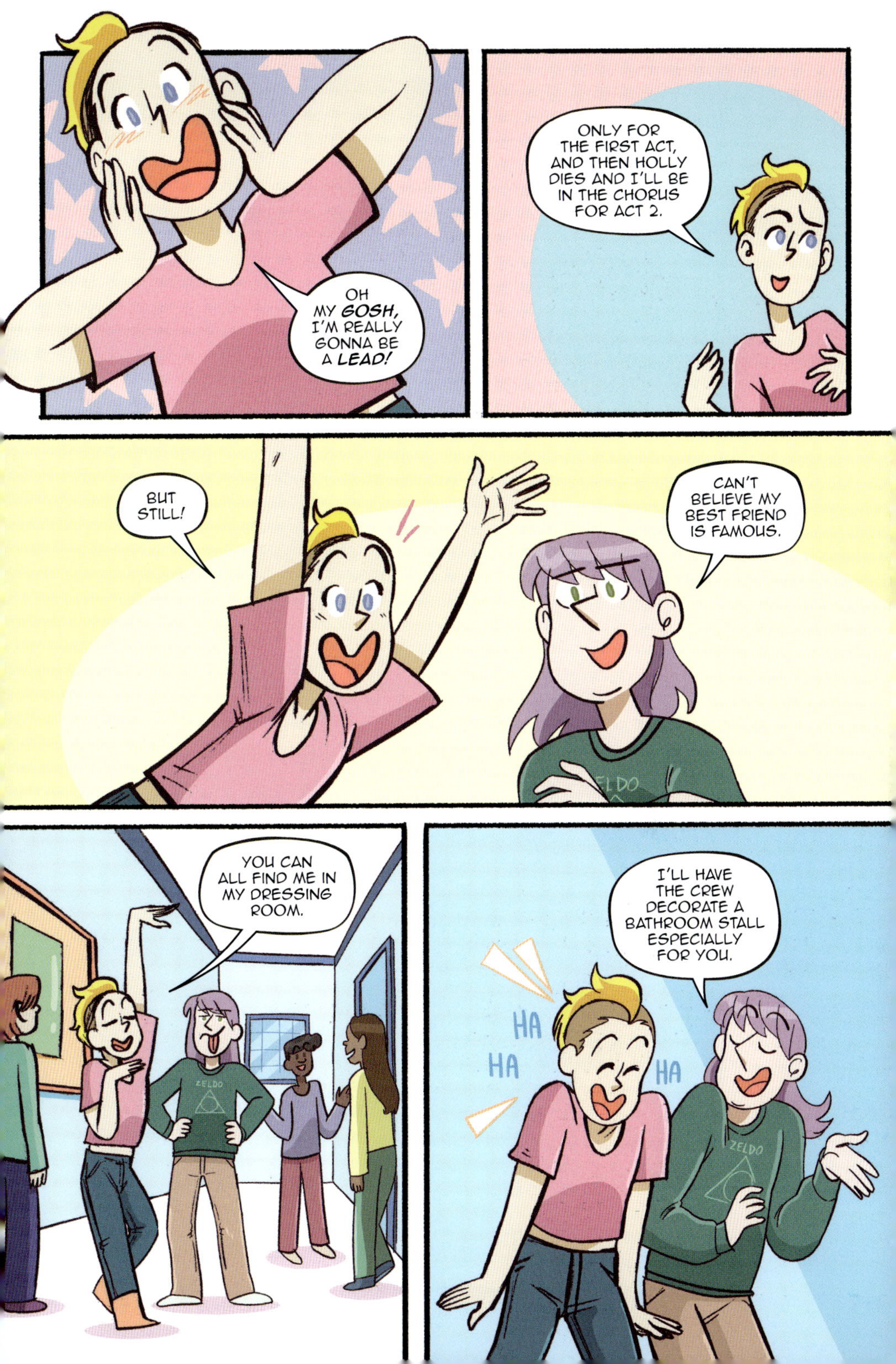
OH MY GOSH, I'M REALLY GONNA BE A LEAD!
ONLY FOR THE FIRST ACT, AND THEN HOLLY DIES AND I'LL BE IN THE CHORUS FOR ACT 2.
BUT STILL!
CAN'T BELIEVE MY BEST FRIEND IS FAMOUS.
ZELDO
YOU CAN ALL FIND ME IN MY DRESSING ROOM.
ZELDO
I'LL HAVE THE CREW DECORATE A BATHROOM STALL ESPECIALLY FOR YOU.
HA
HA
HA
ZELDO

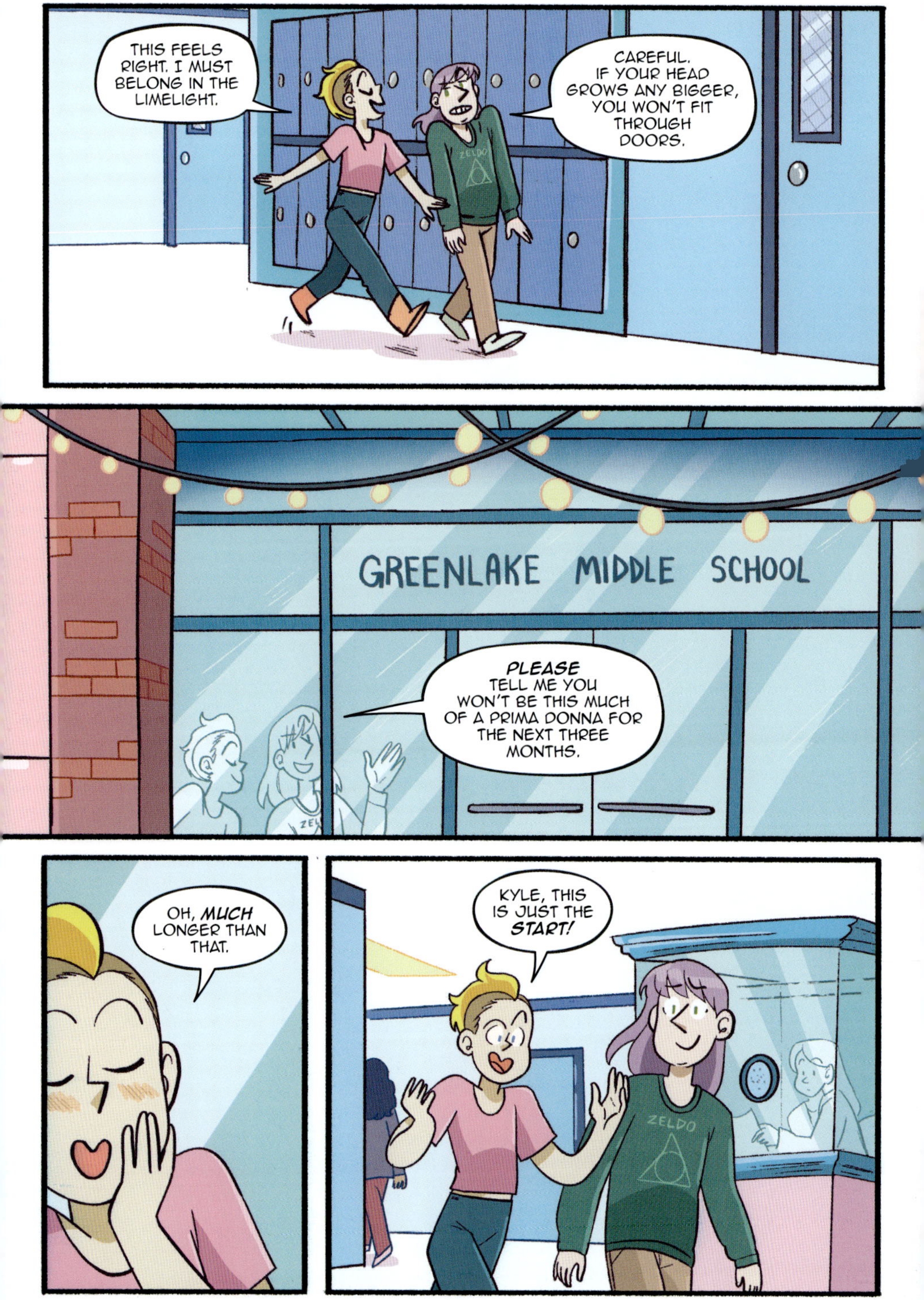
THIS FEELS RIGHT. I MUST BELONG IN THE LIMELIGHT.
CAREFUL. IF YOUR HEAD GROWS ANY BIGGER, YOU WON'T FIT THROUGH DOORS.
GREENLAKE MIDDLE SCHOOL
PLEASE TELL ME YOU WON'T BE THIS MUCH OF A PRIMA DONNA FOR THE NEXT THREE MONTHS.
OH, *MUCH* LONGER THAN THAT.
KYLE, THIS IS JUST THE *START!*

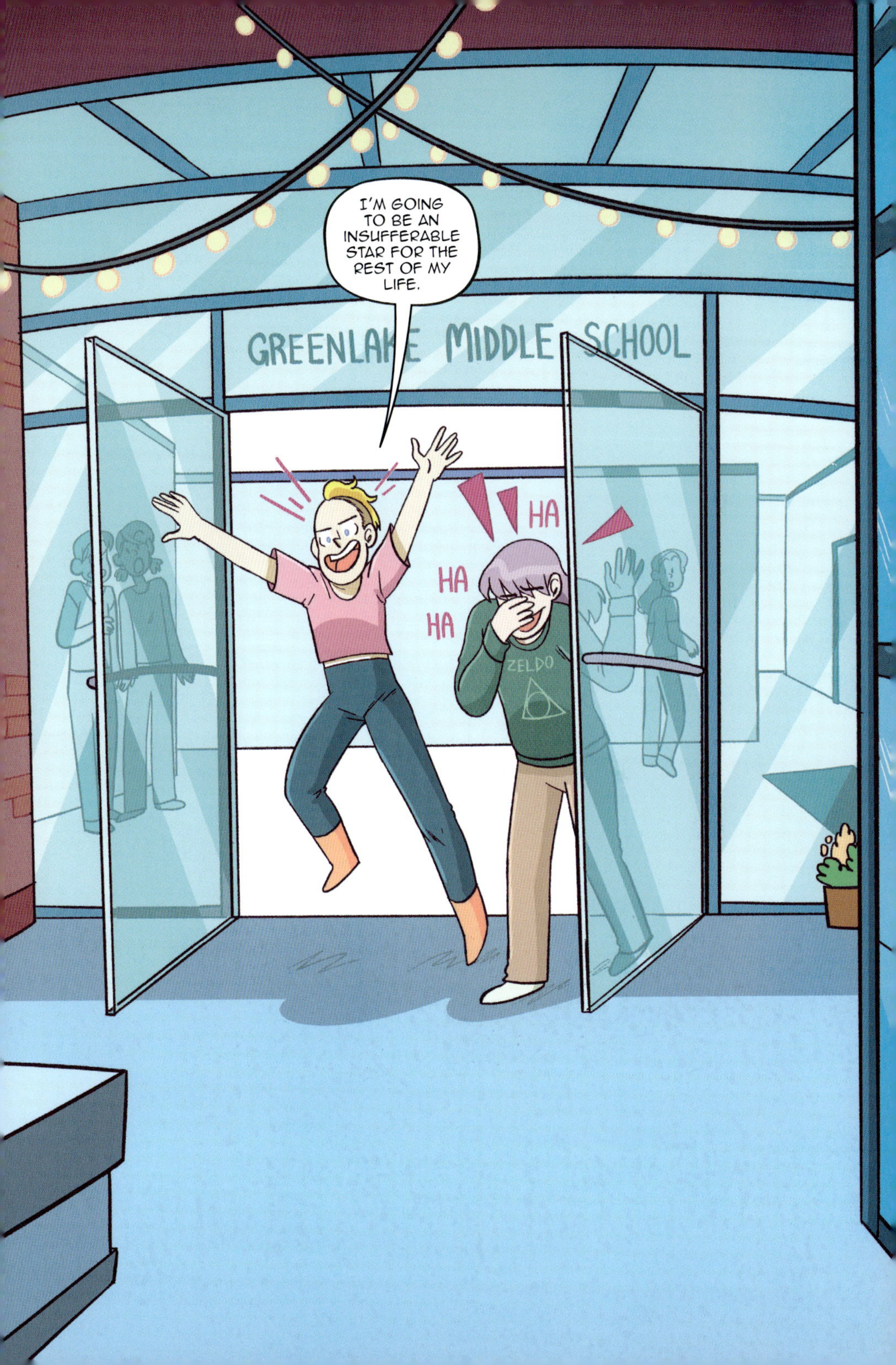
I'M GOING TO BE AN INSUFFERABLE STAR FOR THE REST OF MY LIFE.
GREENLAKE MIDDLE SCHOOL
HA
HA
HA
ZELDO

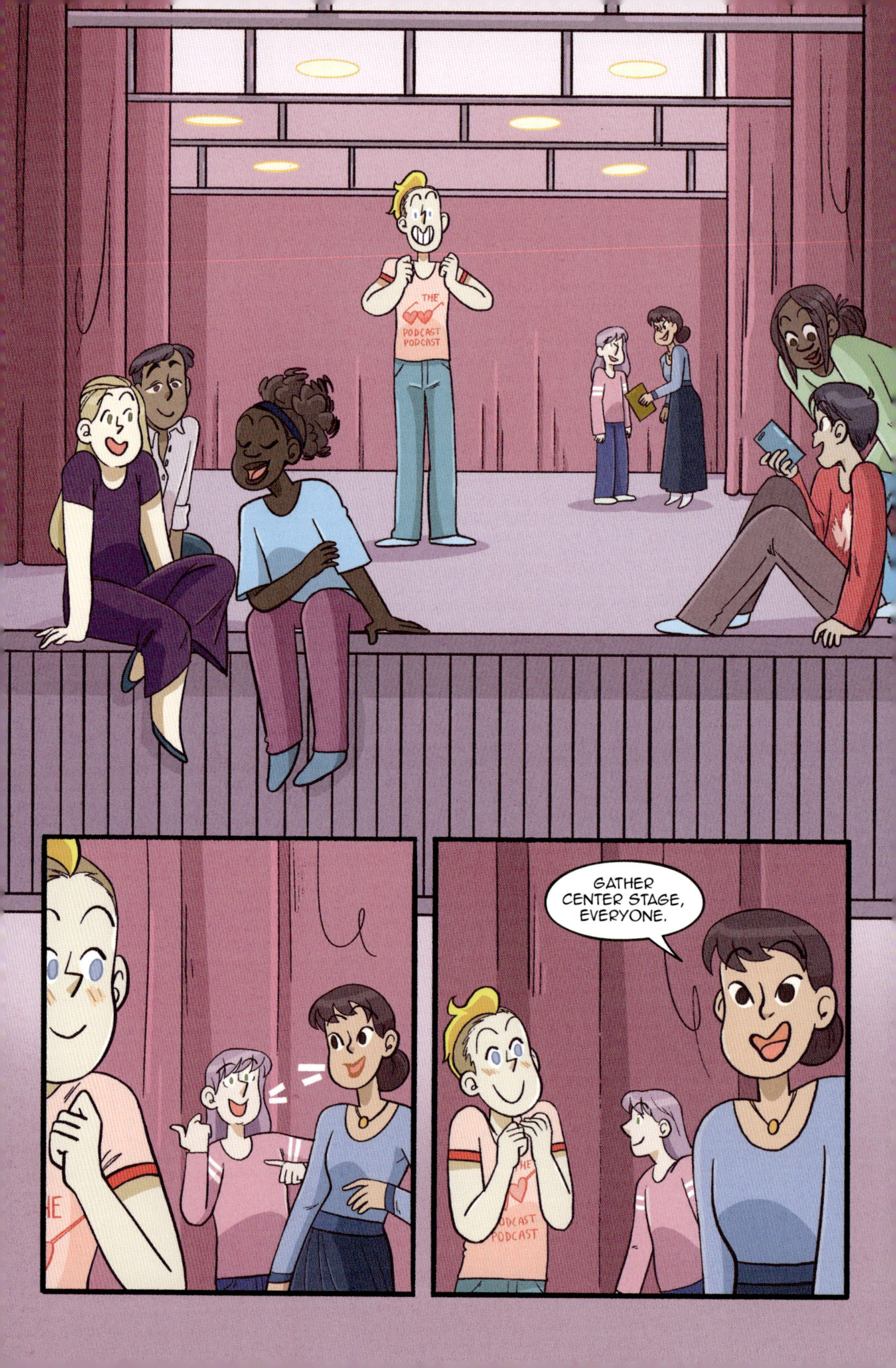
THE PODCAST PODCAST
GATHER CENTER STAGE, EVERYONE.

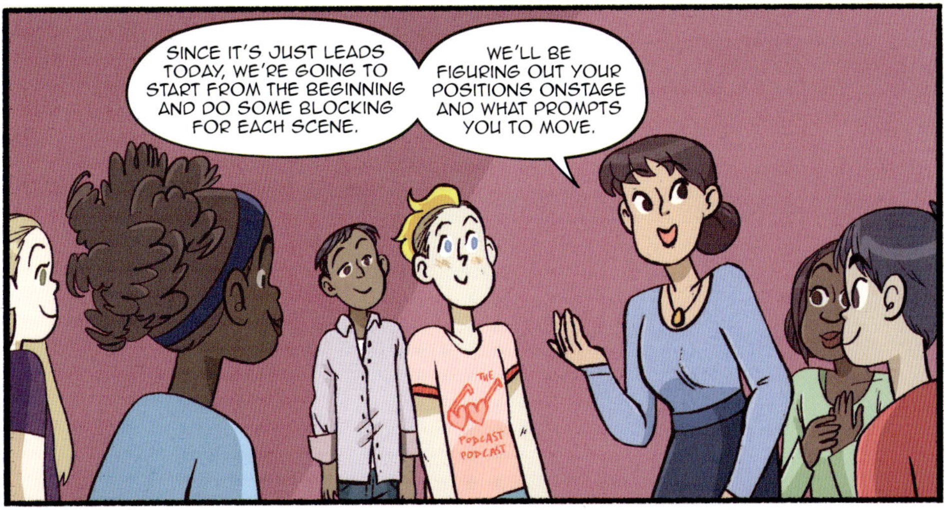
SINCE IT'S JUST LEADS TODAY, WE'RE GOING TO START FROM THE BEGINNING AND DO SOME BLOCKING FOR EACH SCENE.
WE'LL BE FIGURING OUT YOUR POSITIONS ONSTAGE AND WHAT PROMPTS YOU TO MOVE.
THE PODCAST PODCAST

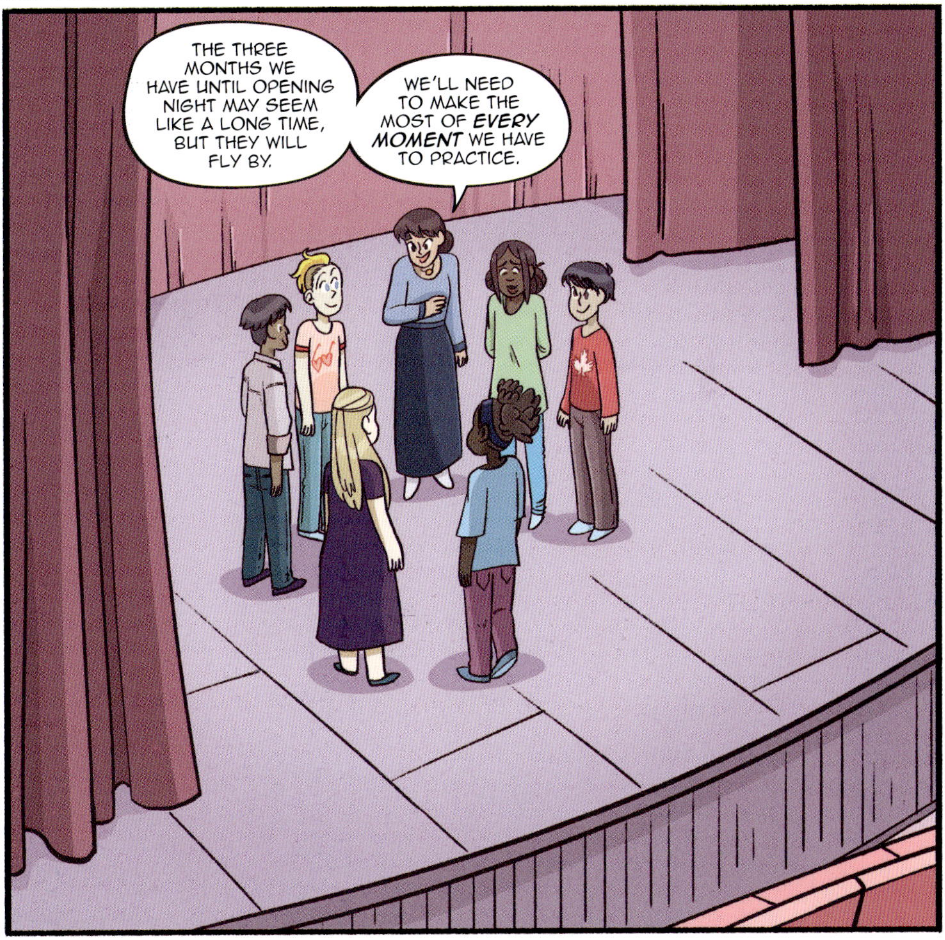
THE THREE MONTHS WE HAVE UNTIL OPENING NIGHT MAY SEEM LIKE A LONG TIME, BUT THEY WILL FLY BY.
WE'LL NEED TO MAKE THE MOST OF ***EVERY MOMENT*** WE HAVE TO PRACTICE.

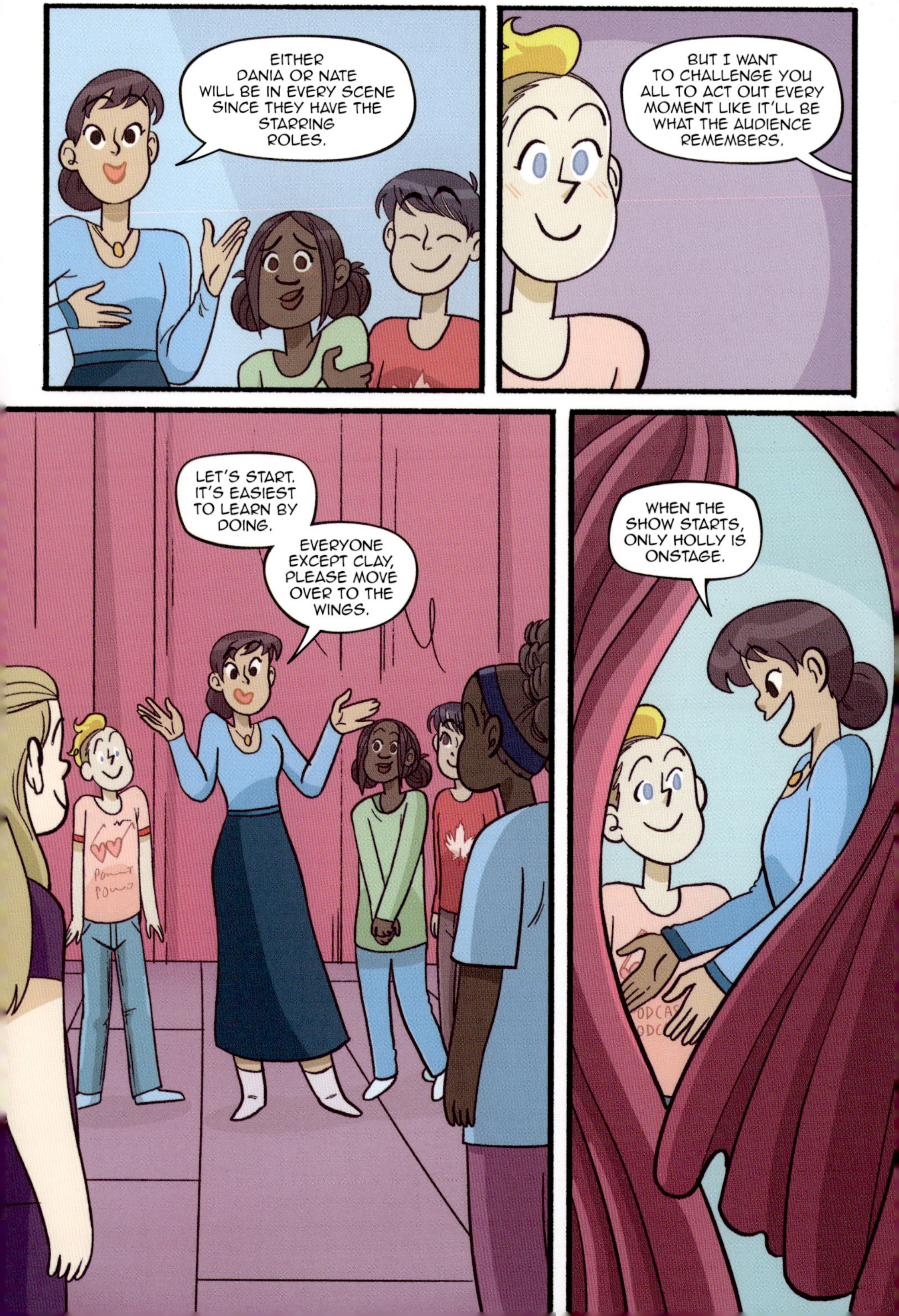
EITHER DANIA OR NATE WILL BE IN EVERY SCENE SINCE THEY HAVE THE STARRING ROLES.
BUT I WANT TO CHALLENGE YOU ALL TO ACT OUT EVERY MOMENT LIKE IT'LL BE WHAT THE AUDIENCE REMEMBERS.
LET'S START. IT'S EASIEST TO LEARN BY DOING.
EVERYONE EXCEPT CLAY, PLEASE MOVE OVER TO THE WINGS.
WHEN THE SHOW STARTS, ONLY HOLLY IS ONSTAGE.

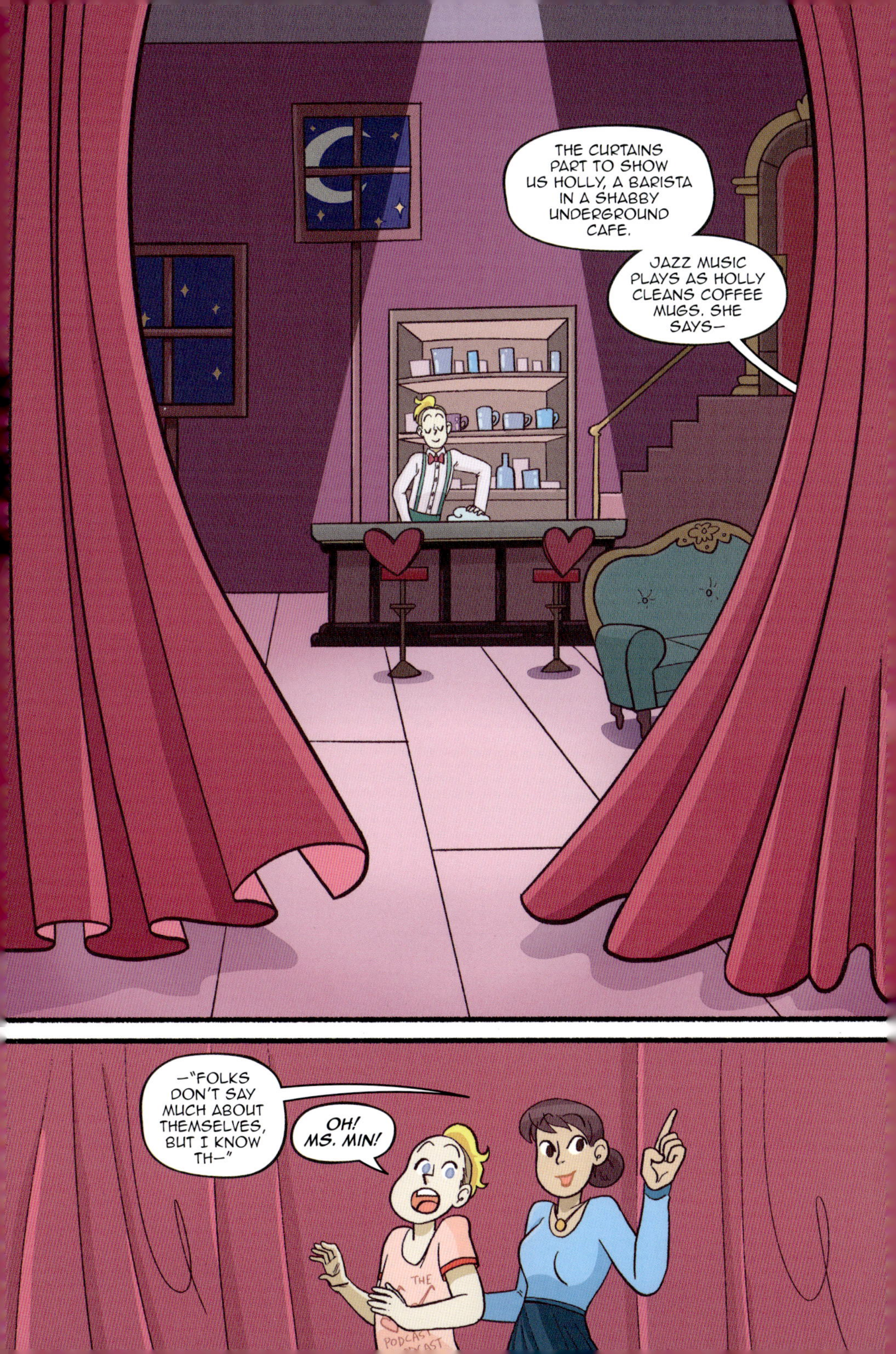
THE CURTAINS PART TO SHOW US HOLLY, A BARISTA IN A SHABBY UNDERGROUND CAFE.
JAZZ MUSIC PLAYS AS HOLLY CLEANS COFFEE MUGS. SHE SAYS—
—"FOLKS DON'T SAY MUCH ABOUT THEMSELVES, BUT I KNOW TH—"
OH! MS. MIN!

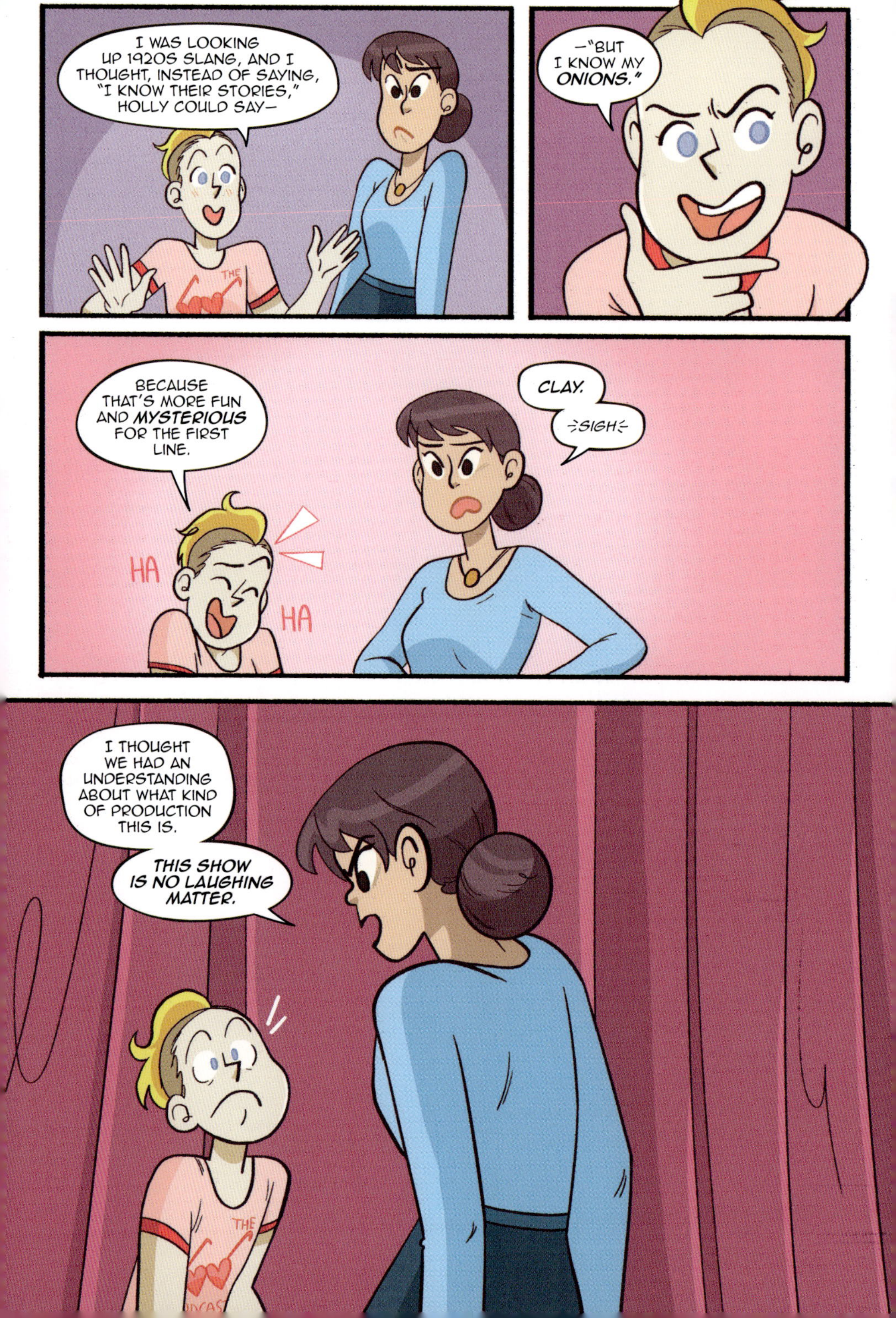
I WAS LOOKING UP 1920S SLANG, AND I THOUGHT, INSTEAD OF SAYING, "I KNOW THEIR STORIES," HOLLY COULD SAY—
—"BUT I KNOW MY *ONIONS.*"
BECAUSE THAT'S MORE FUN AND *MYSTERIOUS* FOR THE FIRST LINE.
HA HA
CLAY.
SIGH
I THOUGHT WE HAD AN UNDERSTANDING ABOUT WHAT KIND OF PRODUCTION THIS IS.
THIS SHOW IS NO LAUGHING MATTER.

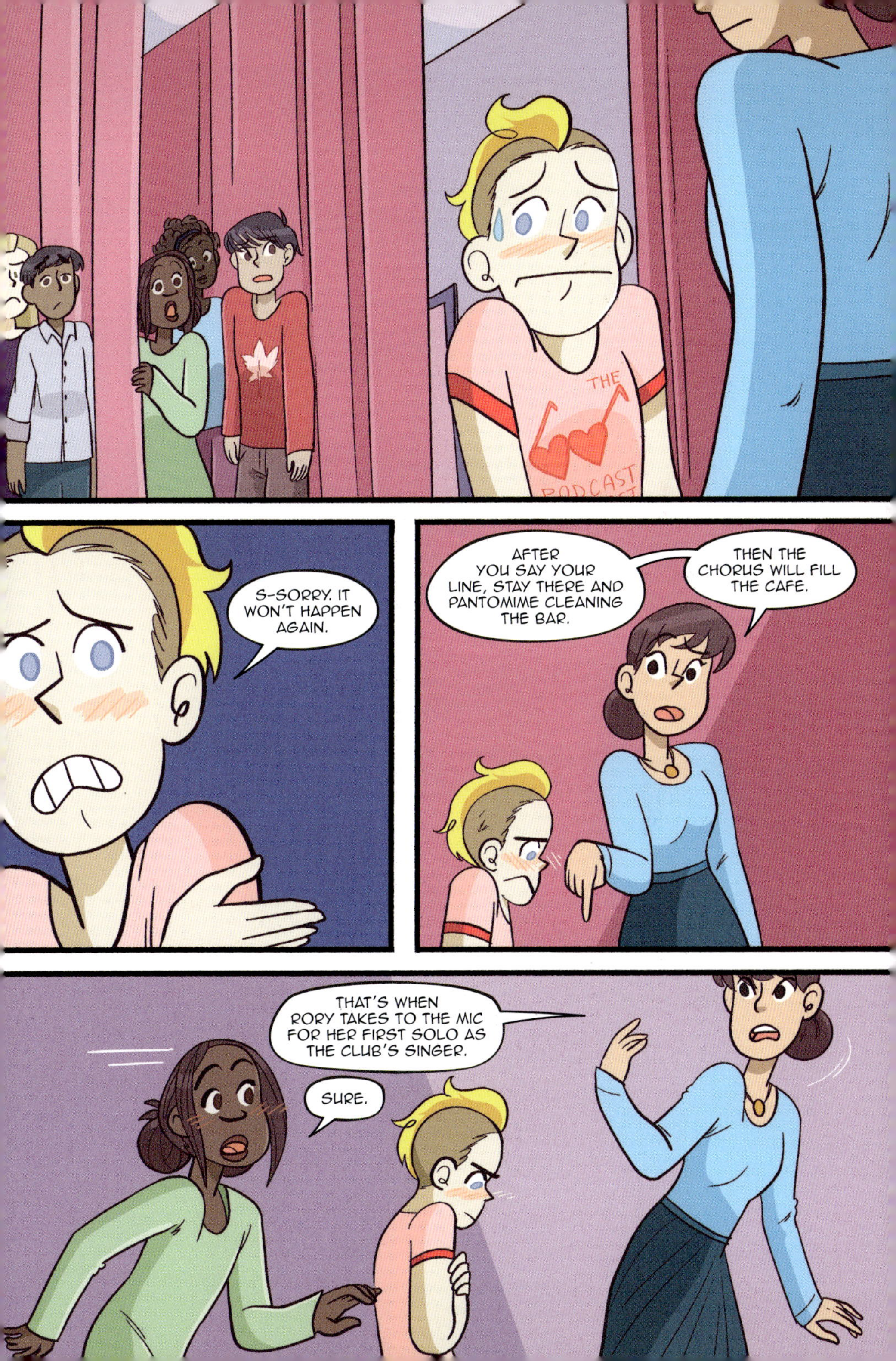
THE
PODCAST
S-SORRY. IT WON'T HAPPEN AGAIN.
AFTER YOU SAY YOUR LINE, STAY THERE AND PANTOMIME CLEANING THE BAR.
THEN THE CHORUS WILL FILL THE CAFE.
THAT'S WHEN RORY TAKES TO THE MIC FOR HER FIRST SOLO AS THE CLUB'S SINGER.
SURE.

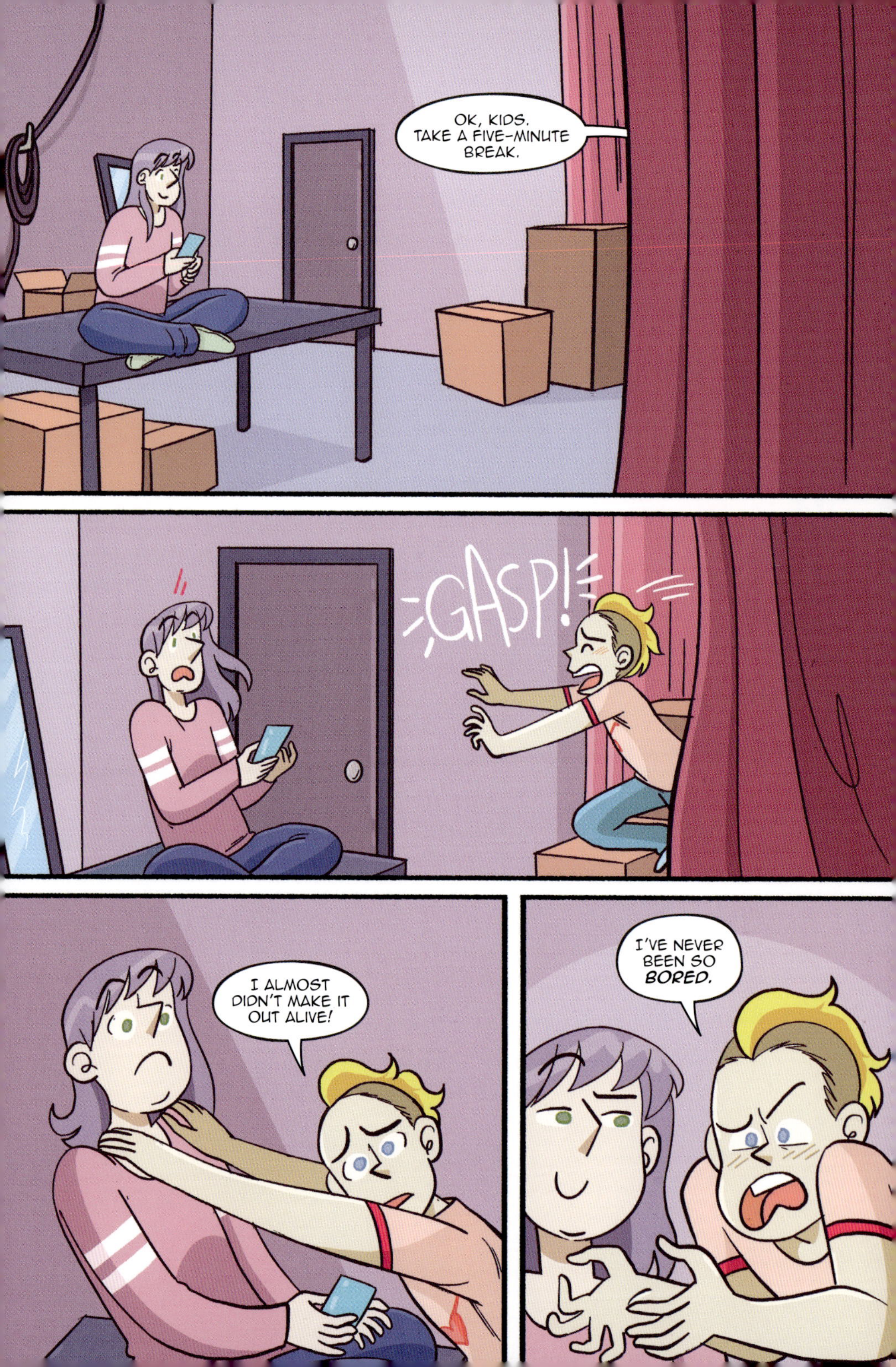
OK, KIDS. TAKE A FIVE-MINUTE BREAK.
GASP!
I ALMOST DIDN'T MAKE IT OUT ALIVE!
I'VE NEVER BEEN SO *BORED.*

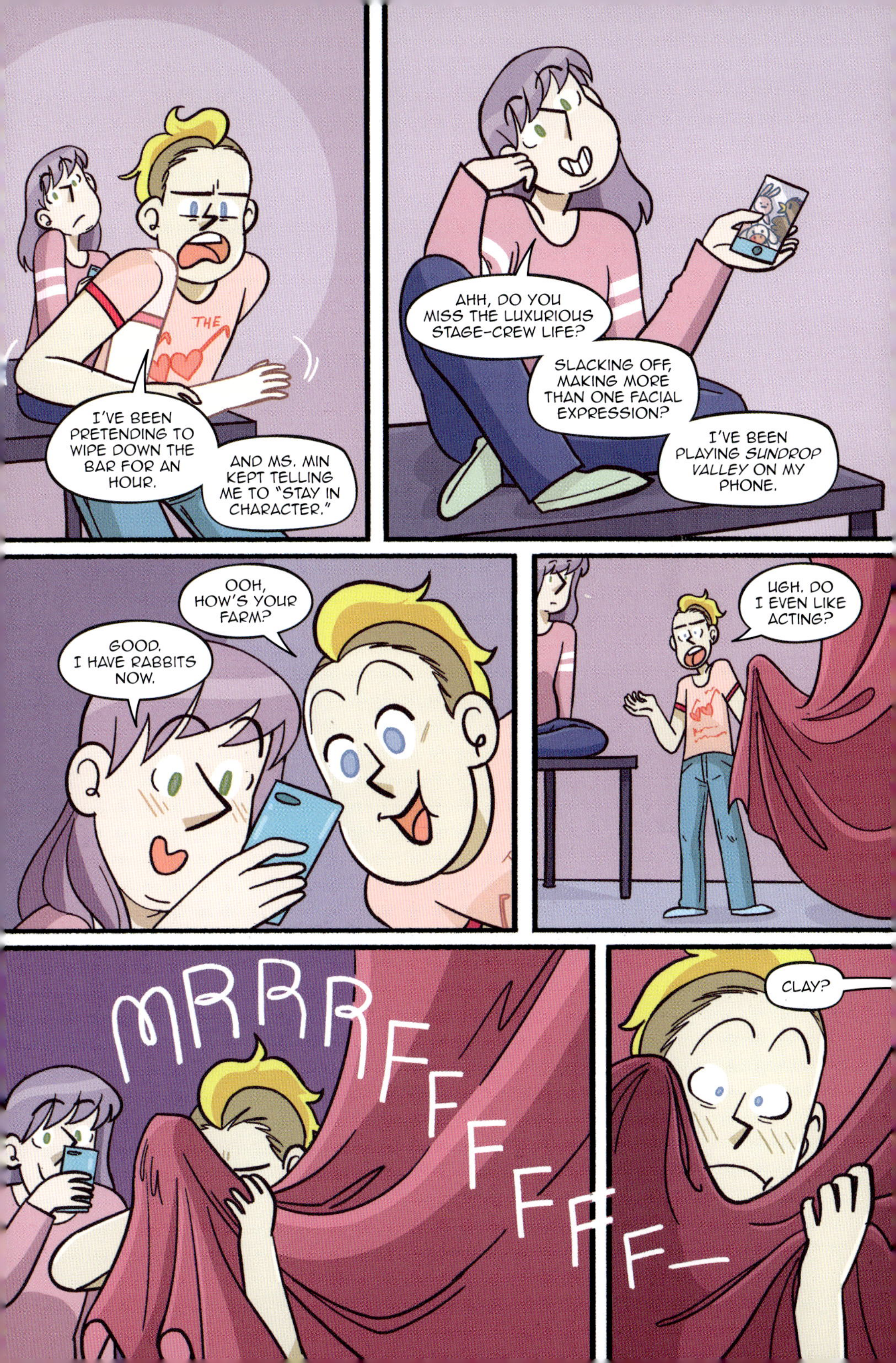
I'VE BEEN PRETENDING TO WIPE DOWN THE BAR FOR AN HOUR.
AND MS. MIN KEPT TELLING ME TO "STAY IN CHARACTER."
AHH, DO YOU MISS THE LUXURIOUS STAGE-CREW LIFE?
SLACKING OFF, MAKING MORE THAN ONE FACIAL EXPRESSION?
I'VE BEEN PLAYING *SUNDROP VALLEY* ON MY PHONE.
OOH, HOW'S YOUR FARM?
GOOD. I HAVE RABBITS NOW.
UGH. DO I EVEN LIKE ACTING?
MRRRFFFFFF—
CLAY?

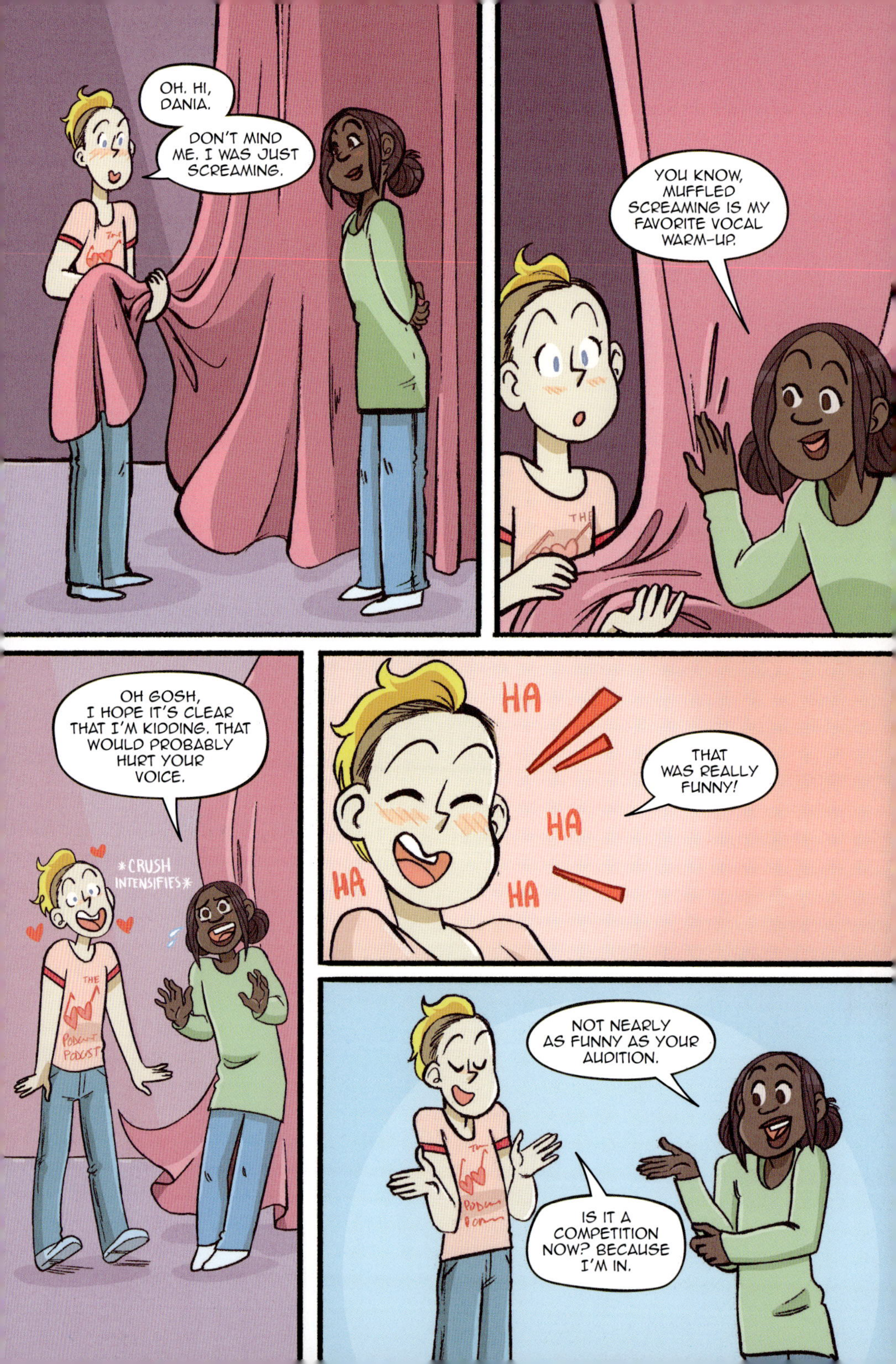
OH. HI, DANIA.
DON'T MIND ME. I WAS JUST SCREAMING.
YOU KNOW, MUFFLED SCREAMING IS MY FAVORITE VOCAL WARM-UP.
OH GOSH, I HOPE IT'S CLEAR THAT I'M KIDDING. THAT WOULD PROBABLY HURT YOUR VOICE.
CRUSH INTENSIFIES
HA
HA
HA
HA
THAT WAS REALLY FUNNY!
NOT NEARLY AS FUNNY AS YOUR AUDITION.
IS IT A COMPETITION NOW? BECAUSE I'M IN.

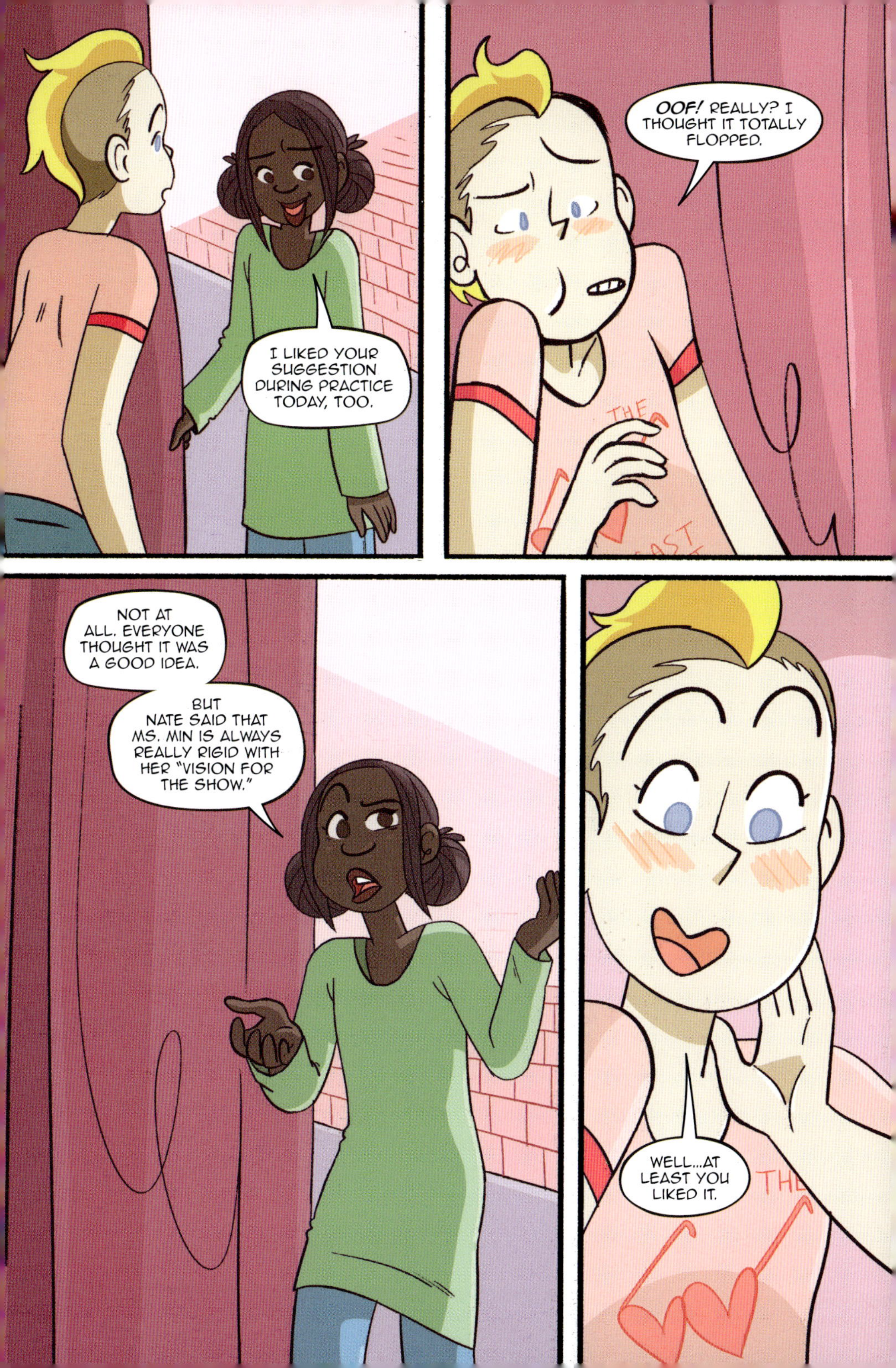
I LIKED YOUR SUGGESTION DURING PRACTICE TODAY, TOO.
OOF! REALLY? I THOUGHT IT TOTALLY FLOPPED.
NOT AT ALL. EVERYONE THOUGHT IT WAS A GOOD IDEA.
BUT NATE SAID THAT MS. MIN IS ALWAYS REALLY RIGID WITH HER "VISION FOR THE SHOW."
WELL...AT LEAST YOU LIKED IT.

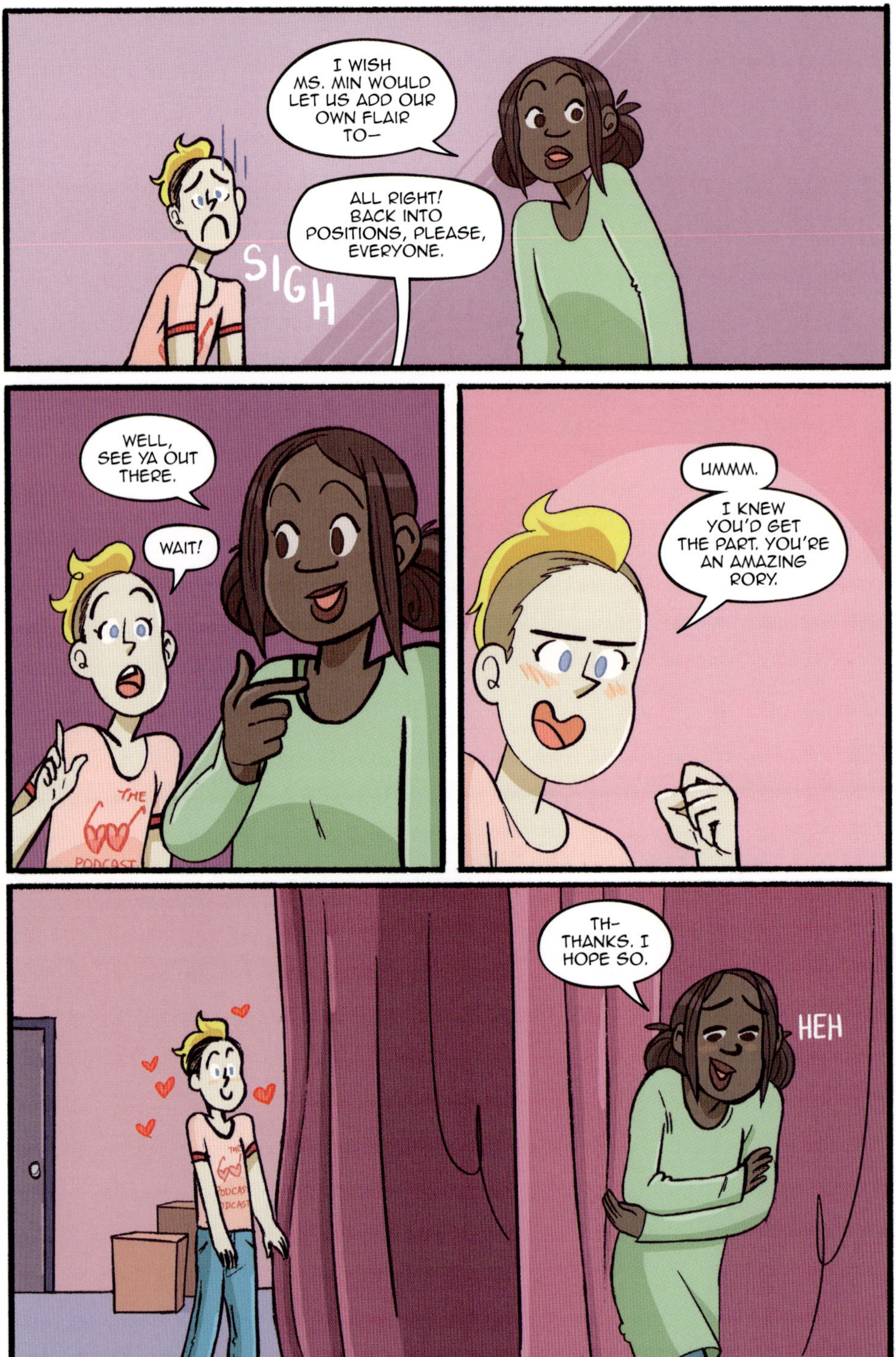

I WISH MS. MIN WOULD LET US ADD OUR OWN FLAIR TO—
SIGH
ALL RIGHT! BACK INTO POSITIONS, PLEASE, EVERYONE.
WELL, SEE YA OUT THERE.
WAIT!
THE PODCAST
UMMM.
I KNEW YOU'D GET THE PART. YOU'RE AN AMAZING RORY.
TH-THANKS. I HOPE SO.
HEH

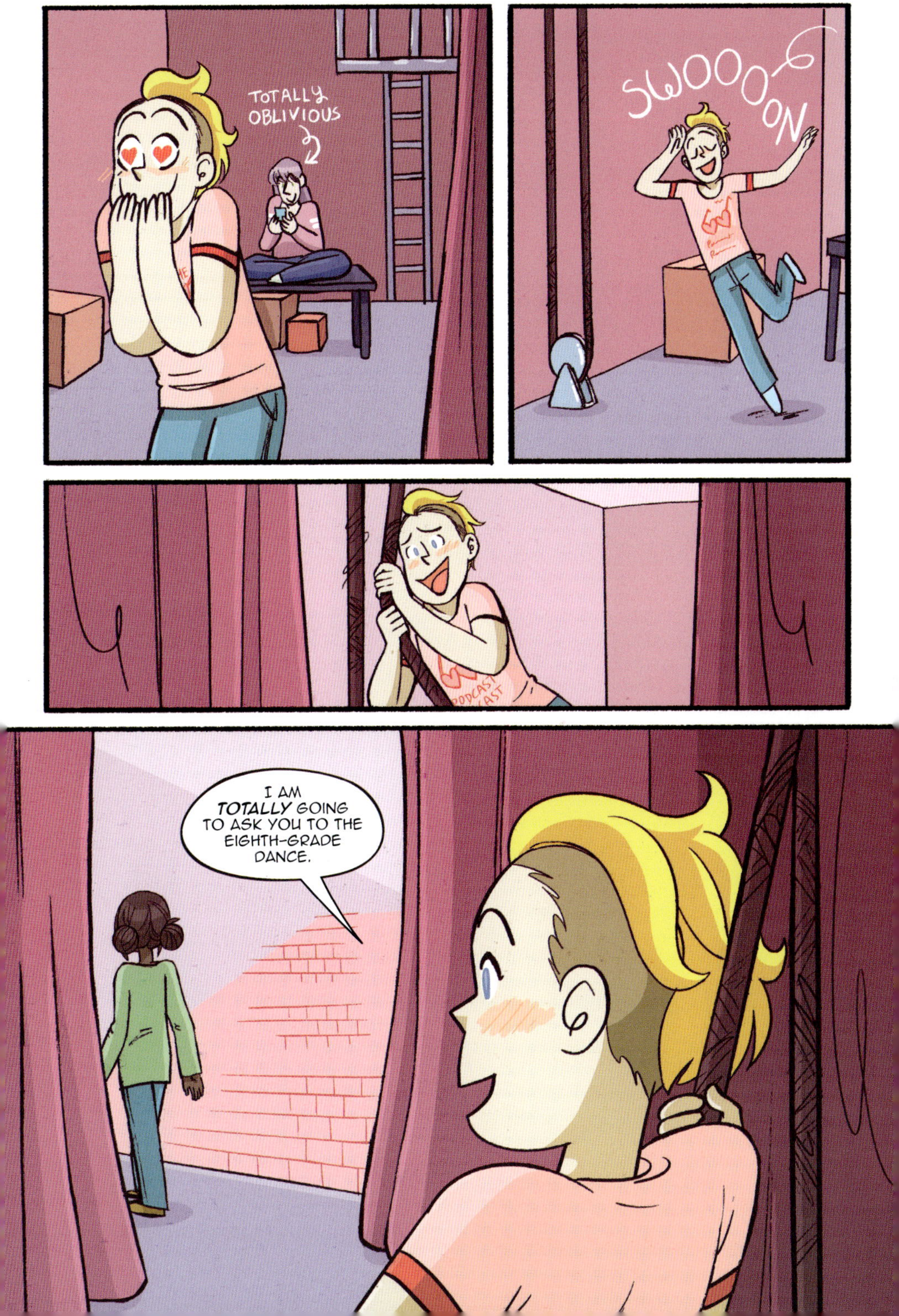
TOTALLY OBLIVIOUS
SWOOOOON
I AM *TOTALLY* GOING TO ASK YOU TO THE EIGHTH-GRADE DANCE.

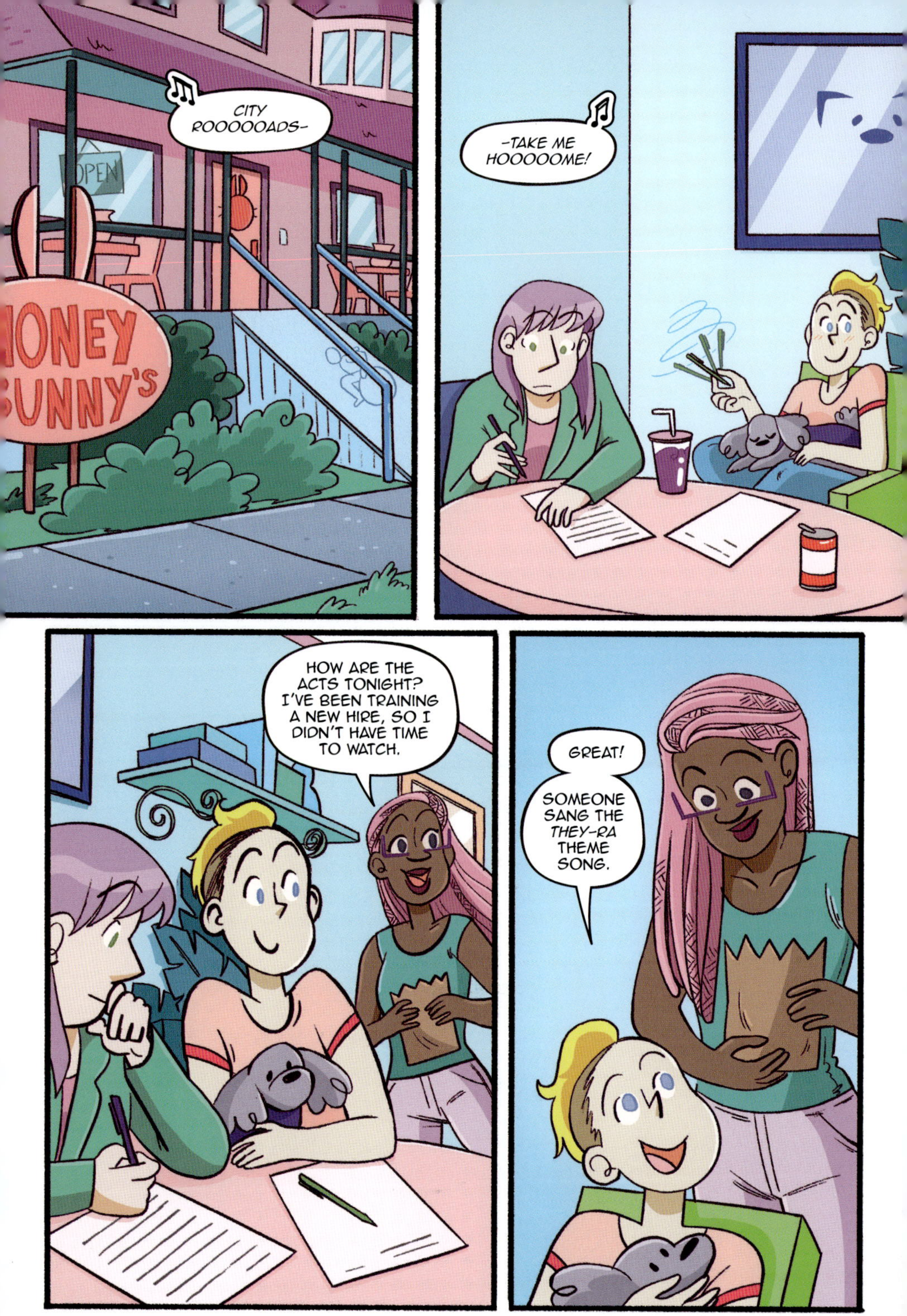
OPEN
HONEY BUNNY'S
CITY ROOOOOADS-
-TAKE ME HOOOOOME!
HOW ARE THE ACTS TONIGHT? I'VE BEEN TRAINING A NEW HIRE, SO I DIDN'T HAVE TIME TO WATCH.
GREAT!
SOMEONE SANG THE *THEY-RA* THEME SONG.

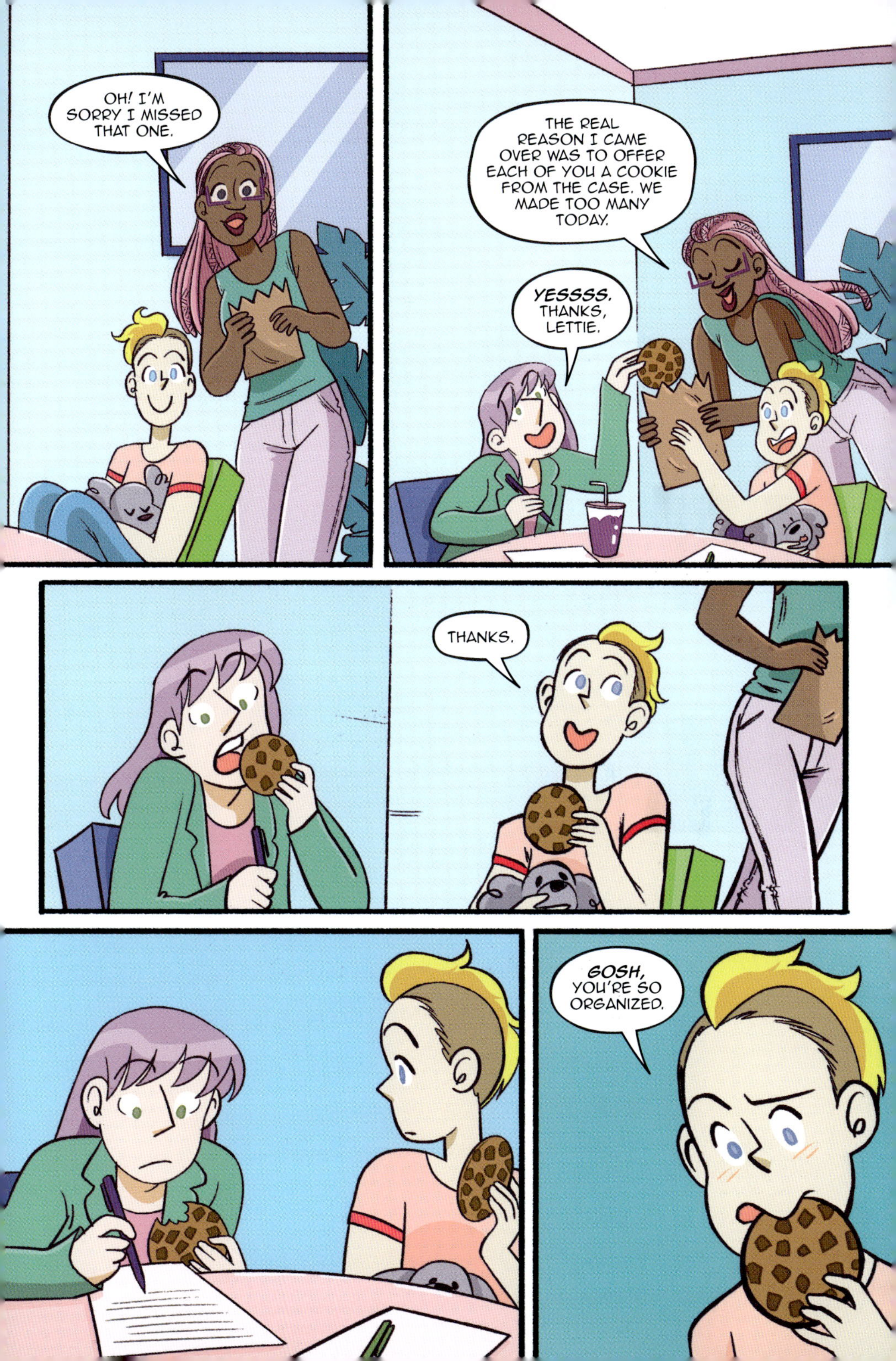
OH! I'M SORRY I MISSED THAT ONE.
THE REAL REASON I CAME OVER WAS TO OFFER EACH OF YOU A COOKIE FROM THE CASE. WE MADE TOO MANY TODAY.
YESSSS. THANKS, LETTIE.
THANKS.
GOSH, YOU'RE SO ORGANIZED.

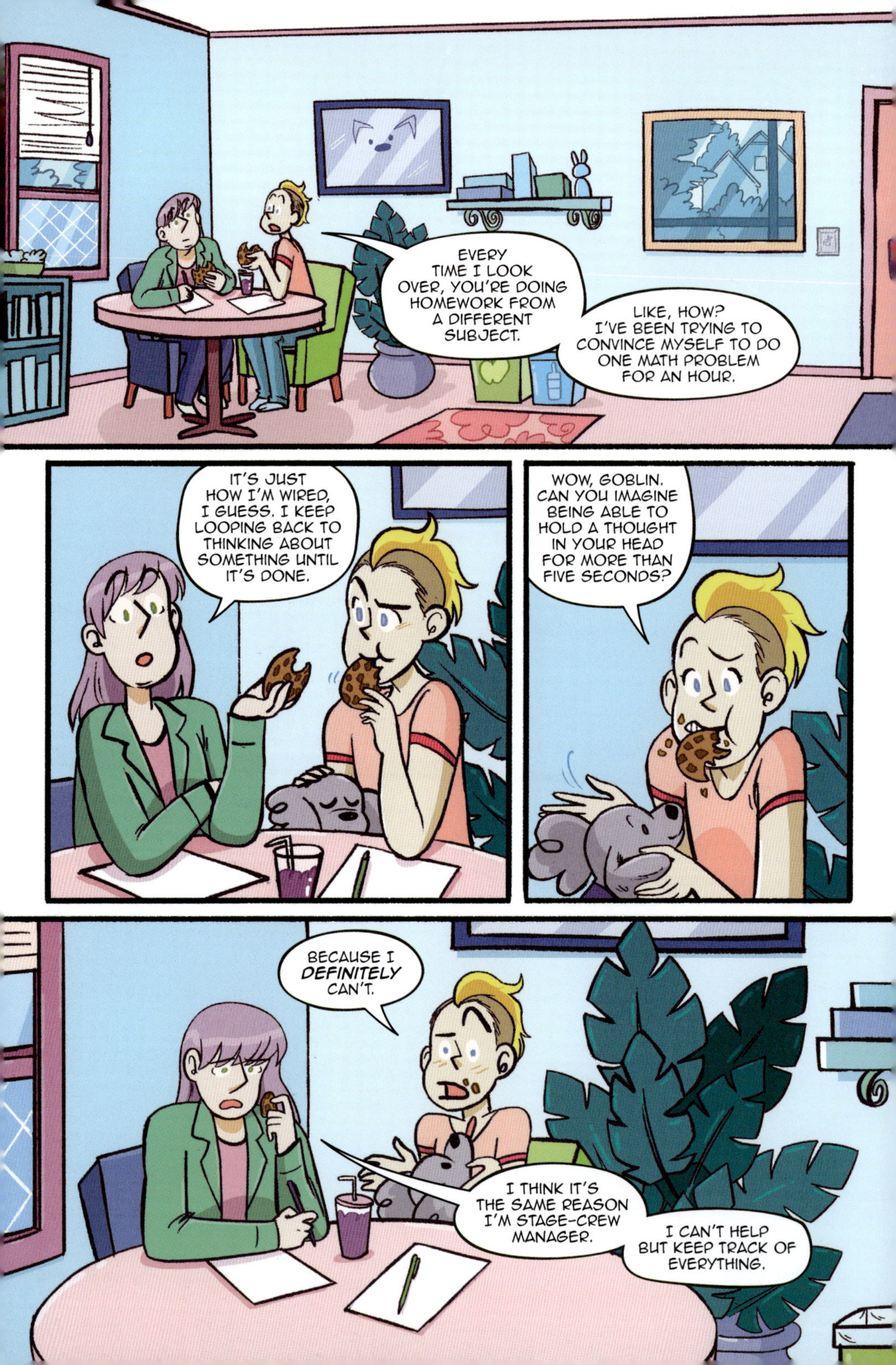
EVERY TIME I LOOK OVER, YOU'RE DOING HOMEWORK FROM A DIFFERENT SUBJECT.
LIKE, HOW? I'VE BEEN TRYING TO CONVINCE MYSELF TO DO ONE MATH PROBLEM FOR AN HOUR.
IT'S JUST HOW I'M WIRED, I GUESS. I KEEP LOOPING BACK TO THINKING ABOUT SOMETHING UNTIL IT'S DONE.
WOW, GOBLIN. CAN YOU IMAGINE BEING ABLE TO HOLD A THOUGHT IN YOUR HEAD FOR MORE THAN FIVE SECONDS?
BECAUSE I *DEFINITELY* CAN'T.
I THINK IT'S THE SAME REASON I'M STAGE-CREW MANAGER.
I CAN'T HELP BUT KEEP TRACK OF EVERYTHING.

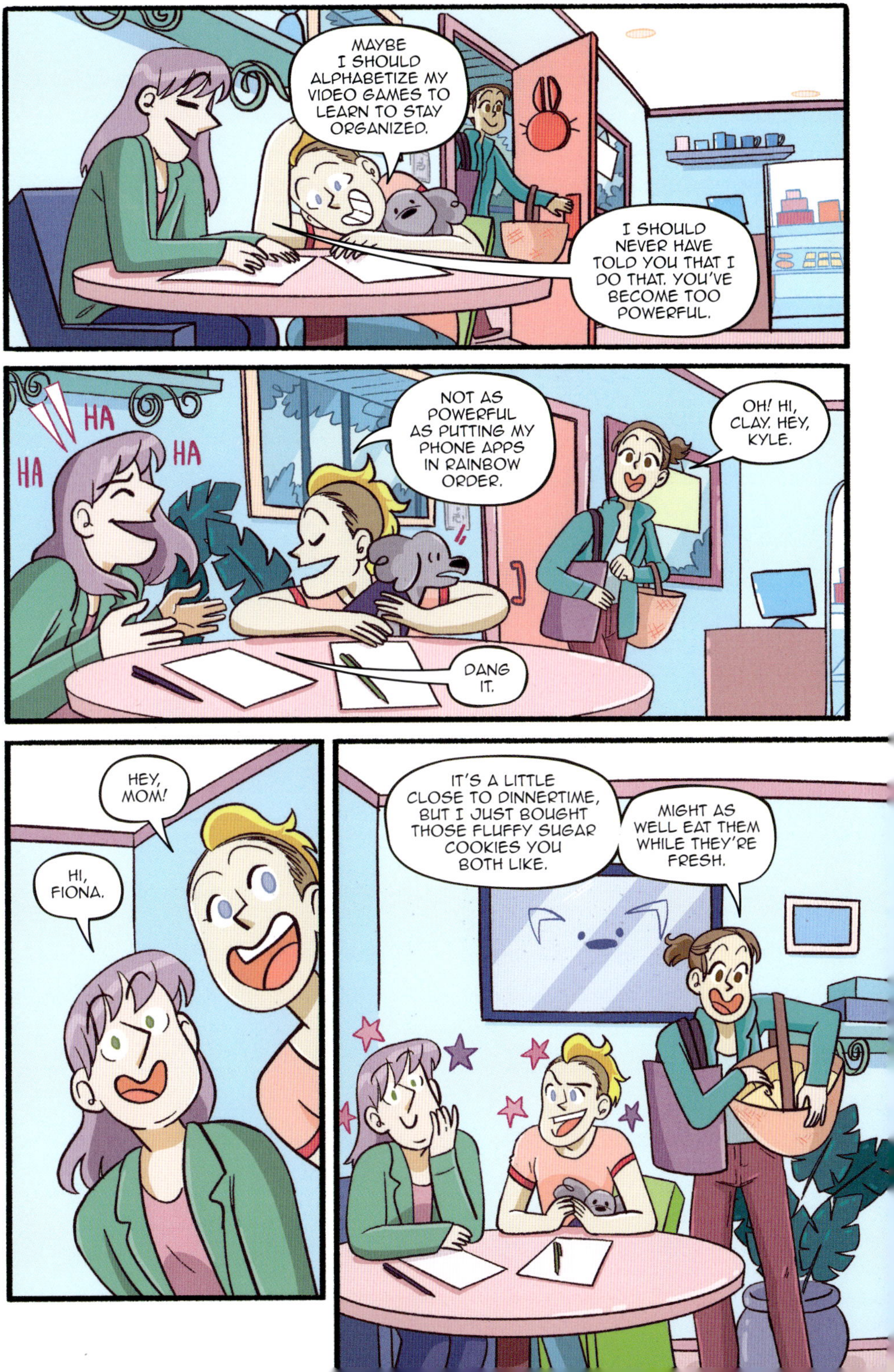
MAYBE I SHOULD ALPHABETIZE MY VIDEO GAMES TO LEARN TO STAY ORGANIZED.
I SHOULD NEVER HAVE TOLD YOU THAT I DO THAT. YOU'VE BECOME TOO POWERFUL.
HA
HA
HA
NOT AS POWERFUL AS PUTTING MY PHONE APPS IN RAINBOW ORDER.
OH! HI, CLAY. HEY, KYLE.
DANG IT.
HEY, MOM!
HI, FIONA.
IT'S A LITTLE CLOSE TO DINNERTIME, BUT I JUST BOUGHT THOSE FLUFFY SUGAR COOKIES YOU BOTH LIKE.
MIGHT AS WELL EAT THEM WHILE THEY'RE FRESH.

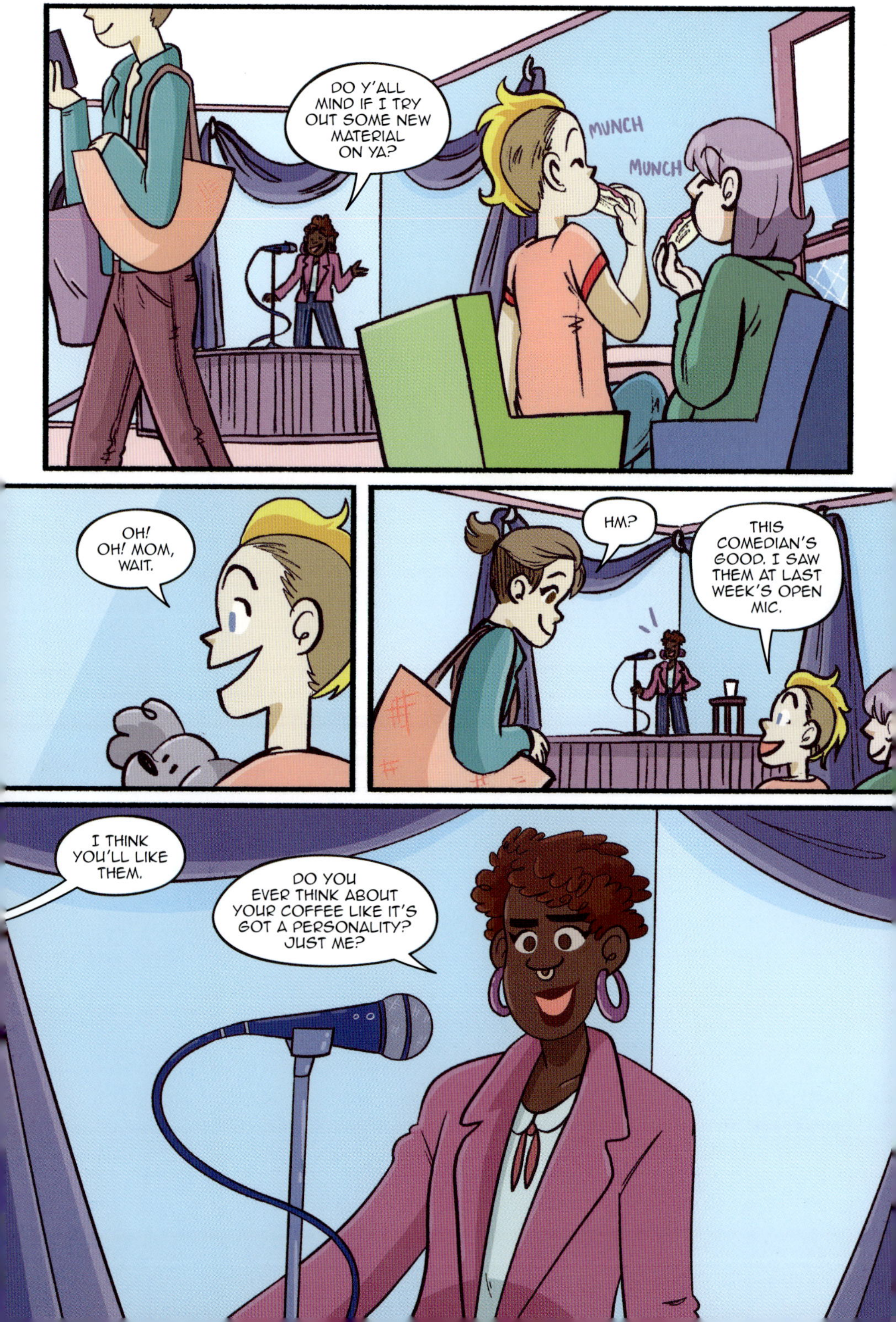
DO Y'ALL MIND IF I TRY OUT SOME NEW MATERIAL ON YA?
MUNCH
MUNCH
OH! OH! MOM, WAIT.
HM?
THIS COMEDIAN'S GOOD. I SAW THEM AT LAST WEEK'S OPEN MIC.
I THINK YOU'LL LIKE THEM.
DO YOU EVER THINK ABOUT YOUR COFFEE LIKE IT'S GOT A PERSONALITY? JUST ME?

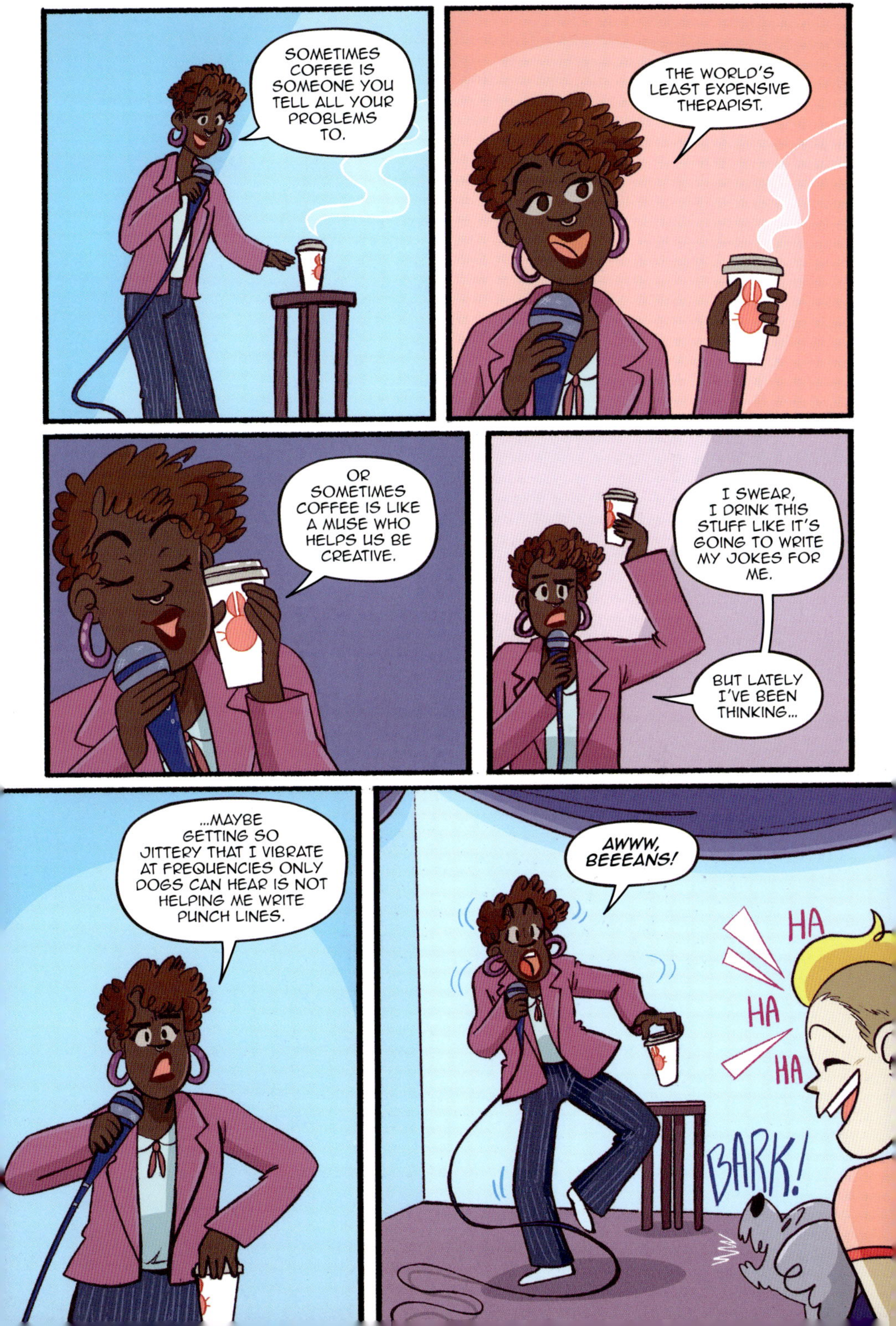
SOMETIMES COFFEE IS SOMEONE YOU TELL ALL YOUR PROBLEMS TO.
THE WORLD'S LEAST EXPENSIVE THERAPIST.
OR SOMETIMES COFFEE IS LIKE A MUSE WHO HELPS US BE CREATIVE.
I SWEAR, I DRINK THIS STUFF LIKE IT'S GOING TO WRITE MY JOKES FOR ME.
BUT LATELY I'VE BEEN THINKING...
...MAYBE GETTING SO JITTERY THAT I VIBRATE AT FREQUENCIES ONLY DOGS CAN HEAR IS NOT HELPING ME WRITE PUNCH LINES.
AWWW, BEEEANS!
HA
HA
HA
BARK!

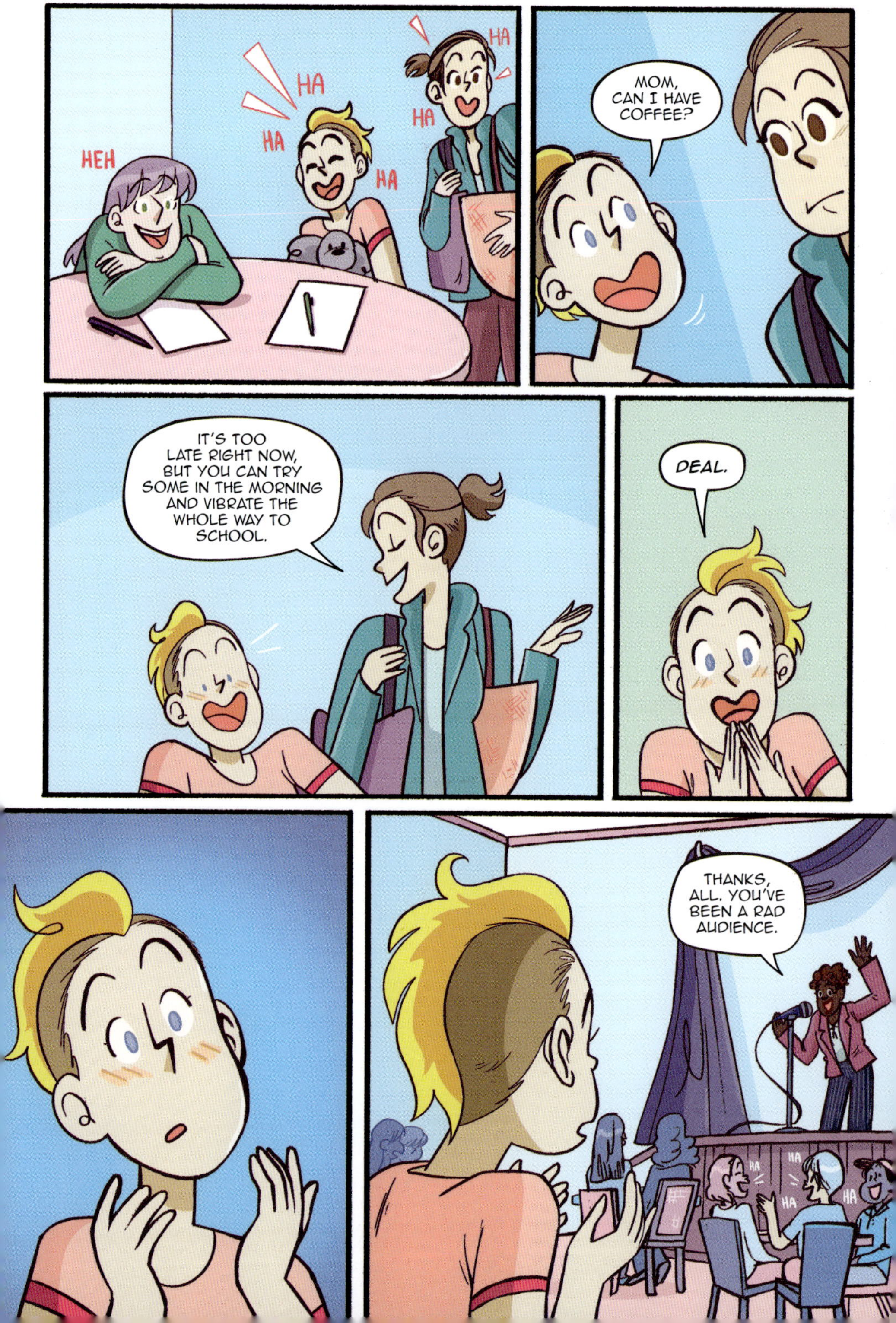
HEH
HA
HA
HA
HA
HA
MOM, CAN I HAVE COFFEE?
IT'S TOO LATE RIGHT NOW, BUT YOU CAN TRY SOME IN THE MORNING AND VIBRATE THE WHOLE WAY TO SCHOOL.
DEAL.
THANKS, ALL. YOU'VE BEEN A RAD AUDIENCE.
HA
HA
HA
HA

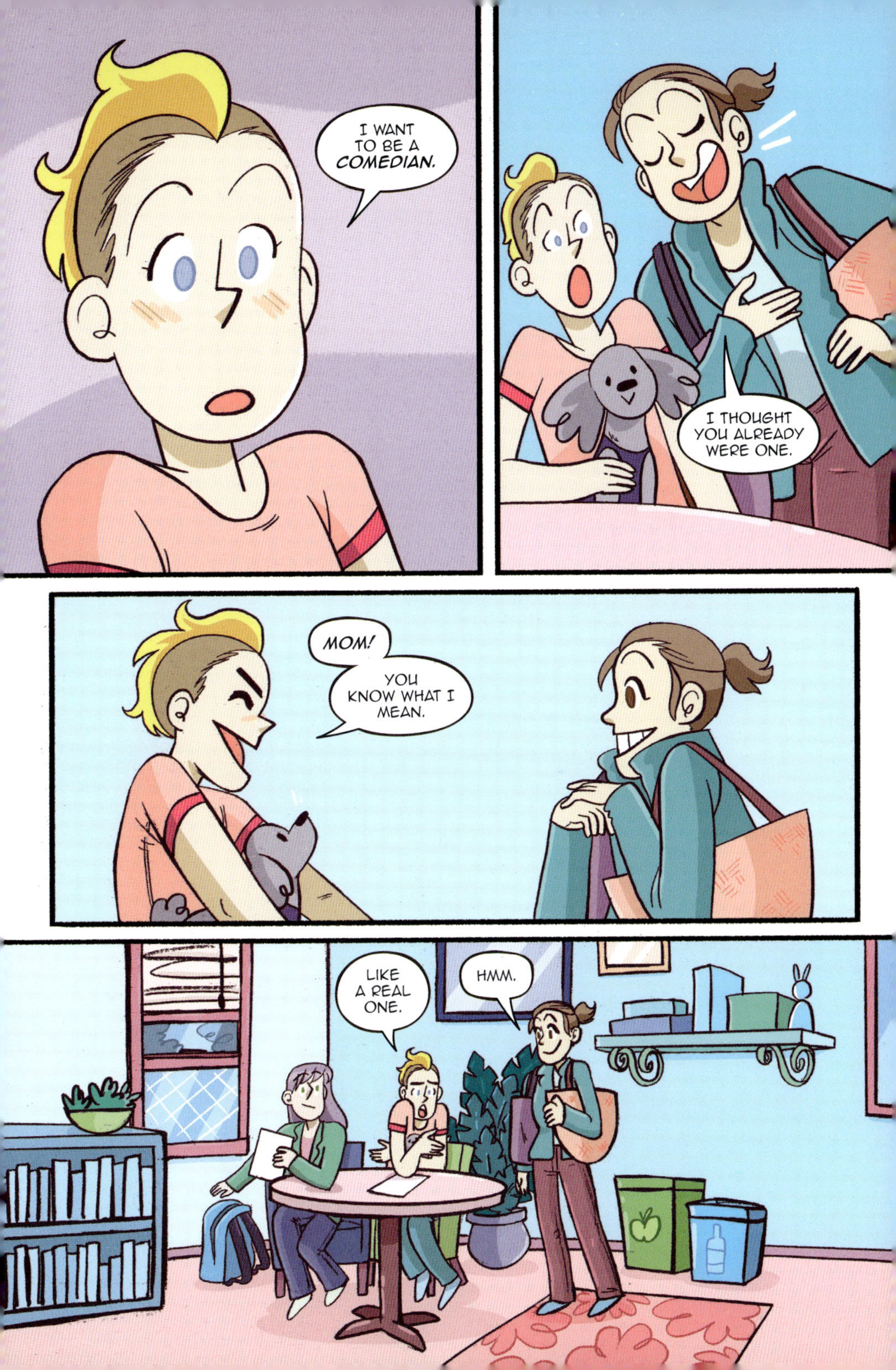
I WANT TO BE A *COMEDIAN.*
I THOUGHT YOU ALREADY WERE ONE.
MOM!
YOU KNOW WHAT I MEAN.
LIKE A REAL ONE.
HMM.

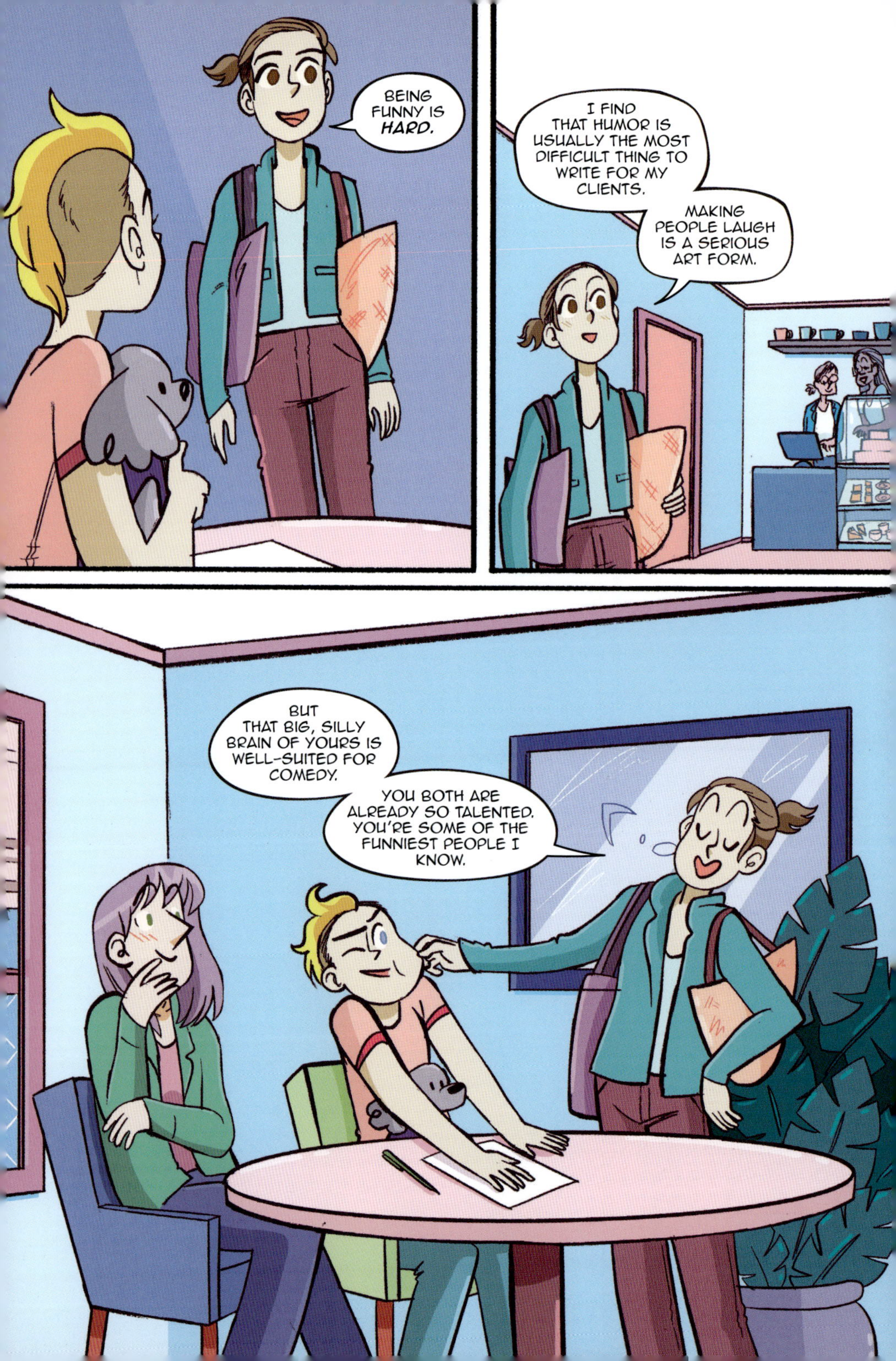
BEING FUNNY IS ***HARD.***
I FIND THAT HUMOR IS USUALLY THE MOST DIFFICULT THING TO WRITE FOR MY CLIENTS.
MAKING PEOPLE LAUGH IS A SERIOUS ART FORM.
BUT THAT BIG, SILLY BRAIN OF YOURS IS WELL-SUITED FOR COMEDY.
YOU BOTH ARE ALREADY SO TALENTED. YOU'RE SOME OF THE FUNNIEST PEOPLE I KNOW.

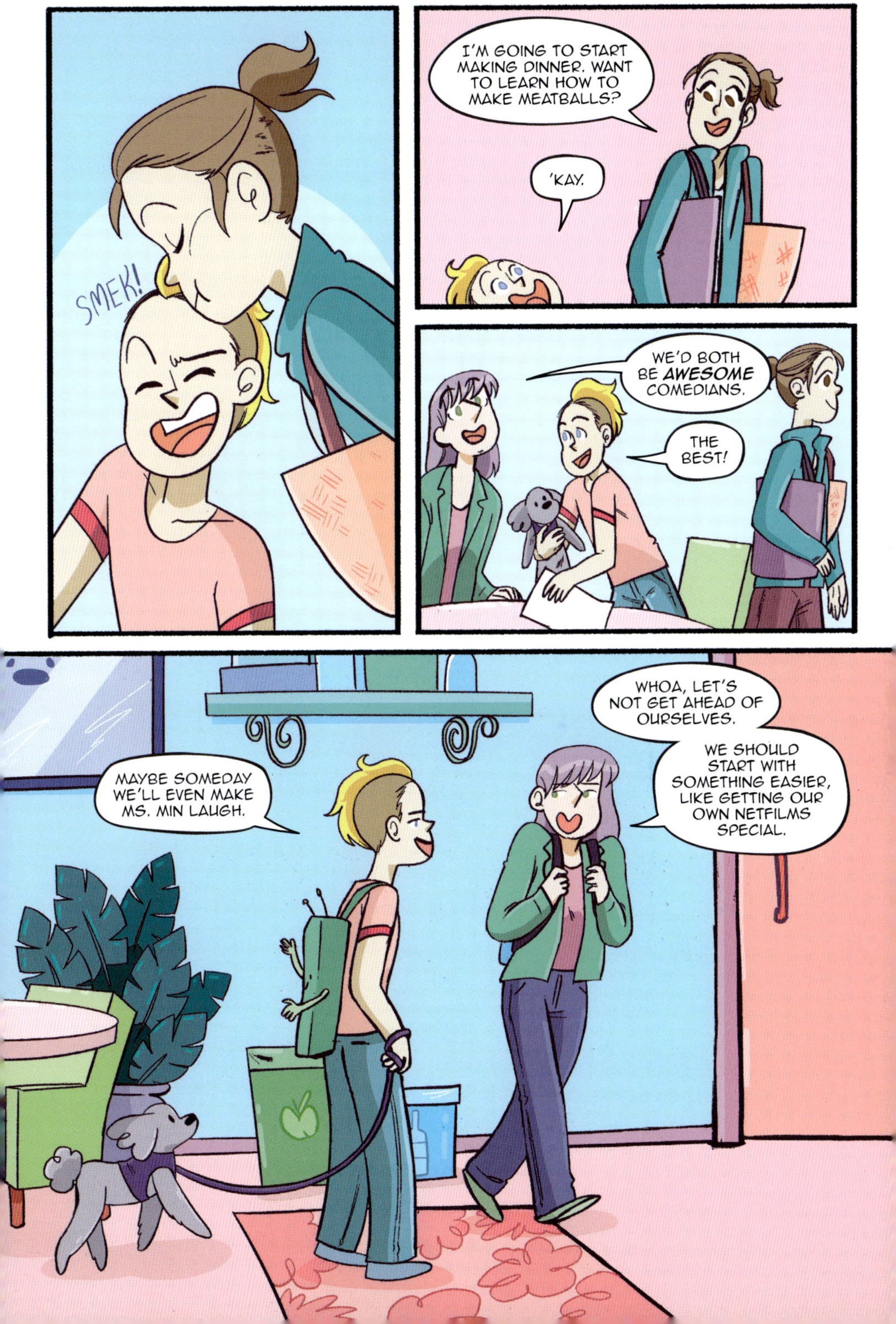
SMEK!
I'M GOING TO START MAKING DINNER. WANT TO LEARN HOW TO MAKE MEATBALLS?
'KAY.
WE'D BOTH BE **AWESOME** COMEDIANS.
THE BEST!
MAYBE SOMEDAY WE'LL EVEN MAKE MS. MIN LAUGH.
WHOA, LET'S NOT GET AHEAD OF OURSELVES.
WE SHOULD START WITH SOMETHING EASIER, LIKE GETTING OUR OWN NETFILMS SPECIAL.

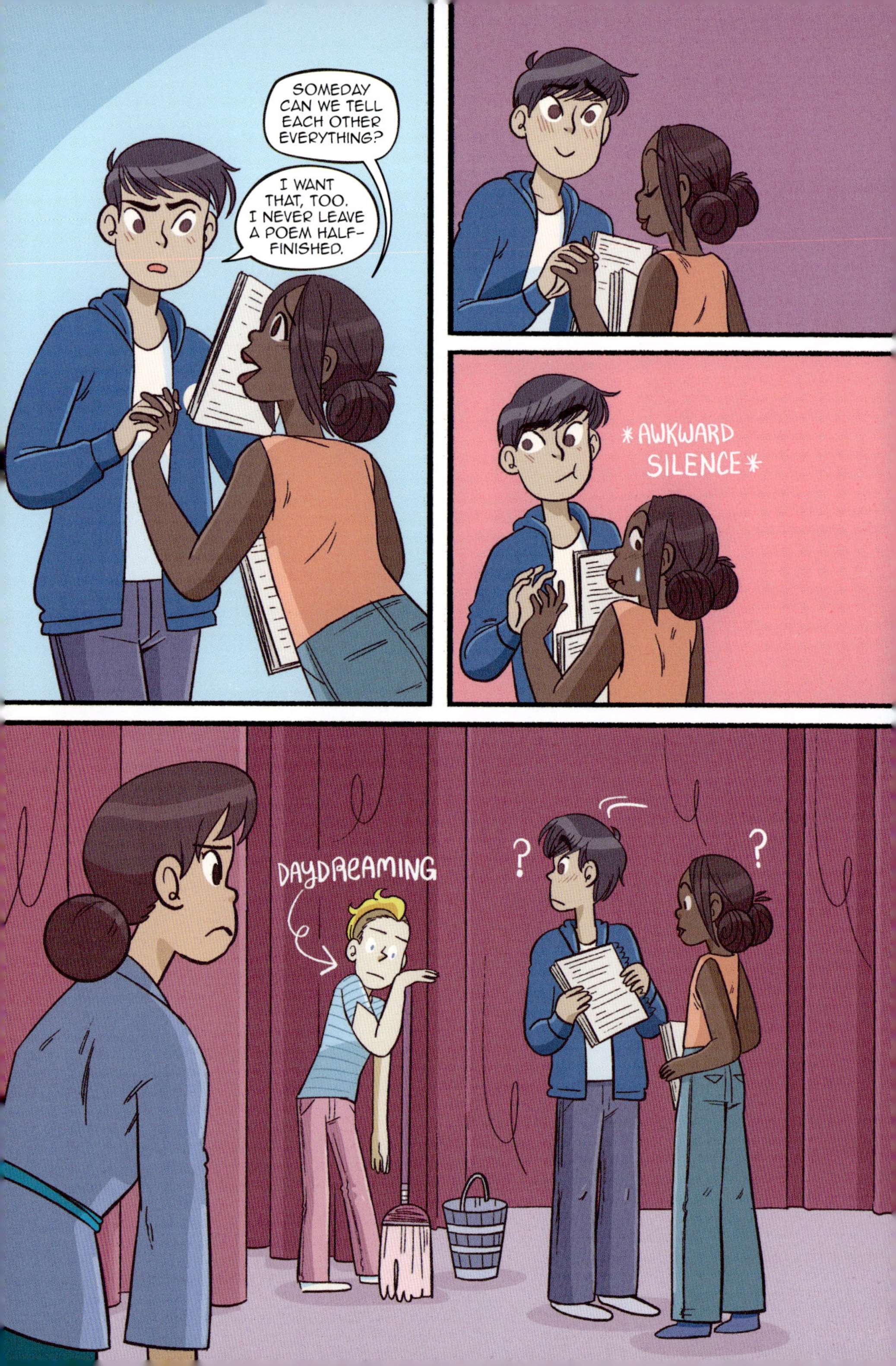
SOMEDAY CAN WE TELL EACH OTHER EVERYTHING?
I WANT THAT, TOO. I NEVER LEAVE A POEM HALF-FINISHED.
AWKWARD SILENCE
DAYDREAMING
?
?

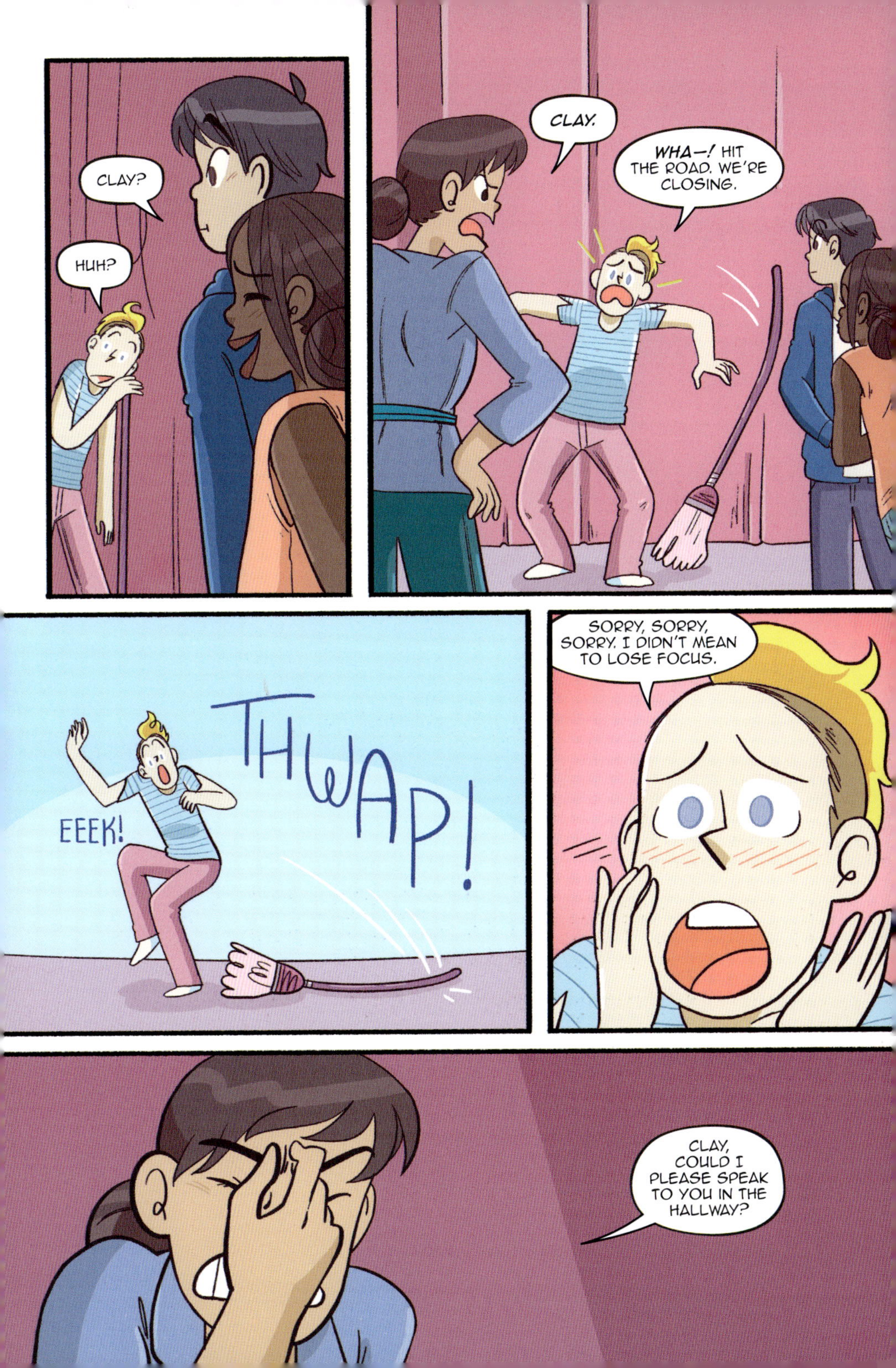
CLAY?
HUH?
CLAY.
WHA—! HIT THE ROAD. WE'RE CLOSING.
THWAP!
EEEK!
SORRY, SORRY, SORRY. I DIDN'T MEAN TO LOSE FOCUS.
CLAY, COULD I PLEASE SPEAK TO YOU IN THE HALLWAY?

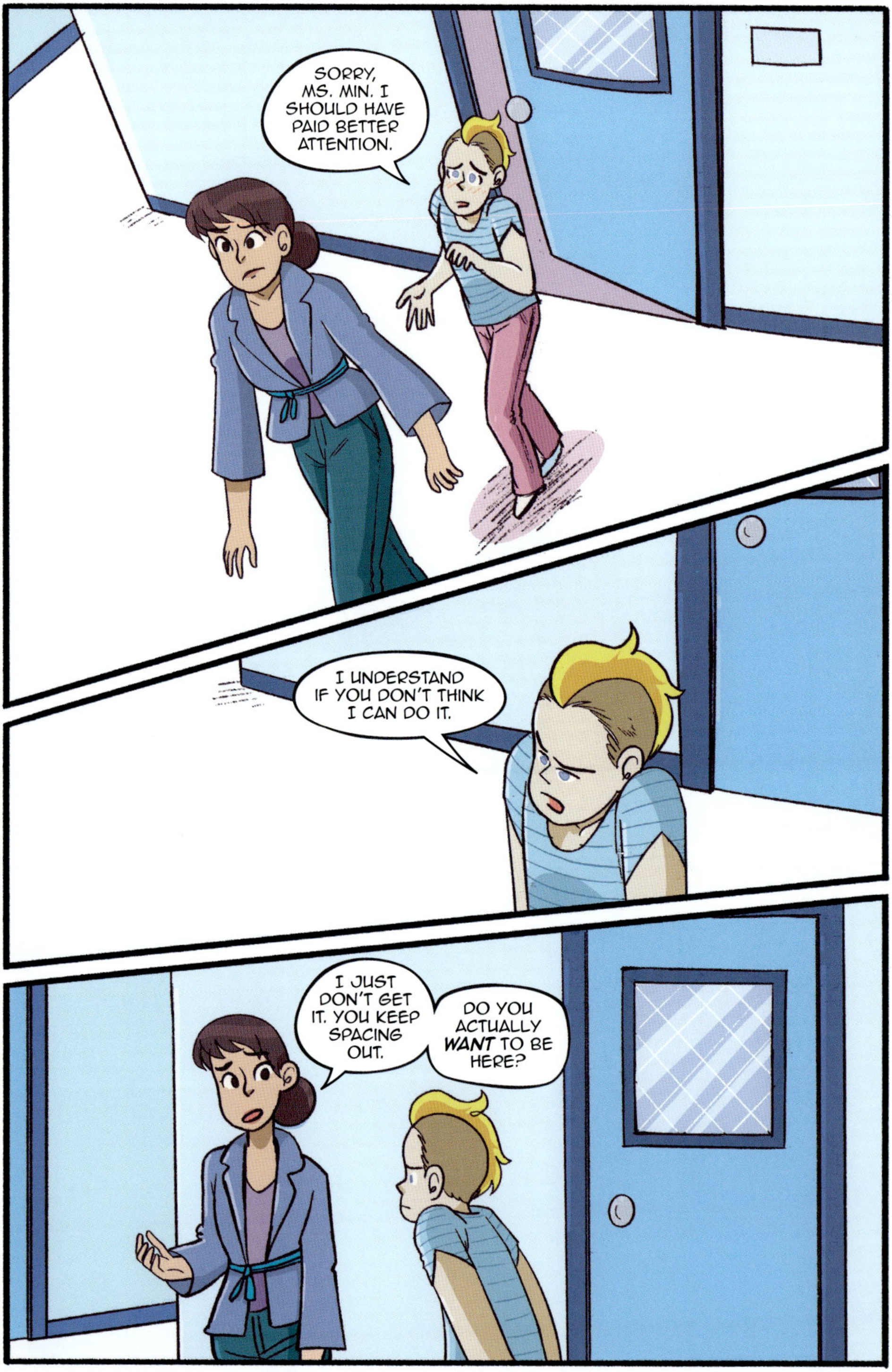
SORRY, MS. MIN. I SHOULD HAVE PAID BETTER ATTENTION.
I UNDERSTAND IF YOU DON'T THINK I CAN DO IT.
I JUST DON'T GET IT. YOU KEEP SPACING OUT.
DO YOU ACTUALLY *WANT* TO BE HERE?

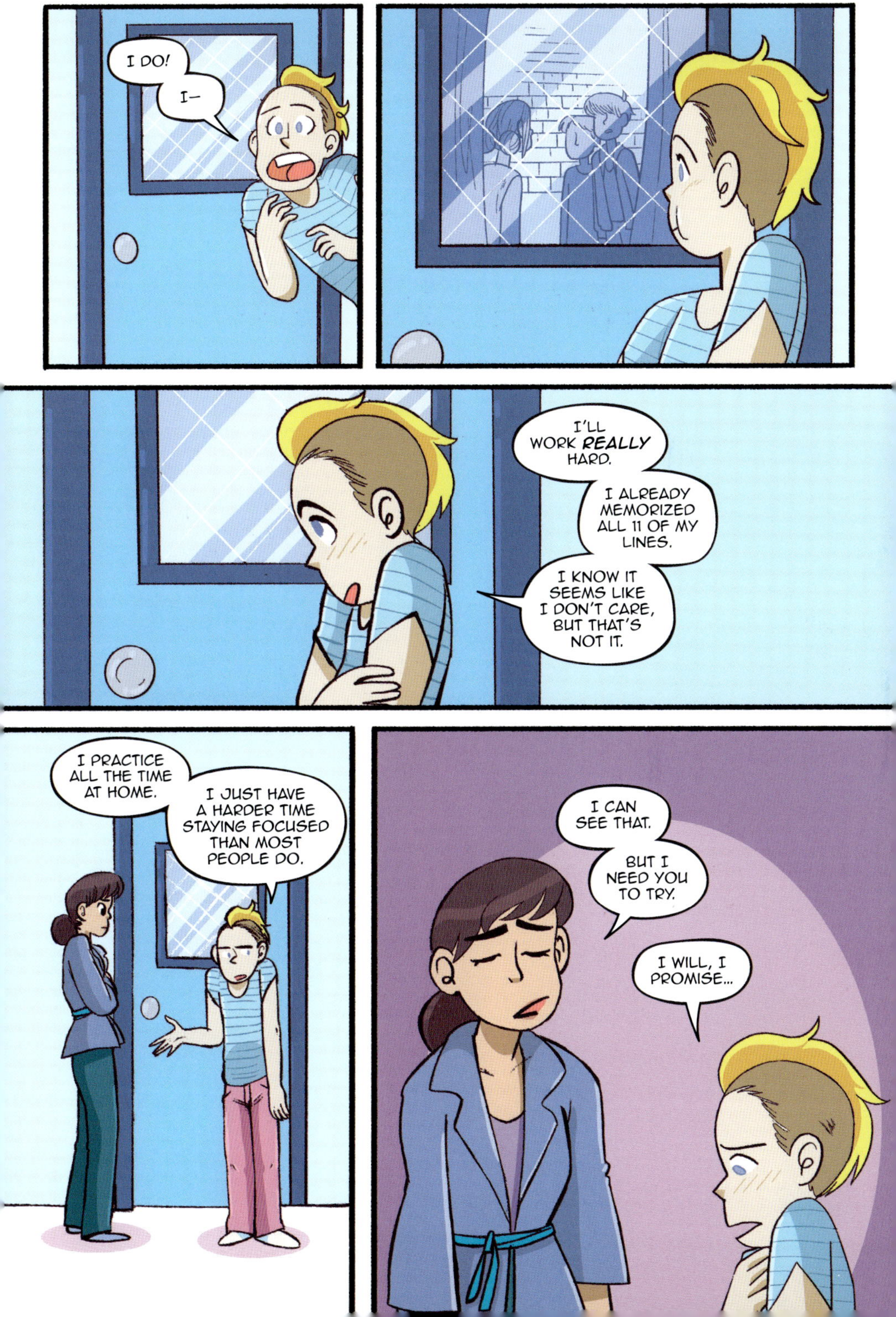

I DO!
I—
I'LL WORK **REALLY** HARD.
I ALREADY MEMORIZED ALL 11 OF MY LINES.
I KNOW IT SEEMS LIKE I DON'T CARE, BUT THAT'S NOT IT.
I PRACTICE ALL THE TIME AT HOME.
I JUST HAVE A HARDER TIME STAYING FOCUSED THAN MOST PEOPLE DO.
I CAN SEE THAT.
BUT I NEED YOU TO TRY.
I WILL, I PROMISE...

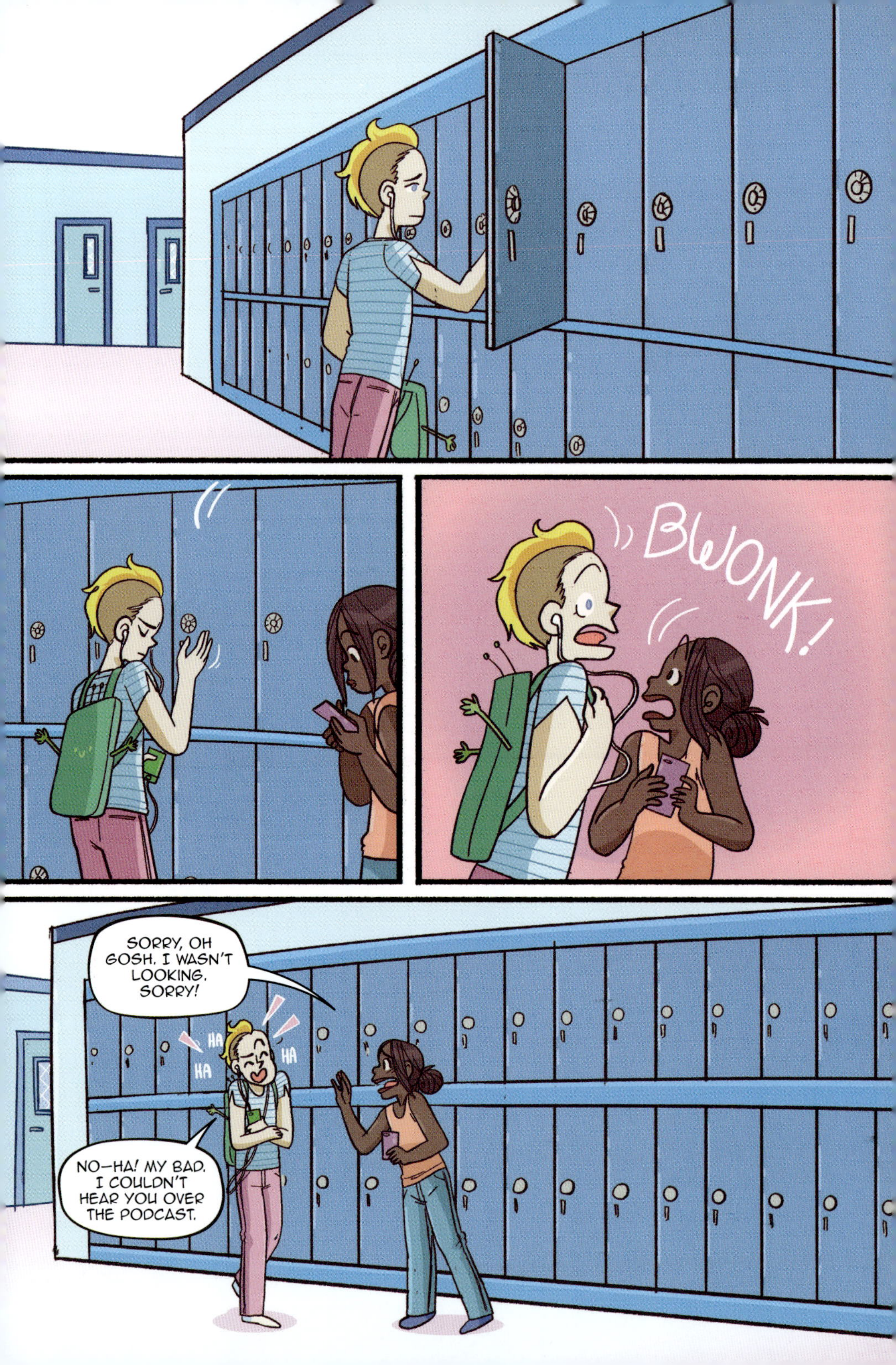

BWONK!
SORRY, OH GOSH. I WASN'T LOOKING. SORRY!
HA
HA
HA
NO—HA! MY BAD. I COULDN'T HEAR YOU OVER THE PODCAST.

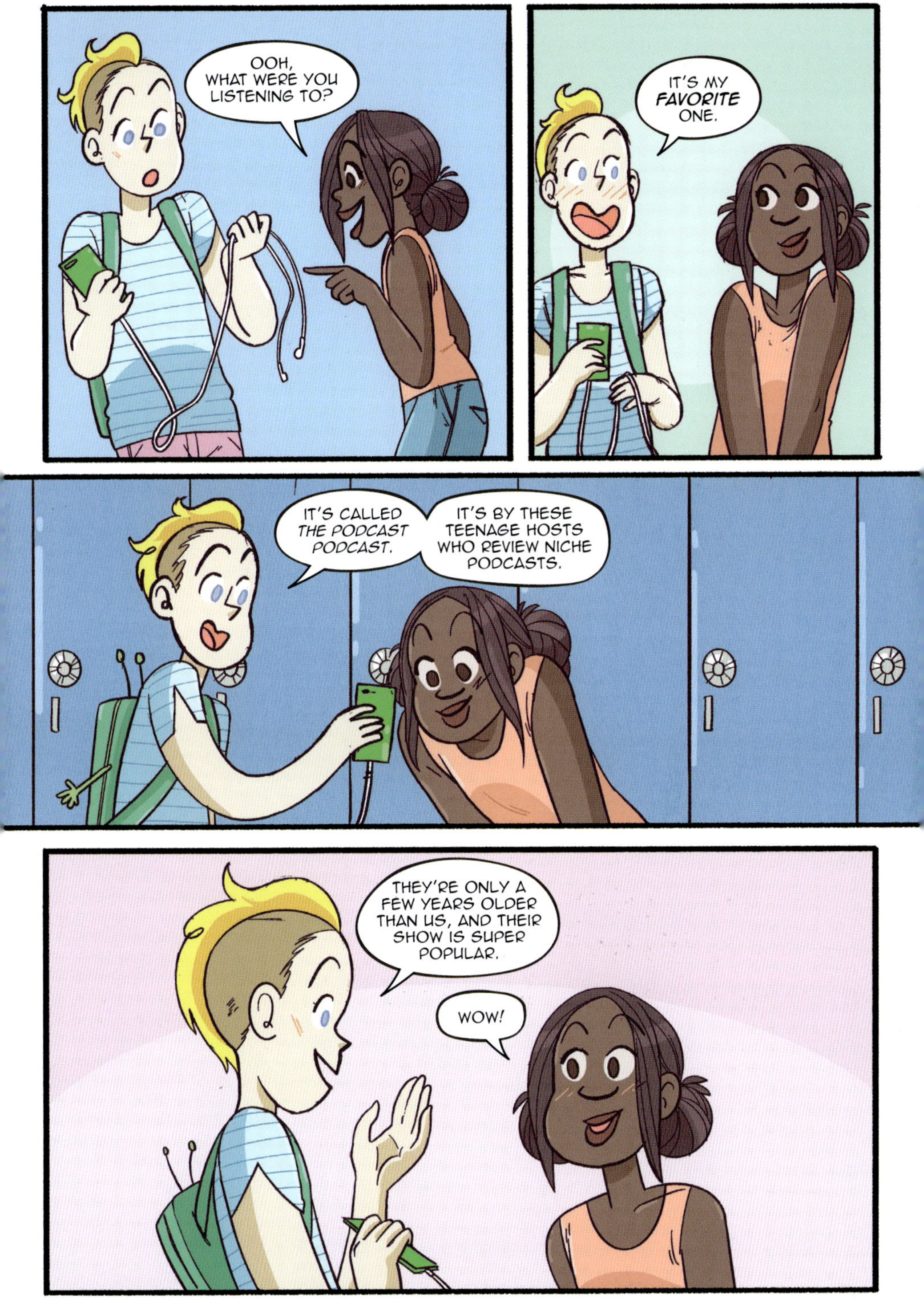
OOH, WHAT WERE YOU LISTENING TO?
IT'S MY *FAVORITE* ONE.
IT'S CALLED *THE PODCAST PODCAST.*
IT'S BY THESE TEENAGE HOSTS WHO REVIEW NICHE PODCASTS.
THEY'RE ONLY A FEW YEARS OLDER THAN US, AND THEIR SHOW IS SUPER POPULAR.
WOW!

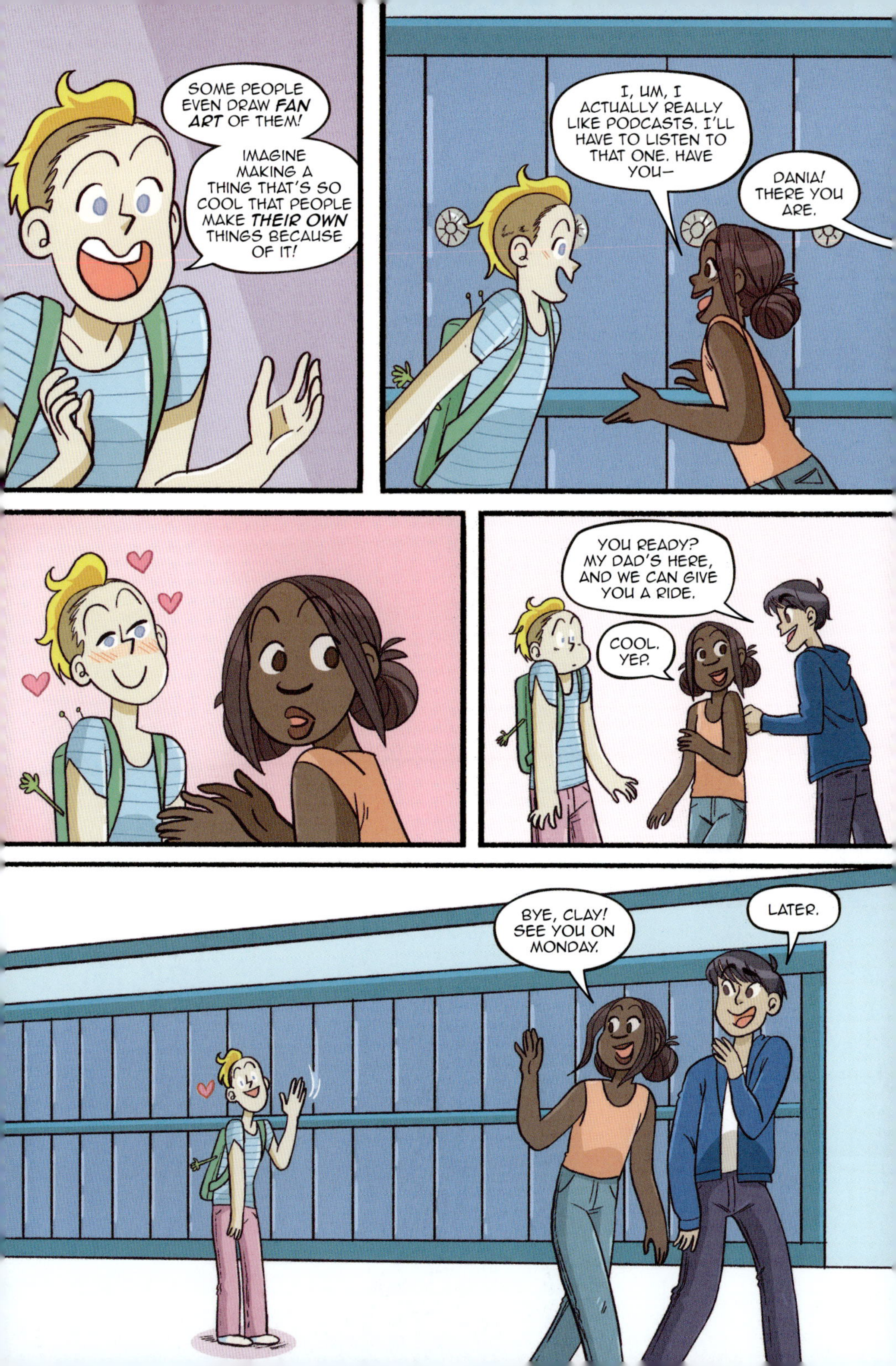
SOME PEOPLE EVEN DRAW **FAN ART** OF THEM!
IMAGINE MAKING A THING THAT'S SO COOL THAT PEOPLE MAKE ***THEIR OWN*** THINGS BECAUSE OF IT!
I, UM, I ACTUALLY REALLY LIKE PODCASTS. I'LL HAVE TO LISTEN TO THAT ONE. HAVE YOU–
DANIA! THERE YOU ARE.
YOU READY? MY DAD'S HERE, AND WE CAN GIVE YOU A RIDE.
COOL. YEP.
BYE, CLAY! SEE YOU ON MONDAY.
LATER.

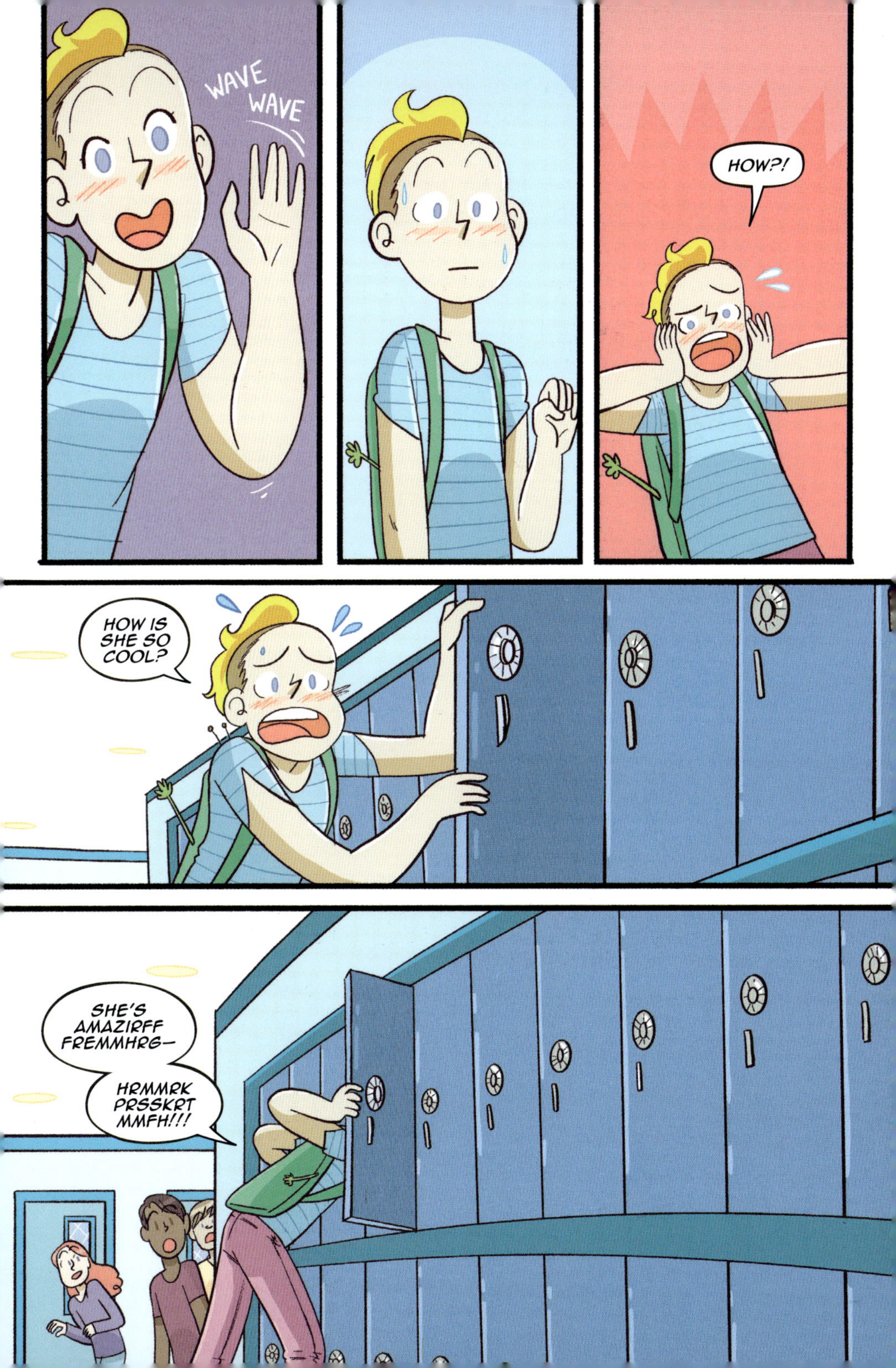
WAVE
WAVE
HOW?!
HOW IS SHE SO COOL?
SHE'S AMAZIRFF FREMMHRG—
HRMMRK PRSSKRT MMFH!!!

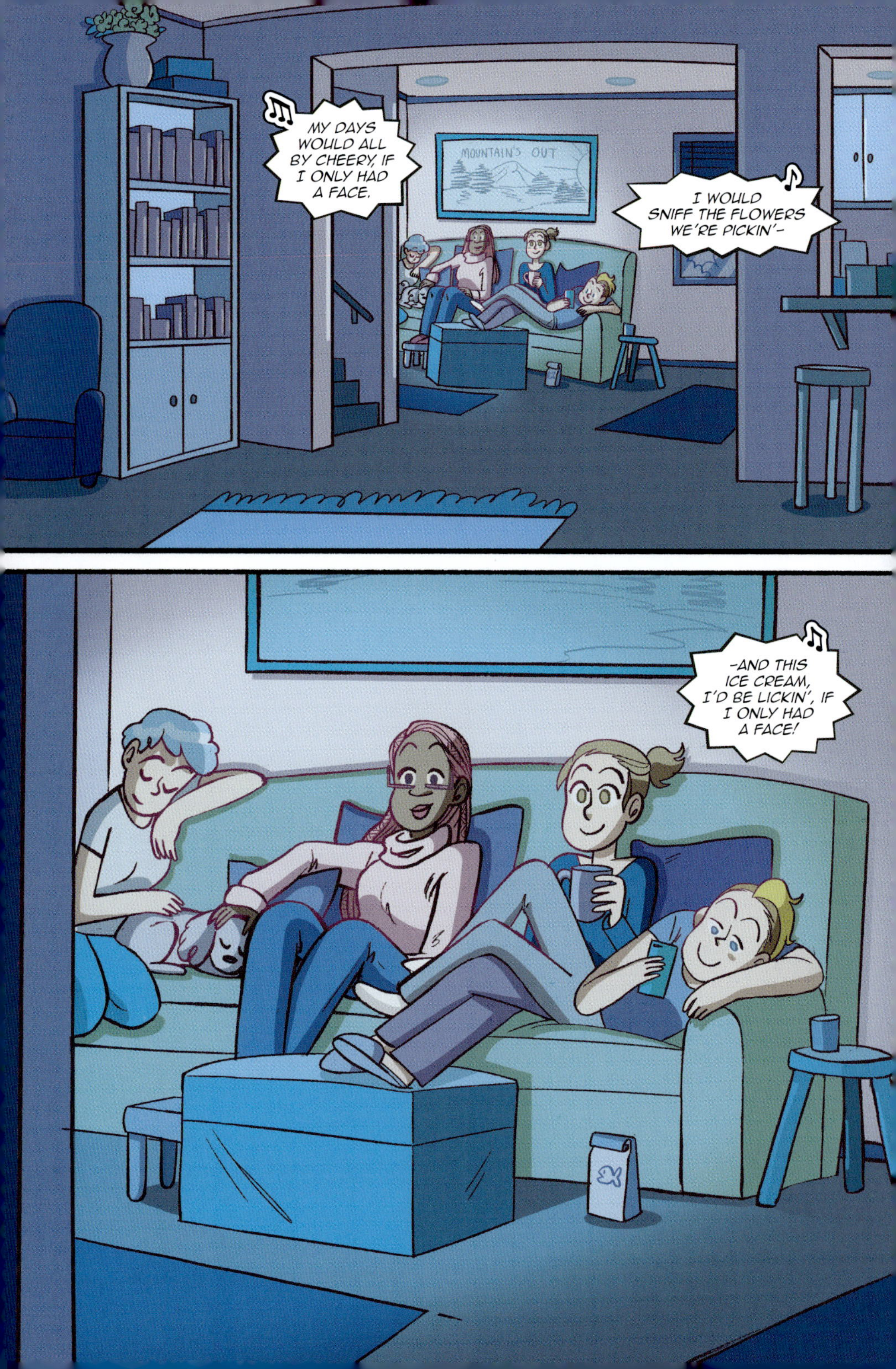
MY DAYS WOULD ALL BY CHEERY, IF I ONLY HAD A FACE.
MOUNTAIN'S OUT
I WOULD SNIFF THE FLOWERS WE'RE PICKIN'-
-AND THIS ICE CREAM, I'D BE LICKIN', IF I ONLY HAD A FACE!

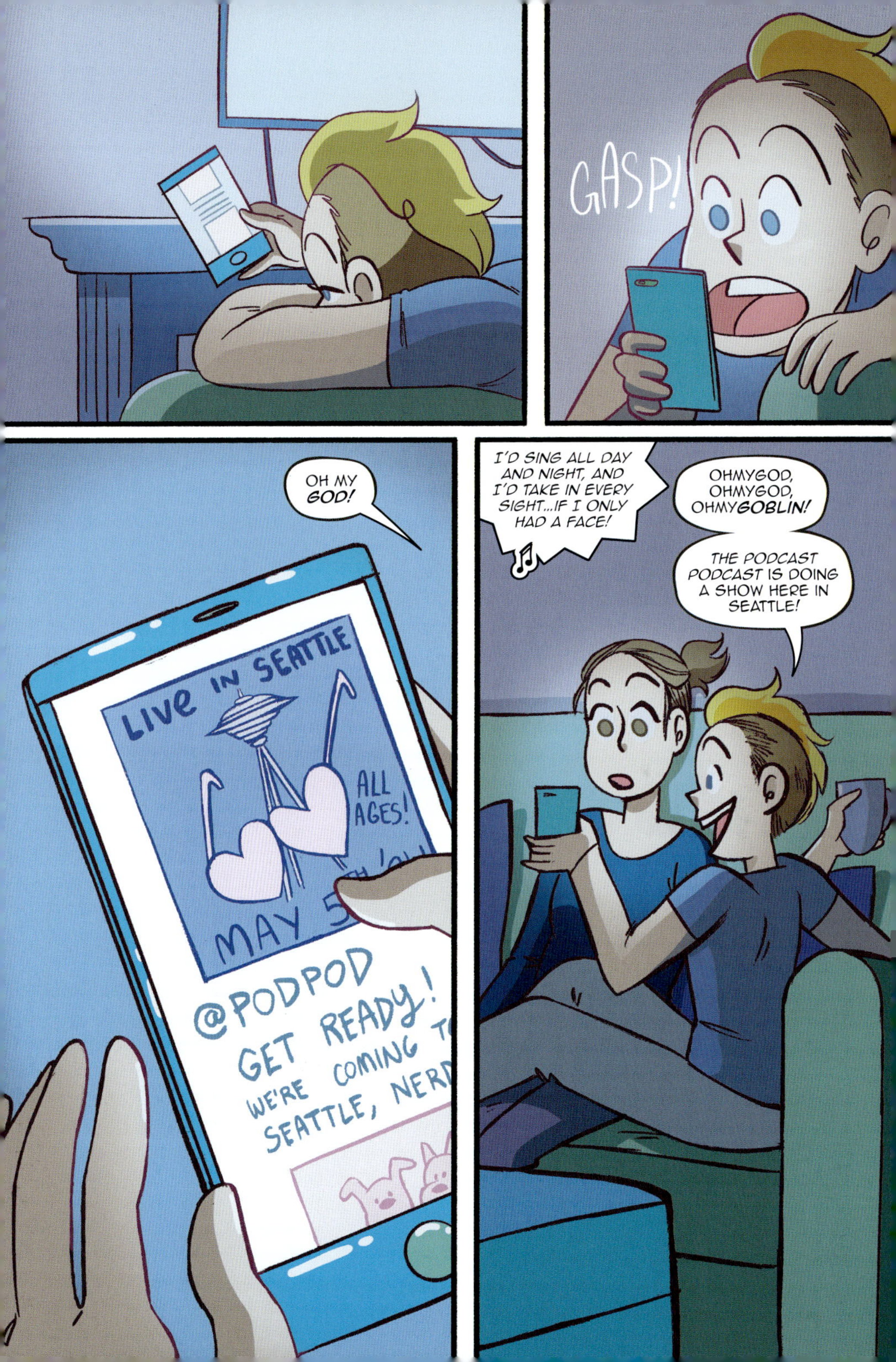
GASP!
OH MY GOD!
LIVE IN SEATTLE
ALL AGES!
MAY 5
@PODPOD
GET READY!
WE'RE COMING T
SEATTLE, NERD
I'D SING ALL DAY AND NIGHT, AND I'D TAKE IN EVERY SIGHT...IF I ONLY HAD A FACE!
OHMYGOD, OHMYGOD, OHMYGOBLIN!
THE PODCAST PODCAST IS DOING A SHOW HERE IN SEATTLE!

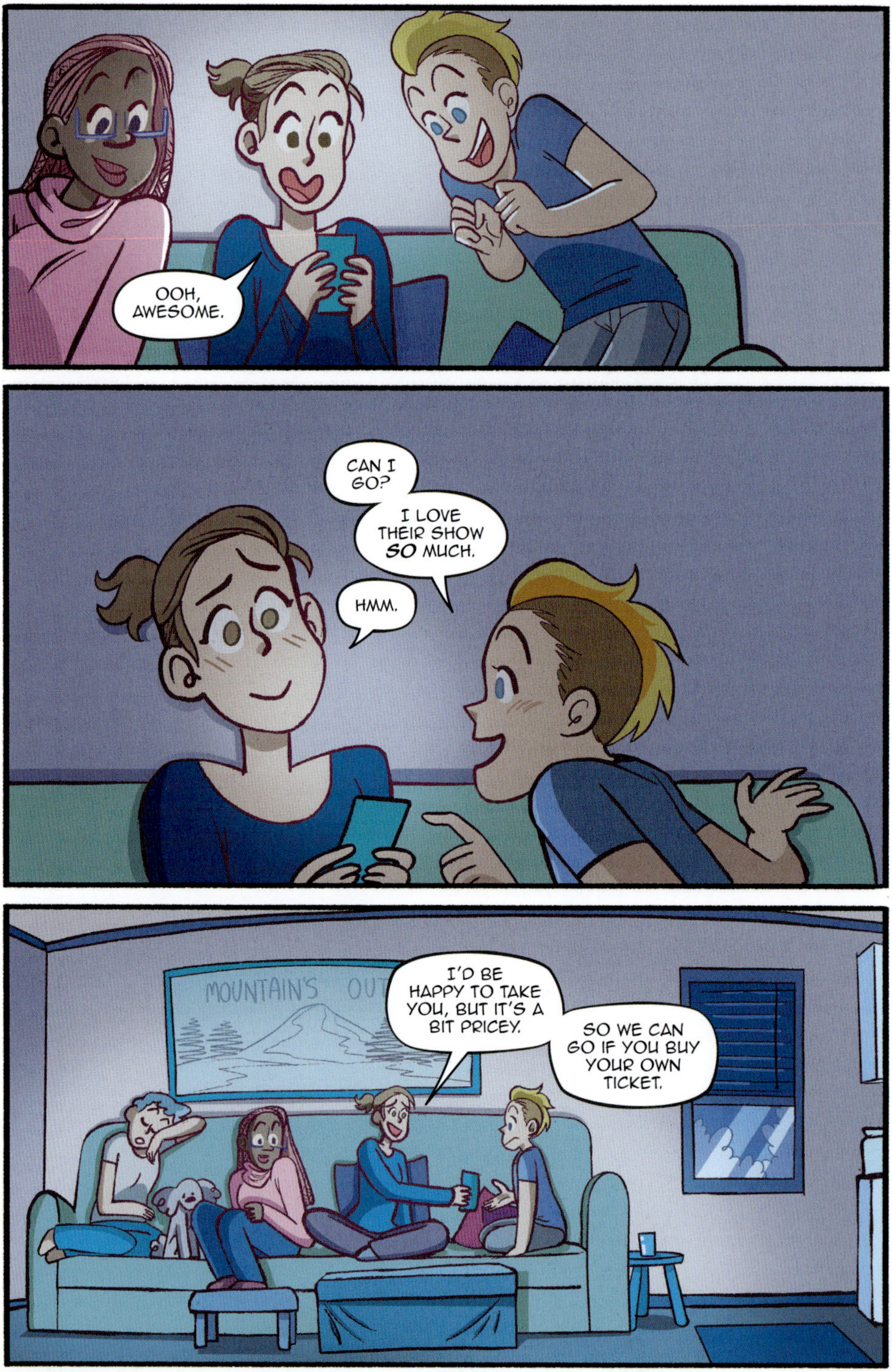
OOH, AWESOME.
CAN I GO?
I LOVE THEIR SHOW SO MUCH.
HMM.
MOUNTAIN'S OUT
I'D BE HAPPY TO TAKE YOU, BUT IT'S A BIT PRICEY.
SO WE CAN GO IF YOU BUY YOUR OWN TICKET.

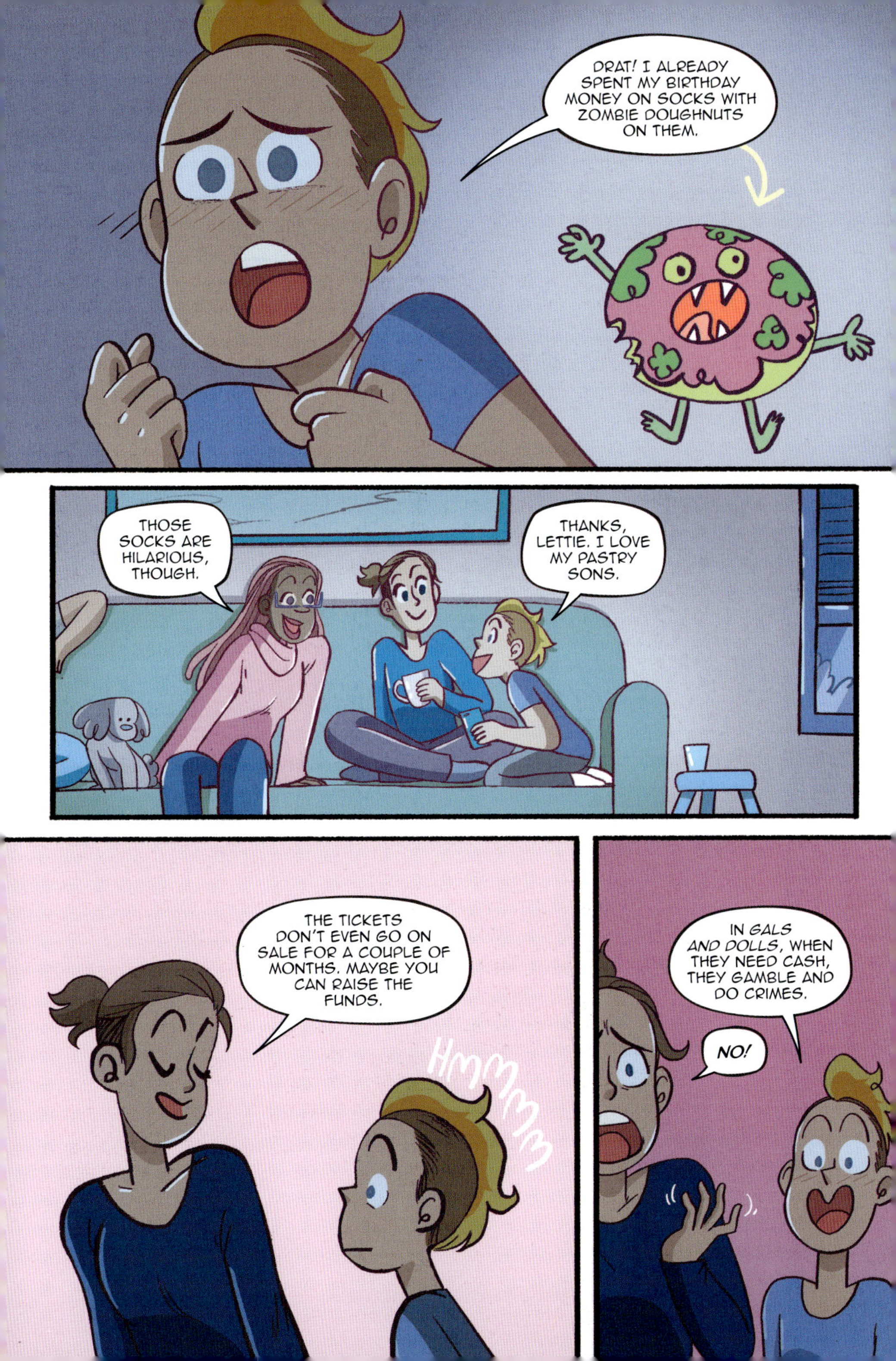
DRAT! I ALREADY SPENT MY BIRTHDAY MONEY ON SOCKS WITH ZOMBIE DOUGHNUTS ON THEM.
THOSE SOCKS ARE HILARIOUS, THOUGH.
THANKS, LETTIE. I LOVE MY PASTRY SONS.
THE TICKETS DON'T EVEN GO ON SALE FOR A COUPLE OF MONTHS. MAYBE YOU CAN RAISE THE FUNDS.
HMMMMM
IN GALS AND DOLLS, WHEN THEY NEED CASH, THEY GAMBLE AND DO CRIMES.
NO!

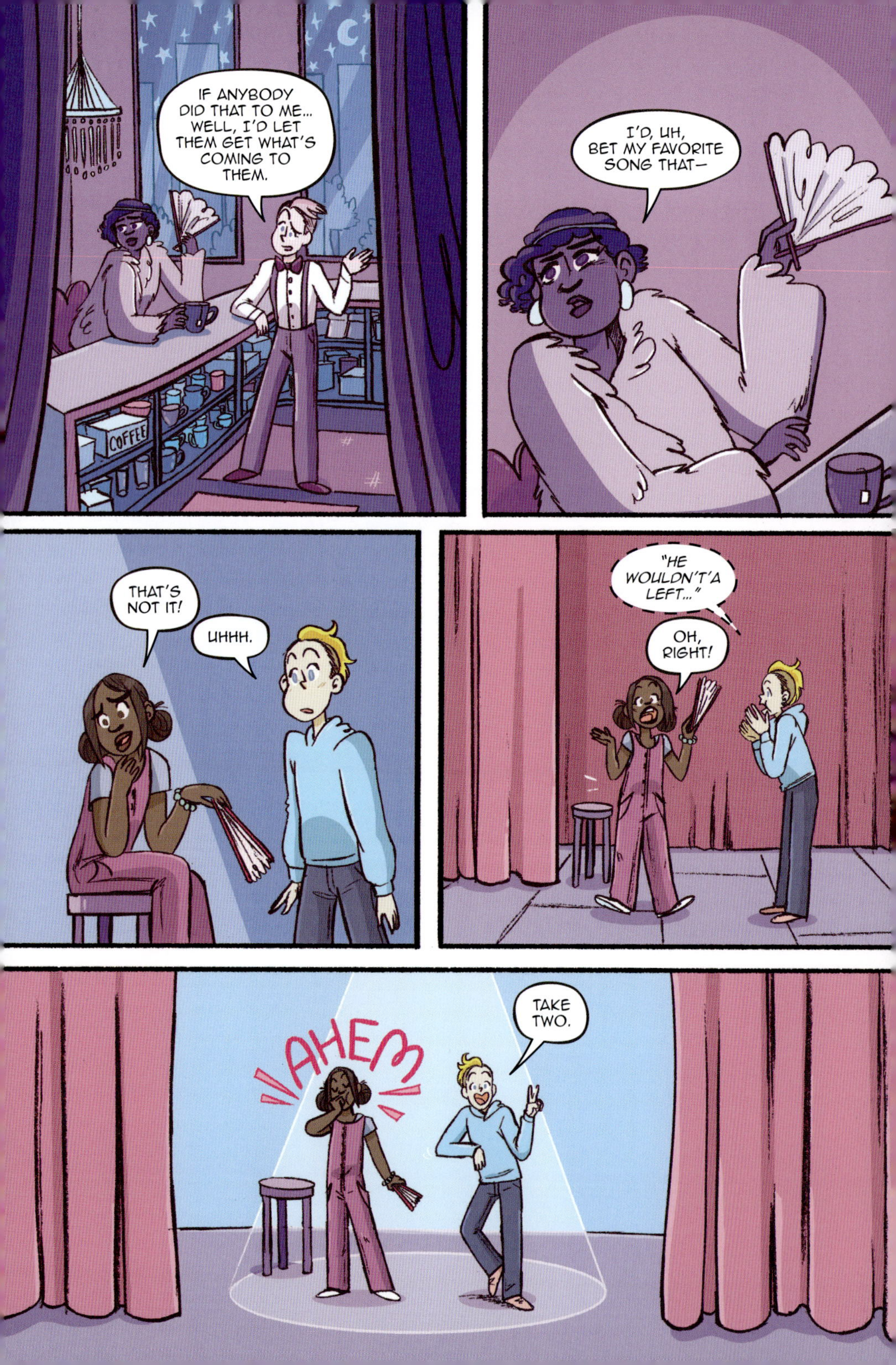
IF ANYBODY DID THAT TO ME... WELL, I'D LET THEM GET WHAT'S COMING TO THEM.
COFFEE
I'D, UH, BET MY FAVORITE SONG THAT—
THAT'S NOT IT!
UHHH.
"HE WOULDN'T'A LEFT..."
OH, RIGHT!
AHEM
TAKE TWO.

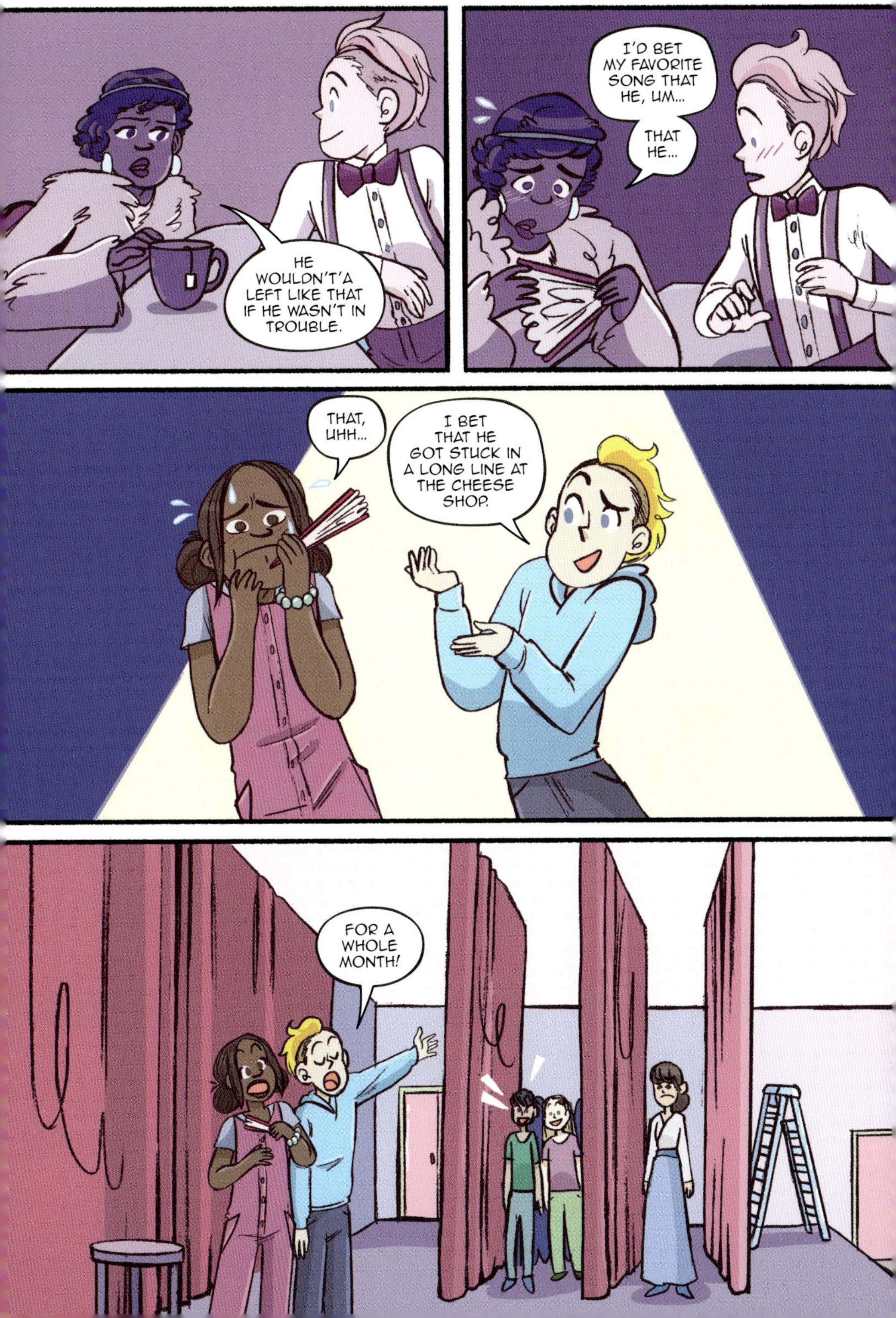
HE WOULDN'T'A LEFT LIKE THAT IF HE WASN'T IN TROUBLE.
I'D BET MY FAVORITE SONG THAT HE, UM...
THAT HE...
THAT, UHH...
I BET THAT HE GOT STUCK IN A LONG LINE AT THE CHEESE SHOP.
FOR A WHOLE MONTH!

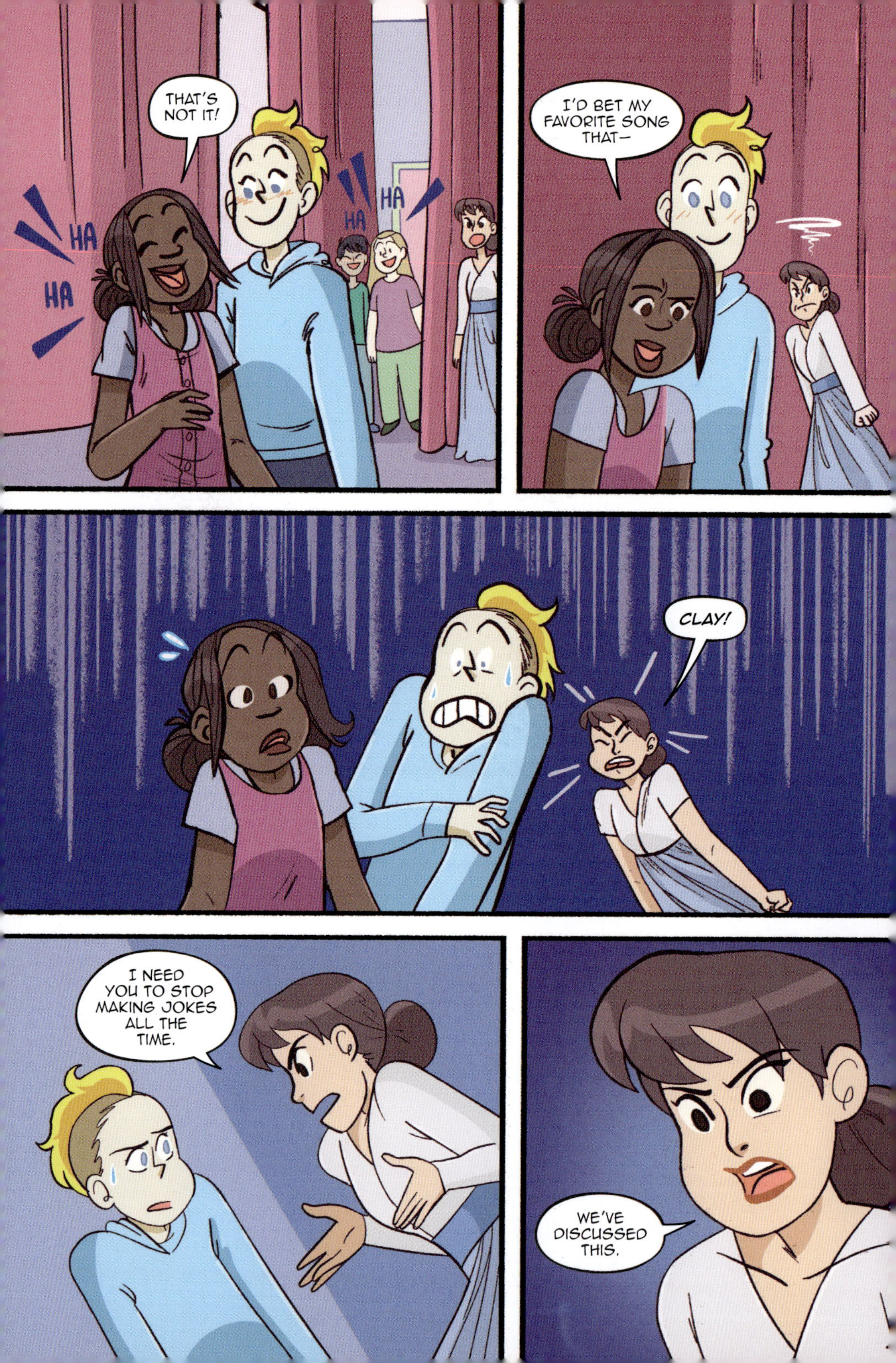

THAT'S NOT IT!
HA
HA
HA
HA
I'D BET MY FAVORITE SONG THAT—
CLAY!
I NEED YOU TO STOP MAKING JOKES ALL THE TIME.
WE'VE DISCUSSED THIS.

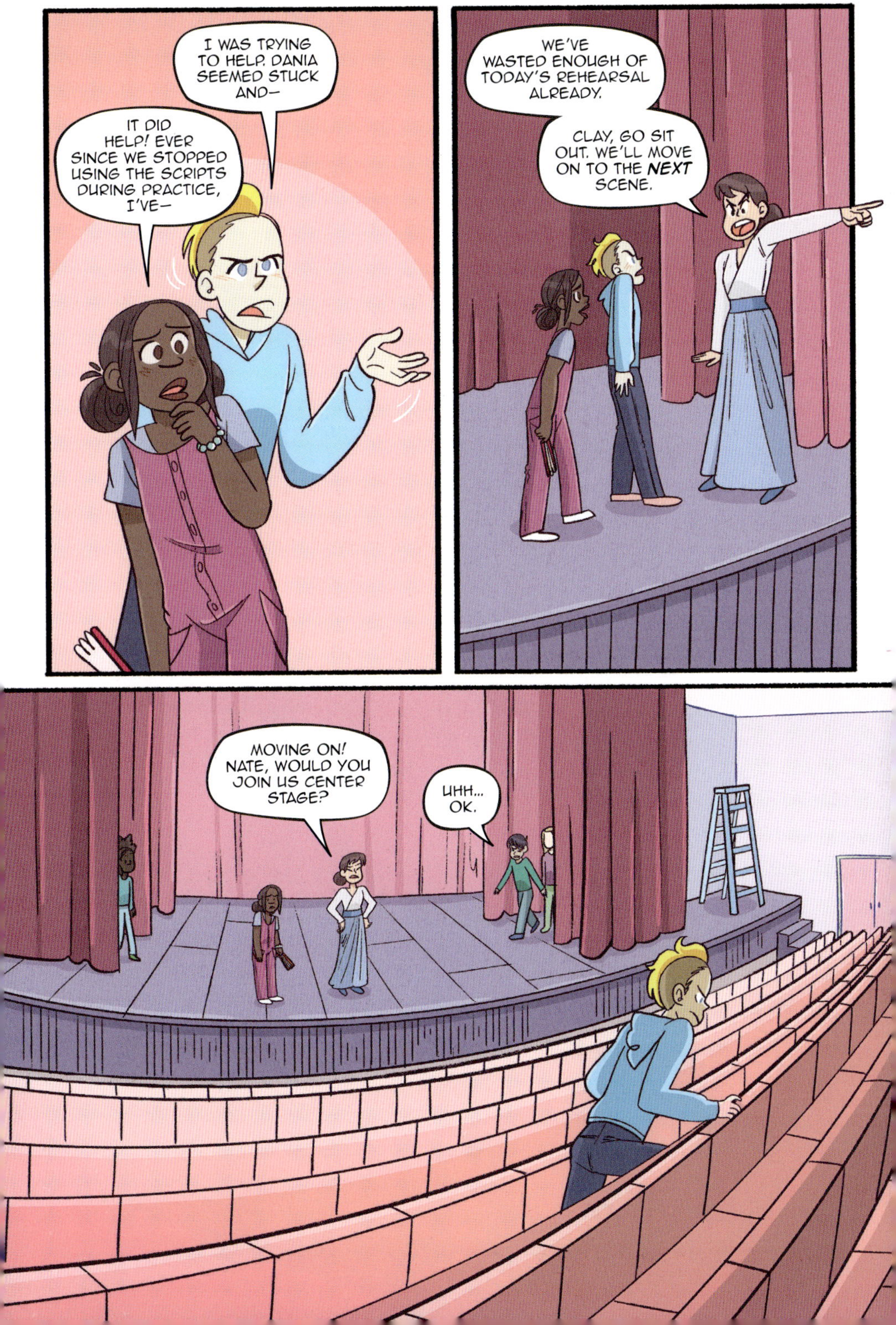
I WAS TRYING TO HELP. DANIA SEEMED STUCK AND—
IT DID HELP! EVER SINCE WE STOPPED USING THE SCRIPTS DURING PRACTICE, I'VE—
WE'VE WASTED ENOUGH OF TODAY'S REHEARSAL ALREADY.
CLAY, GO SIT OUT. WE'LL MOVE ON TO THE NEXT SCENE.
MOVING ON! NATE, WOULD YOU JOIN US CENTER STAGE?
UHH... OK.

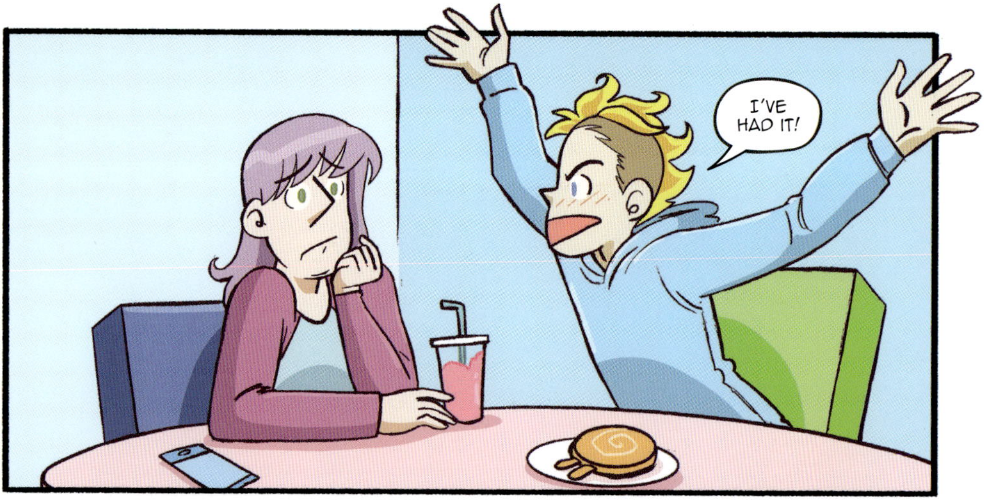
I'VE HAD IT!

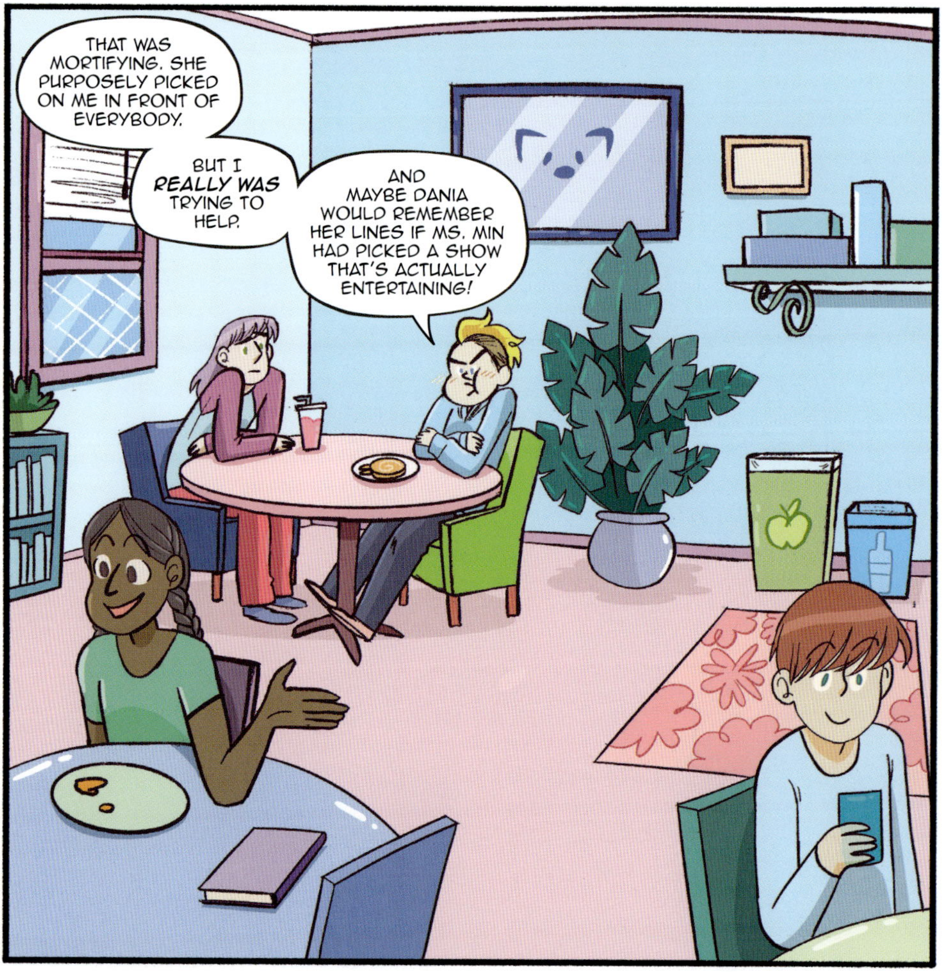
THAT WAS MORTIFYING. SHE PURPOSELY PICKED ON ME IN FRONT OF EVERYBODY.
BUT I **REALLY WAS** TRYING TO HELP.
AND MAYBE DANIA WOULD REMEMBER HER LINES IF MS. MIN HAD PICKED A SHOW THAT'S ACTUALLY ENTERTAINING!

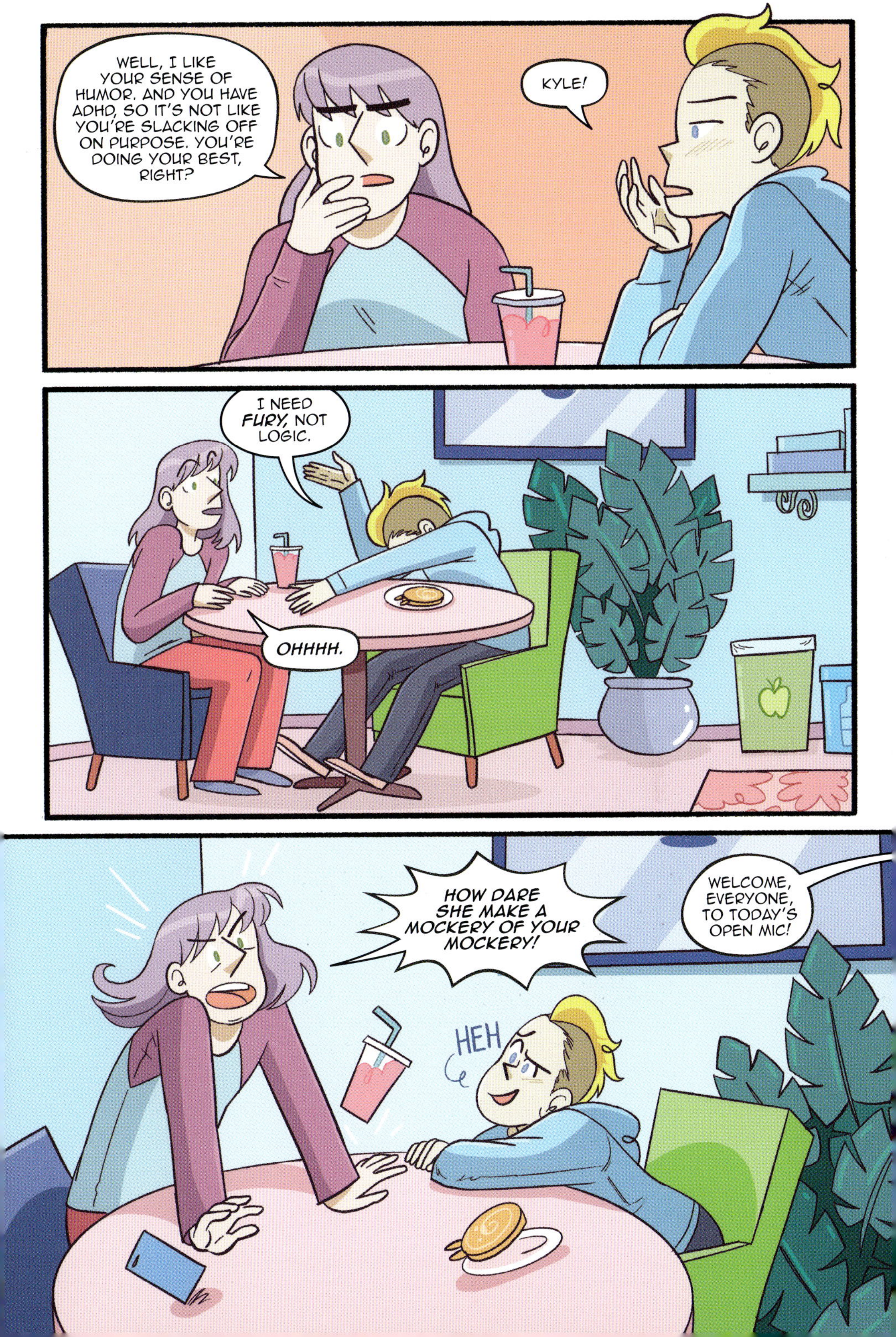
WELL, I LIKE YOUR SENSE OF HUMOR. AND YOU HAVE ADHD, SO IT'S NOT LIKE YOU'RE SLACKING OFF ON PURPOSE. YOU'RE DOING YOUR BEST, RIGHT?
KYLE!
I NEED FURY, NOT LOGIC.
OHHHH.
HOW DARE SHE MAKE A MOCKERY OF YOUR MOCKERY!
WELCOME, EVERYONE, TO TODAY'S OPEN MIC!
HEH

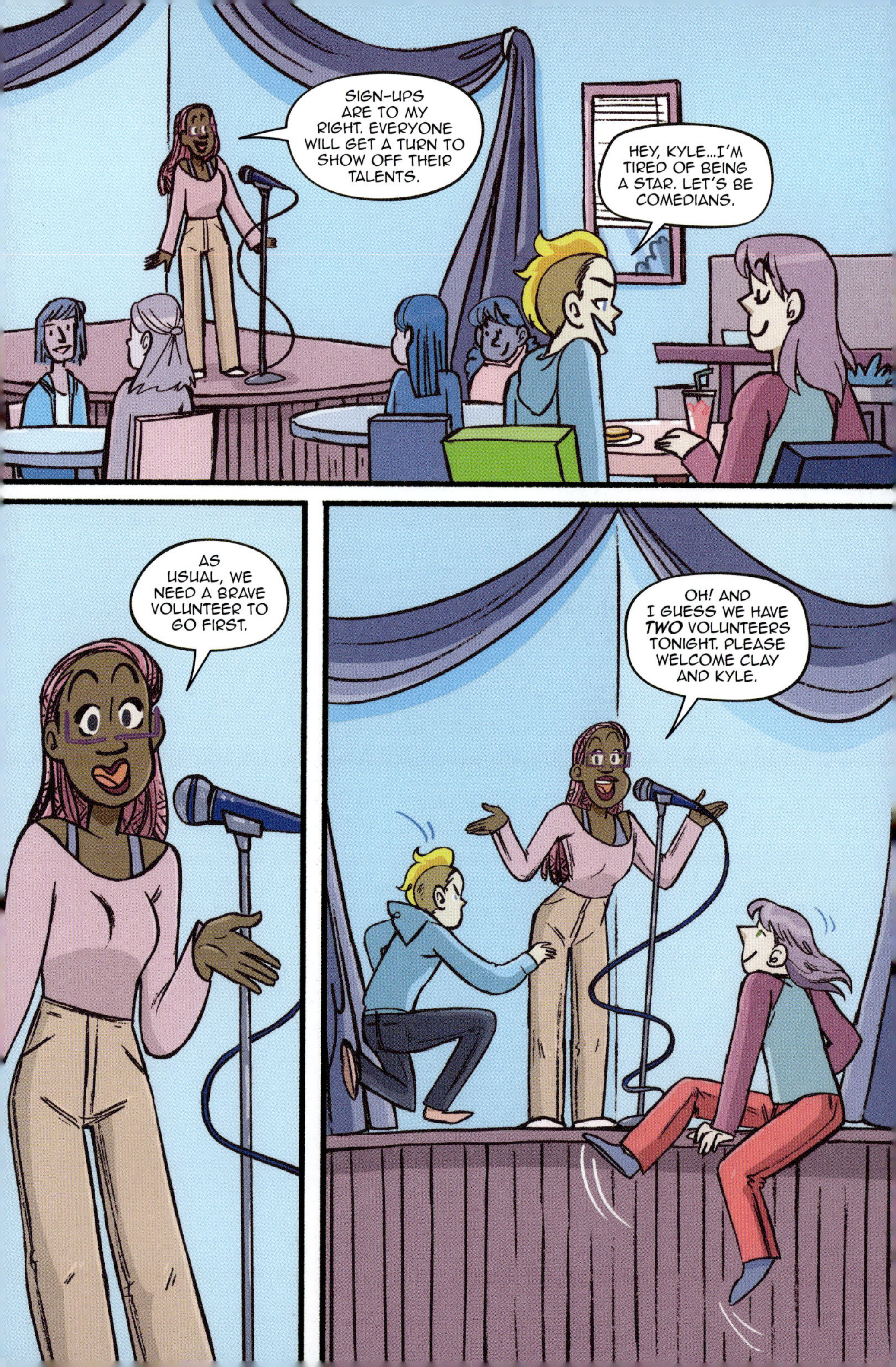
SIGN-UPS ARE TO MY RIGHT. EVERYONE WILL GET A TURN TO SHOW OFF THEIR TALENTS.
HEY, KYLE...I'M TIRED OF BEING A STAR. LET'S BE COMEDIANS.
AS USUAL, WE NEED A BRAVE VOLUNTEER TO GO FIRST.
OH! AND I GUESS WE HAVE **TWO** VOLUNTEERS TONIGHT. PLEASE WELCOME CLAY AND KYLE.

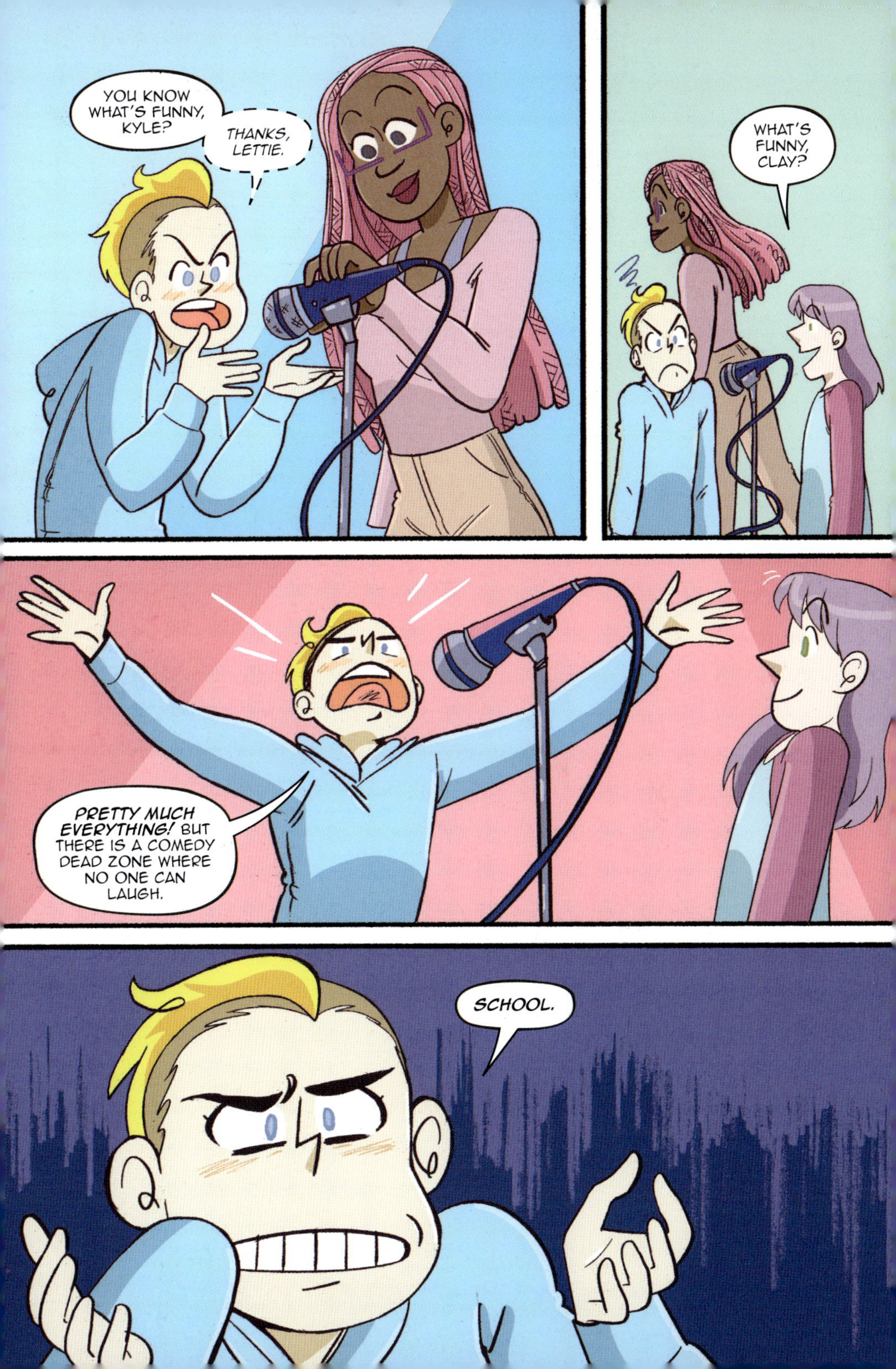

YOU KNOW WHAT'S FUNNY, KYLE?
THANKS, LETTIE.
WHAT'S FUNNY, CLAY?
PRETTY MUCH EVERYTHING! BUT THERE IS A COMEDY DEAD ZONE WHERE NO ONE CAN LAUGH.
SCHOOL.

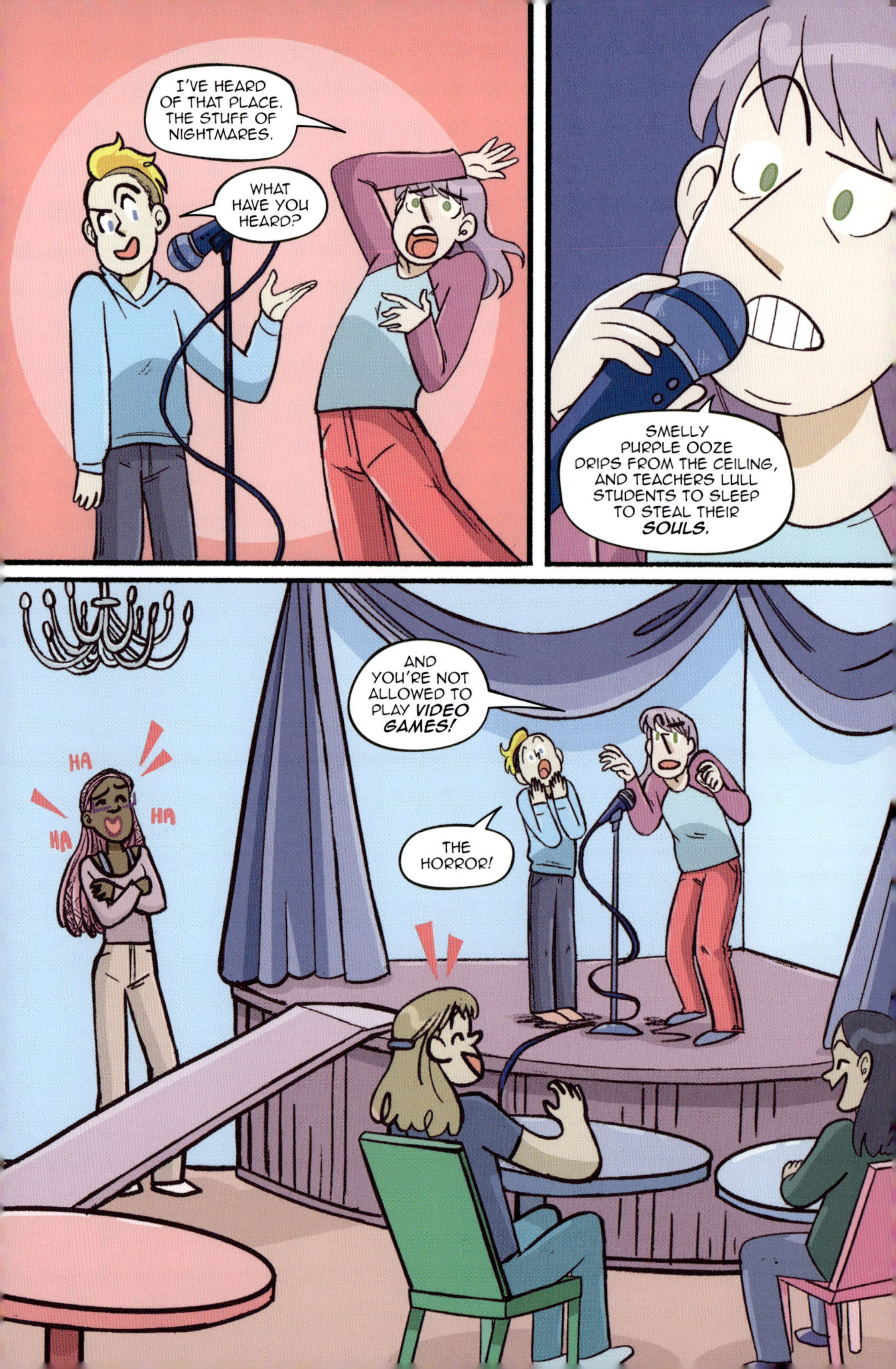

I'VE HEARD OF THAT PLACE. THE STUFF OF NIGHTMARES.
WHAT HAVE YOU HEARD?
SMELLY PURPLE OOZE DRIPS FROM THE CEILING, AND TEACHERS LULL STUDENTS TO SLEEP TO STEAL THEIR *SOULS.*
AND YOU'RE NOT ALLOWED TO PLAY *VIDEO GAMES!*
THE HORROR!
HA
HA
HA

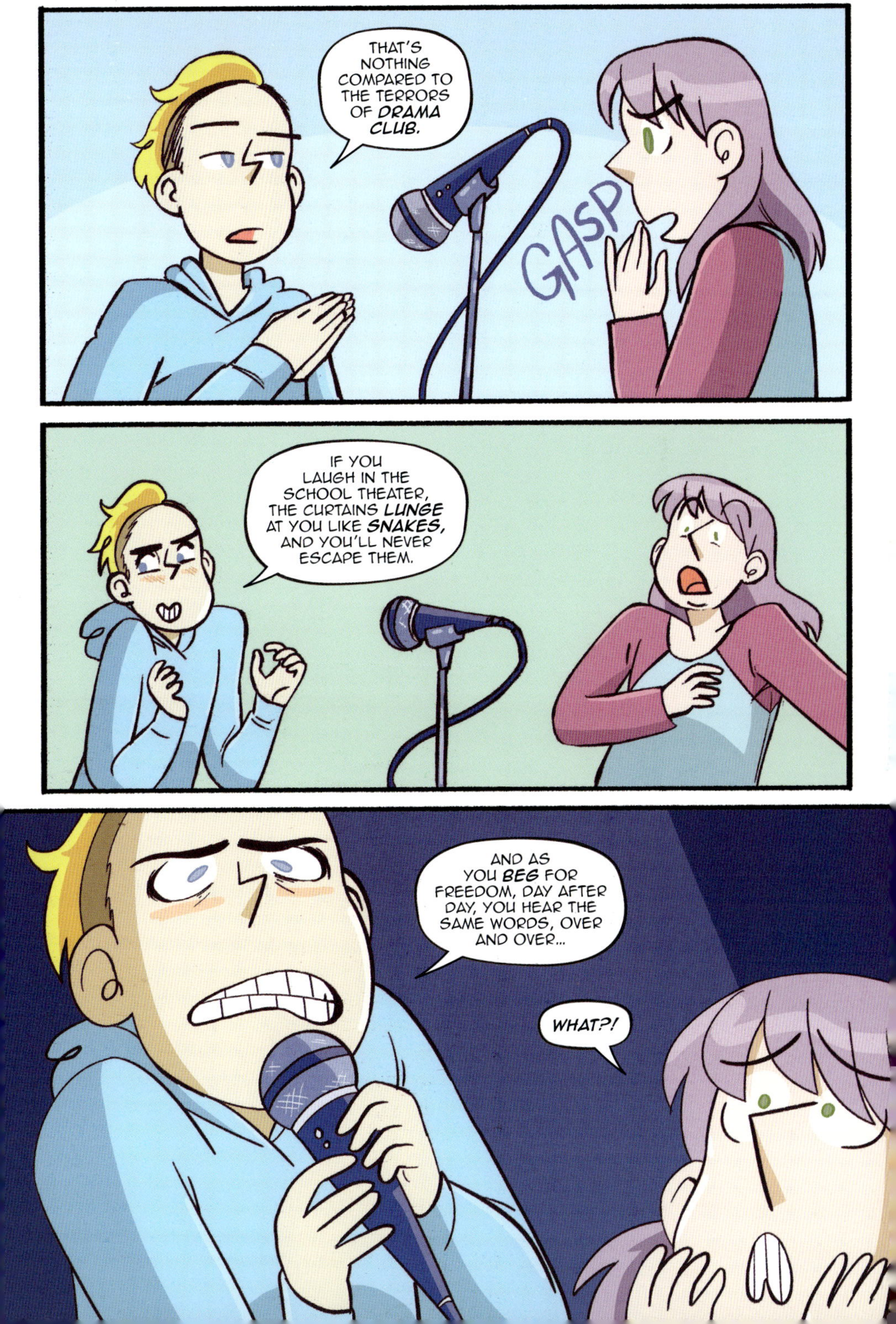
THAT'S NOTHING COMPARED TO THE TERRORS OF DRAMA CLUB.
GASP
IF YOU LAUGH IN THE SCHOOL THEATER, THE CURTAINS LUNGE AT YOU LIKE SNAKES, AND YOU'LL NEVER ESCAPE THEM.
AND AS YOU BEG FOR FREEDOM, DAY AFTER DAY, YOU HEAR THE SAME WORDS, OVER AND OVER...
WHAT?!

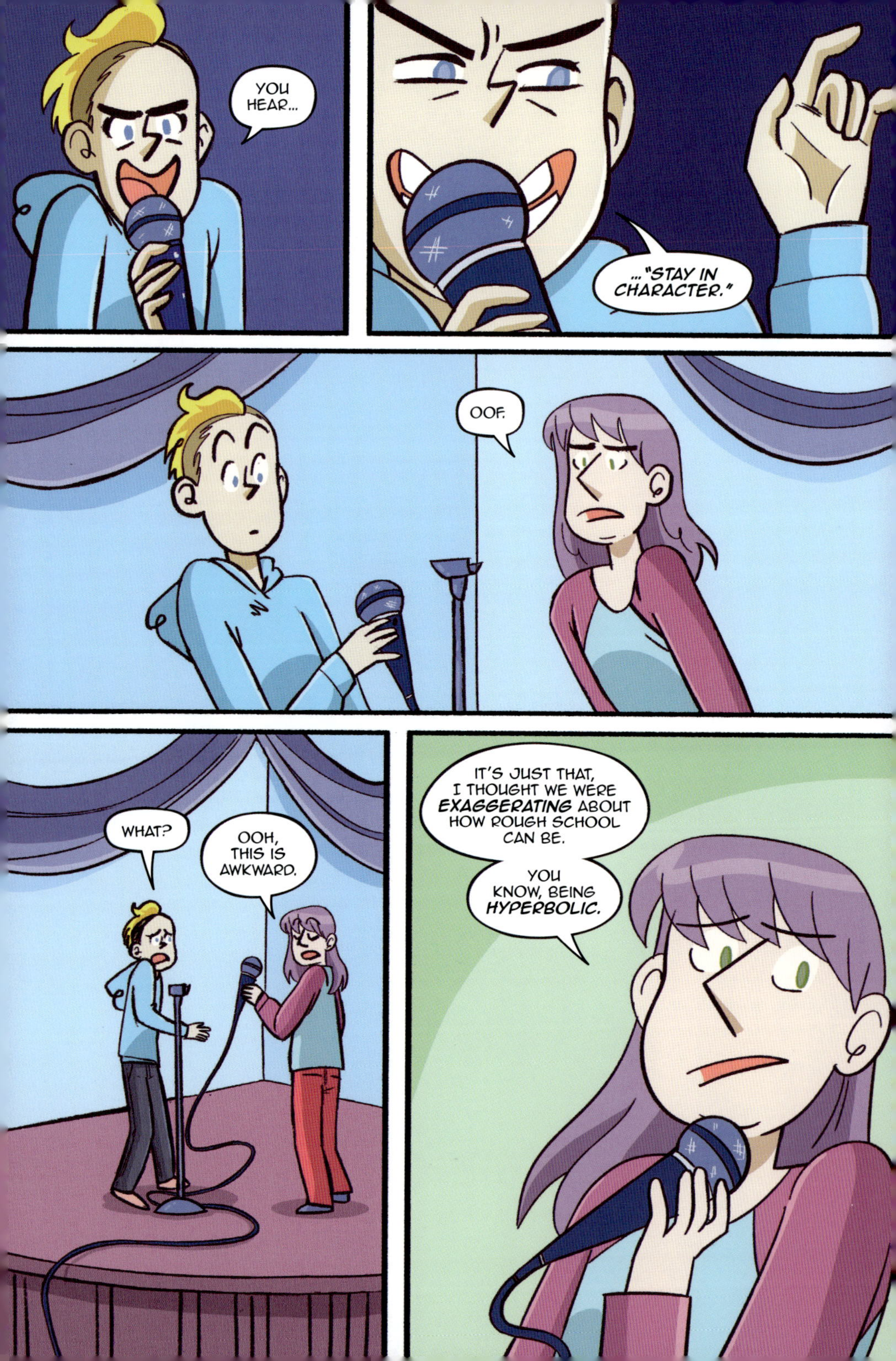
YOU HEAR...
..."STAY IN CHARACTER."
OOF.
WHAT?
OOH, THIS IS AWKWARD.
IT'S JUST THAT, I THOUGHT WE WERE EXAGGERATING ABOUT HOW ROUGH SCHOOL CAN BE.
YOU KNOW, BEING HYPERBOLIC.

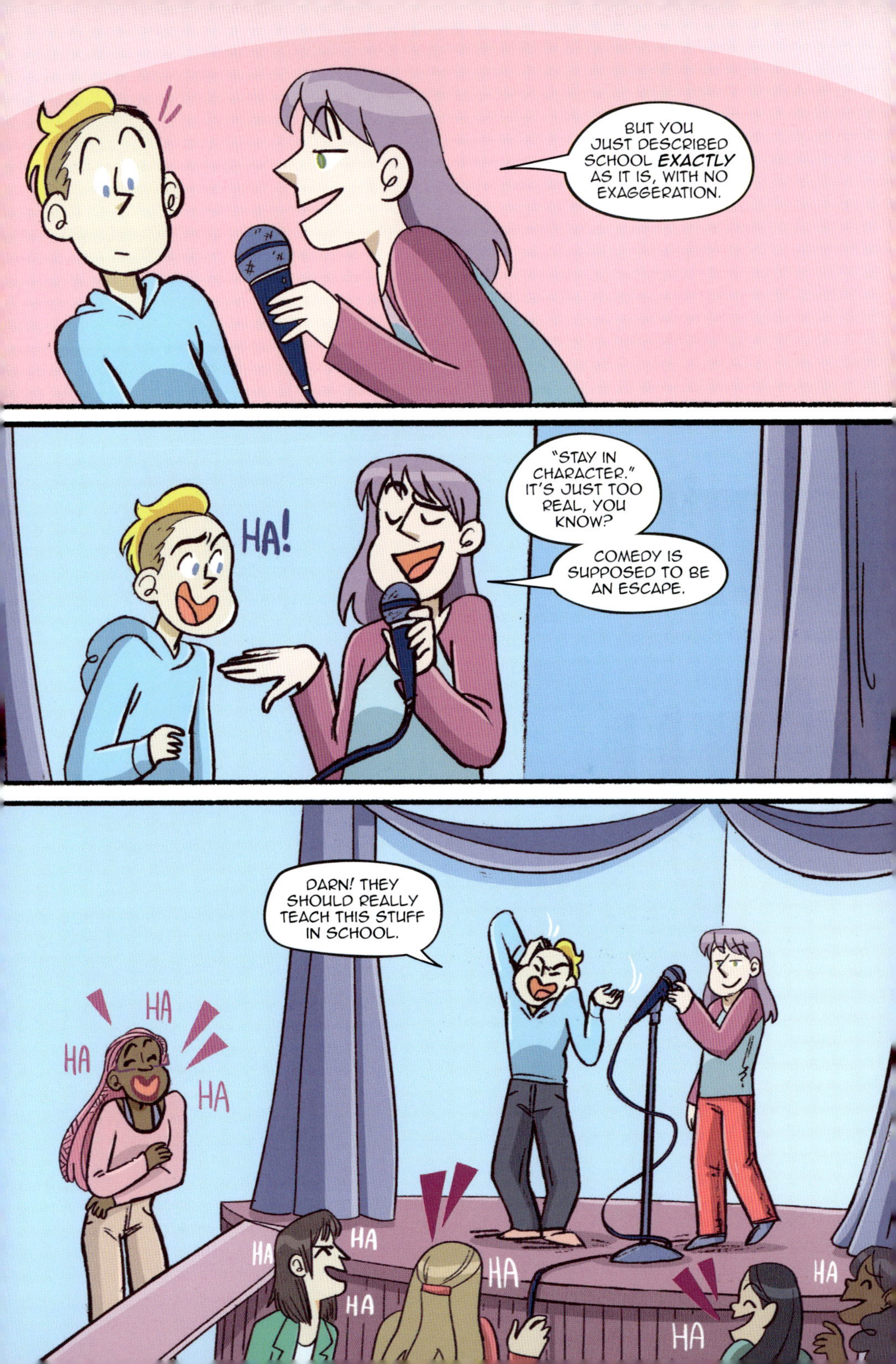
BUT YOU JUST DESCRIBED SCHOOL **EXACTLY** AS IT IS, WITH NO EXAGGERATION.
HA!
"STAY IN CHARACTER." IT'S JUST TOO REAL, YOU KNOW?
COMEDY IS SUPPOSED TO BE AN ESCAPE.
DARN! THEY SHOULD REALLY TEACH THIS STUFF IN SCHOOL.
HA
HA
HA
HA
HA
HA
HA
HA
HA

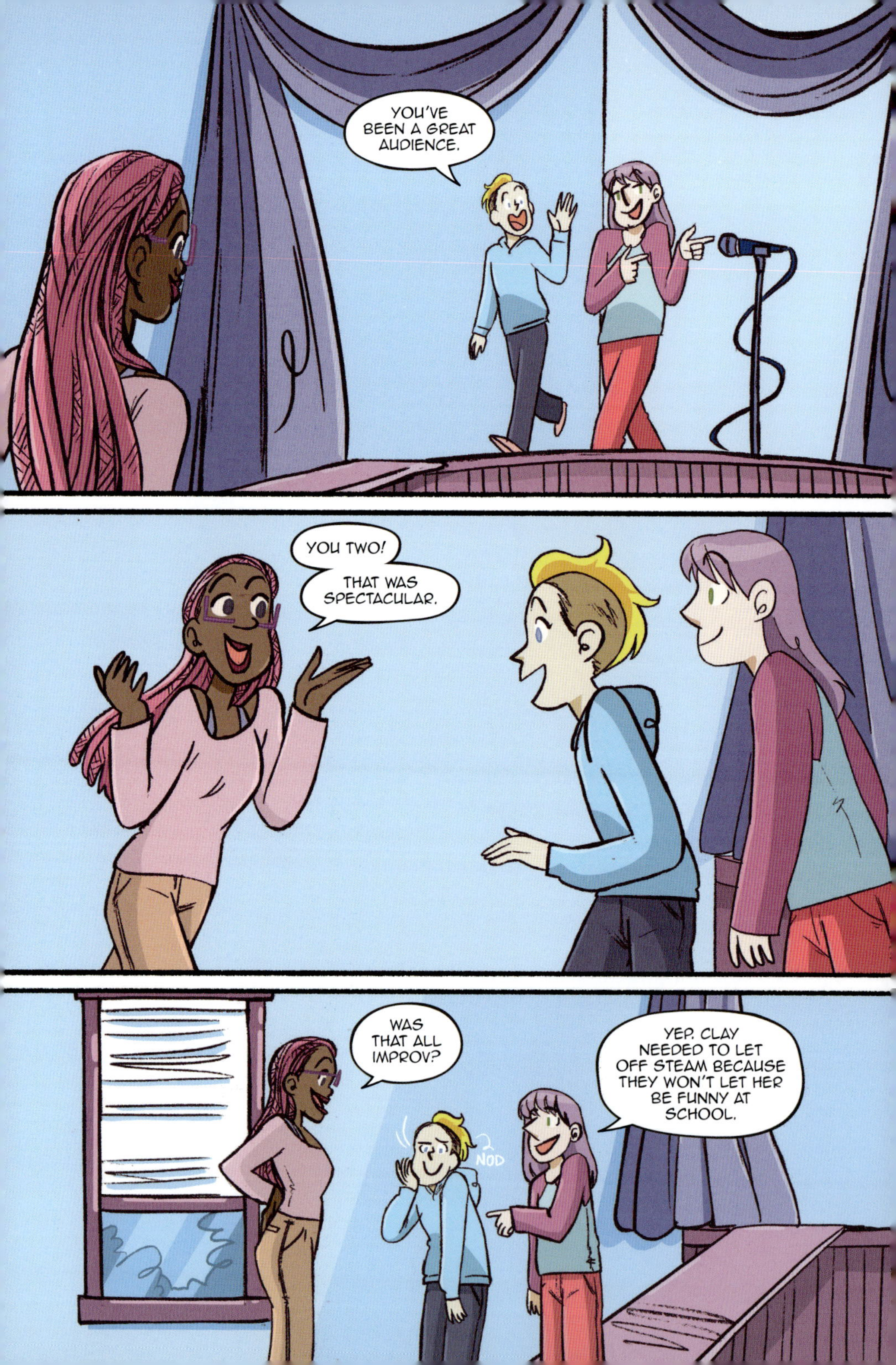
YOU'VE BEEN A GREAT AUDIENCE.
YOU TWO!
THAT WAS SPECTACULAR.
WAS THAT ALL IMPROV?
YEP. CLAY NEEDED TO LET OFF STEAM BECAUSE THEY WON'T LET HER BE FUNNY AT SCHOOL.
NOD

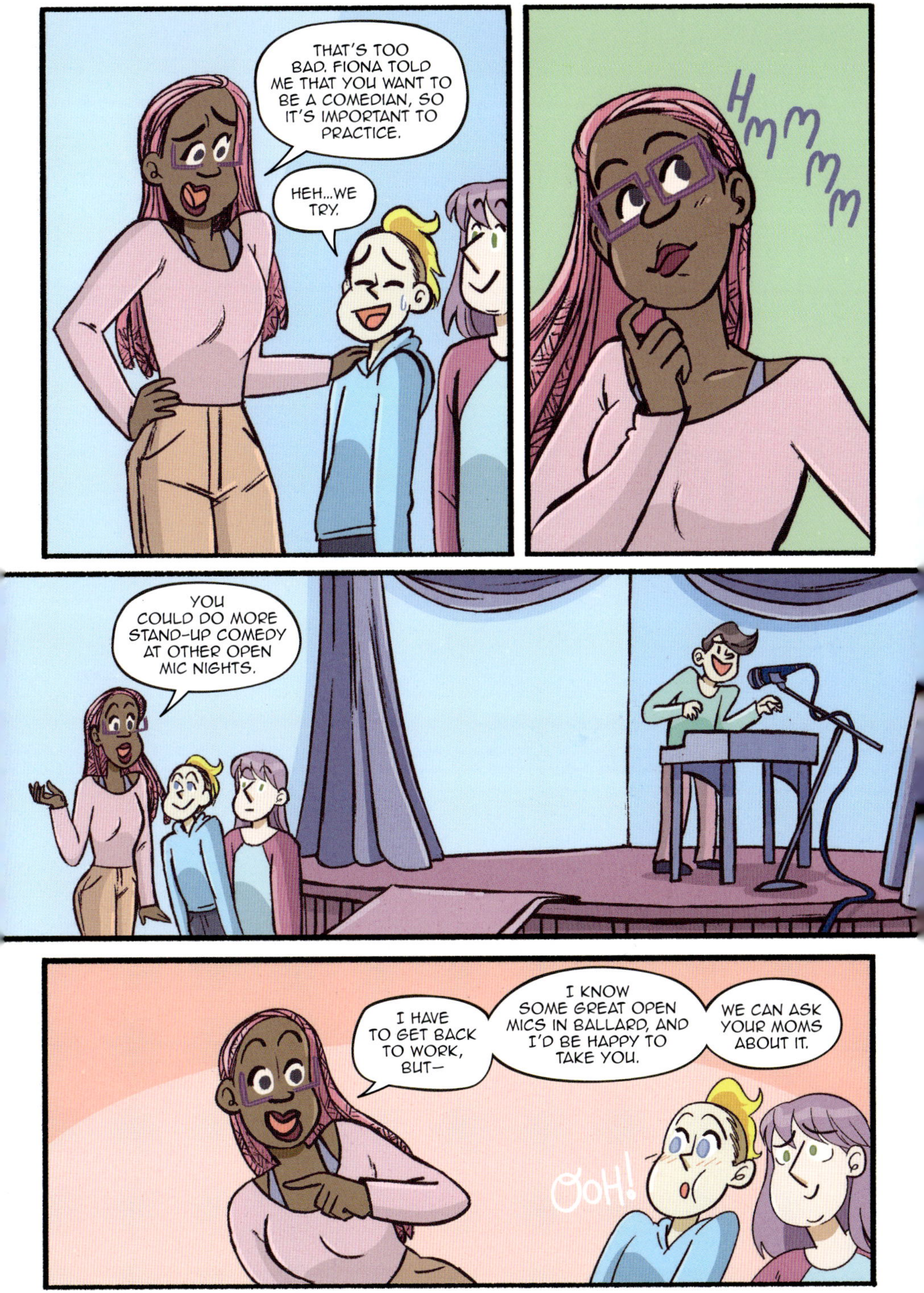
THAT'S TOO BAD. FIONA TOLD ME THAT YOU WANT TO BE A COMEDIAN, SO IT'S IMPORTANT TO PRACTICE.
HEH...WE TRY.
HMMMM
YOU COULD DO MORE STAND-UP COMEDY AT OTHER OPEN MIC NIGHTS.
I HAVE TO GET BACK TO WORK, BUT—
I KNOW SOME GREAT OPEN MICS IN BALLARD, AND I'D BE HAPPY TO TAKE YOU.
WE CAN ASK YOUR MOMS ABOUT IT.
OOH!

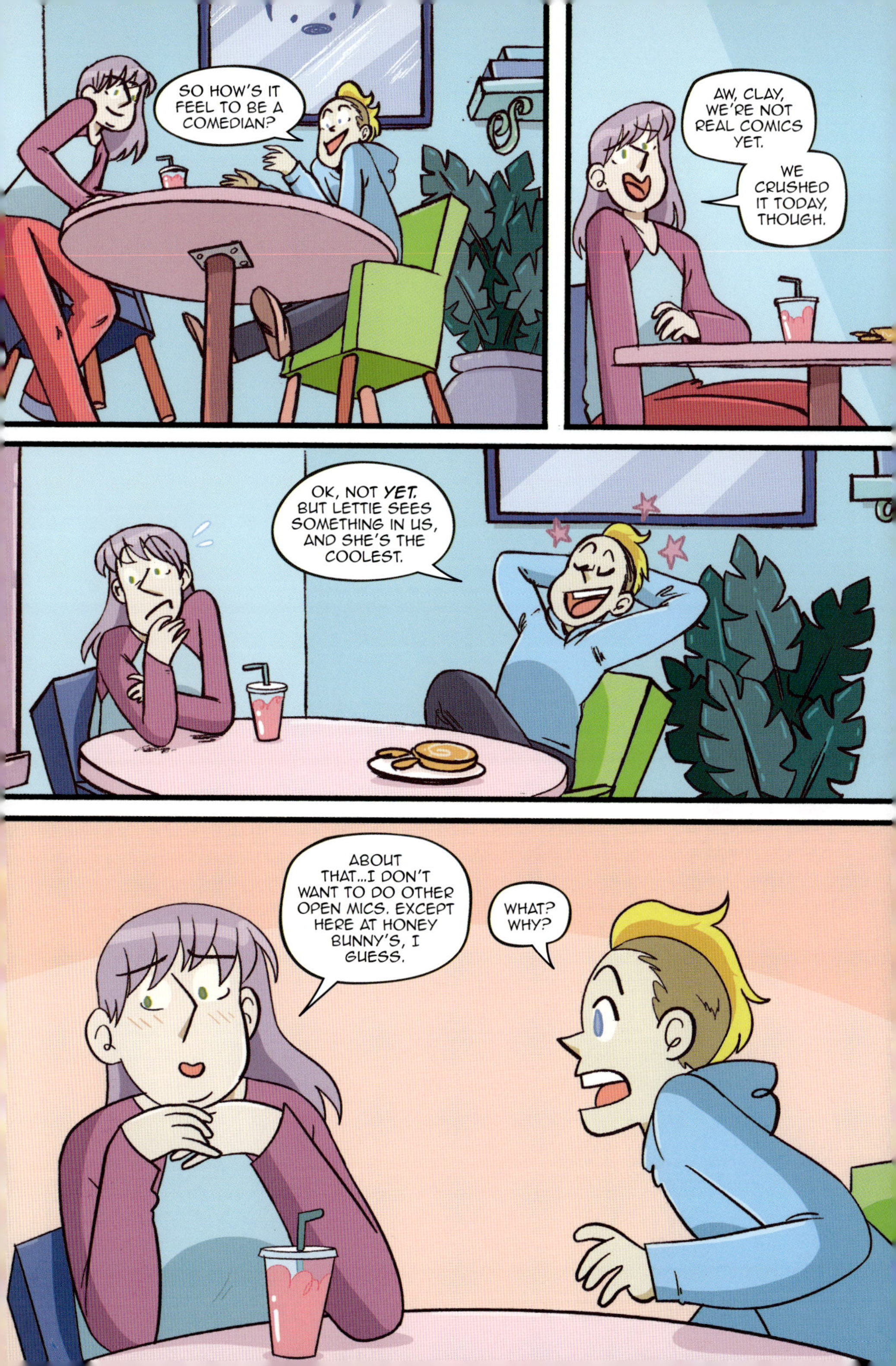
SO HOW'S IT FEEL TO BE A COMEDIAN?
AW, CLAY, WE'RE NOT REAL COMICS YET.
WE CRUSHED IT TODAY, THOUGH.
OK, NOT *YET.* BUT LETTIE SEES SOMETHING IN US, AND SHE'S THE COOLEST.
ABOUT THAT...I DON'T WANT TO DO OTHER OPEN MICS. EXCEPT HERE AT HONEY BUNNY'S, I GUESS.
WHAT? WHY?

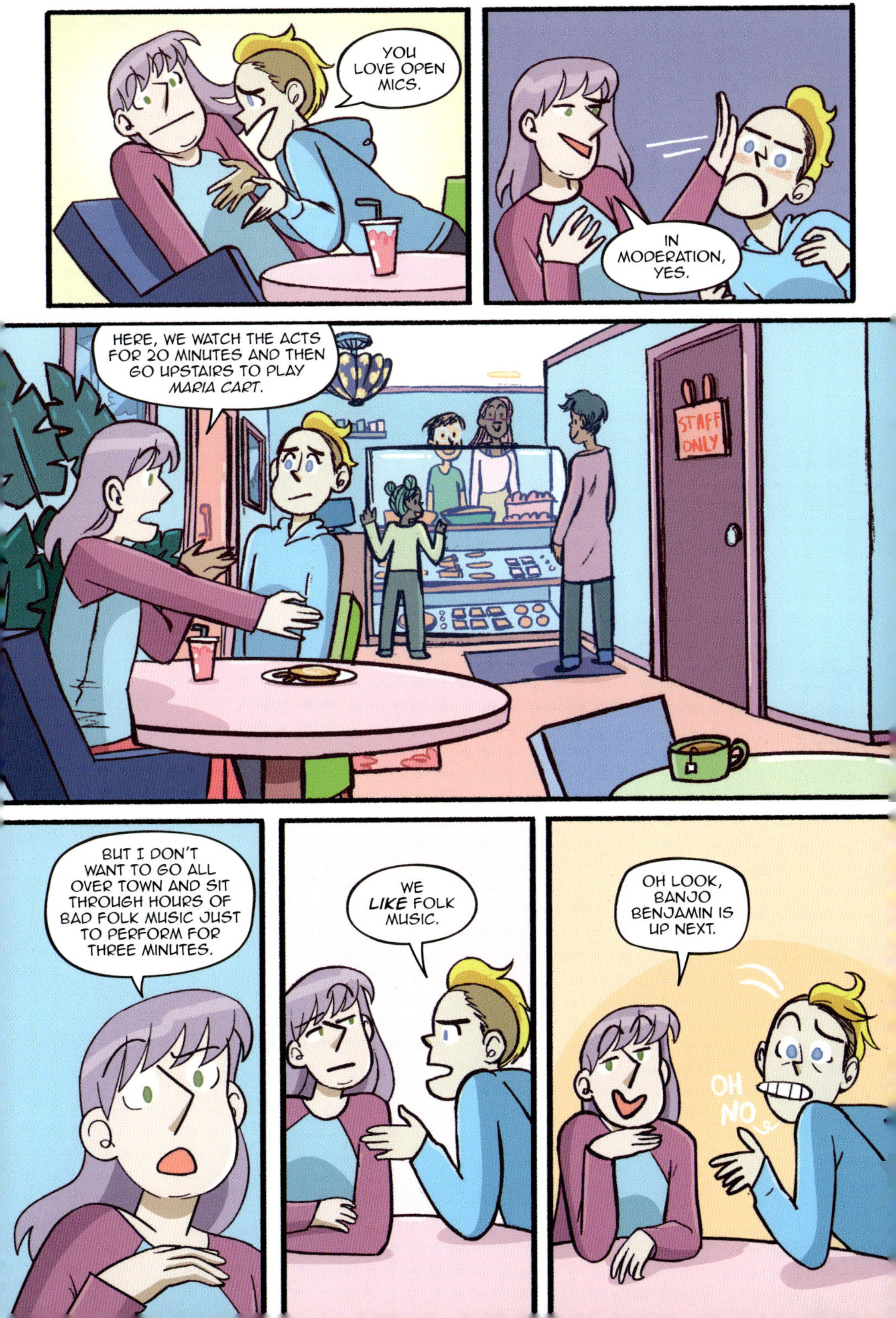
YOU LOVE OPEN MICS.
IN MODERATION, YES.
HERE, WE WATCH THE ACTS FOR 20 MINUTES AND THEN GO UPSTAIRS TO PLAY *MARIA CART.*
STAFF ONLY
BUT I DON'T WANT TO GO ALL OVER TOWN AND SIT THROUGH HOURS OF BAD FOLK MUSIC JUST TO PERFORM FOR THREE MINUTES.
WE ***LIKE*** FOLK MUSIC.
OH LOOK, BANJO BENJAMIN IS UP NEXT.
OH NO

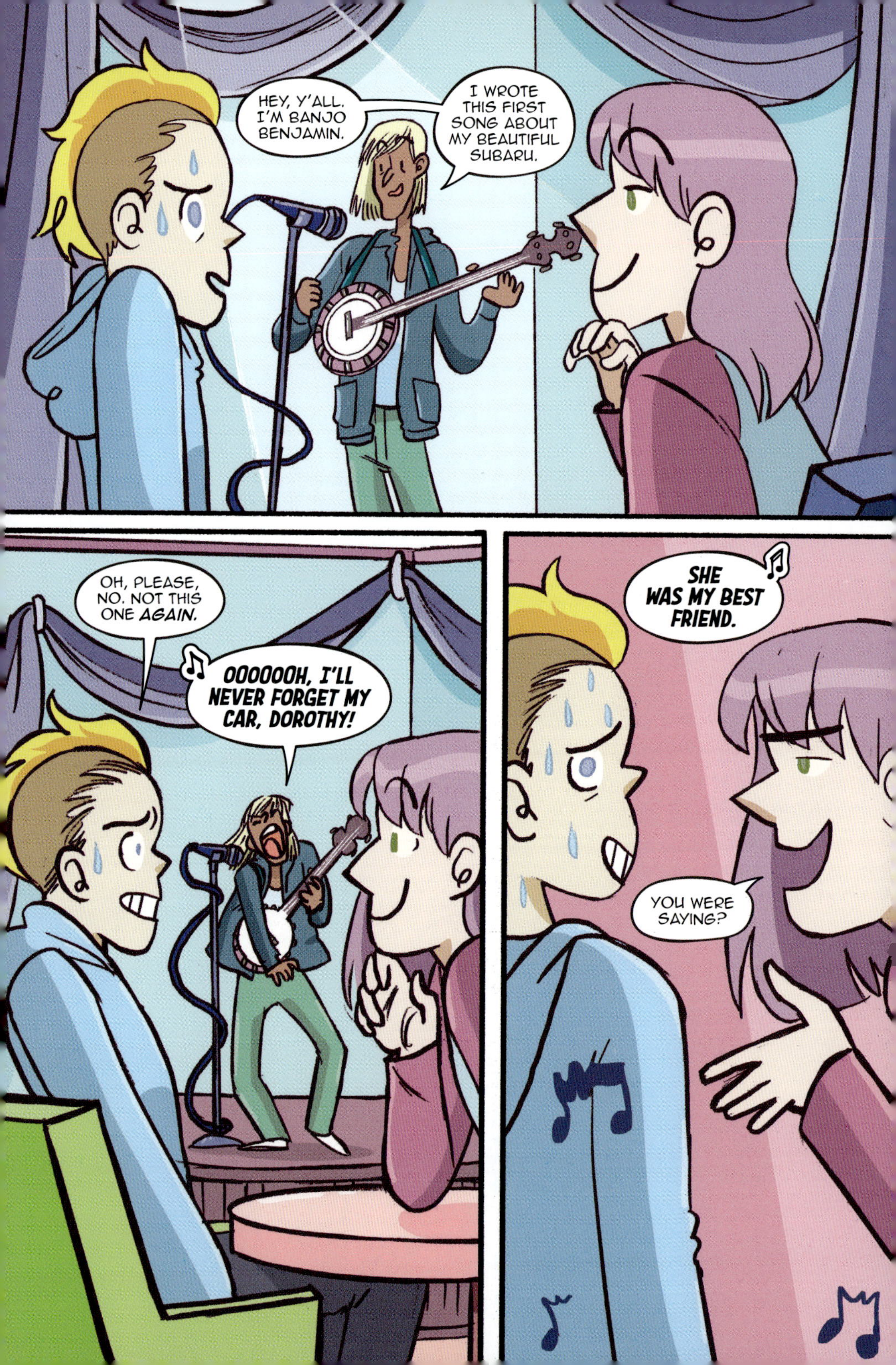
HEY, Y'ALL. I'M BANJO BENJAMIN.
I WROTE THIS FIRST SONG ABOUT MY BEAUTIFUL SUBARU.
OH, PLEASE, NO. NOT THIS ONE *AGAIN*.
OOOOOOH, I'LL NEVER FORGET MY CAR, DOROTHY!
SHE WAS MY BEST FRIEND.
YOU WERE SAYING?

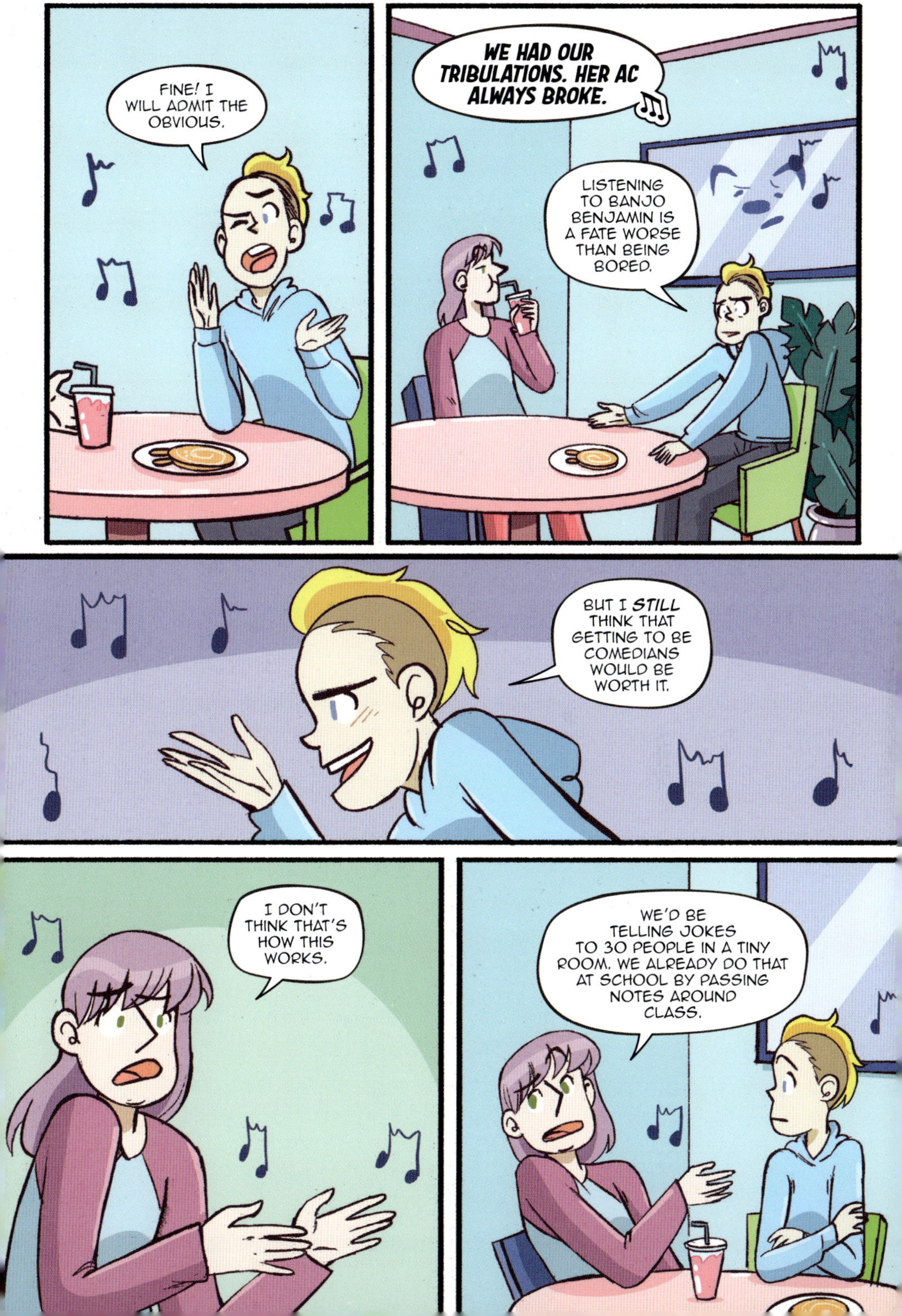
FINE! I WILL ADMIT THE OBVIOUS.
WE HAD OUR TRIBULATIONS. HER AC ALWAYS BROKE.
LISTENING TO BANJO BENJAMIN IS A FATE WORSE THAN BEING BORED.
BUT I STILL THINK THAT GETTING TO BE COMEDIANS WOULD BE WORTH IT.
I DON'T THINK THAT'S HOW THIS WORKS.
WE'D BE TELLING JOKES TO 30 PEOPLE IN A TINY ROOM. WE ALREADY DO THAT AT SCHOOL BY PASSING NOTES AROUND CLASS.

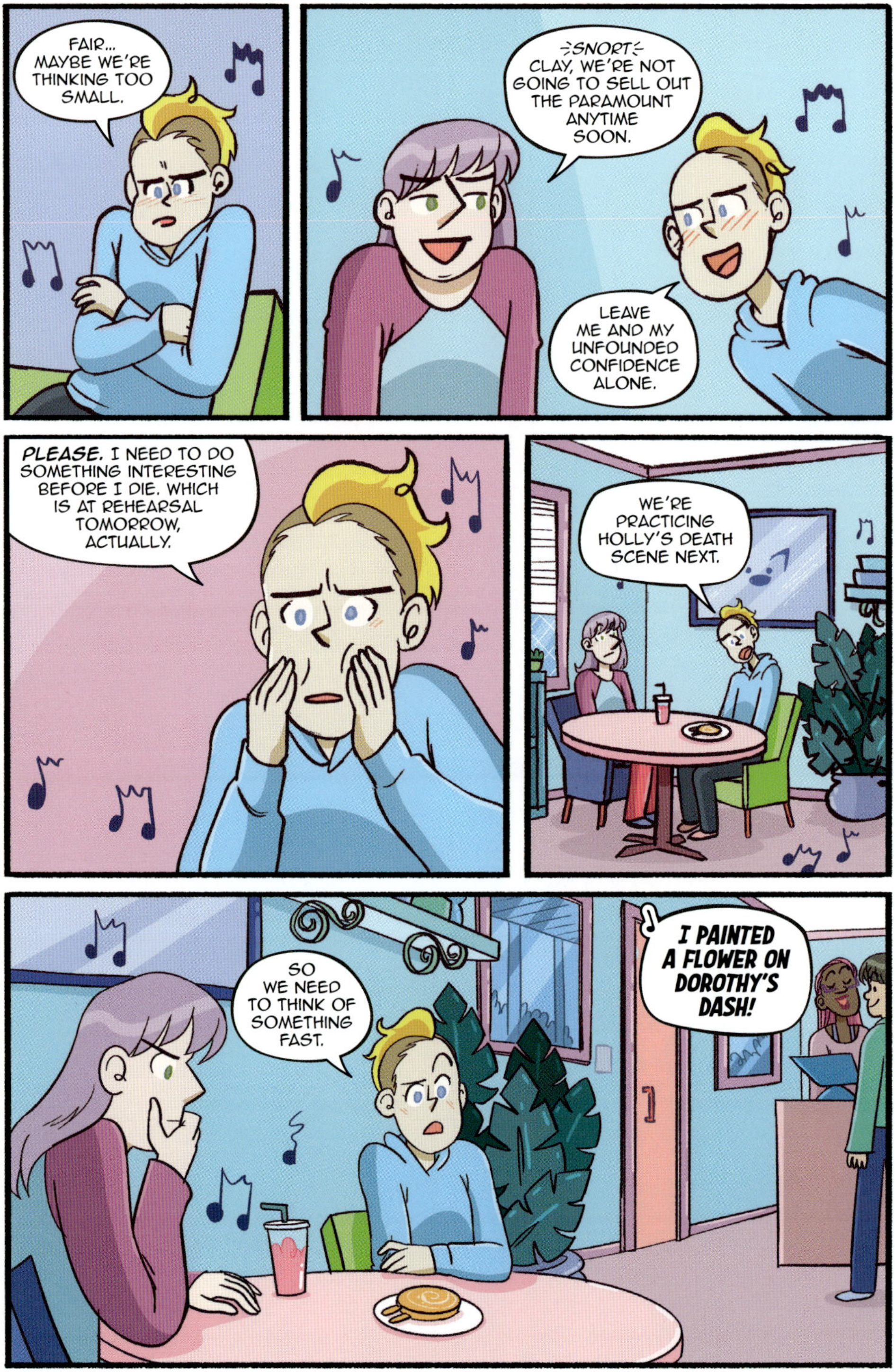

FAIR... MAYBE WE'RE THINKING TOO SMALL.
-SNORT- CLAY, WE'RE NOT GOING TO SELL OUT THE PARAMOUNT ANYTIME SOON.
LEAVE ME AND MY UNFOUNDED CONFIDENCE ALONE.
PLEASE. I NEED TO DO SOMETHING INTERESTING BEFORE I DIE. WHICH IS AT REHEARSAL TOMORROW, ACTUALLY.
WE'RE PRACTICING HOLLY'S DEATH SCENE NEXT.
SO WE NEED TO THINK OF SOMETHING FAST.
I PAINTED A FLOWER ON DOROTHY'S DASH!

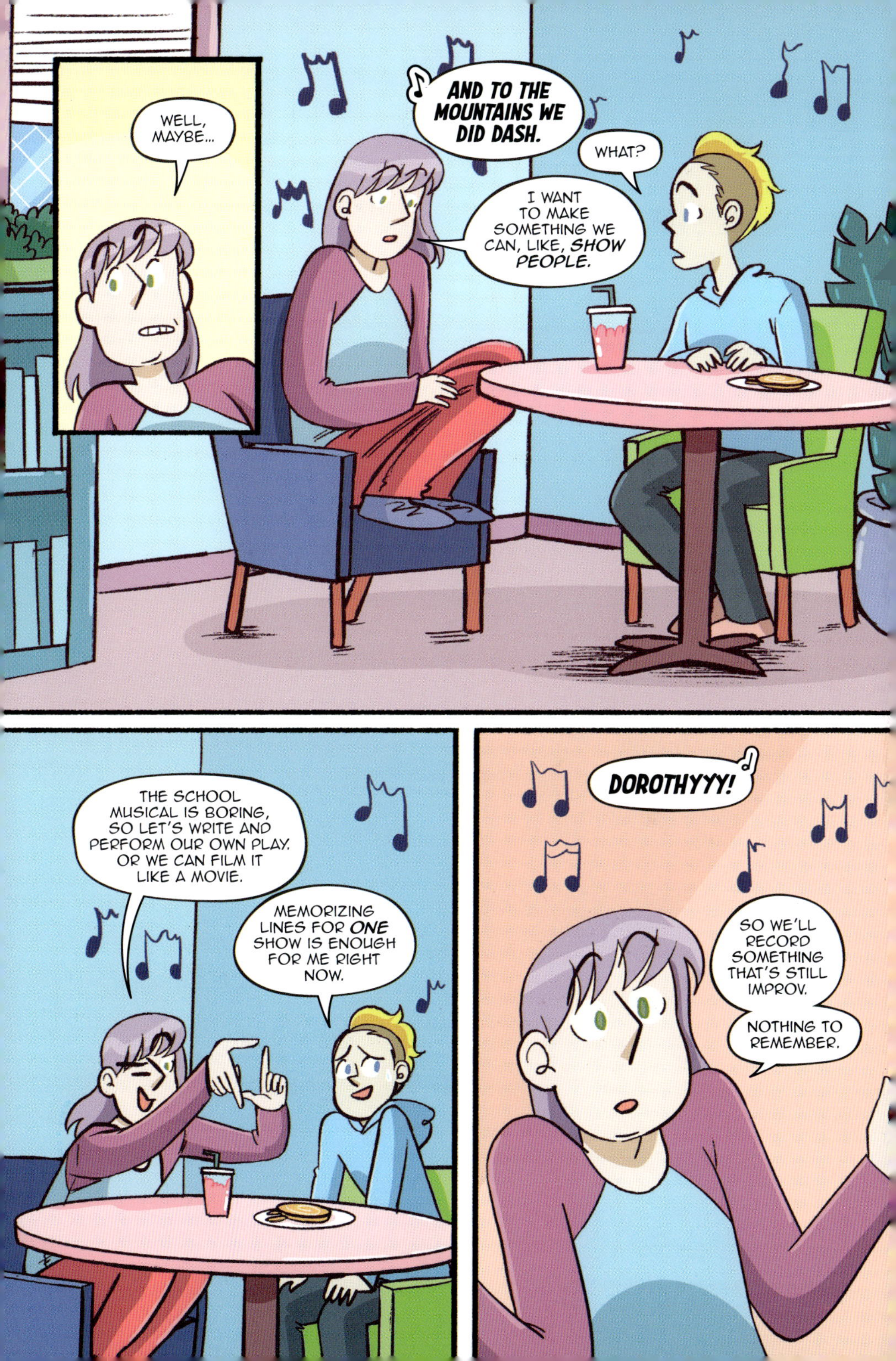
WELL, MAYBE...
AND TO THE MOUNTAINS WE DID DASH.
I WANT TO MAKE SOMETHING WE CAN, LIKE, *SHOW PEOPLE.*
WHAT?
THE SCHOOL MUSICAL IS BORING, SO LET'S WRITE AND PERFORM OUR OWN PLAY. OR WE CAN FILM IT LIKE A MOVIE.
MEMORIZING LINES FOR *ONE* SHOW IS ENOUGH FOR ME RIGHT NOW.
DOROTHYYY!
SO WE'LL RECORD SOMETHING THAT'S STILL IMPROV.
NOTHING TO REMEMBER.

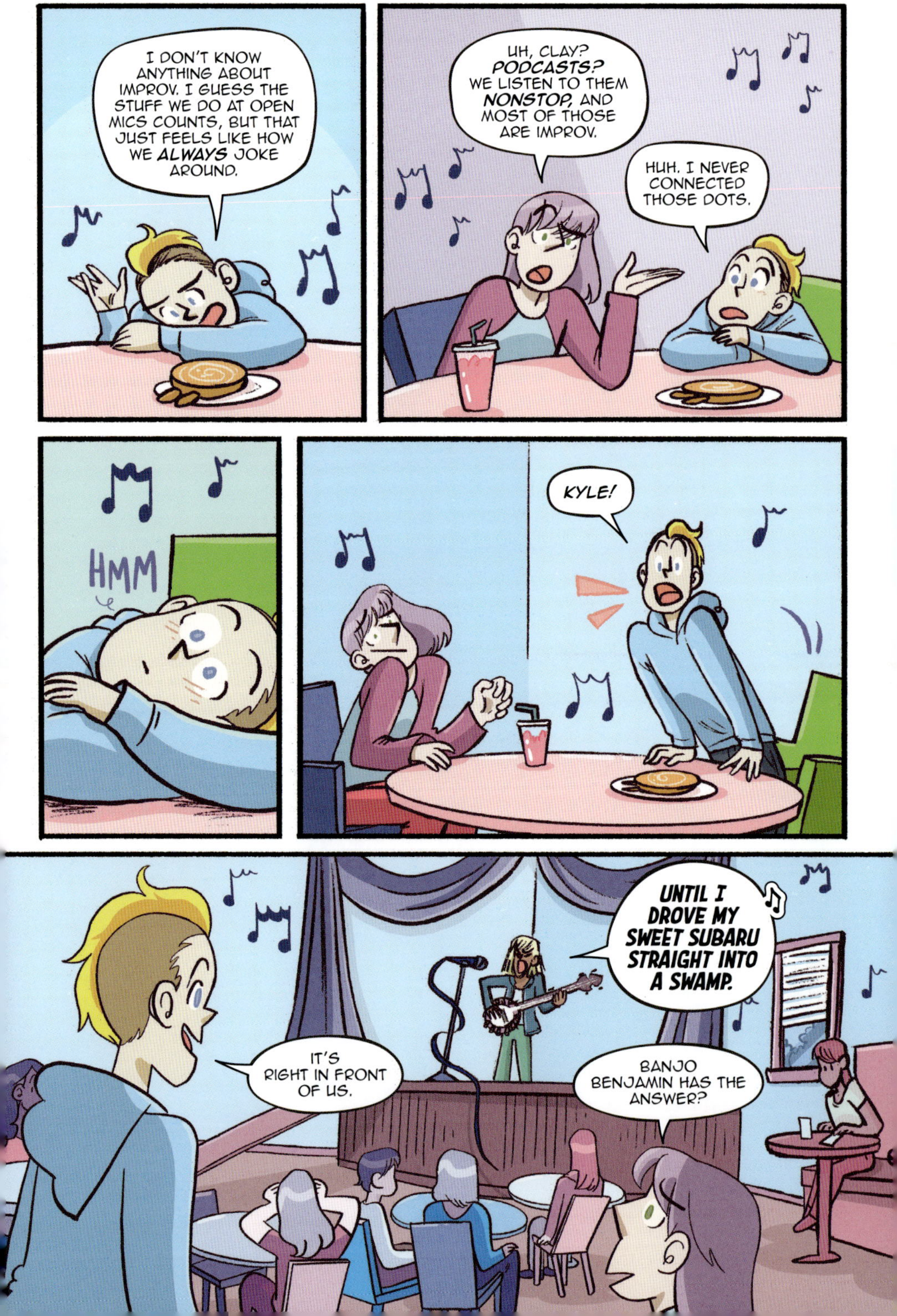
I DON'T KNOW ANYTHING ABOUT IMPROV. I GUESS THE STUFF WE DO AT OPEN MICS COUNTS, BUT THAT JUST FEELS LIKE HOW WE ALWAYS JOKE AROUND.
UH, CLAY? PODCASTS? WE LISTEN TO THEM NONSTOP, AND MOST OF THOSE ARE IMPROV.
HUH. I NEVER CONNECTED THOSE DOTS.
HMM
KYLE!
UNTIL I DROVE MY SWEET SUBARU STRAIGHT INTO A SWAMP.
IT'S RIGHT IN FRONT OF US.
BANJO BENJAMIN HAS THE ANSWER?

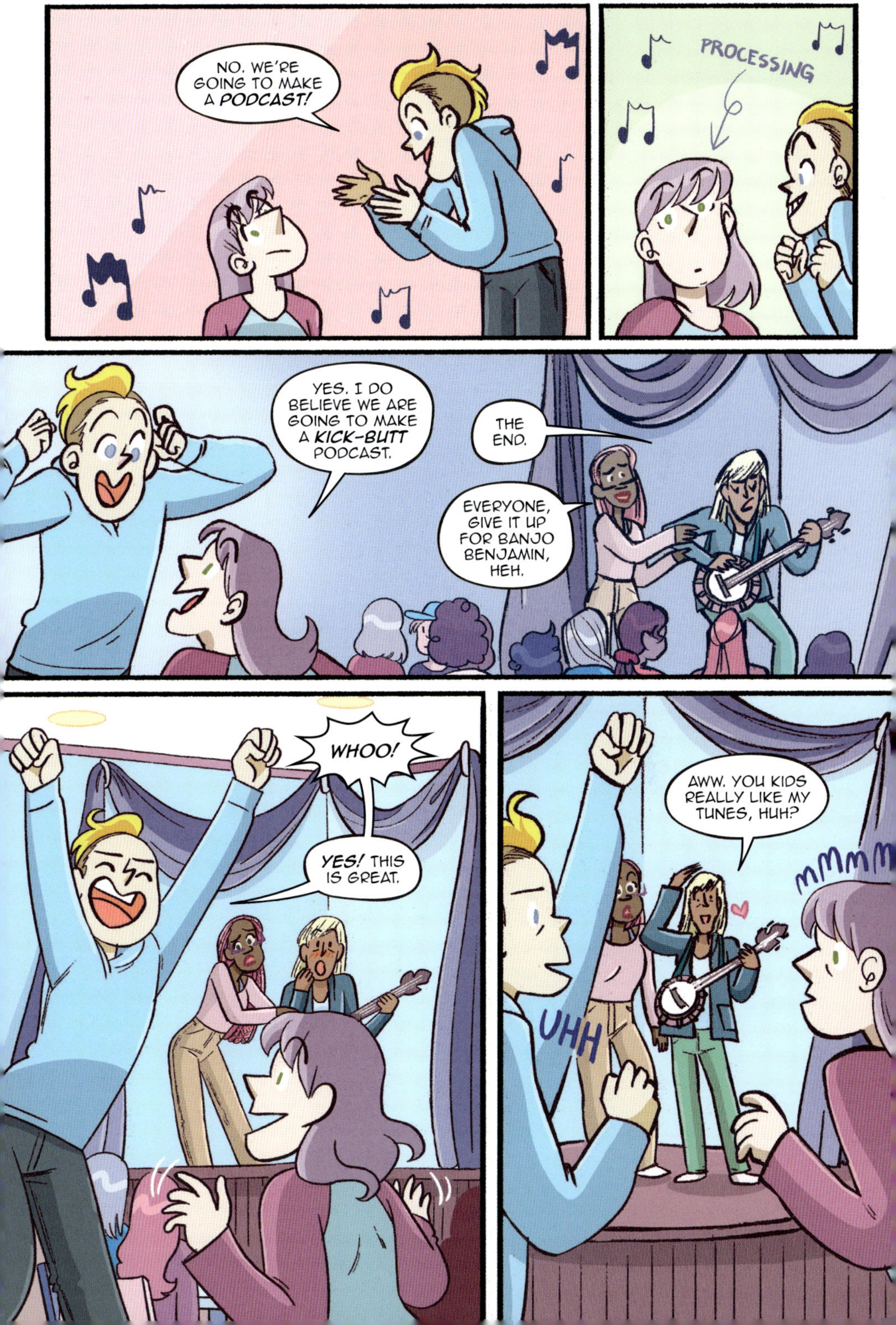
NO. WE'RE GOING TO MAKE A *PODCAST!*
PROCESSING
YES. I DO BELIEVE WE ARE GOING TO MAKE A ***KICK-BUTT*** PODCAST.
THE END.
EVERYONE, GIVE IT UP FOR BANJO BENJAMIN, HEH.
WHOO!
YES! THIS IS GREAT.
AWW. YOU KIDS REALLY LIKE MY TUNES, HUH?
UHH
MMMM

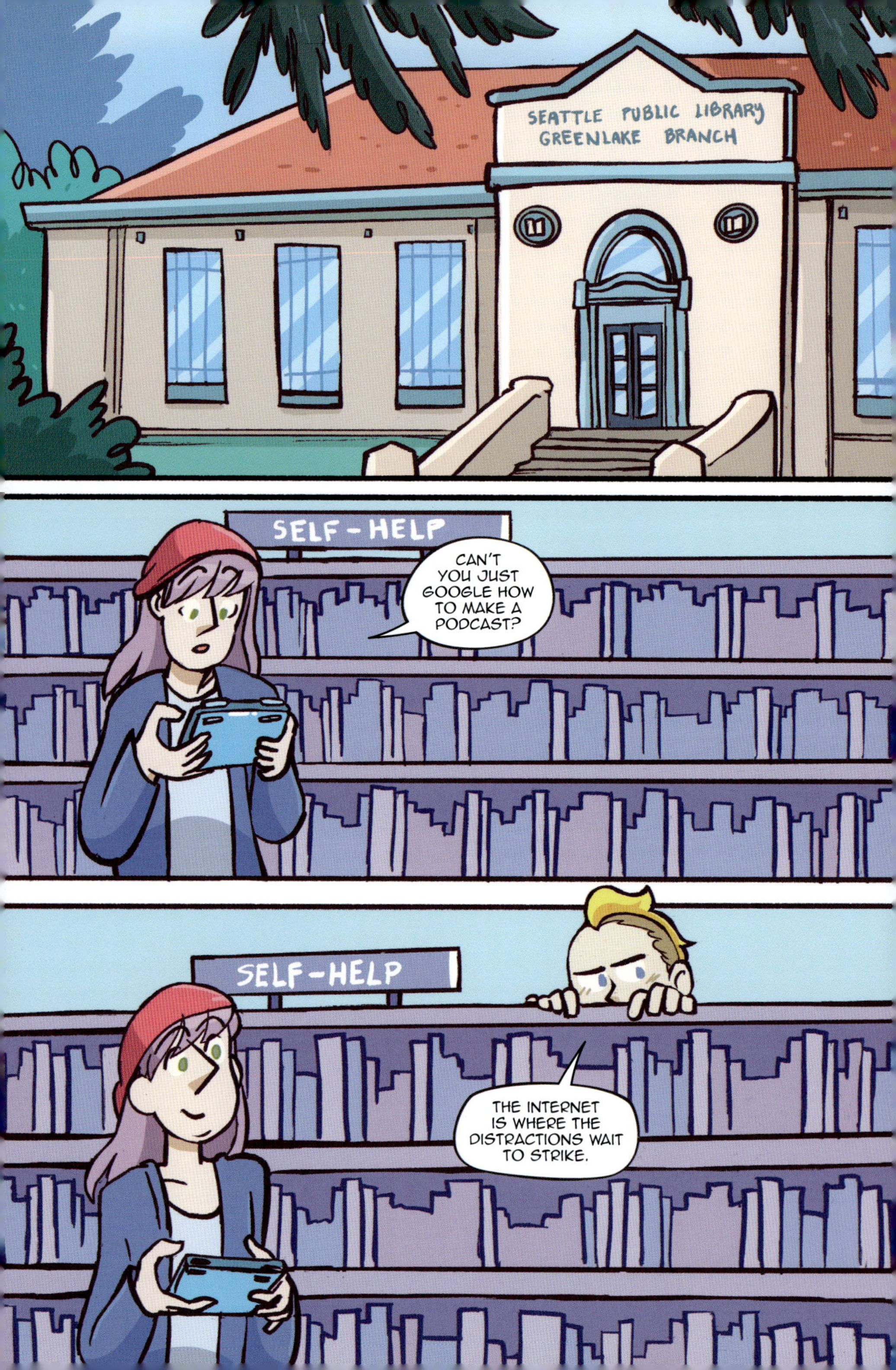
SEATTLE PUBLIC LIBRARY
GREENLAKE BRANCH
SELF-HELP
CAN'T YOU JUST GOOGLE HOW TO MAKE A PODCAST?
SELF-HELP
THE INTERNET IS WHERE THE DISTRACTIONS WAIT TO STRIKE.

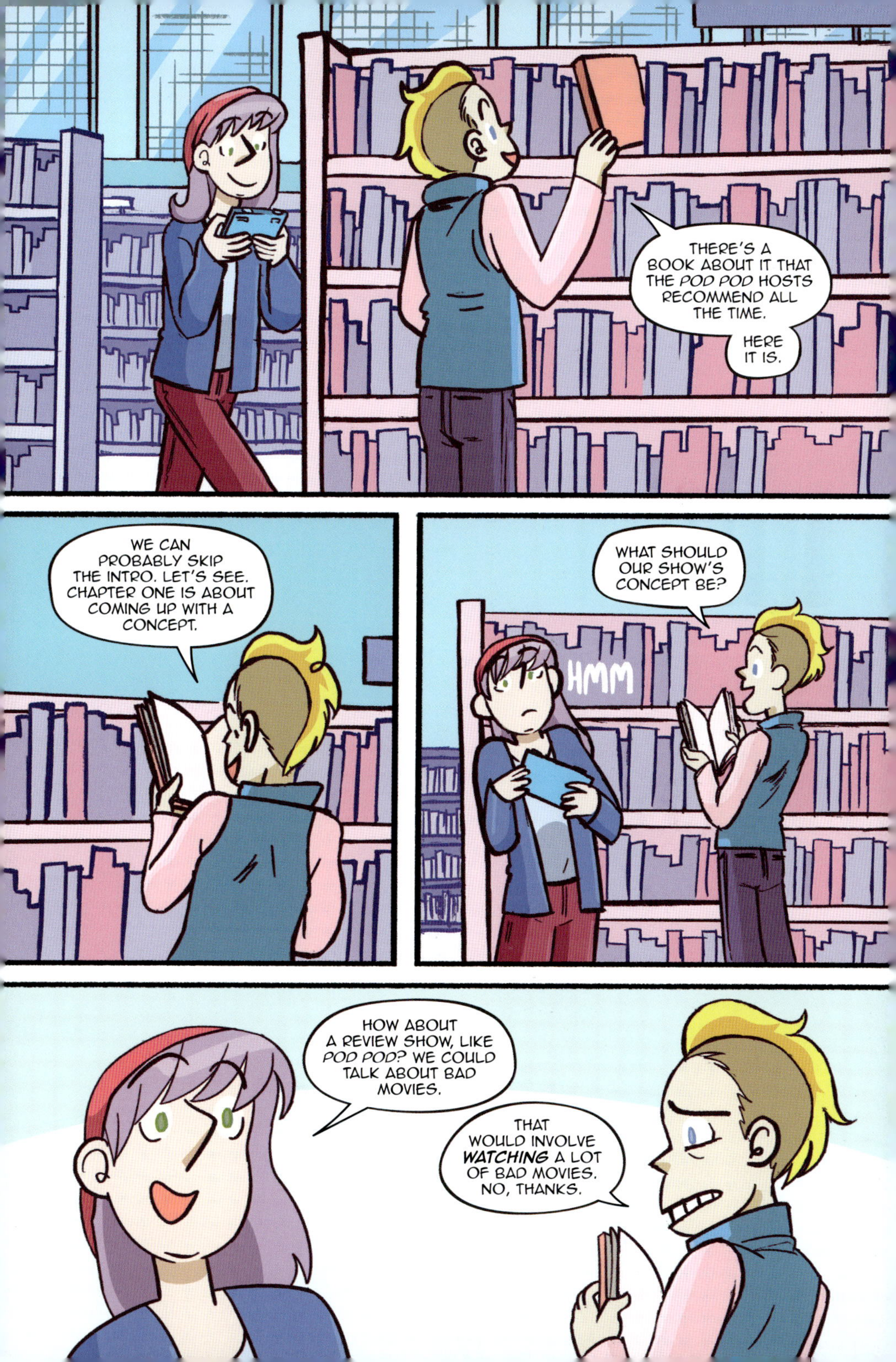
THERE'S A BOOK ABOUT IT THAT THE *POD POD* HOSTS RECOMMEND ALL THE TIME.
HERE IT IS.
WE CAN PROBABLY SKIP THE INTRO. LET'S SEE. CHAPTER ONE IS ABOUT COMING UP WITH A CONCEPT.
WHAT SHOULD OUR SHOW'S CONCEPT BE?
HMM
HOW ABOUT A REVIEW SHOW, LIKE *POD POD*? WE COULD TALK ABOUT BAD MOVIES.
THAT WOULD INVOLVE ***WATCHING*** A LOT OF BAD MOVIES. NO, THANKS.

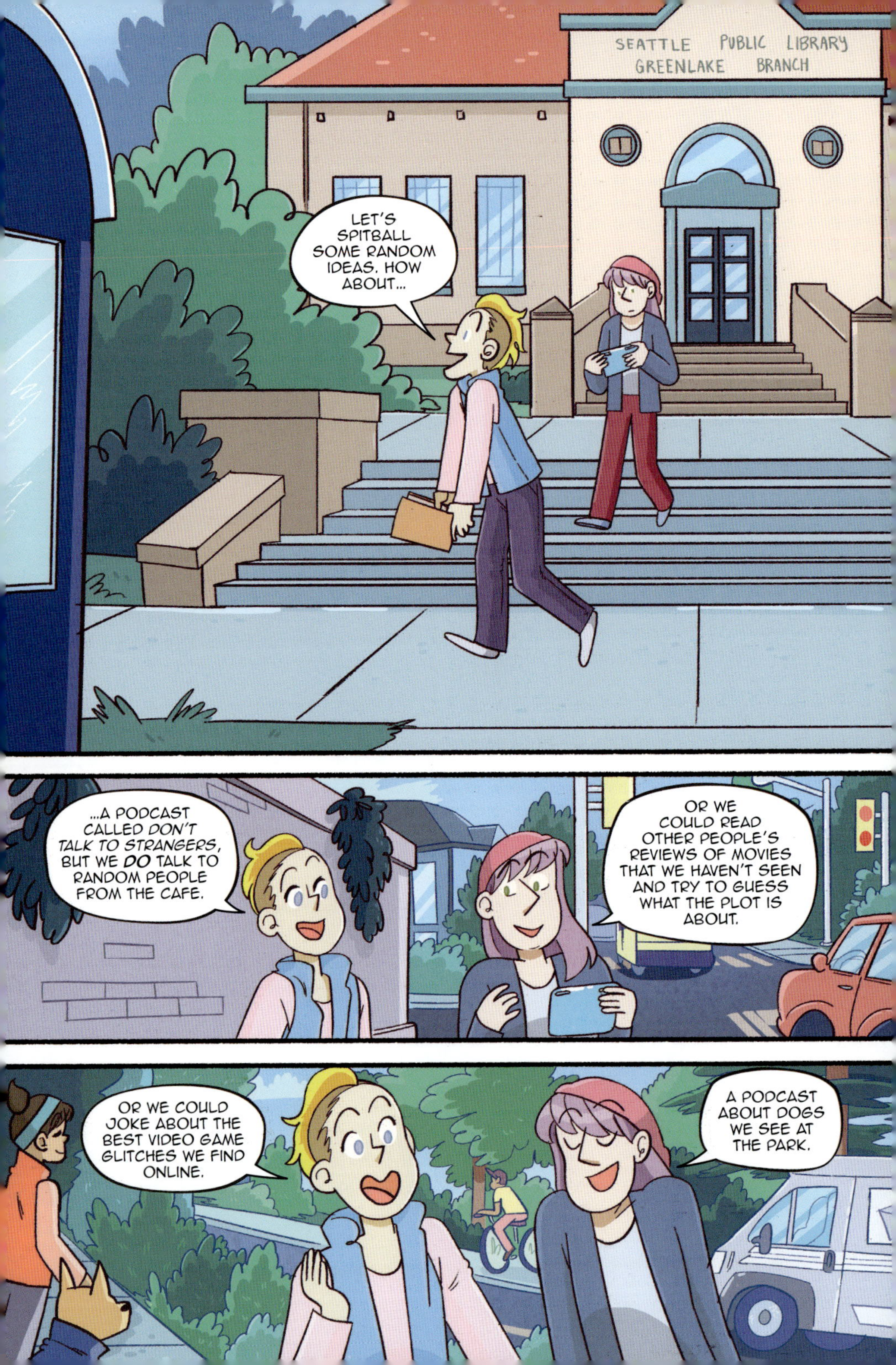
SEATTLE PUBLIC LIBRARY GREENLAKE BRANCH
LET'S SPITBALL SOME RANDOM IDEAS. HOW ABOUT...
...A PODCAST CALLED *DON'T TALK TO STRANGERS*, BUT WE ***DO*** TALK TO RANDOM PEOPLE FROM THE CAFE.
OR WE COULD READ OTHER PEOPLE'S REVIEWS OF MOVIES THAT WE HAVEN'T SEEN AND TRY TO GUESS WHAT THE PLOT IS ABOUT.
OR WE COULD JOKE ABOUT THE BEST VIDEO GAME GLITCHES WE FIND ONLINE.
A PODCAST ABOUT DOGS WE SEE AT THE PARK.

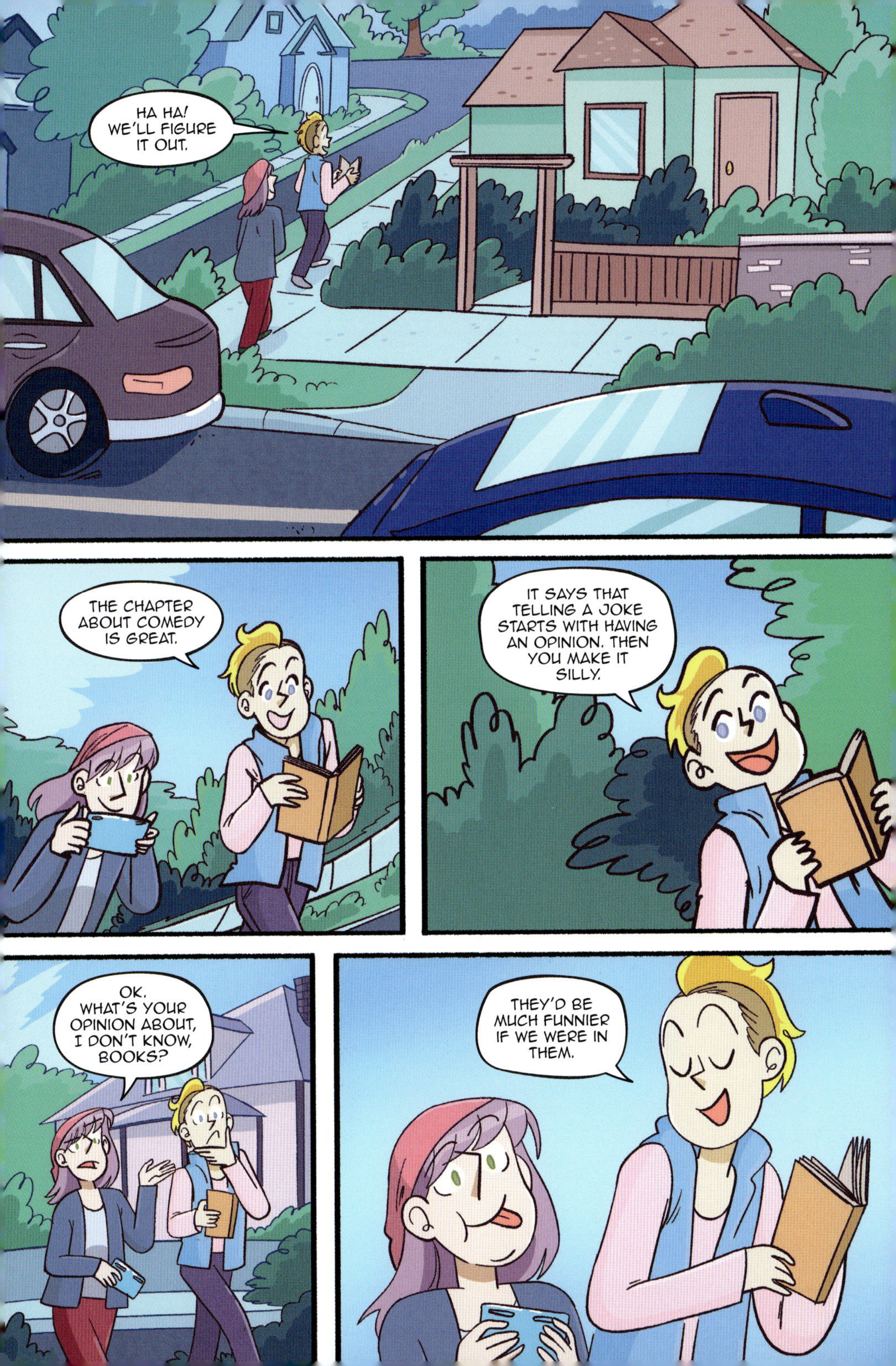
HA HA! WE'LL FIGURE IT OUT.
THE CHAPTER ABOUT COMEDY IS GREAT.
IT SAYS THAT TELLING A JOKE STARTS WITH HAVING AN OPINION. THEN YOU MAKE IT SILLY.
OK. WHAT'S YOUR OPINION ABOUT, I DON'T KNOW, BOOKS?
THEY'D BE MUCH FUNNIER IF WE WERE IN THEM.

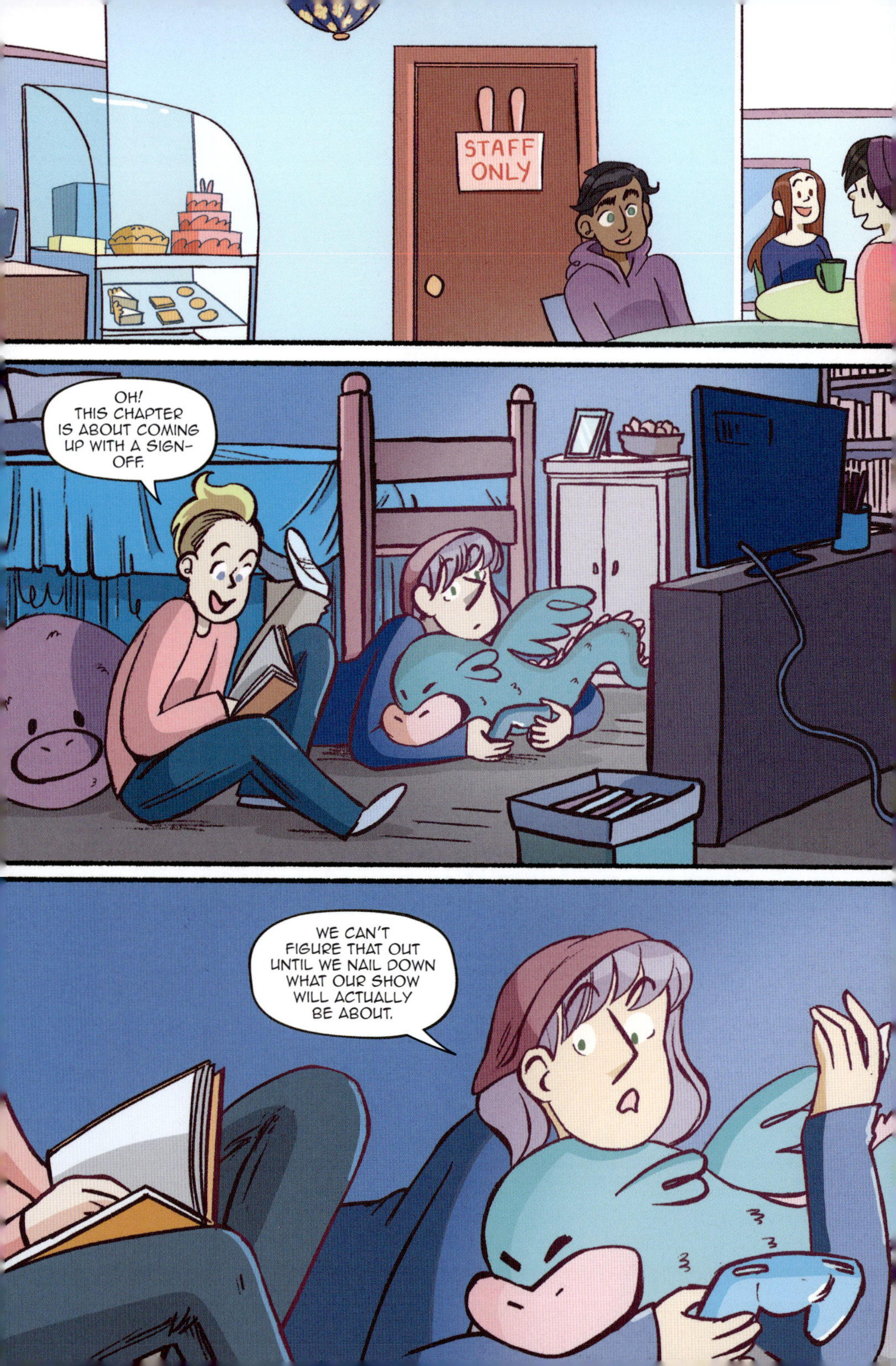
STAFF ONLY
OH! THIS CHAPTER IS ABOUT COMING UP WITH A SIGN-OFF.
WE CAN'T FIGURE THAT OUT UNTIL WE NAIL DOWN WHAT OUR SHOW WILL ACTUALLY BE ABOUT.

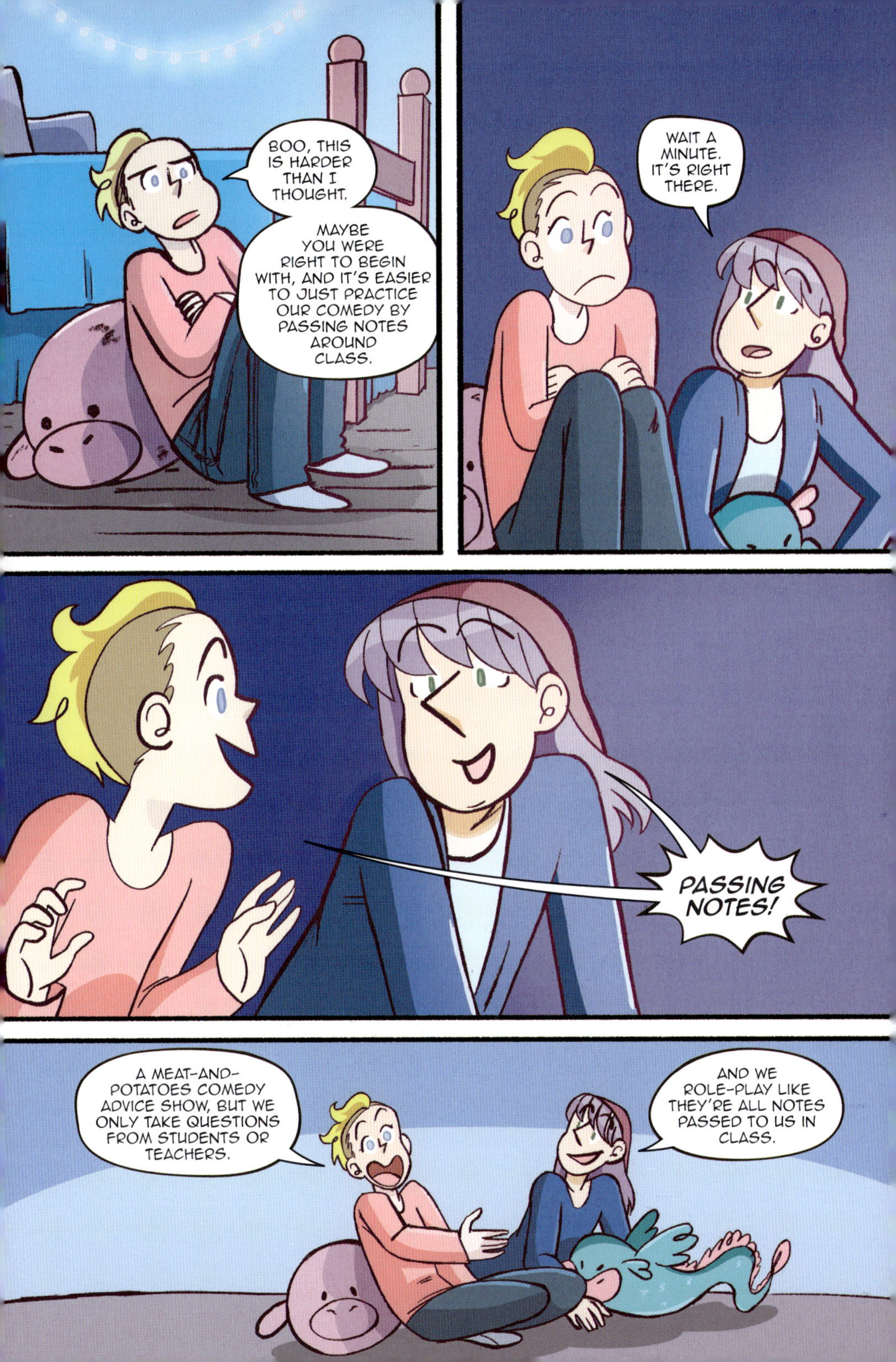
BOO, THIS IS HARDER THAN I THOUGHT.
MAYBE YOU WERE RIGHT TO BEGIN WITH, AND IT'S EASIER TO JUST PRACTICE OUR COMEDY BY PASSING NOTES AROUND CLASS.
WAIT A MINUTE. IT'S RIGHT THERE.
PASSING NOTES!
A MEAT-AND-POTATOES COMEDY ADVICE SHOW, BUT WE ONLY TAKE QUESTIONS FROM STUDENTS OR TEACHERS.
AND WE ROLE-PLAY LIKE THEY'RE ALL NOTES PASSED TO US IN CLASS.

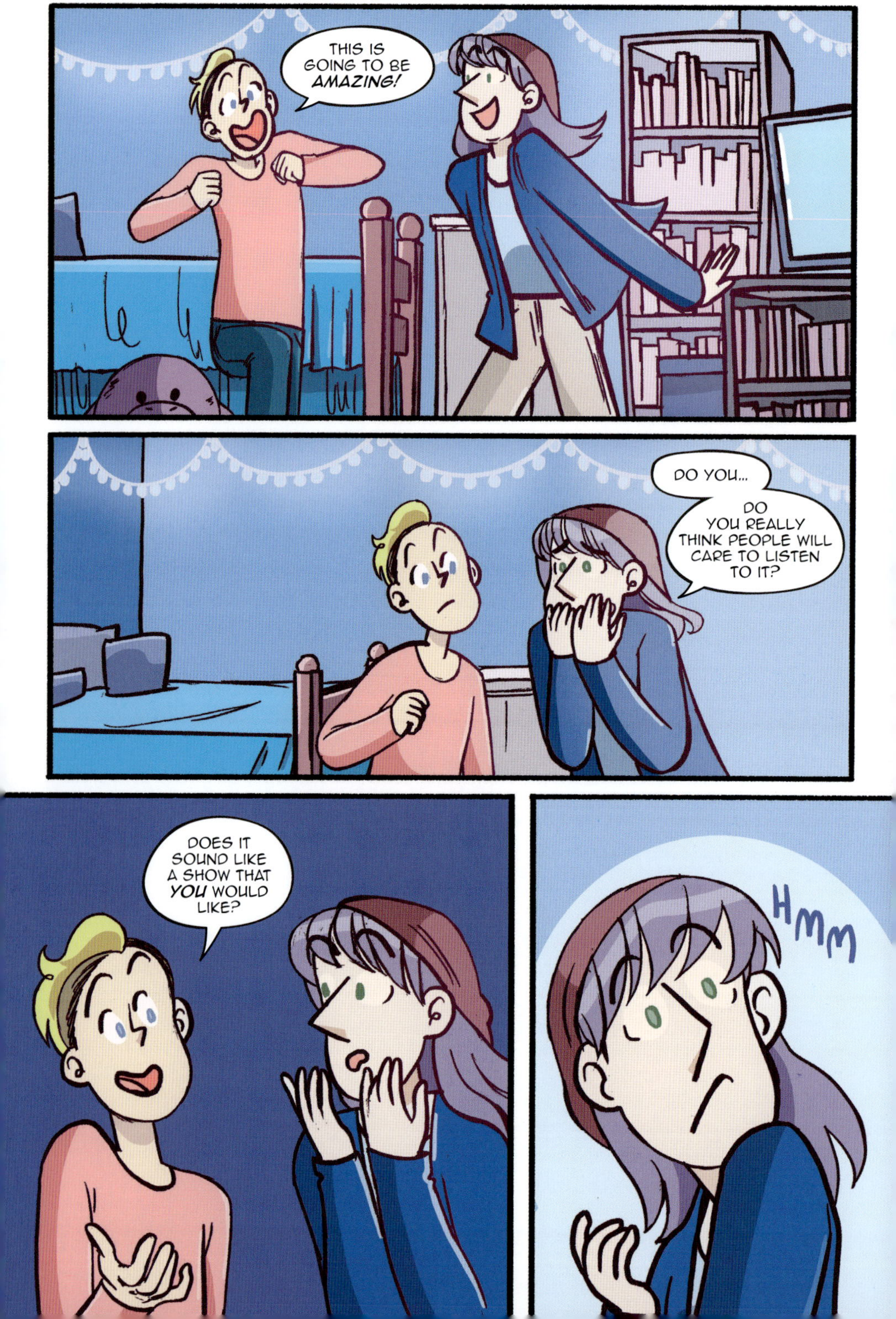
THIS IS GOING TO BE *AMAZING!*
DO YOU...
DO YOU REALLY THINK PEOPLE WILL CARE TO LISTEN TO IT?
DOES IT SOUND LIKE A SHOW THAT *YOU* WOULD LIKE?
HMM

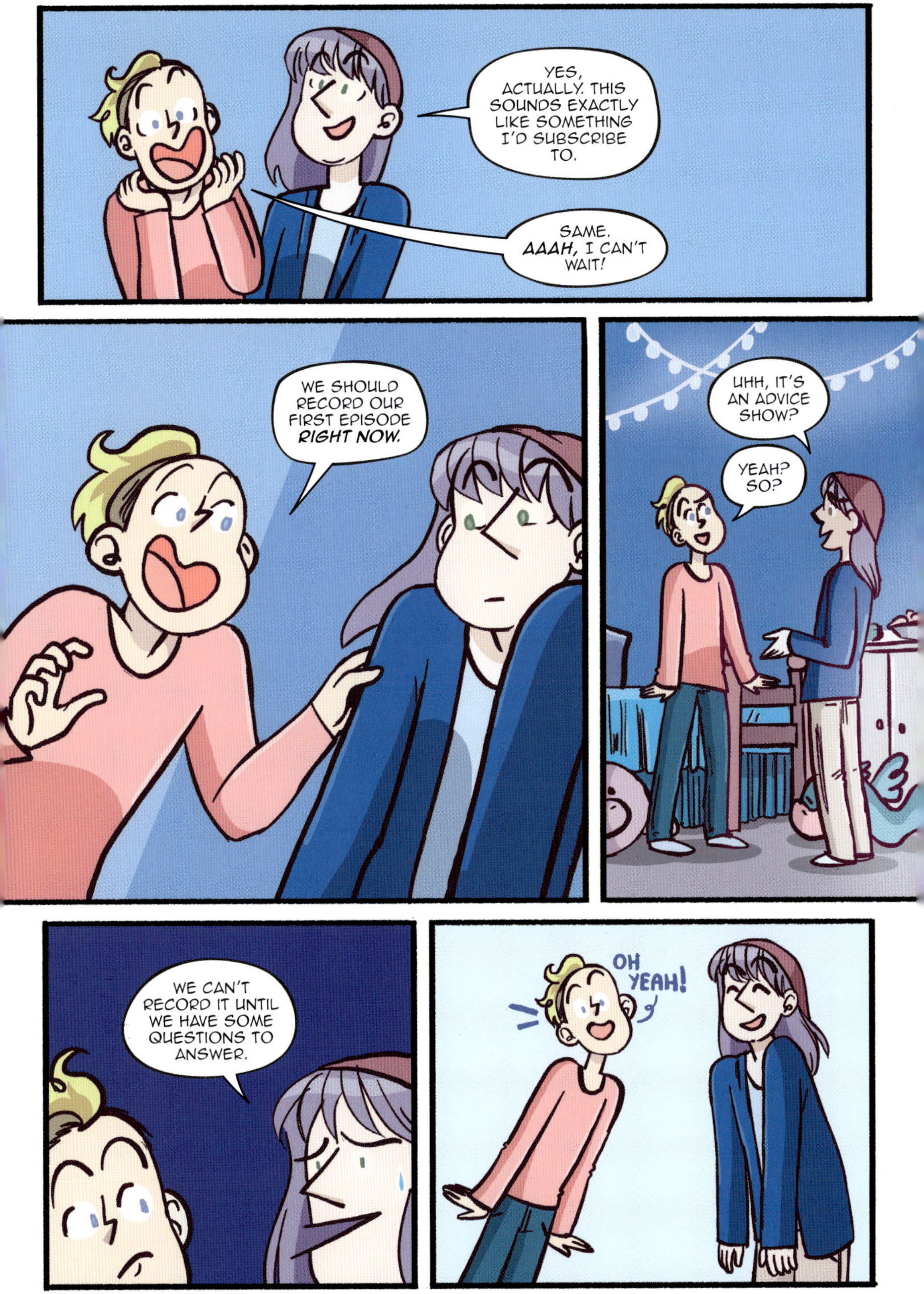
YES, ACTUALLY. THIS SOUNDS EXACTLY LIKE SOMETHING I'D SUBSCRIBE TO.
SAME. **AAAH,** I CAN'T WAIT!
WE SHOULD RECORD OUR FIRST EPISODE ***RIGHT NOW.***
UHH, IT'S AN ADVICE SHOW?
YEAH? SO?
WE CAN'T RECORD IT UNTIL WE HAVE SOME QUESTIONS TO ANSWER.
OH YEAH!

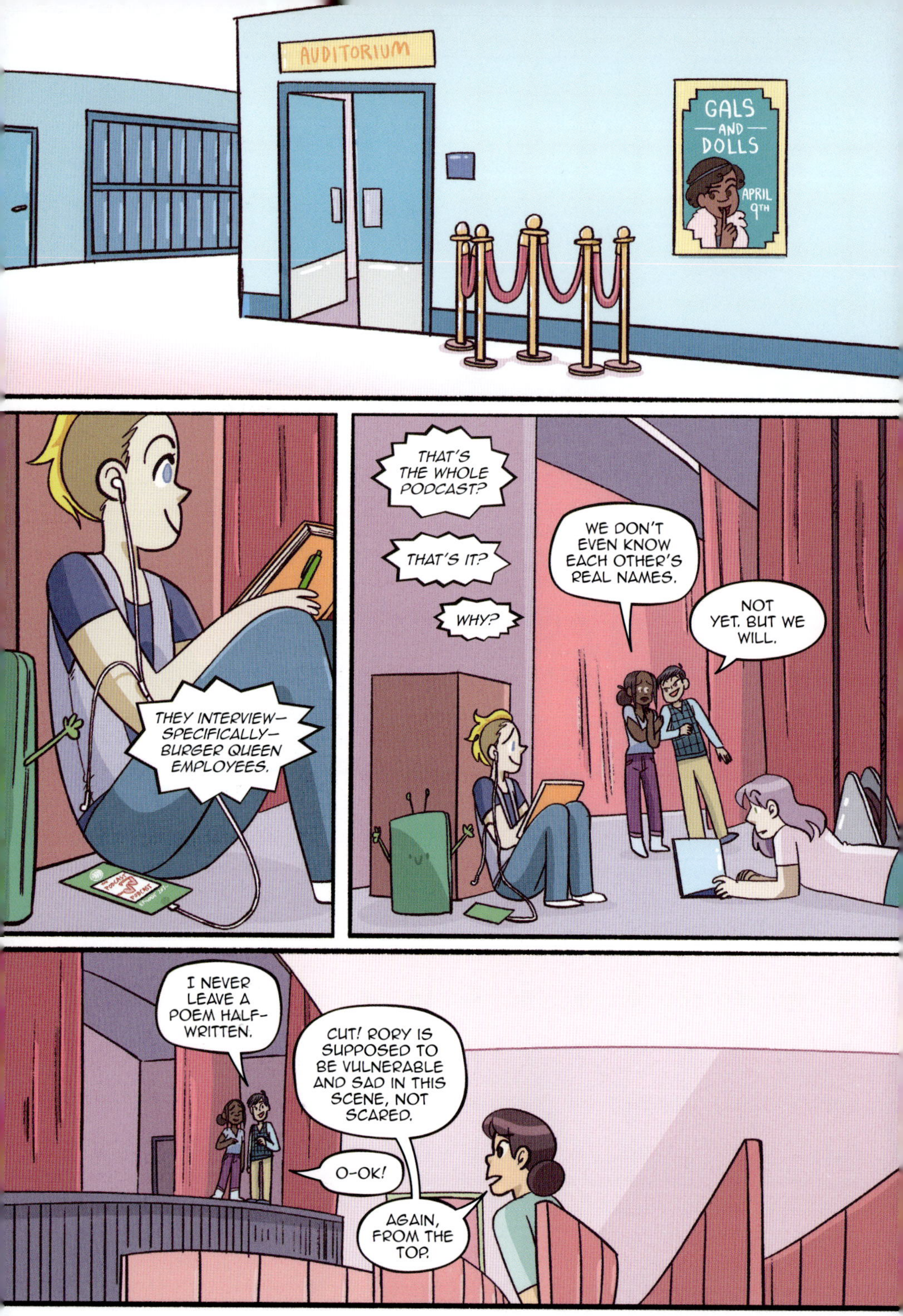
AUDITORIUM
GALS AND DOLLS
APRIL 9TH
THEY INTERVIEW—SPECIFICALLY—BURGER QUEEN EMPLOYEES.
THAT'S THE WHOLE PODCAST?
THAT'S IT?
WHY?
WE DON'T EVEN KNOW EACH OTHER'S REAL NAMES.
NOT YET. BUT WE WILL.
I NEVER LEAVE A POEM HALF-WRITTEN.
CUT! RORY IS SUPPOSED TO BE VULNERABLE AND SAD IN THIS SCENE, NOT SCARED.
O-OK!
AGAIN, FROM THE TOP.

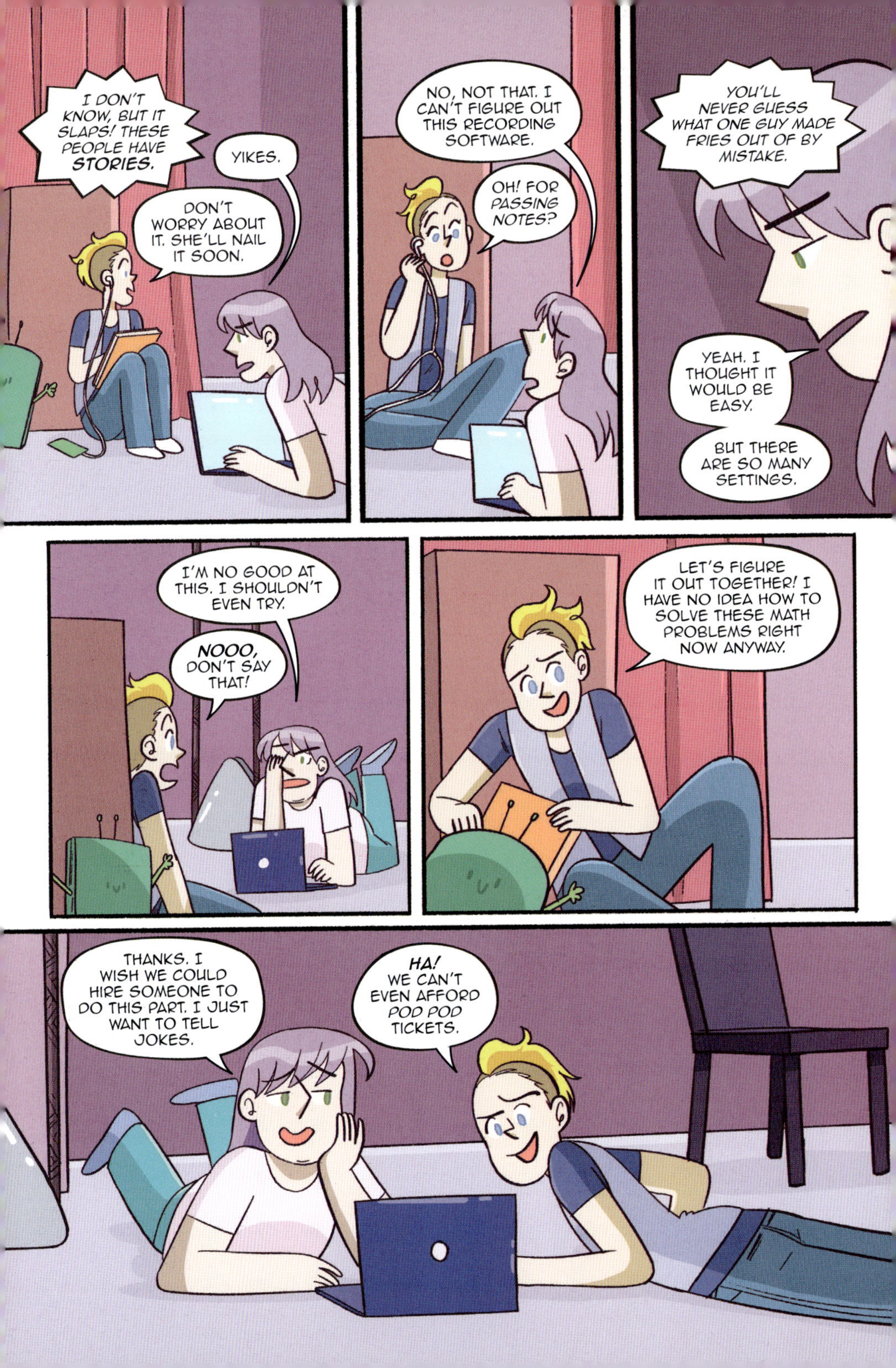
I DON'T KNOW, BUT IT SLAPS! THESE PEOPLE HAVE **STORIES.**
YIKES.
DON'T WORRY ABOUT IT. SHE'LL NAIL IT SOON.
NO, NOT THAT. I CAN'T FIGURE OUT THIS RECORDING SOFTWARE.
OH! FOR PASSING NOTES?
YOU'LL NEVER GUESS WHAT ONE GUY MADE FRIES OUT OF BY MISTAKE.
YEAH. I THOUGHT IT WOULD BE EASY.
BUT THERE ARE SO MANY SETTINGS.
I'M NO GOOD AT THIS. I SHOULDN'T EVEN TRY.
NOOO, DON'T SAY THAT!
LET'S FIGURE IT OUT TOGETHER! I HAVE NO IDEA HOW TO SOLVE THESE MATH PROBLEMS RIGHT NOW ANYWAY.
THANKS. I WISH WE COULD HIRE SOMEONE TO DO THIS PART. I JUST WANT TO TELL JOKES.
HA! WE CAN'T EVEN AFFORD *POD POD* TICKETS.

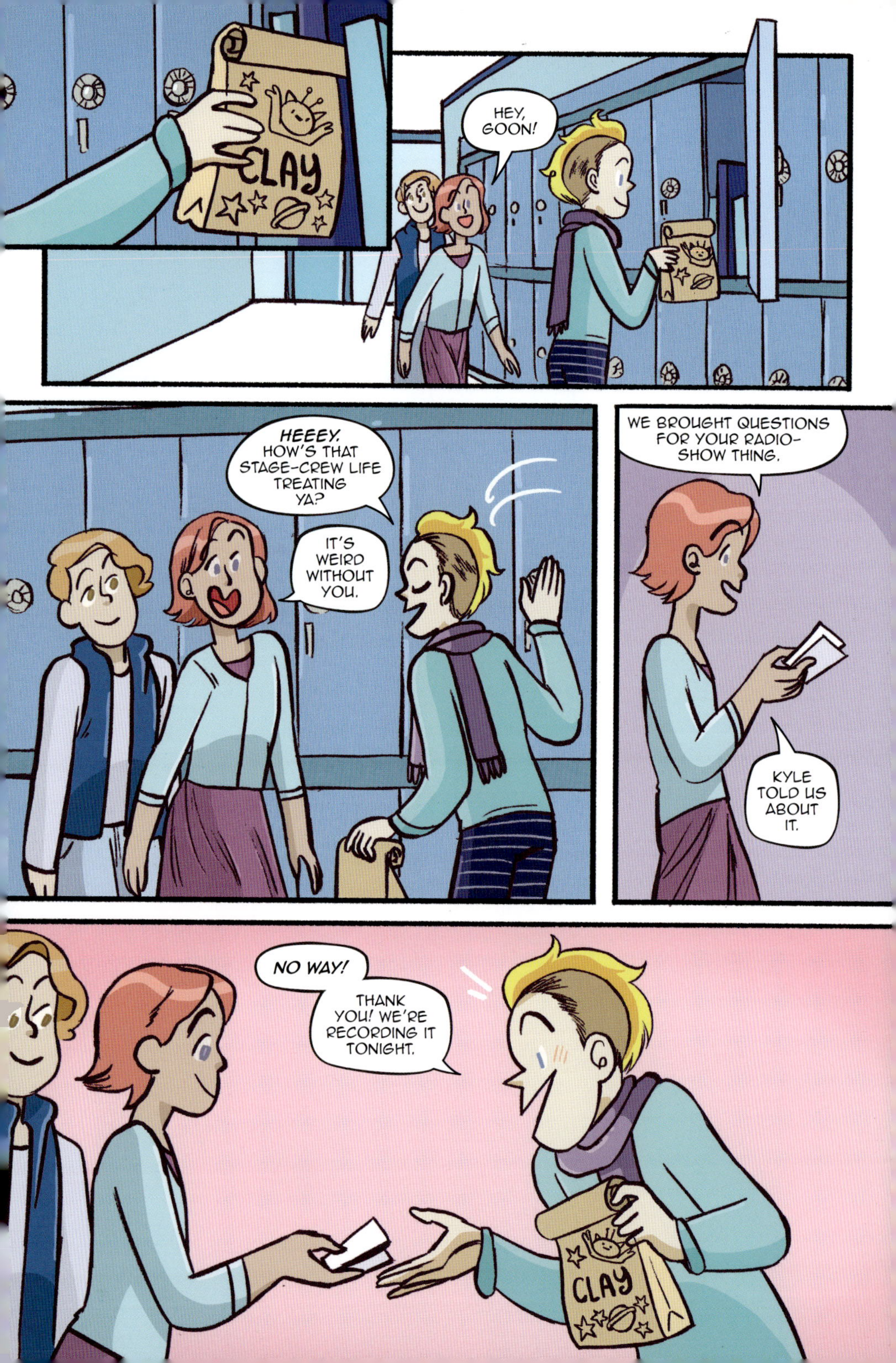
CLAY
HEY, GOON!
HEEEY. HOW'S THAT STAGE-CREW LIFE TREATING YA?
IT'S WEIRD WITHOUT YOU.
WE BROUGHT QUESTIONS FOR YOUR RADIO-SHOW THING.
KYLE TOLD US ABOUT IT.
NO WAY!
THANK YOU! WE'RE RECORDING IT TONIGHT.
CLAY

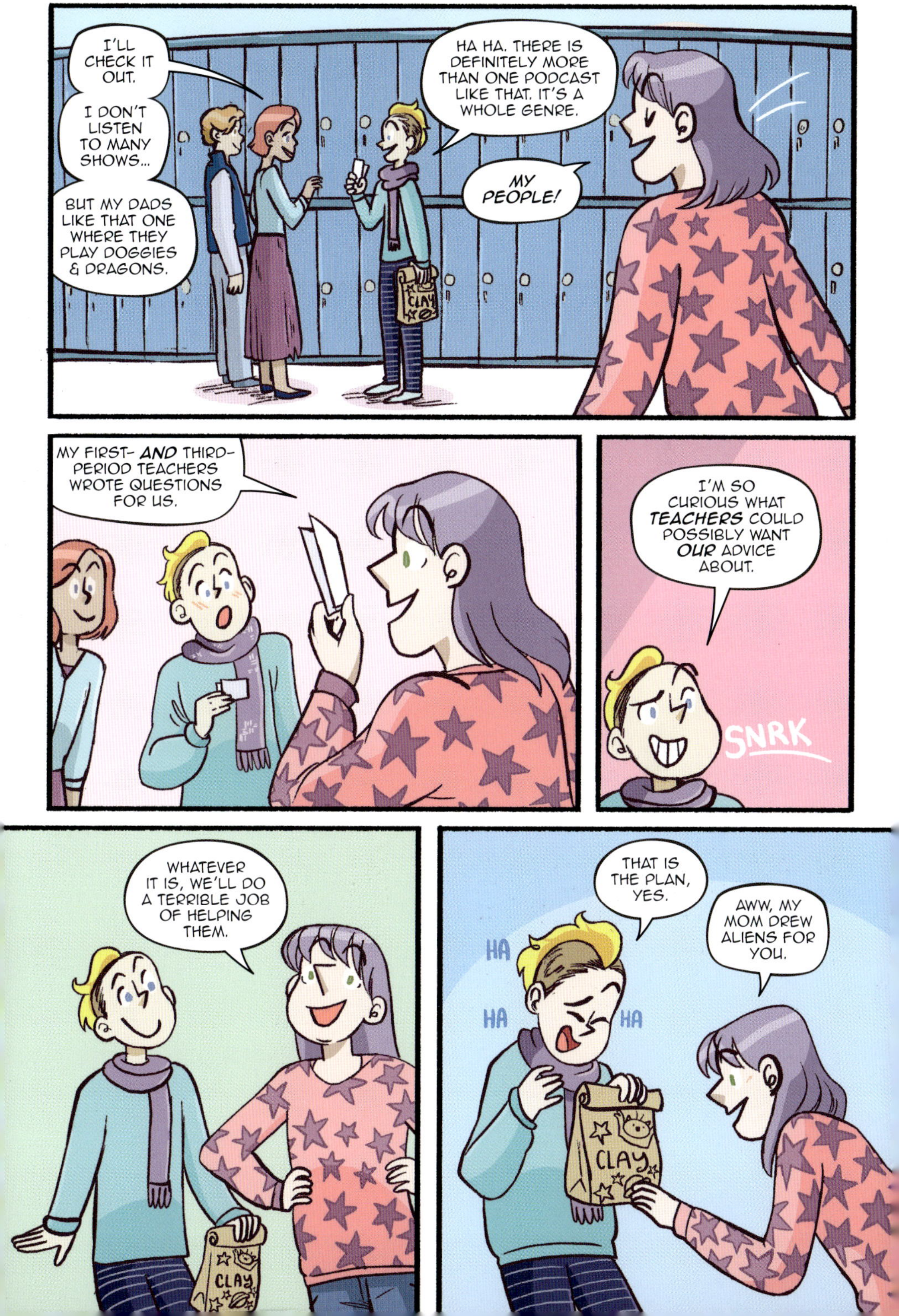
I'LL CHECK IT OUT.
I DON'T LISTEN TO MANY SHOWS...
BUT MY DADS LIKE THAT ONE WHERE THEY PLAY DOGGIES & DRAGONS.
HA HA. THERE IS DEFINITELY MORE THAN ONE PODCAST LIKE THAT. IT'S A WHOLE GENRE.
MY PEOPLE!
CLAY
MY FIRST- AND THIRD-PERIOD TEACHERS WROTE QUESTIONS FOR US.
I'M SO CURIOUS WHAT TEACHERS COULD POSSIBLY WANT OUR ADVICE ABOUT.
SNRK
WHATEVER IT IS, WE'LL DO A TERRIBLE JOB OF HELPING THEM.
CLAY
THAT IS THE PLAN, YES.
HA
HA
HA
AWW, MY MOM DREW ALIENS FOR YOU.
CLAY

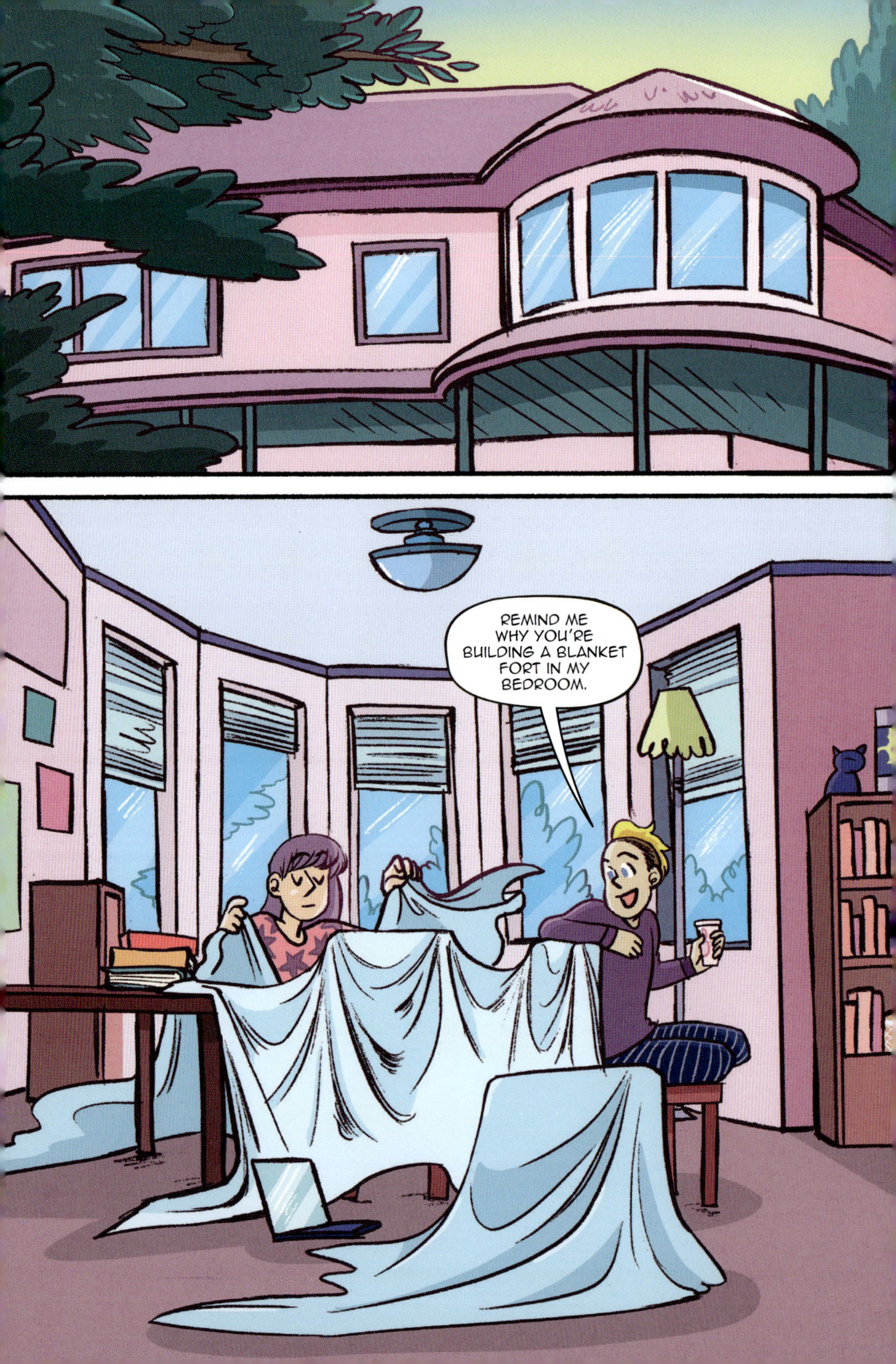
REMIND ME WHY YOU'RE BUILDING A BLANKET FORT IN MY BEDROOM.

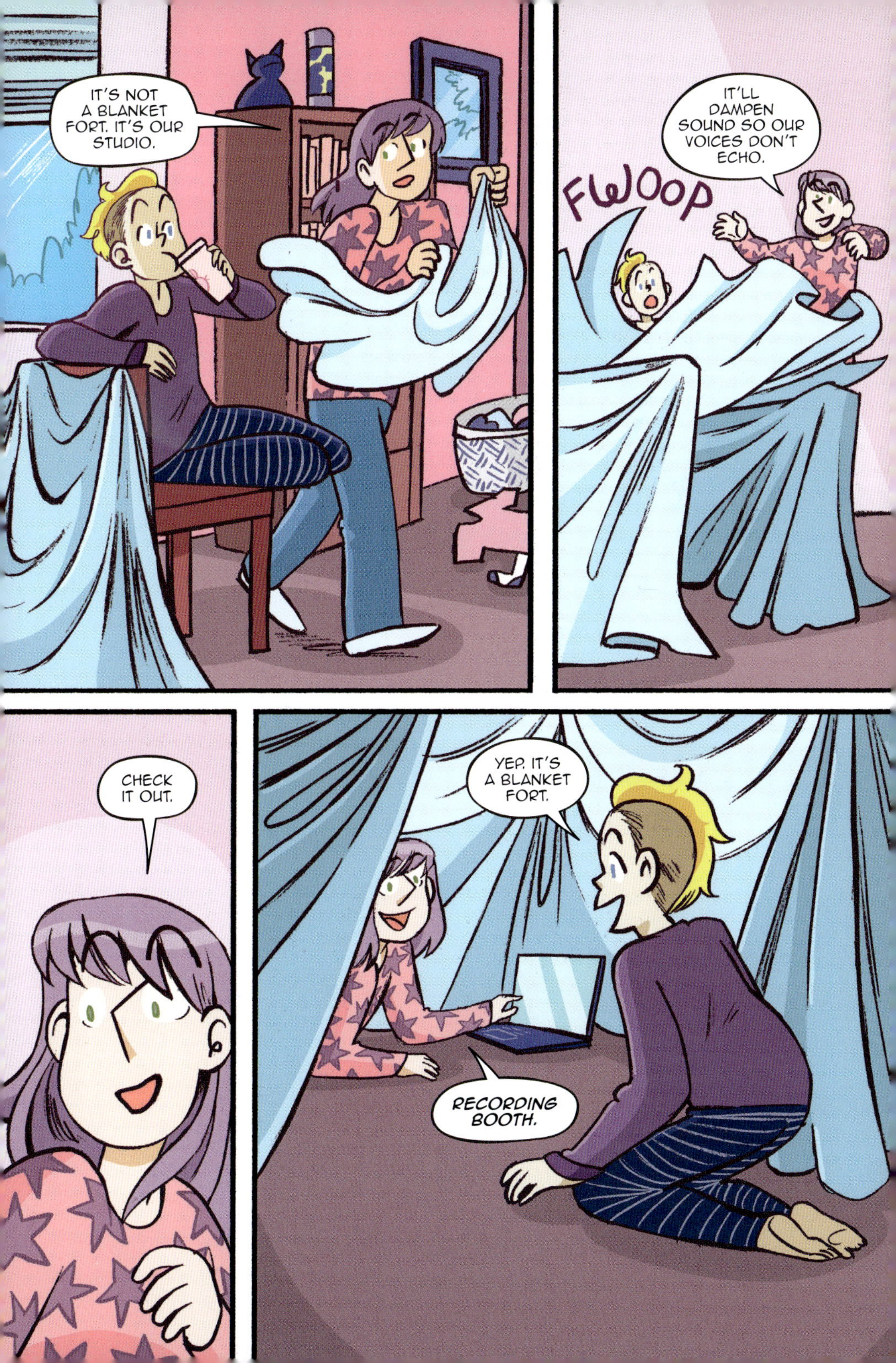
IT'S NOT A BLANKET FORT. IT'S OUR STUDIO.
IT'LL DAMPEN SOUND SO OUR VOICES DON'T ECHO.
FWOOP
CHECK IT OUT.
YEP. IT'S A BLANKET FORT.
RECORDING BOOTH.

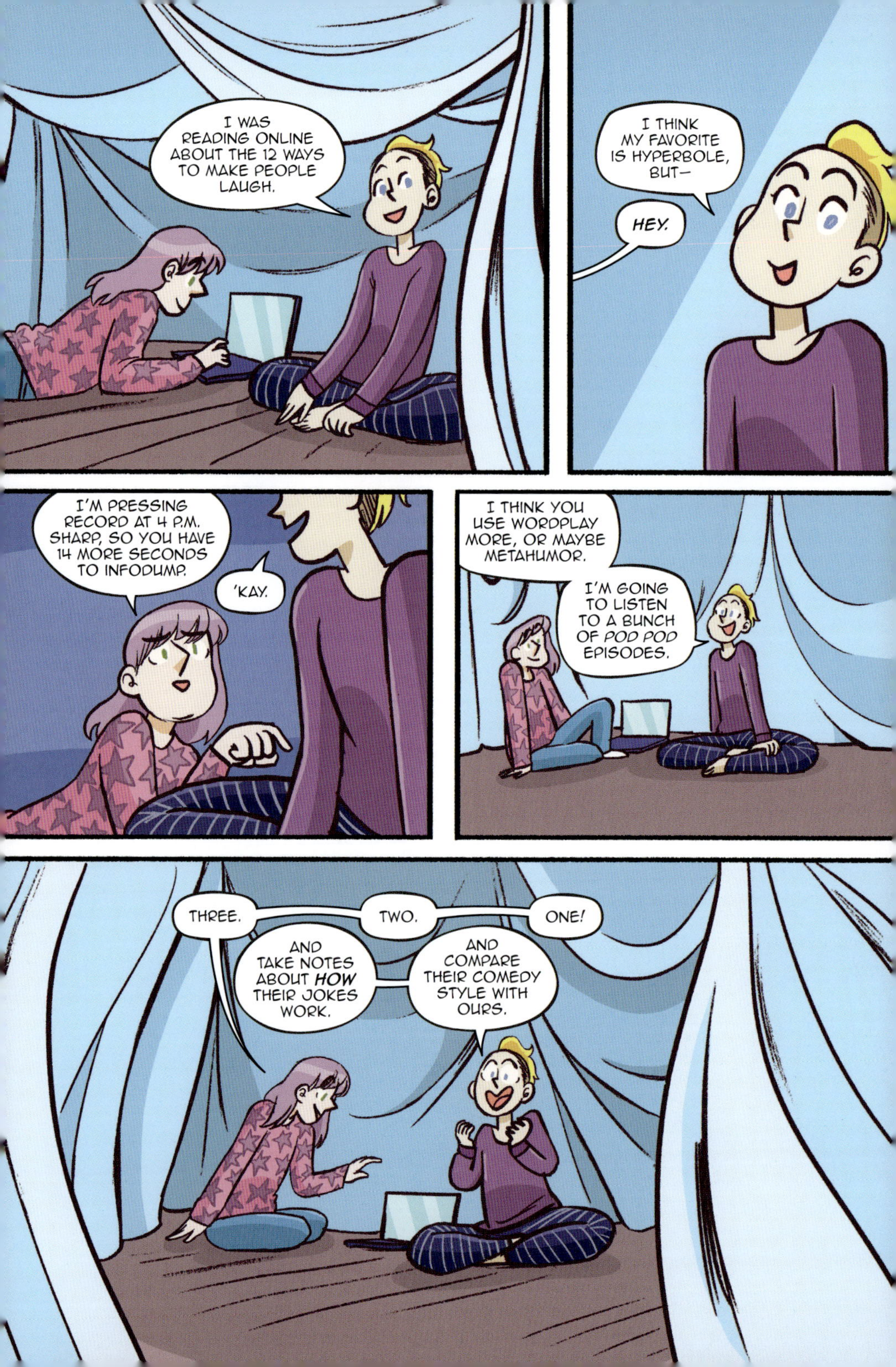
I WAS READING ONLINE ABOUT THE 12 WAYS TO MAKE PEOPLE LAUGH.
I THINK MY FAVORITE IS HYPERBOLE, BUT—
HEY.
I'M PRESSING RECORD AT 4 P.M. SHARP, SO YOU HAVE 14 MORE SECONDS TO INFODUMP.
'KAY.
I THINK YOU USE WORDPLAY MORE, OR MAYBE METAHUMOR.
I'M GOING TO LISTEN TO A BUNCH OF *POD POD* EPISODES.
AND TAKE NOTES ABOUT ***HOW*** THEIR JOKES WORK.
AND COMPARE THEIR COMEDY STYLE WITH OURS.
THREE.
TWO.
ONE!

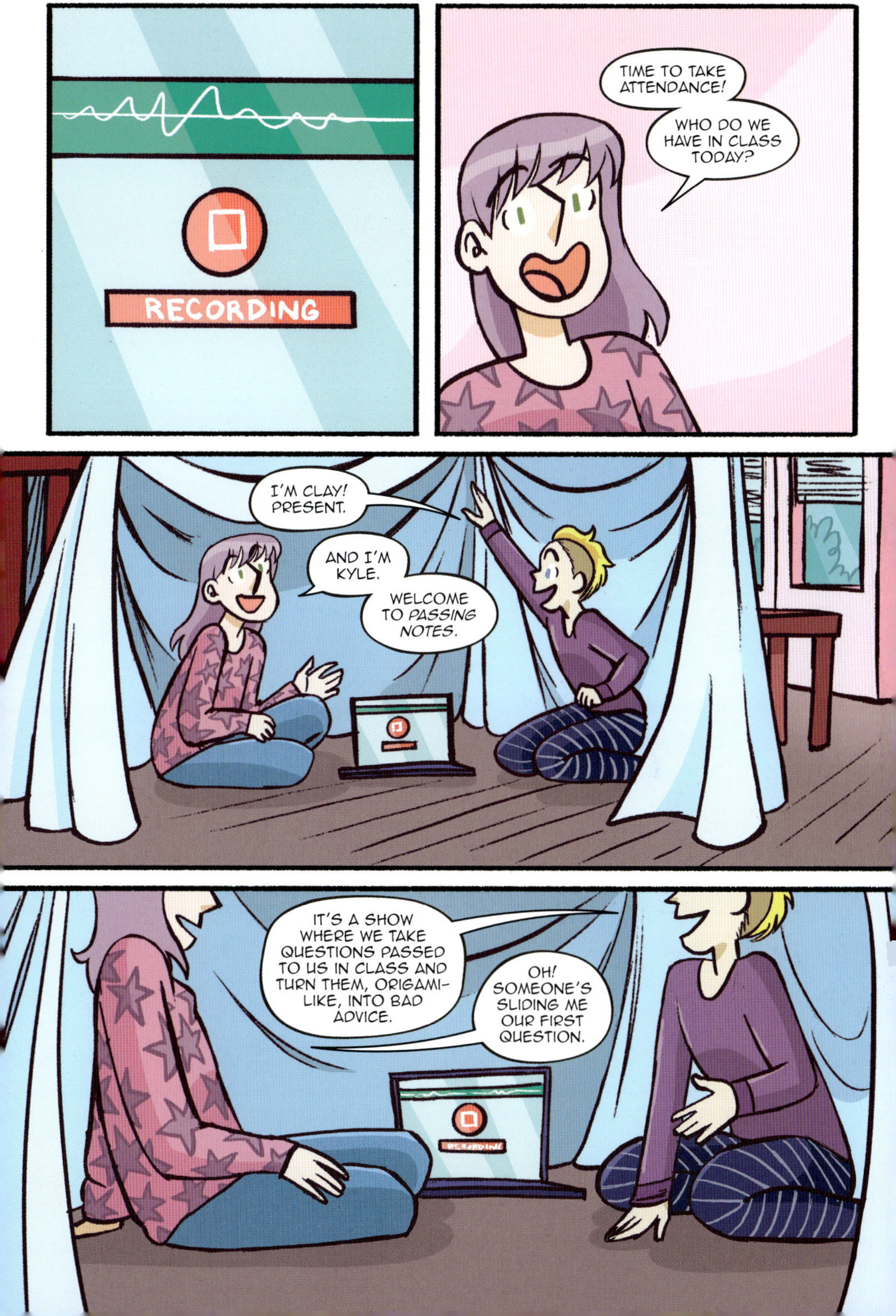
RECORDING
TIME TO TAKE ATTENDANCE!
WHO DO WE HAVE IN CLASS TODAY?
I'M CLAY! PRESENT.
AND I'M KYLE.
WELCOME TO PASSING NOTES.
IT'S A SHOW WHERE WE TAKE QUESTIONS PASSED TO US IN CLASS AND TURN THEM, ORIGAMI-LIKE, INTO BAD ADVICE.
OH! SOMEONE'S SLIDING ME OUR FIRST QUESTION.

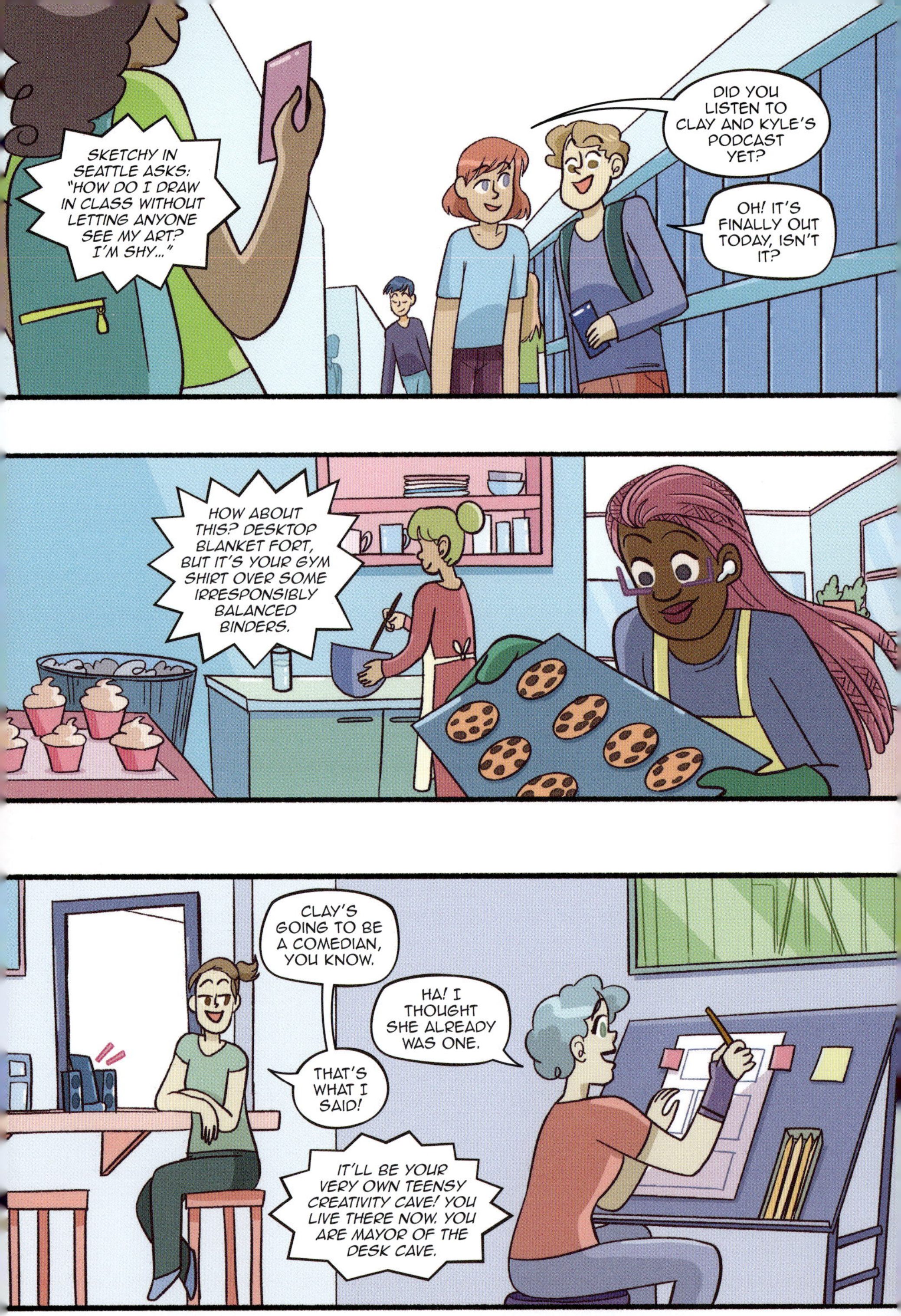
SKETCHY IN SEATTLE ASKS: "HOW DO I DRAW IN CLASS WITHOUT LETTING ANYONE SEE MY ART? I'M SHY..."
DID YOU LISTEN TO CLAY AND KYLE'S PODCAST YET?
OH! IT'S FINALLY OUT TODAY, ISN'T IT?
HOW ABOUT THIS? DESKTOP BLANKET FORT, BUT IT'S YOUR GYM SHIRT OVER SOME IRRESPONSIBLY BALANCED BINDERS.
CLAY'S GOING TO BE A COMEDIAN, YOU KNOW.
HA! I THOUGHT SHE ALREADY WAS ONE.
THAT'S WHAT I SAID!
IT'LL BE YOUR VERY OWN TEENSY CREATIVITY CAVE! YOU LIVE THERE NOW. YOU ARE MAYOR OF THE DESK CAVE.

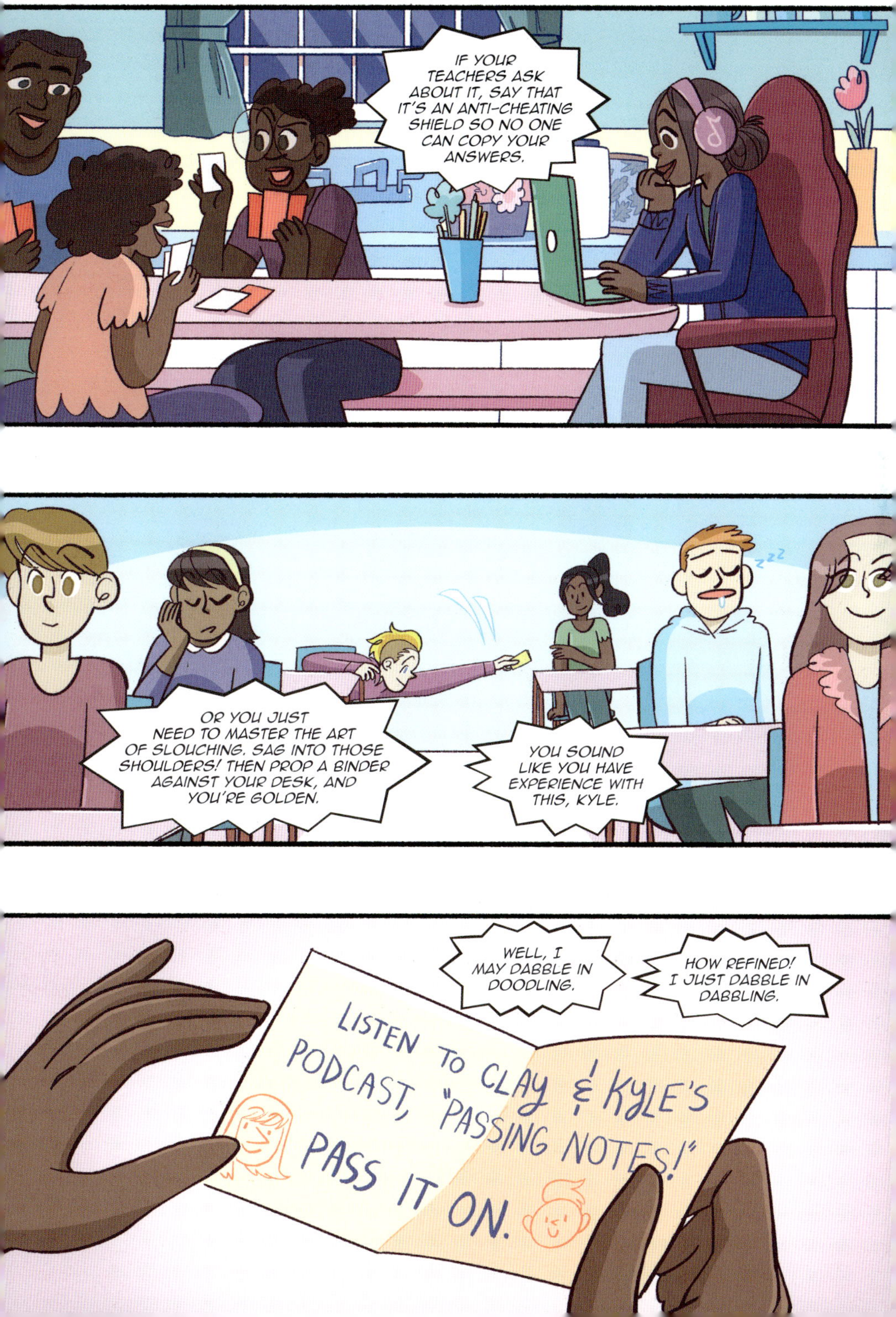
IF YOUR TEACHERS ASK ABOUT IT, SAY THAT IT'S AN ANTI-CHEATING SHIELD SO NO ONE CAN COPY YOUR ANSWERS.
OR YOU JUST NEED TO MASTER THE ART OF SLOUCHING. SAG INTO THOSE SHOULDERS! THEN PROP A BINDER AGAINST YOUR DESK, AND YOU'RE GOLDEN.
YOU SOUND LIKE YOU HAVE EXPERIENCE WITH THIS, KYLE.
WELL, I MAY DABBLE IN DOODLING.
HOW REFINED! I JUST DABBLE IN DABBLING.
LISTEN TO CLAY & KYLE'S PODCAST, "PASSING NOTES!"
PASS IT ON.

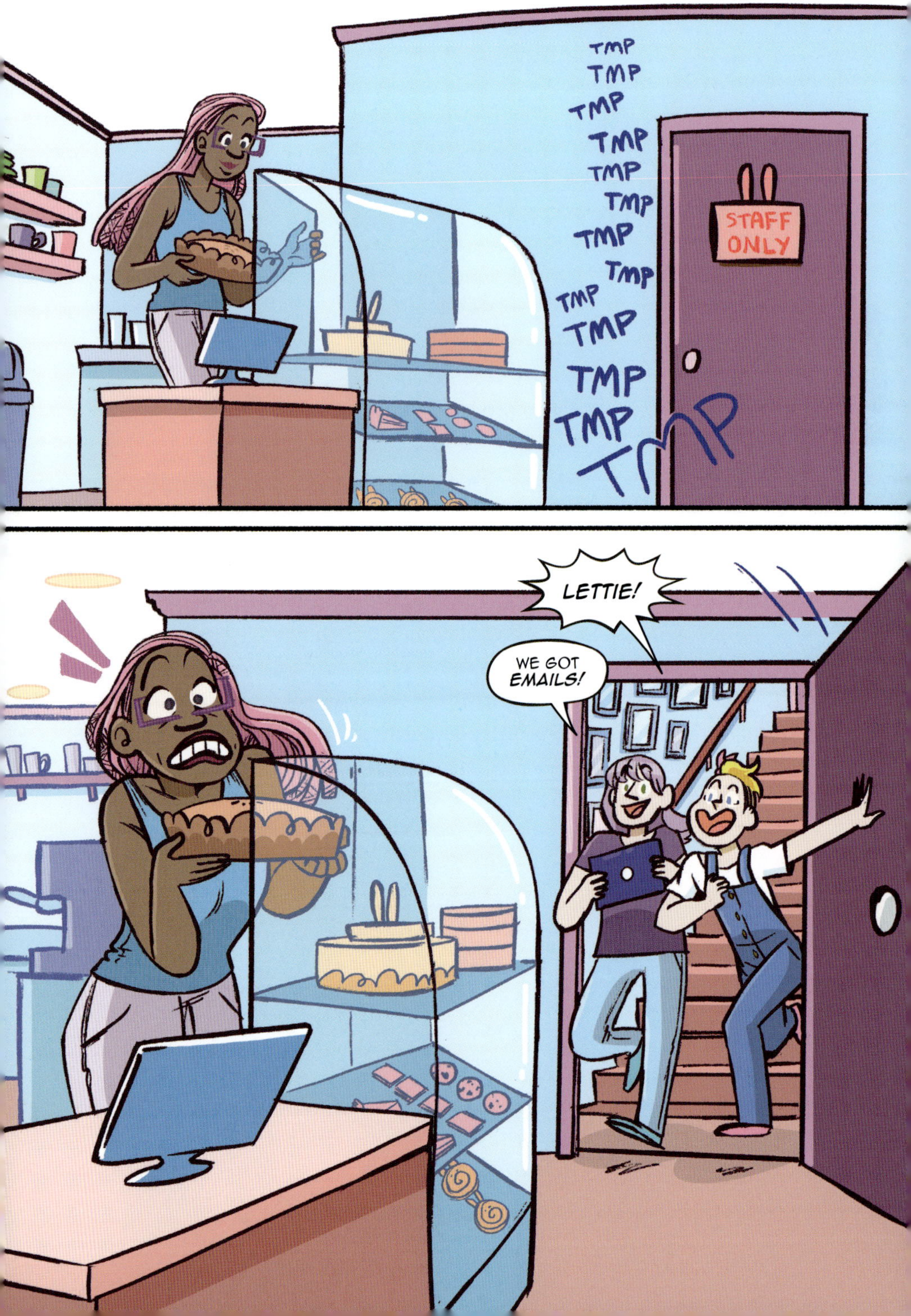
TMP
TMP
TMP
TMP
TMP
TMP
TMP
TMP
TMP
TMP
TMP
TMP
TMP
STAFF ONLY
LETTIE!
WE GOT EMAILS!

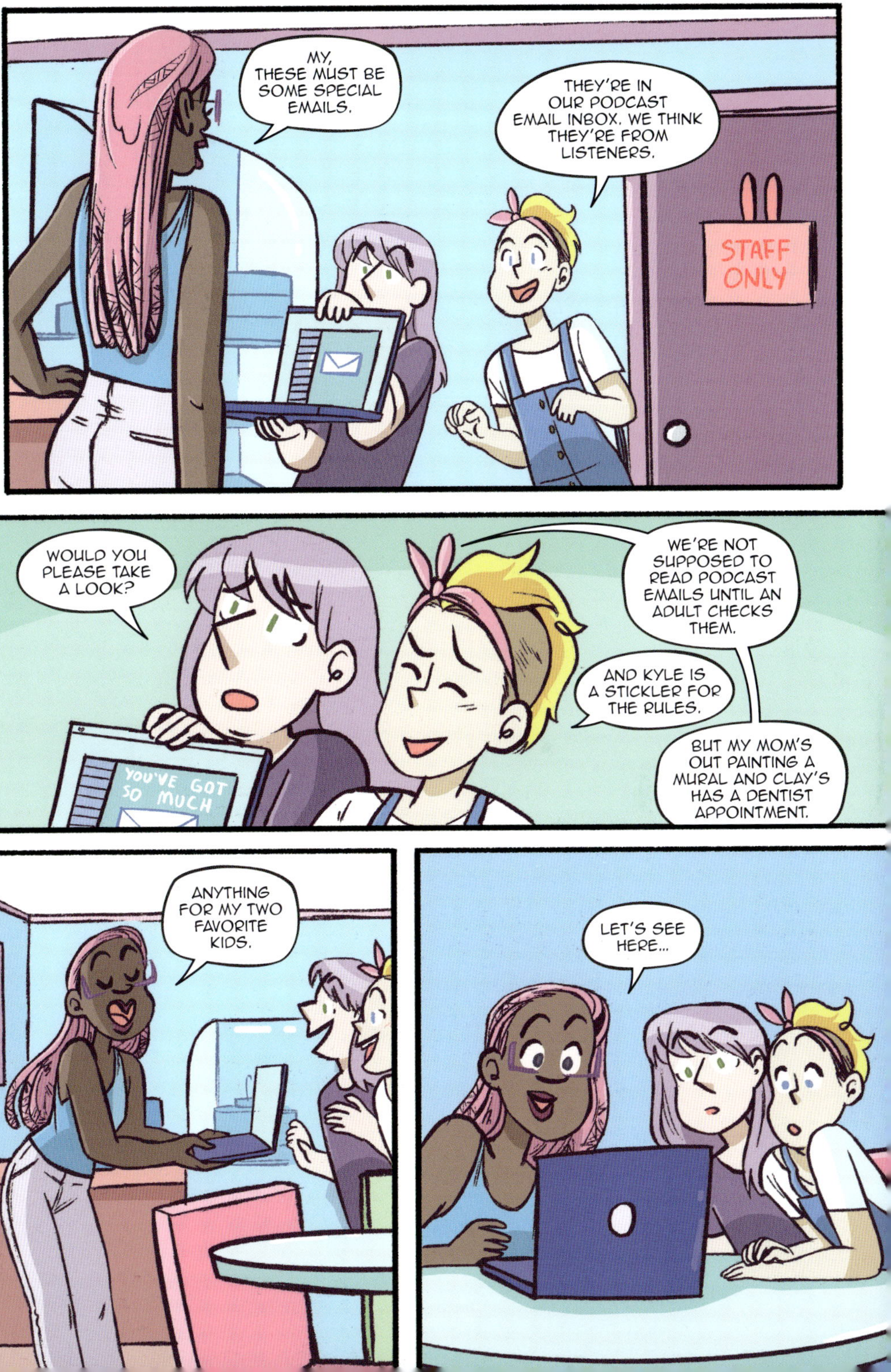
MY, THESE MUST BE SOME SPECIAL EMAILS.
THEY'RE IN OUR PODCAST EMAIL INBOX. WE THINK THEY'RE FROM LISTENERS.
STAFF ONLY
WOULD YOU PLEASE TAKE A LOOK?
WE'RE NOT SUPPOSED TO READ PODCAST EMAILS UNTIL AN ADULT CHECKS THEM.
AND KYLE IS A STICKLER FOR THE RULES.
BUT MY MOM'S OUT PAINTING A MURAL AND CLAY'S HAS A DENTIST APPOINTMENT.
YOU'VE GOT SO MUCH
ANYTHING FOR MY TWO FAVORITE KIDS.
LET'S SEE HERE...

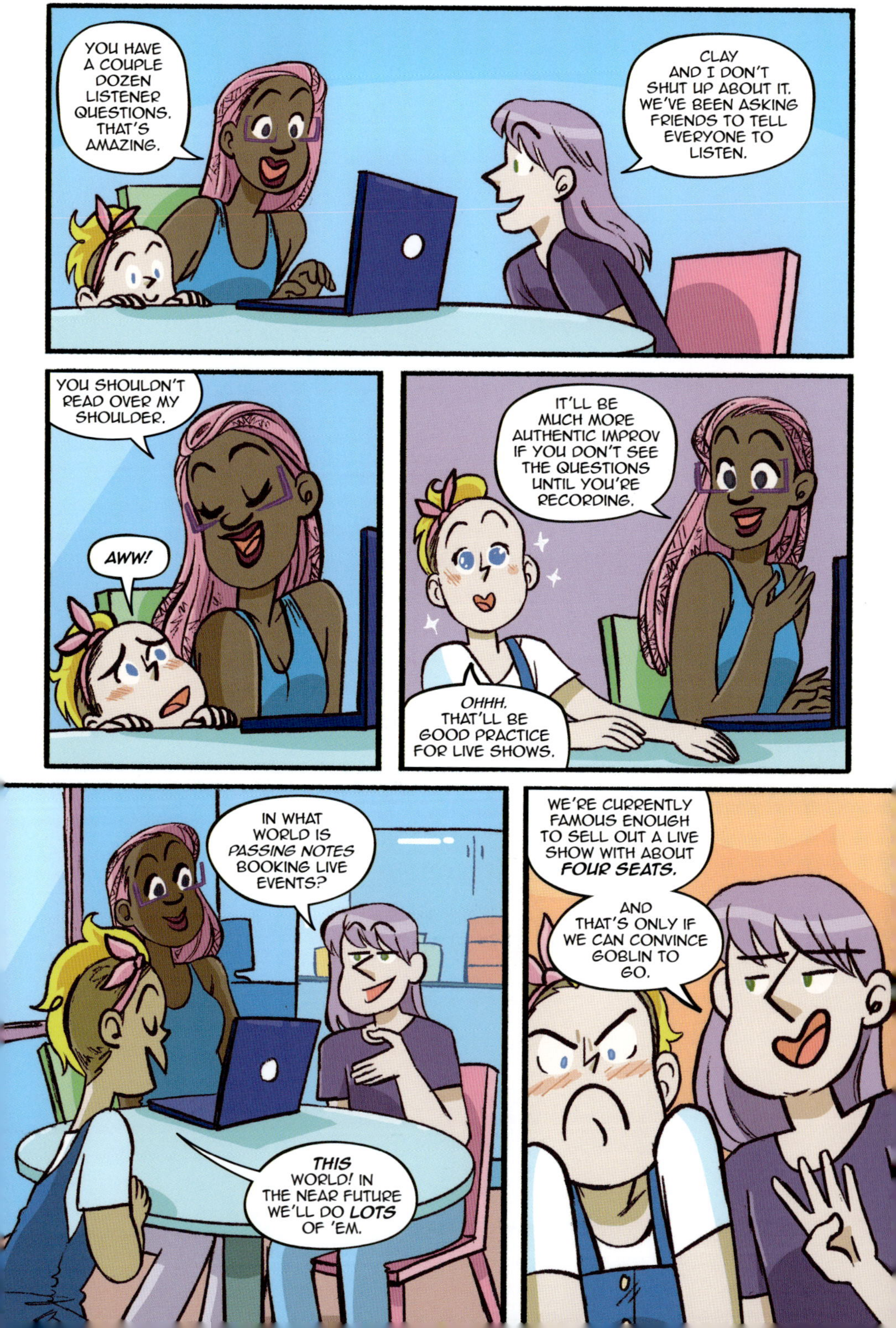
YOU HAVE A COUPLE DOZEN LISTENER QUESTIONS. THAT'S AMAZING.
CLAY AND I DON'T SHUT UP ABOUT IT. WE'VE BEEN ASKING FRIENDS TO TELL EVERYONE TO LISTEN.
YOU SHOULDN'T READ OVER MY SHOULDER.
AWW!
IT'LL BE MUCH MORE AUTHENTIC IMPROV IF YOU DON'T SEE THE QUESTIONS UNTIL YOU'RE RECORDING.
OHHH. THAT'LL BE GOOD PRACTICE FOR LIVE SHOWS.
IN WHAT WORLD IS PASSING NOTES BOOKING LIVE EVENTS?
THIS WORLD! IN THE NEAR FUTURE WE'LL DO LOTS OF 'EM.
WE'RE CURRENTLY FAMOUS ENOUGH TO SELL OUT A LIVE SHOW WITH ABOUT FOUR SEATS.
AND THAT'S ONLY IF WE CAN CONVINCE GOBLIN TO GO.

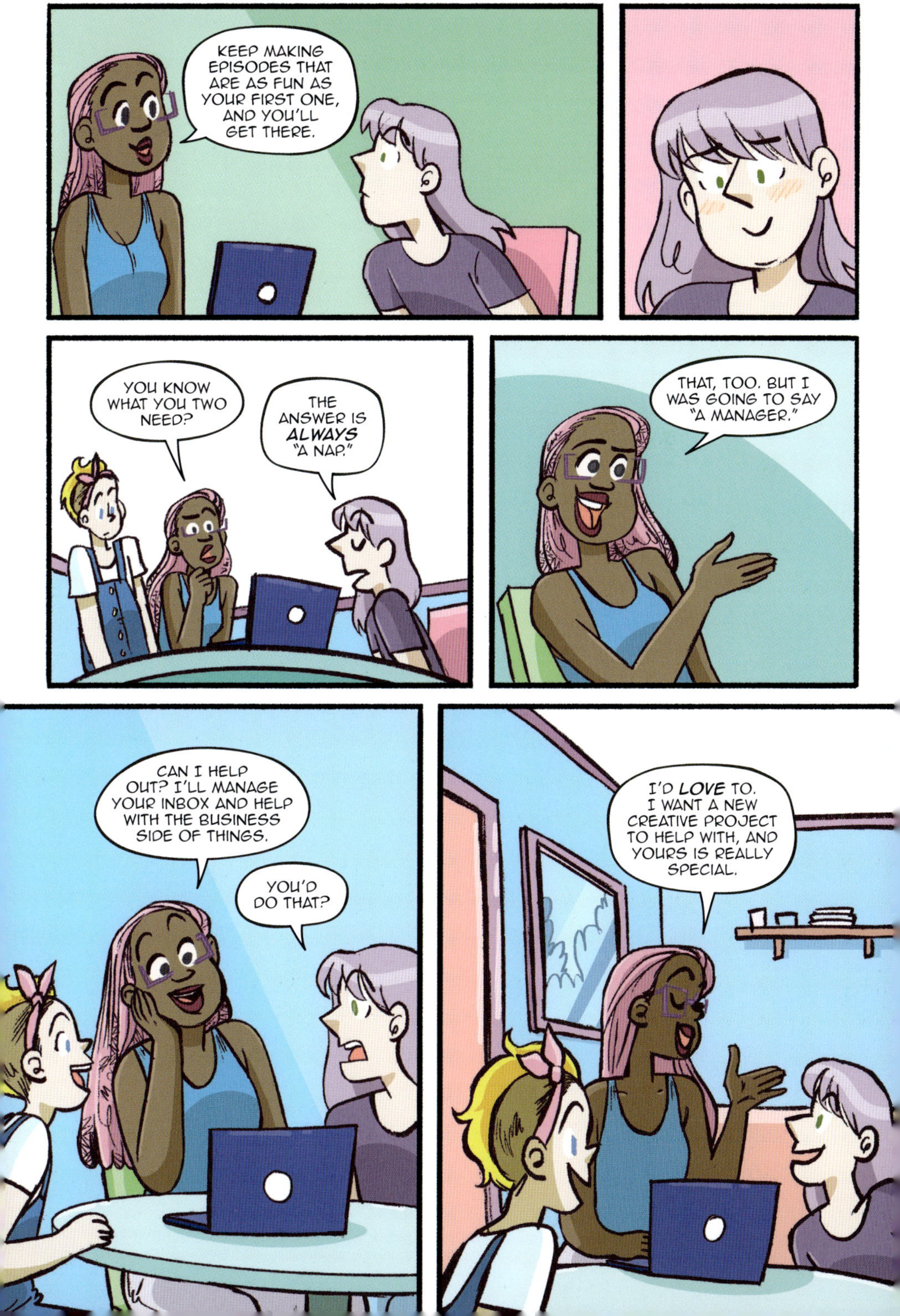
KEEP MAKING EPISODES THAT ARE AS FUN AS YOUR FIRST ONE, AND YOU'LL GET THERE.
YOU KNOW WHAT YOU TWO NEED?
THE ANSWER IS **ALWAYS** "A NAP."
THAT, TOO. BUT I WAS GOING TO SAY "A MANAGER."
CAN I HELP OUT? I'LL MANAGE YOUR INBOX AND HELP WITH THE BUSINESS SIDE OF THINGS.
YOU'D DO THAT?
I'D **LOVE** TO. I WANT A NEW CREATIVE PROJECT TO HELP WITH, AND YOURS IS REALLY SPECIAL.

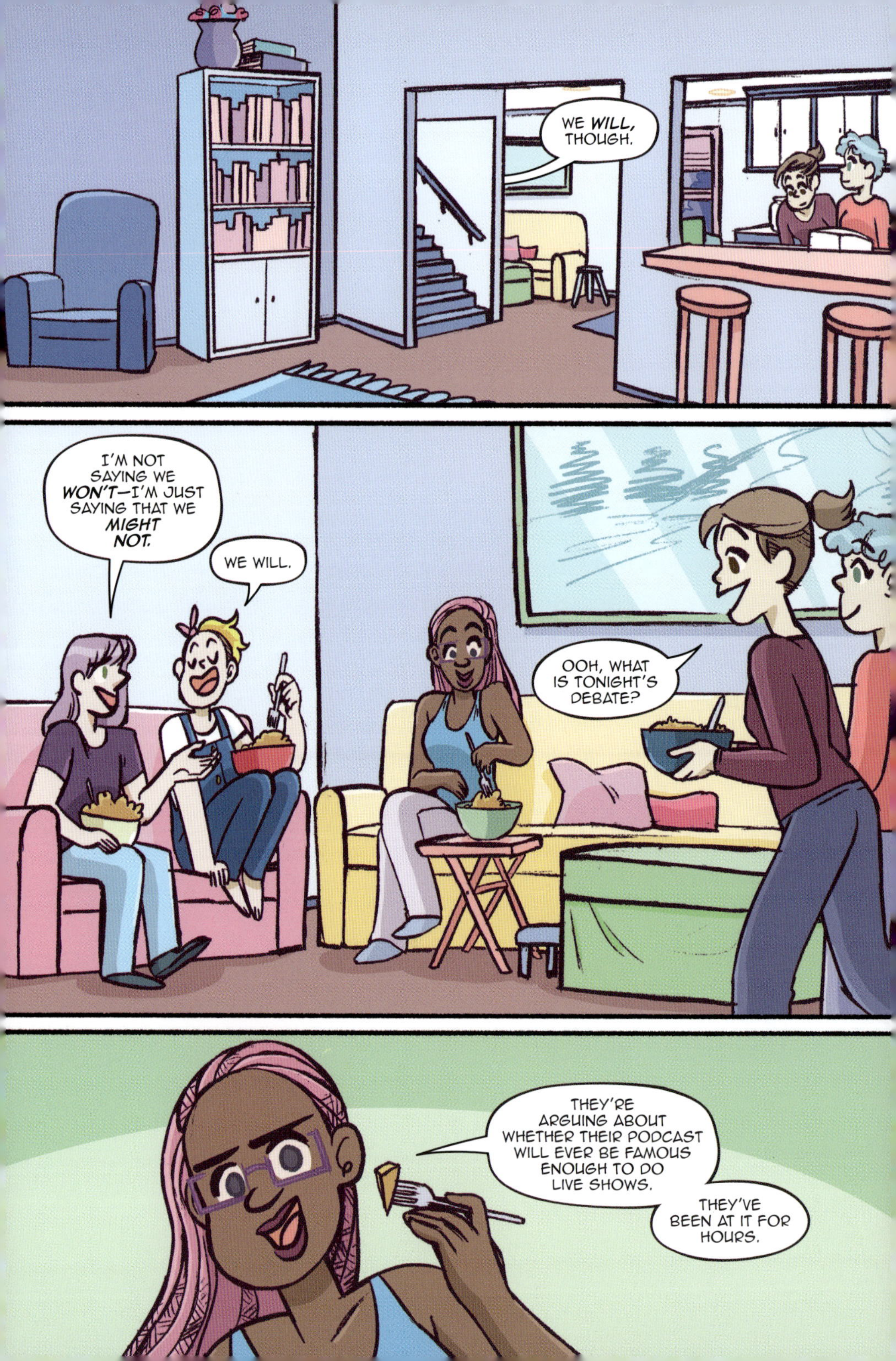
WE *WILL*, THOUGH.
I'M NOT SAYING WE *WON'T*—I'M JUST SAYING THAT WE *MIGHT NOT.*
WE WILL.
OOH, WHAT IS TONIGHT'S DEBATE?
THEY'RE ARGUING ABOUT WHETHER THEIR PODCAST WILL EVER BE FAMOUS ENOUGH TO DO LIVE SHOWS.
THEY'VE BEEN AT IT FOR HOURS.

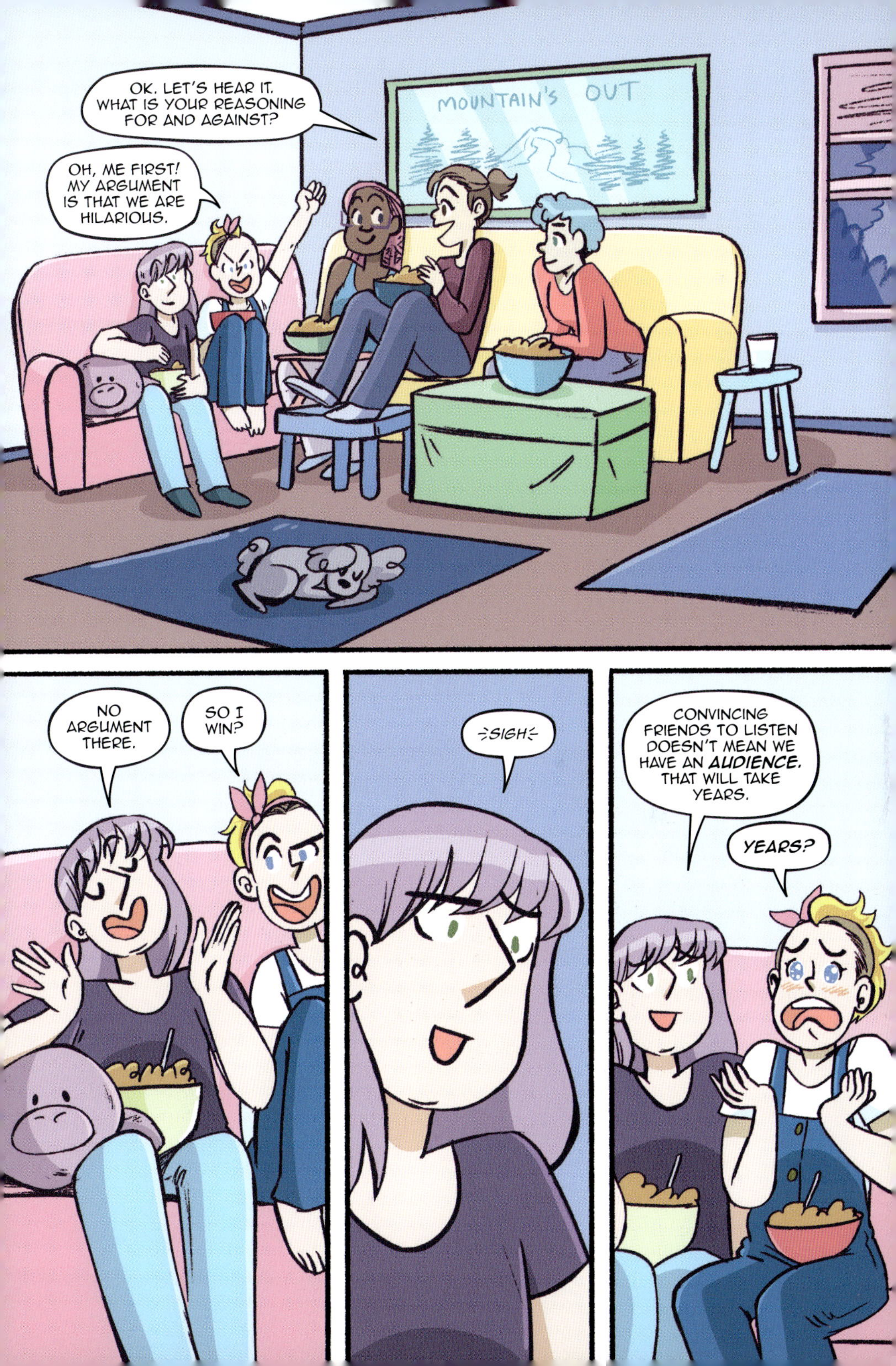

OK. LET'S HEAR IT. WHAT IS YOUR REASONING FOR AND AGAINST?
OH, ME FIRST! MY ARGUMENT IS THAT WE ARE HILARIOUS.
MOUNTAIN'S OUT
NO ARGUMENT THERE.
SO I WIN?
SIGH
CONVINCING FRIENDS TO LISTEN DOESN'T MEAN WE HAVE AN AUDIENCE. THAT WILL TAKE YEARS.
YEARS?

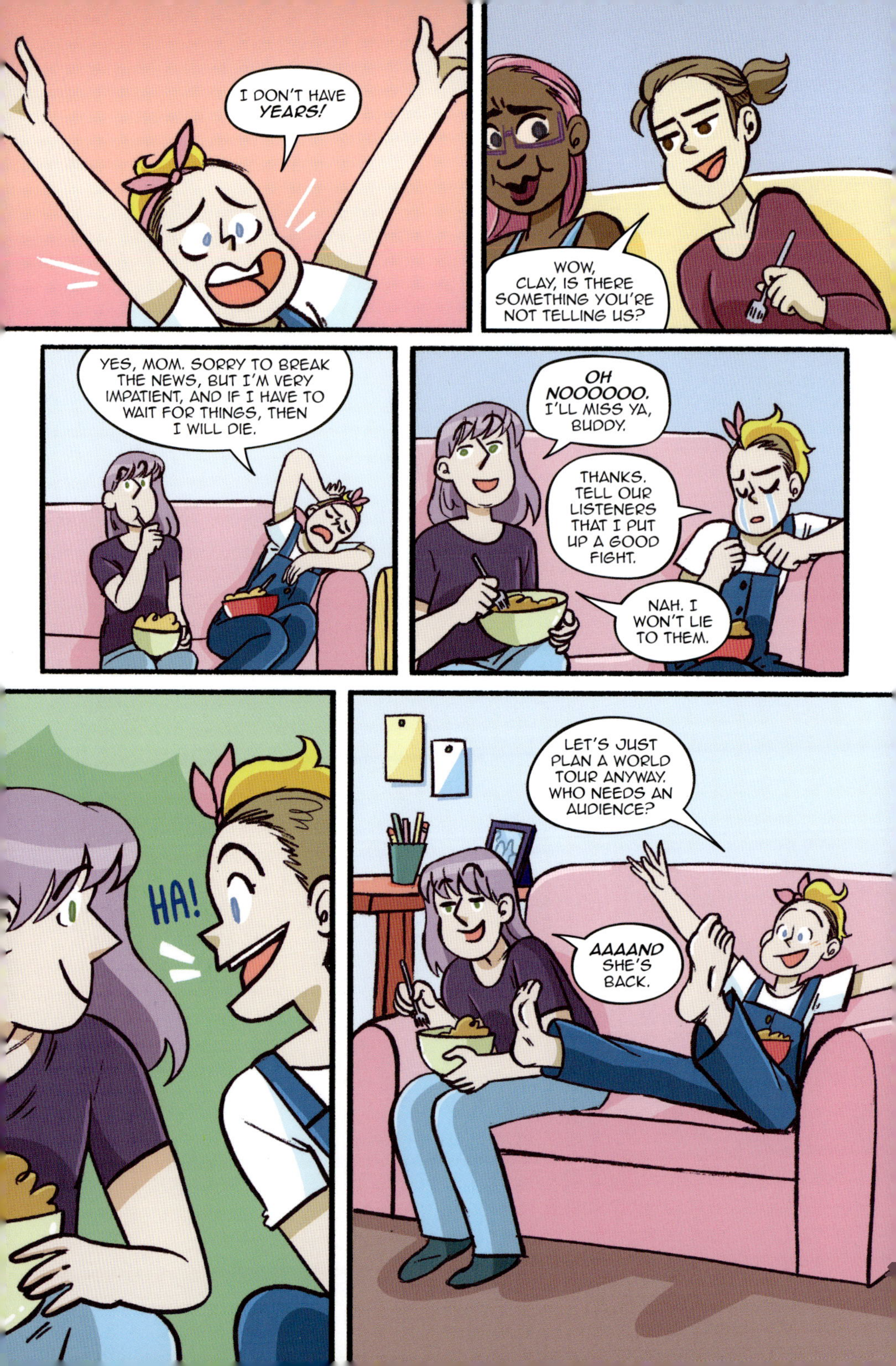
I DON'T HAVE *YEARS!*
WOW, CLAY, IS THERE SOMETHING YOU'RE NOT TELLING US?
YES, MOM. SORRY TO BREAK THE NEWS, BUT I'M VERY IMPATIENT, AND IF I HAVE TO WAIT FOR THINGS, THEN I WILL DIE.
OH NOOOOOO. I'LL MISS YA, BUDDY.
THANKS. TELL OUR LISTENERS THAT I PUT UP A GOOD FIGHT.
NAH. I WON'T LIE TO THEM.
HA!
LET'S JUST PLAN A WORLD TOUR ANYWAY. WHO NEEDS AN AUDIENCE?
AAAAND SHE'S BACK.

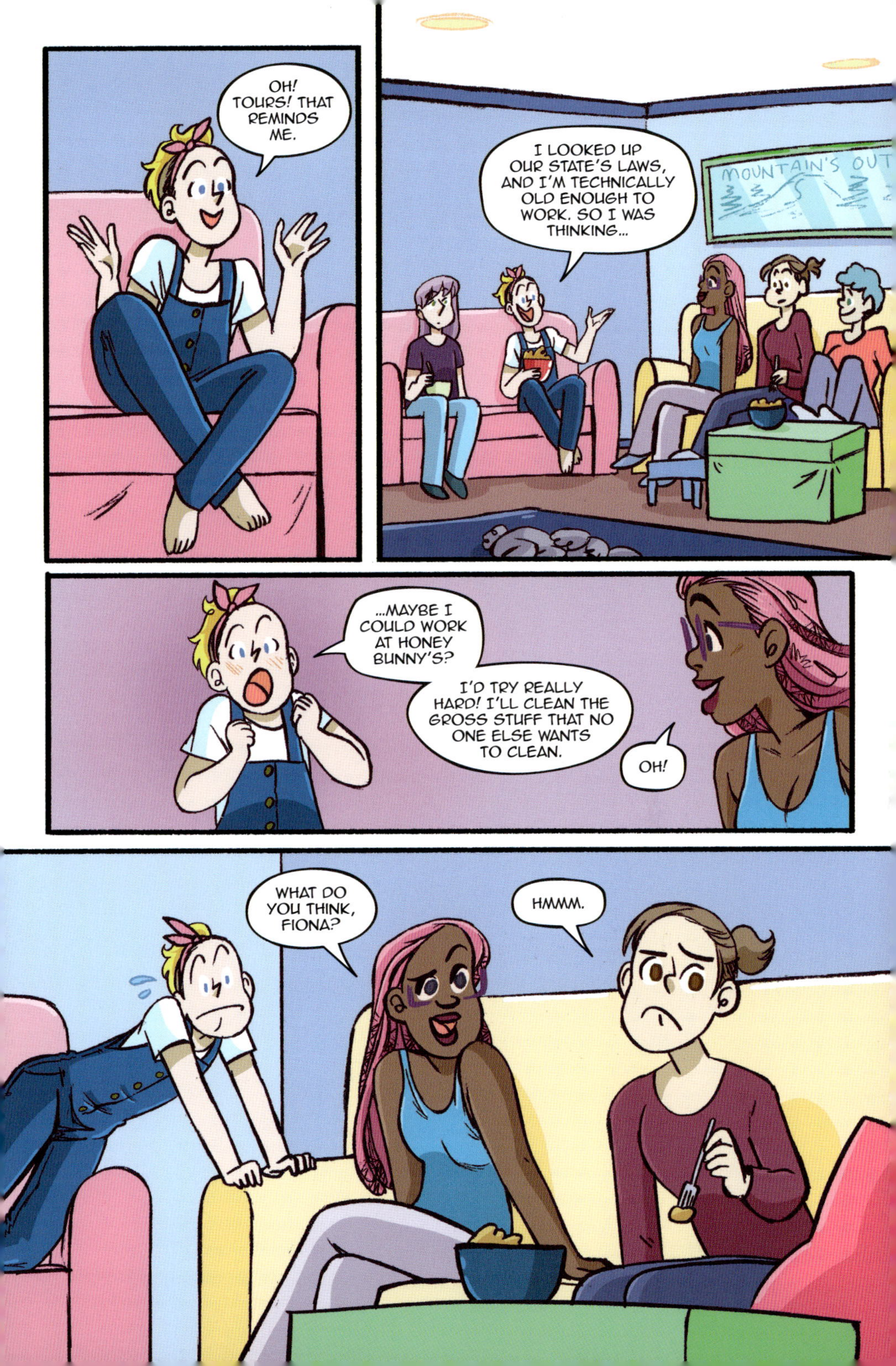
OH! TOURS! THAT REMINDS ME.
I LOOKED UP OUR STATE'S LAWS, AND I'M TECHNICALLY OLD ENOUGH TO WORK. SO I WAS THINKING...
MOUNTAIN'S OUT
...MAYBE I COULD WORK AT HONEY BUNNY'S?
I'D TRY REALLY HARD! I'LL CLEAN THE GROSS STUFF THAT NO ONE ELSE WANTS TO CLEAN.
OH!
WHAT DO YOU THINK, FIONA?
HMMM.

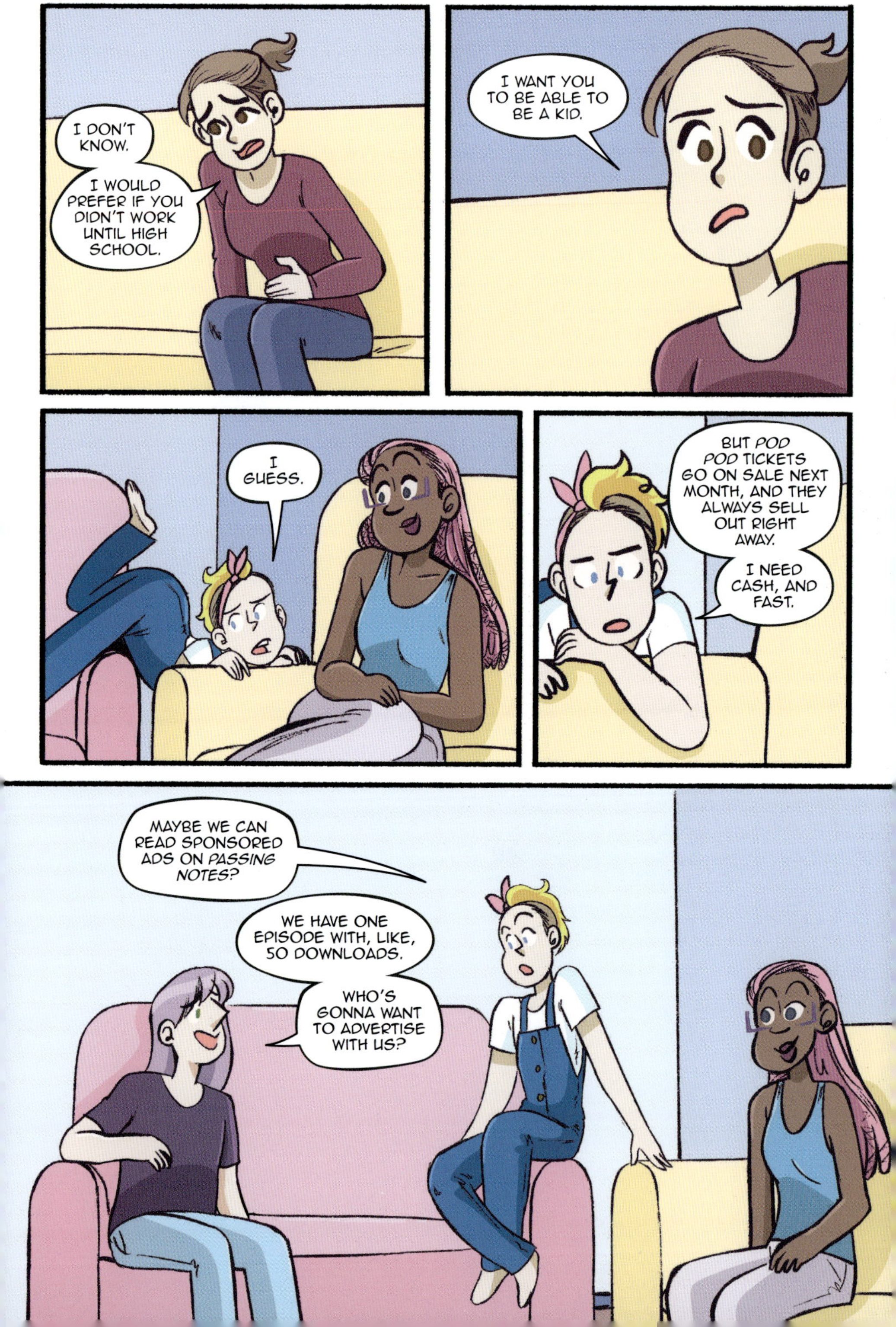
I DON'T KNOW.
I WOULD PREFER IF YOU DIDN'T WORK UNTIL HIGH SCHOOL.
I WANT YOU TO BE ABLE TO BE A KID.
I GUESS.
BUT *POD POD* TICKETS GO ON SALE NEXT MONTH, AND THEY ALWAYS SELL OUT RIGHT AWAY.
I NEED CASH, AND FAST.
MAYBE WE CAN READ SPONSORED ADS ON *PASSING NOTES*?
WE HAVE ONE EPISODE WITH, LIKE, 50 DOWNLOADS.
WHO'S GONNA WANT TO ADVERTISE WITH US?

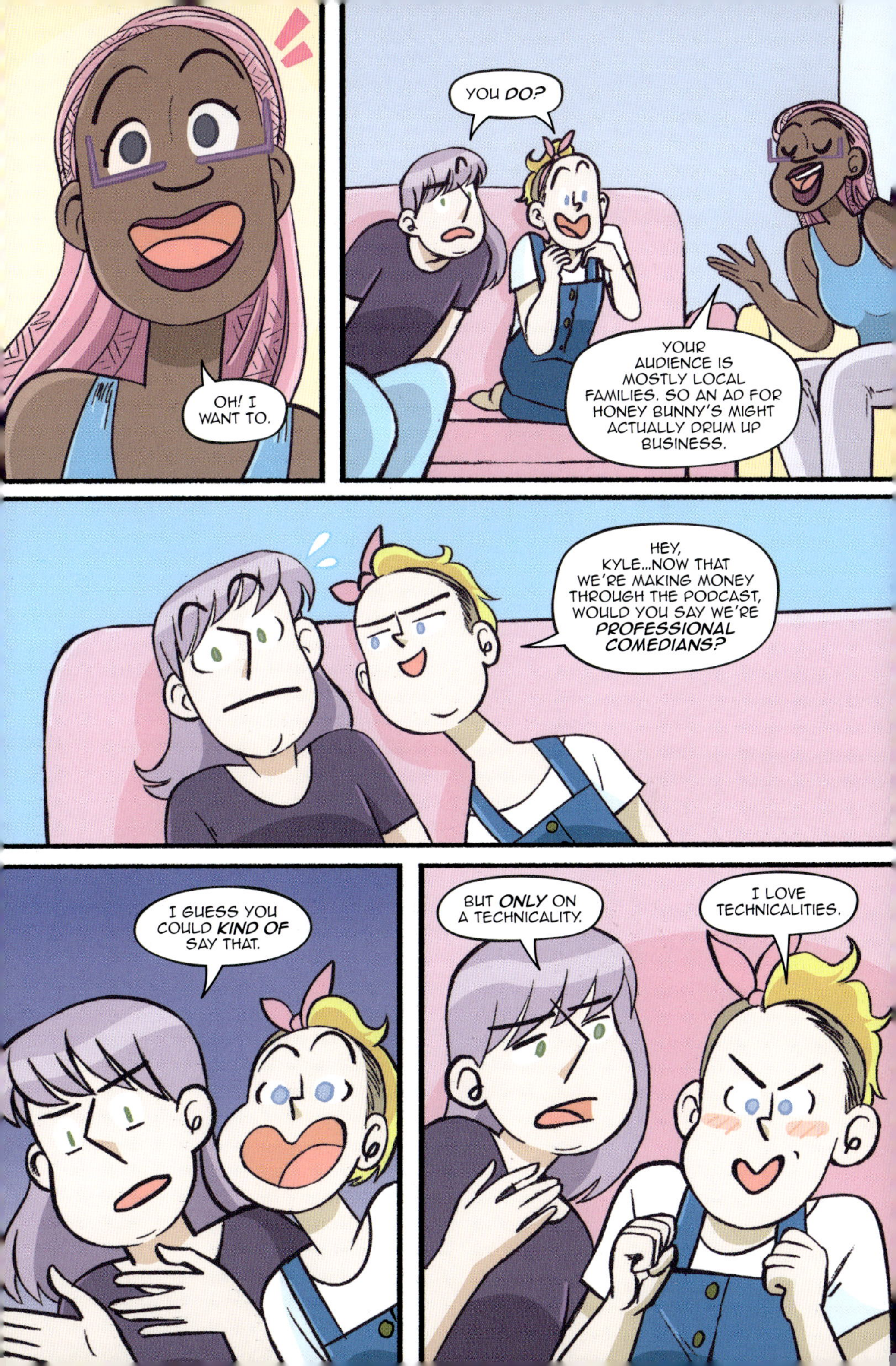

OH! I WANT TO.
YOU *DO?*
YOUR AUDIENCE IS MOSTLY LOCAL FAMILIES. SO AN AD FOR HONEY BUNNY'S MIGHT ACTUALLY DRUM UP BUSINESS.
HEY, KYLE...NOW THAT WE'RE MAKING MONEY THROUGH THE PODCAST, WOULD YOU SAY WE'RE ***PROFESSIONAL COMEDIANS?***
I GUESS YOU COULD ***KIND OF*** SAY THAT.
BUT ***ONLY*** ON A TECHNICALITY.
I LOVE TECHNICALITIES.

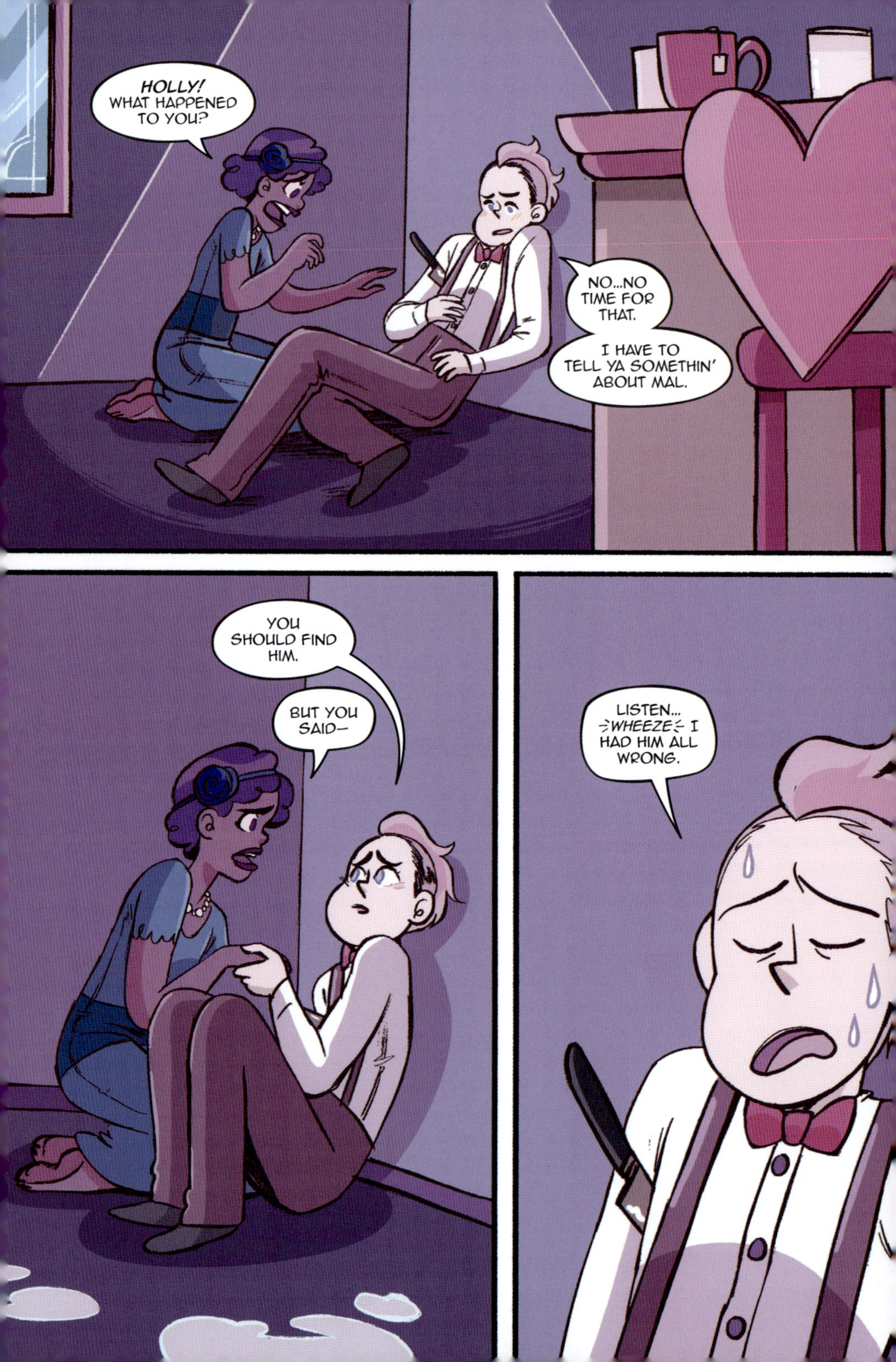
HOLLY! WHAT HAPPENED TO YOU?
NO...NO TIME FOR THAT.
I HAVE TO TELL YA SOMETHIN' ABOUT MAL.
YOU SHOULD FIND HIM.
BUT YOU SAID—
LISTEN... ⩦WHEEZE⩦ I HAD HIM ALL WRONG.

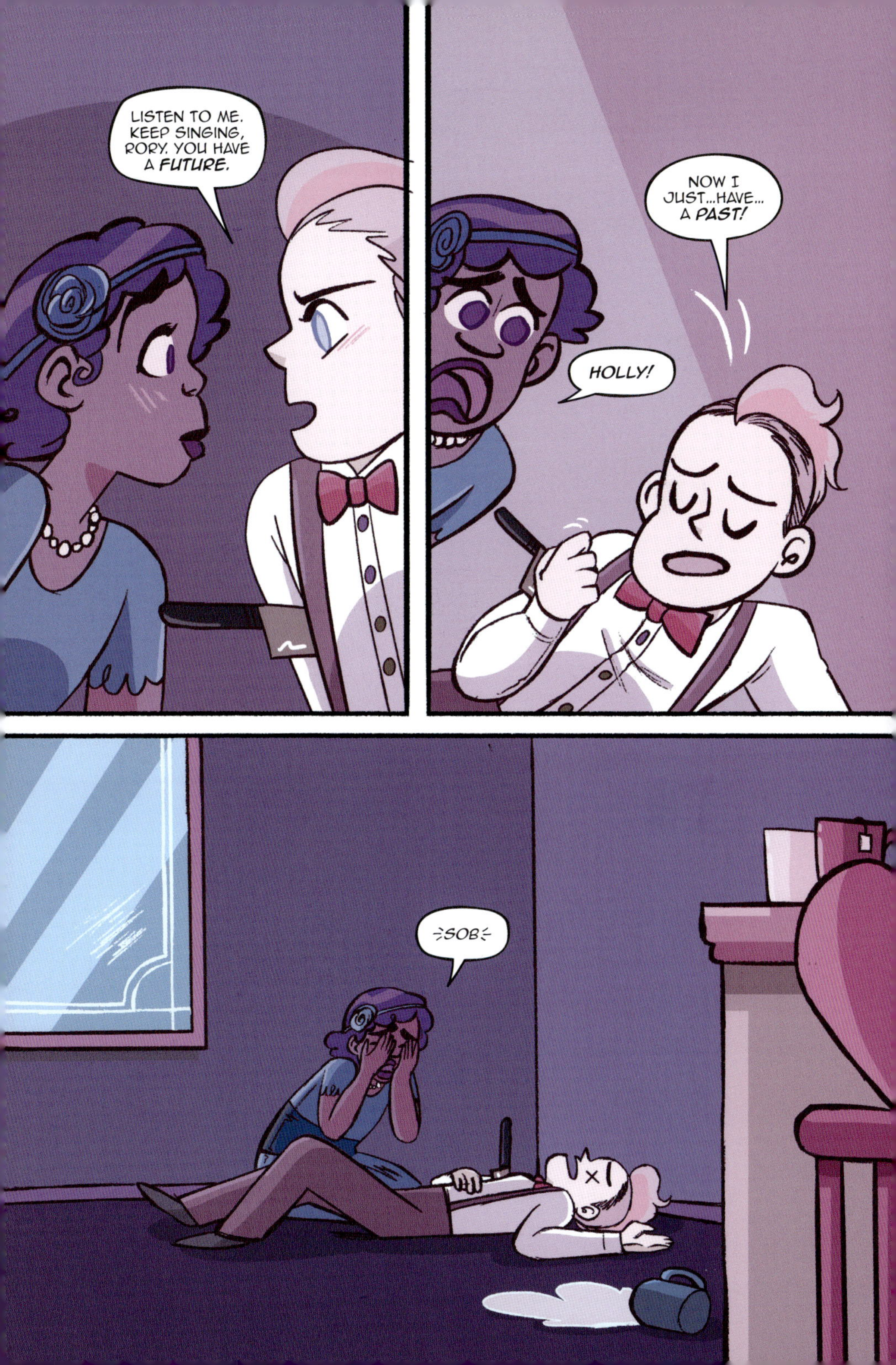
LISTEN TO ME. KEEP SINGING, RORY. YOU HAVE A *FUTURE*.
NOW I JUST...HAVE... A *PAST!*
HOLLY!
⁼SOB⁼

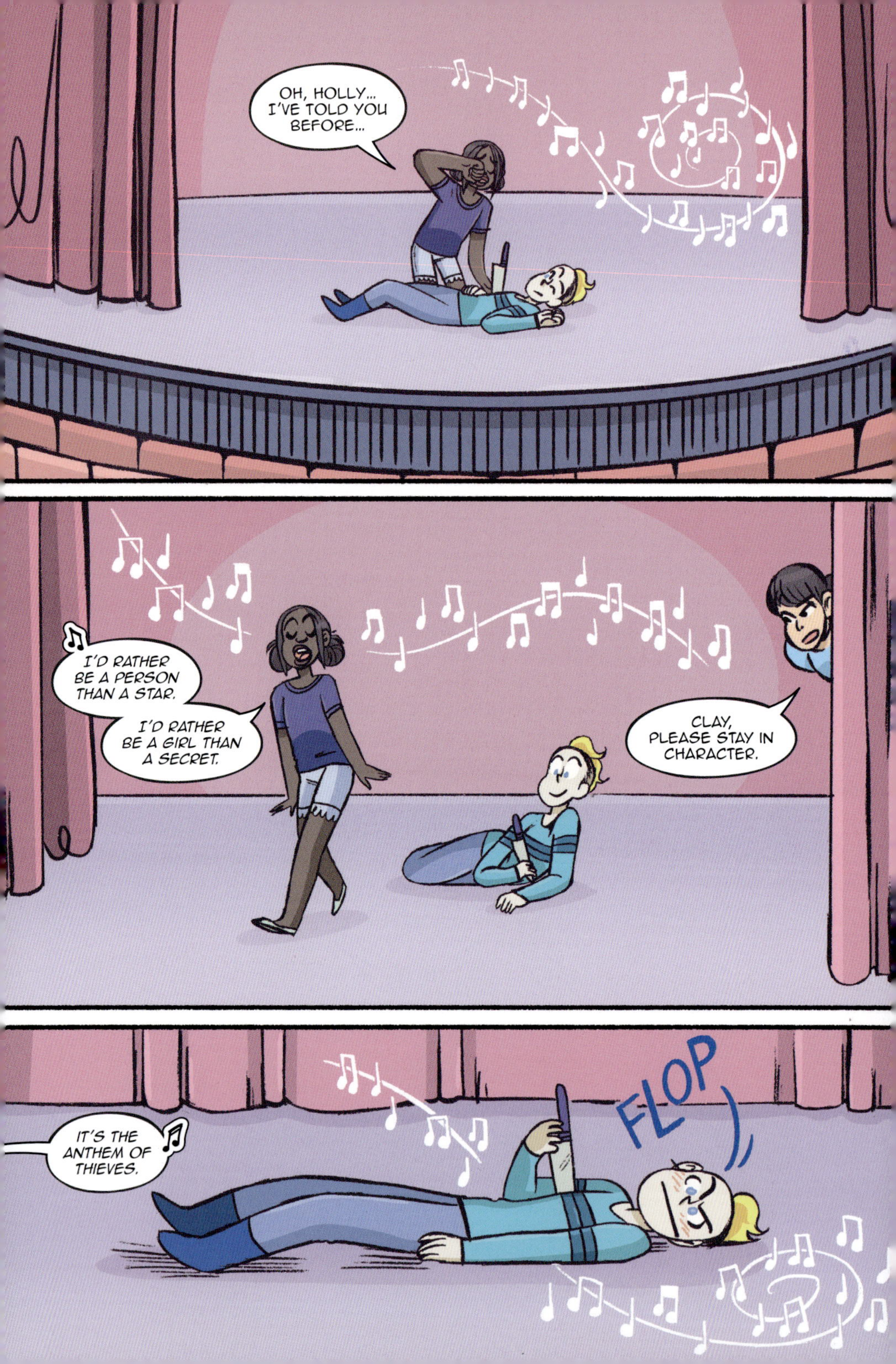

OH, HOLLY... I'VE TOLD YOU BEFORE...
I'D RATHER BE A PERSON THAN A STAR.
I'D RATHER BE A GIRL THAN A SECRET.
CLAY, PLEASE STAY IN CHARACTER.
IT'S THE ANTHEM OF THIEVES.
FLOP

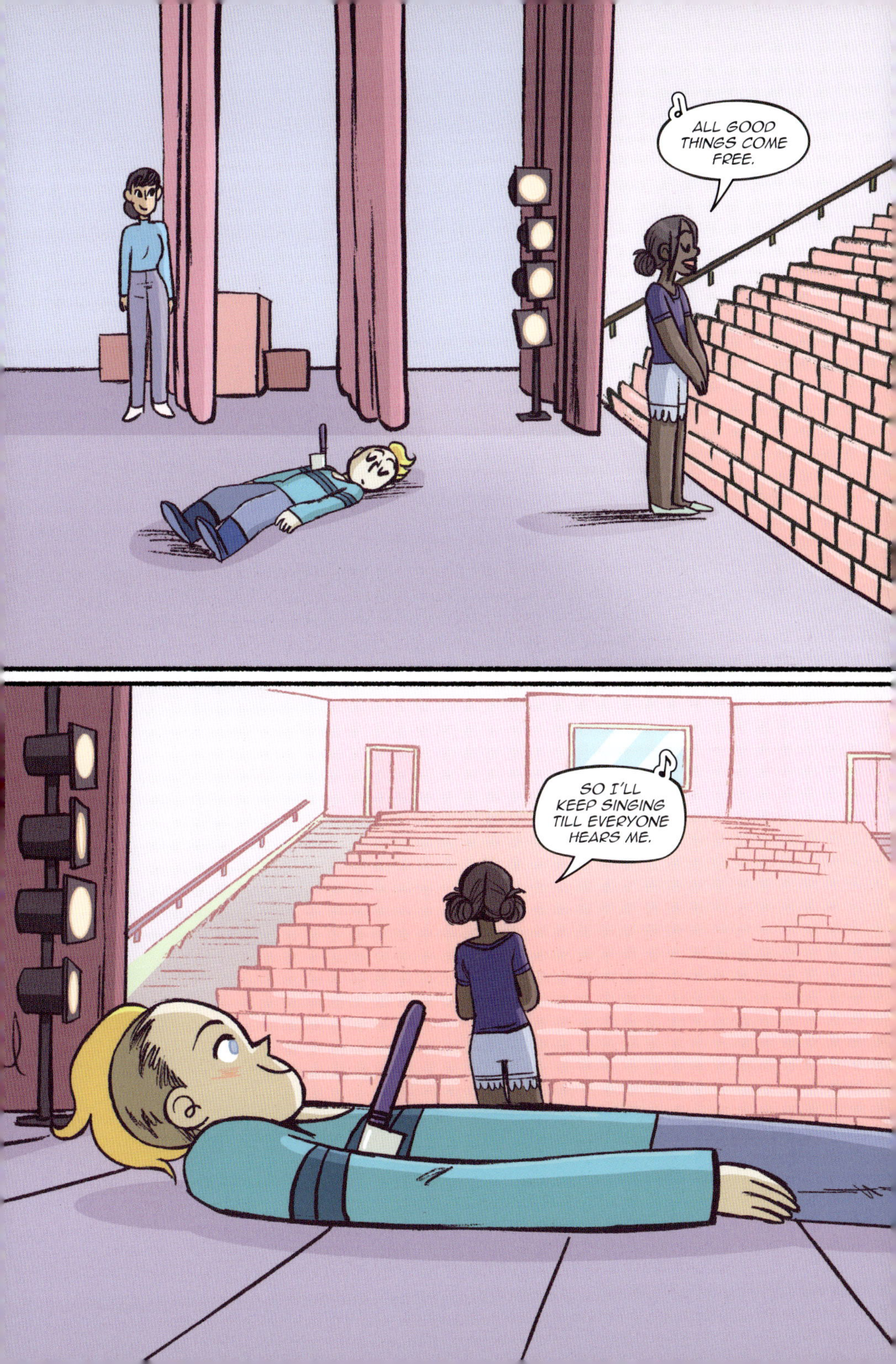
ALL GOOD THINGS COME FREE.
SO I'LL KEEP SINGING TILL EVERYONE HEARS ME.

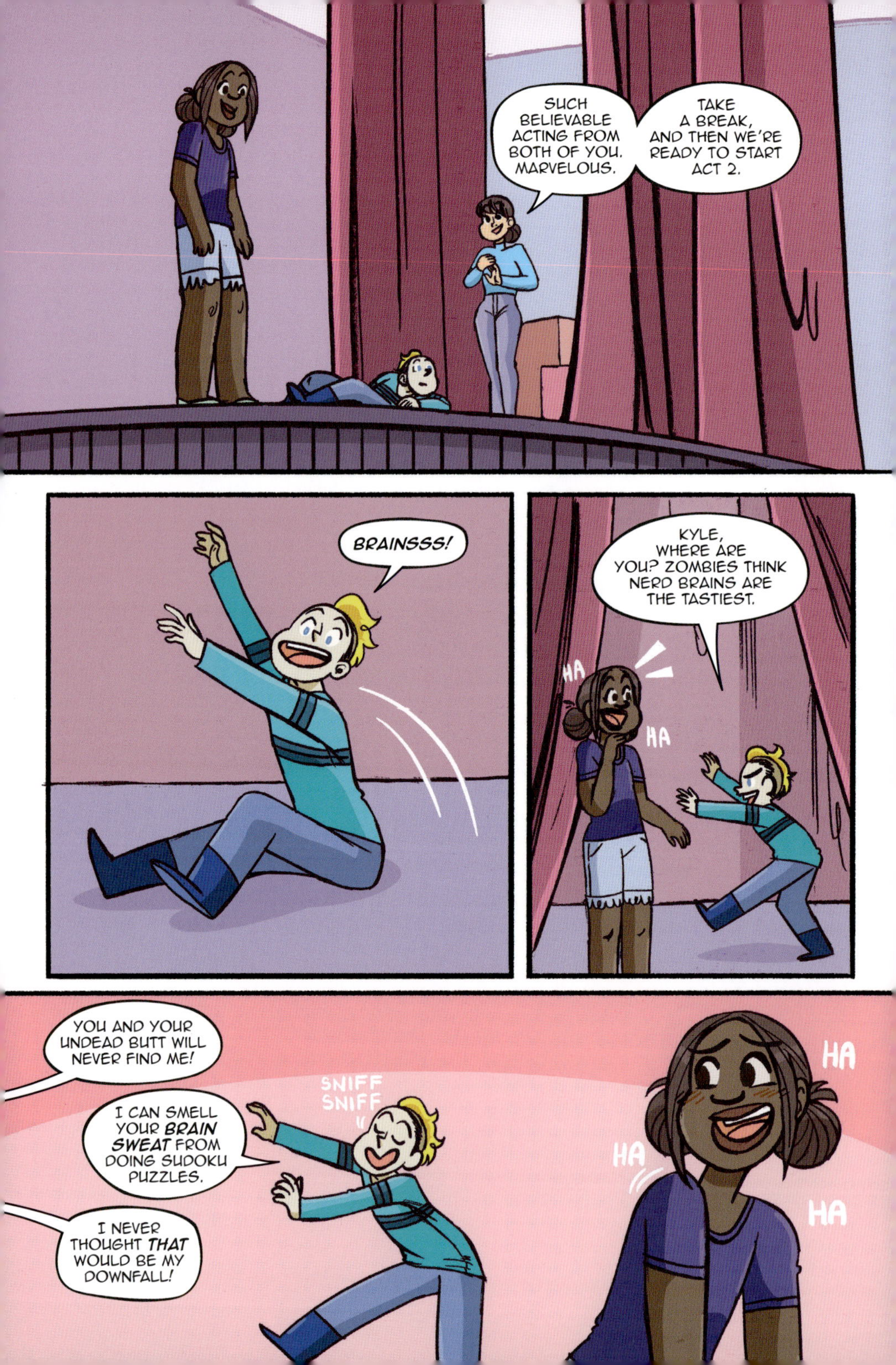
SUCH BELIEVABLE ACTING FROM BOTH OF YOU. MARVELOUS.
TAKE A BREAK, AND THEN WE'RE READY TO START ACT 2.
BRAINSSS!
KYLE, WHERE ARE YOU? ZOMBIES THINK NERD BRAINS ARE THE TASTIEST.
HA
HA
YOU AND YOUR UNDEAD BUTT WILL NEVER FIND ME!
SNIFF SNIFF
I CAN SMELL YOUR BRAIN SWEAT FROM DOING SUDOKU PUZZLES.
I NEVER THOUGHT THAT WOULD BE MY DOWNFALL!
HA
HA
HA

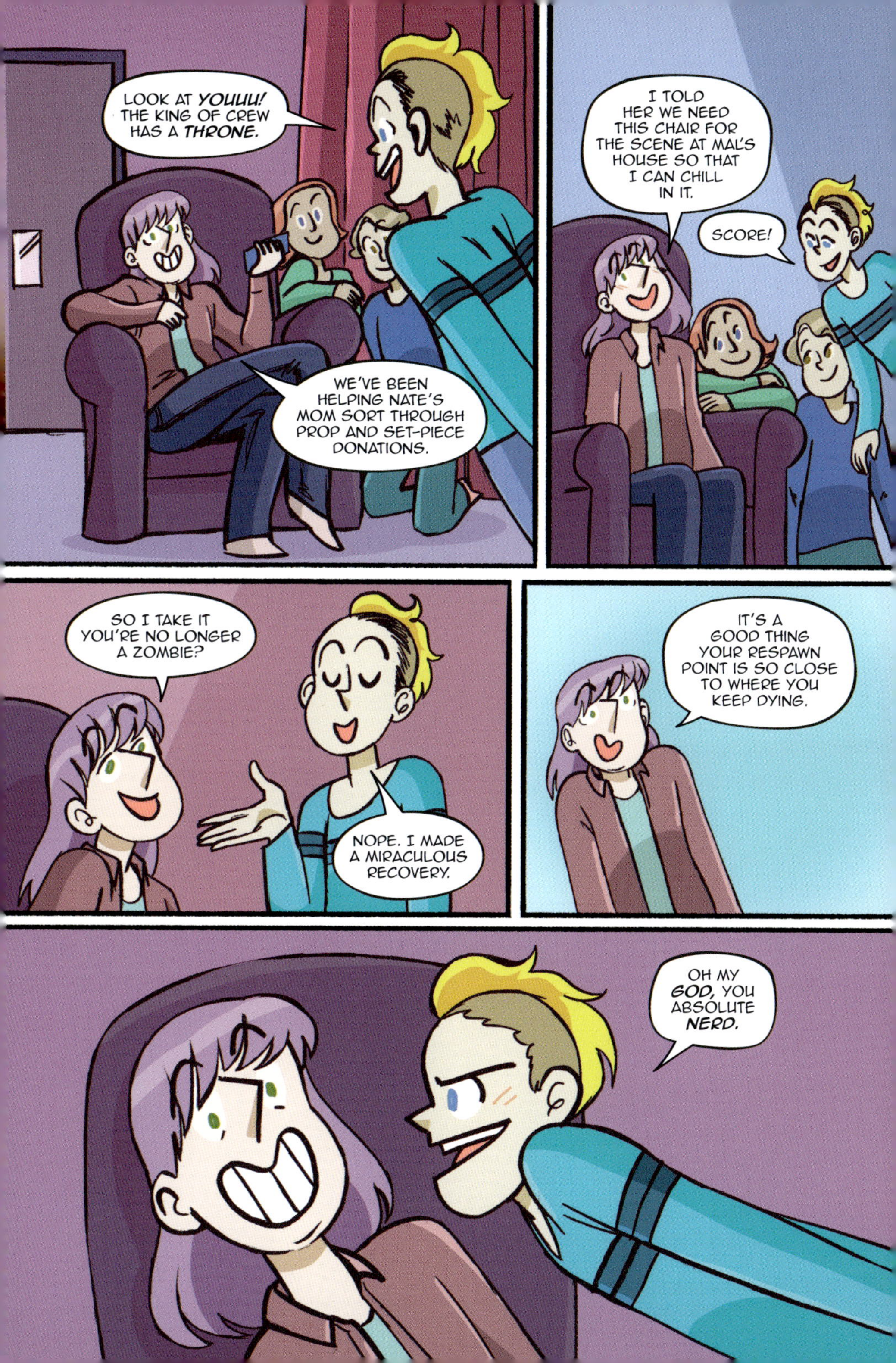
LOOK AT YOUUU! THE KING OF CREW HAS A THRONE.
WE'VE BEEN HELPING NATE'S MOM SORT THROUGH PROP AND SET-PIECE DONATIONS.
I TOLD HER WE NEED THIS CHAIR FOR THE SCENE AT MAL'S HOUSE SO THAT I CAN CHILL IN IT.
SCORE!
SO I TAKE IT YOU'RE NO LONGER A ZOMBIE?
NOPE. I MADE A MIRACULOUS RECOVERY.
IT'S A GOOD THING YOUR RESPAWN POINT IS SO CLOSE TO WHERE YOU KEEP DYING.
OH MY GOD, YOU ABSOLUTE NERD.

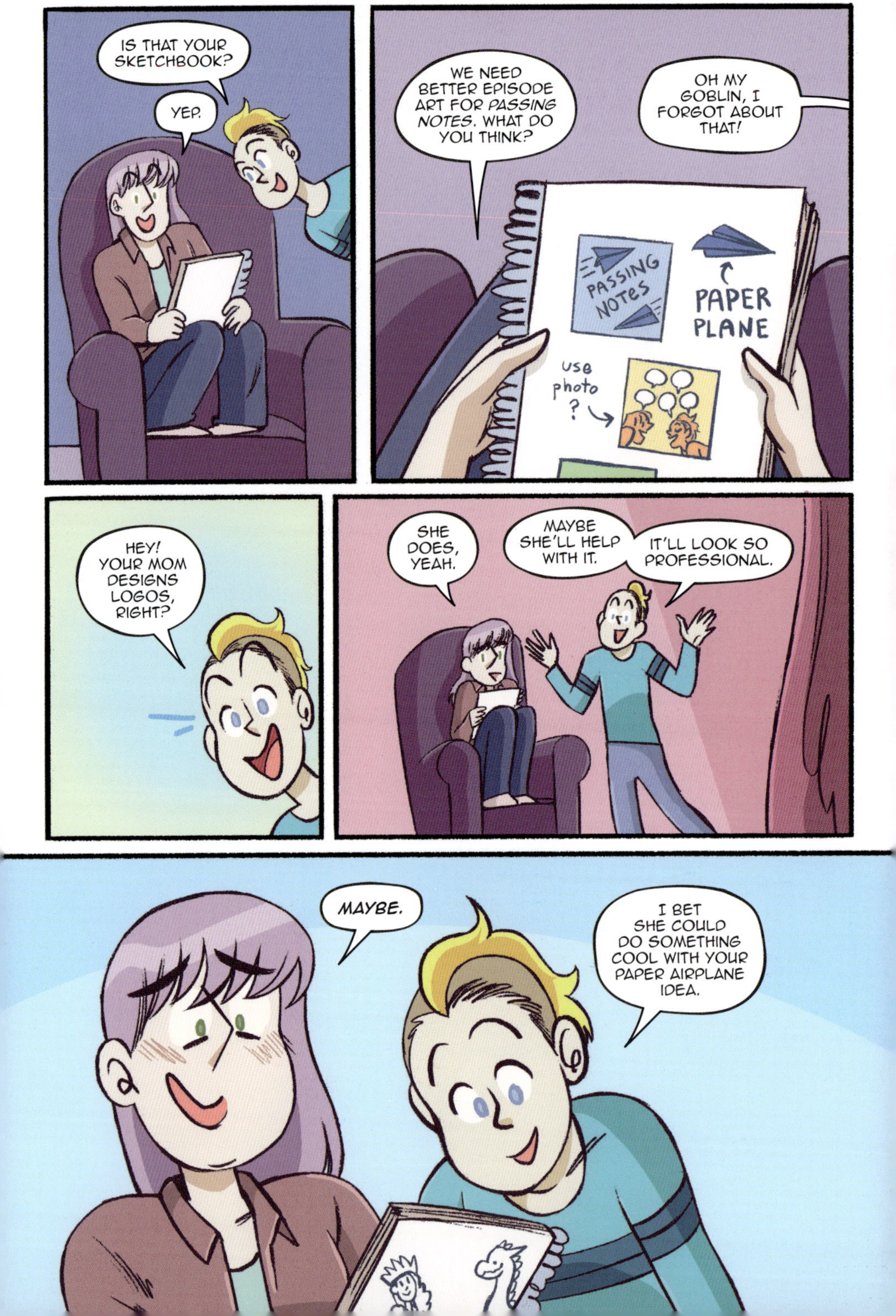
IS THAT YOUR SKETCHBOOK?
YEP.
WE NEED BETTER EPISODE ART FOR *PASSING NOTES*. WHAT DO YOU THINK?
OH MY GOBLIN, I FORGOT ABOUT THAT!
PASSING NOTES
PAPER PLANE
use photo ?
HEY! YOUR MOM DESIGNS LOGOS, RIGHT?
SHE DOES, YEAH.
MAYBE SHE'LL HELP WITH IT.
IT'LL LOOK SO PROFESSIONAL.
MAYBE.
I BET SHE COULD DO SOMETHING COOL WITH YOUR PAPER AIRPLANE IDEA.

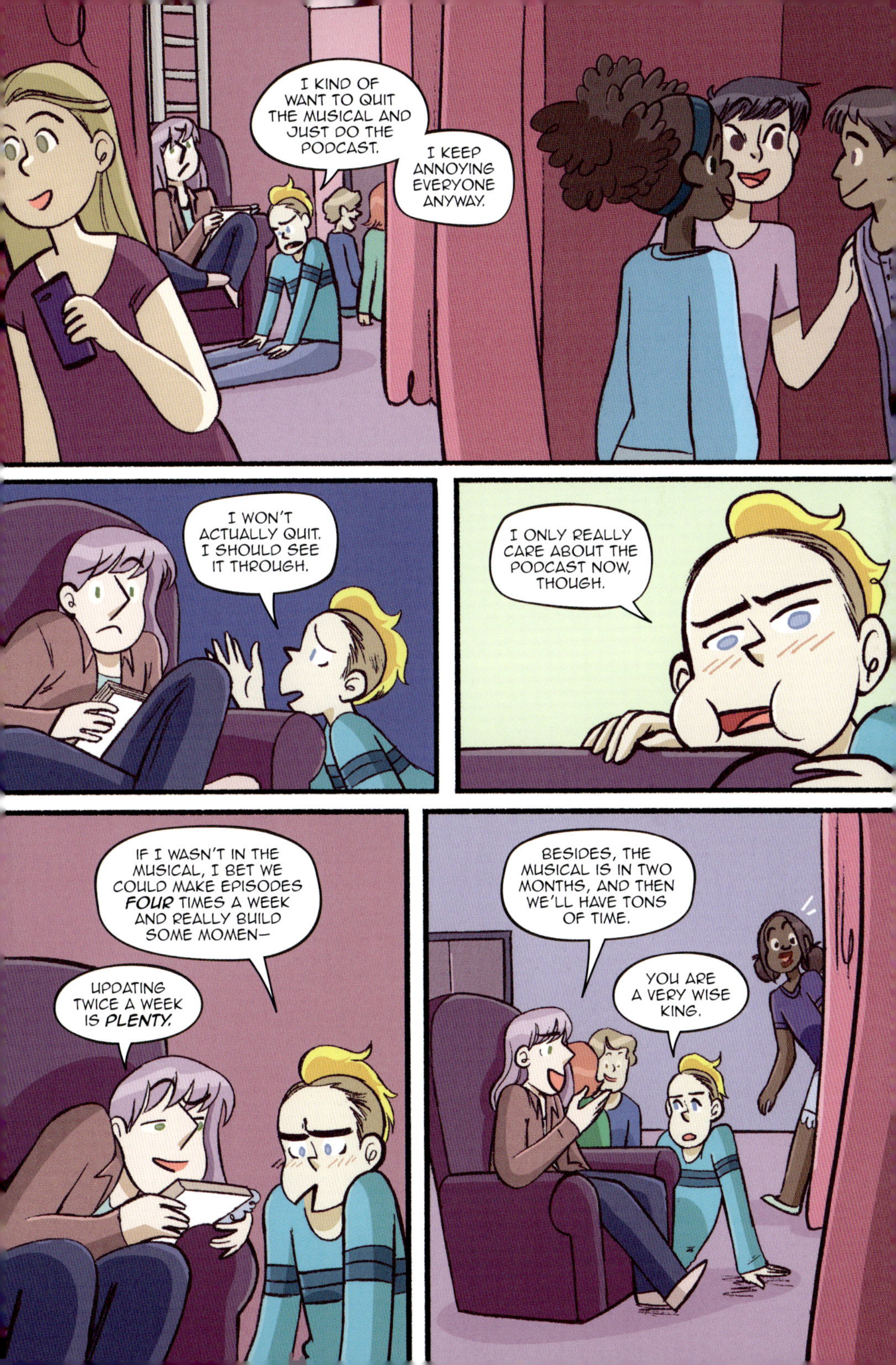
I KIND OF WANT TO QUIT THE MUSICAL AND JUST DO THE PODCAST.
I KEEP ANNOYING EVERYONE ANYWAY.
I WON'T ACTUALLY QUIT. I SHOULD SEE IT THROUGH.
I ONLY REALLY CARE ABOUT THE PODCAST NOW, THOUGH.
IF I WASN'T IN THE MUSICAL, I BET WE COULD MAKE EPISODES ***FOUR*** TIMES A WEEK AND REALLY BUILD SOME MOMEN—
UPDATING TWICE A WEEK IS ***PLENTY.***
BESIDES, THE MUSICAL IS IN TWO MONTHS, AND THEN WE'LL HAVE TONS OF TIME.
YOU ARE A VERY WISE KING.

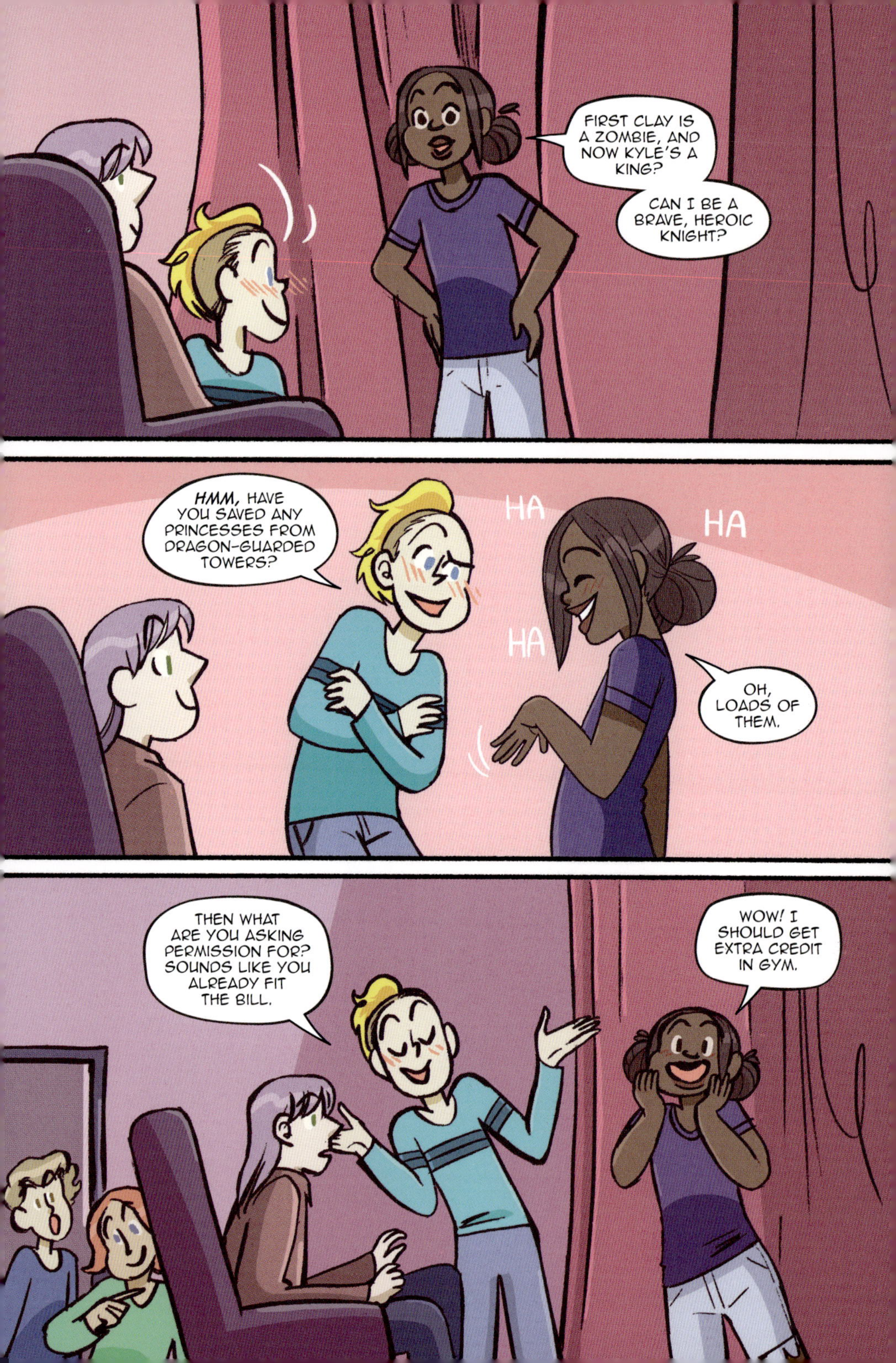
FIRST CLAY IS A ZOMBIE, AND NOW KYLE'S A KING?
CAN I BE A BRAVE, HEROIC KNIGHT?
HMM, HAVE YOU SAVED ANY PRINCESSES FROM DRAGON-GUARDED TOWERS?
HA
HA
HA
OH, LOADS OF THEM.
THEN WHAT ARE YOU ASKING PERMISSION FOR? SOUNDS LIKE YOU ALREADY FIT THE BILL.
WOW! I SHOULD GET EXTRA CREDIT IN GYM.

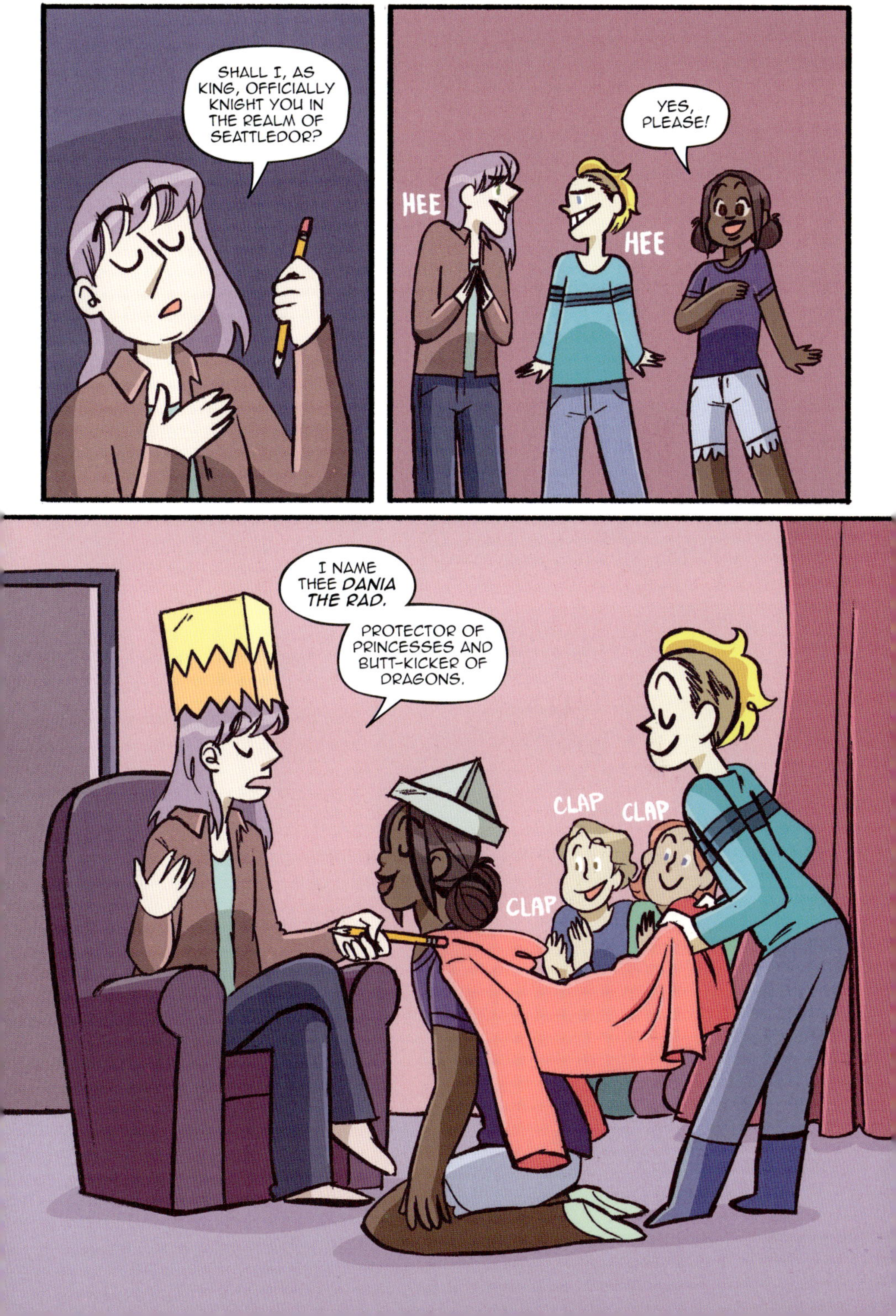
SHALL I, AS KING, OFFICIALLY KNIGHT YOU IN THE REALM OF SEATTLEDOR?
HEE
HEE
YES, PLEASE!
I NAME THEE *DANIA THE RAD.*
PROTECTOR OF PRINCESSES AND BUTT-KICKER OF DRAGONS.
CLAP
CLAP
CLAP

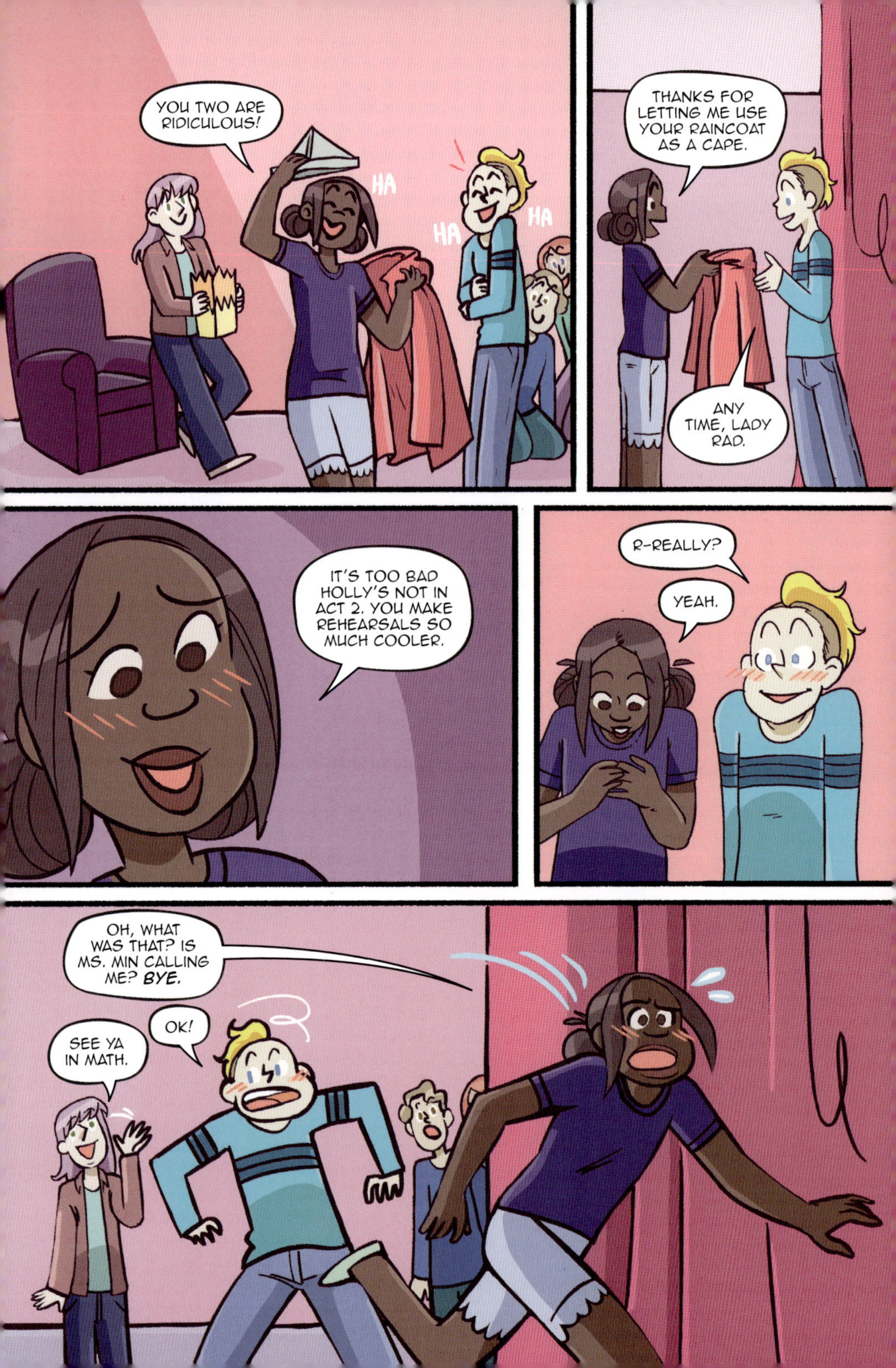
YOU TWO ARE RIDICULOUS!
HA
HA
HA
THANKS FOR LETTING ME USE YOUR RAINCOAT AS A CAPE.
ANY TIME, LADY RAD.
IT'S TOO BAD HOLLY'S NOT IN ACT 2. YOU MAKE REHEARSALS SO MUCH COOLER.
R-REALLY?
YEAH.
OH, WHAT WAS THAT? IS MS. MIN CALLING ME? BYE.
OK!
SEE YA IN MATH.

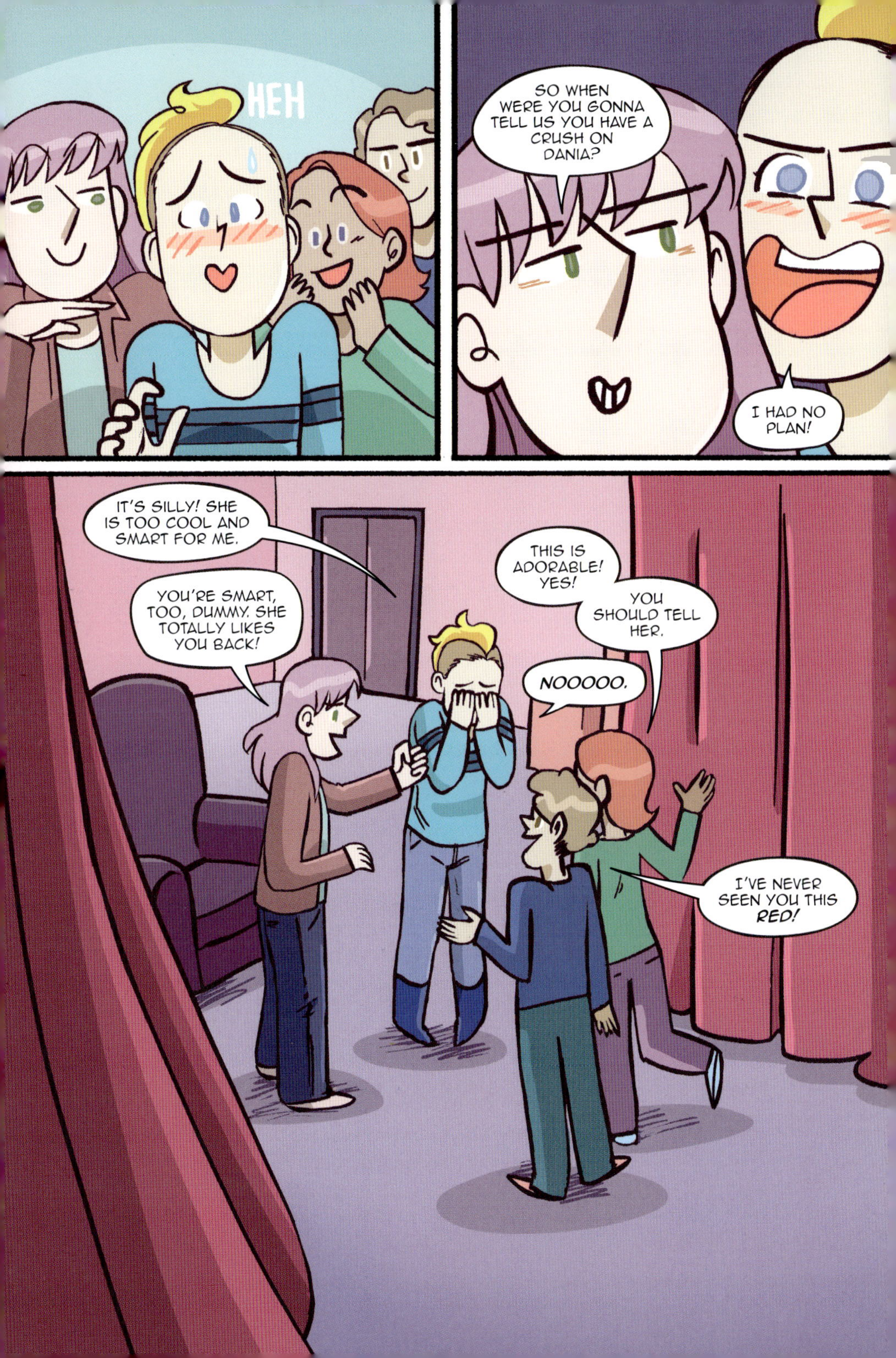
HEH
SO WHEN WERE YOU GONNA TELL US YOU HAVE A CRUSH ON DANIA?
I HAD NO PLAN!
IT'S SILLY! SHE IS TOO COOL AND SMART FOR ME.
YOU'RE SMART, TOO, DUMMY. SHE TOTALLY LIKES YOU BACK!
THIS IS ADORABLE! YES!
YOU SHOULD TELL HER.
NOOOOO.
I'VE NEVER SEEN YOU THIS RED!

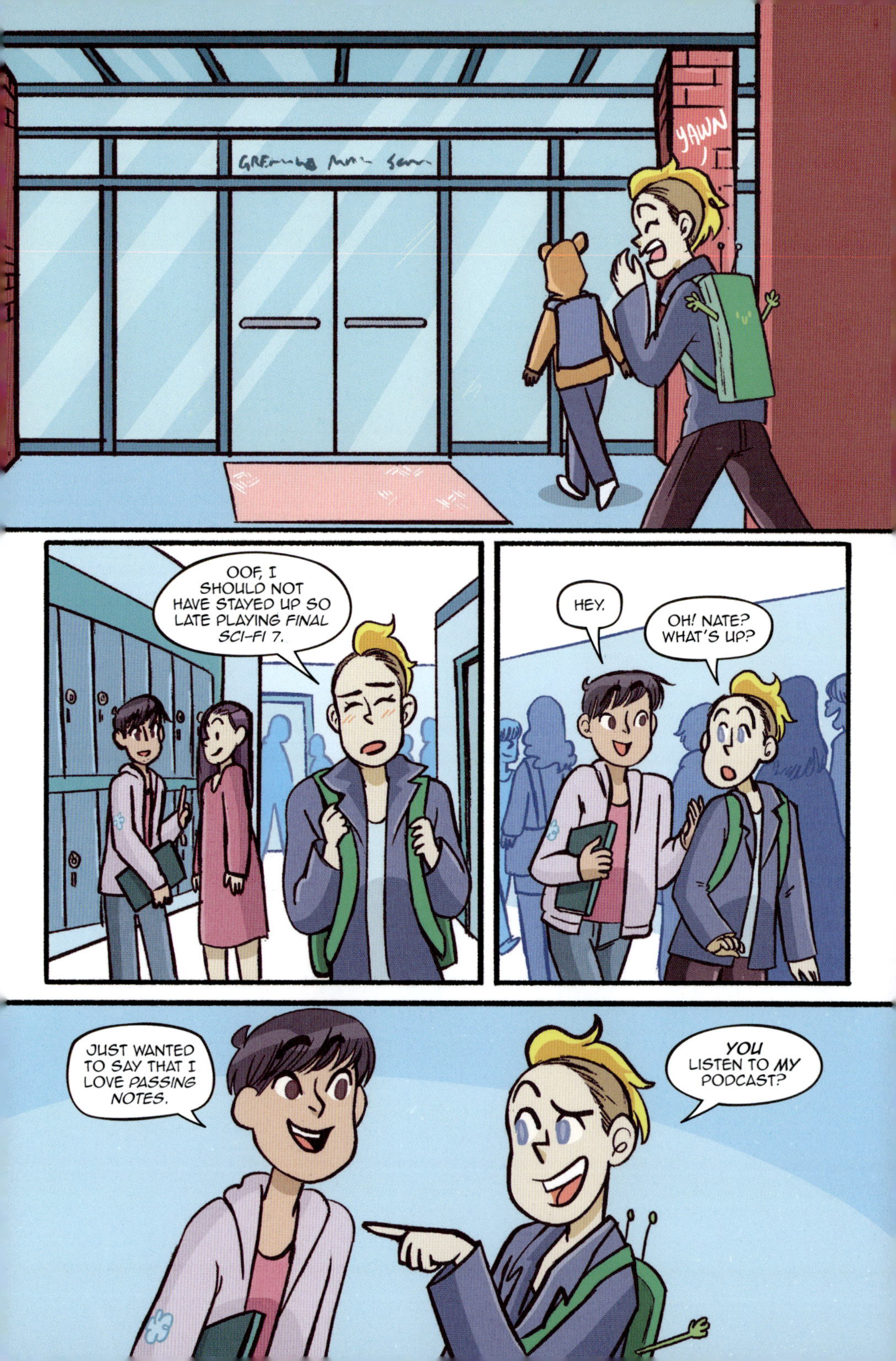
YAWN
OOF, I SHOULD NOT HAVE STAYED UP SO LATE PLAYING *FINAL SCI-FI 7.*
HEY.
OH! NATE? WHAT'S UP?
JUST WANTED TO SAY THAT I LOVE *PASSING NOTES.*
YOU LISTEN TO *MY* PODCAST?

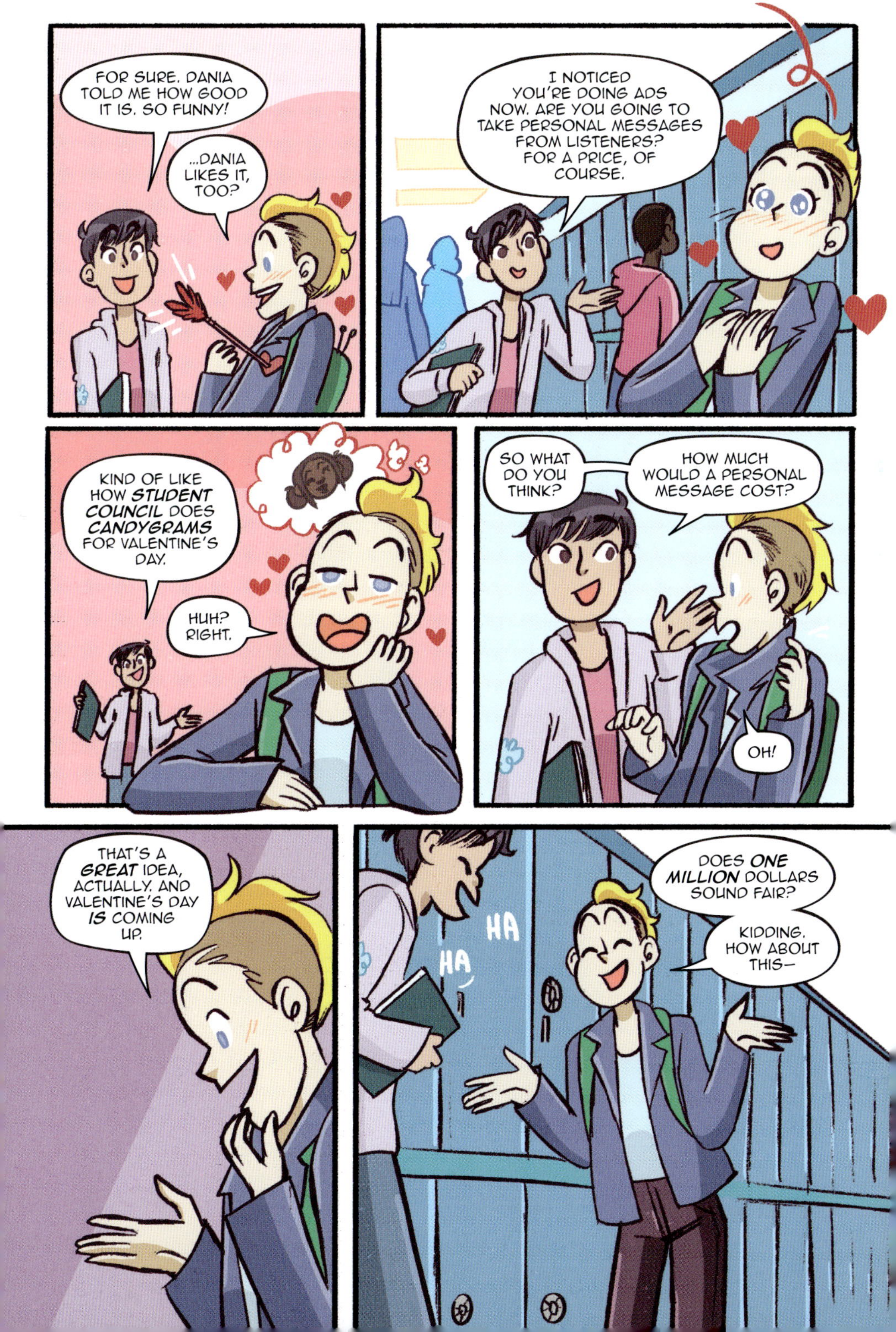
FOR SURE. DANIA TOLD ME HOW GOOD IT IS. SO FUNNY!
...DANIA LIKES IT, TOO?
I NOTICED YOU'RE DOING ADS NOW. ARE YOU GOING TO TAKE PERSONAL MESSAGES FROM LISTENERS? FOR A PRICE, OF COURSE.
KIND OF LIKE HOW **STUDENT COUNCIL** DOES **CANDYGRAMS** FOR VALENTINE'S DAY.
HUH? RIGHT.
SO WHAT DO YOU THINK?
HOW MUCH WOULD A PERSONAL MESSAGE COST?
OH!
THAT'S A **GREAT** IDEA, ACTUALLY. AND VALENTINE'S DAY **IS** COMING UP.
HA
HA
DOES **ONE MILLION** DOLLARS SOUND FAIR?
KIDDING. HOW ABOUT THIS—

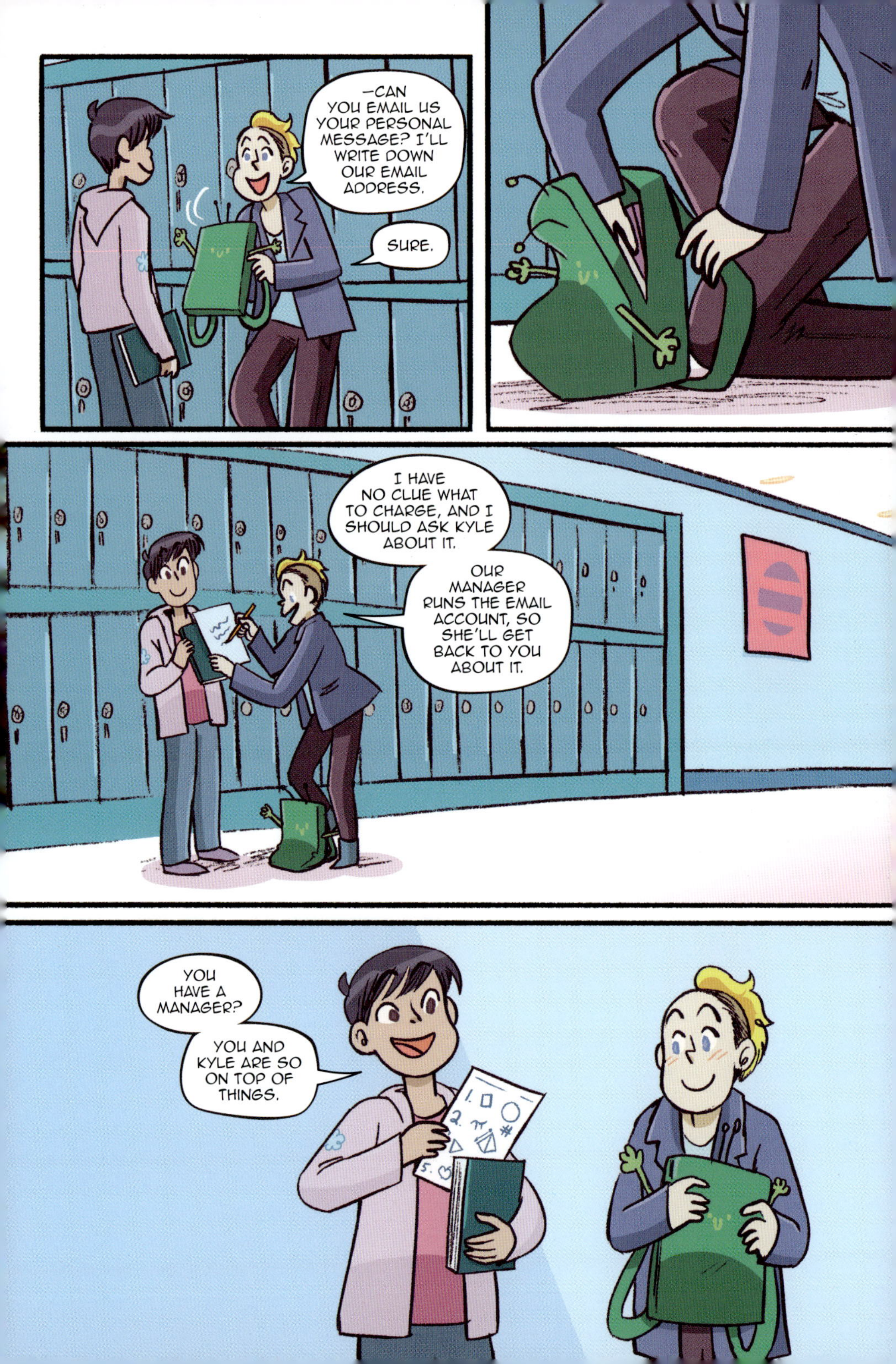
—CAN YOU EMAIL US YOUR PERSONAL MESSAGE? I'LL WRITE DOWN OUR EMAIL ADDRESS.
SURE.
I HAVE NO CLUE WHAT TO CHARGE, AND I SHOULD ASK KYLE ABOUT IT.
OUR MANAGER RUNS THE EMAIL ACCOUNT, SO SHE'LL GET BACK TO YOU ABOUT IT.
YOU HAVE A MANAGER?
YOU AND KYLE ARE SO ON TOP OF THINGS.

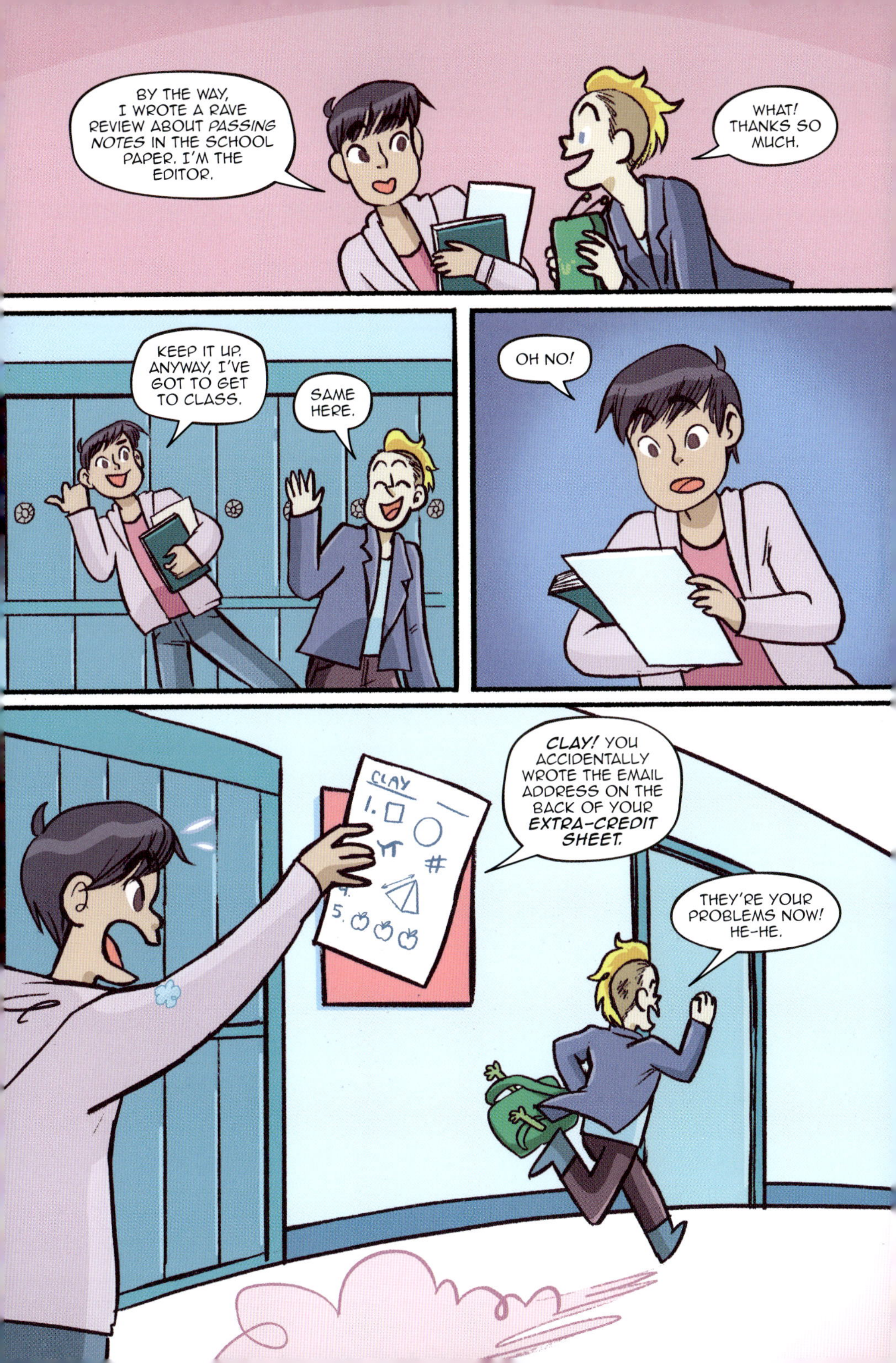
BY THE WAY, I WROTE A RAVE REVIEW ABOUT *PASSING NOTES* IN THE SCHOOL PAPER. I'M THE EDITOR.
WHAT! THANKS SO MUCH.
KEEP IT UP. ANYWAY, I'VE GOT TO GET TO CLASS.
SAME HERE.
OH NO!
CLAY
1.
4.
5.
CLAY! YOU ACCIDENTALLY WROTE THE EMAIL ADDRESS ON THE BACK OF YOUR **EXTRA-CREDIT SHEET.**
THEY'RE YOUR PROBLEMS NOW! HE-HE.

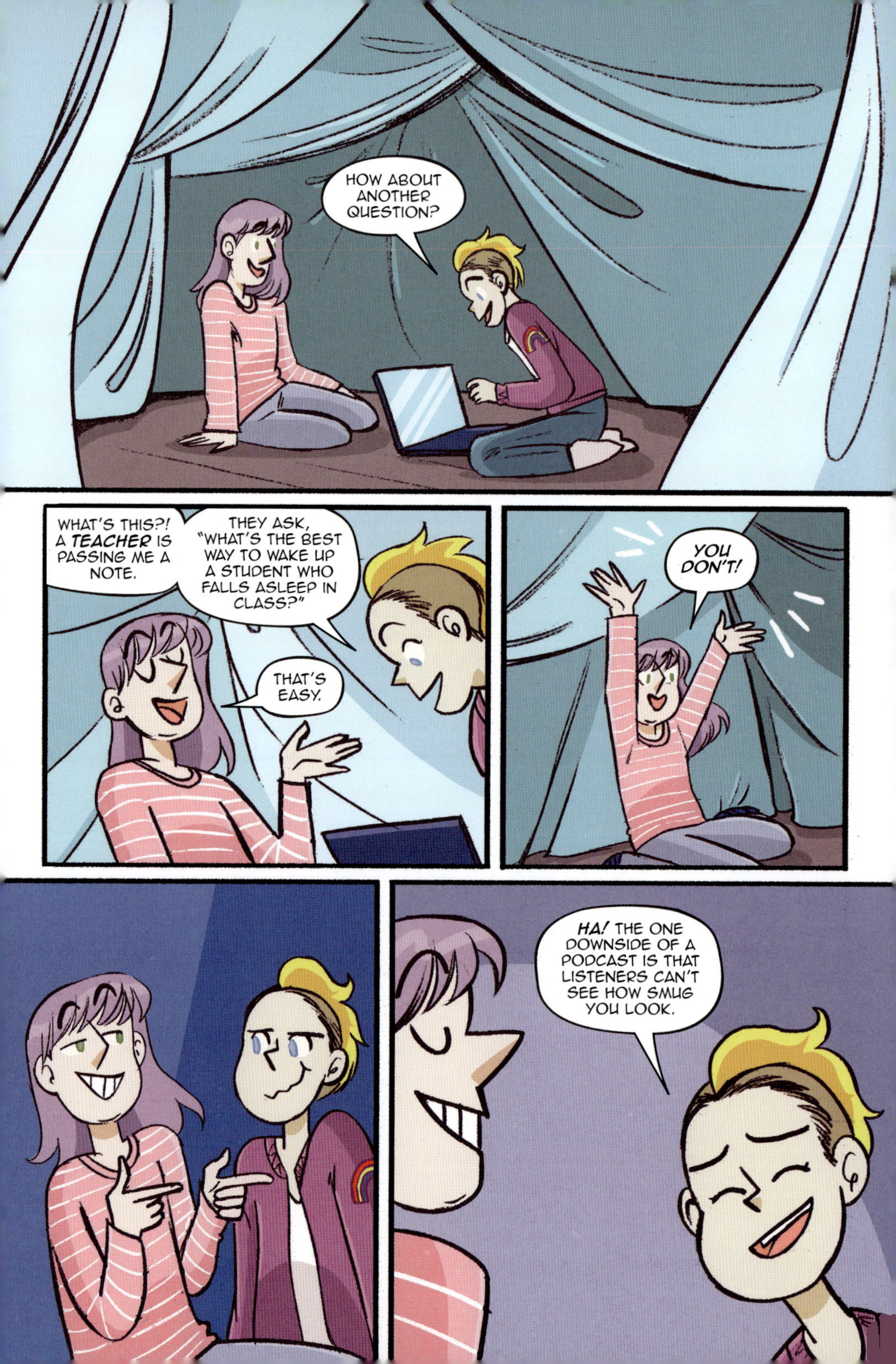
HOW ABOUT ANOTHER QUESTION?
WHAT'S THIS?! A **TEACHER** IS PASSING ME A NOTE.
THEY ASK, "WHAT'S THE BEST WAY TO WAKE UP A STUDENT WHO FALLS ASLEEP IN CLASS?"
THAT'S EASY.
YOU DON'T!
HA! THE ONE DOWNSIDE OF A PODCAST IS THAT LISTENERS CAN'T SEE HOW SMUG YOU LOOK.

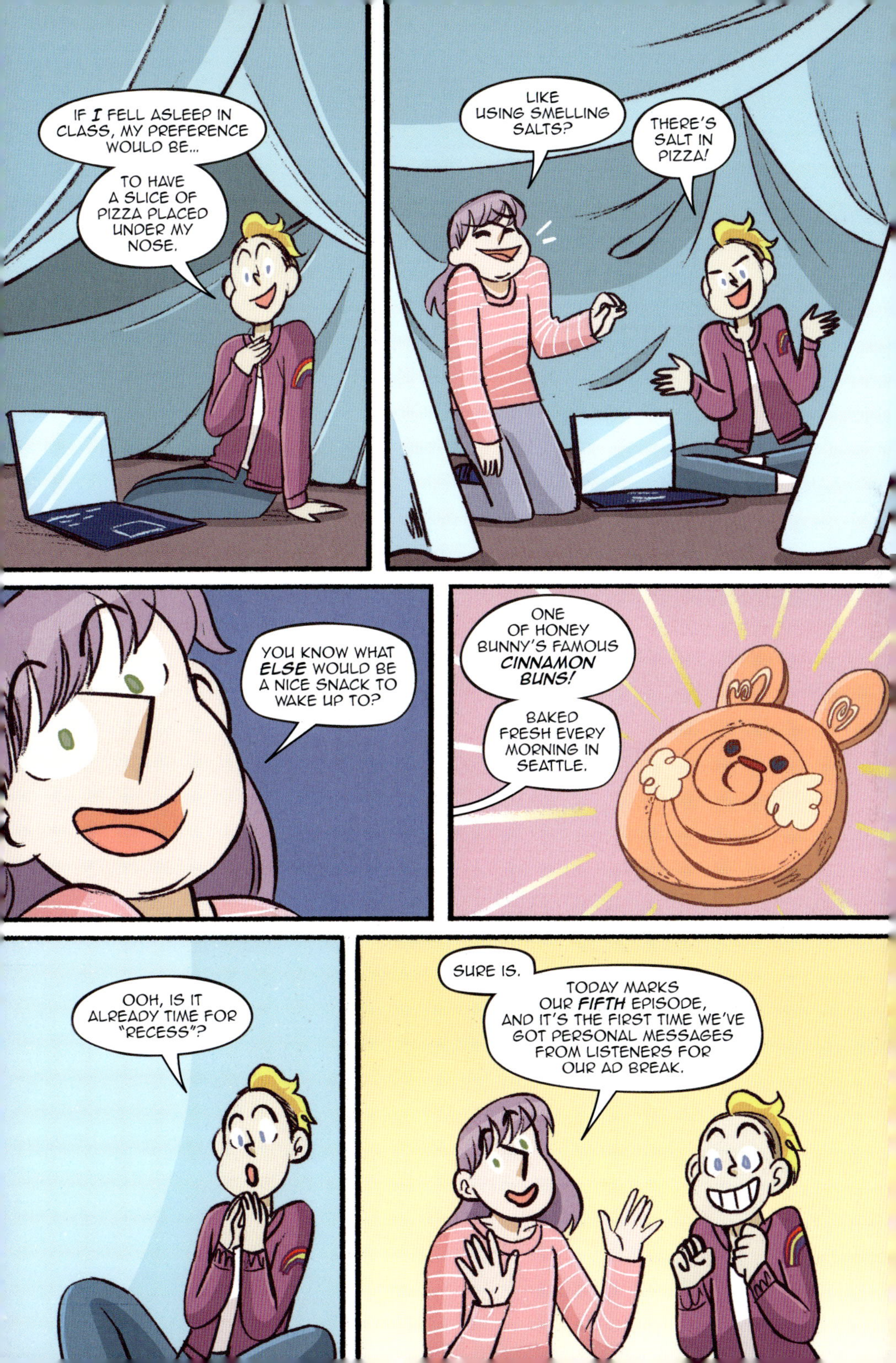
IF *I* FELL ASLEEP IN CLASS, MY PREFERENCE WOULD BE...
TO HAVE A SLICE OF PIZZA PLACED UNDER MY NOSE.
LIKE USING SMELLING SALTS?
THERE'S SALT IN PIZZA!
YOU KNOW WHAT *ELSE* WOULD BE A NICE SNACK TO WAKE UP TO?
ONE OF HONEY BUNNY'S FAMOUS ***CINNAMON BUNS!***
BAKED FRESH EVERY MORNING IN SEATTLE.
OOH, IS IT ALREADY TIME FOR "RECESS"?
SURE IS.
TODAY MARKS OUR *FIFTH* EPISODE, AND IT'S THE FIRST TIME WE'VE GOT PERSONAL MESSAGES FROM LISTENERS FOR OUR AD BREAK.

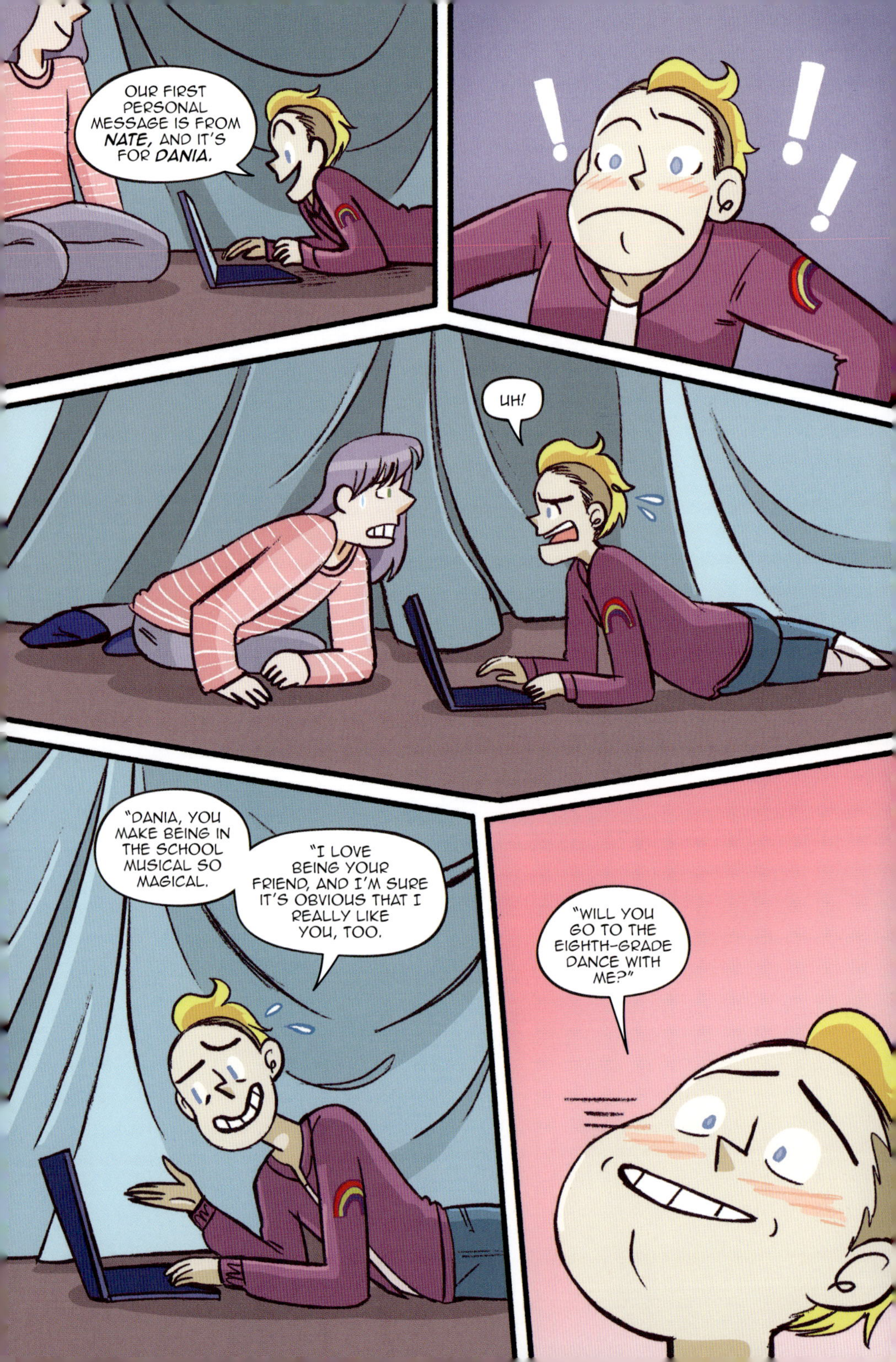
OUR FIRST PERSONAL MESSAGE IS FROM NATE, AND IT'S FOR DANIA.
!
!
!
UH!
"DANIA, YOU MAKE BEING IN THE SCHOOL MUSICAL SO MAGICAL.
"I LOVE BEING YOUR FRIEND, AND I'M SURE IT'S OBVIOUS THAT I REALLY LIKE YOU, TOO.
"WILL YOU GO TO THE EIGHTH-GRADE DANCE WITH ME?"

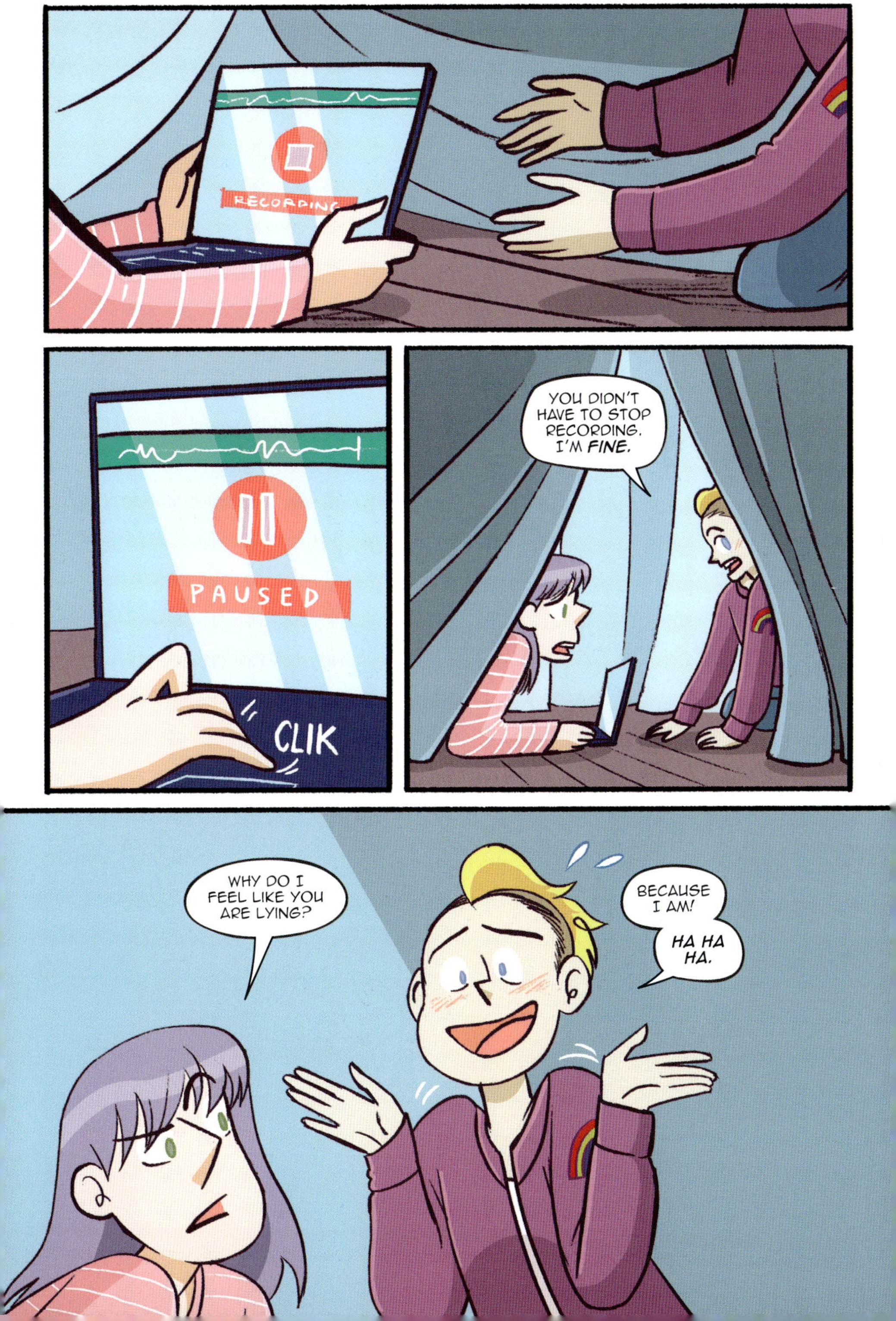
RECORDING
PAUSED
CLIK
YOU DIDN'T HAVE TO STOP RECORDING. I'M FINE.
WHY DO I FEEL LIKE YOU ARE LYING?
BECAUSE I AM!
HA HA HA.

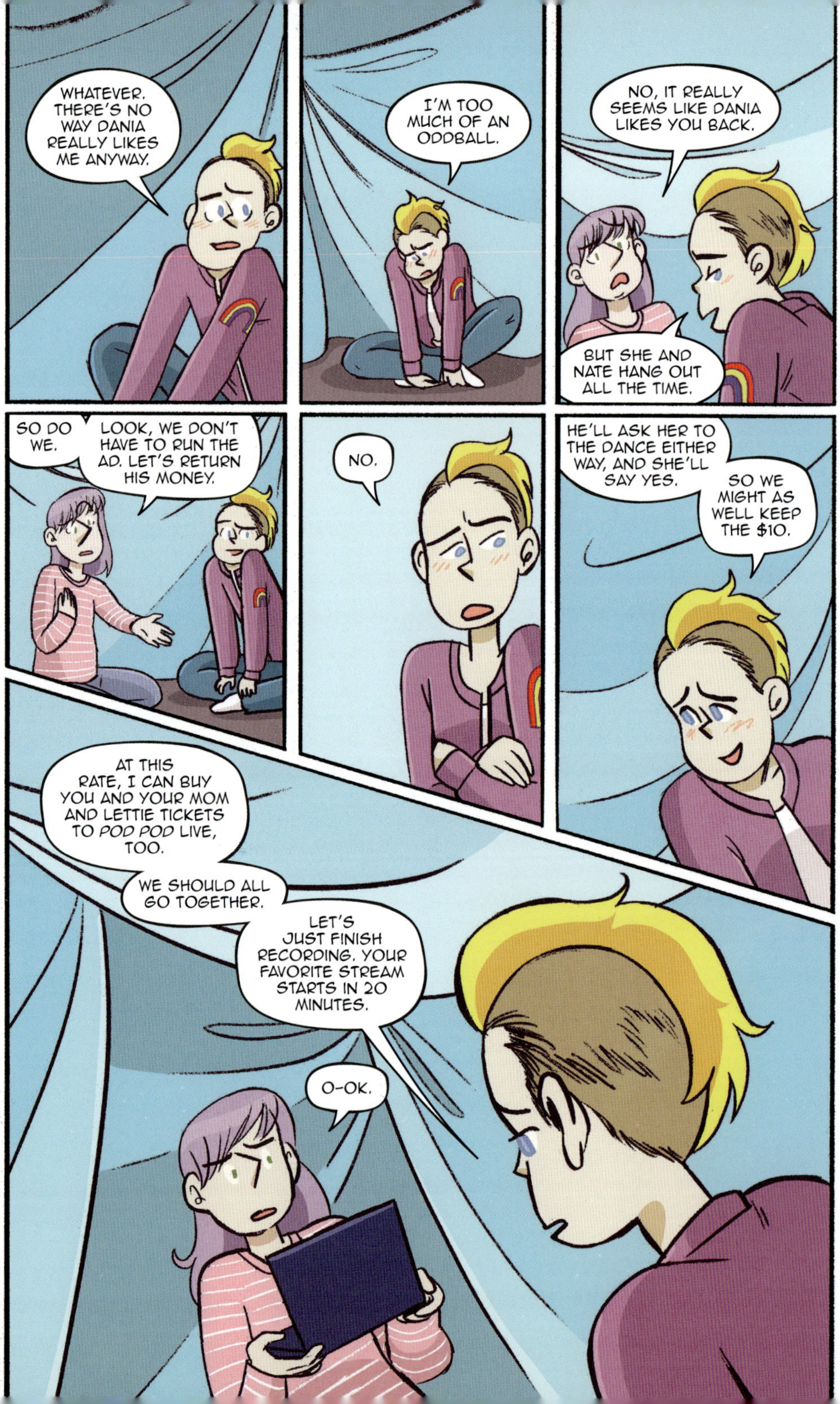
WHATEVER. THERE'S NO WAY DANIA REALLY LIKES ME ANYWAY.
I'M TOO MUCH OF AN ODDBALL.
NO, IT REALLY SEEMS LIKE DANIA LIKES YOU BACK.
BUT SHE AND NATE HANG OUT ALL THE TIME.
SO DO WE.
LOOK, WE DON'T HAVE TO RUN THE AD. LET'S RETURN HIS MONEY.
NO.
HE'LL ASK HER TO THE DANCE EITHER WAY, AND SHE'LL SAY YES.
SO WE MIGHT AS WELL KEEP THE $10.
AT THIS RATE, I CAN BUY YOU AND YOUR MOM AND LETTIE TICKETS TO *POD POD* LIVE, TOO.
WE SHOULD ALL GO TOGETHER.
LET'S JUST FINISH RECORDING. YOUR FAVORITE STREAM STARTS IN 20 MINUTES.
O-OK.

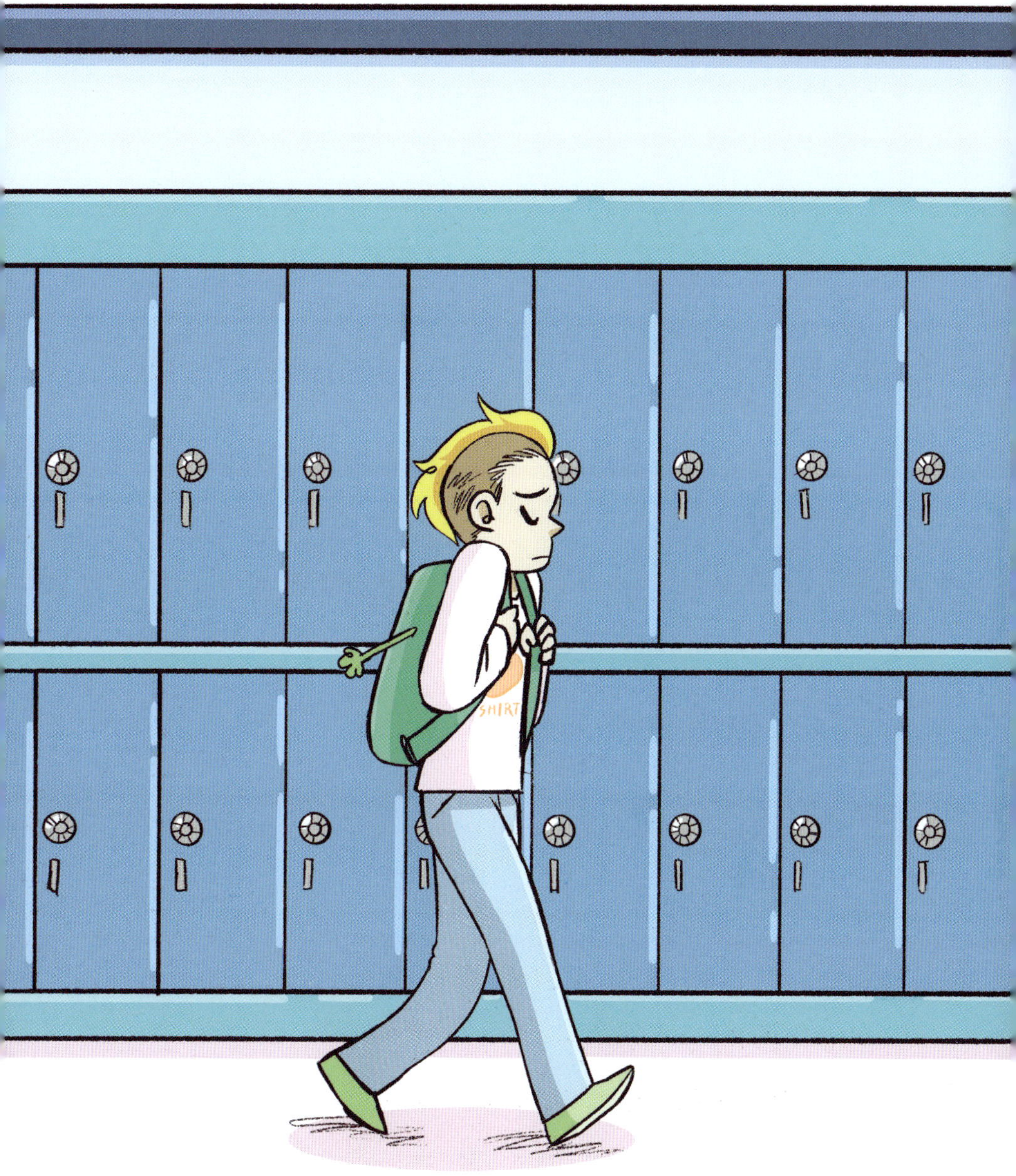
SHIRT

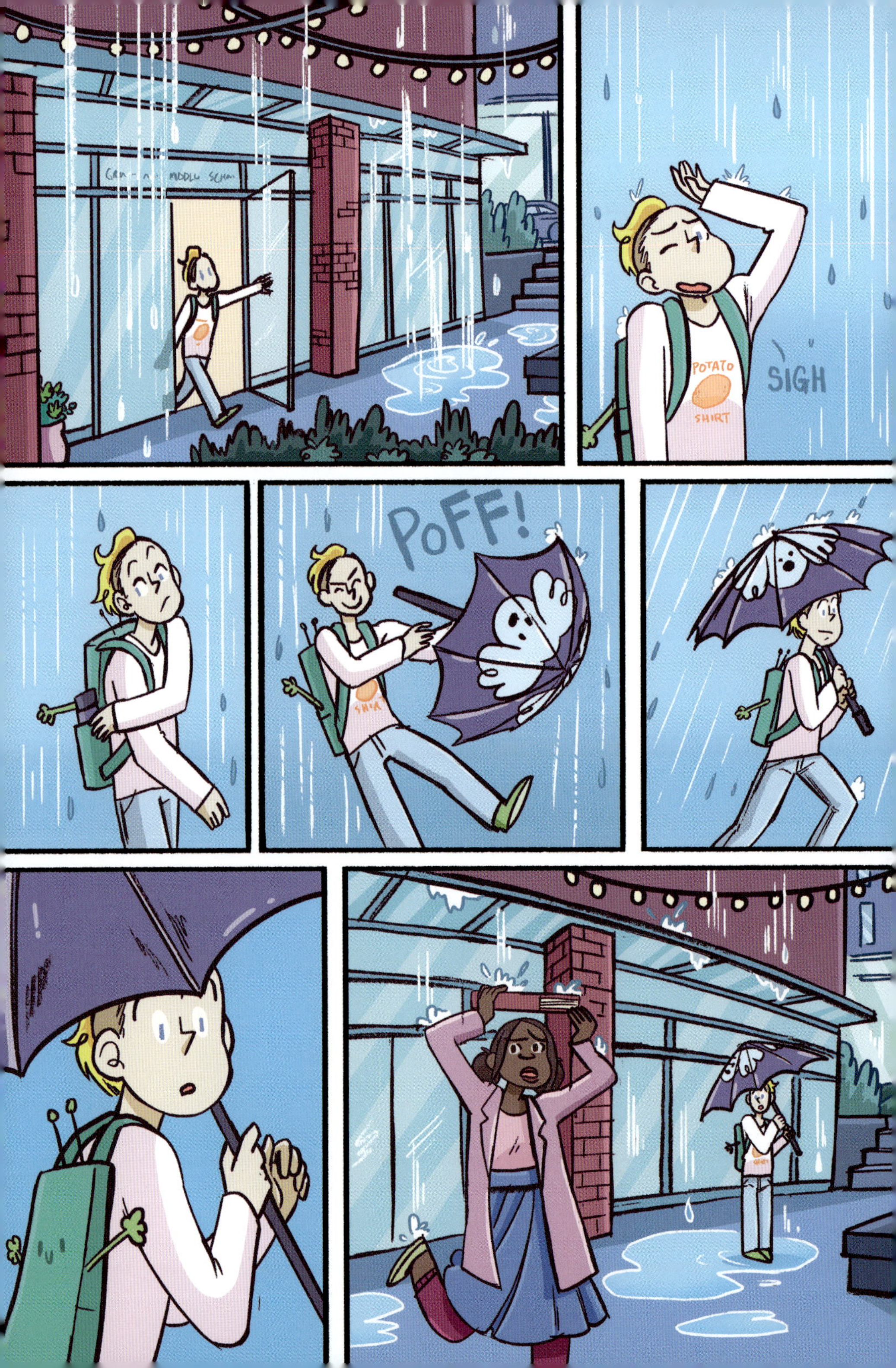

POTATO
SHIRT
SIGH
PoFF!

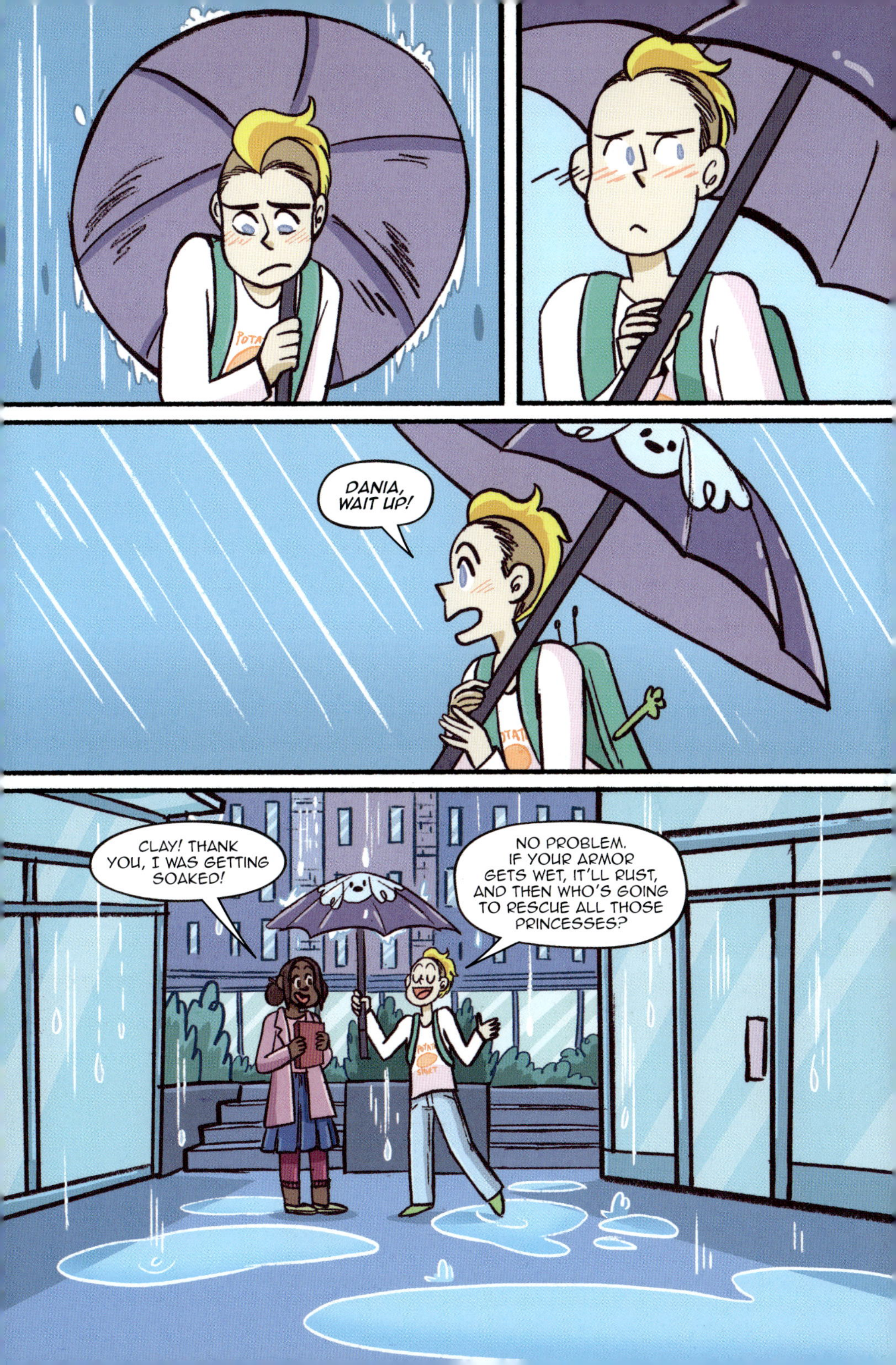
DANIA, WAIT UP!
CLAY! THANK YOU, I WAS GETTING SOAKED!
NO PROBLEM. IF YOUR ARMOR GETS WET, IT'LL RUST, AND THEN WHO'S GOING TO RESCUE ALL THOSE PRINCESSES?

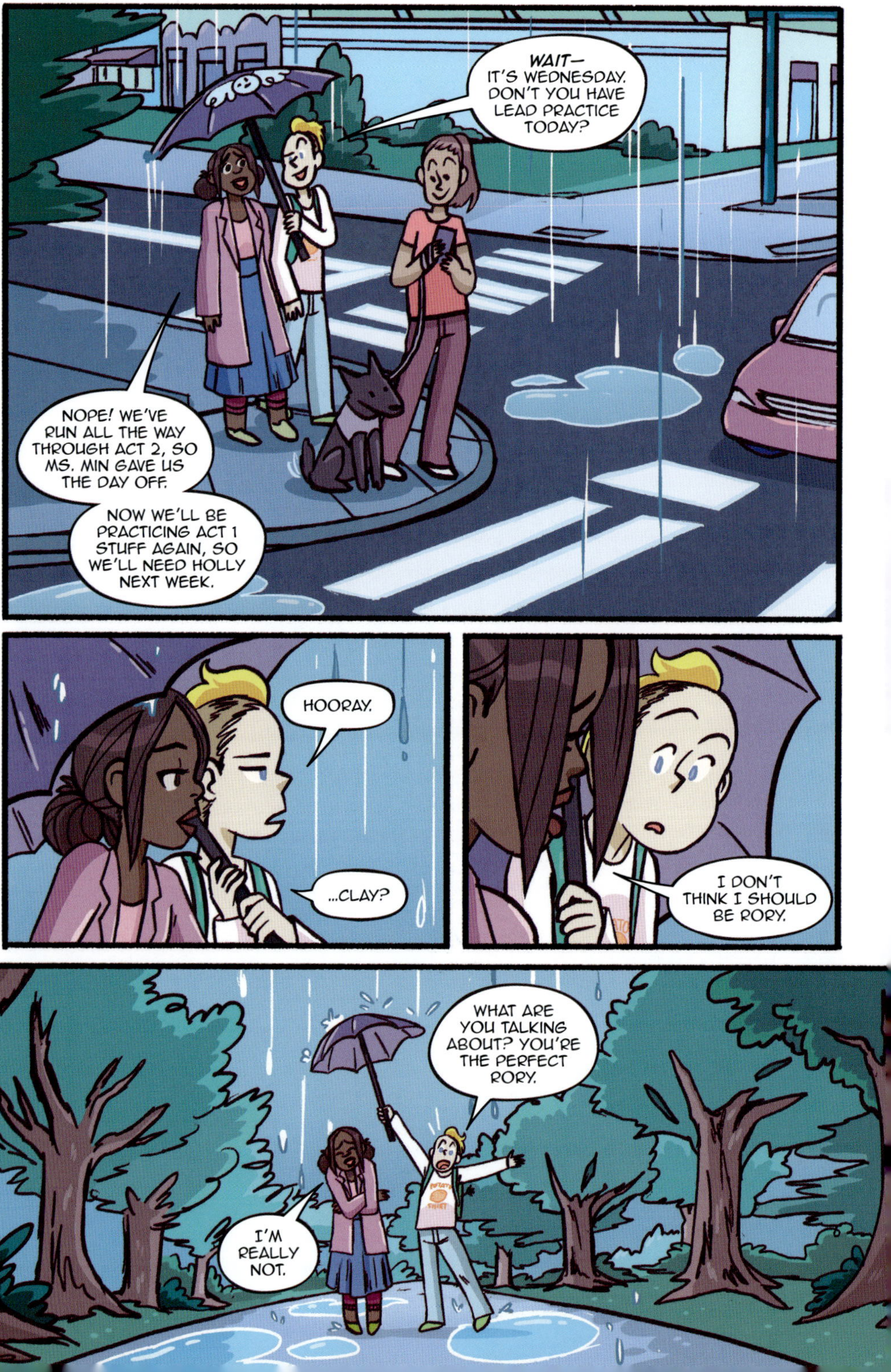

WAIT—
IT'S WEDNESDAY. DON'T YOU HAVE LEAD PRACTICE TODAY?
NOPE! WE'VE RUN ALL THE WAY THROUGH ACT 2, SO MS. MIN GAVE US THE DAY OFF.
NOW WE'LL BE PRACTICING ACT 1 STUFF AGAIN, SO WE'LL NEED HOLLY NEXT WEEK.
HOORAY.
...CLAY?
I DON'T THINK I SHOULD BE RORY.
WHAT ARE YOU TALKING ABOUT? YOU'RE THE PERFECT RORY.
I'M REALLY NOT.

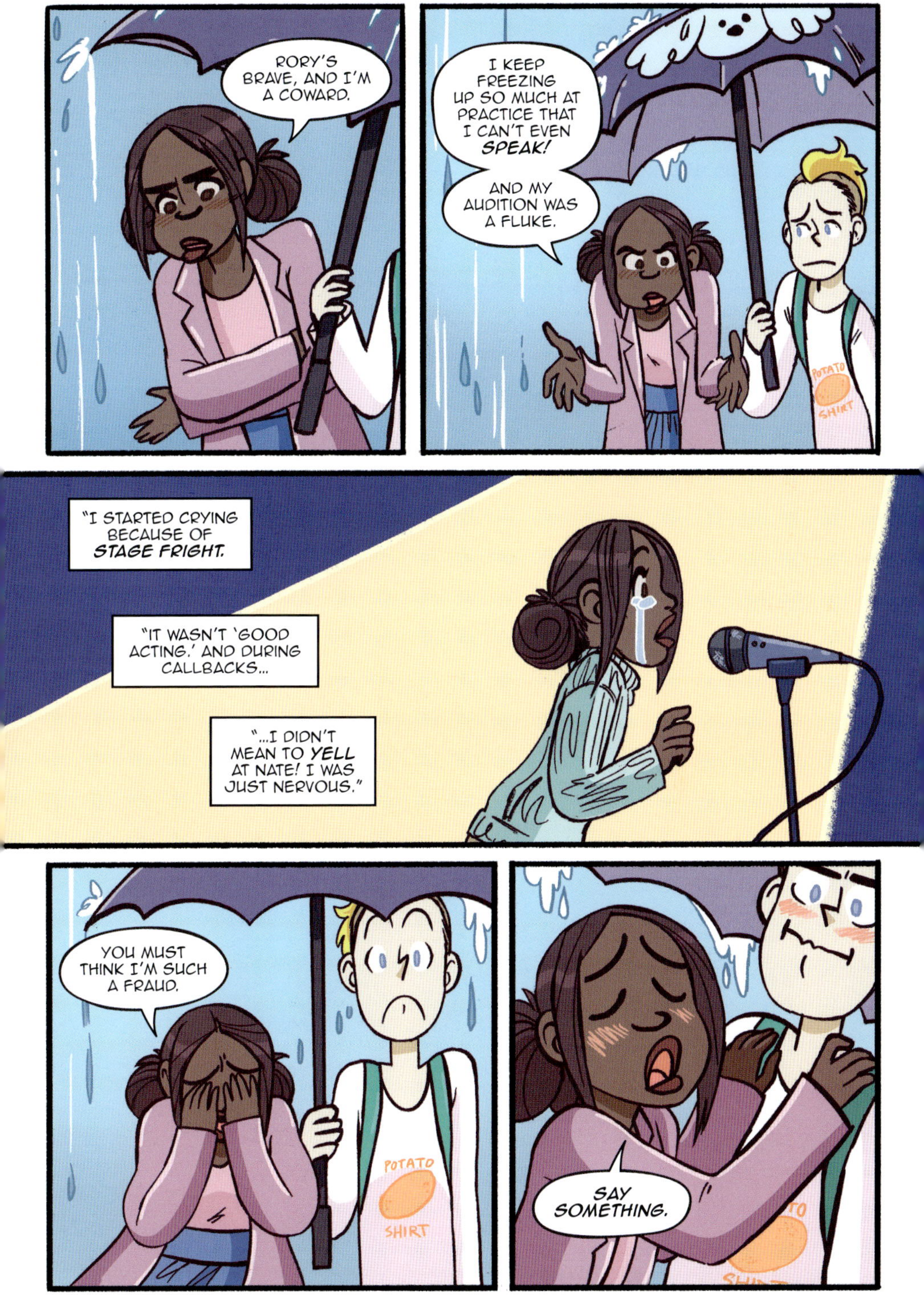
RORY'S BRAVE, AND I'M A COWARD.
I KEEP FREEZING UP SO MUCH AT PRACTICE THAT I CAN'T EVEN *SPEAK!*
AND MY AUDITION WAS A FLUKE.
POTATO SHIRT
"I STARTED CRYING BECAUSE OF *STAGE FRIGHT.*
"IT WASN'T 'GOOD ACTING.' AND DURING CALLBACKS...
"...I DIDN'T MEAN TO *YELL* AT NATE! I WAS JUST NERVOUS."
YOU MUST THINK I'M SUCH A FRAUD.
POTATO SHIRT
SAY SOMETHING.

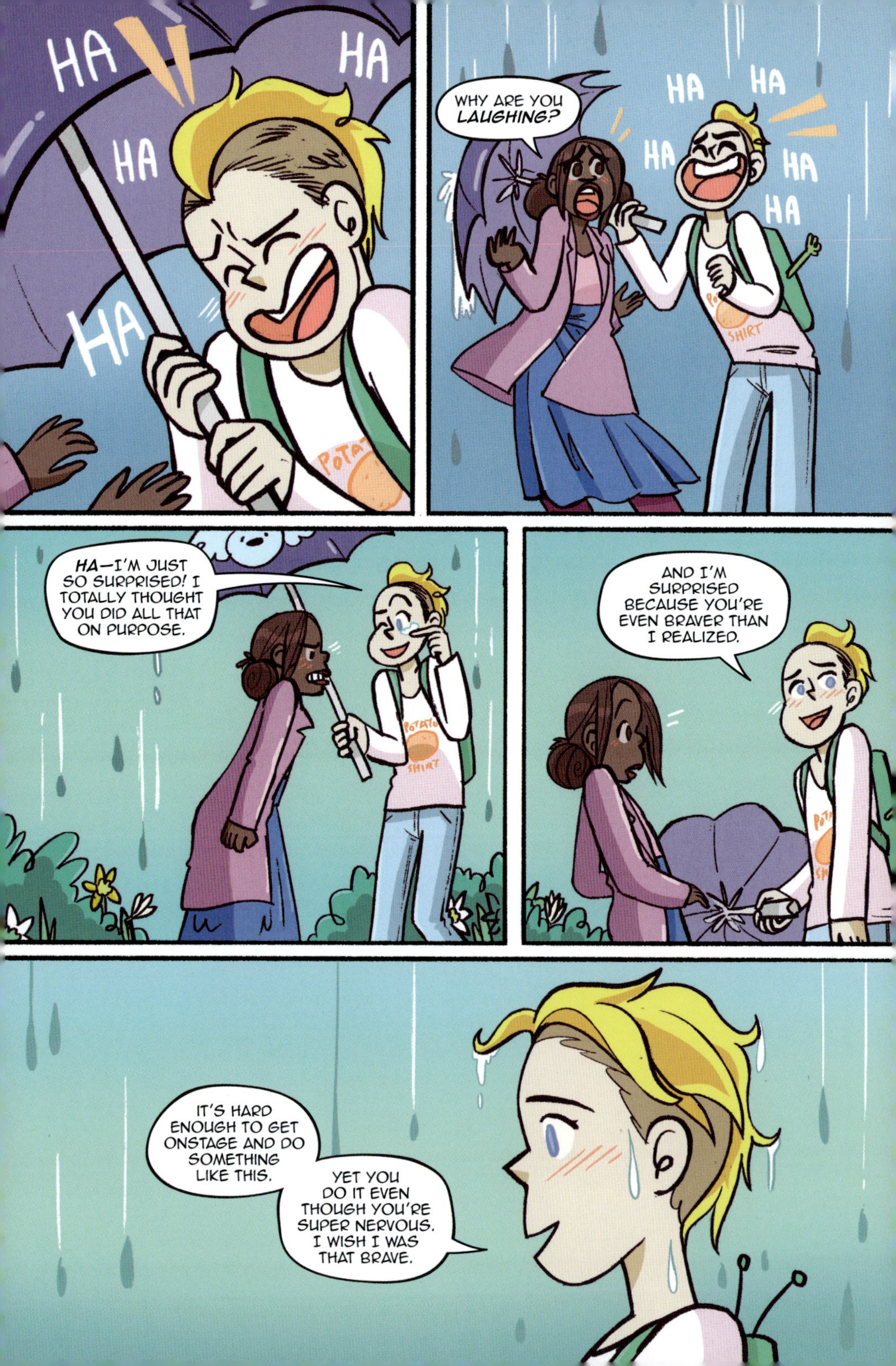
HA
HA
HA
HA
WHY ARE YOU LAUGHING?
HA
HA
HA
HA
HA
HA—I'M JUST SO SURPRISED! I TOTALLY THOUGHT YOU DID ALL THAT ON PURPOSE.
AND I'M SURPRISED BECAUSE YOU'RE EVEN BRAVER THAN I REALIZED.
IT'S HARD ENOUGH TO GET ONSTAGE AND DO SOMETHING LIKE THIS.
YET YOU DO IT EVEN THOUGH YOU'RE SUPER NERVOUS. I WISH I WAS THAT BRAVE.

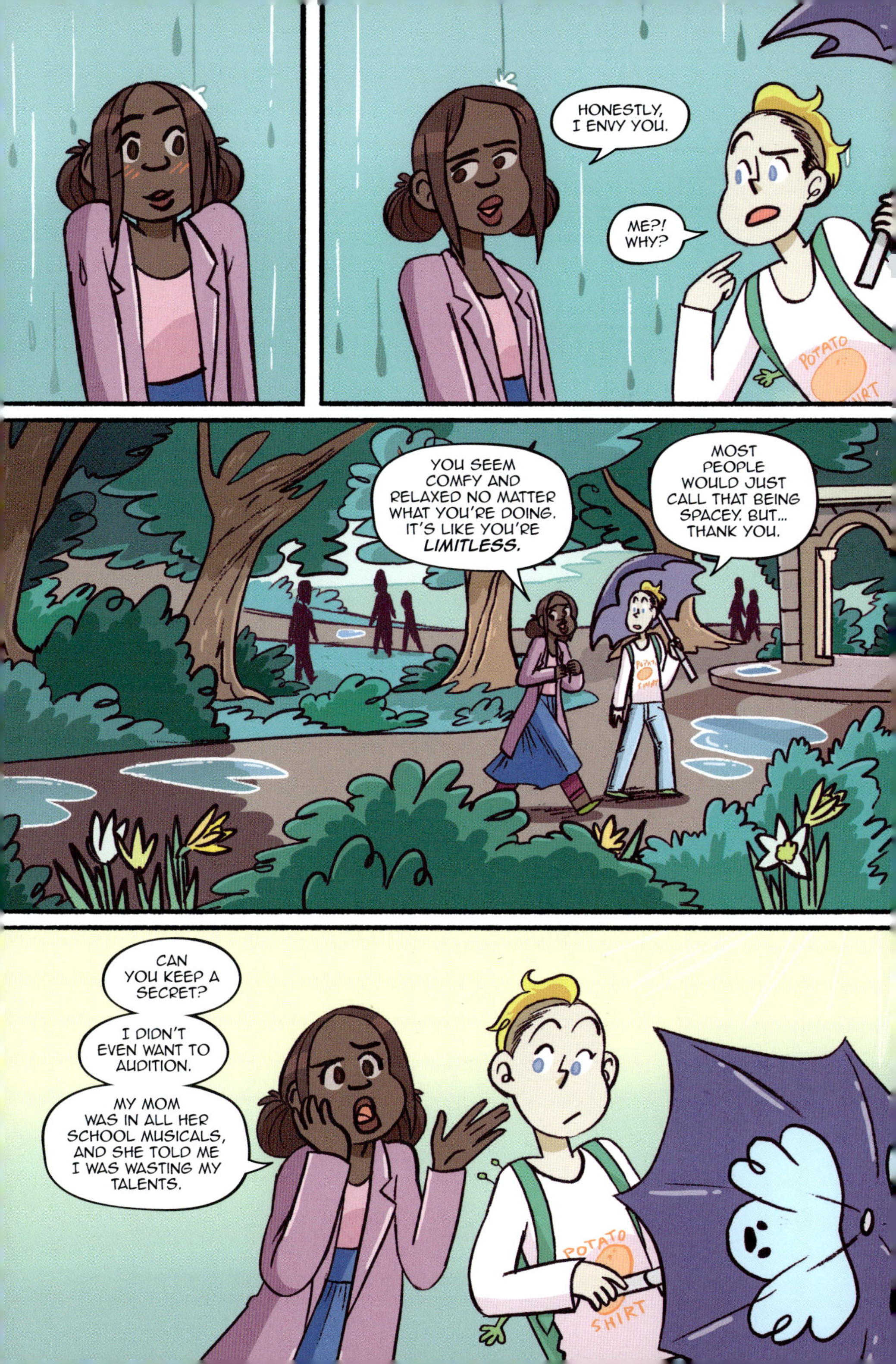
HONESTLY, I ENVY YOU.
ME?! WHY?
YOU SEEM COMFY AND RELAXED NO MATTER WHAT YOU'RE DOING. IT'S LIKE YOU'RE *LIMITLESS.*
MOST PEOPLE WOULD JUST CALL THAT BEING SPACEY. BUT... THANK YOU.
CAN YOU KEEP A SECRET?
I DIDN'T EVEN WANT TO AUDITION.
MY MOM WAS IN ALL HER SCHOOL MUSICALS, AND SHE TOLD ME I WAS WASTING MY TALENTS.
POTATO SHIRT

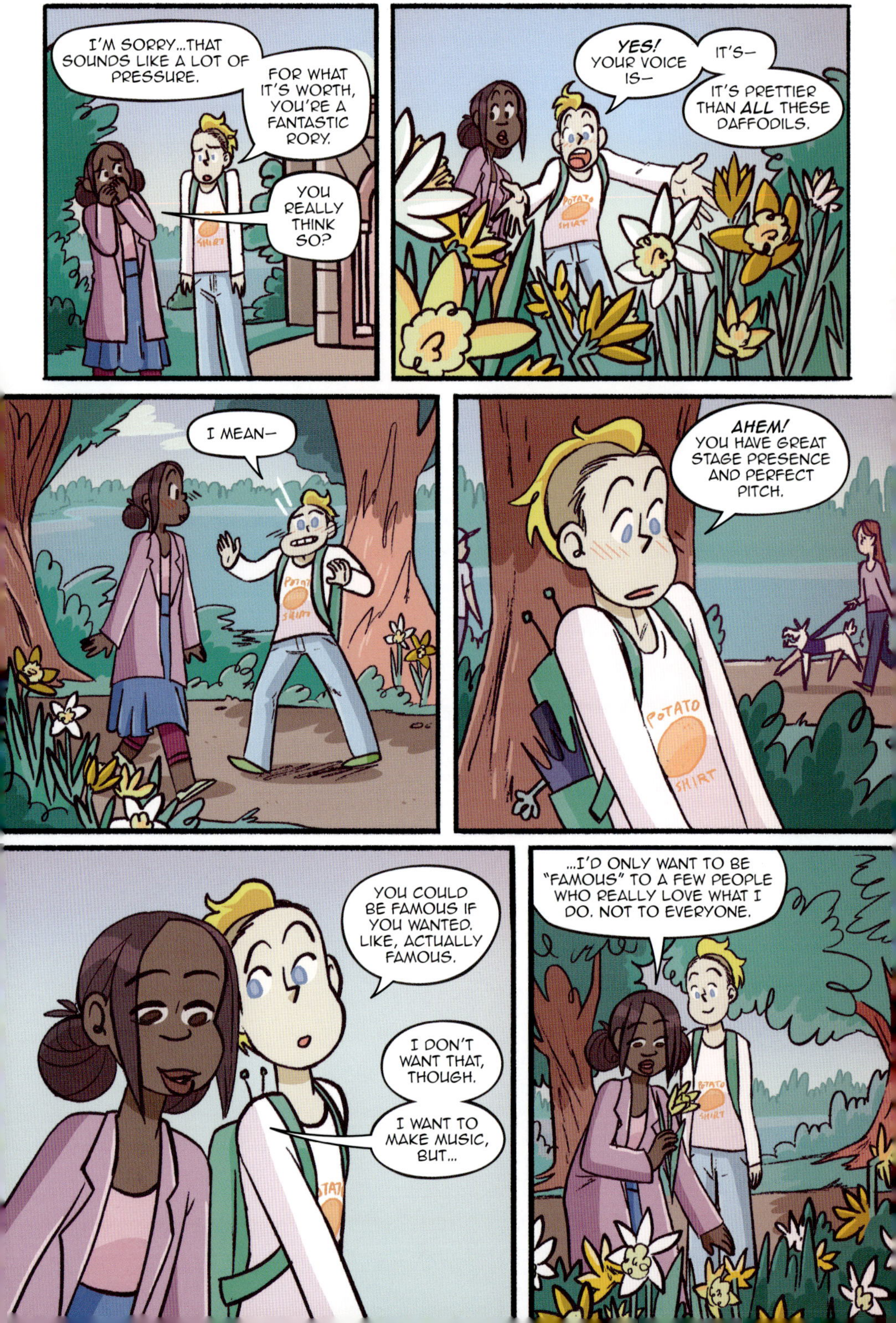
I'M SORRY...THAT SOUNDS LIKE A LOT OF PRESSURE.
FOR WHAT IT'S WORTH, YOU'RE A FANTASTIC RORY.
YOU REALLY THINK SO?
POTATO SHIRT
YES! YOUR VOICE IS—
IT'S—
IT'S PRETTIER THAN ALL THESE DAFFODILS.
I MEAN—
AHEM! YOU HAVE GREAT STAGE PRESENCE AND PERFECT PITCH.
YOU COULD BE FAMOUS IF YOU WANTED. LIKE, ACTUALLY FAMOUS.
I DON'T WANT THAT, THOUGH.
I WANT TO MAKE MUSIC, BUT...
...I'D ONLY WANT TO BE "FAMOUS" TO A FEW PEOPLE WHO REALLY LOVE WHAT I DO. NOT TO EVERYONE.

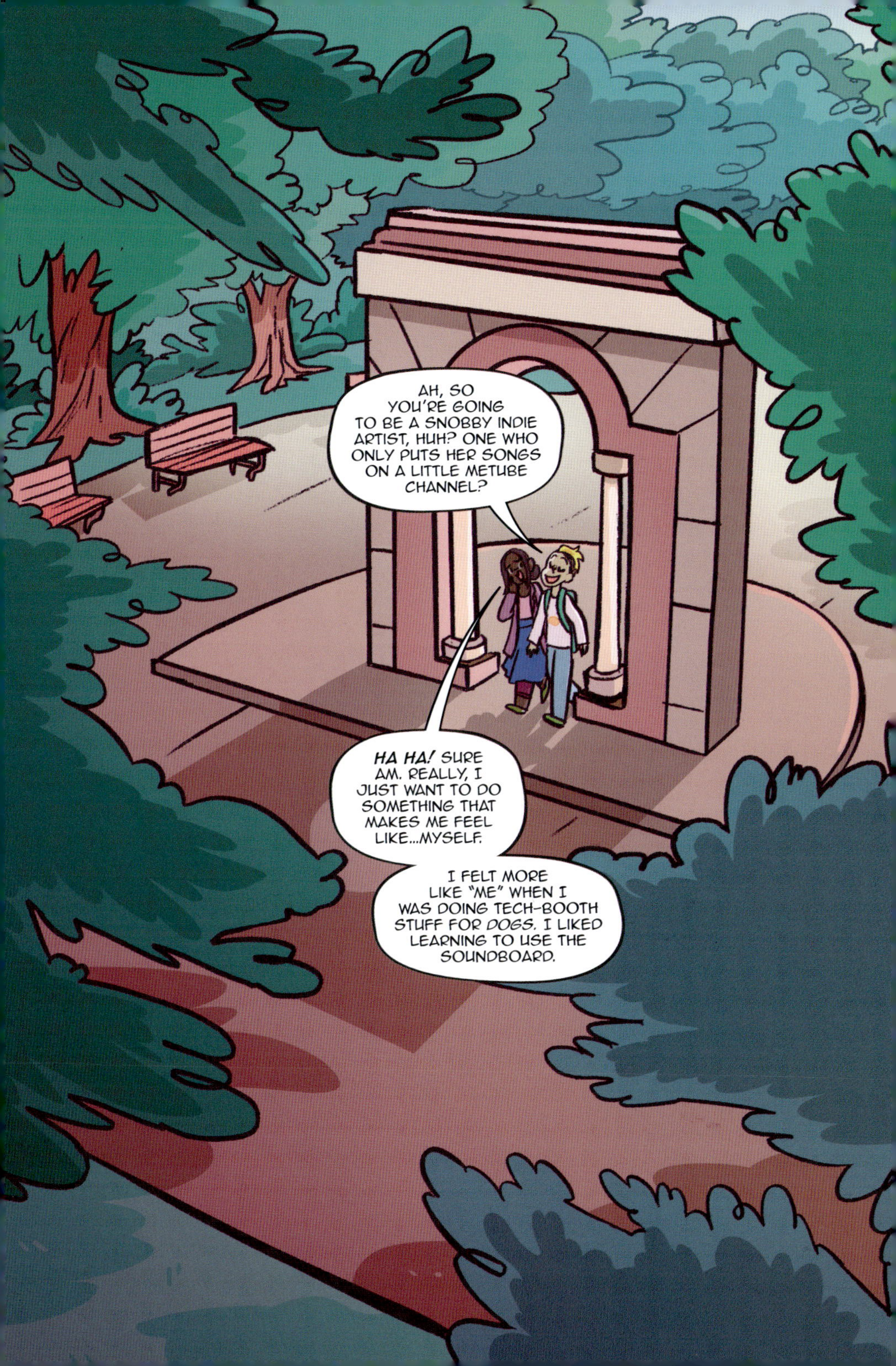
AH, SO YOU'RE GOING TO BE A SNOBBY INDIE ARTIST, HUH? ONE WHO ONLY PUTS HER SONGS ON A LITTLE METUBE CHANNEL?
HA HA! SURE AM. REALLY, I JUST WANT TO DO SOMETHING THAT MAKES ME FEEL LIKE...MYSELF.
I FELT MORE LIKE "ME" WHEN I WAS DOING TECH-BOOTH STUFF FOR *DOGS*. I LIKED LEARNING TO USE THE SOUNDBOARD.

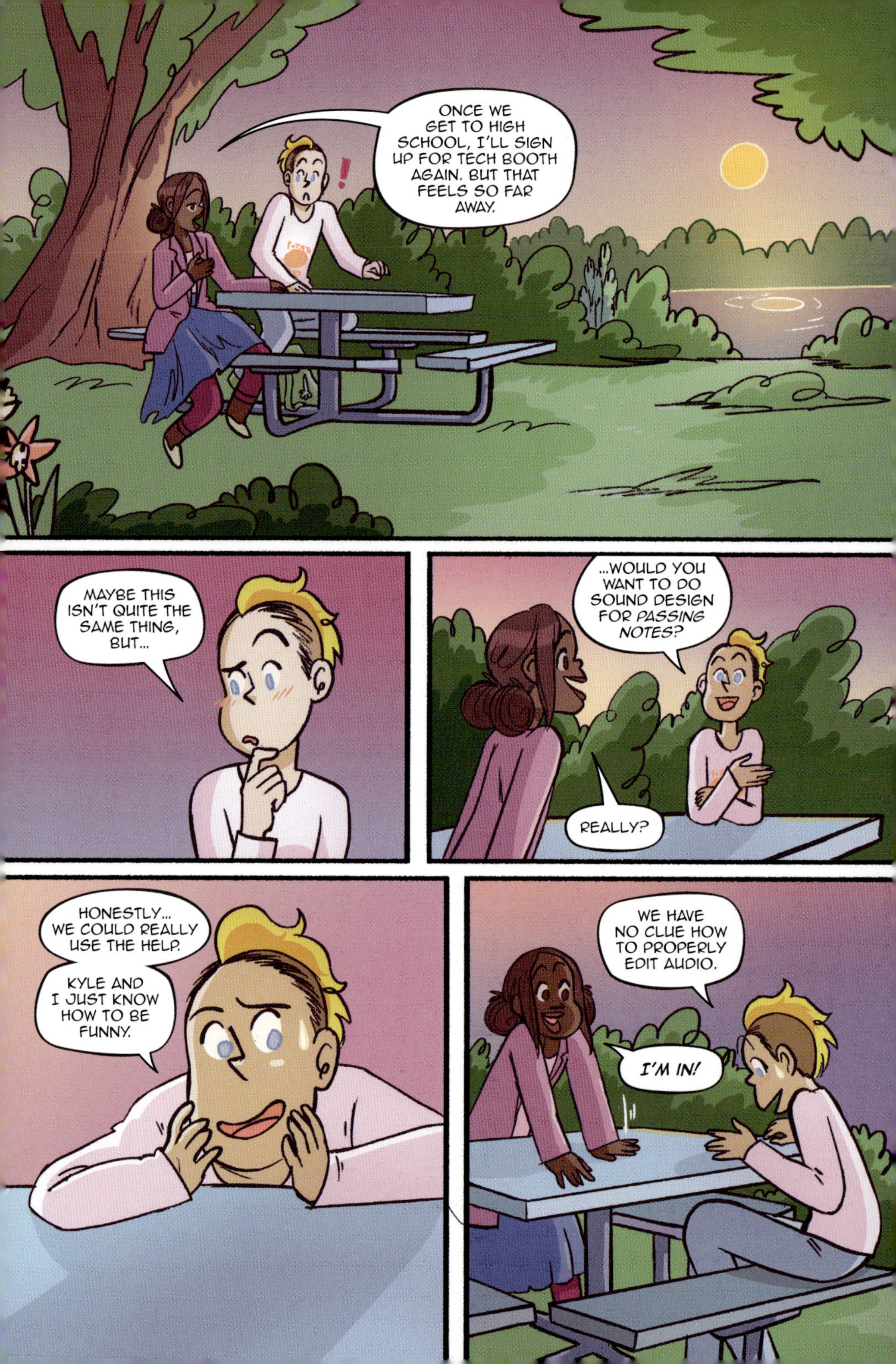
ONCE WE GET TO HIGH SCHOOL, I'LL SIGN UP FOR TECH BOOTH AGAIN. BUT THAT FEELS SO FAR AWAY.
!
MAYBE THIS ISN'T QUITE THE SAME THING, BUT...
...WOULD YOU WANT TO DO SOUND DESIGN FOR *PASSING NOTES*?
REALLY?
HONESTLY... WE COULD REALLY USE THE HELP.
KYLE AND I JUST KNOW HOW TO BE FUNNY.
WE HAVE NO CLUE HOW TO PROPERLY EDIT AUDIO.
I'M IN!

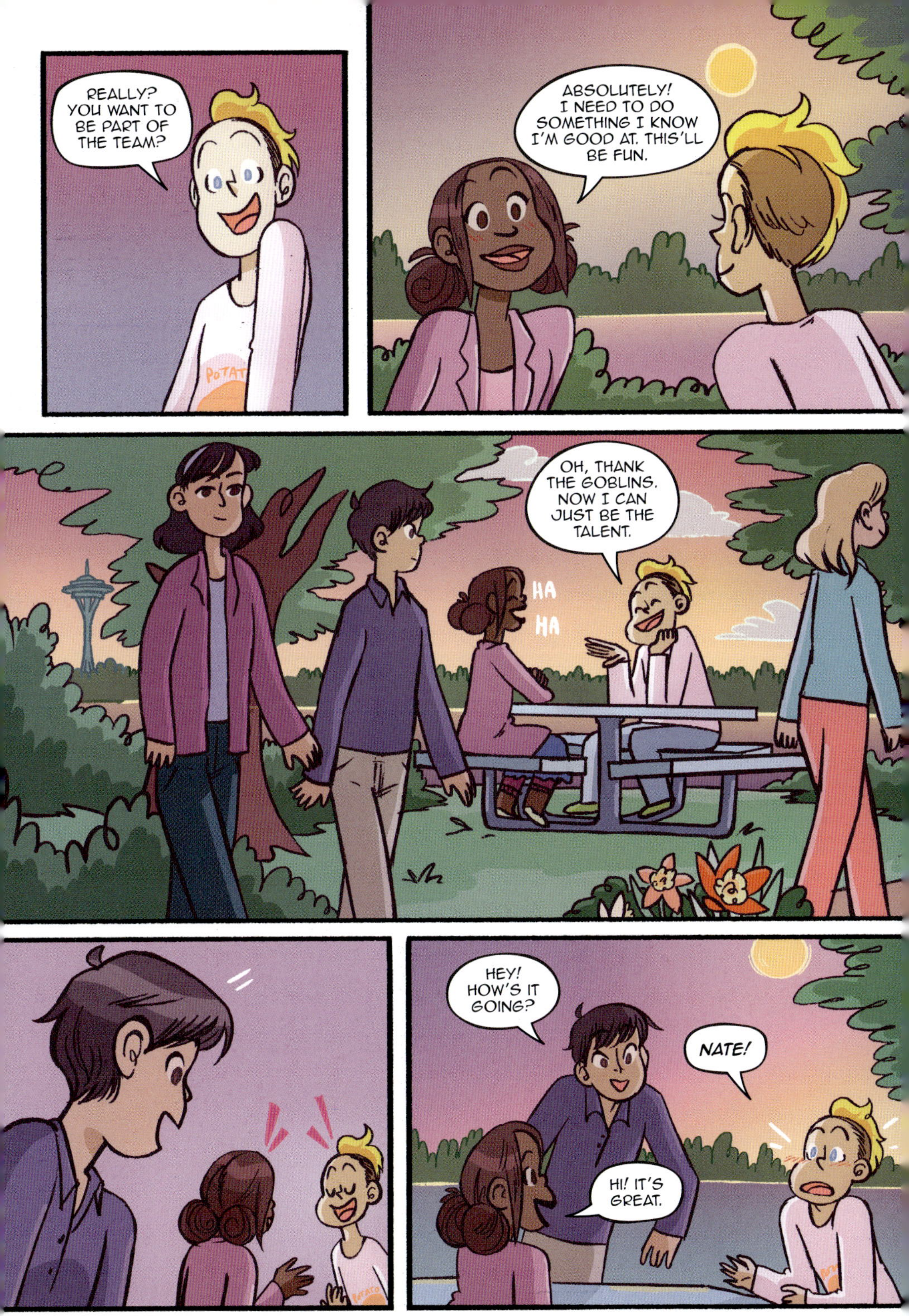
REALLY? YOU WANT TO BE PART OF THE TEAM?
ABSOLUTELY! I NEED TO DO SOMETHING I KNOW I'M GOOD AT. THIS'LL BE FUN.
OH, THANK THE GOBLINS. NOW I CAN JUST BE THE TALENT.
HA HA
HEY! HOW'S IT GOING?
NATE!
HI! IT'S GREAT.

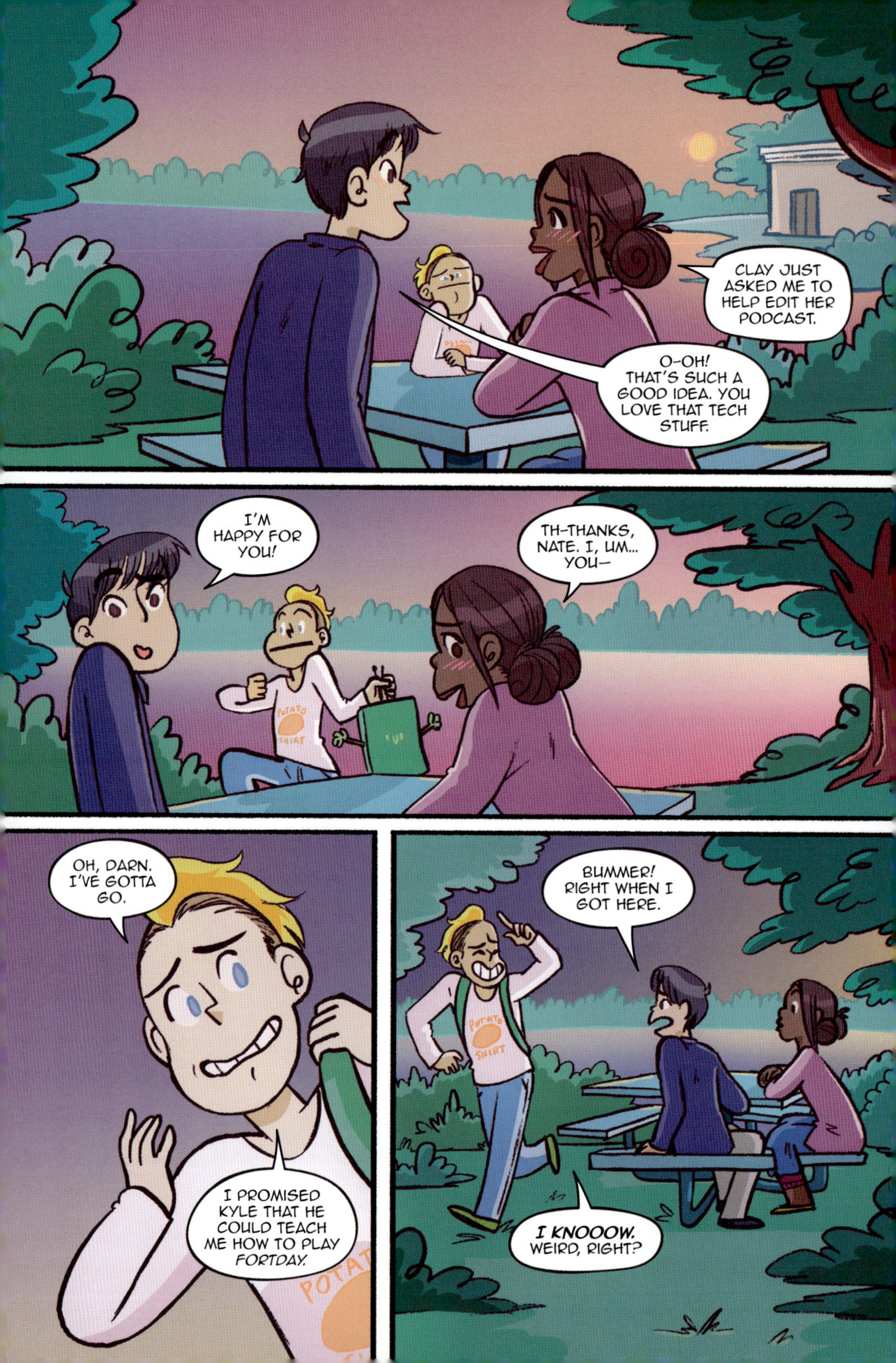
CLAY JUST ASKED ME TO HELP EDIT HER PODCAST.
O-OH! THAT'S SUCH A GOOD IDEA. YOU LOVE THAT TECH STUFF.
I'M HAPPY FOR YOU!
TH-THANKS, NATE. I, UM... YOU—
POTATO SHIRT
OH, DARN. I'VE GOTTA GO.
I PROMISED KYLE THAT HE COULD TEACH ME HOW TO PLAY *FORTDAY.*
BUMMER! RIGHT WHEN I GOT HERE.
I KNOOOW. WEIRD, RIGHT?

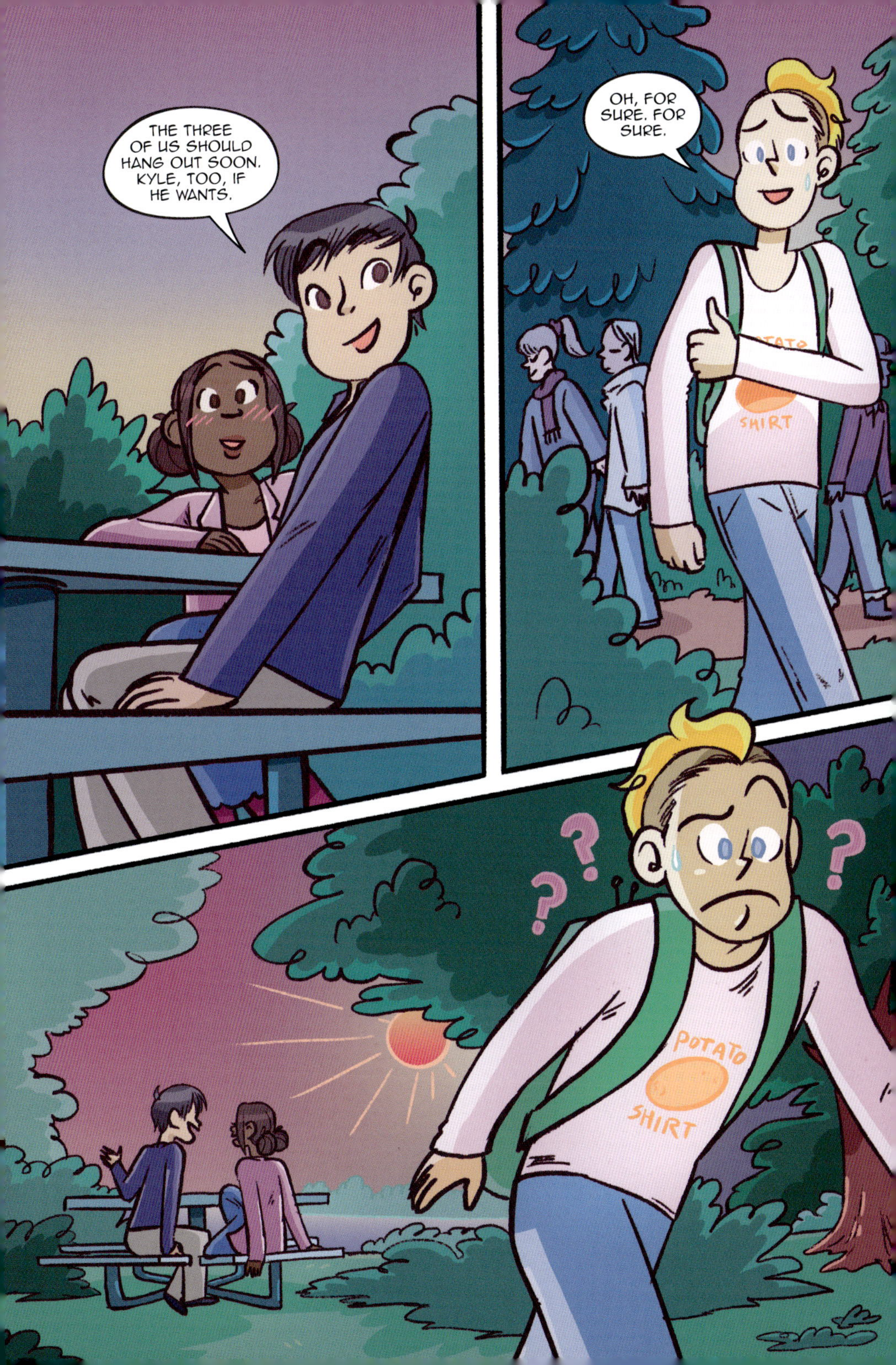
THE THREE OF US SHOULD HANG OUT SOON. KYLE, TOO, IF HE WANTS.
OH, FOR SURE. FOR SURE.
POTATO SHIRT
?
?
?
POTATO SHIRT

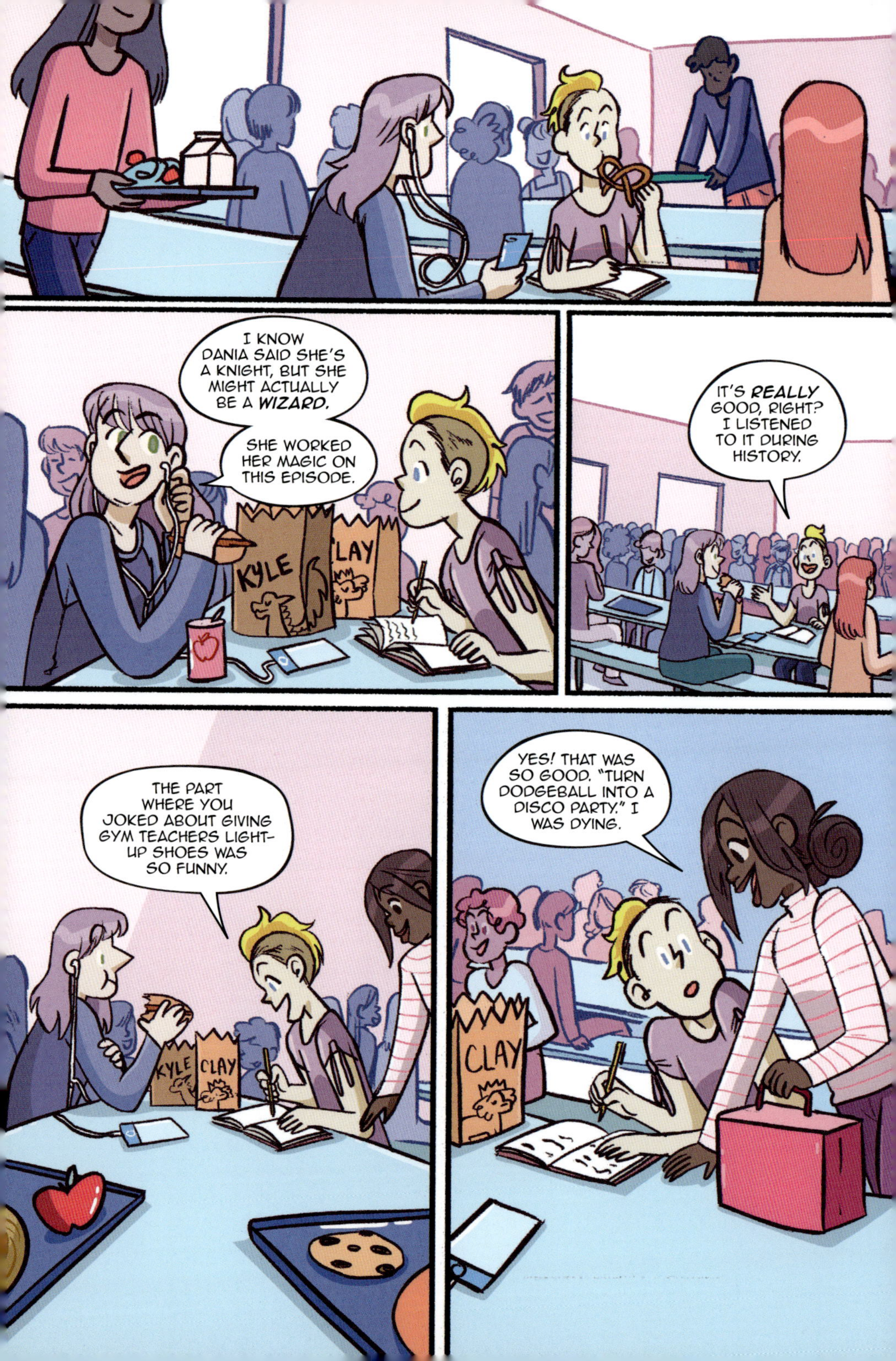
I KNOW DANIA SAID SHE'S A KNIGHT, BUT SHE MIGHT ACTUALLY BE A *WIZARD.*
SHE WORKED HER MAGIC ON THIS EPISODE.
KYLE
CLAY
IT'S ***REALLY*** GOOD, RIGHT? I LISTENED TO IT DURING HISTORY.
THE PART WHERE YOU JOKED ABOUT GIVING GYM TEACHERS LIGHT-UP SHOES WAS SO FUNNY.
KYLE
CLAY
YES! THAT WAS SO GOOD. "TURN DODGEBALL INTO A DISCO PARTY." I WAS DYING.
CLAY

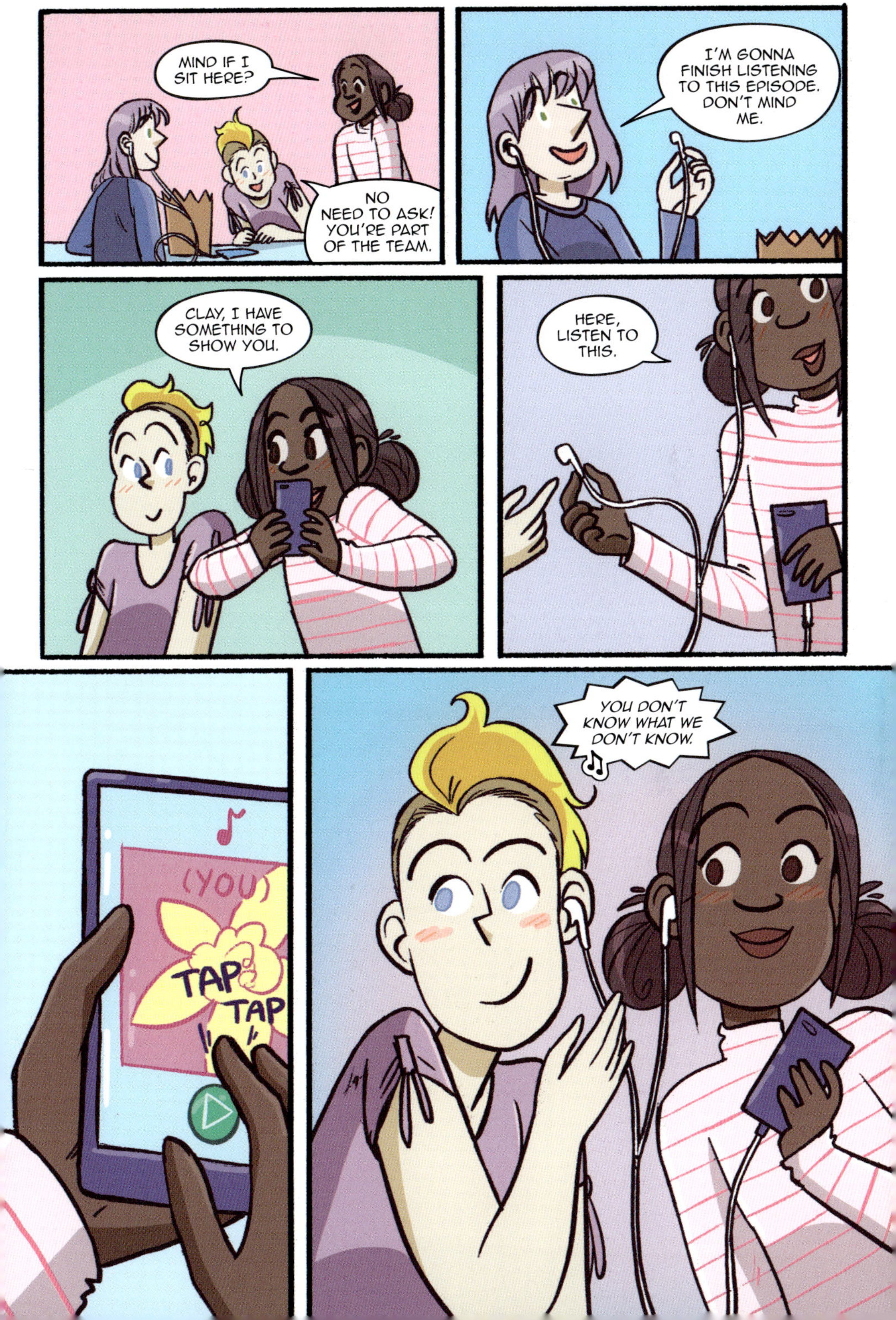
MIND IF I SIT HERE?
NO NEED TO ASK! YOU'RE PART OF THE TEAM.
I'M GONNA FINISH LISTENING TO THIS EPISODE. DON'T MIND ME.
CLAY, I HAVE SOMETHING TO SHOW YOU.
HERE, LISTEN TO THIS.
(YOU)
TAP TAP
YOU DON'T KNOW WHAT WE DON'T KNOW.

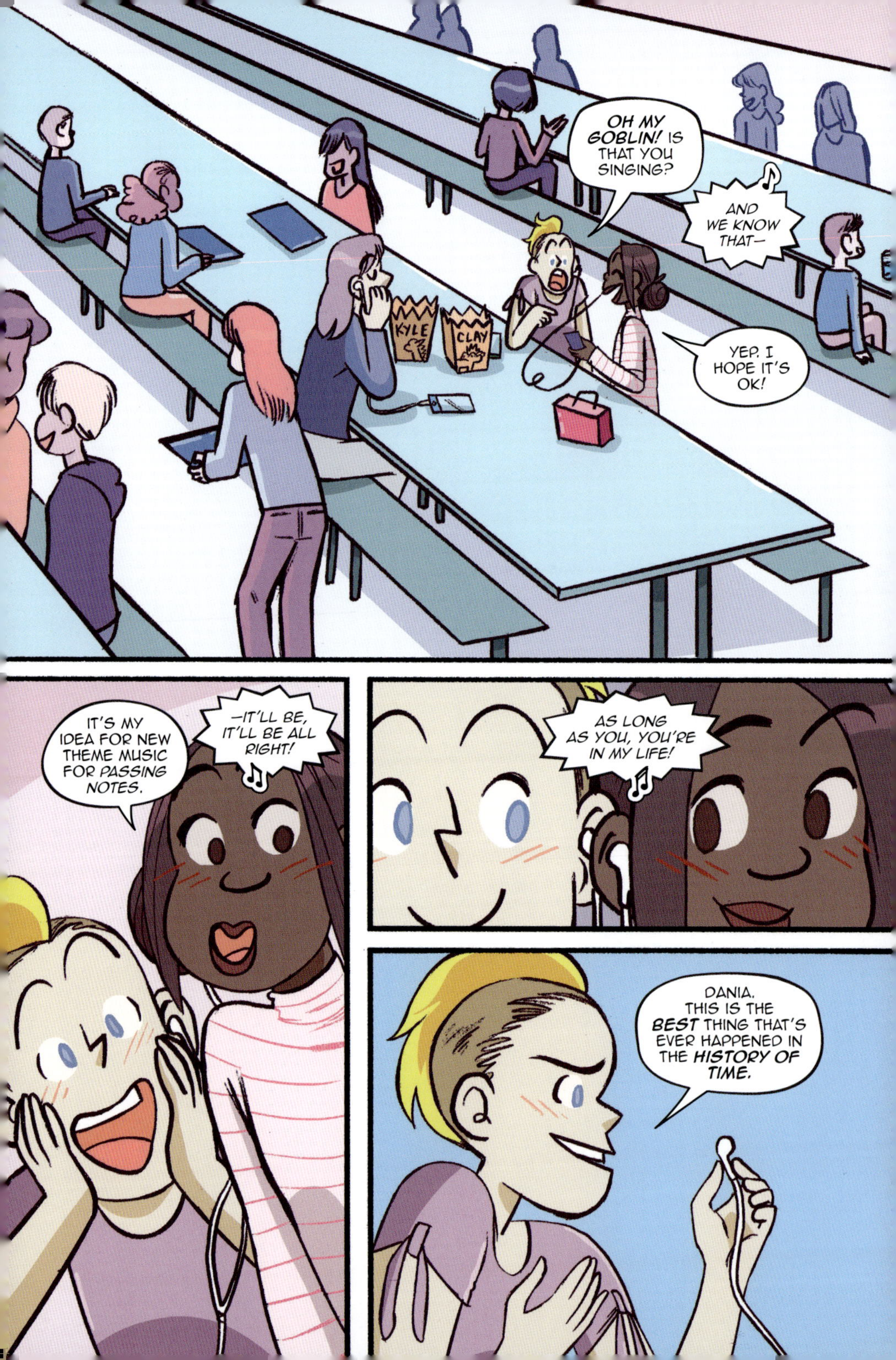

OH MY GOBLIN! IS THAT YOU SINGING?
AND WE KNOW THAT—
KYLE
CLAY
YEP. I HOPE IT'S OK!
IT'S MY IDEA FOR NEW THEME MUSIC FOR PASSING NOTES.
—IT'LL BE, IT'LL BE ALL RIGHT!
AS LONG AS YOU, YOU'RE IN MY LIFE!
DANIA. THIS IS THE BEST THING THAT'S EVER HAPPENED IN THE HISTORY OF TIME.

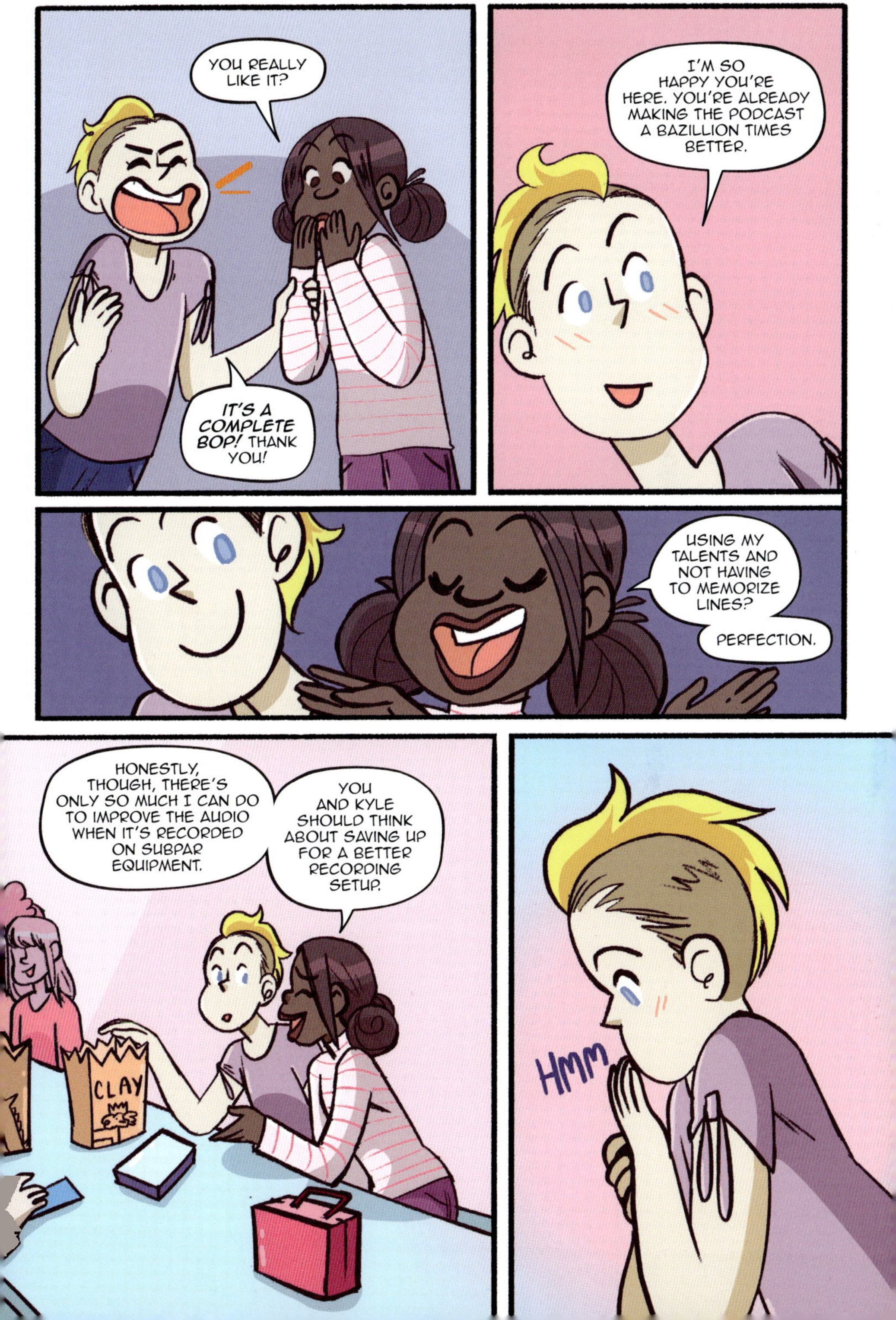
YOU REALLY LIKE IT?
IT'S A COMPLETE BOP! THANK YOU!
I'M SO HAPPY YOU'RE HERE. YOU'RE ALREADY MAKING THE PODCAST A BAZILLION TIMES BETTER.
USING MY TALENTS AND NOT HAVING TO MEMORIZE LINES?
PERFECTION.
HONESTLY, THOUGH, THERE'S ONLY SO MUCH I CAN DO TO IMPROVE THE AUDIO WHEN IT'S RECORDED ON SUBPAR EQUIPMENT.
YOU AND KYLE SHOULD THINK ABOUT SAVING UP FOR A BETTER RECORDING SETUP.
CLAY
HMM

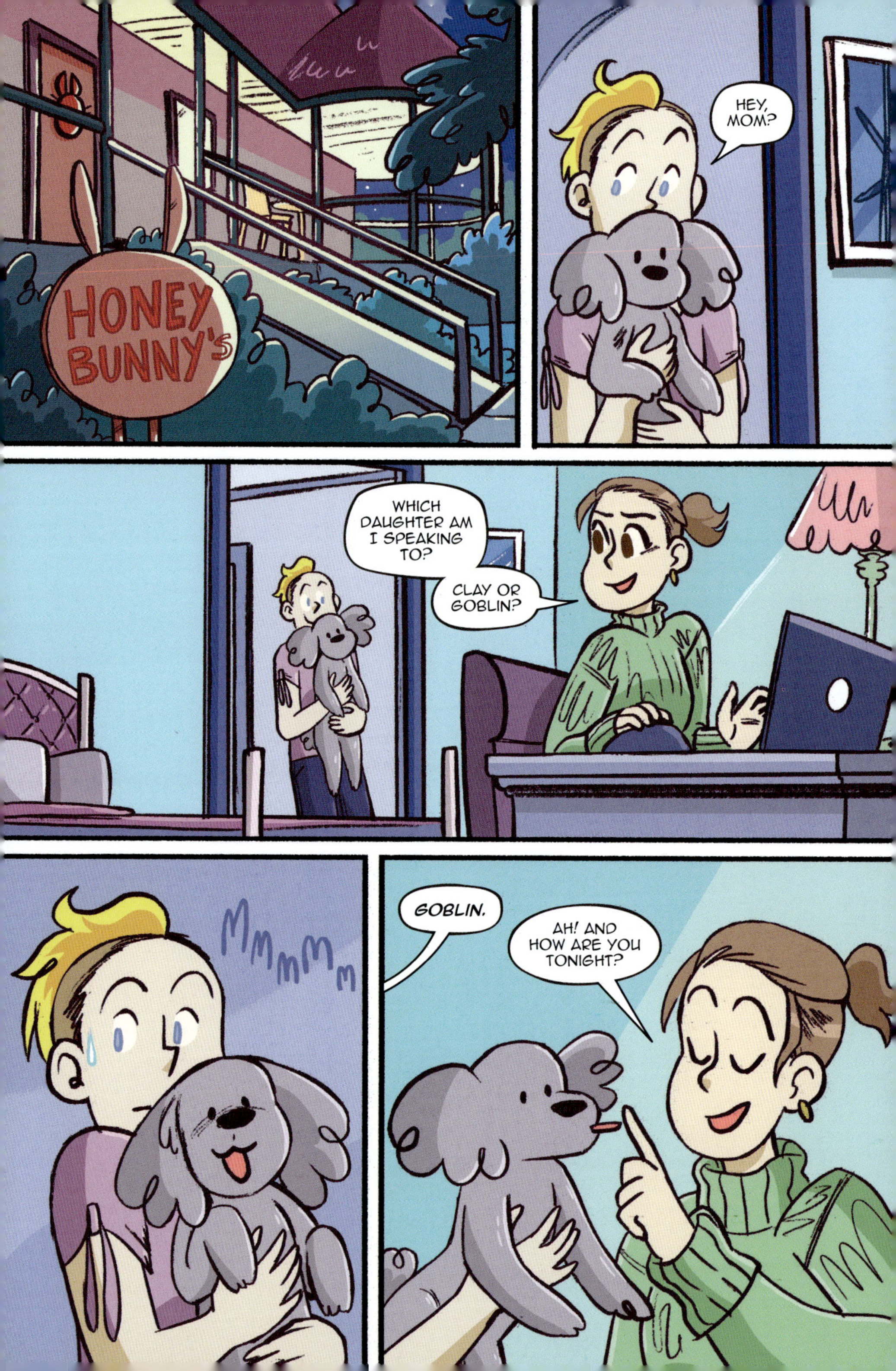

HONEY BUNNY'S
HEY, MOM?
WHICH DAUGHTER AM I SPEAKING TO?
CLAY OR GOBLIN?
MMMMM
GOBLIN.
AH! AND HOW ARE YOU TONIGHT?

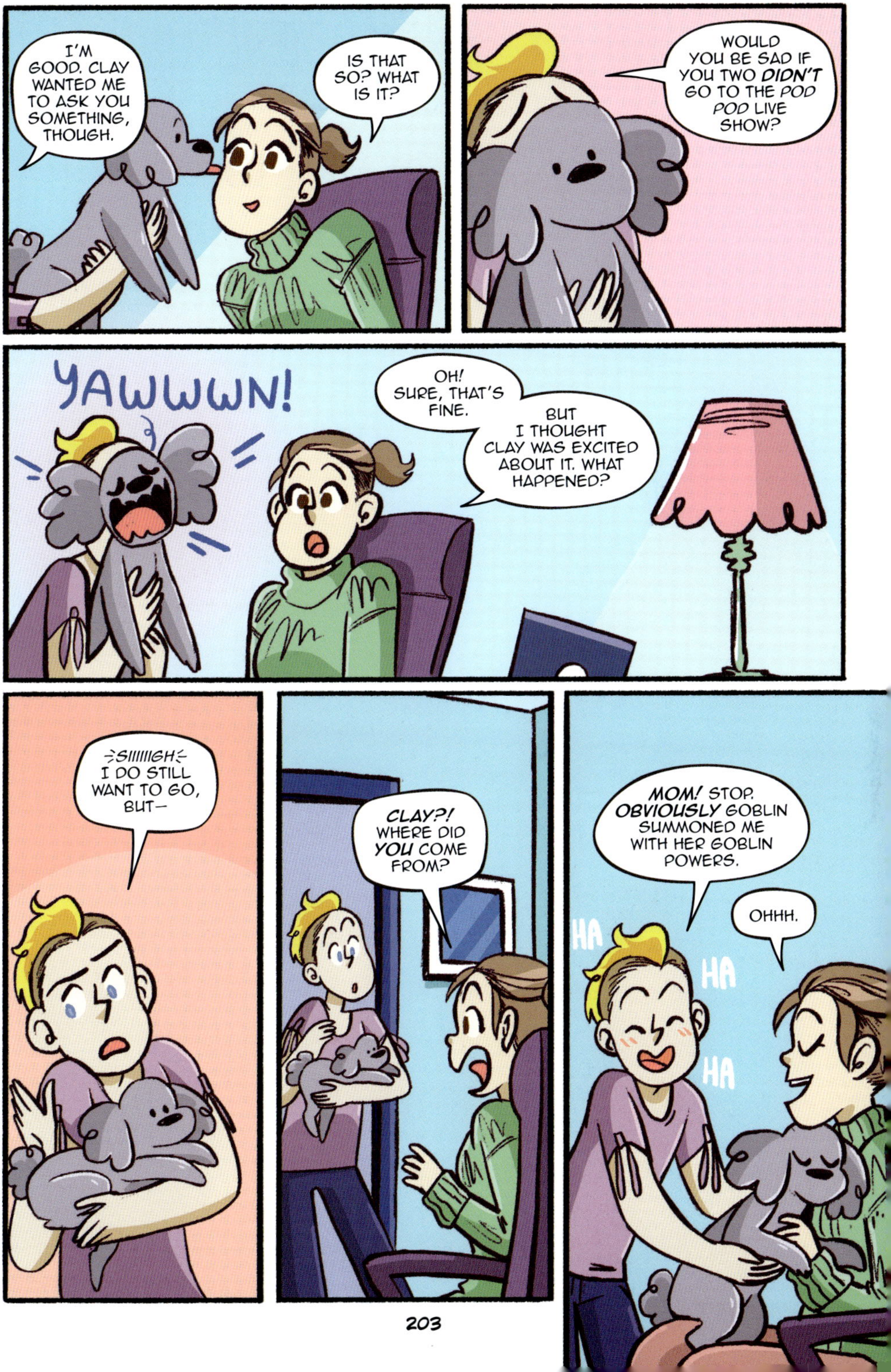
I'M GOOD. CLAY WANTED ME TO ASK YOU SOMETHING, THOUGH.
IS THAT SO? WHAT IS IT?
WOULD YOU BE SAD IF YOU TWO *DIDN'T* GO TO THE *POD POD* LIVE SHOW?
YAWWWN!
OH! SURE, THAT'S FINE.
BUT I THOUGHT CLAY WAS EXCITED ABOUT IT. WHAT HAPPENED?
SIIIIIGH
I DO STILL WANT TO GO, BUT—
CLAY?! WHERE DID *YOU* COME FROM?
MOM! STOP. ***OBVIOUSLY*** GOBLIN SUMMONED ME WITH HER GOBLIN POWERS.
HA
HA
HA
OHHH.

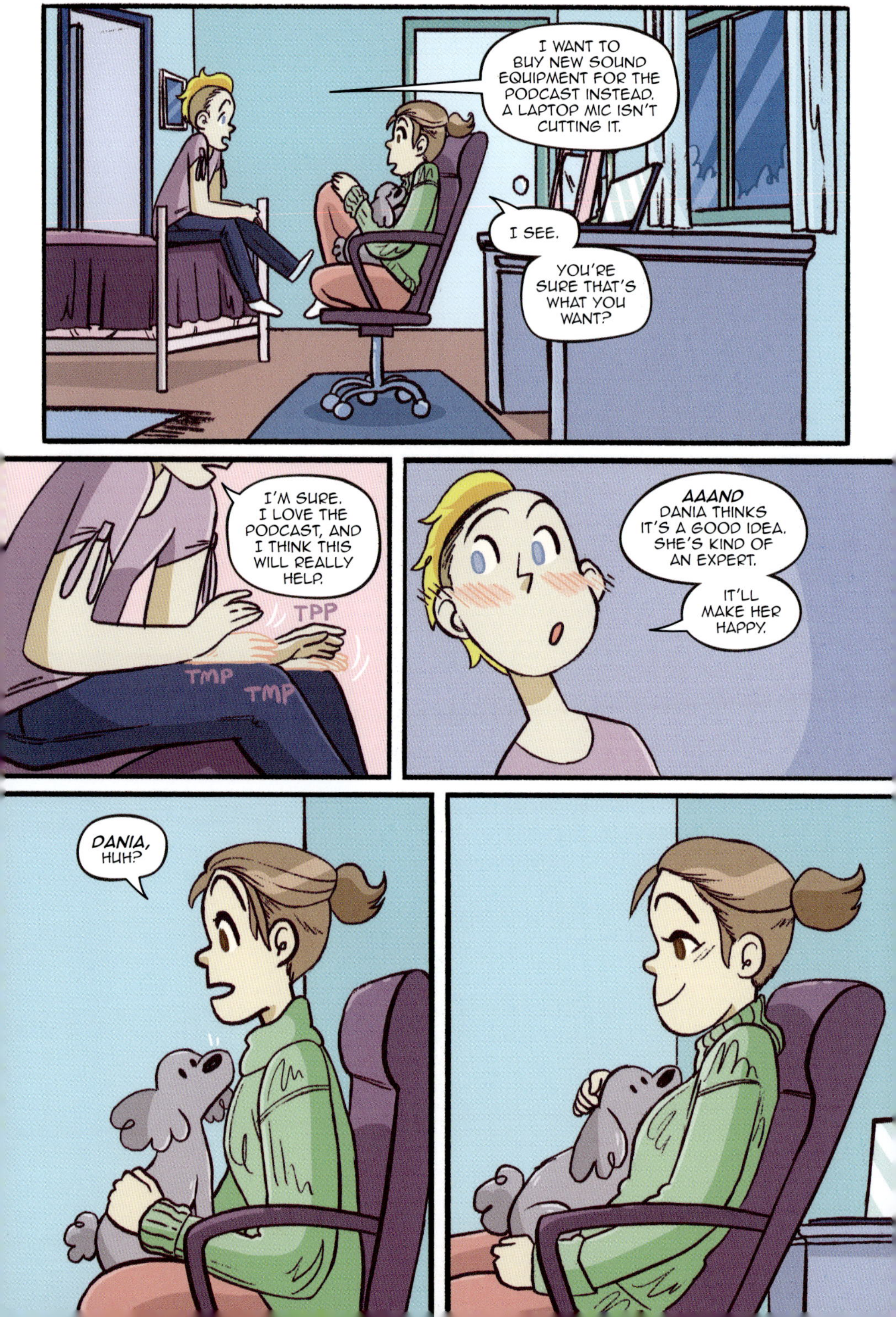
I WANT TO BUY NEW SOUND EQUIPMENT FOR THE PODCAST INSTEAD. A LAPTOP MIC ISN'T CUTTING IT.
I SEE.
YOU'RE SURE THAT'S WHAT YOU WANT?
I'M SURE. I LOVE THE PODCAST, AND I THINK THIS WILL REALLY HELP.
TPP
TMP
TMP
AAAND DANIA THINKS IT'S A GOOD IDEA. SHE'S KIND OF AN EXPERT.
IT'LL MAKE HER HAPPY.
DANIA, HUH?

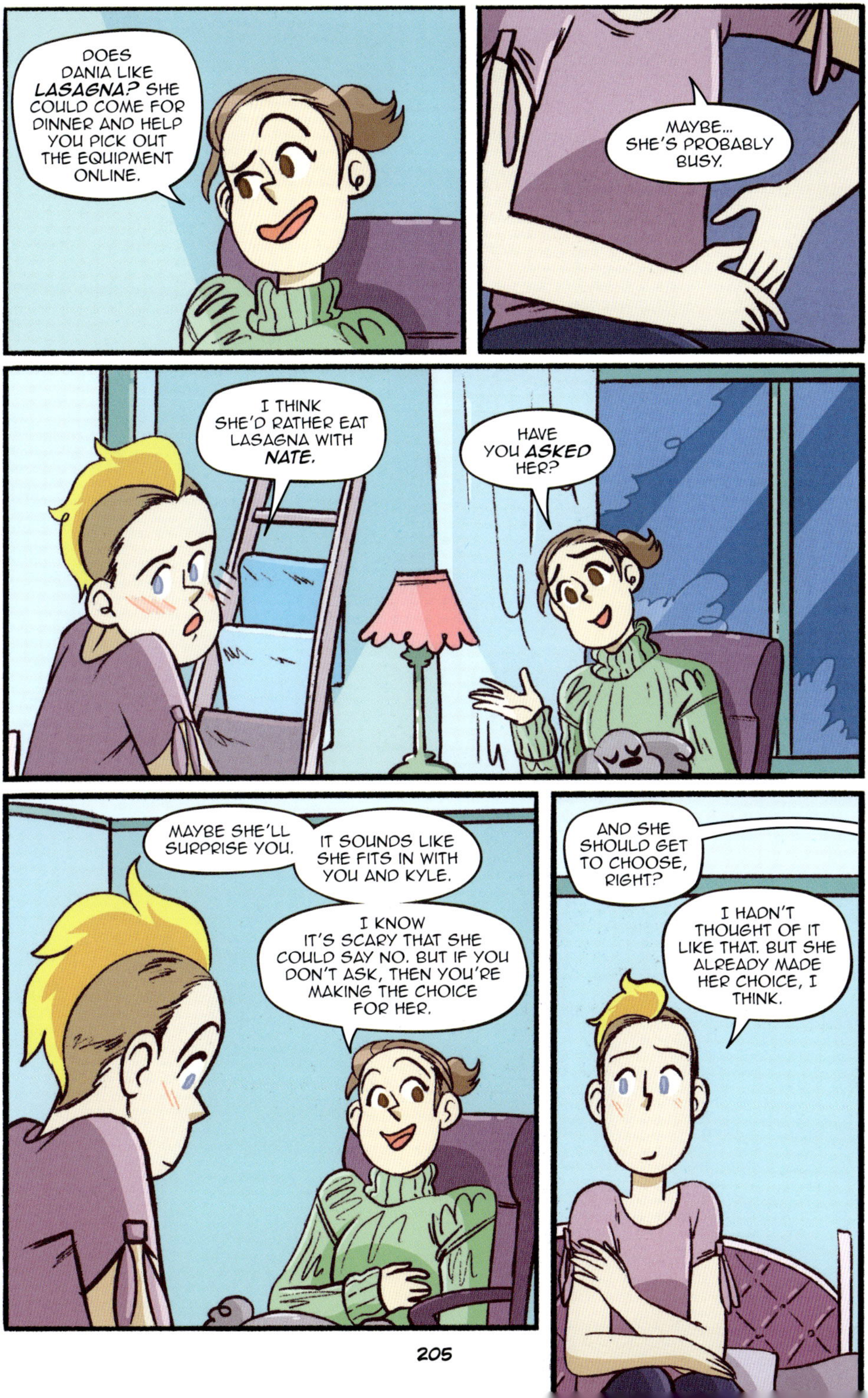
DOES DANIA LIKE LASAGNA? SHE COULD COME FOR DINNER AND HELP YOU PICK OUT THE EQUIPMENT ONLINE.
MAYBE... SHE'S PROBABLY BUSY.
I THINK SHE'D RATHER EAT LASAGNA WITH NATE.
HAVE YOU ASKED HER?
MAYBE SHE'LL SURPRISE YOU.
IT SOUNDS LIKE SHE FITS IN WITH YOU AND KYLE.
I KNOW IT'S SCARY THAT SHE COULD SAY NO. BUT IF YOU DON'T ASK, THEN YOU'RE MAKING THE CHOICE FOR HER.
AND SHE SHOULD GET TO CHOOSE, RIGHT?
I HADN'T THOUGHT OF IT LIKE THAT. BUT SHE ALREADY MADE HER CHOICE, I THINK.

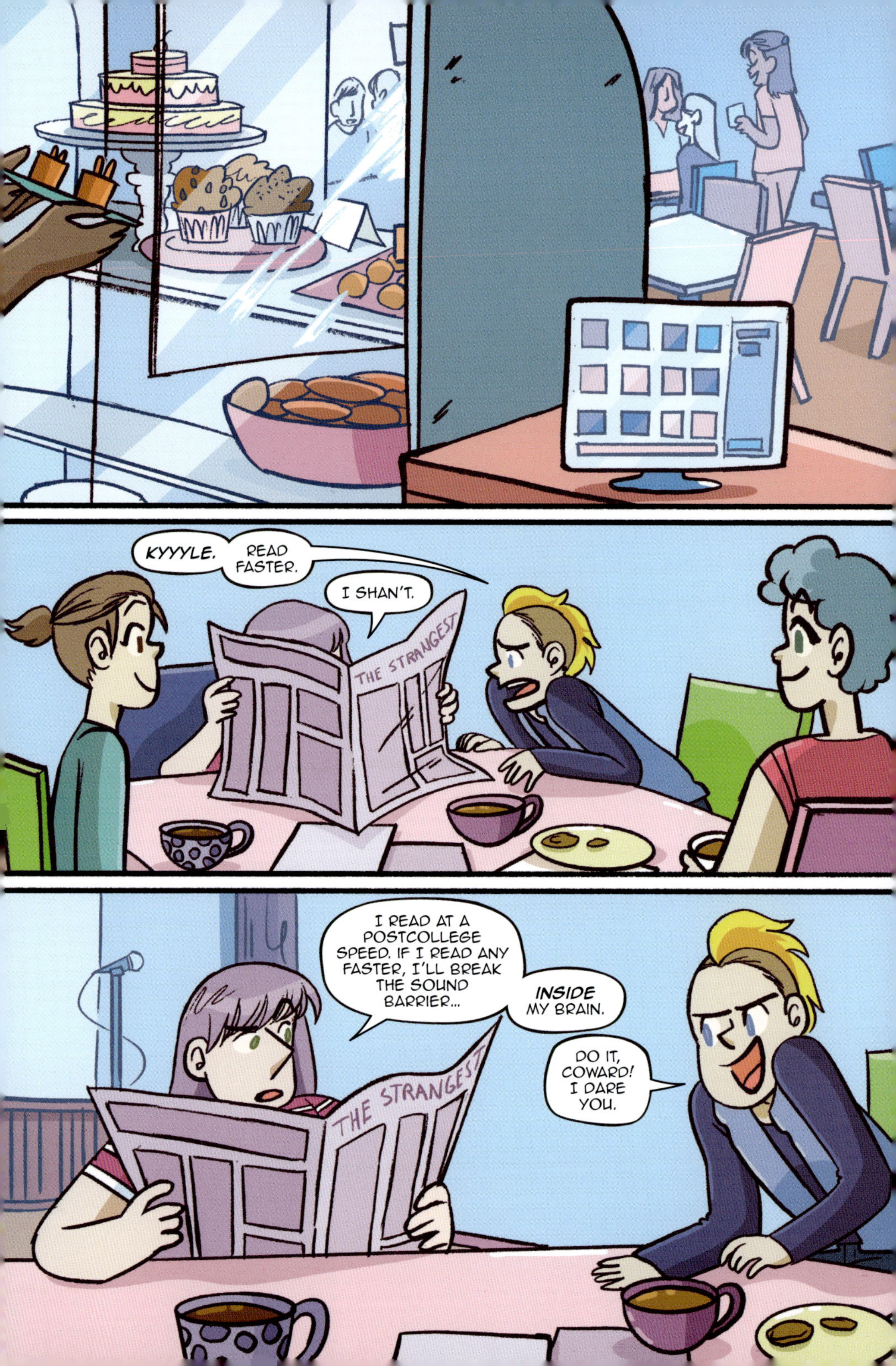
KYYYLE.
READ FASTER.
I SHAN'T.
THE STRANGEST
I READ AT A POSTCOLLEGE SPEED. IF I READ ANY FASTER, I'LL BREAK THE SOUND BARRIER...
INSIDE MY BRAIN.
THE STRANGEST
DO IT, COWARD! I DARE YOU.

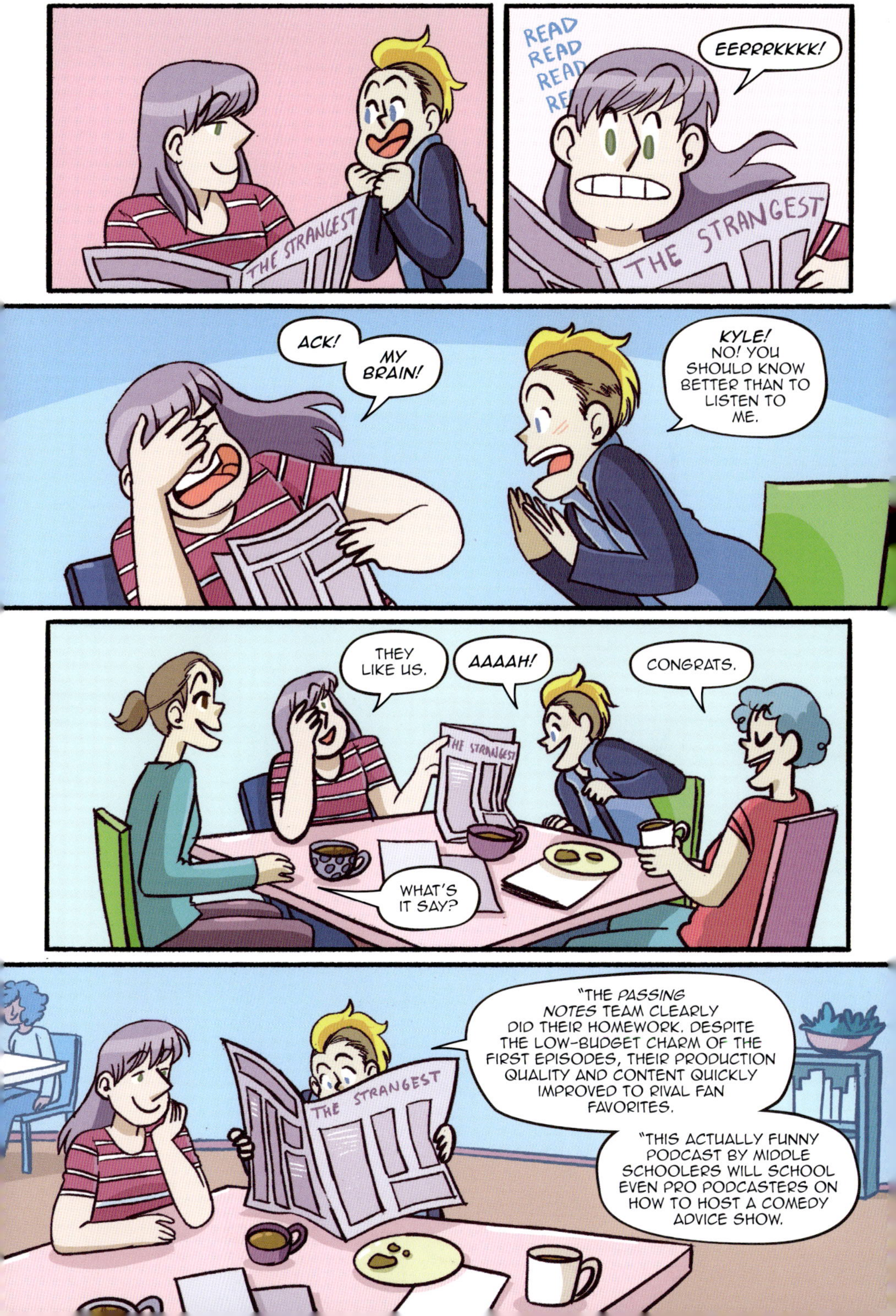
THE STRANGEST
READ READ READ RE
EERRRKKKK!
THE STRANGEST
ACK!
MY BRAIN!
KYLE! NO! YOU SHOULD KNOW BETTER THAN TO LISTEN TO ME.
THEY LIKE US.
AAAAH!
CONGRATS.
THE STRANGEST
WHAT'S IT SAY?
THE STRANGEST
"THE PASSING NOTES TEAM CLEARLY DID THEIR HOMEWORK. DESPITE THE LOW-BUDGET CHARM OF THE FIRST EPISODES, THEIR PRODUCTION QUALITY AND CONTENT QUICKLY IMPROVED TO RIVAL FAN FAVORITES.
"THIS ACTUALLY FUNNY PODCAST BY MIDDLE SCHOOLERS WILL SCHOOL EVEN PRO PODCASTERS ON HOW TO HOST A COMEDY ADVICE SHOW.

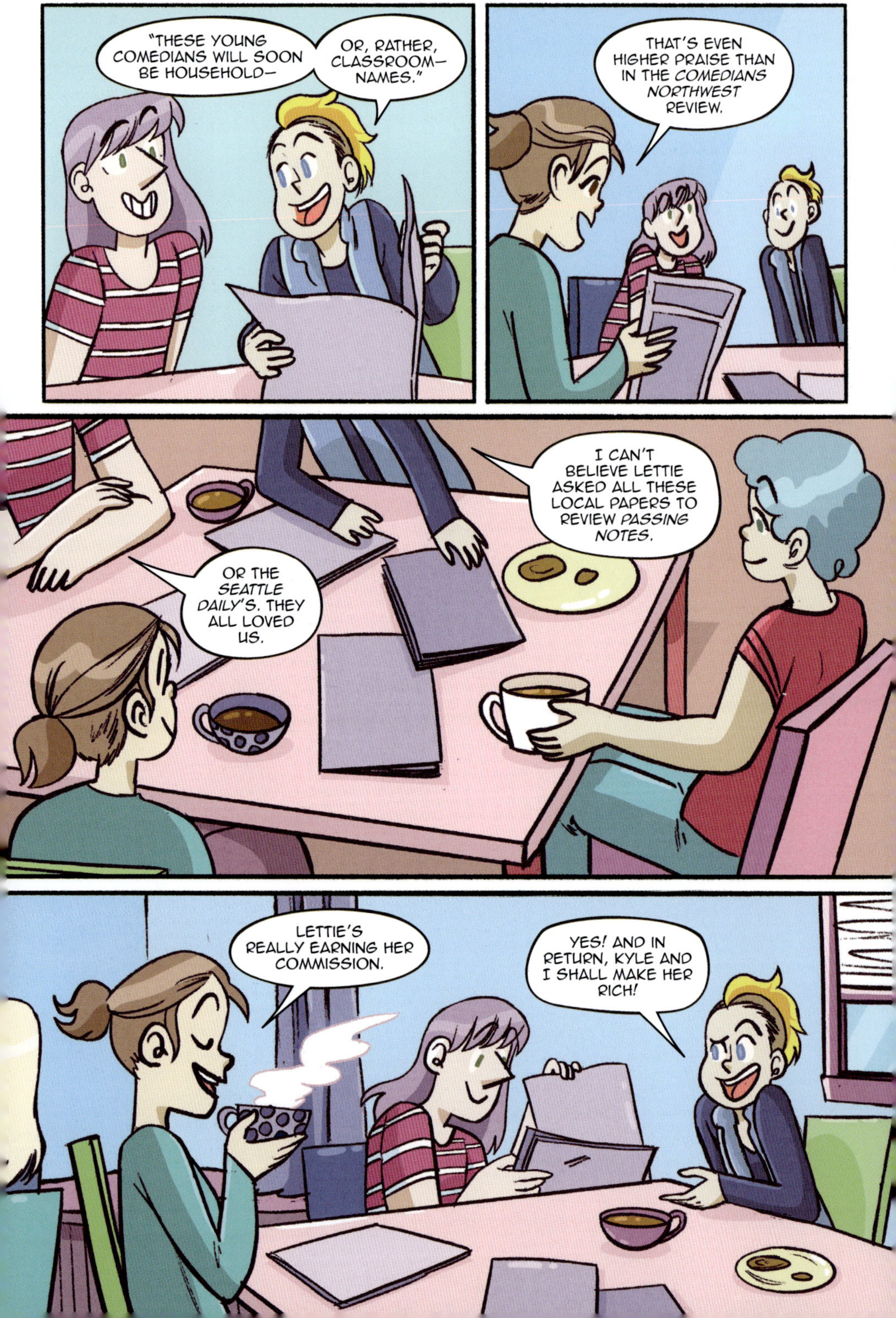
"THESE YOUNG COMEDIANS WILL SOON BE HOUSEHOLD—
OR, RATHER, CLASSROOM—NAMES."
THAT'S EVEN HIGHER PRAISE THAN IN THE *COMEDIANS NORTHWEST REVIEW*.
I CAN'T BELIEVE LETTIE ASKED ALL THESE LOCAL PAPERS TO REVIEW *PASSING NOTES*.
OR THE *SEATTLE DAILY*'S. THEY ALL LOVED US.
LETTIE'S REALLY EARNING HER COMMISSION.
YES! AND IN RETURN, KYLE AND I SHALL MAKE HER RICH!

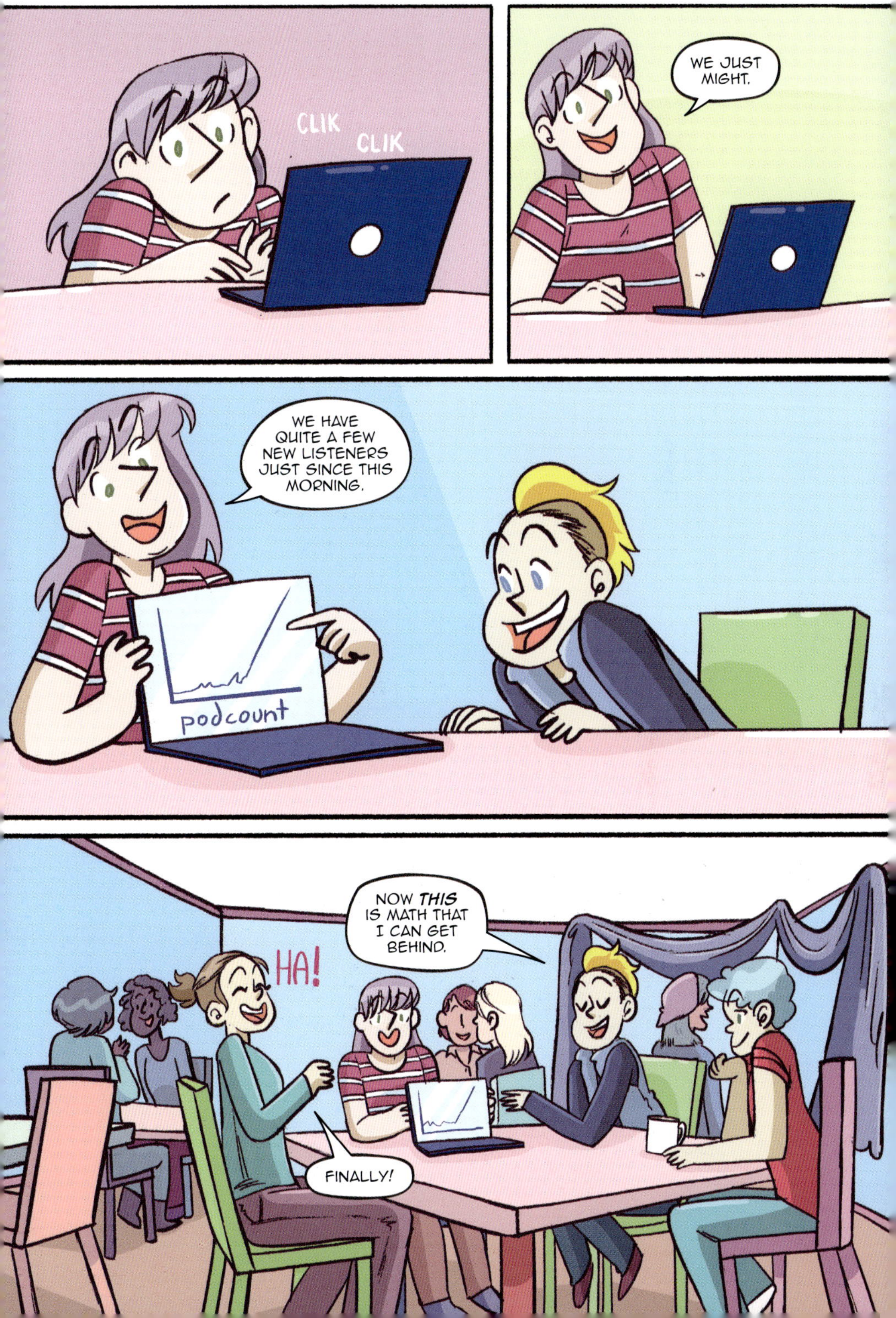
CLIK
CLIK
WE JUST MIGHT.
WE HAVE QUITE A FEW NEW LISTENERS JUST SINCE THIS MORNING.
podcount
NOW *THIS* IS MATH THAT I CAN GET BEHIND.
HA!
FINALLY!

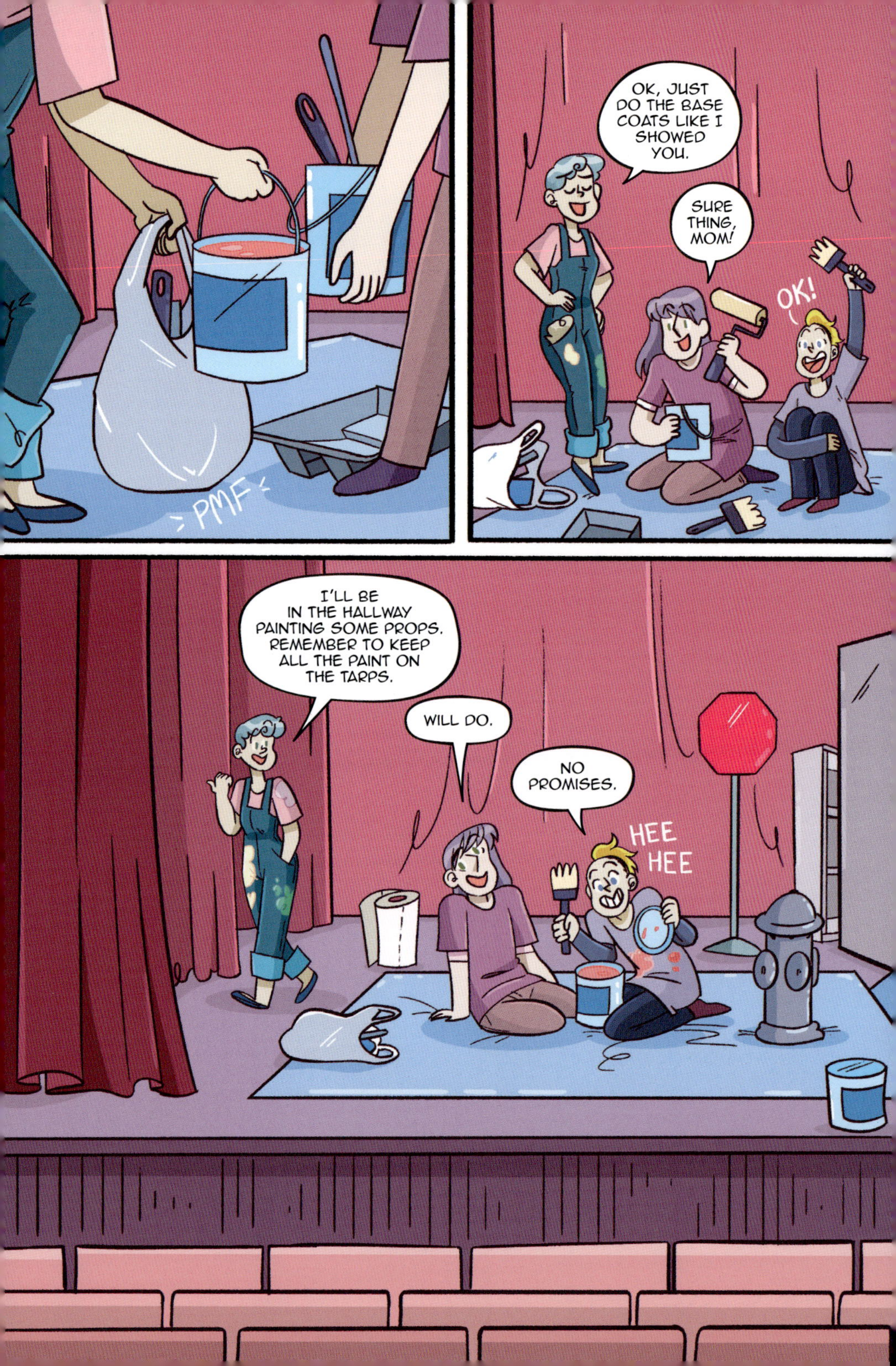

PMF
OK, JUST DO THE BASE COATS LIKE I SHOWED YOU.
SURE THING, MOM!
OK!
I'LL BE IN THE HALLWAY PAINTING SOME PROPS. REMEMBER TO KEEP ALL THE PAINT ON THE TARPS.
WILL DO.
NO PROMISES.
HEE HEE

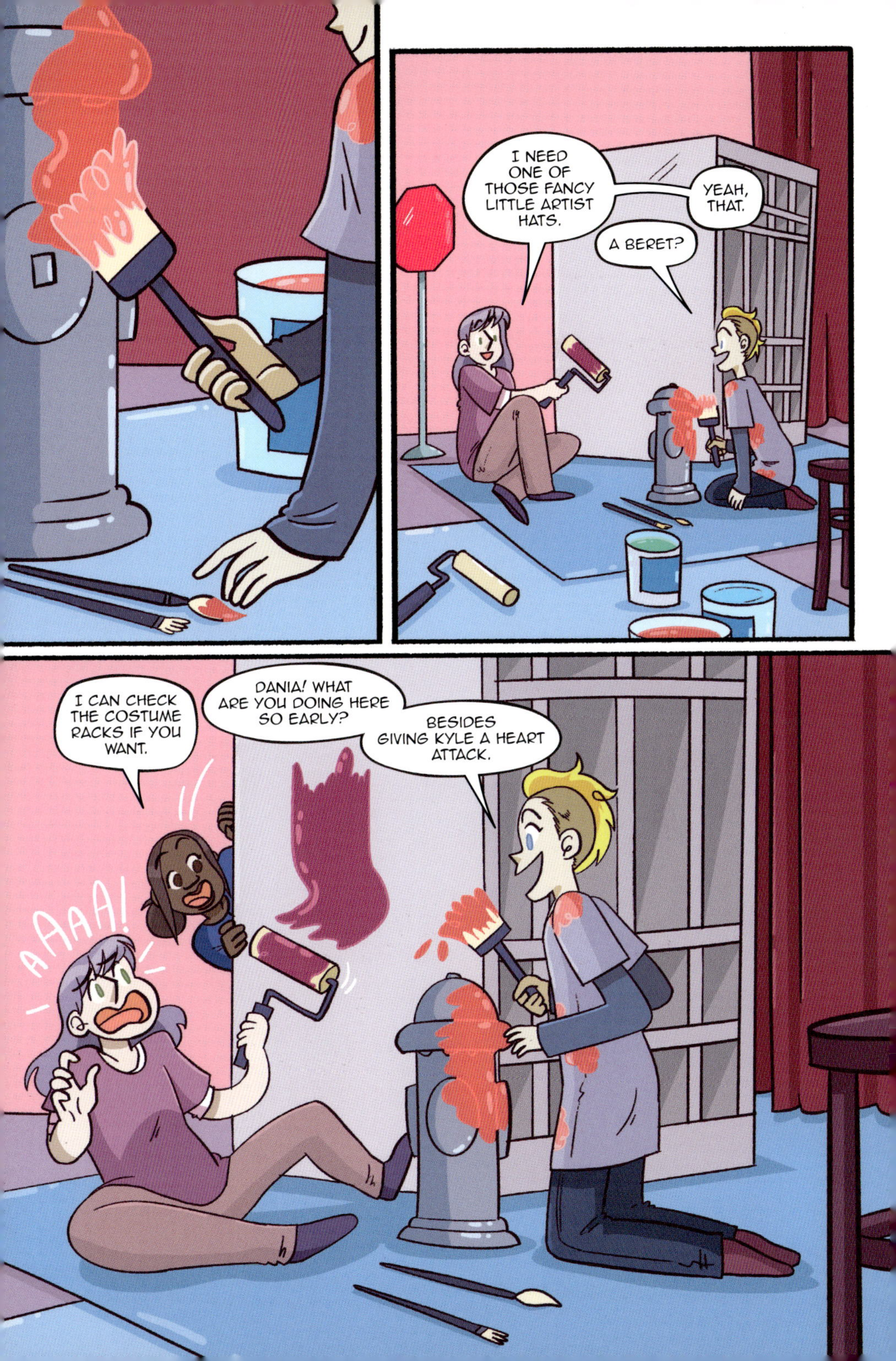
I NEED ONE OF THOSE FANCY LITTLE ARTIST HATS.
A BERET?
YEAH, THAT.
I CAN CHECK THE COSTUME RACKS IF YOU WANT.
DANIA! WHAT ARE YOU DOING HERE SO EARLY?
BESIDES GIVING KYLE A HEART ATTACK.
AAAA!

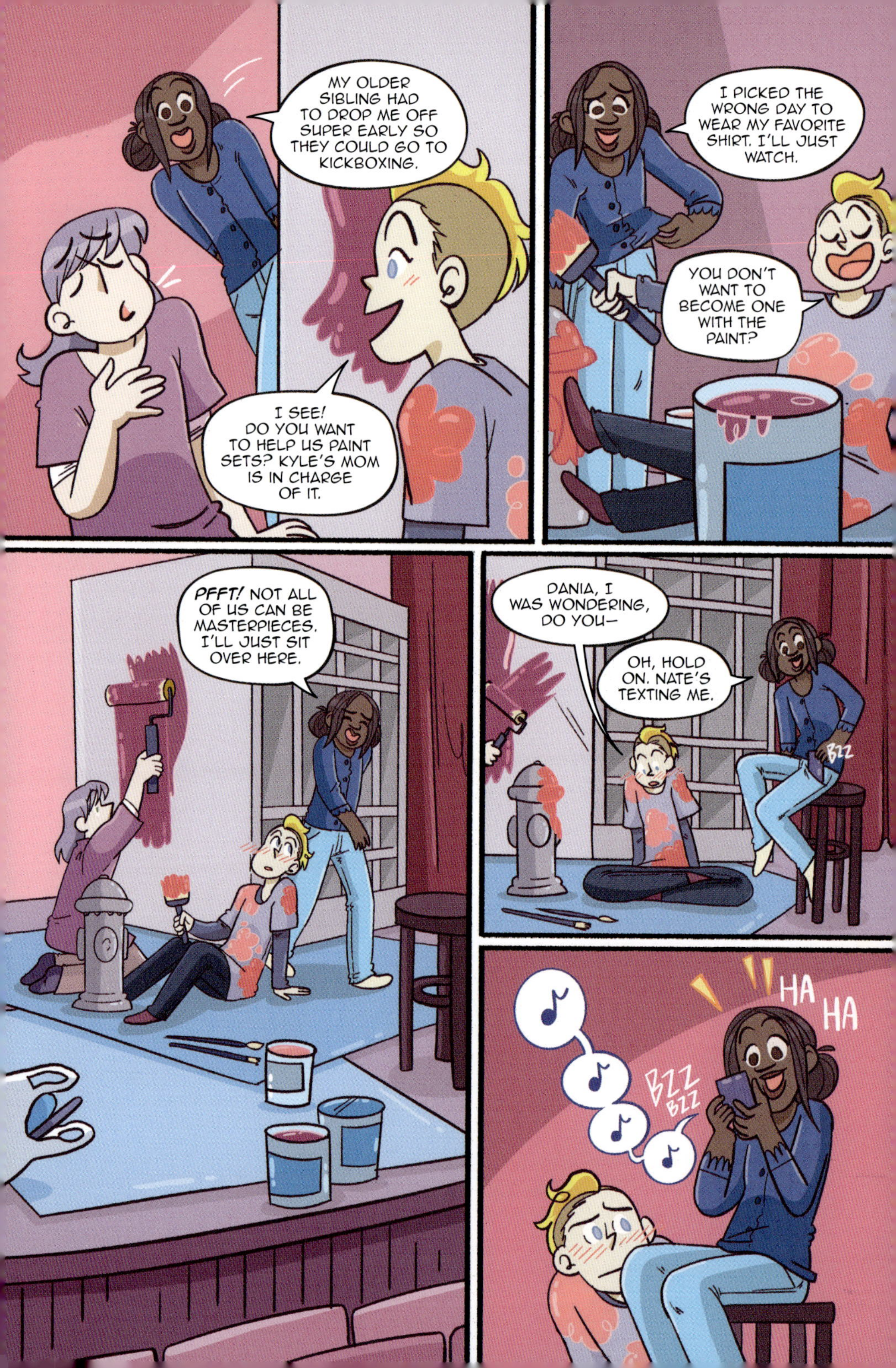
MY OLDER SIBLING HAD TO DROP ME OFF SUPER EARLY SO THEY COULD GO TO KICKBOXING.
I SEE! DO YOU WANT TO HELP US PAINT SETS? KYLE'S MOM IS IN CHARGE OF IT.
I PICKED THE WRONG DAY TO WEAR MY FAVORITE SHIRT. I'LL JUST WATCH.
YOU DON'T WANT TO BECOME ONE WITH THE PAINT?
PFFT! NOT ALL OF US CAN BE MASTERPIECES. I'LL JUST SIT OVER HERE.
DANIA, I WAS WONDERING, DO YOU—
OH, HOLD ON. NATE'S TEXTING ME.
BZZ
HA HA
BZZ BZZ

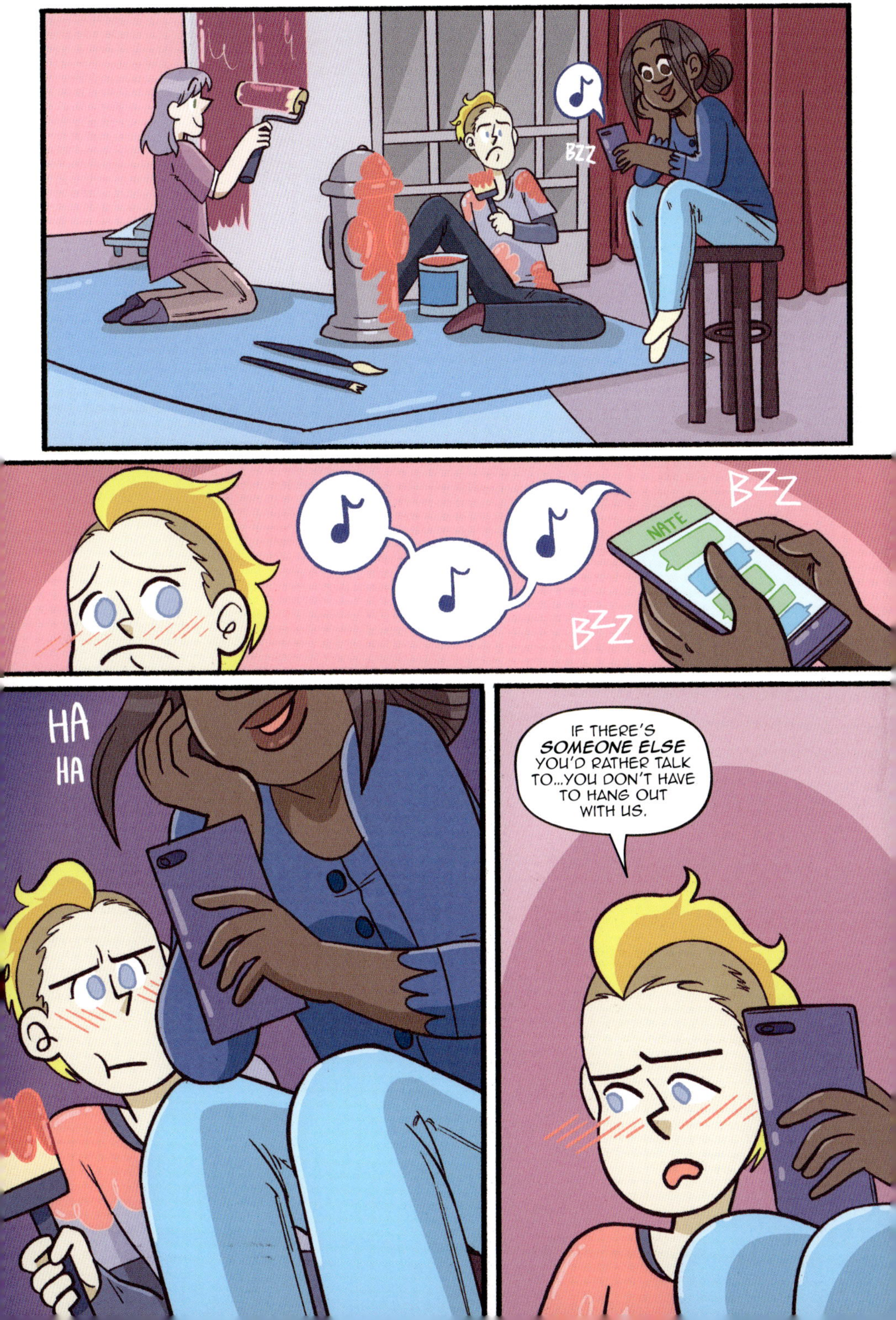
BZZ
BZZ
NATE
BZZ
HA
HA
IF THERE'S *SOMEONE ELSE* YOU'D RATHER TALK TO...YOU DON'T HAVE TO HANG OUT WITH US.

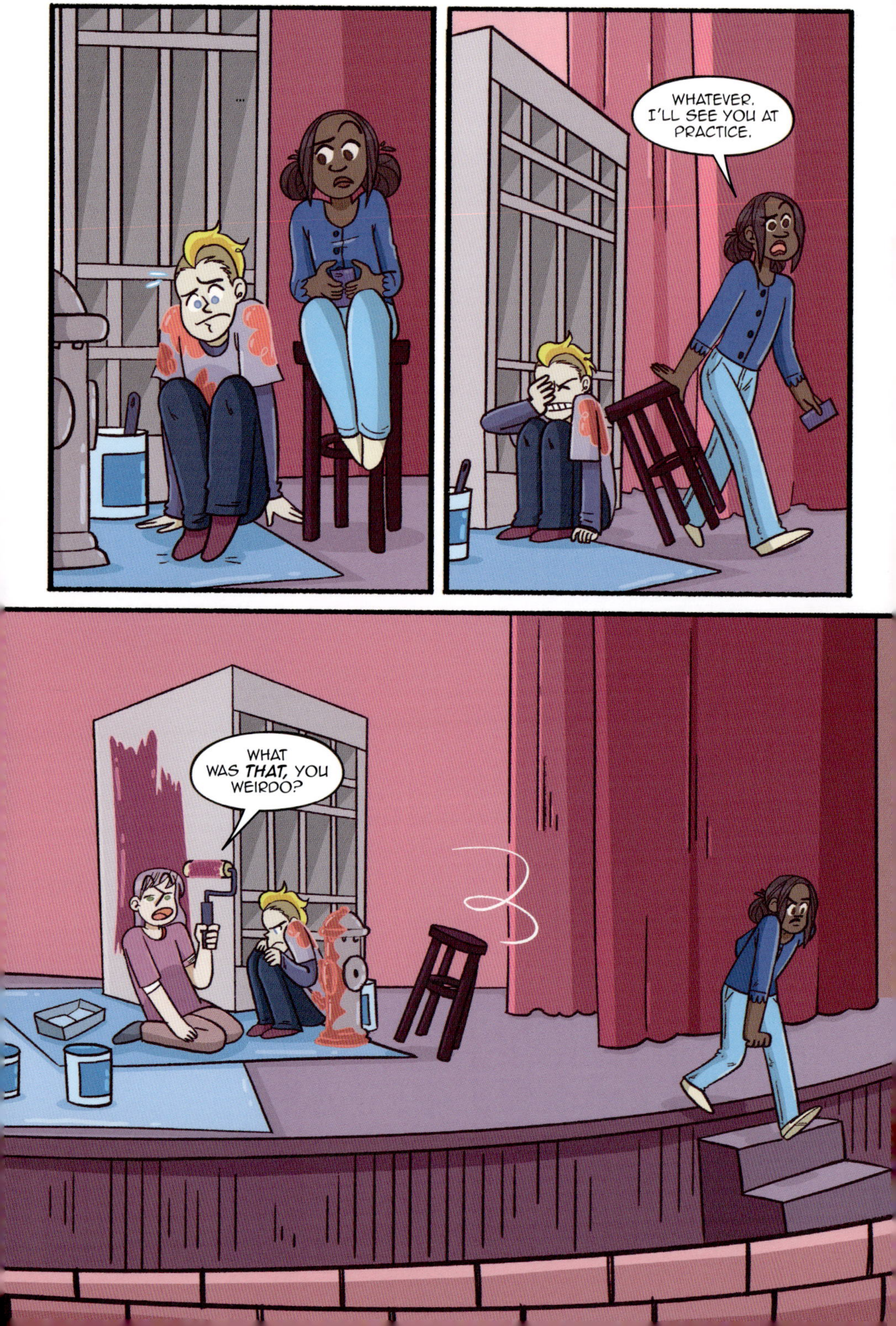
...
WHATEVER. I'LL SEE YOU AT PRACTICE.
WHAT WAS ***THAT,*** YOU WEIRDO?

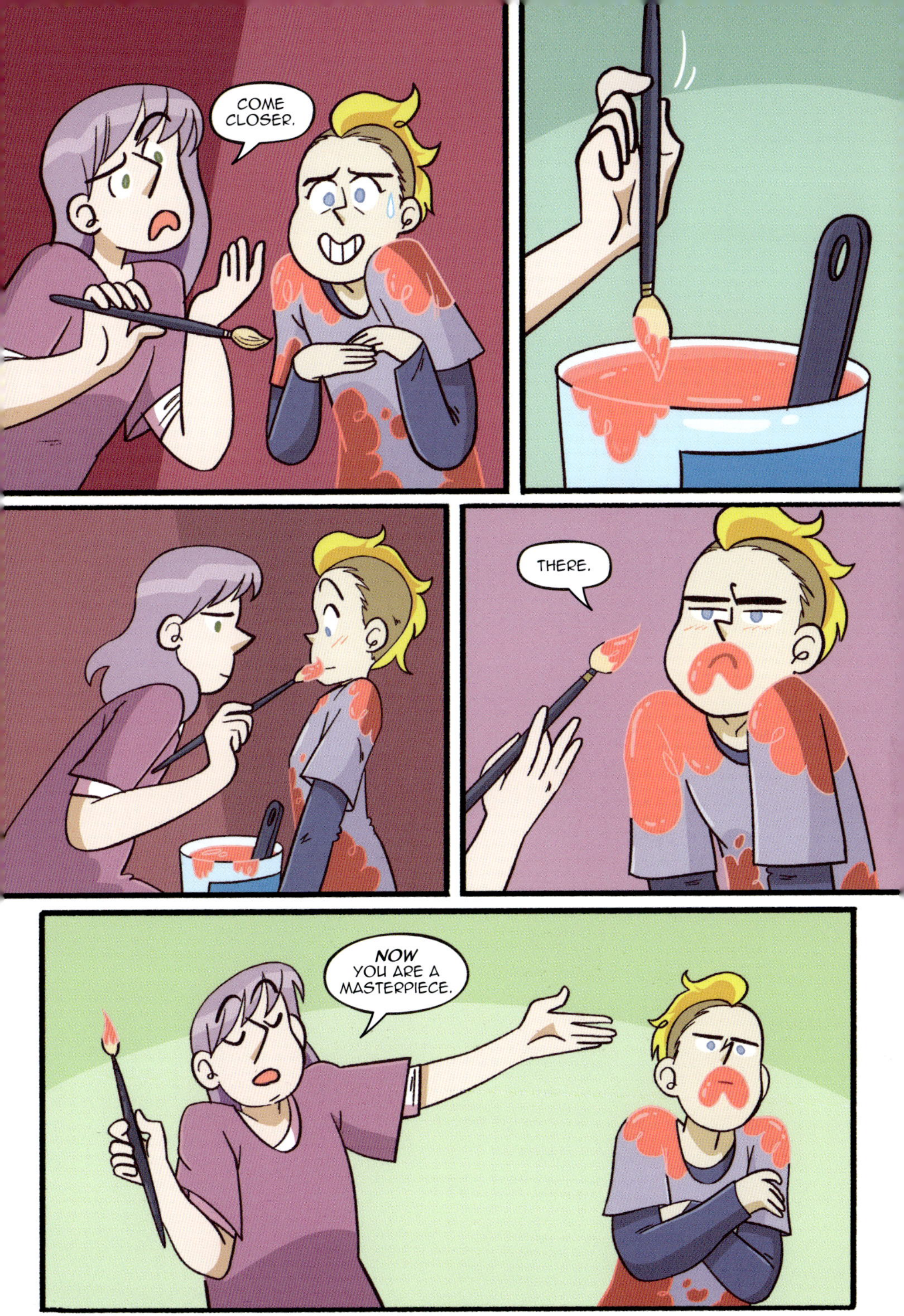
COME CLOSER.
THERE.
NOW YOU ARE A MASTERPIECE.

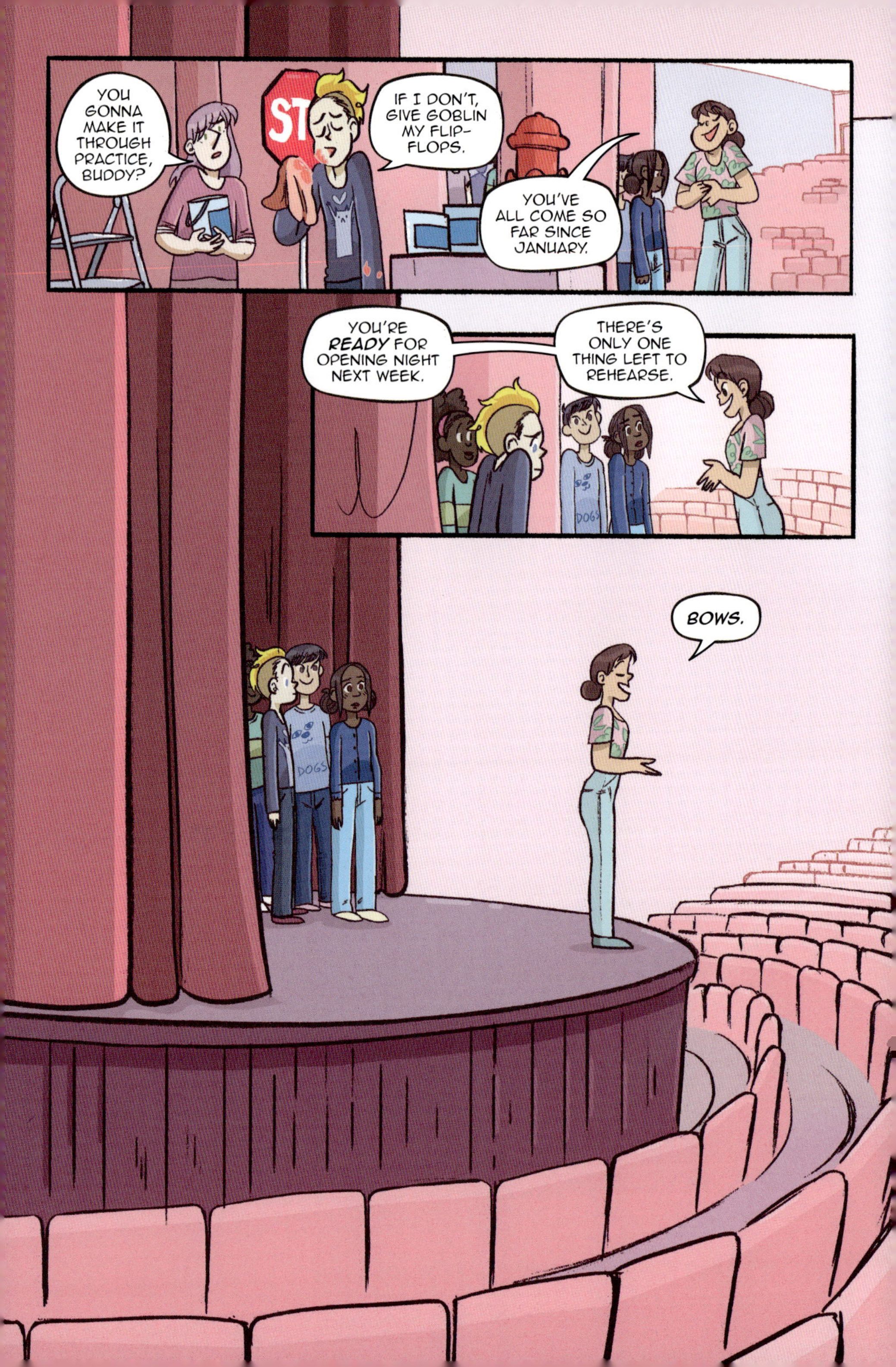
YOU GONNA MAKE IT THROUGH PRACTICE, BUDDY?
ST
IF I DON'T, GIVE GOBLIN MY FLIP-FLOPS.
YOU'VE ALL COME SO FAR SINCE JANUARY.
YOU'RE *READY* FOR OPENING NIGHT NEXT WEEK.
THERE'S ONLY ONE THING LEFT TO REHEARSE.
DOGS
BOWS.

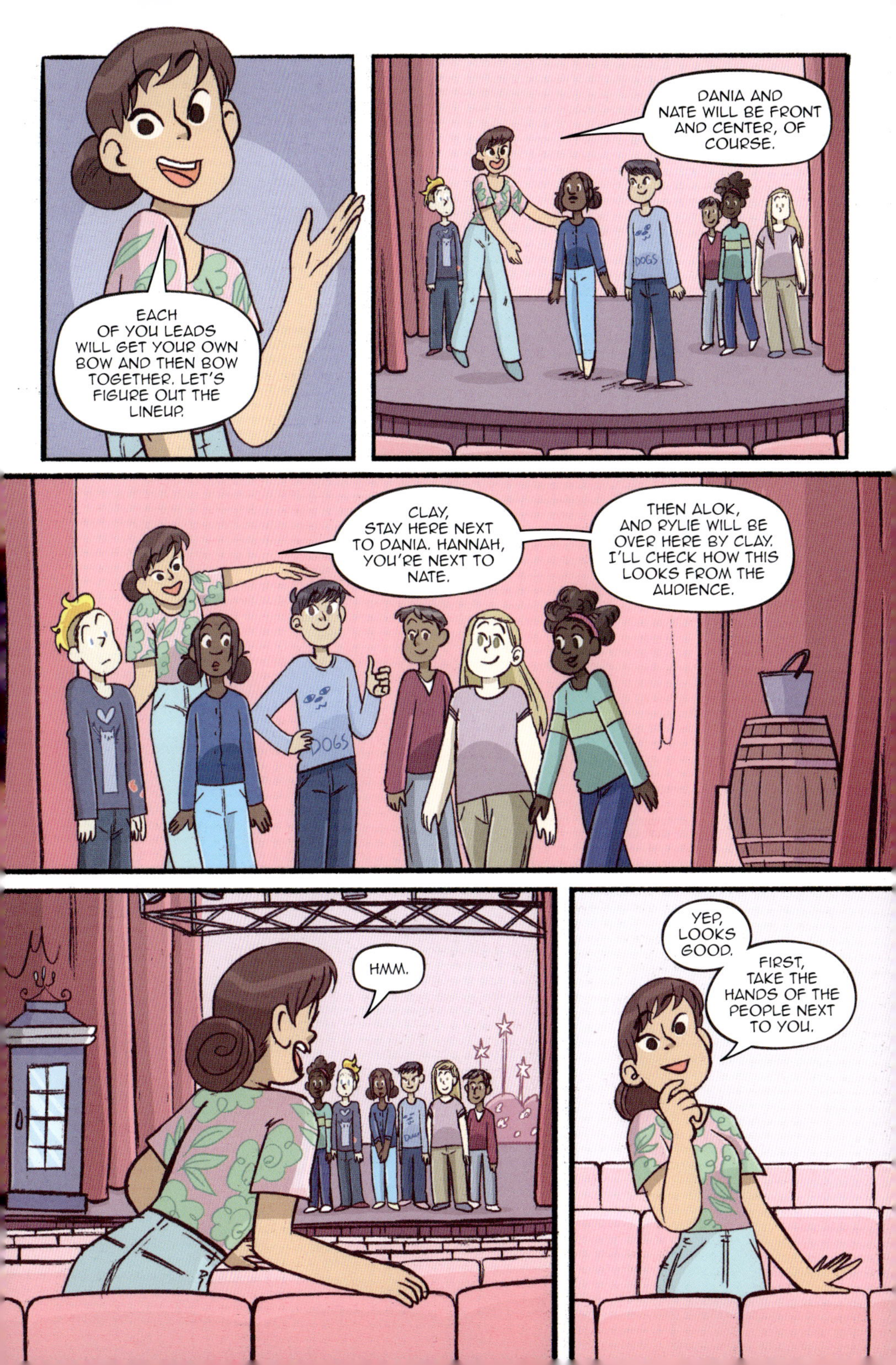
EACH OF YOU LEADS WILL GET YOUR OWN BOW AND THEN BOW TOGETHER. LET'S FIGURE OUT THE LINEUP.
DANIA AND NATE WILL BE FRONT AND CENTER, OF COURSE.
CLAY, STAY HERE NEXT TO DANIA. HANNAH, YOU'RE NEXT TO NATE.
THEN ALOK, AND RYLIE WILL BE OVER HERE BY CLAY. I'LL CHECK HOW THIS LOOKS FROM THE AUDIENCE.
HMM.
YEP, LOOKS GOOD.
FIRST, TAKE THE HANDS OF THE PEOPLE NEXT TO YOU.

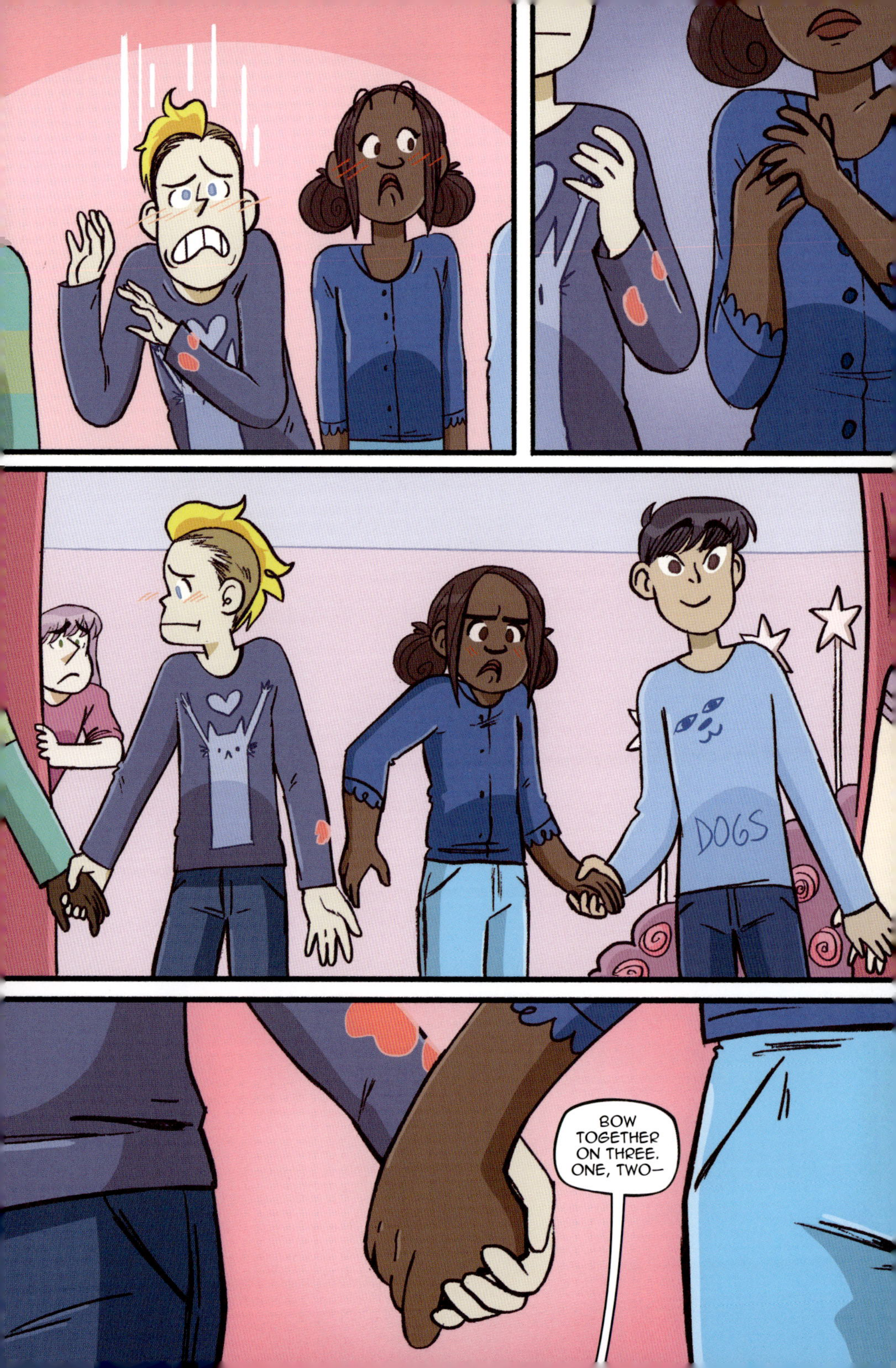
DOGS
BOW TOGETHER ON THREE. ONE, TWO—

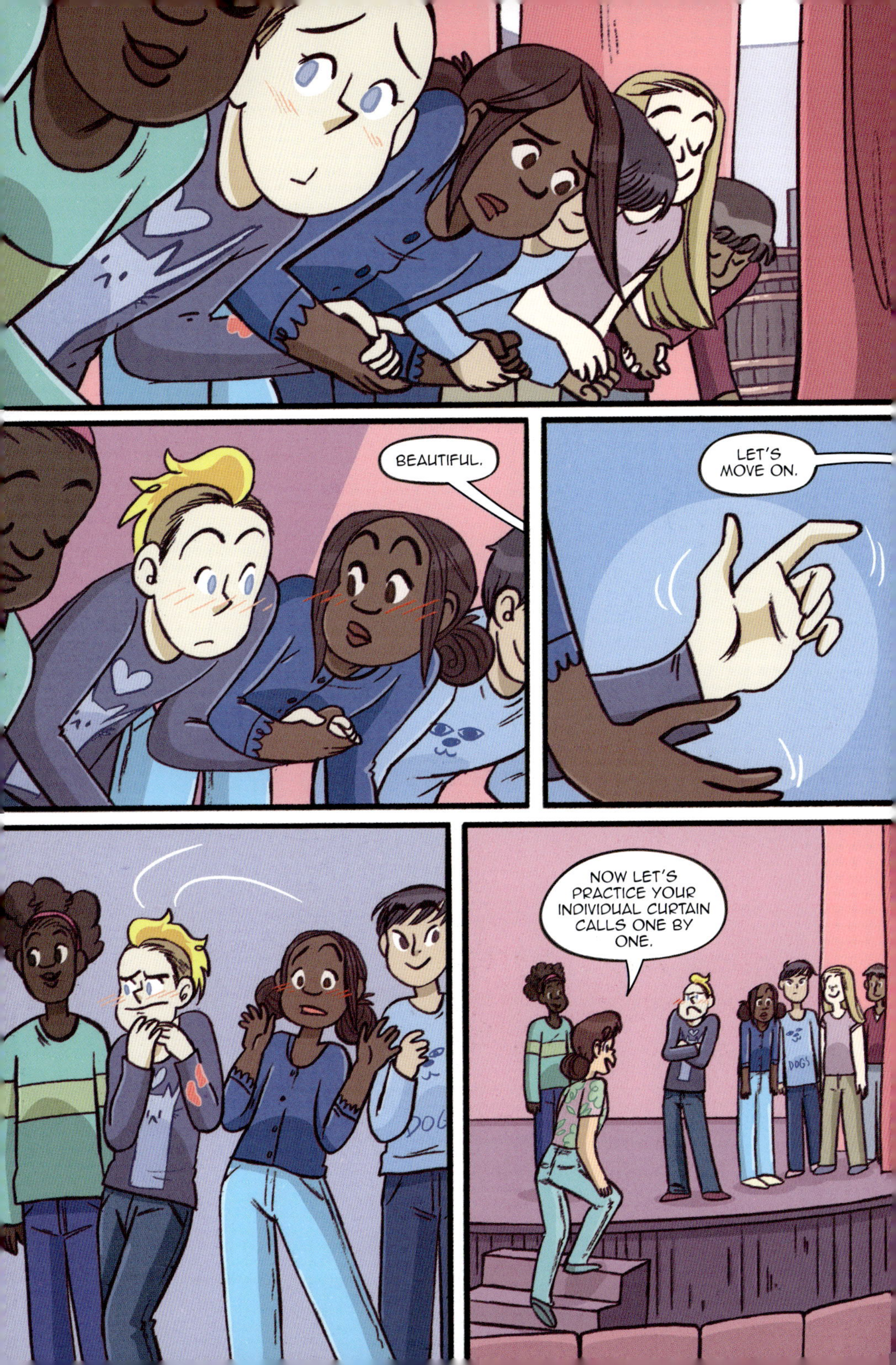
BEAUTIFUL.
LET'S MOVE ON.
NOW LET'S PRACTICE YOUR INDIVIDUAL CURTAIN CALLS ONE BY ONE.

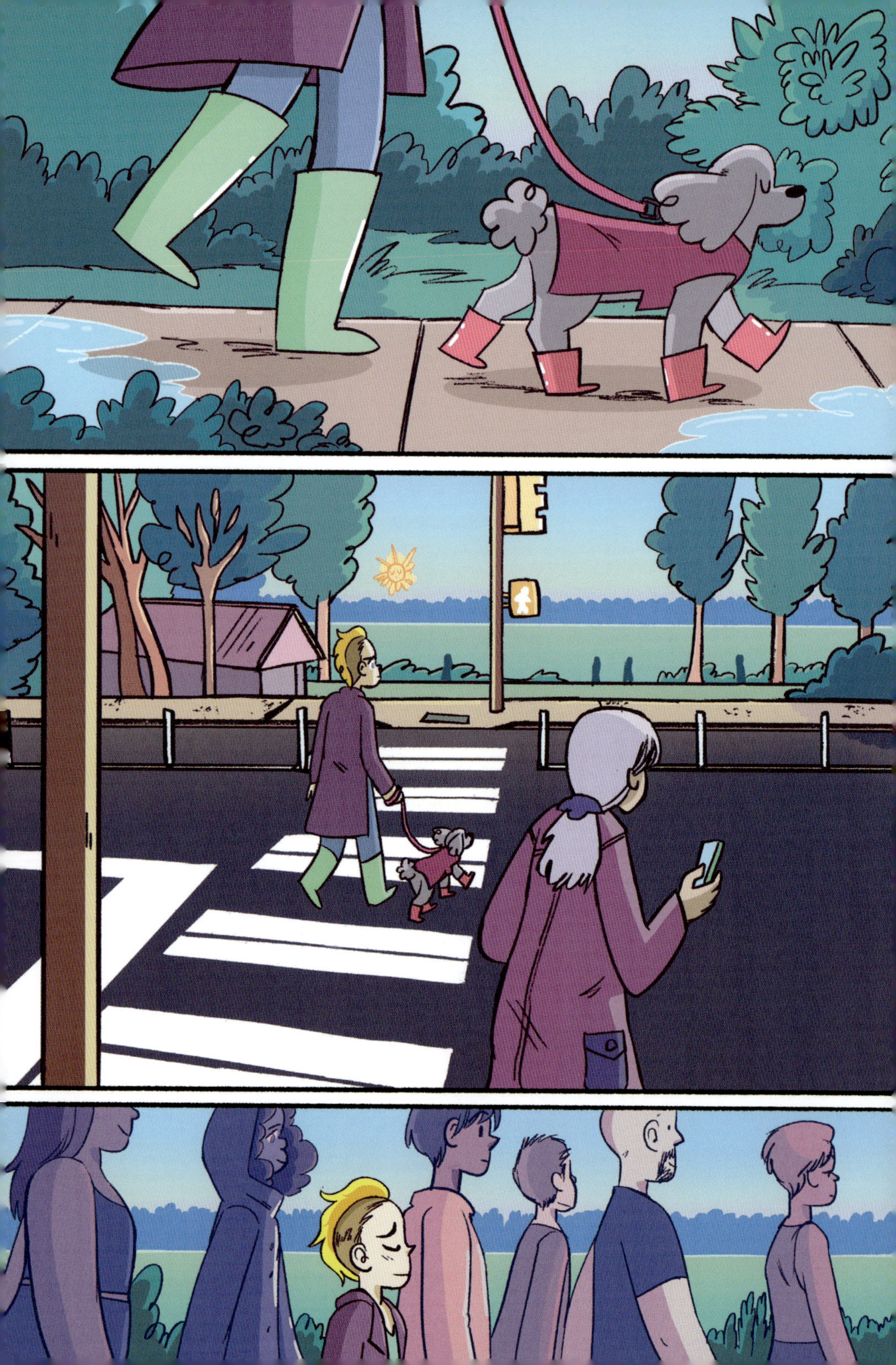

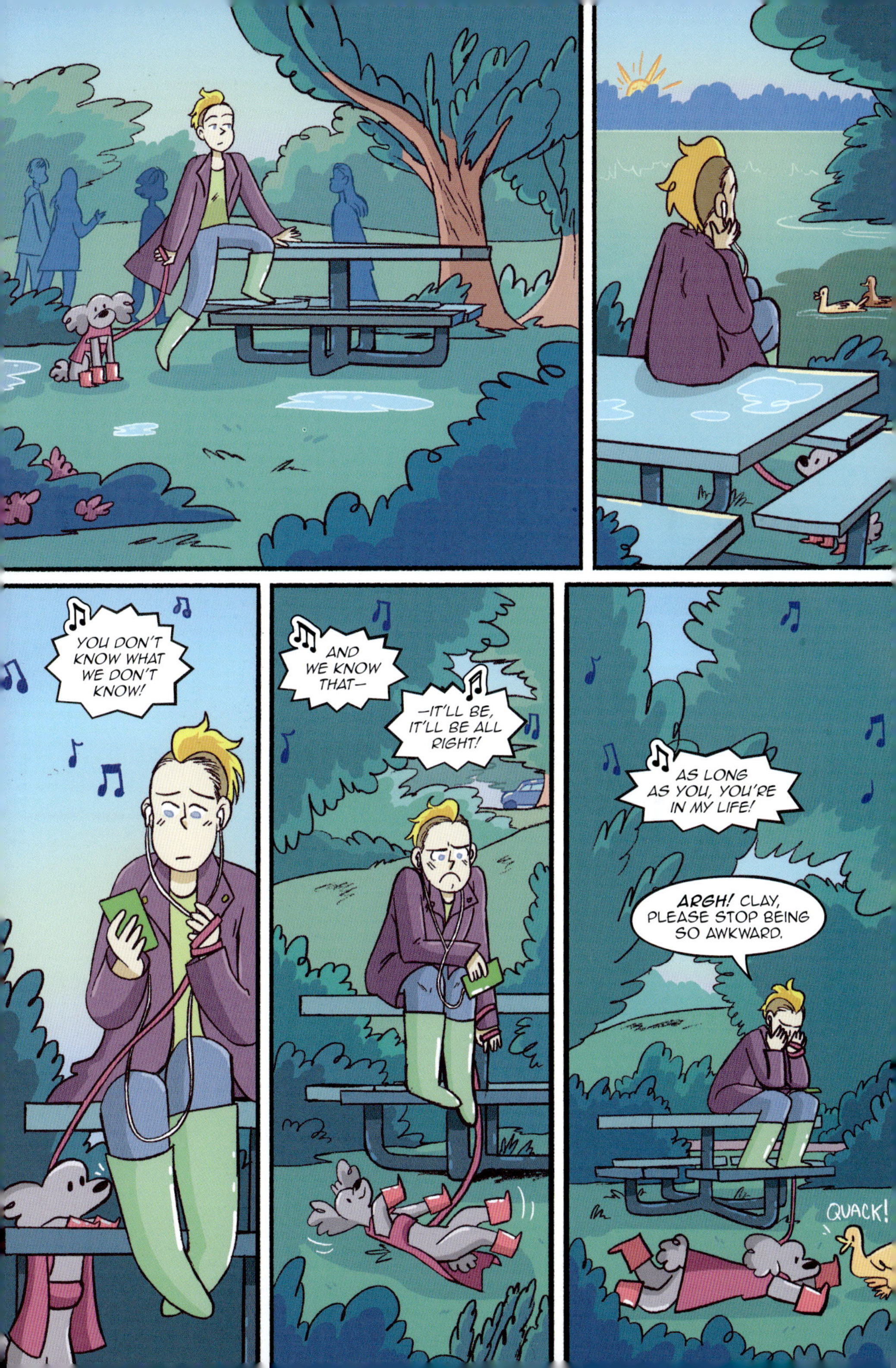
YOU DON'T KNOW WHAT WE DON'T KNOW!
AND WE KNOW THAT—
—IT'LL BE, IT'LL BE ALL RIGHT!
AS LONG AS YOU, YOU'RE IN MY LIFE!
ARGH! CLAY, PLEASE STOP BEING SO AWKWARD.
QUACK!

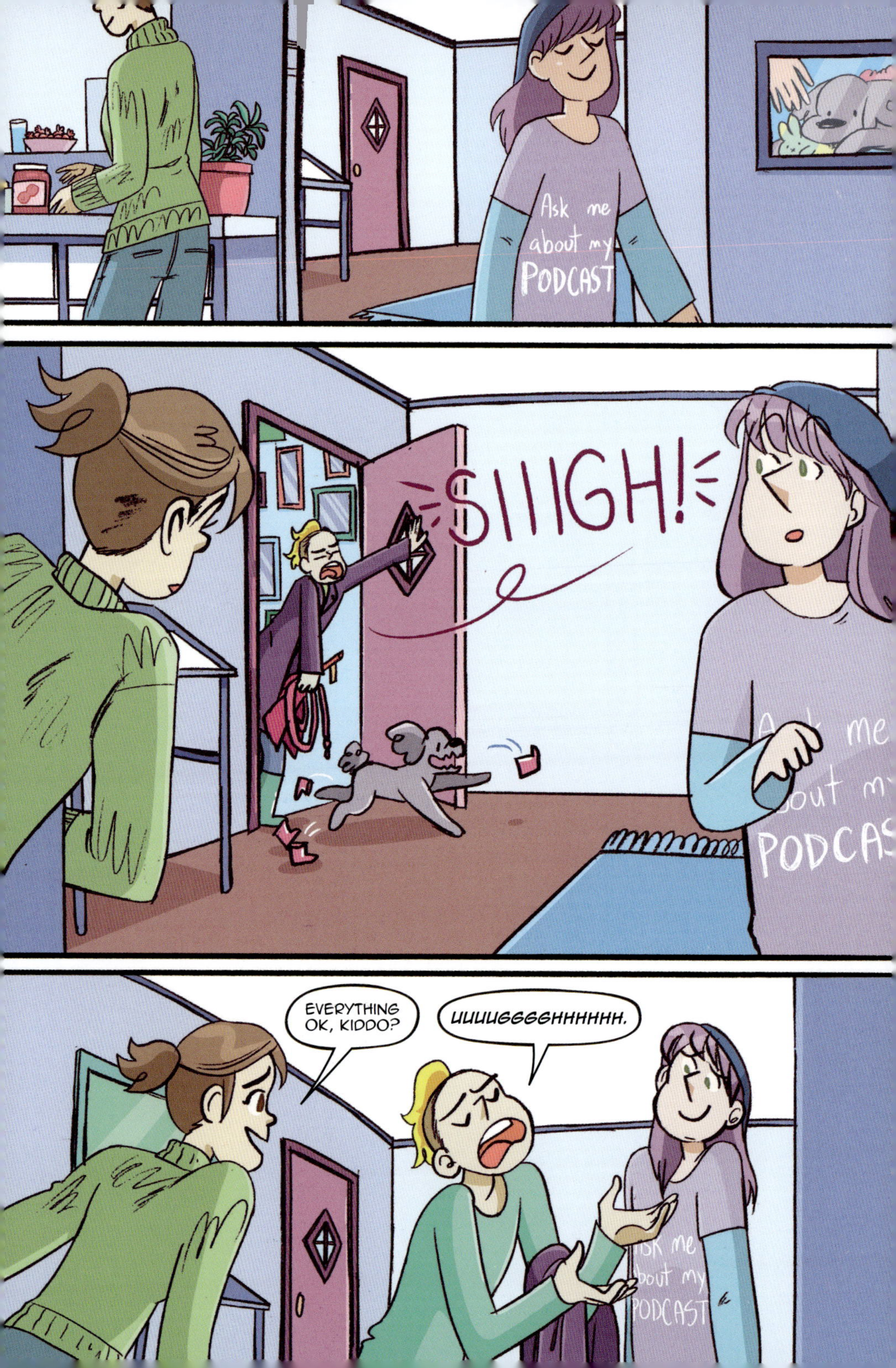

Ask me about my PODCAST
SIIIGH!
EVERYTHING OK, KIDDO?
UUUUGGGGHHHHHH.

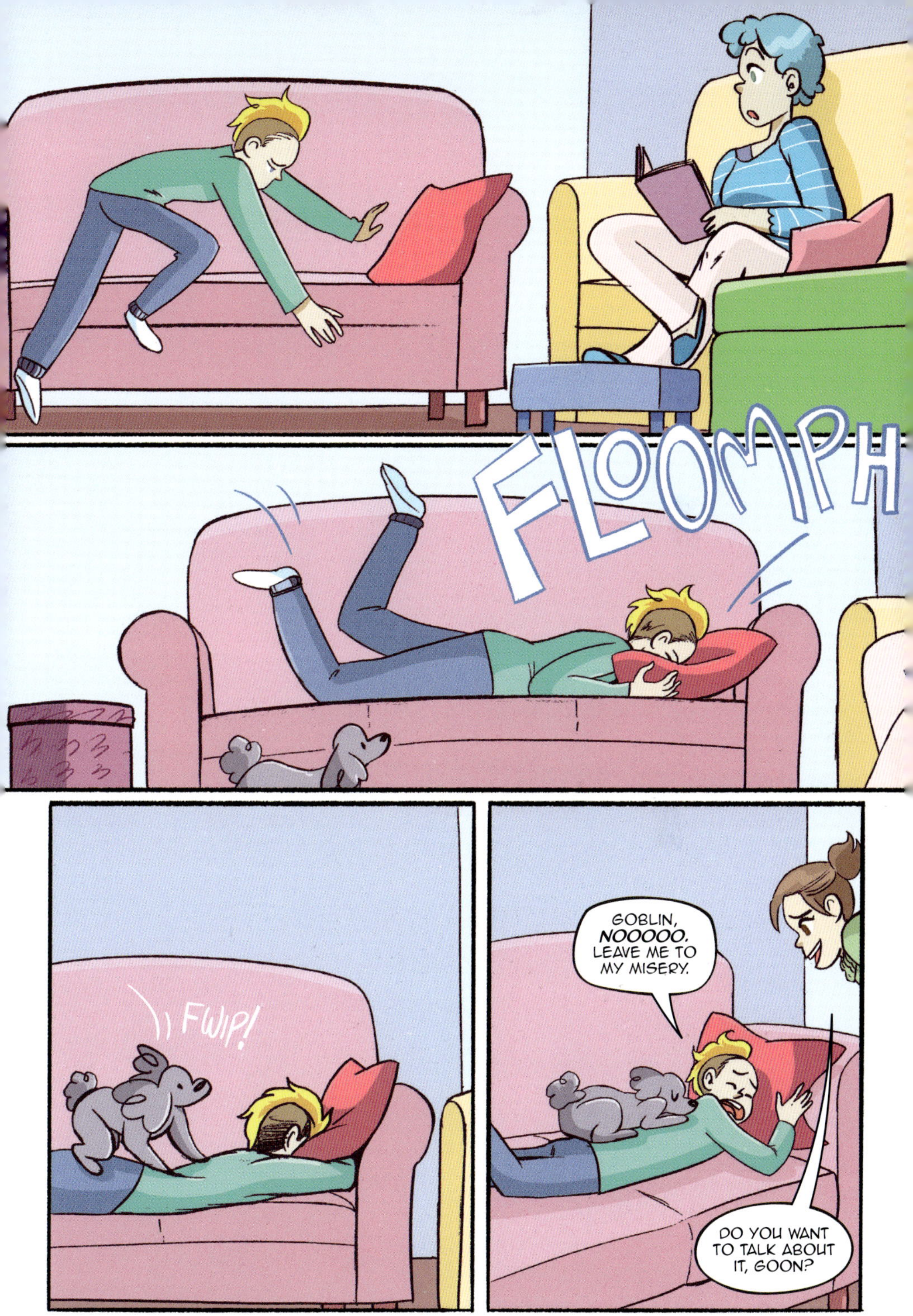
FLOOMPH
FWIP!
GOBLIN, **NOOOOO.** LEAVE ME TO MY MISERY.
DO YOU WANT TO TALK ABOUT IT, GOON?

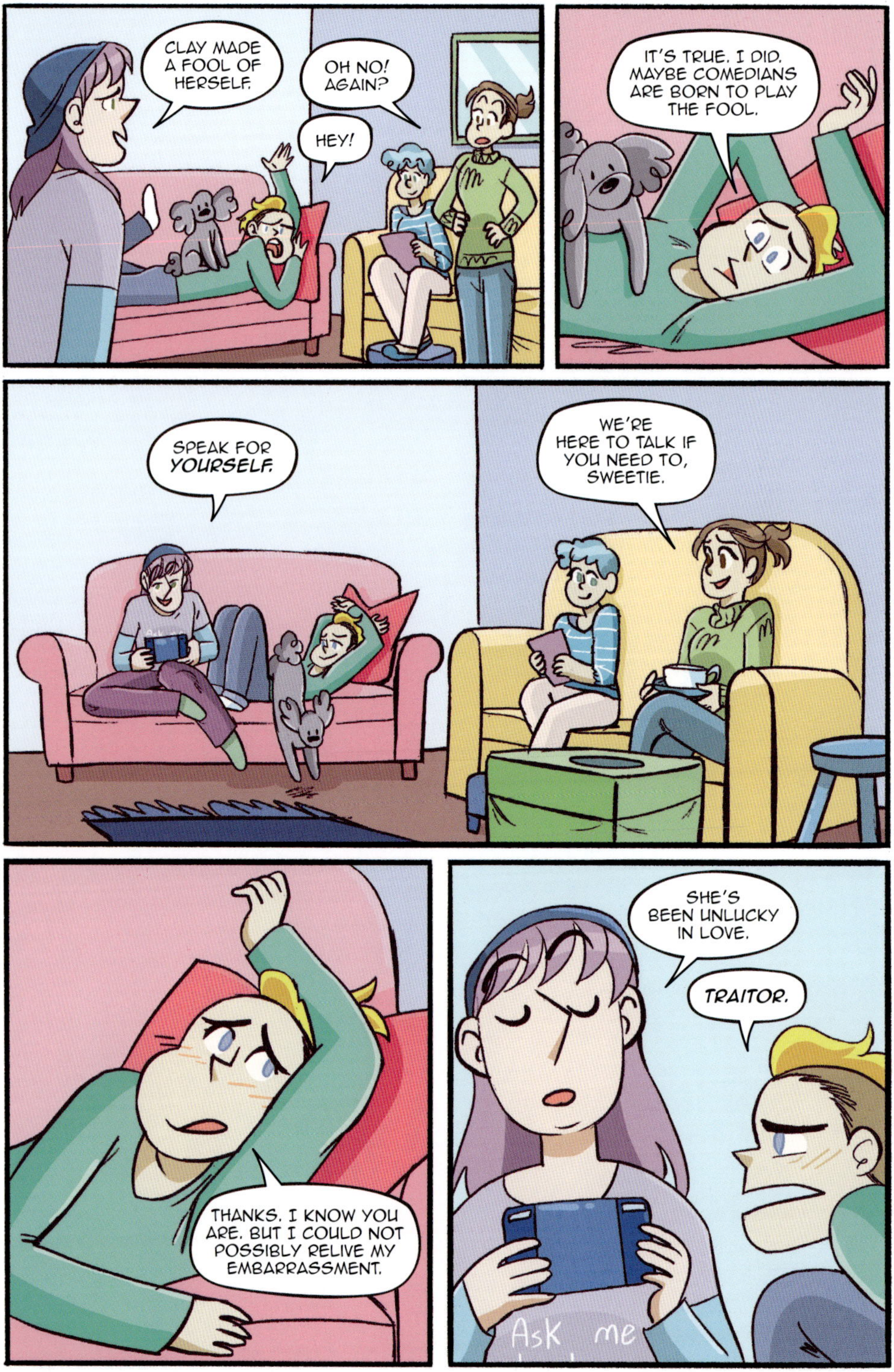
CLAY MADE A FOOL OF HERSELF.
OH NO! AGAIN?
HEY!
IT'S TRUE. I DID. MAYBE COMEDIANS ARE BORN TO PLAY THE FOOL.
SPEAK FOR *YOURSELF.*
WE'RE HERE TO TALK IF YOU NEED TO, SWEETIE.
THANKS. I KNOW YOU ARE. BUT I COULD NOT POSSIBLY RELIVE MY EMBARRASSMENT.
SHE'S BEEN UNLUCKY IN LOVE.
TRAITOR.
Ask me

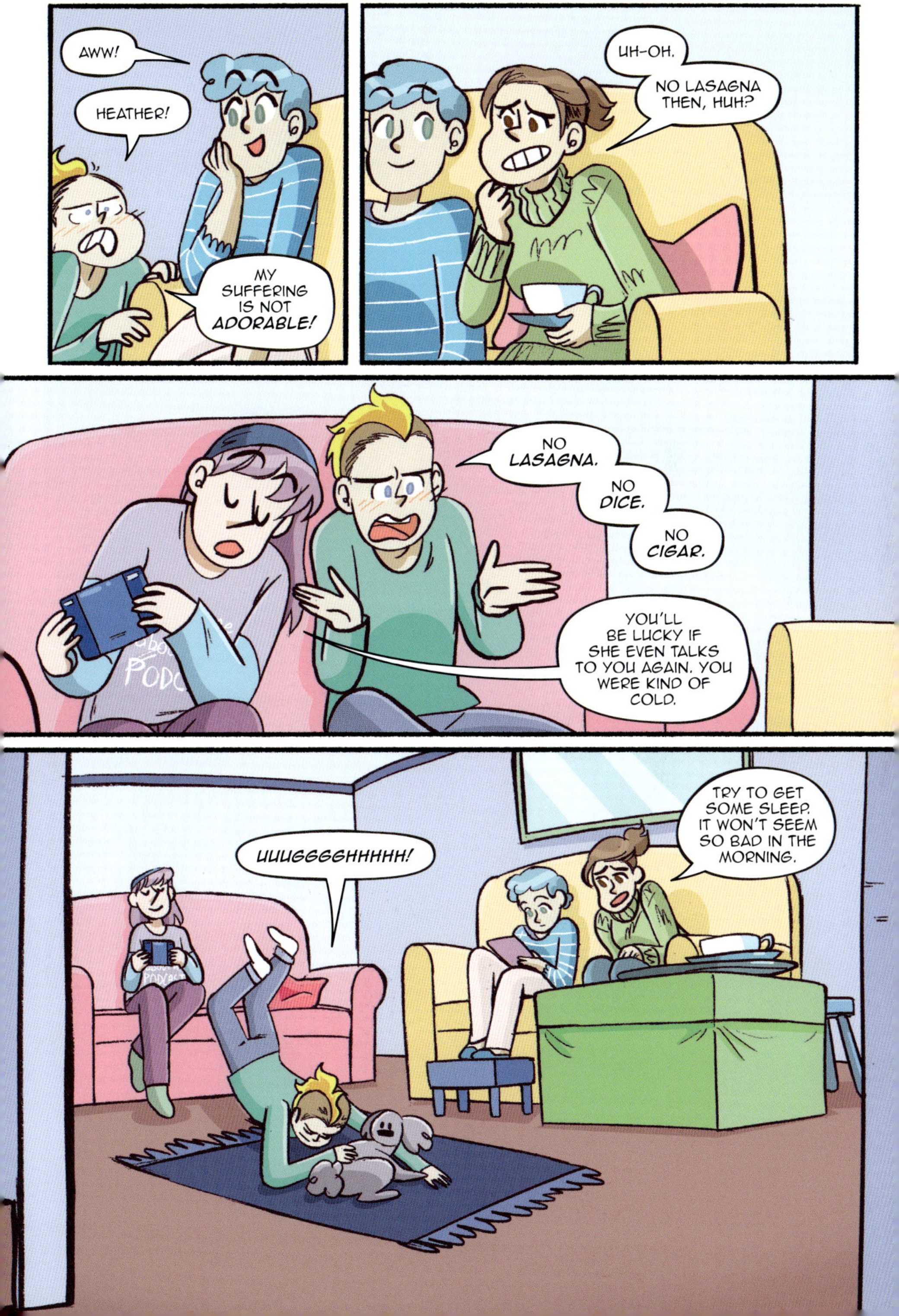

AWW!
HEATHER!
MY SUFFERING IS NOT ADORABLE!
UH-OH.
NO LASAGNA THEN, HUH?
NO LASAGNA.
NO DICE.
NO CIGAR.
YOU'LL BE LUCKY IF SHE EVEN TALKS TO YOU AGAIN. YOU WERE KIND OF COLD.
UUUGGGGHHHHH!
TRY TO GET SOME SLEEP. IT WON'T SEEM SO BAD IN THE MORNING.

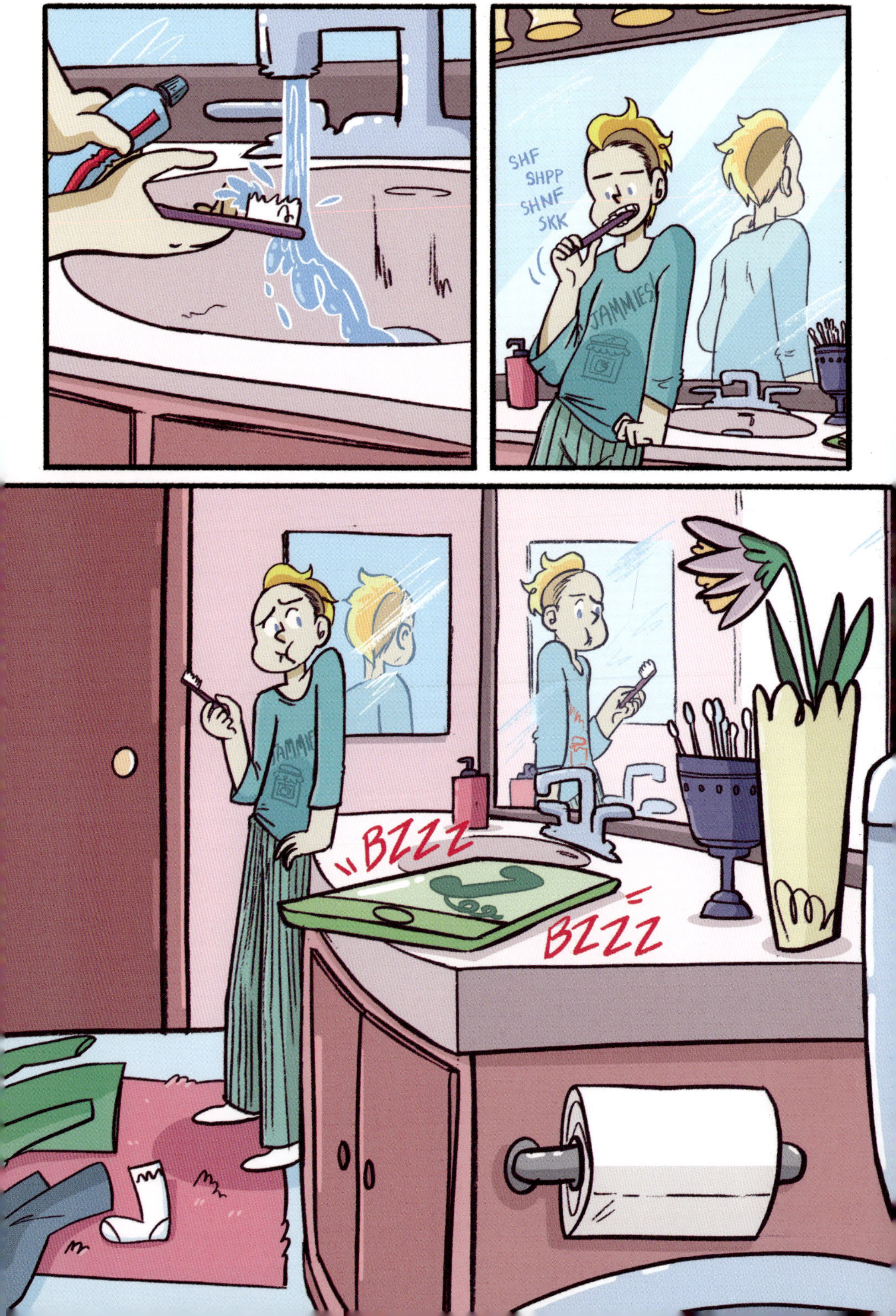
SHF
SHPP
SHNF
SKK
JAMMIES!
BZZZ
BZZZ

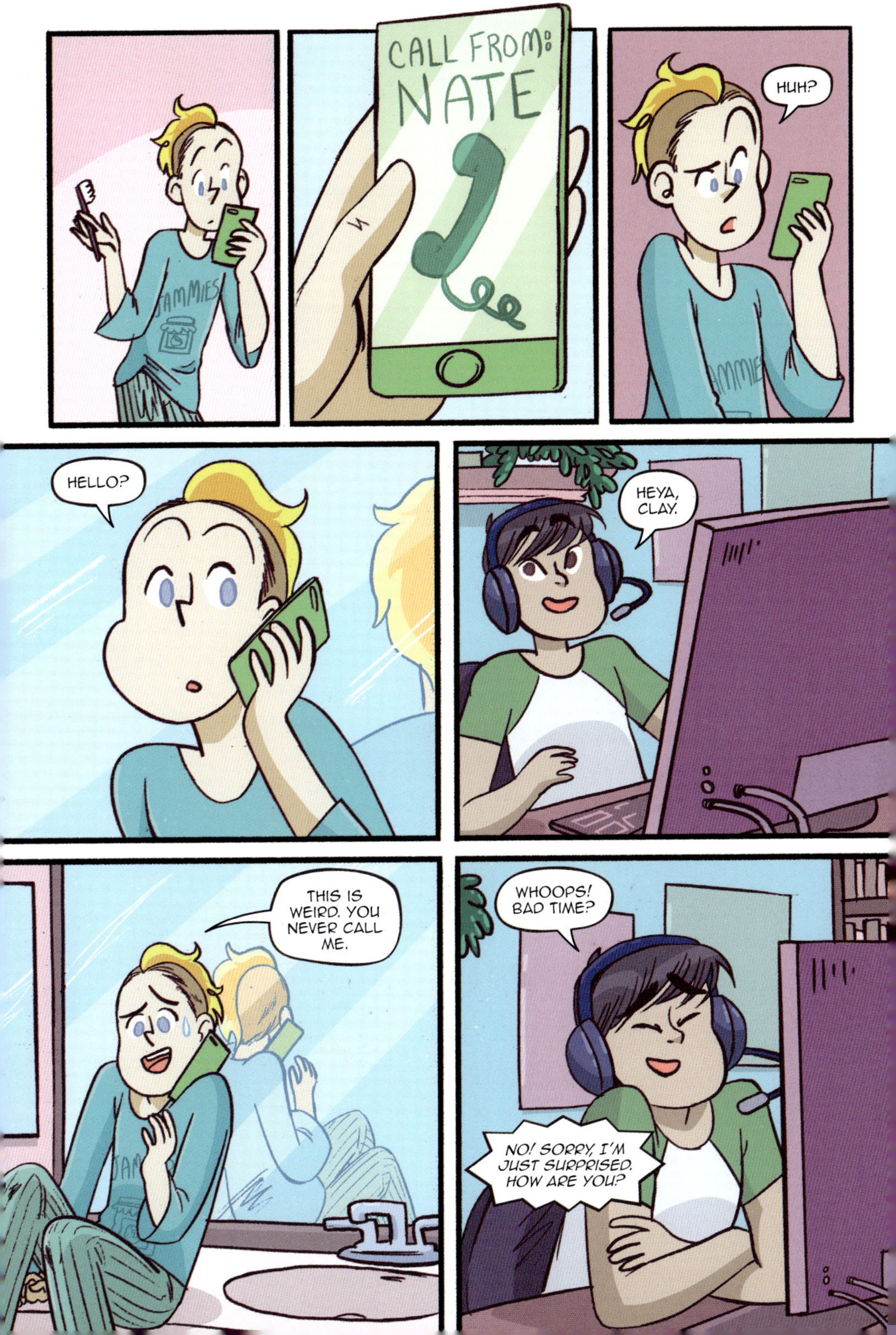
CALL FROM:
NATE
HUH?
HELLO?
HEYA, CLAY.
THIS IS WEIRD. YOU NEVER CALL ME.
WHOOPS! BAD TIME?
NO! SORRY, I'M JUST SURPRISED. HOW ARE YOU?

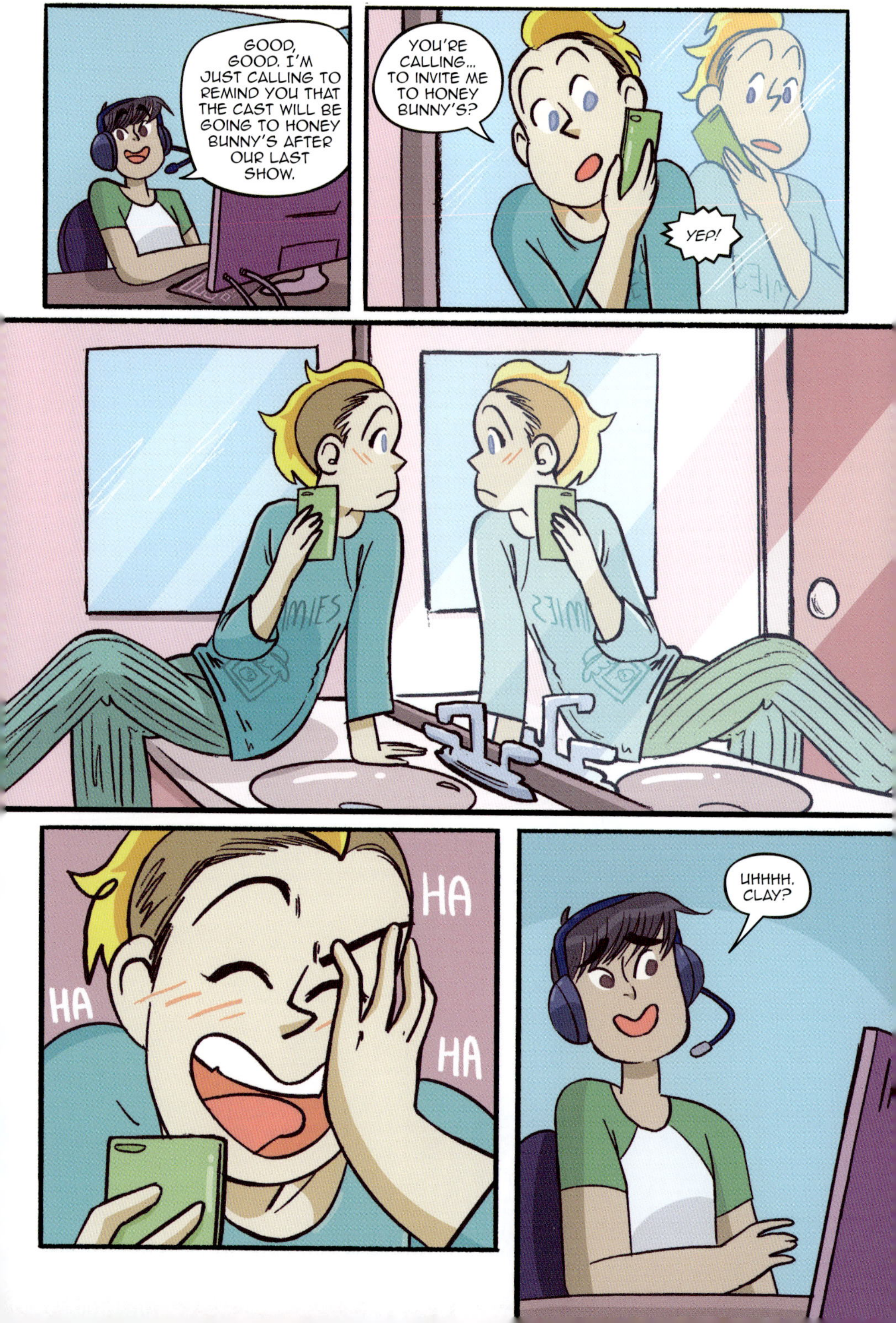
GOOD, GOOD. I'M JUST CALLING TO REMIND YOU THAT THE CAST WILL BE GOING TO HONEY BUNNY'S AFTER OUR LAST SHOW.
YOU'RE CALLING... TO INVITE ME TO HONEY BUNNY'S?
YEP!
HA
HA
HA
UHHHH. CLAY?

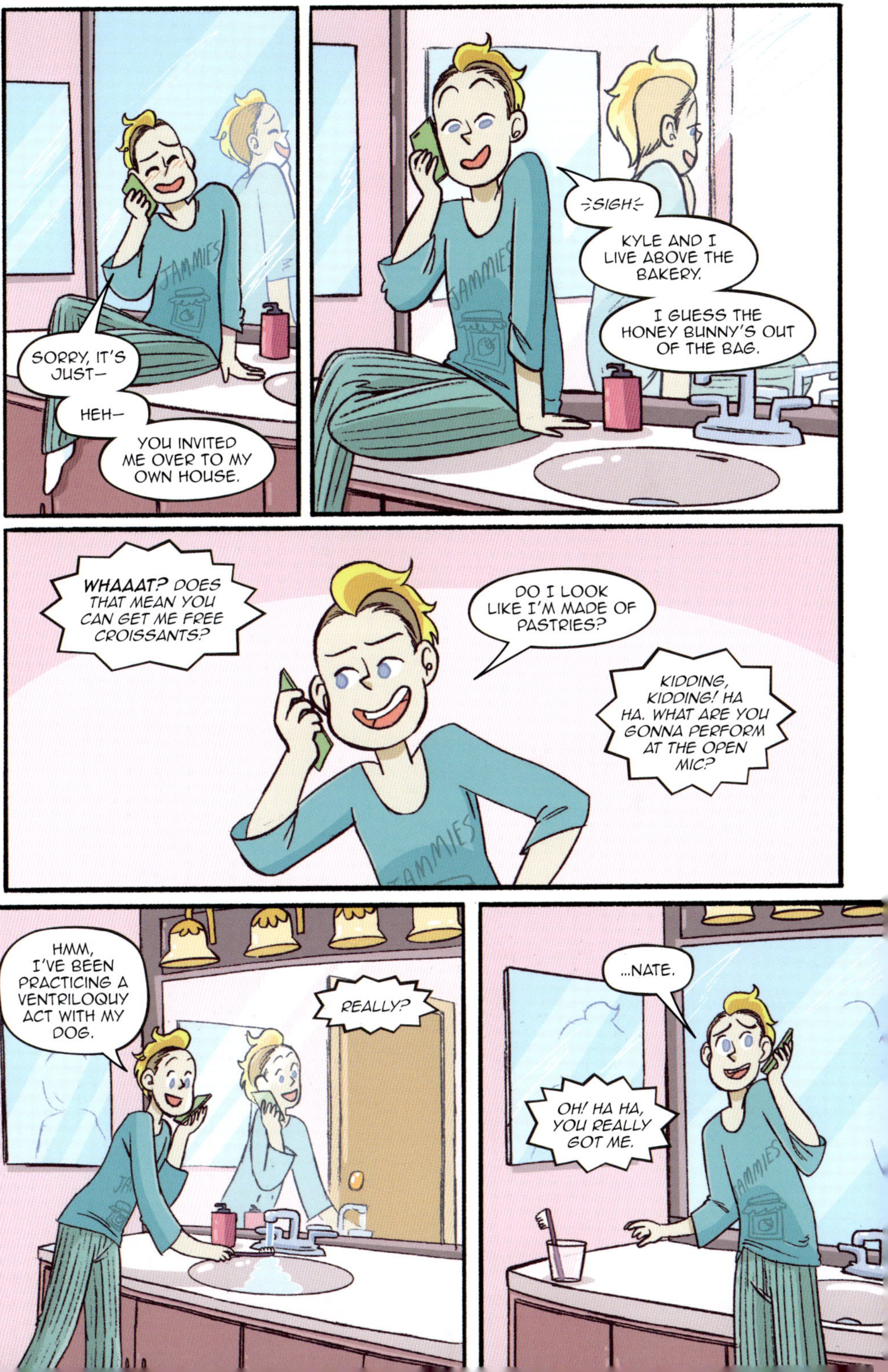
SORRY, IT'S JUST—
HEH—
YOU INVITED ME OVER TO MY OWN HOUSE.
JAMMIES
-SIGH-
KYLE AND I LIVE ABOVE THE BAKERY.
I GUESS THE HONEY BUNNY'S OUT OF THE BAG.
WHAAAT? DOES THAT MEAN YOU CAN GET ME FREE CROISSANTS?
DO I LOOK LIKE I'M MADE OF PASTRIES?
KIDDING, KIDDING! HA HA. WHAT ARE YOU GONNA PERFORM AT THE OPEN MIC?
HMM, I'VE BEEN PRACTICING A VENTRILOQUY ACT WITH MY DOG.
REALLY?
...NATE.
OH! HA HA, YOU REALLY GOT ME.

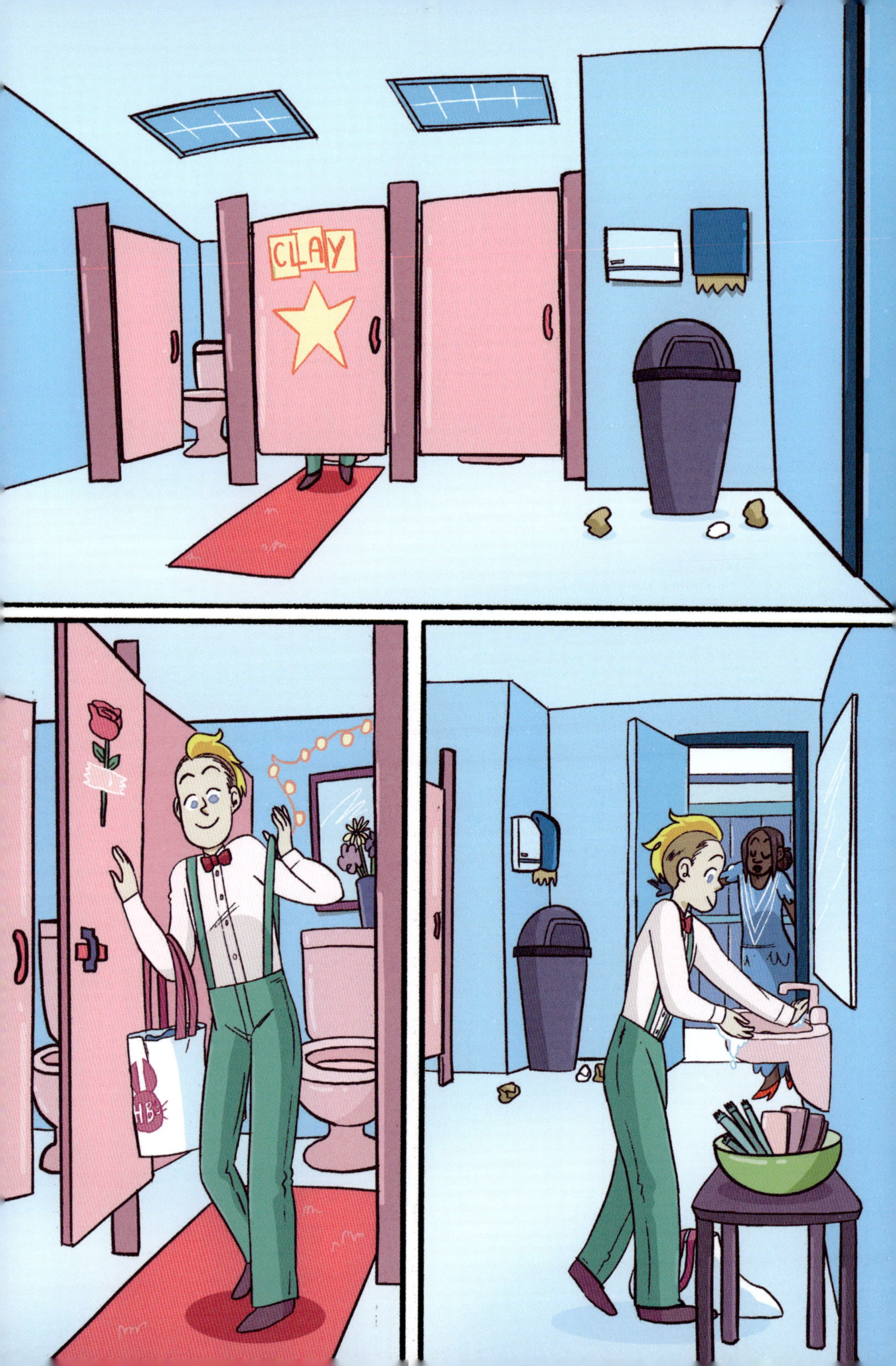
CLAY

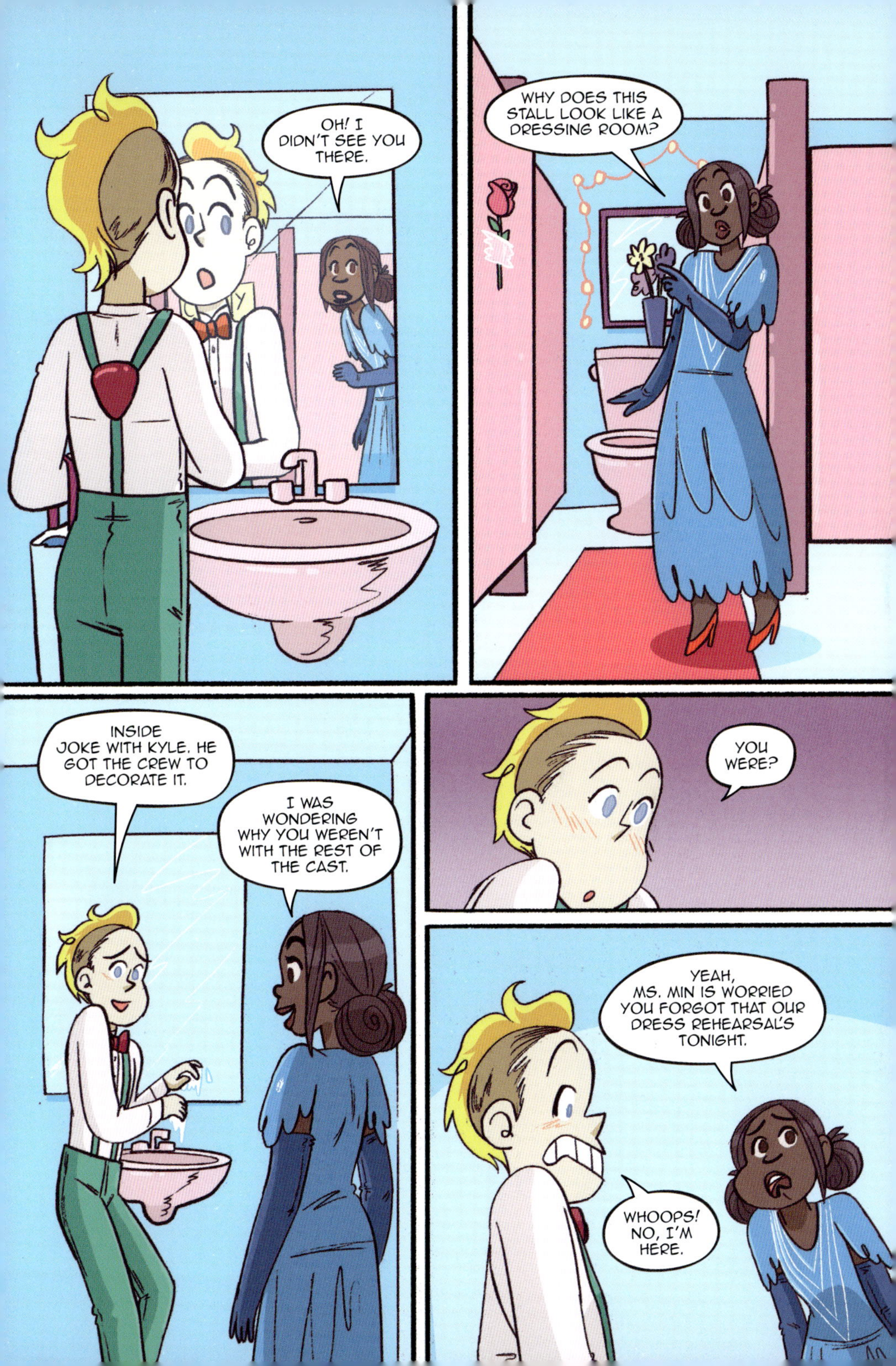
OH! I DIDN'T SEE YOU THERE.
WHY DOES THIS STALL LOOK LIKE A DRESSING ROOM?
INSIDE JOKE WITH KYLE. HE GOT THE CREW TO DECORATE IT.
I WAS WONDERING WHY YOU WEREN'T WITH THE REST OF THE CAST.
YOU WERE?
YEAH, MS. MIN IS WORRIED YOU FORGOT THAT OUR DRESS REHEARSAL'S TONIGHT.
WHOOPS! NO, I'M HERE.

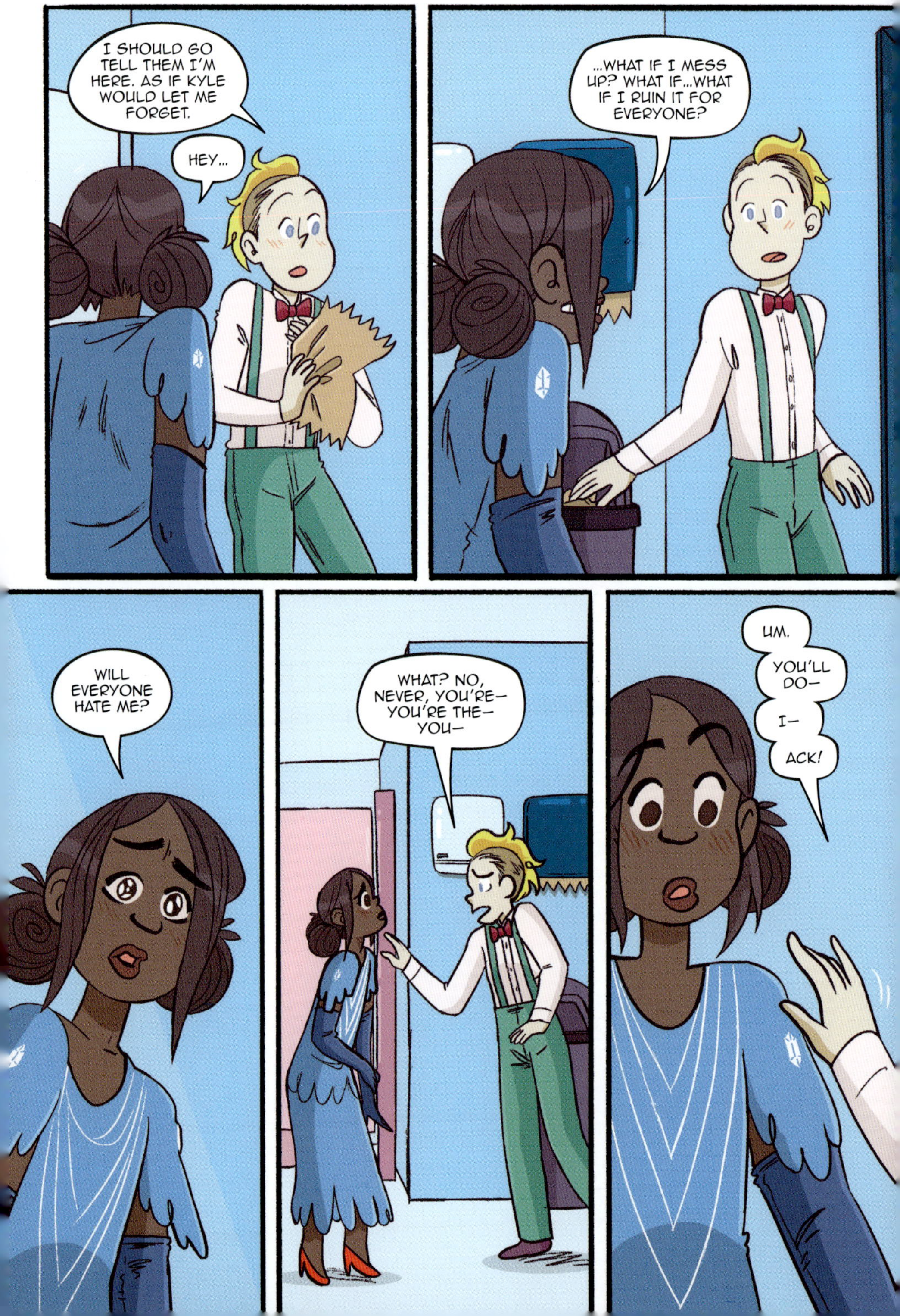

I SHOULD GO TELL THEM I'M HERE. AS IF KYLE WOULD LET ME FORGET.
HEY...
...WHAT IF I MESS UP? WHAT IF...WHAT IF I RUIN IT FOR EVERYONE?
WILL EVERYONE HATE ME?
WHAT? NO, NEVER, YOU'RE— YOU'RE THE— YOU—
UM.
YOU'LL DO—
I—
ACK!

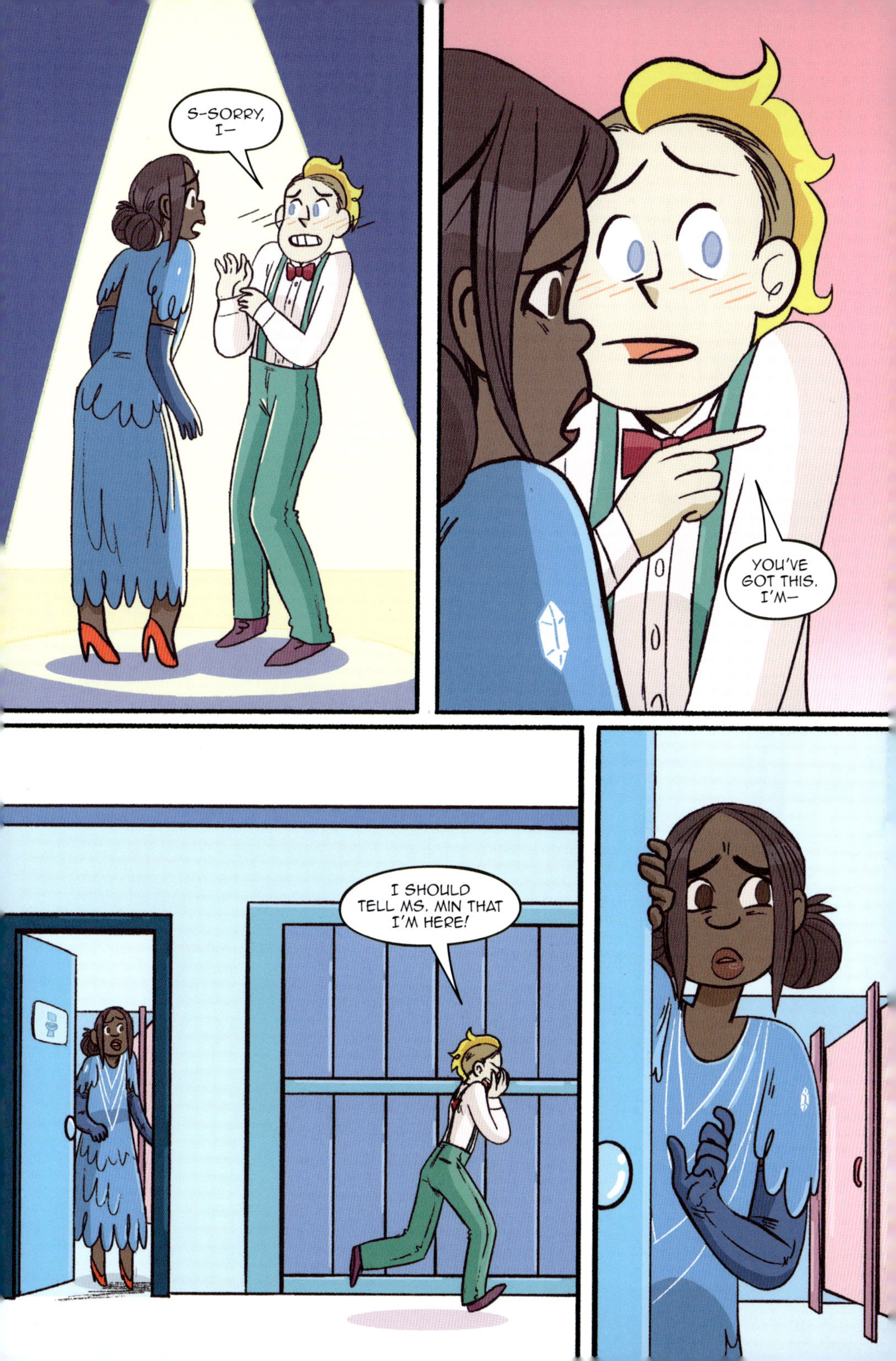
S-SORRY, I—
YOU'VE GOT THIS. I'M—
I SHOULD TELL MS. MIN THAT I'M HERE!

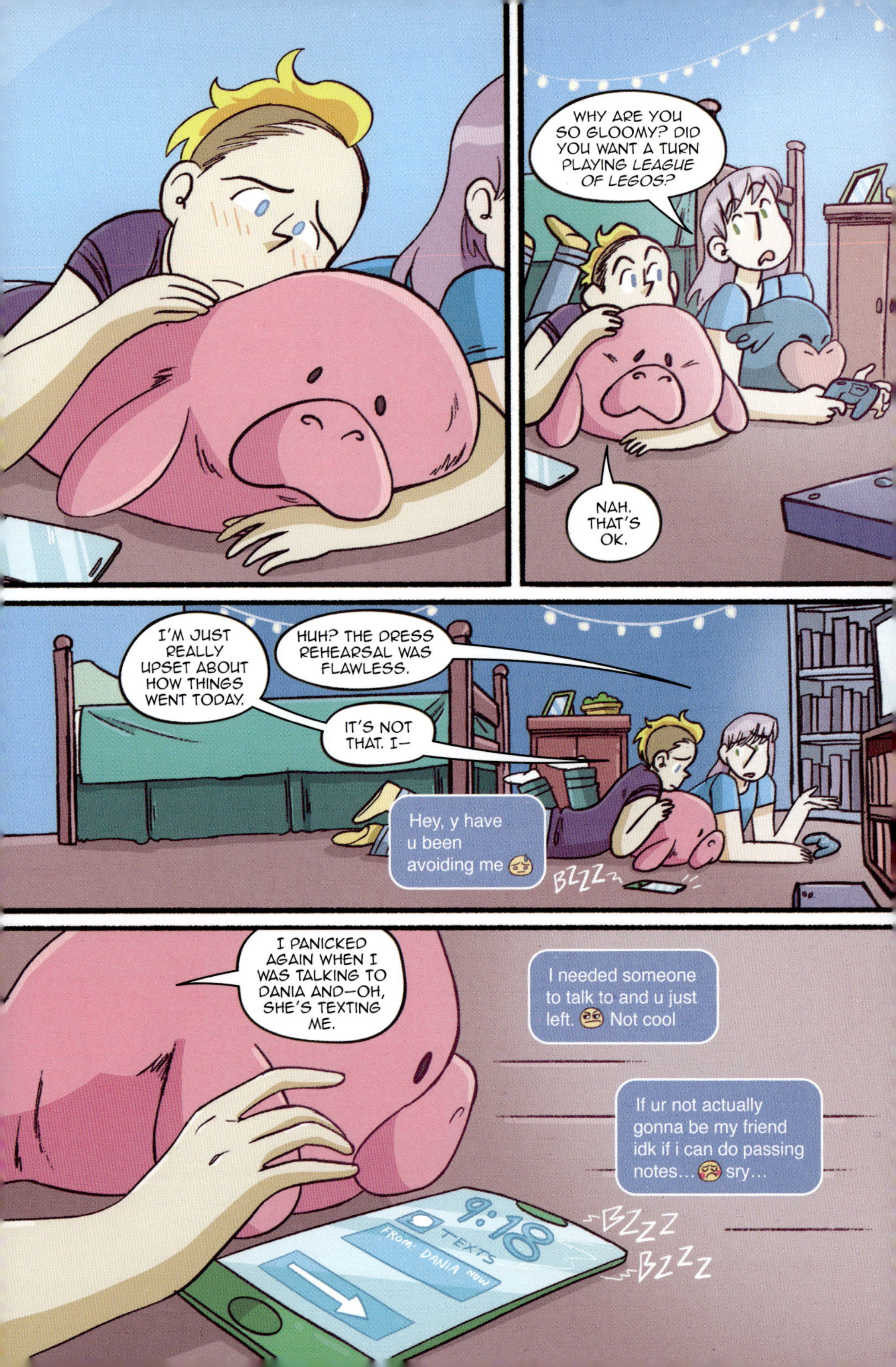
WHY ARE YOU SO GLOOMY? DID YOU WANT A TURN PLAYING LEAGUE OF LEGOS?
NAH. THAT'S OK.
I'M JUST REALLY UPSET ABOUT HOW THINGS WENT TODAY.
HUH? THE DRESS REHEARSAL WAS FLAWLESS.
IT'S NOT THAT. I—
Hey, y have u been avoiding me
BZZZ
I PANICKED AGAIN WHEN I WAS TALKING TO DANIA AND—OH, SHE'S TEXTING ME.
I needed someone to talk to and u just left. Not cool
If ur not actually gonna be my friend idk if i can do passing notes... sry...
9:18
TEXTS
FROM: DANIA NOW
BZZZ
BZZZ

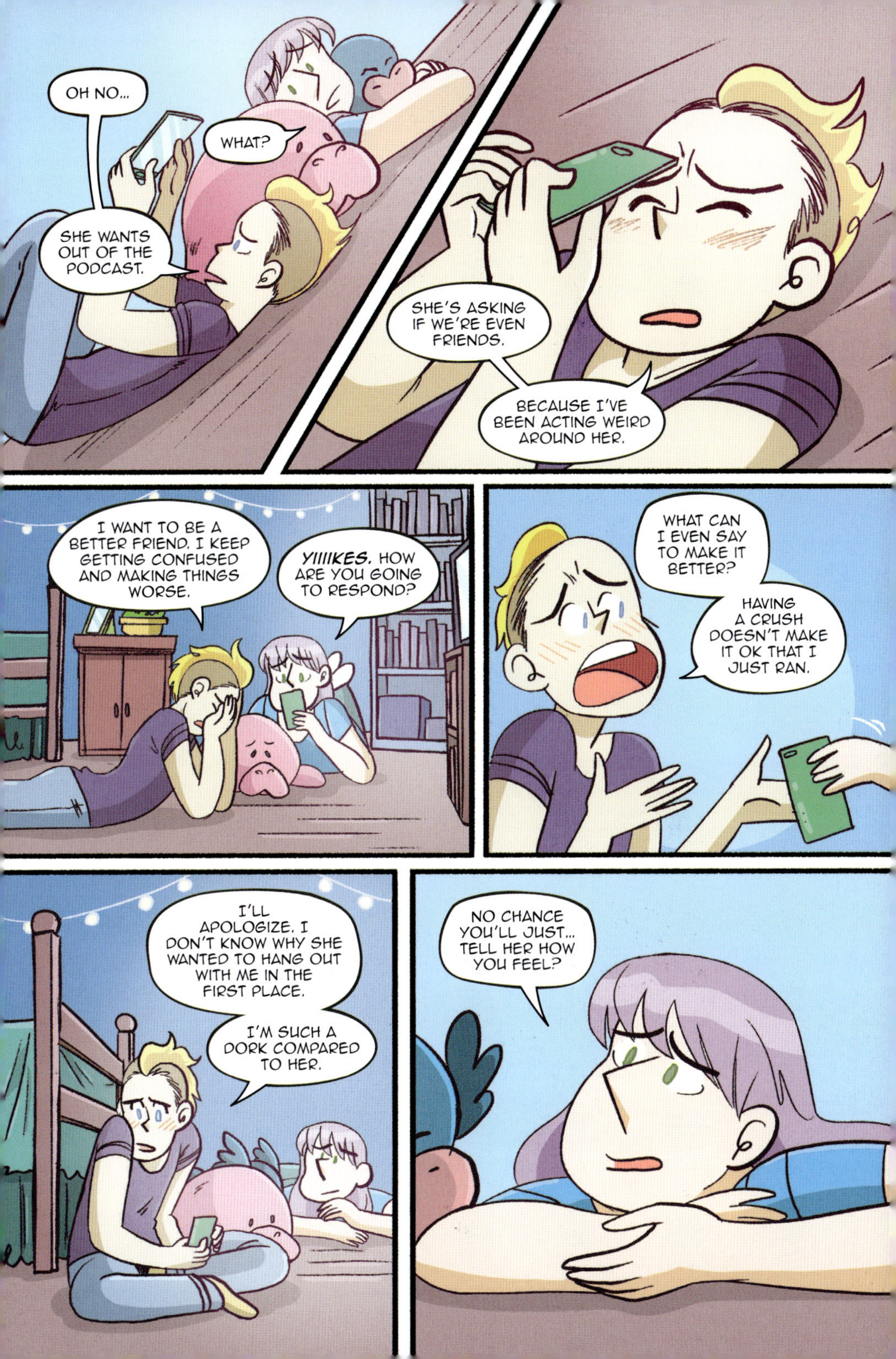
OH NO...
WHAT?
SHE WANTS OUT OF THE PODCAST.
SHE'S ASKING IF WE'RE EVEN FRIENDS.
BECAUSE I'VE BEEN ACTING WEIRD AROUND HER.
I WANT TO BE A BETTER FRIEND. I KEEP GETTING CONFUSED AND MAKING THINGS WORSE.
YIIIIKES. HOW ARE YOU GOING TO RESPOND?
WHAT CAN I EVEN SAY TO MAKE IT BETTER?
HAVING A CRUSH DOESN'T MAKE IT OK THAT I JUST RAN.
I'LL APOLOGIZE. I DON'T KNOW WHY SHE WANTED TO HANG OUT WITH ME IN THE FIRST PLACE.
I'M SUCH A DORK COMPARED TO HER.
NO CHANCE YOU'LL JUST... TELL HER HOW YOU FEEL?

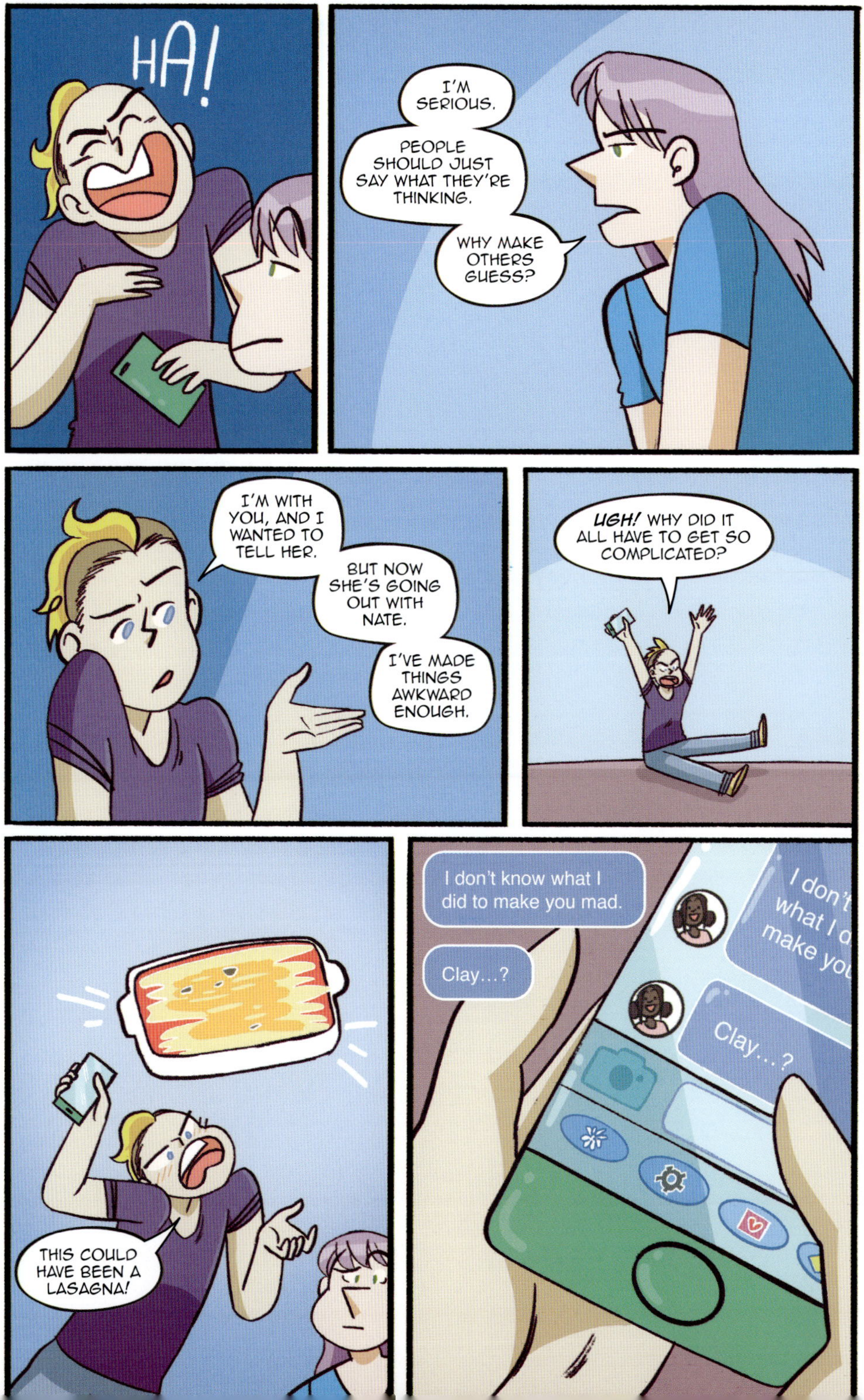
HA!
I'M SERIOUS.
PEOPLE SHOULD JUST SAY WHAT THEY'RE THINKING.
WHY MAKE OTHERS GUESS?
I'M WITH YOU, AND I WANTED TO TELL HER.
BUT NOW SHE'S GOING OUT WITH NATE.
I'VE MADE THINGS AWKWARD ENOUGH.
UGH! WHY DID IT ALL HAVE TO GET SO COMPLICATED?
THIS COULD HAVE BEEN A LASAGNA!
I don't know what I did to make you mad.
Clay…?

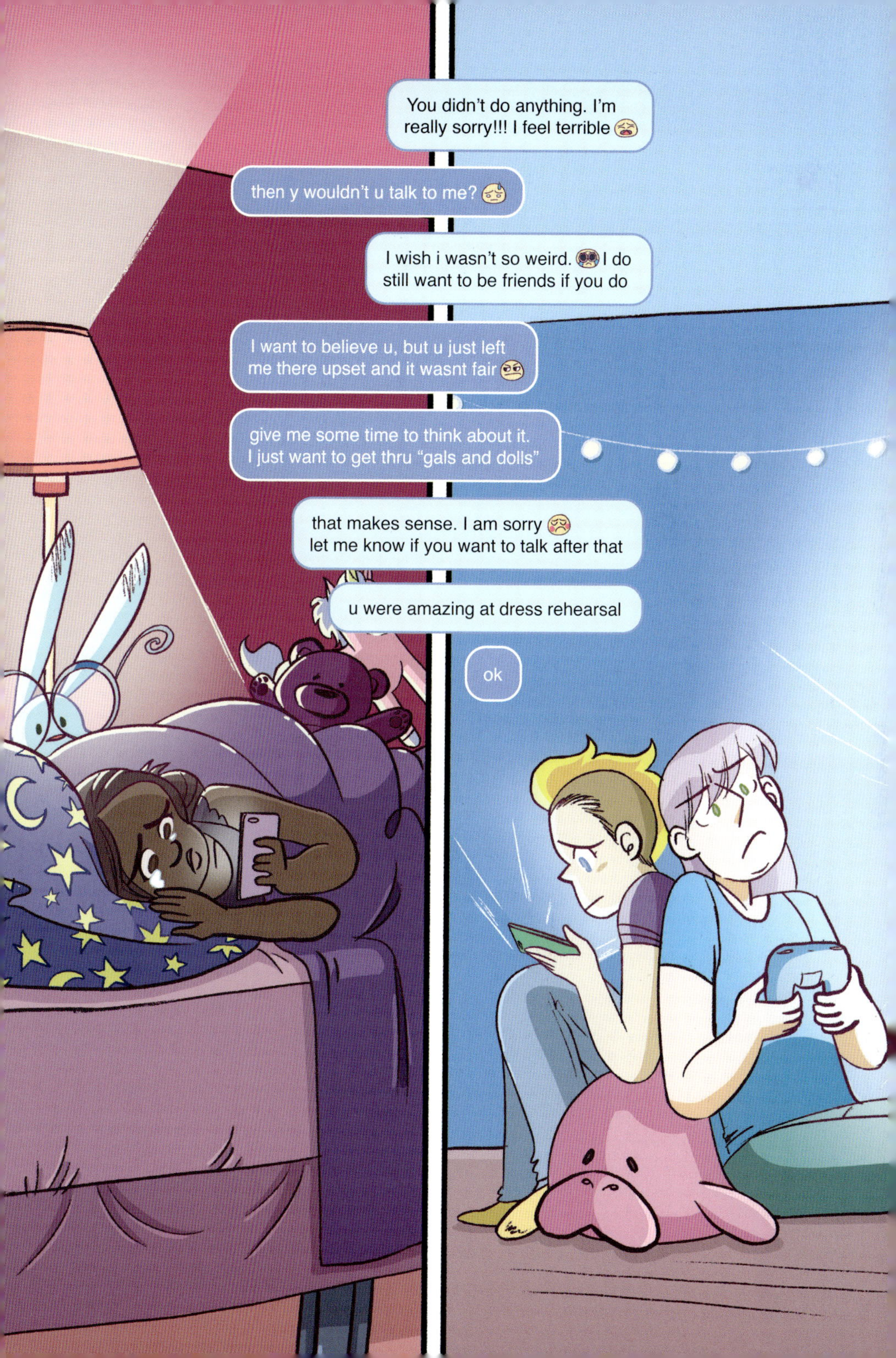
You didn't do anything. I'm really sorry!!! I feel terrible
then y wouldn't u talk to me?
I wish i wasn't so weird. I do still want to be friends if you do
I want to believe u, but u just left me there upset and it wasnt fair
give me some time to think about it. I just want to get thru "gals and dolls"
that makes sense. I am sorry
let me know if you want to talk after that
u were amazing at dress rehearsal
ok

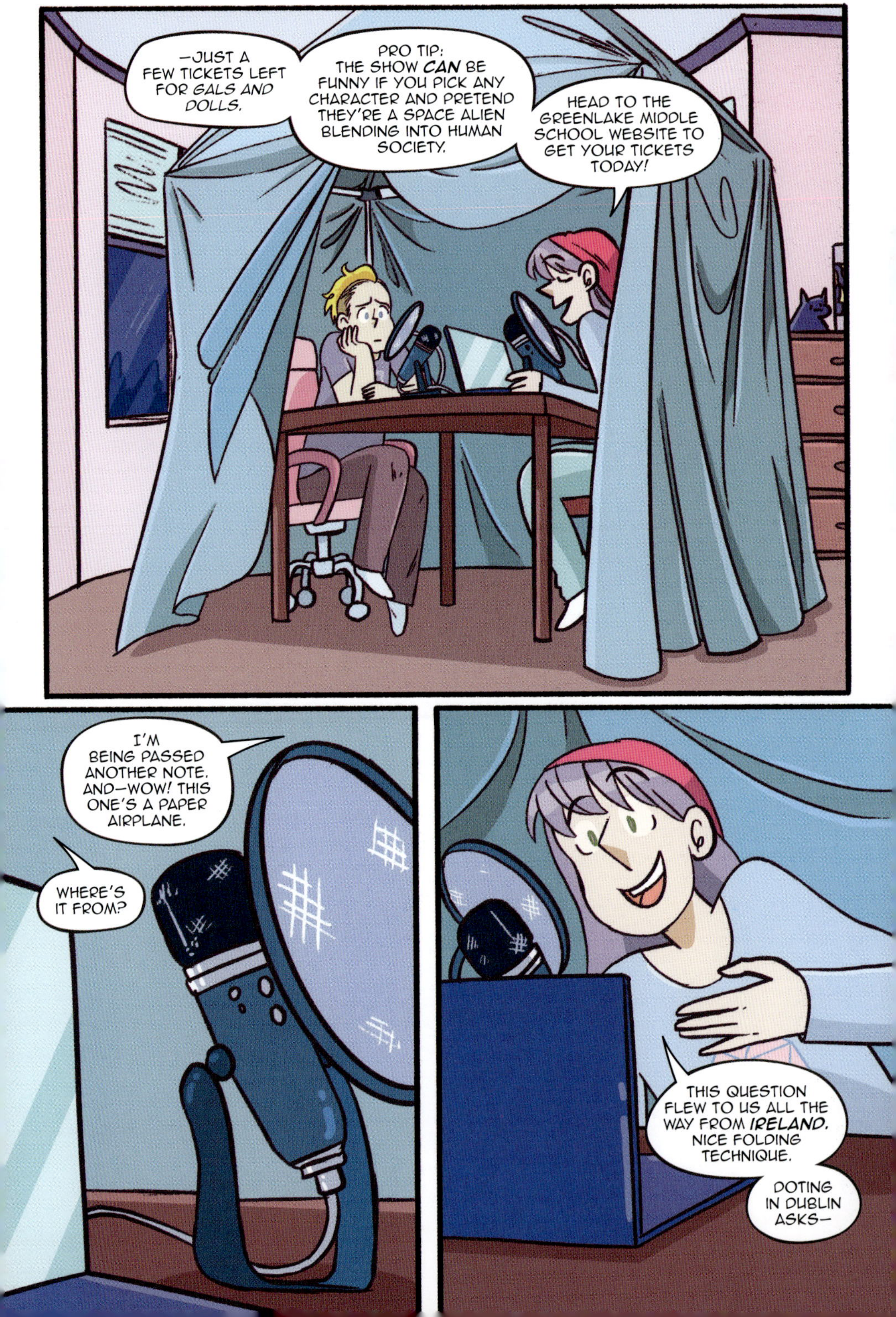
—JUST A FEW TICKETS LEFT FOR GALS AND DOLLS.
PRO TIP: THE SHOW **CAN** BE FUNNY IF YOU PICK ANY CHARACTER AND PRETEND THEY'RE A SPACE ALIEN BLENDING INTO HUMAN SOCIETY.
HEAD TO THE GREENLAKE MIDDLE SCHOOL WEBSITE TO GET YOUR TICKETS TODAY!
I'M BEING PASSED ANOTHER NOTE. AND—WOW! THIS ONE'S A PAPER AIRPLANE.
WHERE'S IT FROM?
THIS QUESTION FLEW TO US ALL THE WAY FROM **IRELAND.** NICE FOLDING TECHNIQUE.
DOTING IN DUBLIN ASKS—

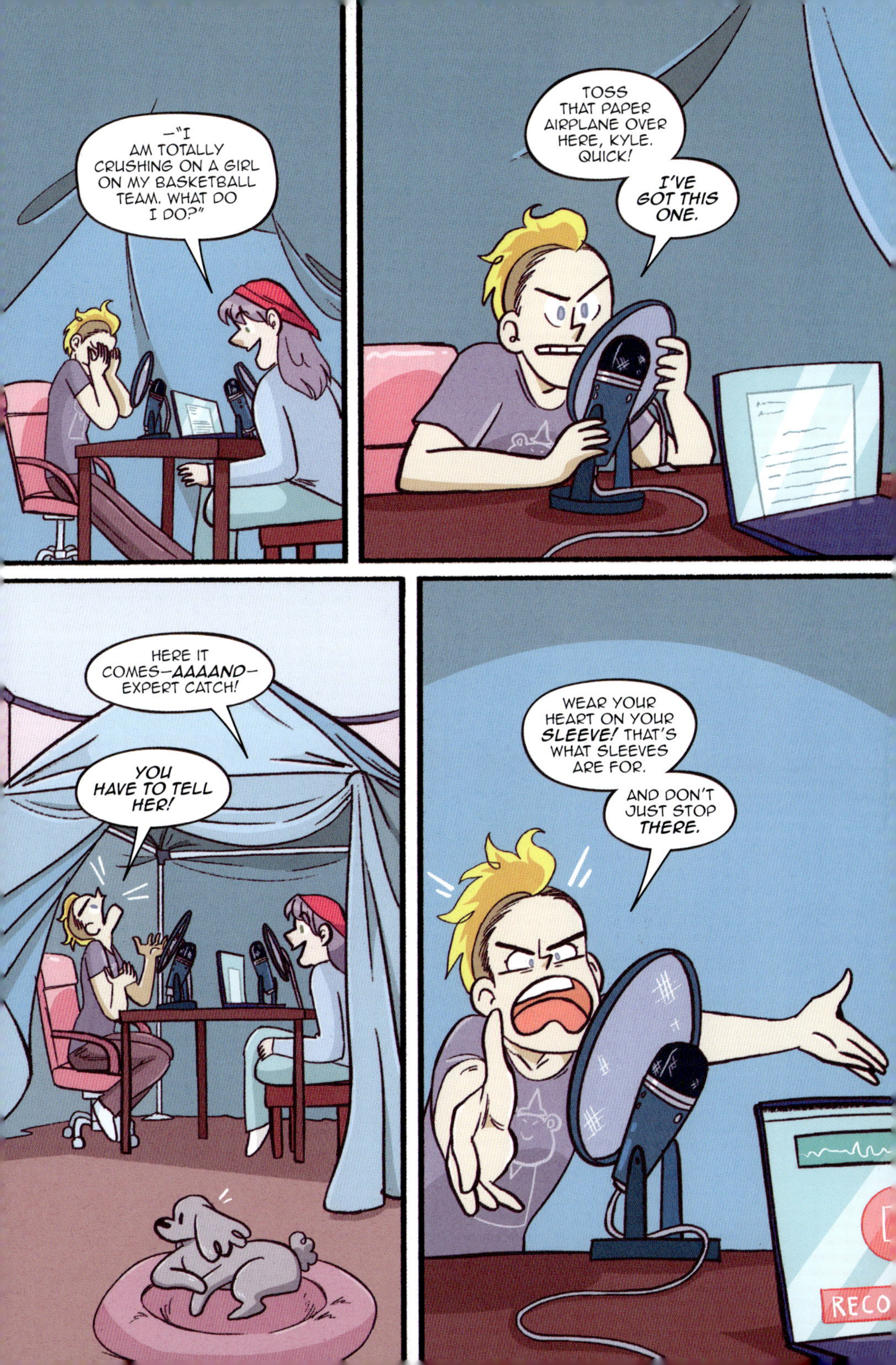

—"I AM TOTALLY CRUSHING ON A GIRL ON MY BASKETBALL TEAM. WHAT DO I DO?"
TOSS THAT PAPER AIRPLANE OVER HERE, KYLE. QUICK!
I'VE GOT THIS ONE.
HERE IT COMES—AAAAND—EXPERT CATCH!
YOU HAVE TO TELL HER!
WEAR YOUR HEART ON YOUR SLEEVE! THAT'S WHAT SLEEVES ARE FOR.
AND DON'T JUST STOP THERE.
RECO

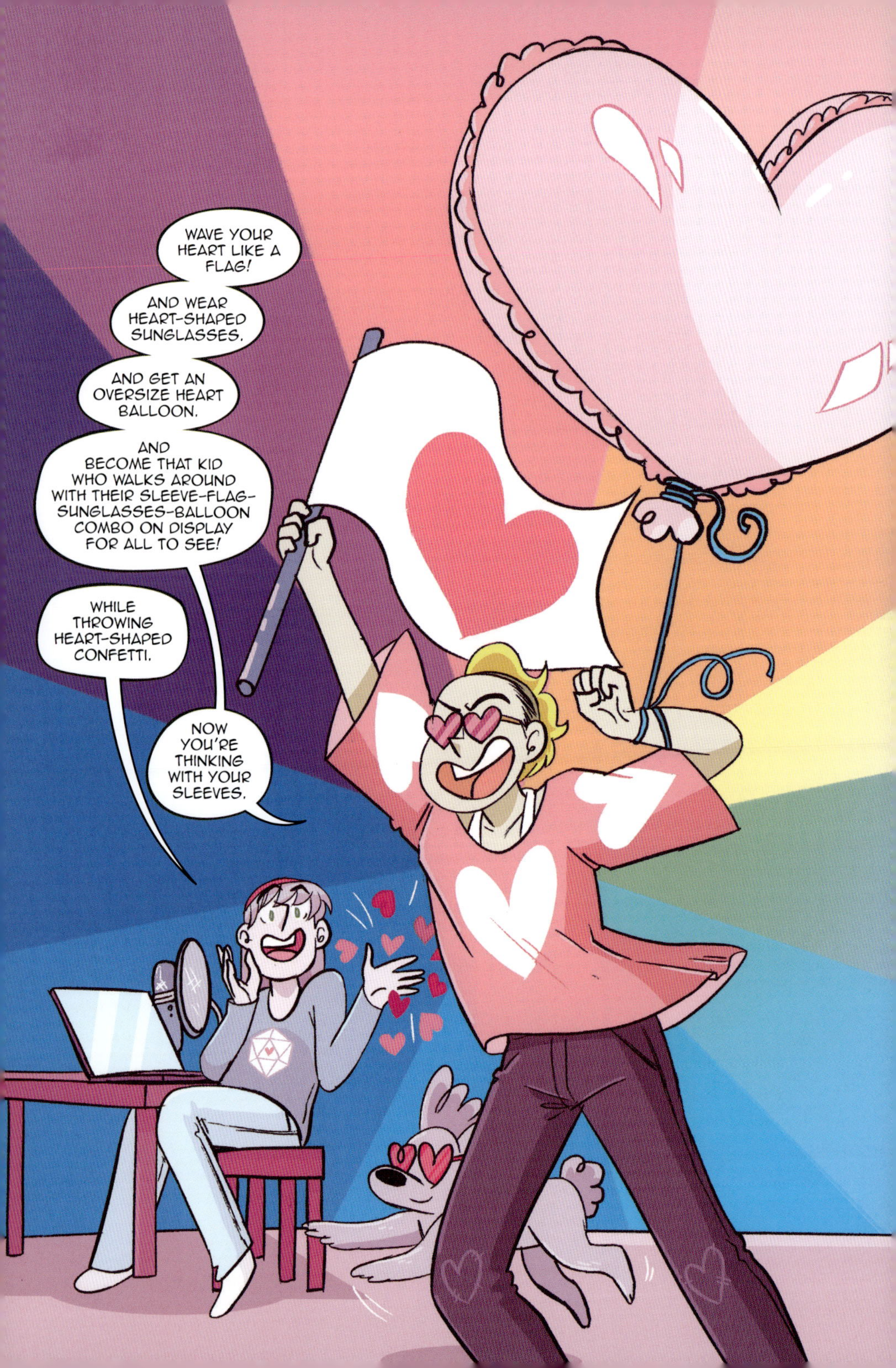

WAVE YOUR HEART LIKE A FLAG!
AND WEAR HEART-SHAPED SUNGLASSES.
AND GET AN OVERSIZE HEART BALLOON.
AND BECOME THAT KID WHO WALKS AROUND WITH THEIR SLEEVE-FLAG-SUNGLASSES-BALLOON COMBO ON DISPLAY FOR ALL TO SEE!
WHILE THROWING HEART-SHAPED CONFETTI.
NOW YOU'RE THINKING WITH YOUR SLEEVES.

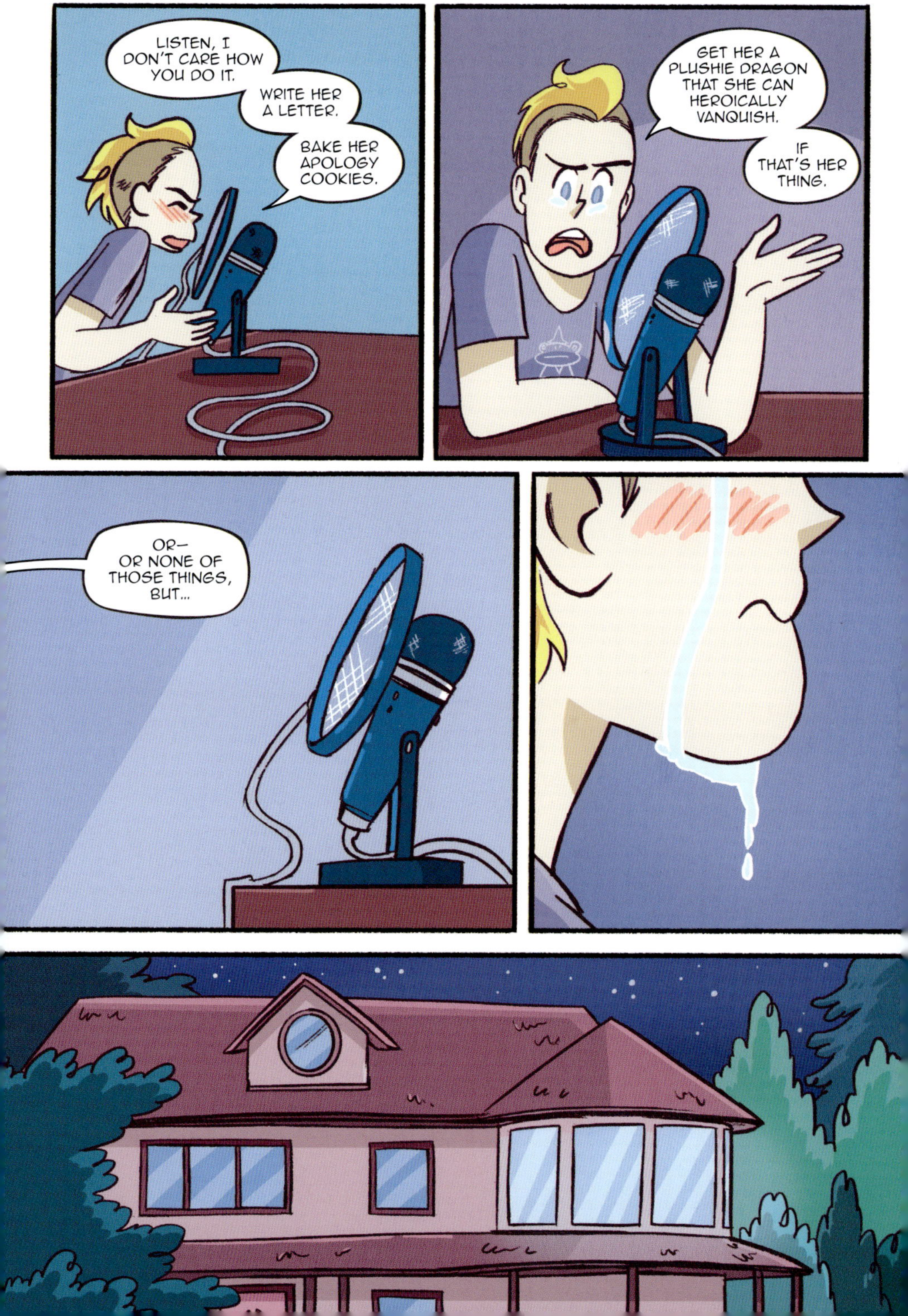
LISTEN, I DON'T CARE HOW YOU DO IT.
WRITE HER A LETTER.
BAKE HER APOLOGY COOKIES.
GET HER A PLUSHIE DRAGON THAT SHE CAN HEROICALLY VANQUISH.
IF THAT'S HER THING.
OR— OR NONE OF THOSE THINGS, BUT...

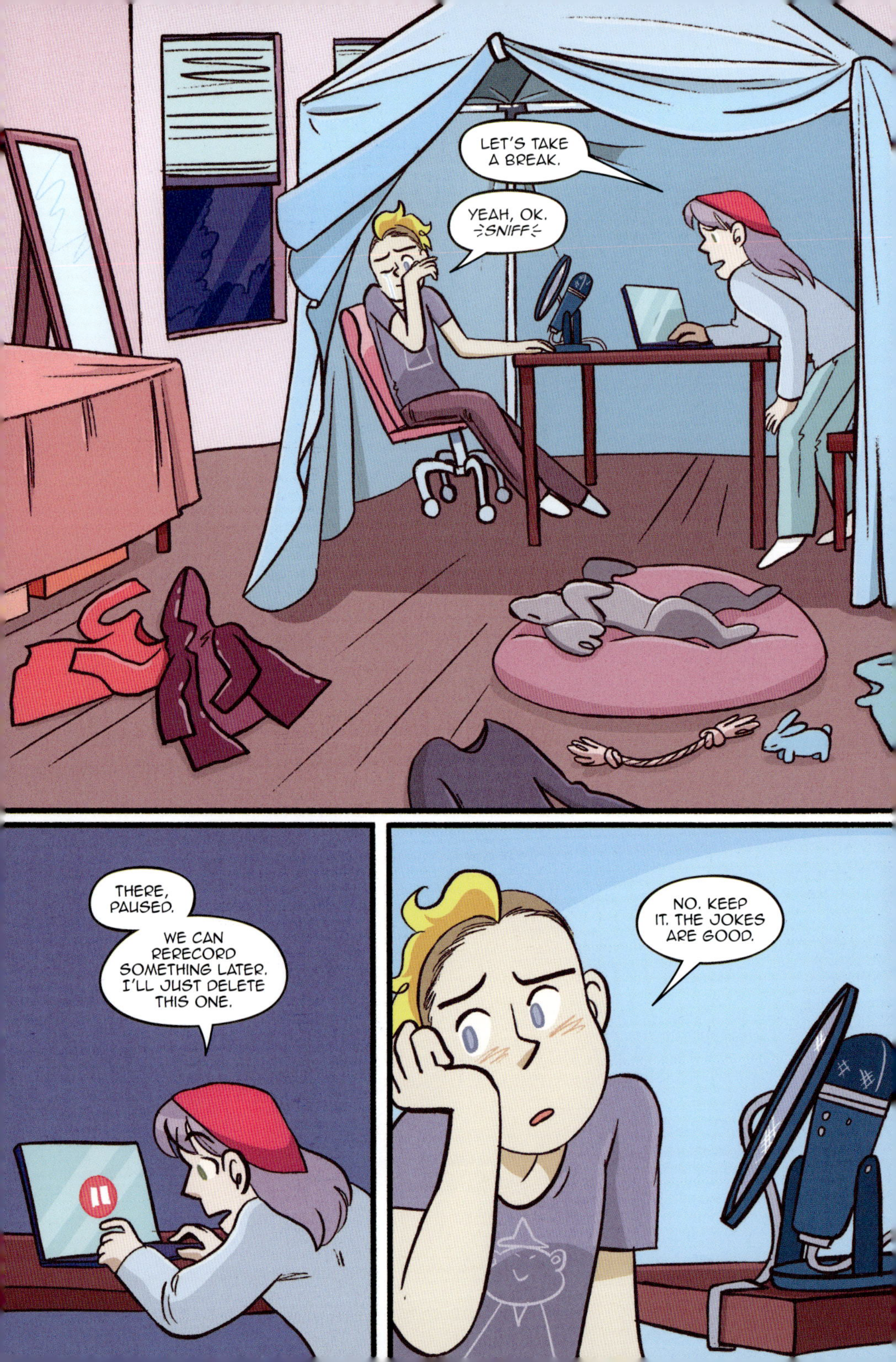
LET'S TAKE A BREAK.
YEAH, OK. SNIFF
THERE, PAUSED.
WE CAN RERECORD SOMETHING LATER. I'LL JUST DELETE THIS ONE.
NO. KEEP IT. THE JOKES ARE GOOD.

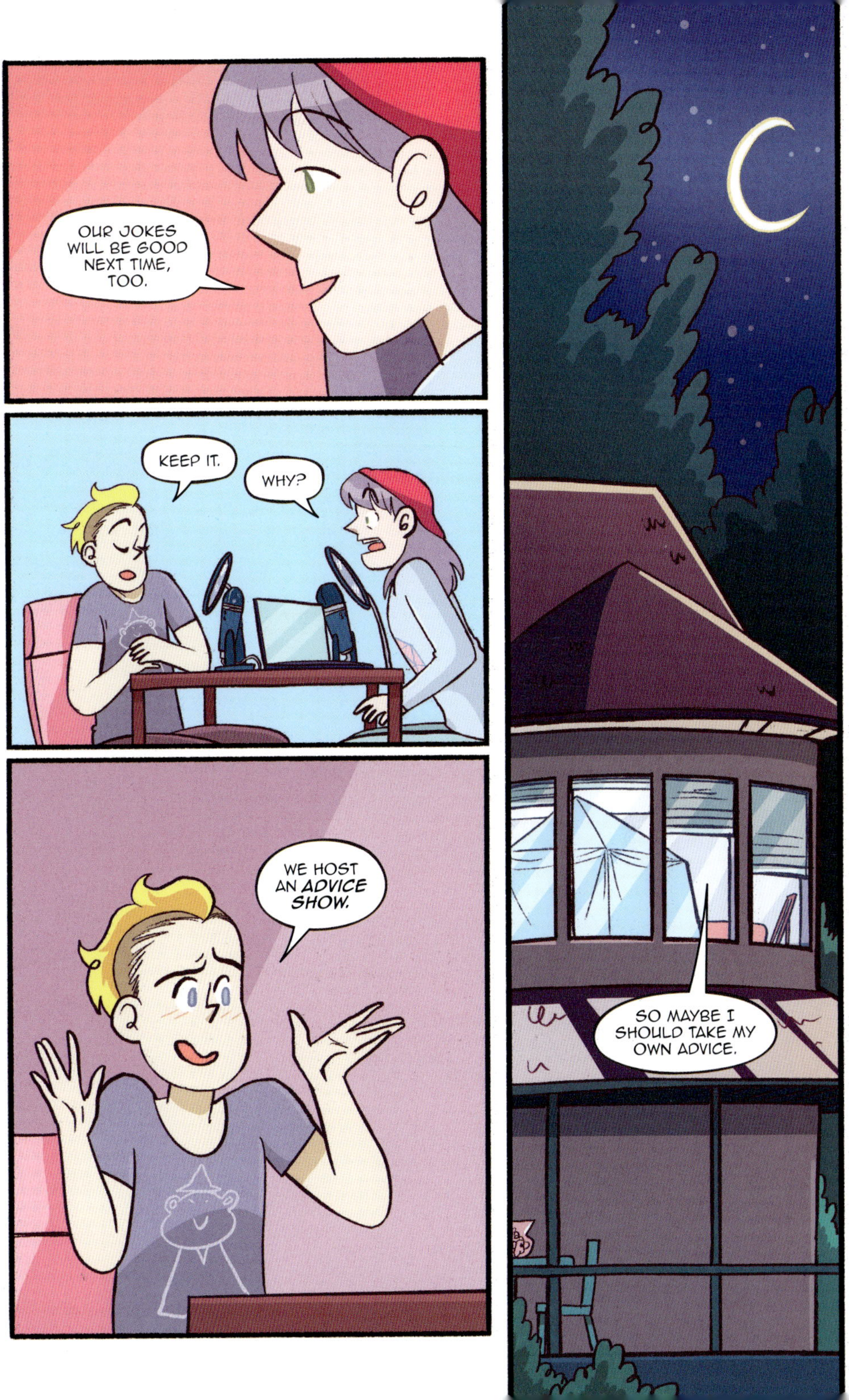
OUR JOKES WILL BE GOOD NEXT TIME, TOO.
KEEP IT.
WHY?
WE HOST AN *ADVICE SHOW.*
SO MAYBE I SHOULD TAKE MY OWN ADVICE.

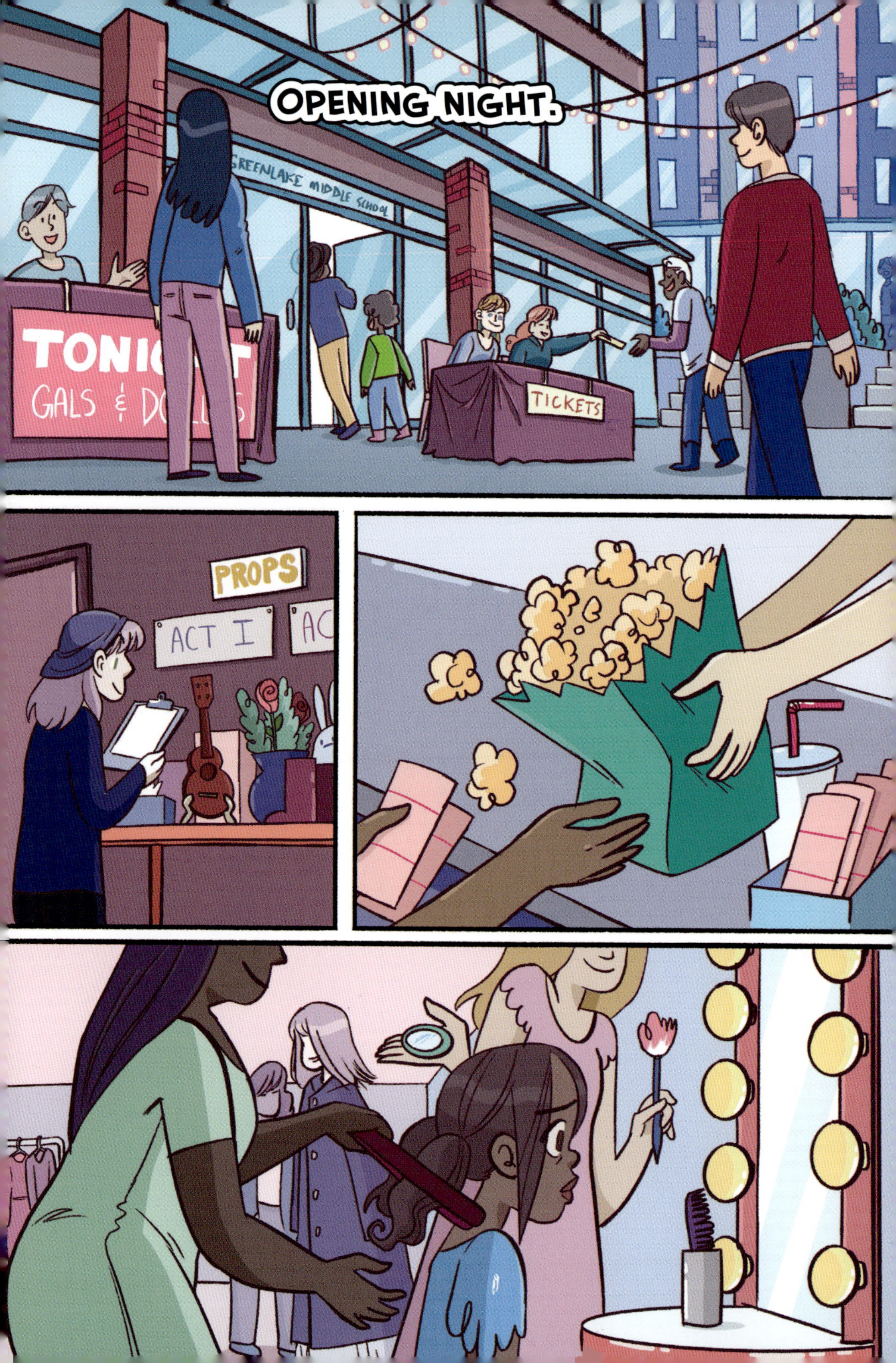

OPENING NIGHT.
GREENLAKE MIDDLE SCHOOL
TICKETS
PROPS
ACT I

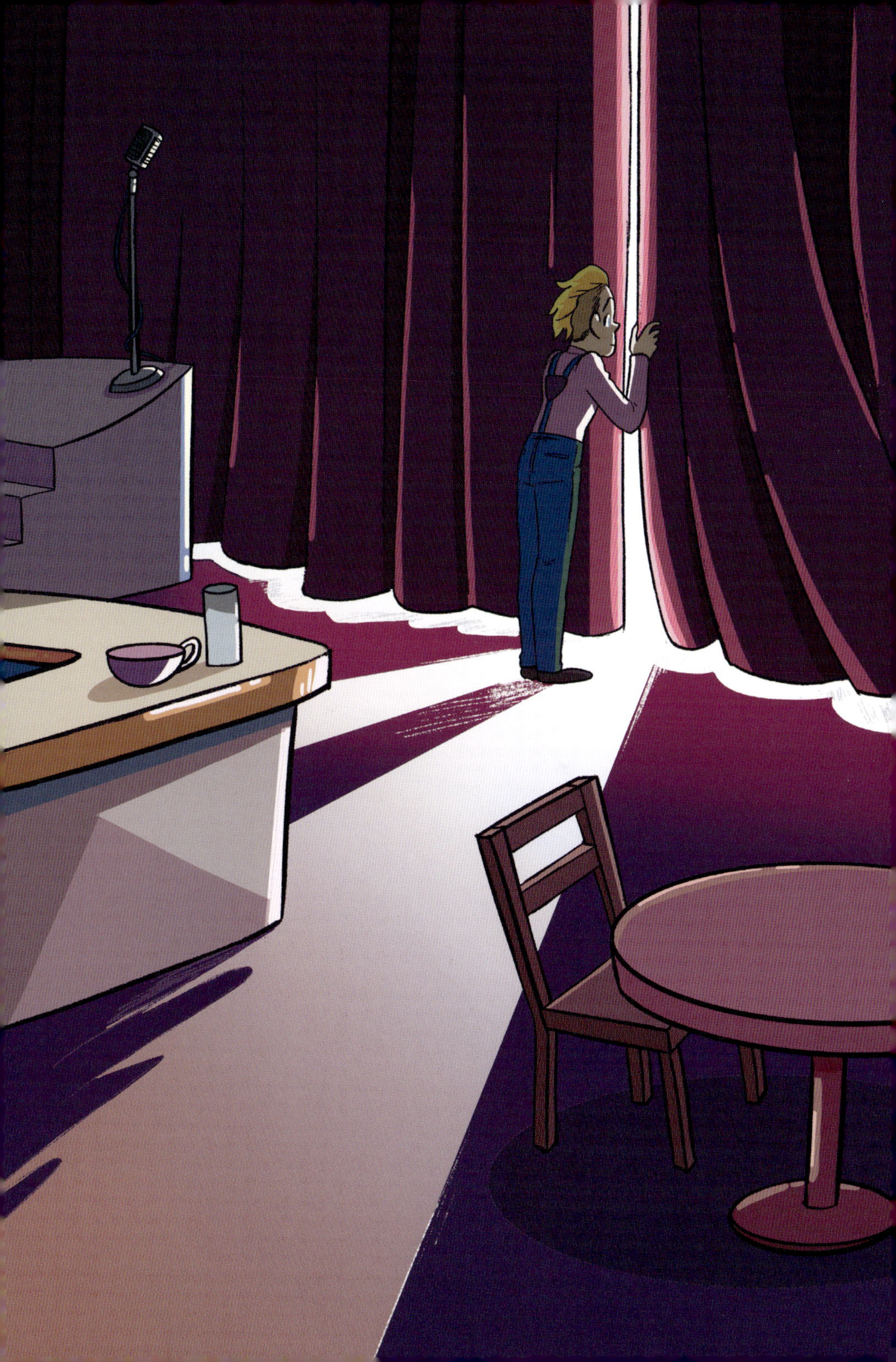

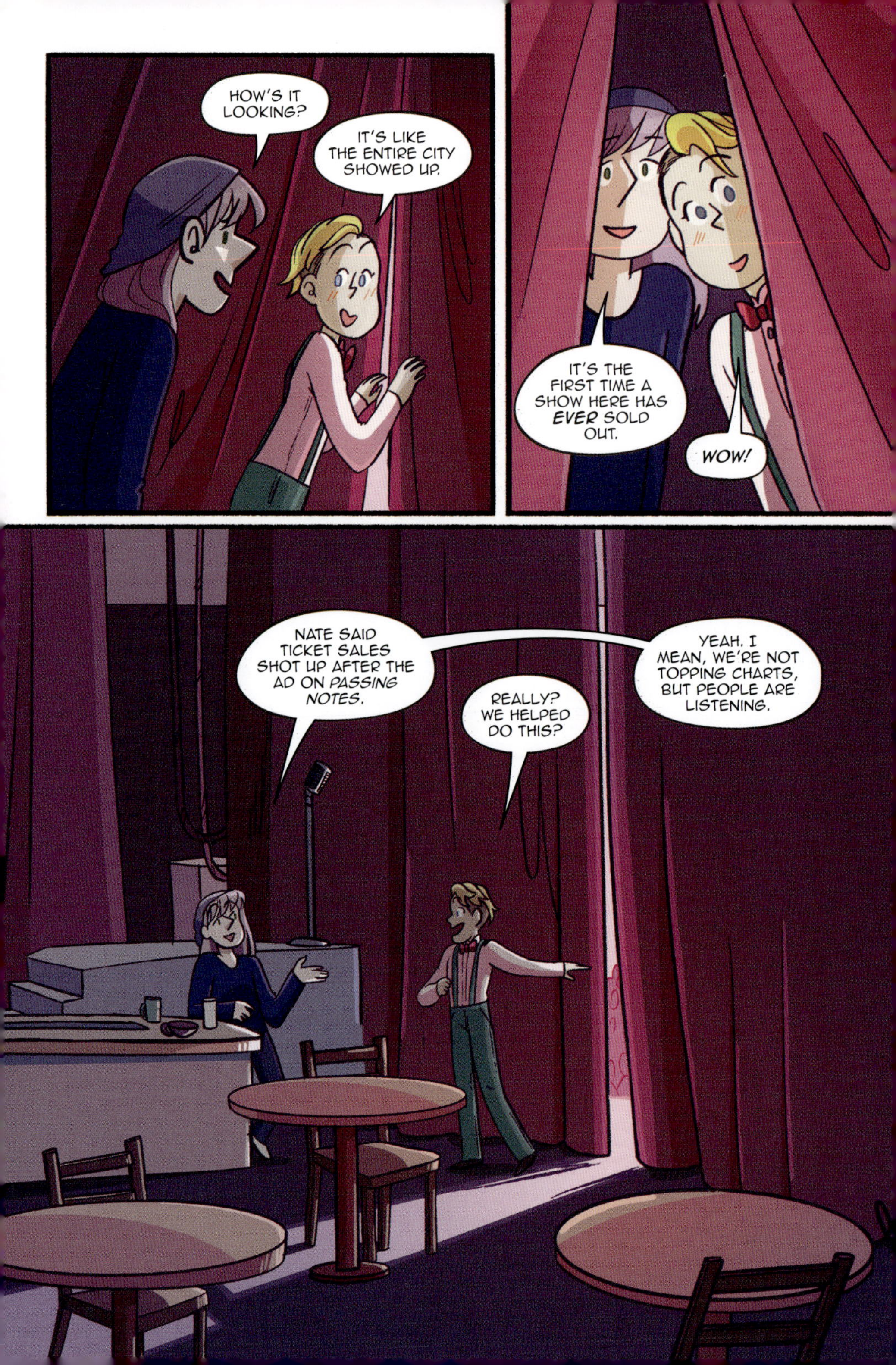
HOW'S IT LOOKING?
IT'S LIKE THE ENTIRE CITY SHOWED UP.
IT'S THE FIRST TIME A SHOW HERE HAS *EVER* SOLD OUT.
WOW!
NATE SAID TICKET SALES SHOT UP AFTER THE AD ON *PASSING NOTES*.
YEAH. I MEAN, WE'RE NOT TOPPING CHARTS, BUT PEOPLE ARE LISTENING.
REALLY? WE HELPED DO THIS?

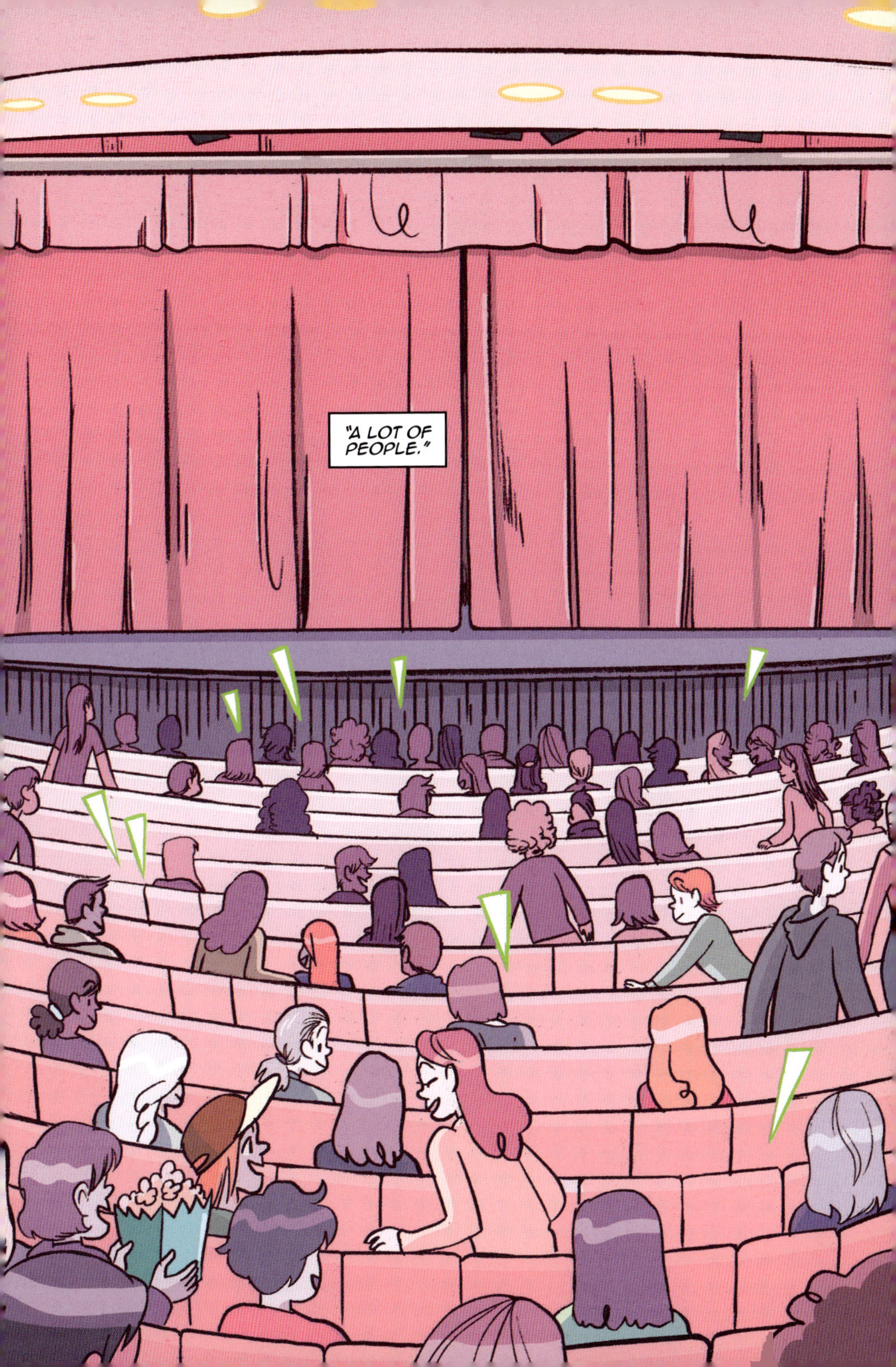
"A LOT OF PEOPLE."

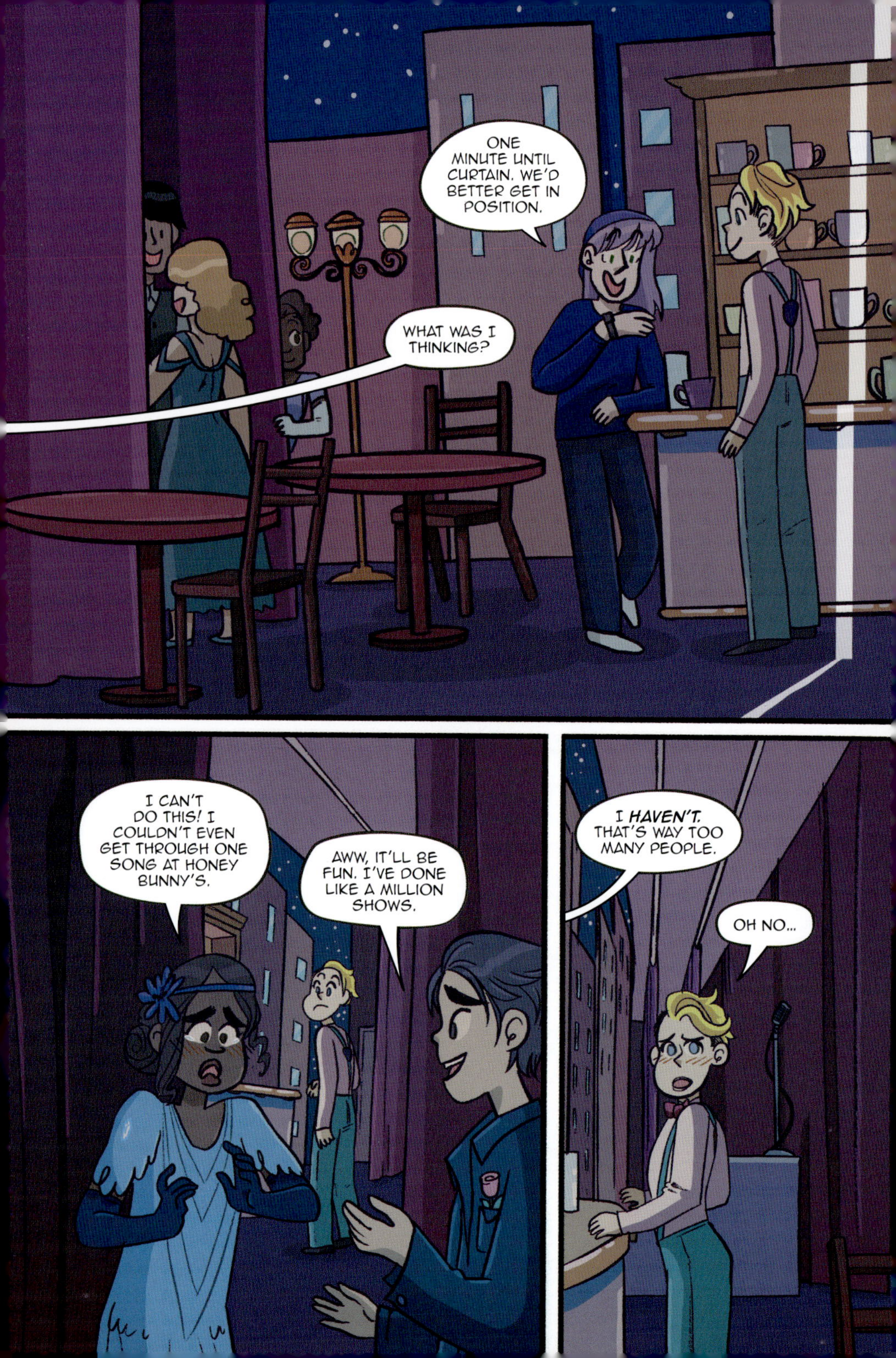
ONE MINUTE UNTIL CURTAIN. WE'D BETTER GET IN POSITION.
WHAT WAS I THINKING?
I CAN'T DO THIS! I COULDN'T EVEN GET THROUGH ONE SONG AT HONEY BUNNY'S.
AWW, IT'LL BE FUN. I'VE DONE LIKE A MILLION SHOWS.
I *HAVEN'T.* THAT'S WAY TOO MANY PEOPLE.
OH NO...

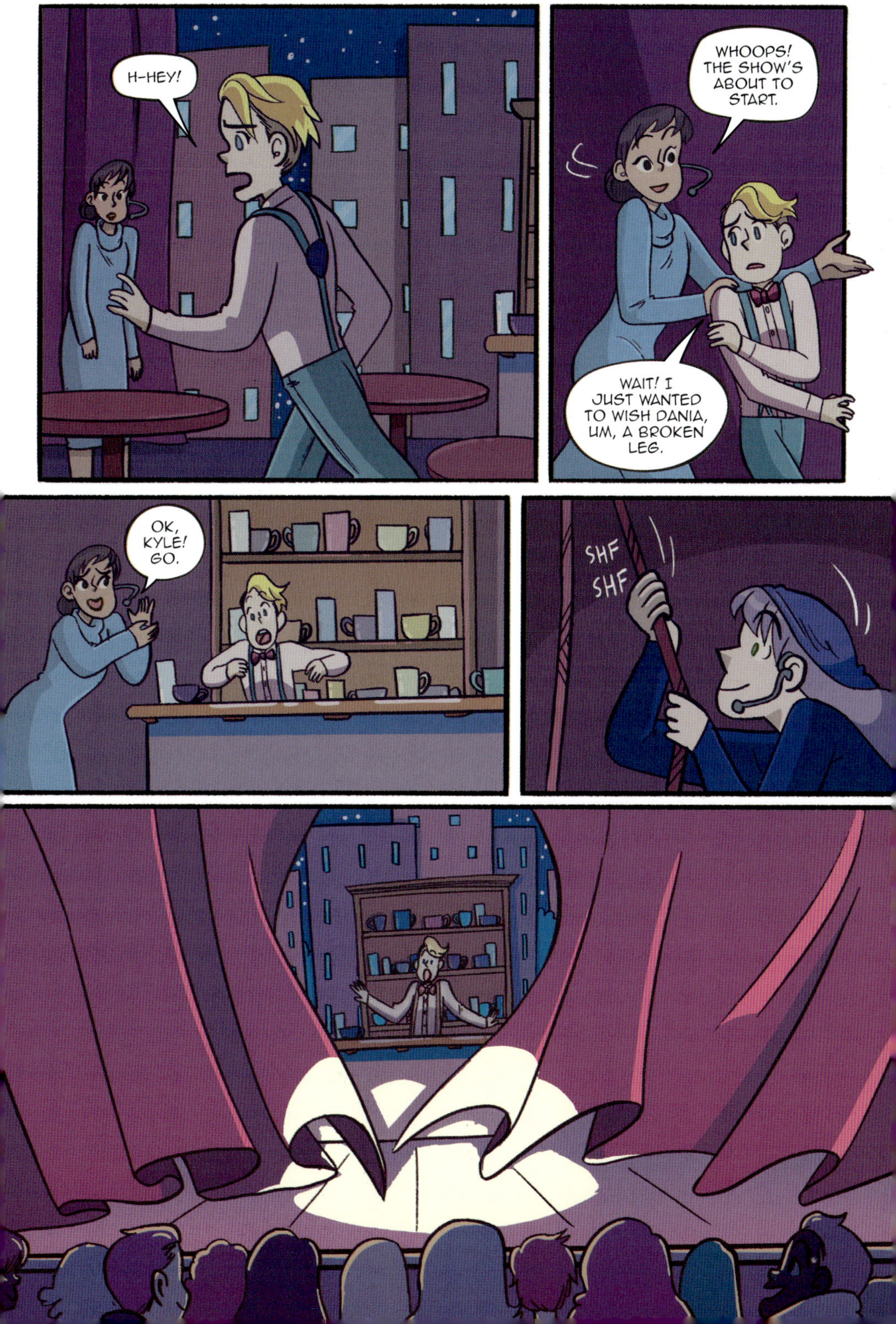
H-HEY!
WHOOPS! THE SHOW'S ABOUT TO START.
WAIT! I JUST WANTED TO WISH DANIA, UM, A BROKEN LEG.
OK, KYLE! GO.
SHF
SHF

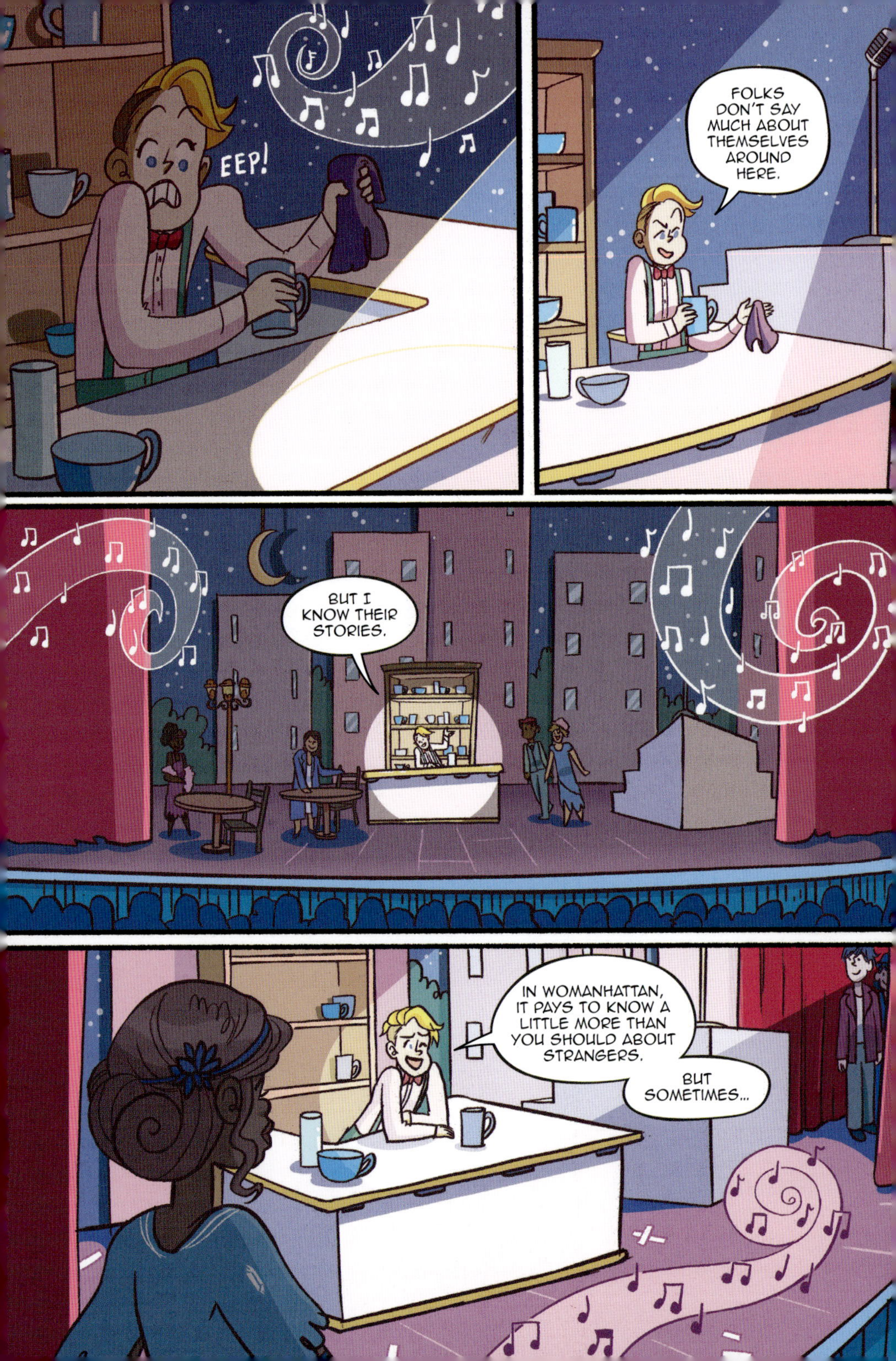

EEP!
FOLKS DON'T SAY MUCH ABOUT THEMSELVES AROUND HERE.
BUT I KNOW THEIR STORIES.
IN WOMANHATTAN, IT PAYS TO KNOW A LITTLE MORE THAN YOU SHOULD ABOUT STRANGERS.
BUT SOMETIMES...

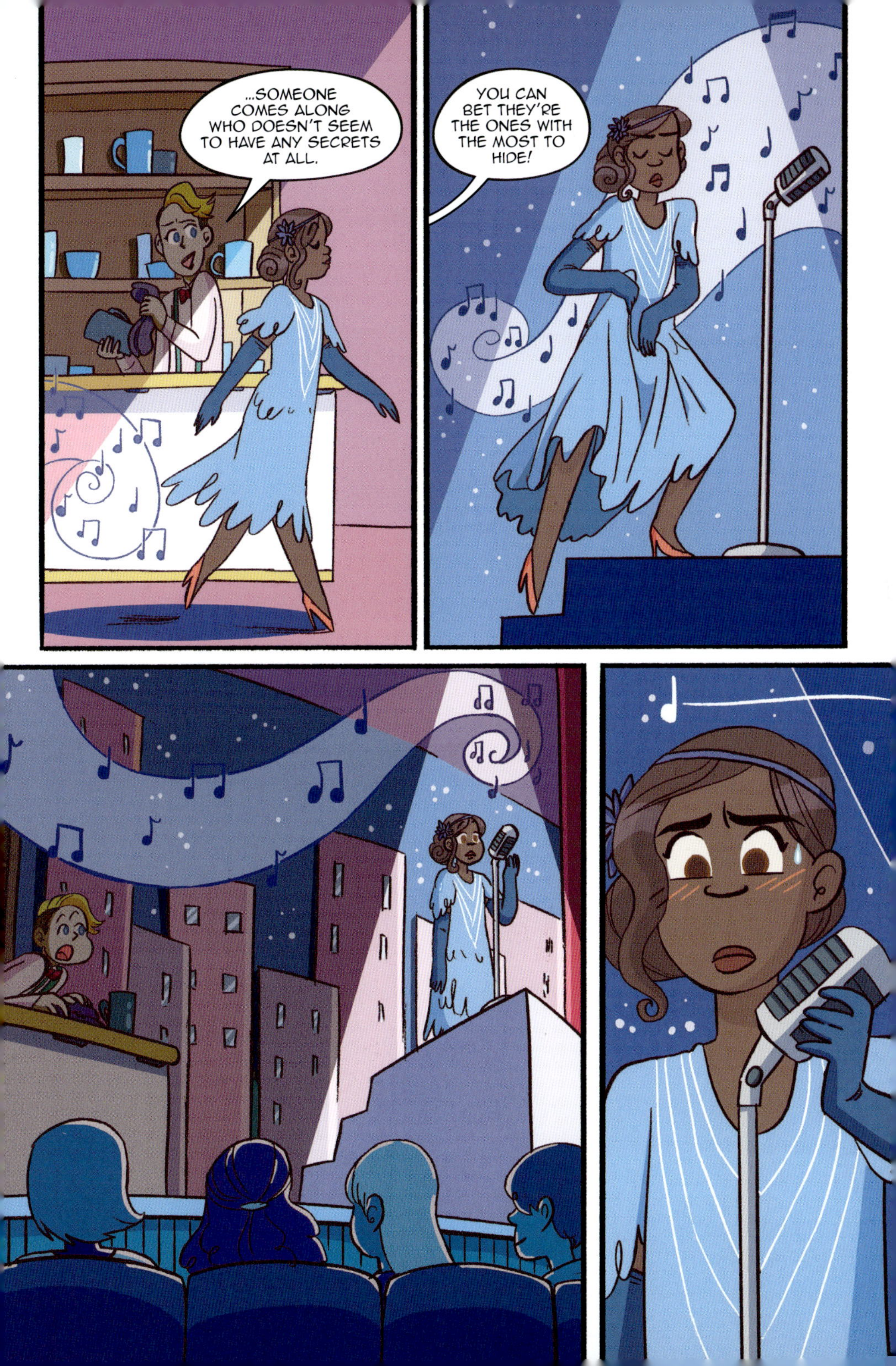
...SOMEONE COMES ALONG WHO DOESN'T SEEM TO HAVE ANY SECRETS AT ALL.
YOU CAN BET THEY'RE THE ONES WITH THE MOST TO HIDE!

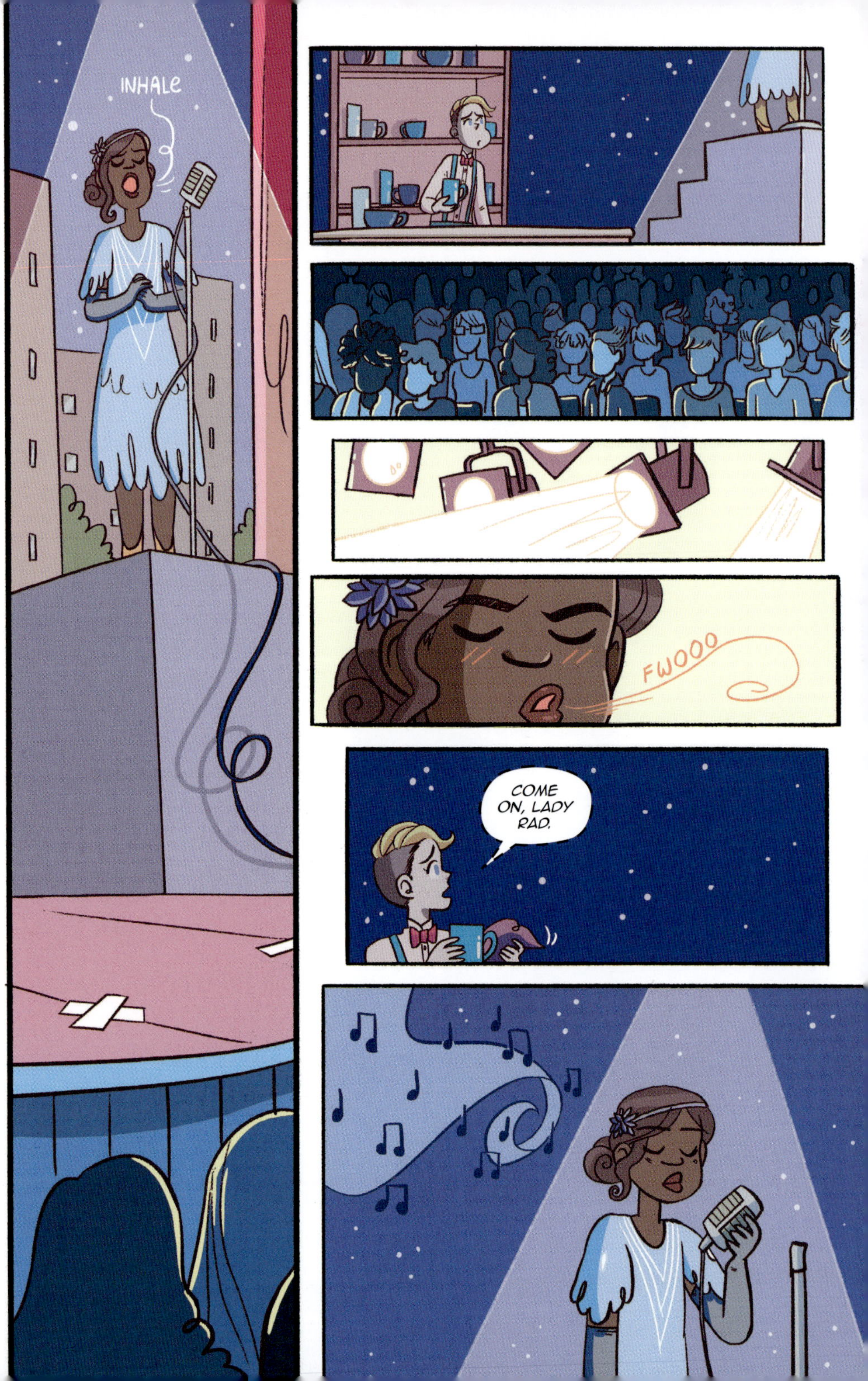
INHALE
FWOOO
COME ON, LADY RAD.

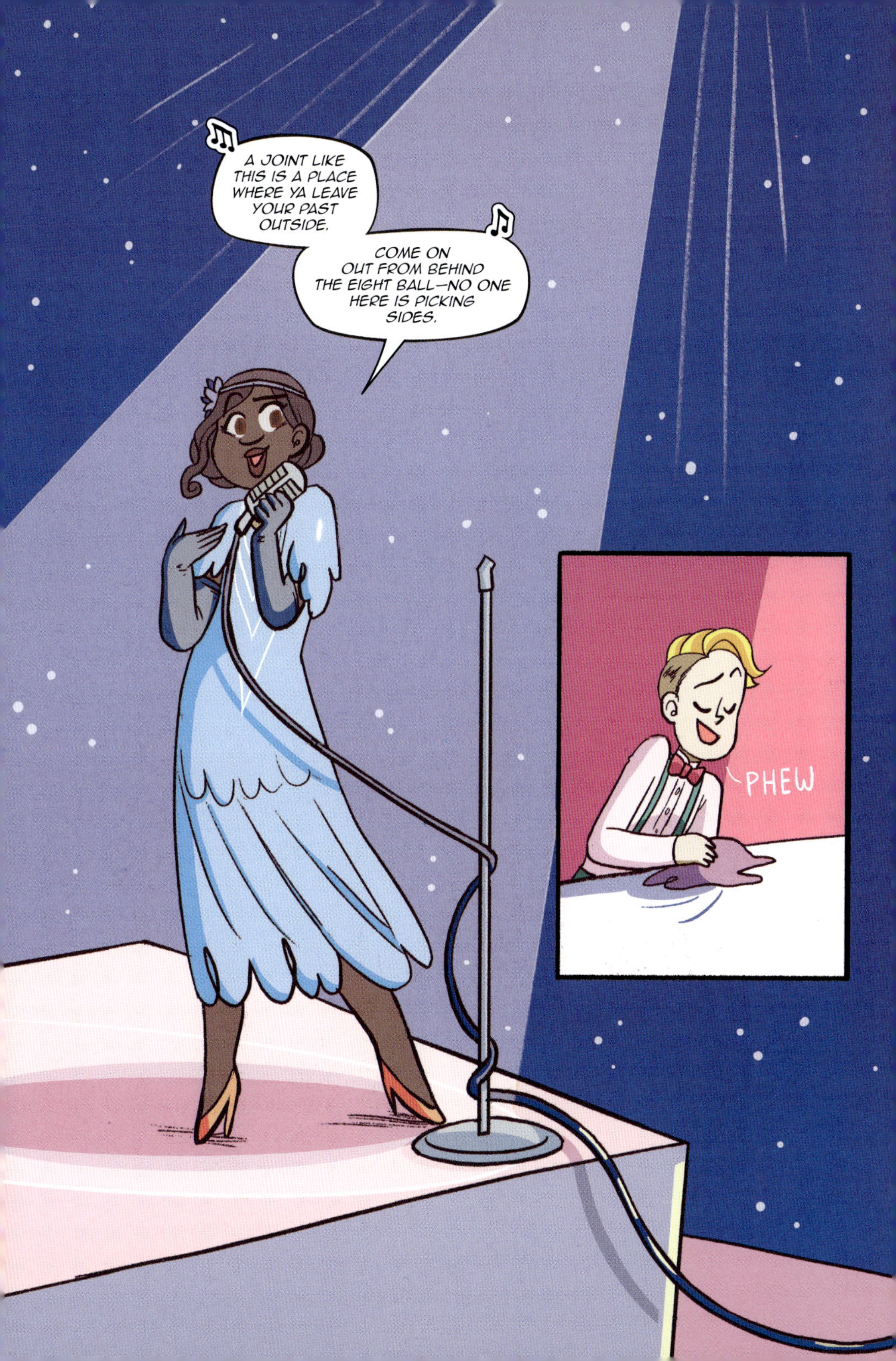
A JOINT LIKE THIS IS A PLACE WHERE YA LEAVE YOUR PAST OUTSIDE.
COME ON OUT FROM BEHIND THE EIGHT BALL—NO ONE HERE IS PICKING SIDES.
PHEW

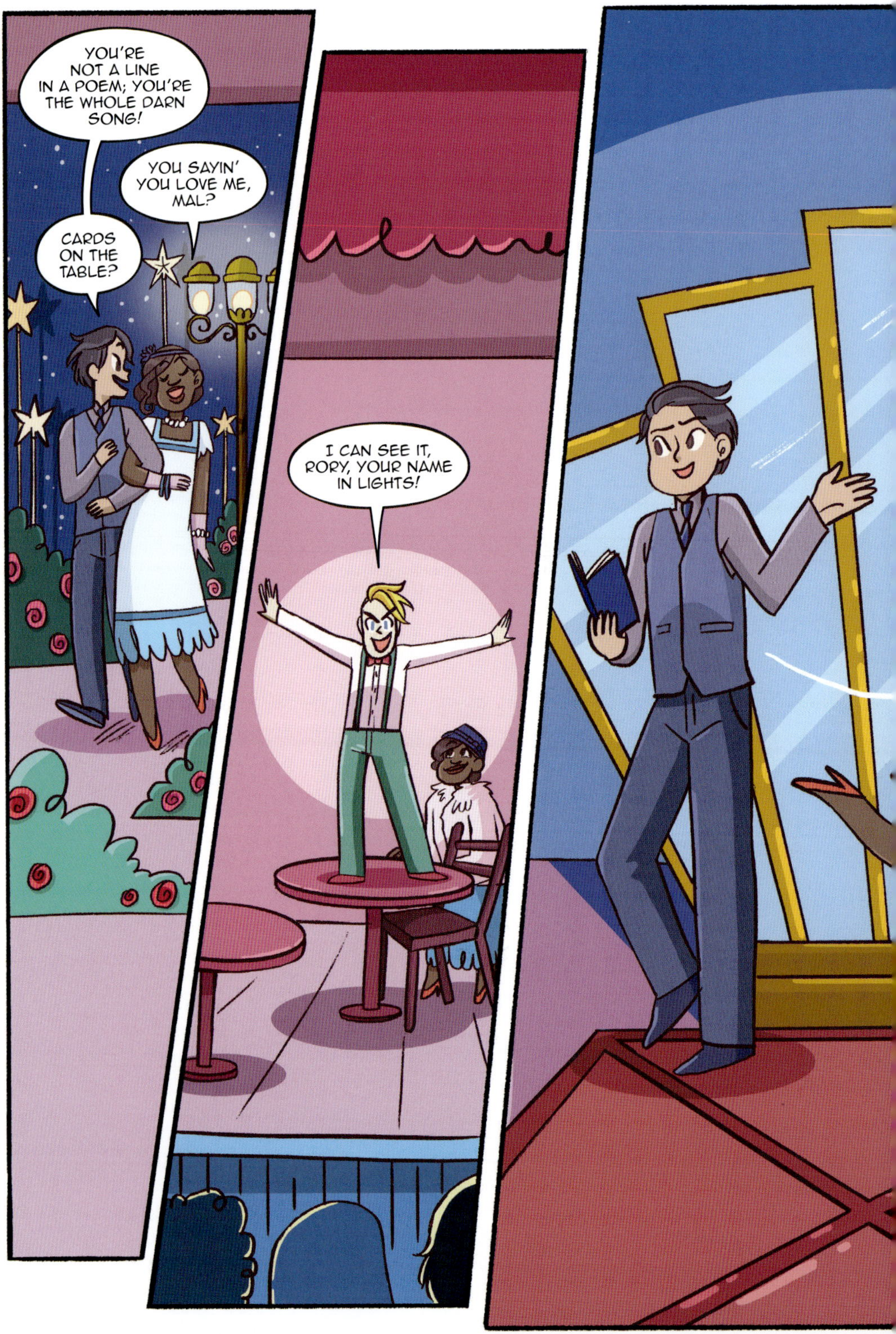
YOU'RE NOT A LINE IN A POEM; YOU'RE THE WHOLE DARN SONG!
YOU SAYIN' YOU LOVE ME, MAL?
CARDS ON THE TABLE?
I CAN SEE IT, RORY, YOUR NAME IN LIGHTS!

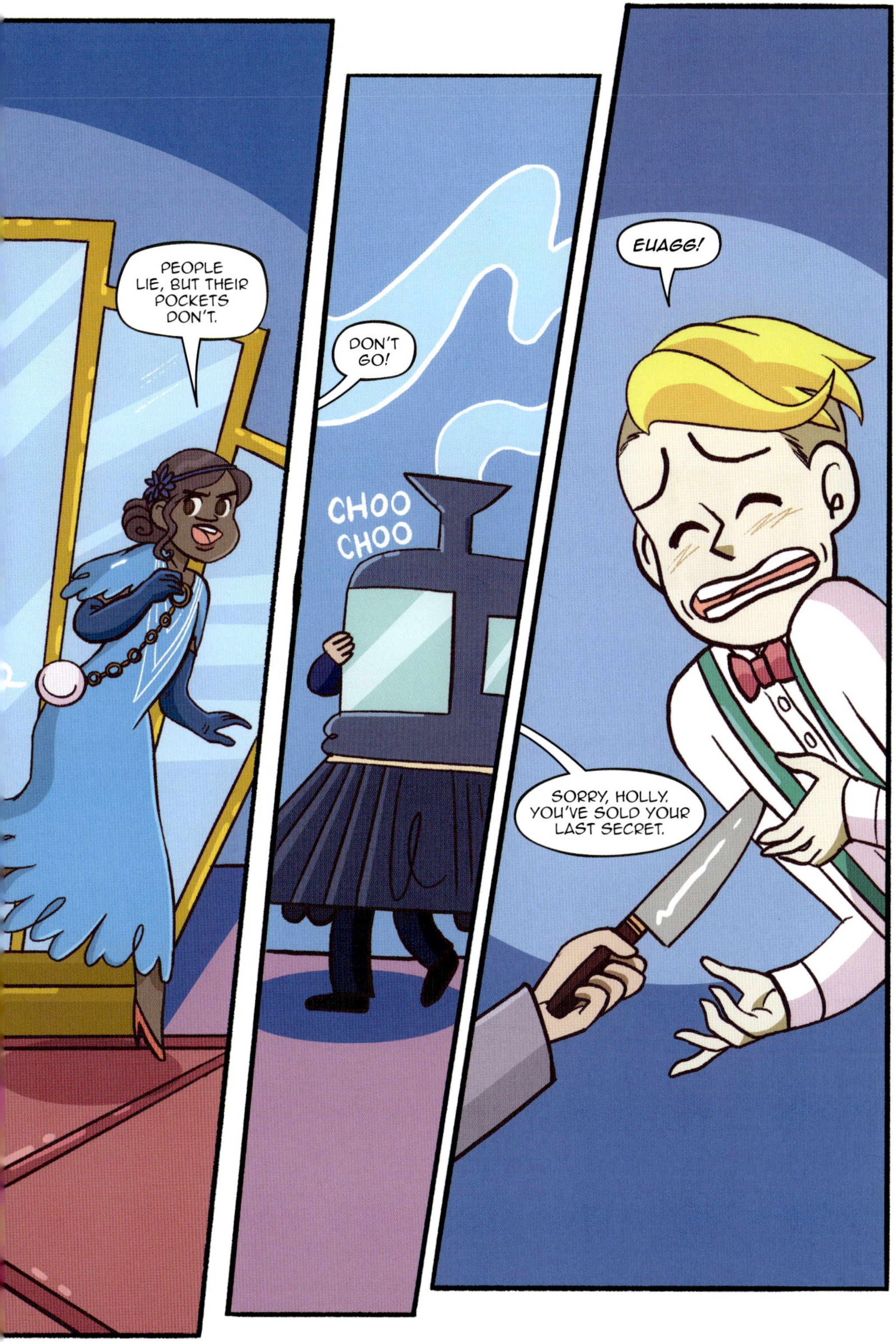
PEOPLE LIE, BUT THEIR POCKETS DON'T.
DON'T GO!
CHOO CHOO
EUAGG!
SORRY, HOLLY. YOU'VE SOLD YOUR LAST SECRET.

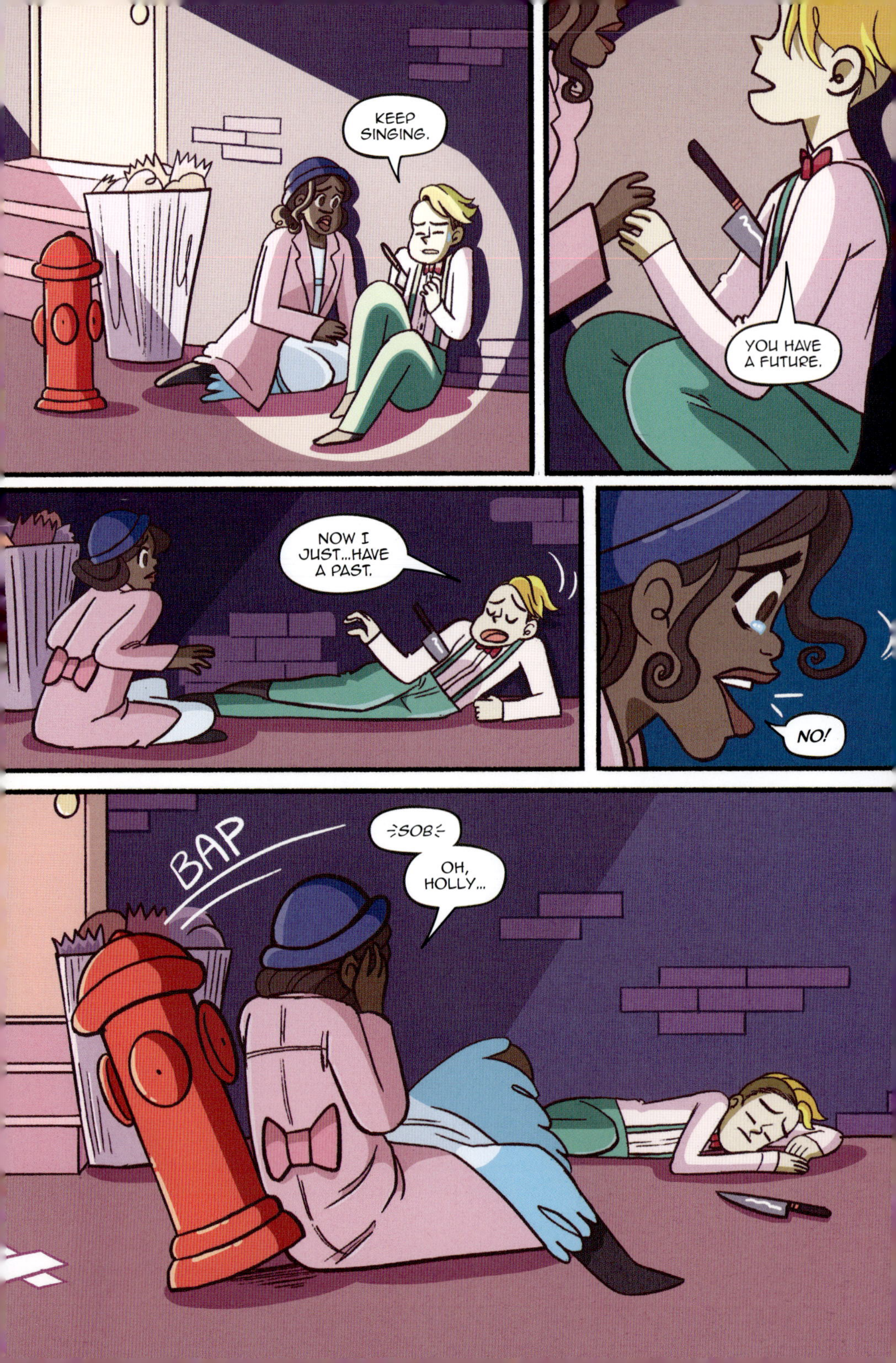
KEEP SINGING.
YOU HAVE A FUTURE.
NOW I JUST...HAVE A PAST.
NO!
BAP
SOB
OH, HOLLY...

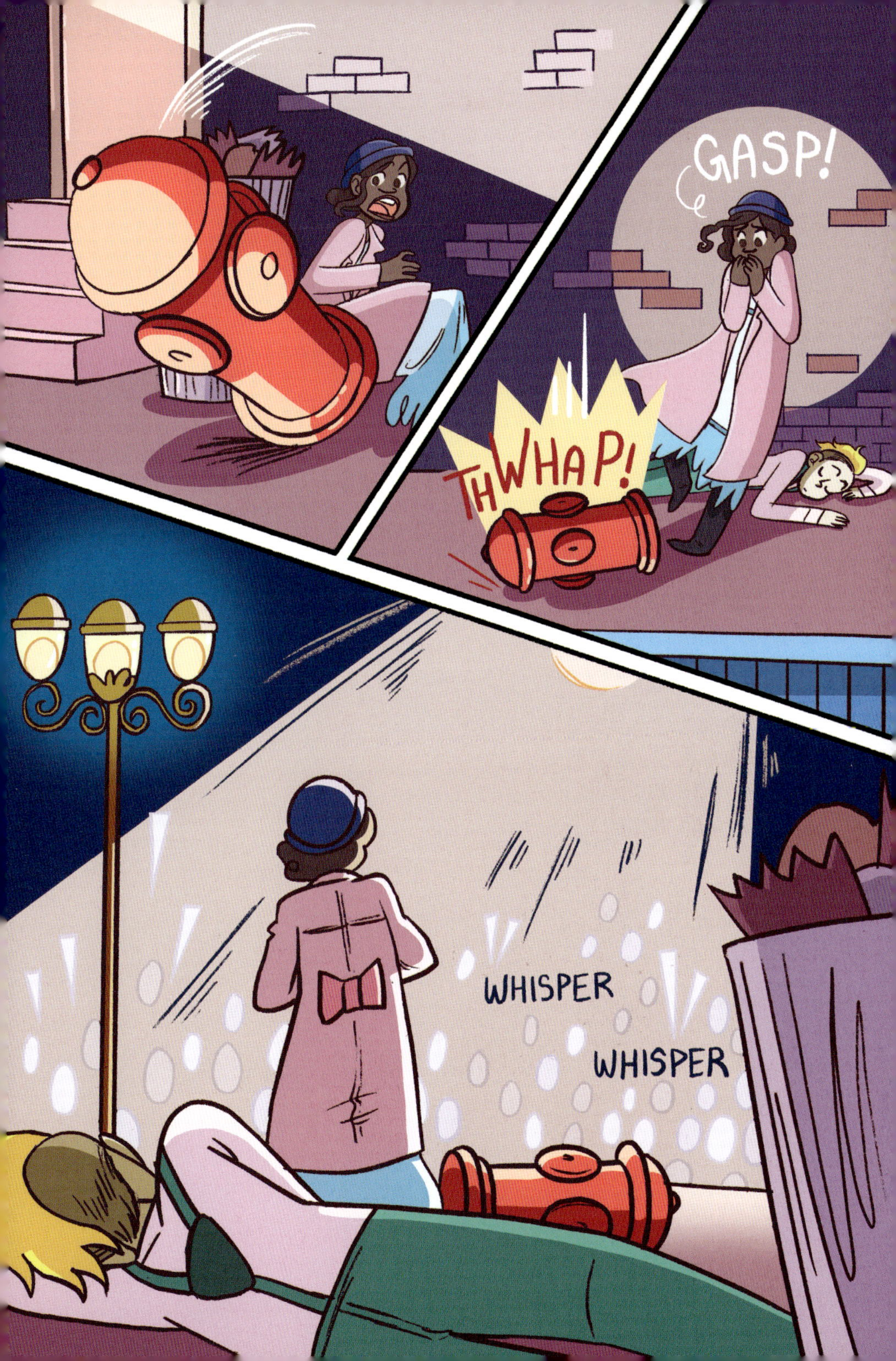
GASP!
THWHAP!
WHISPER
WHISPER

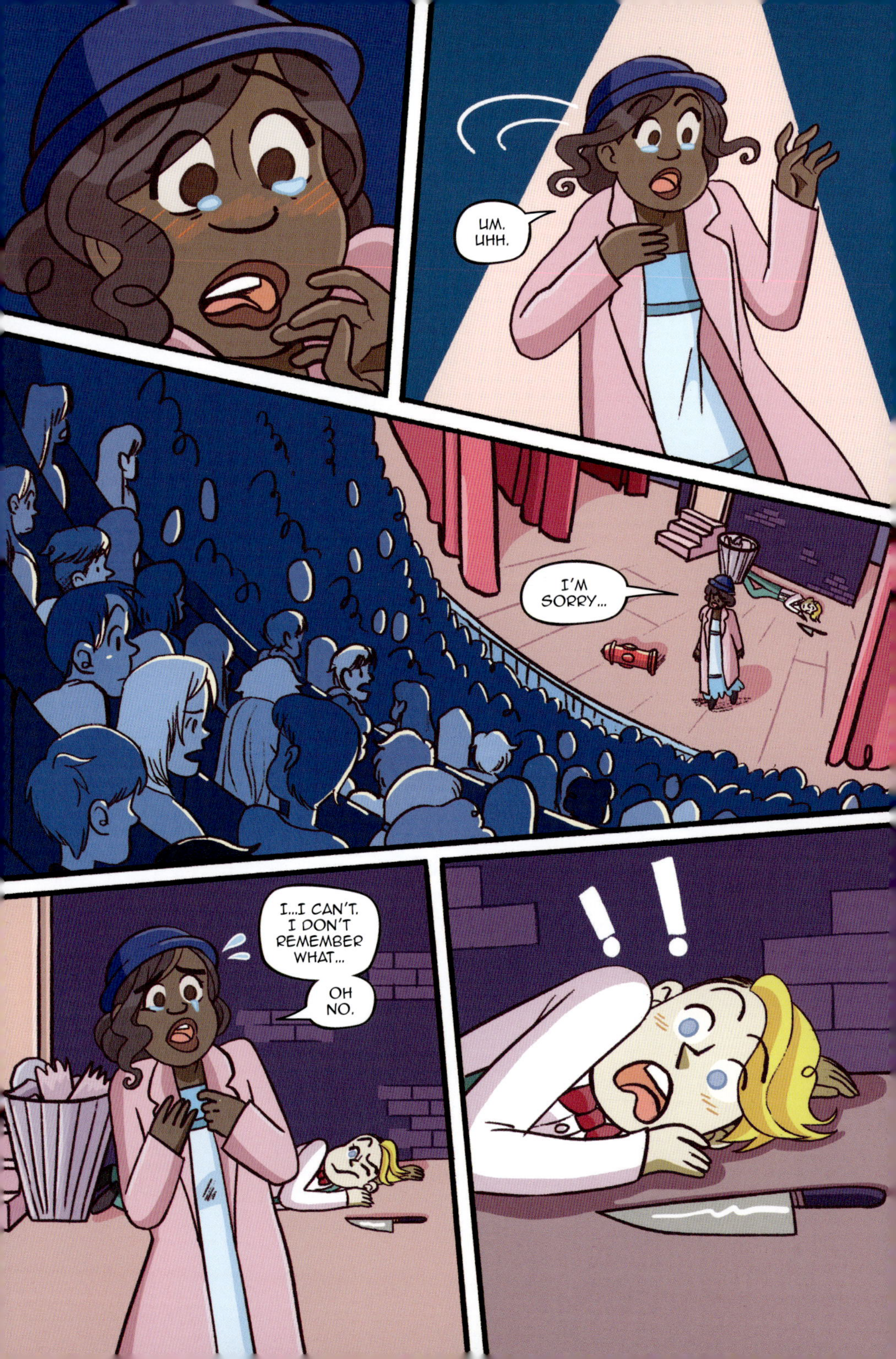
UM. UHH.
I'M SORRY...
I...I CAN'T. I DON'T REMEMBER WHAT...
OH NO.
!!

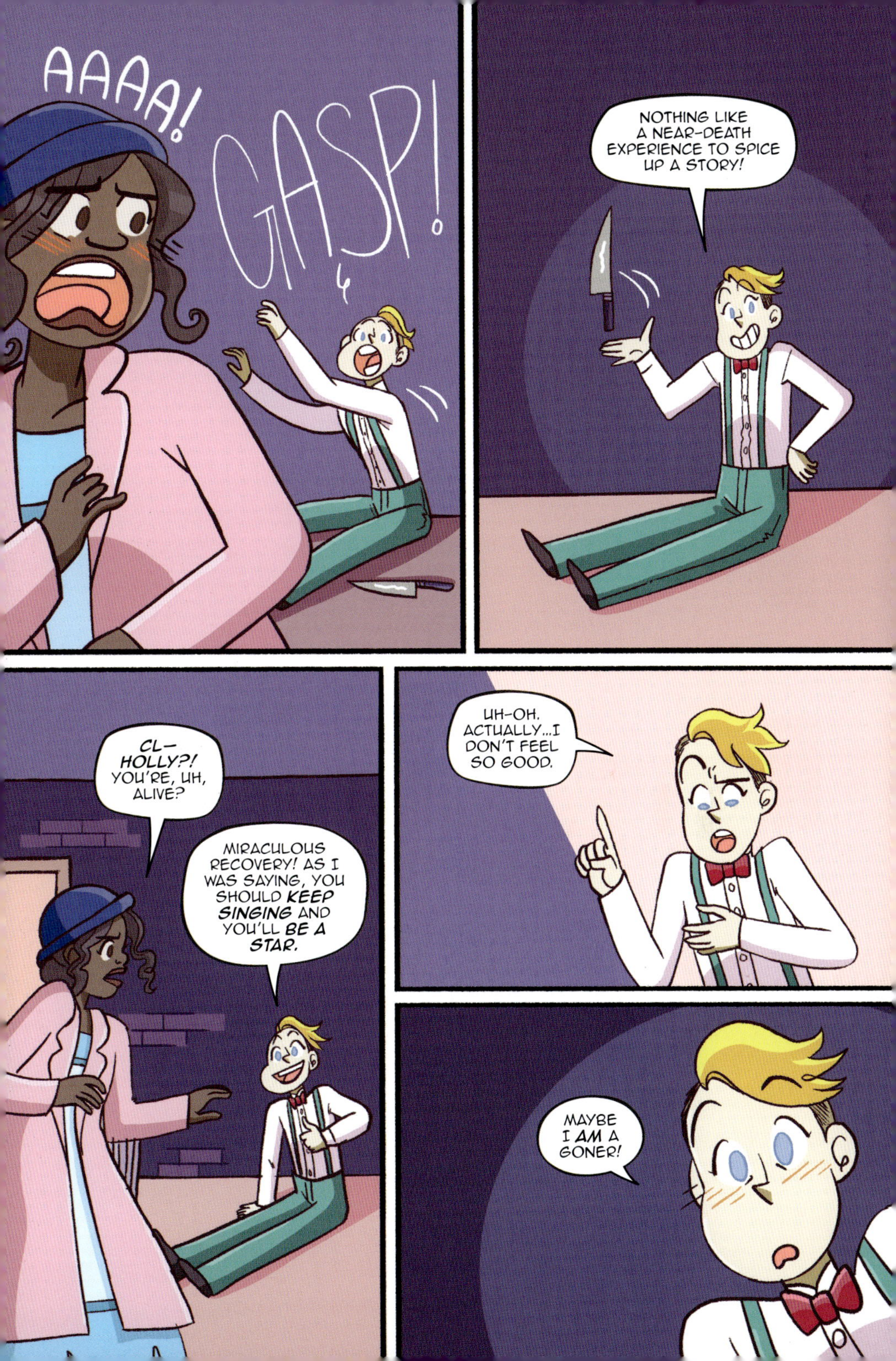
AAAA!
GASP!
NOTHING LIKE A NEAR-DEATH EXPERIENCE TO SPICE UP A STORY!
CL— HOLLY?! YOU'RE, UH, ALIVE?
MIRACULOUS RECOVERY! AS I WAS SAYING, YOU SHOULD KEEP SINGING AND YOU'LL BE A STAR.
UH-OH. ACTUALLY...I DON'T FEEL SO GOOD.
MAYBE I AM A GONER!

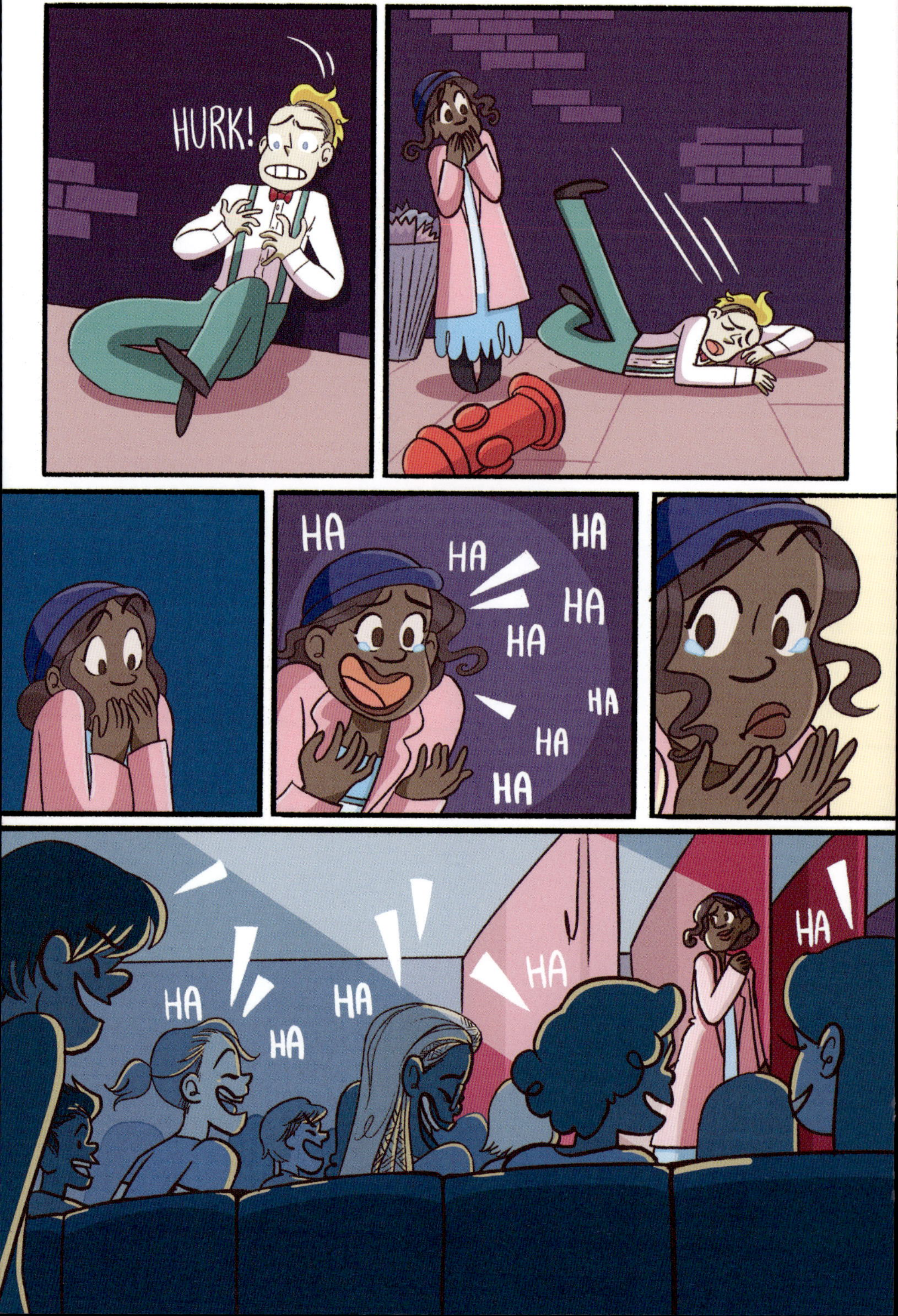
HURK!
HA
HA
HA
HA
HA
HA
HA
HA
HA
HA
HA
HA
HA
HA

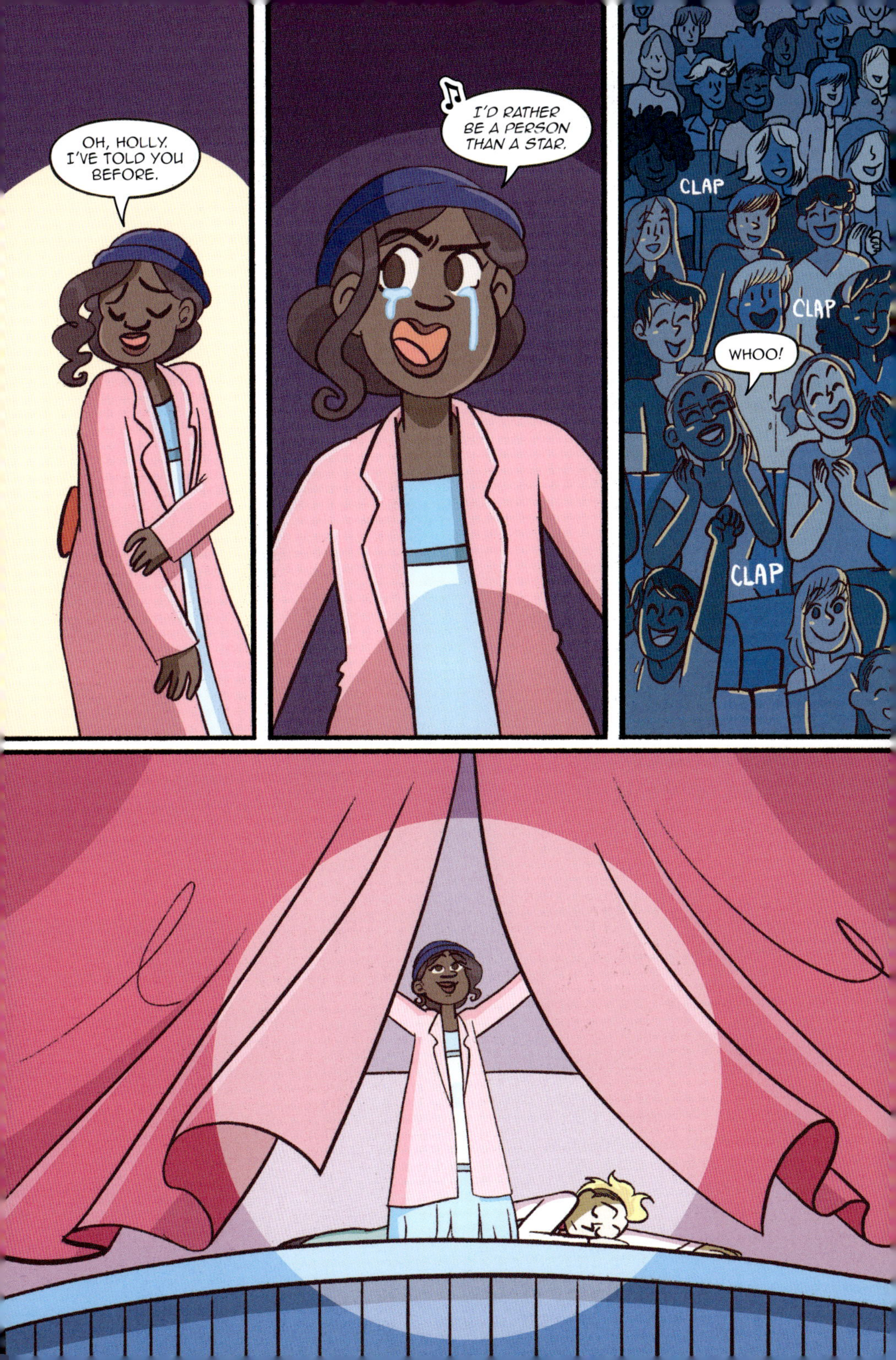
OH, HOLLY. I'VE TOLD YOU BEFORE.
I'D RATHER BE A PERSON THAN A STAR.
CLAP
CLAP
WHOO!
CLAP

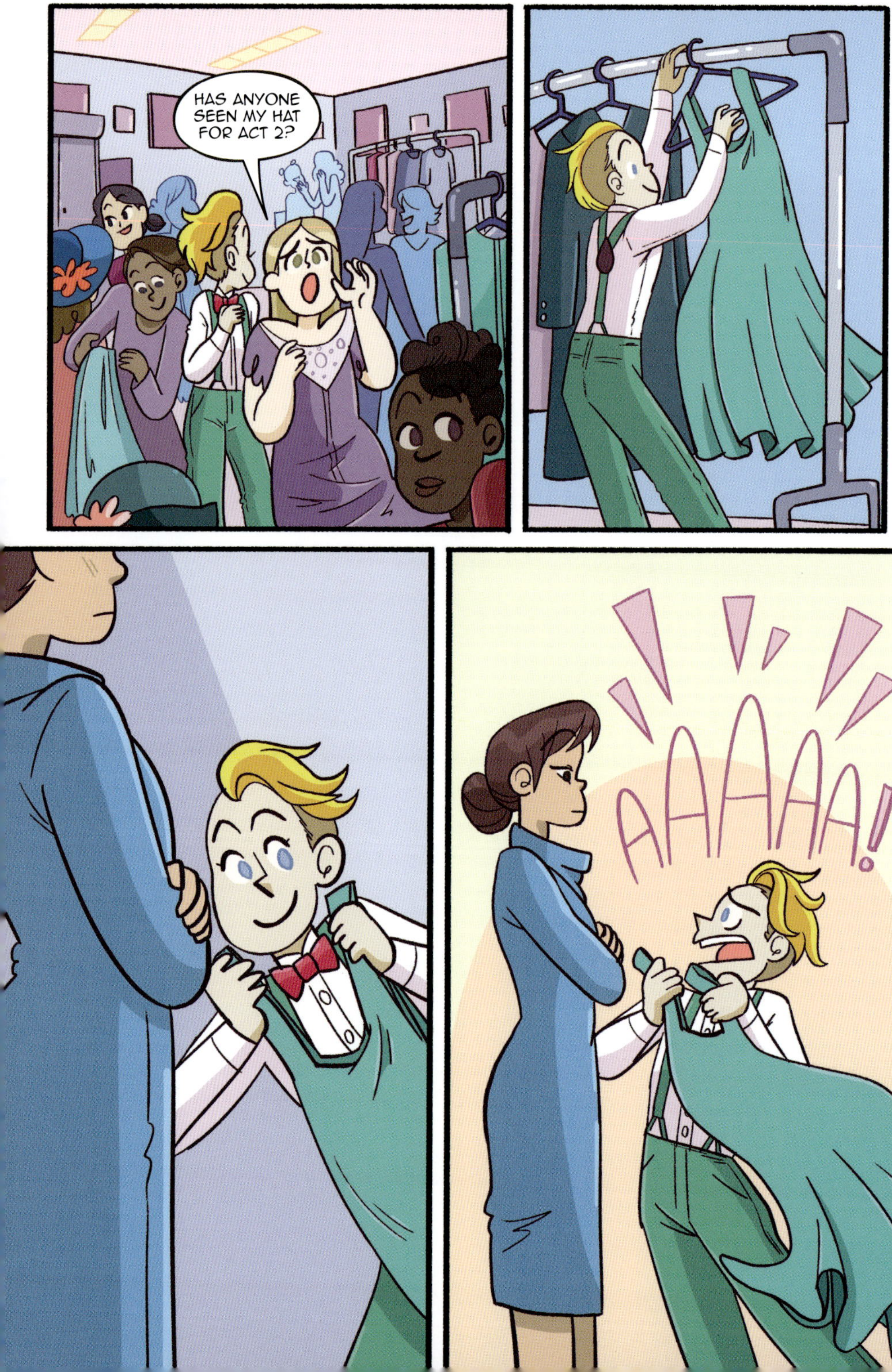
HAS ANYONE SEEN MY HAT FOR ACT 2?
AAAAA!

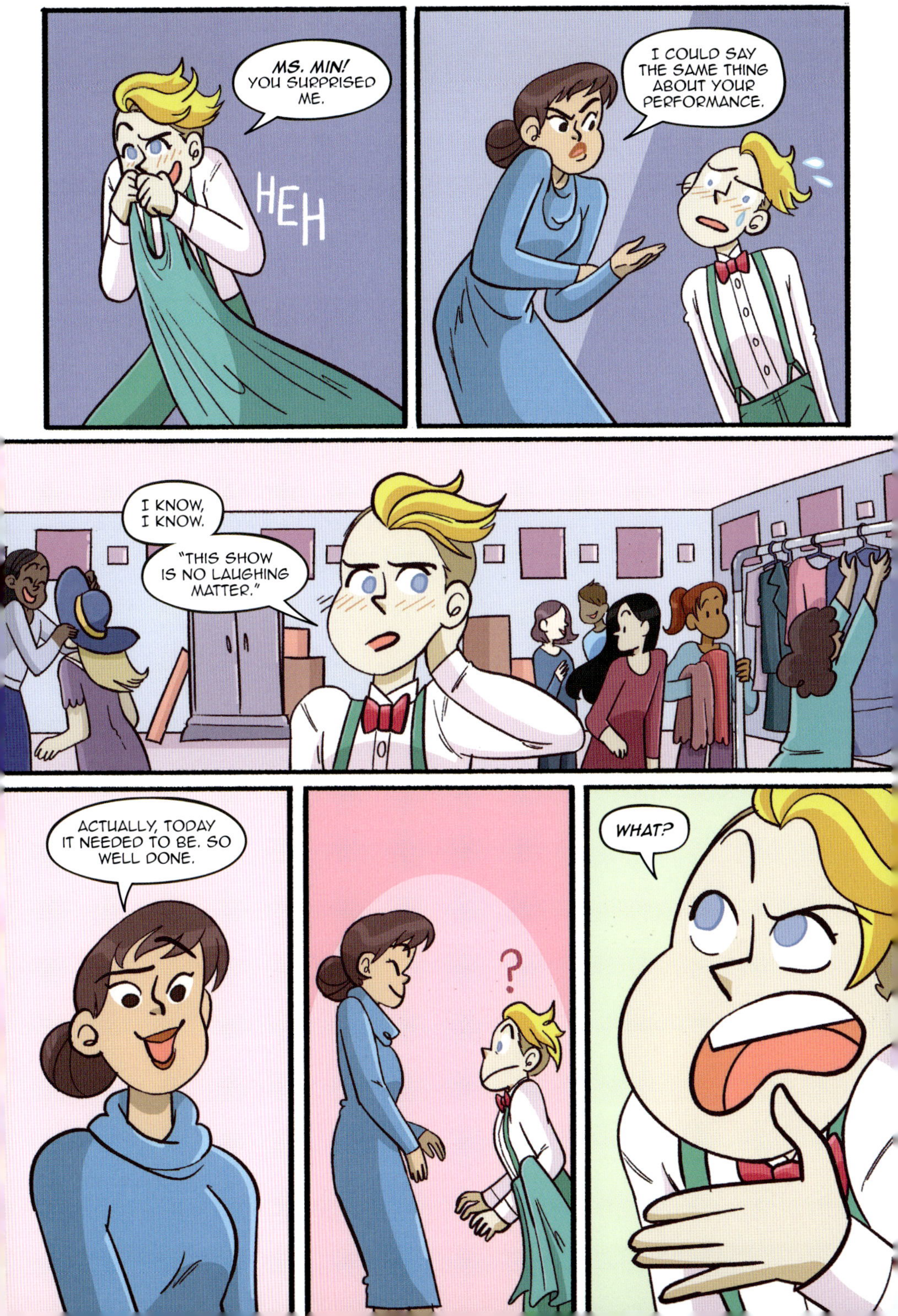
MS. MIN! YOU SURPRISED ME.
HEH
I COULD SAY THE SAME THING ABOUT YOUR PERFORMANCE.
I KNOW, I KNOW.
"THIS SHOW IS NO LAUGHING MATTER."
ACTUALLY, TODAY IT NEEDED TO BE. SO WELL DONE.
?
WHAT?

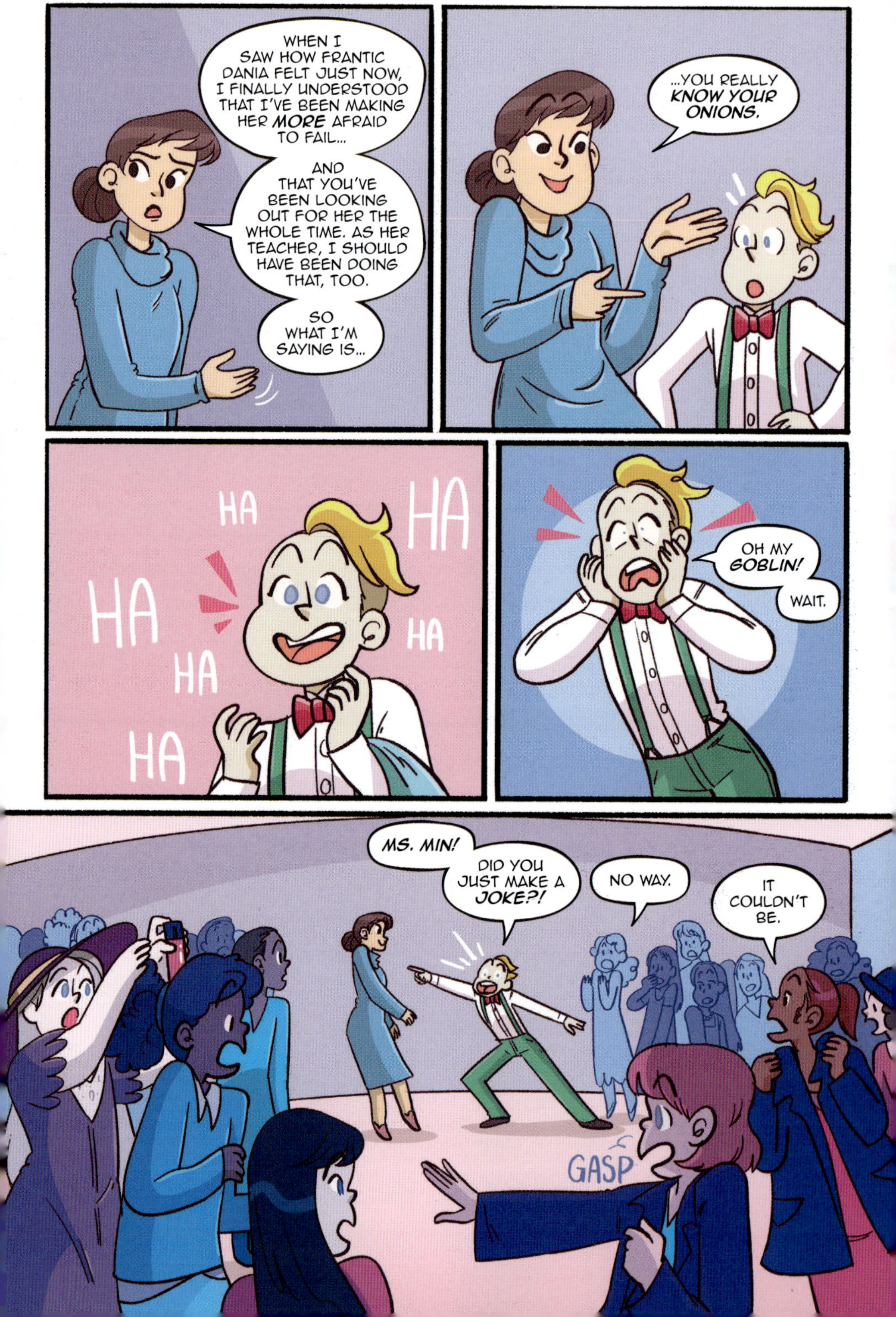
WHEN I SAW HOW FRANTIC DANIA FELT JUST NOW, I FINALLY UNDERSTOOD THAT I'VE BEEN MAKING HER MORE AFRAID TO FAIL...
AND THAT YOU'VE BEEN LOOKING OUT FOR HER THE WHOLE TIME. AS HER TEACHER, I SHOULD HAVE BEEN DOING THAT, TOO.
SO WHAT I'M SAYING IS...
...YOU REALLY KNOW YOUR ONIONS.
HA
HA
HA
HA
HA
HA
OH MY GOBLIN!
WAIT.
MS. MIN!
DID YOU JUST MAKE A JOKE?!
NO WAY.
IT COULDN'T BE.
GASP

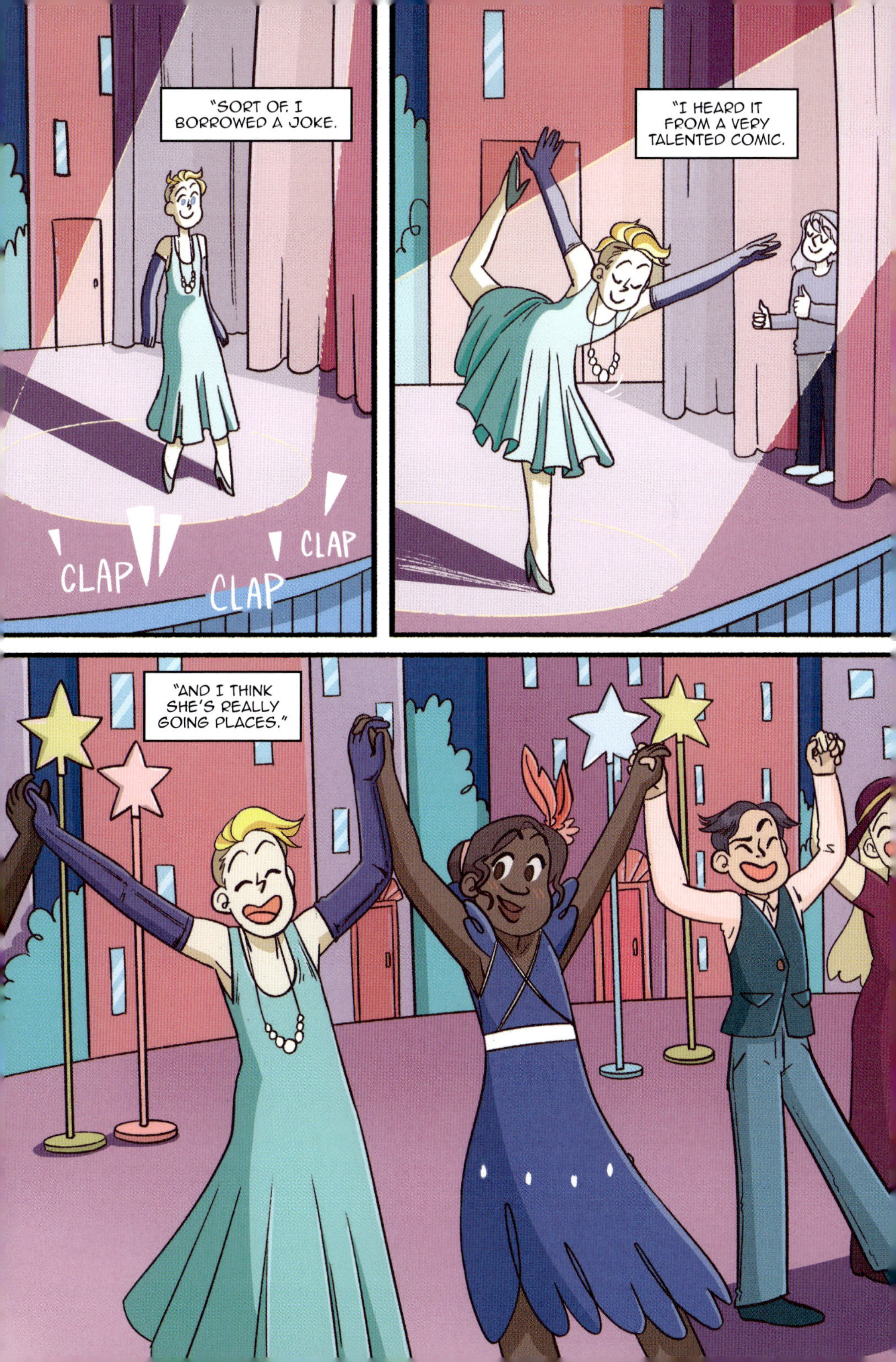
"SORT OF. I BORROWED A JOKE.
CLAP
CLAP
CLAP
"I HEARD IT FROM A VERY TALENTED COMIC.
"AND I THINK SHE'S REALLY GOING PLACES."

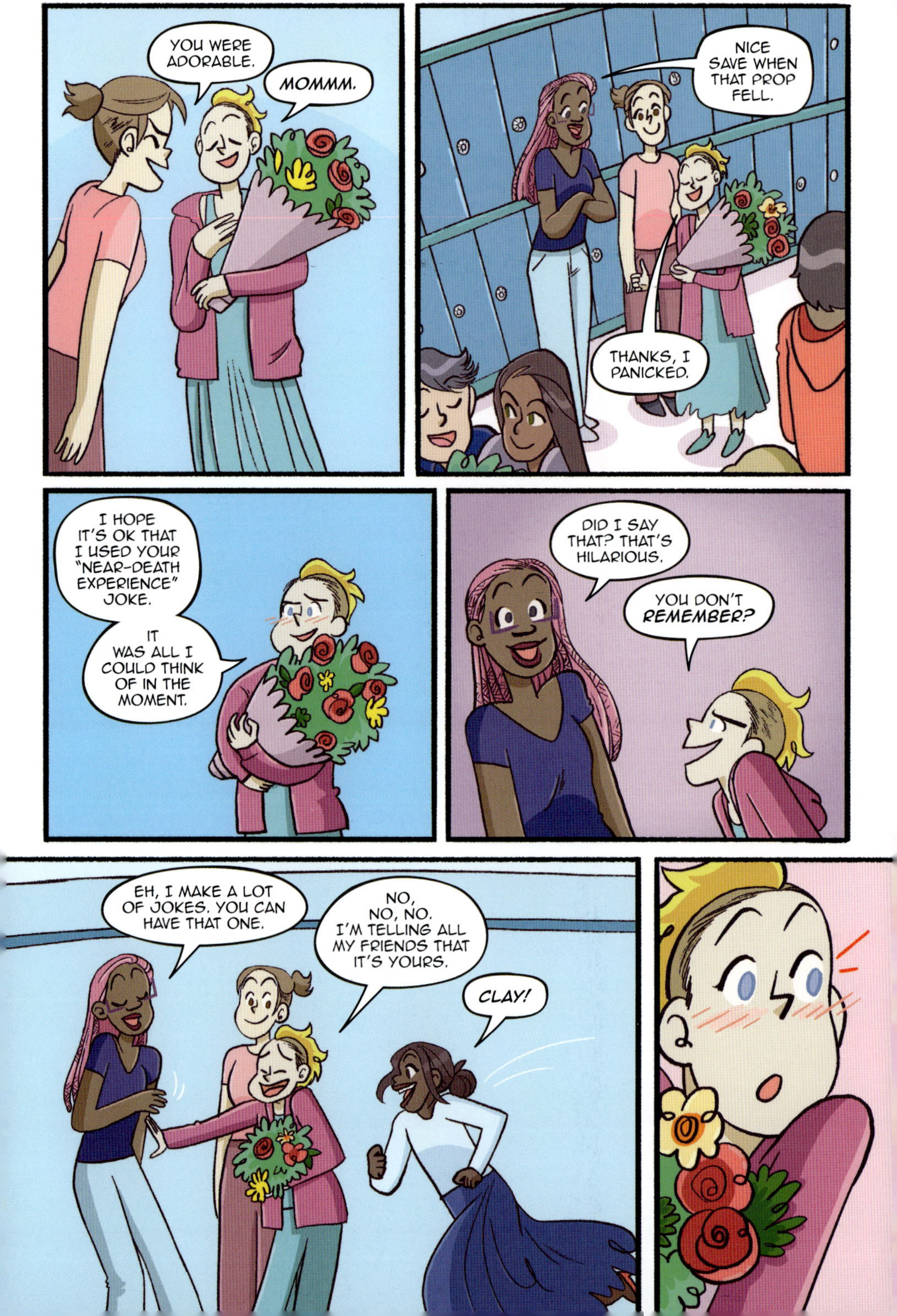
YOU WERE ADORABLE.
MOMMM.
NICE SAVE WHEN THAT PROP FELL.
THANKS, I PANICKED.
I HOPE IT'S OK THAT I USED YOUR "NEAR-DEATH EXPERIENCE" JOKE.
IT WAS ALL I COULD THINK OF IN THE MOMENT.
DID I SAY THAT? THAT'S HILARIOUS.
YOU DON'T REMEMBER?
EH, I MAKE A LOT OF JOKES. YOU CAN HAVE THAT ONE.
NO, NO, NO. I'M TELLING ALL MY FRIENDS THAT IT'S YOURS.
CLAY!

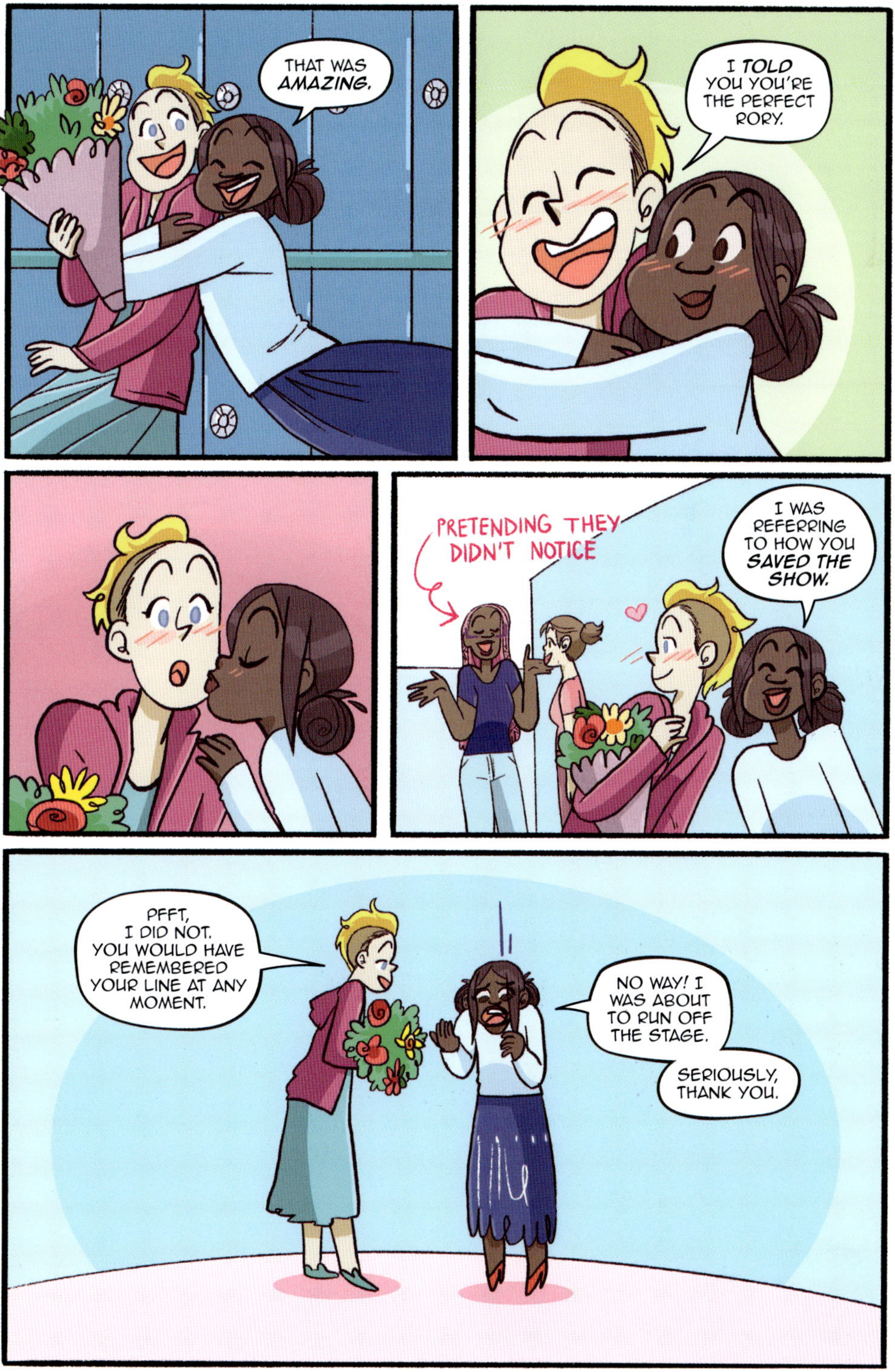
THAT WAS *AMAZING.*
I *TOLD* YOU YOU'RE THE PERFECT RORY.
PRETENDING THEY DIDN'T NOTICE
I WAS REFERRING TO HOW YOU *SAVED THE SHOW.*
PFFT, I DID NOT. YOU WOULD HAVE REMEMBERED YOUR LINE AT ANY MOMENT.
NO WAY! I WAS ABOUT TO RUN OFF THE STAGE.
SERIOUSLY, THANK YOU.

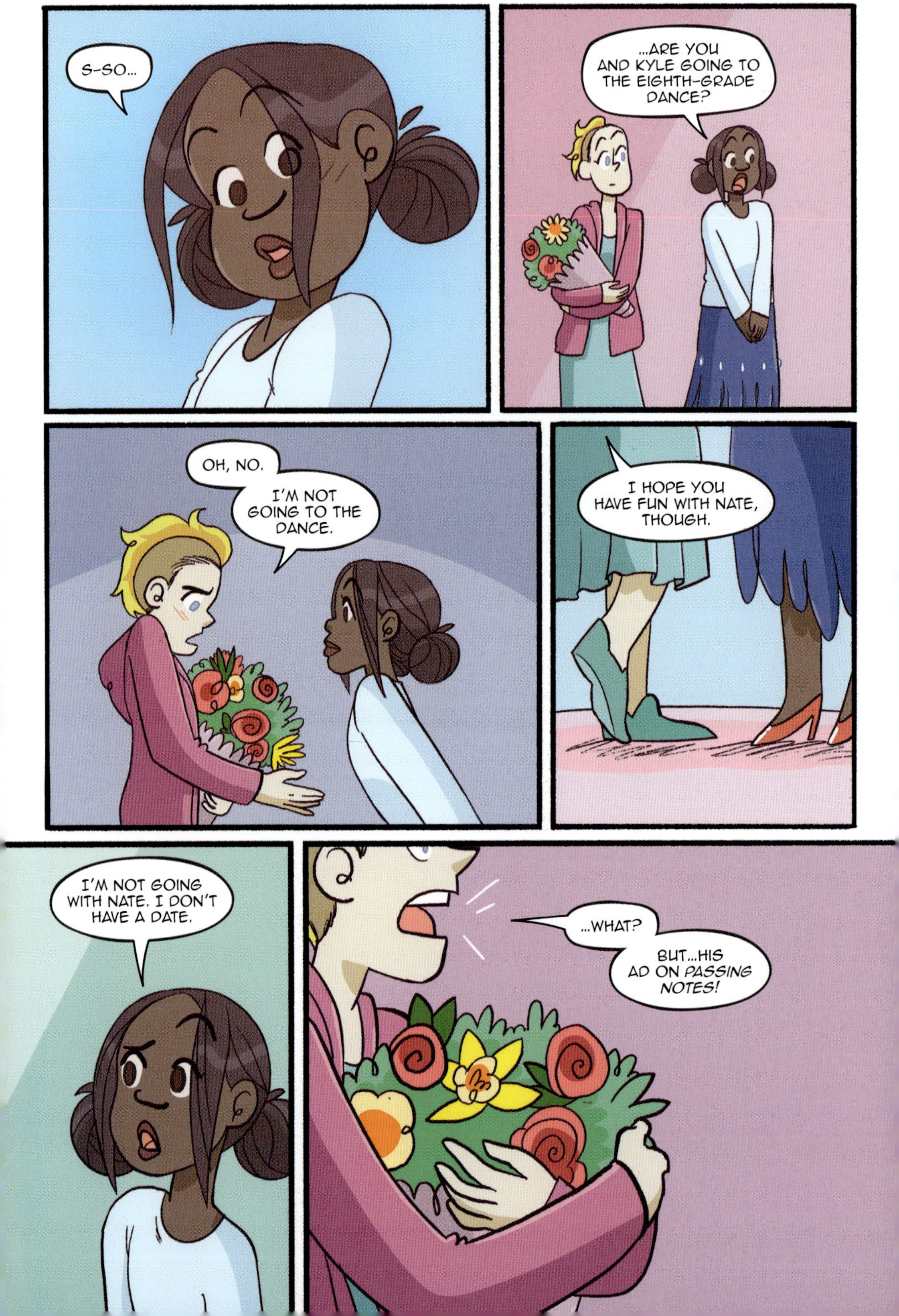
S-SO...
...ARE YOU AND KYLE GOING TO THE EIGHTH-GRADE DANCE?
OH, NO.
I'M NOT GOING TO THE DANCE.
I HOPE YOU HAVE FUN WITH NATE, THOUGH.
I'M NOT GOING WITH NATE. I DON'T HAVE A DATE.
...WHAT?
BUT...HIS AD ON *PASSING NOTES!*

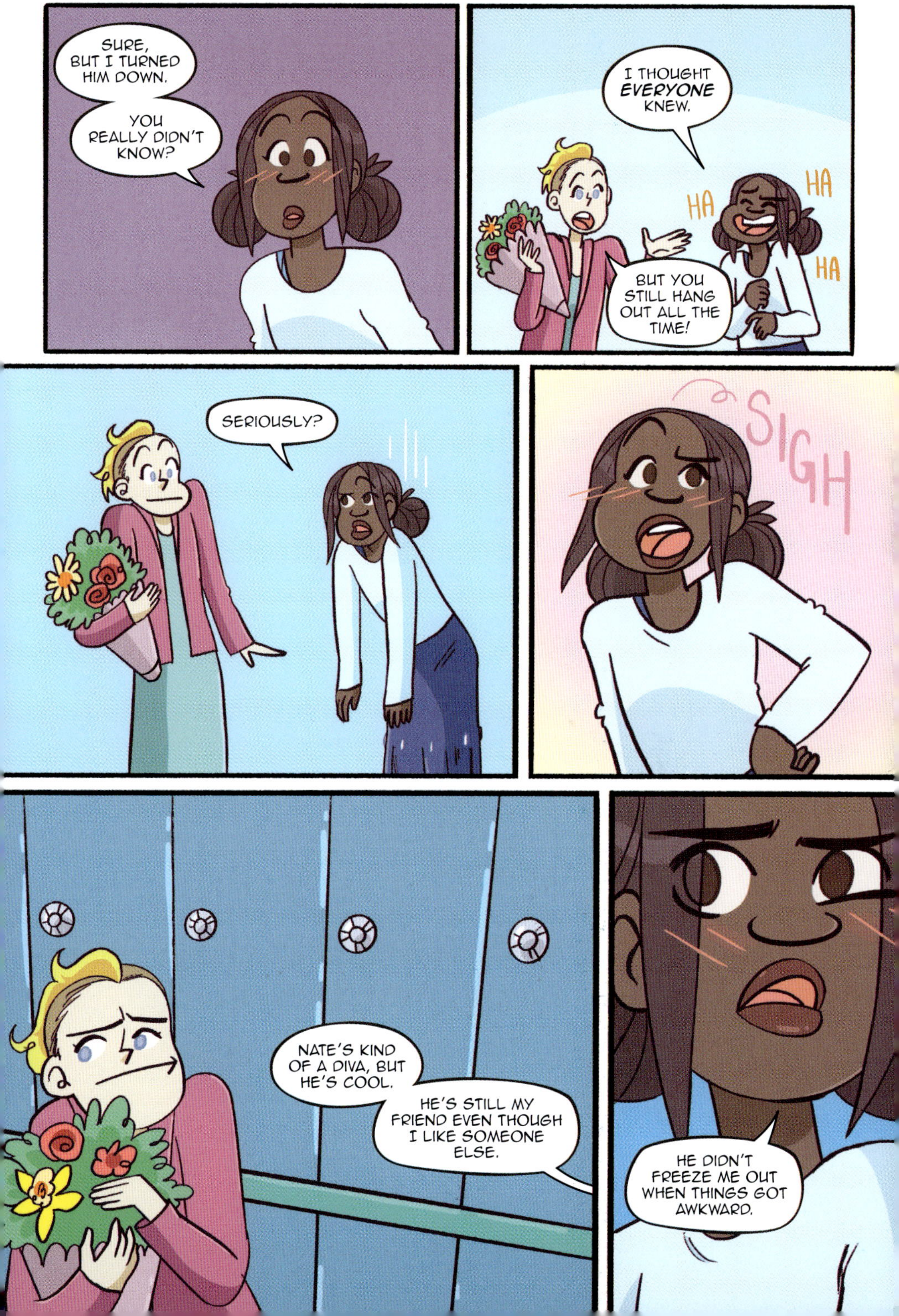
SURE, BUT I TURNED HIM DOWN.
YOU REALLY DIDN'T KNOW?
I THOUGHT *EVERYONE* KNEW.
HA
HA
HA
BUT YOU STILL HANG OUT ALL THE TIME!
SERIOUSLY?
SIGH
NATE'S KIND OF A DIVA, BUT HE'S COOL.
HE'S STILL MY FRIEND EVEN THOUGH I LIKE SOMEONE ELSE.
HE DIDN'T FREEZE ME OUT WHEN THINGS GOT AWKWARD.

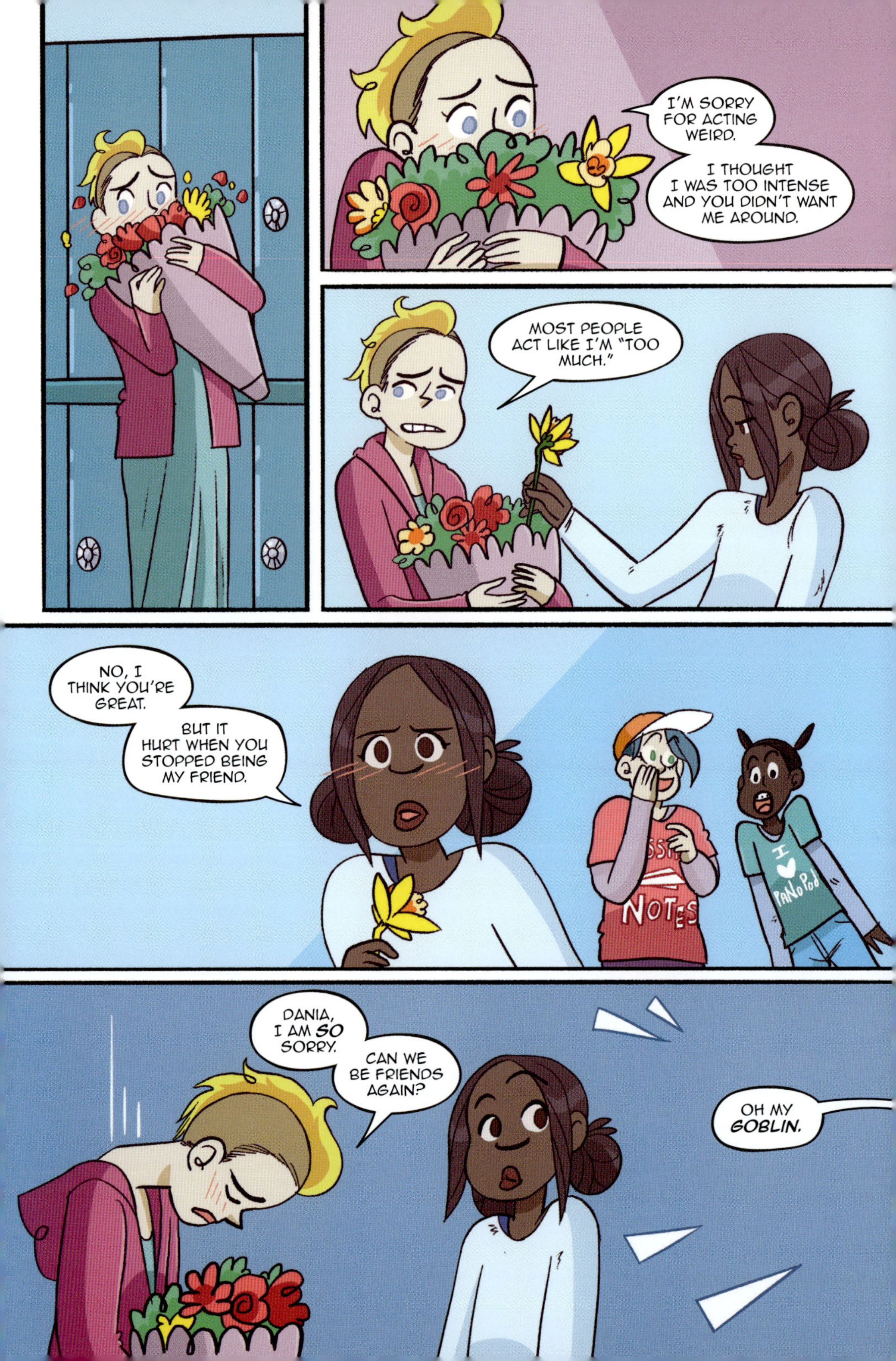
I'M SORRY FOR ACTING WEIRD.
I THOUGHT I WAS TOO INTENSE AND YOU DIDN'T WANT ME AROUND.
MOST PEOPLE ACT LIKE I'M "TOO MUCH."
NO, I THINK YOU'RE GREAT.
BUT IT HURT WHEN YOU STOPPED BEING MY FRIEND.
DANIA, I AM *SO* SORRY.
CAN WE BE FRIENDS AGAIN?
OH MY *GOBLIN.*

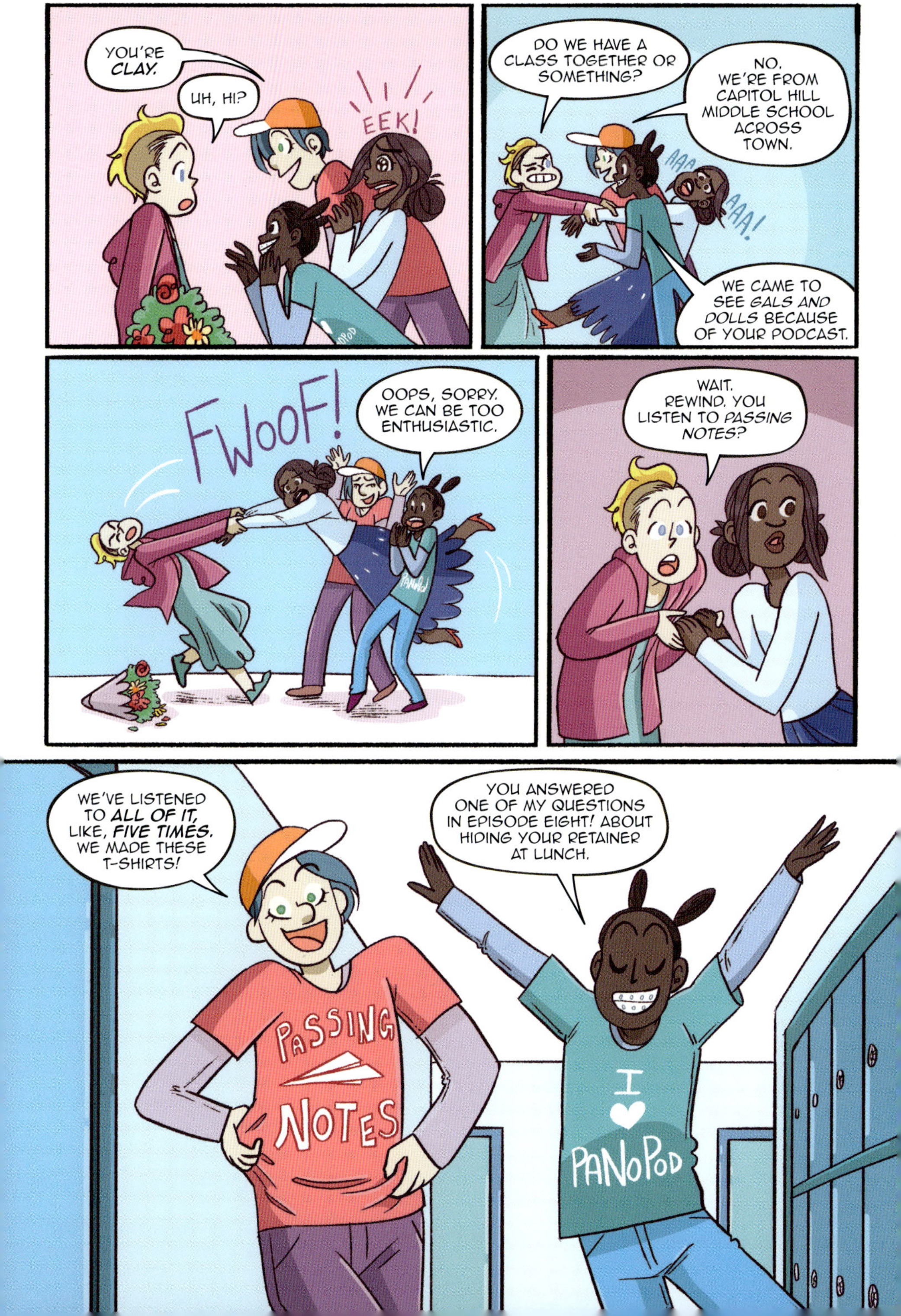
YOU'RE CLAY.
UH, HI?
EEK!
DO WE HAVE A CLASS TOGETHER OR SOMETHING?
NO. WE'RE FROM CAPITOL HILL MIDDLE SCHOOL ACROSS TOWN.
AAA AAA!
WE CAME TO SEE GALS AND DOLLS BECAUSE OF YOUR PODCAST.
FWOOF!
OOPS, SORRY. WE CAN BE TOO ENTHUSIASTIC.
PANOPOD
WAIT. REWIND. YOU LISTEN TO PASSING NOTES?
WE'VE LISTENED TO ALL OF IT, LIKE, FIVE TIMES. WE MADE THESE T-SHIRTS!
YOU ANSWERED ONE OF MY QUESTIONS IN EPISODE EIGHT! ABOUT HIDING YOUR RETAINER AT LUNCH.
PASSING NOTES
I ♥ PANOPOD

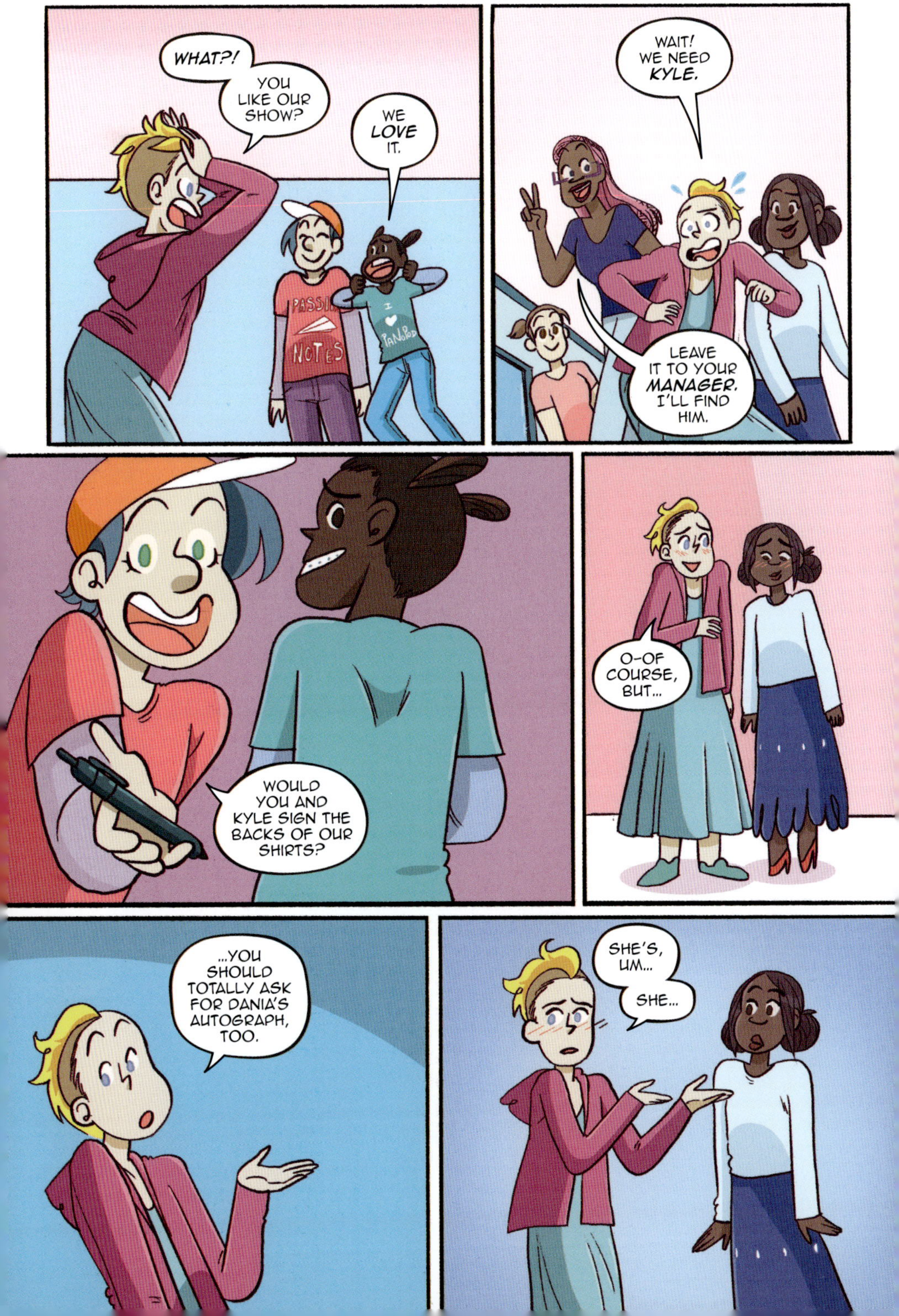
WHAT?!
YOU LIKE OUR SHOW?
WE LOVE IT.
PASSING NOTES
I ♥ PanoPod
WAIT! WE NEED KYLE.
LEAVE IT TO YOUR MANAGER. I'LL FIND HIM.
WOULD YOU AND KYLE SIGN THE BACKS OF OUR SHIRTS?
O-OF COURSE, BUT...
...YOU SHOULD TOTALLY ASK FOR DANIA'S AUTOGRAPH, TOO.
SHE'S, UM...
SHE...

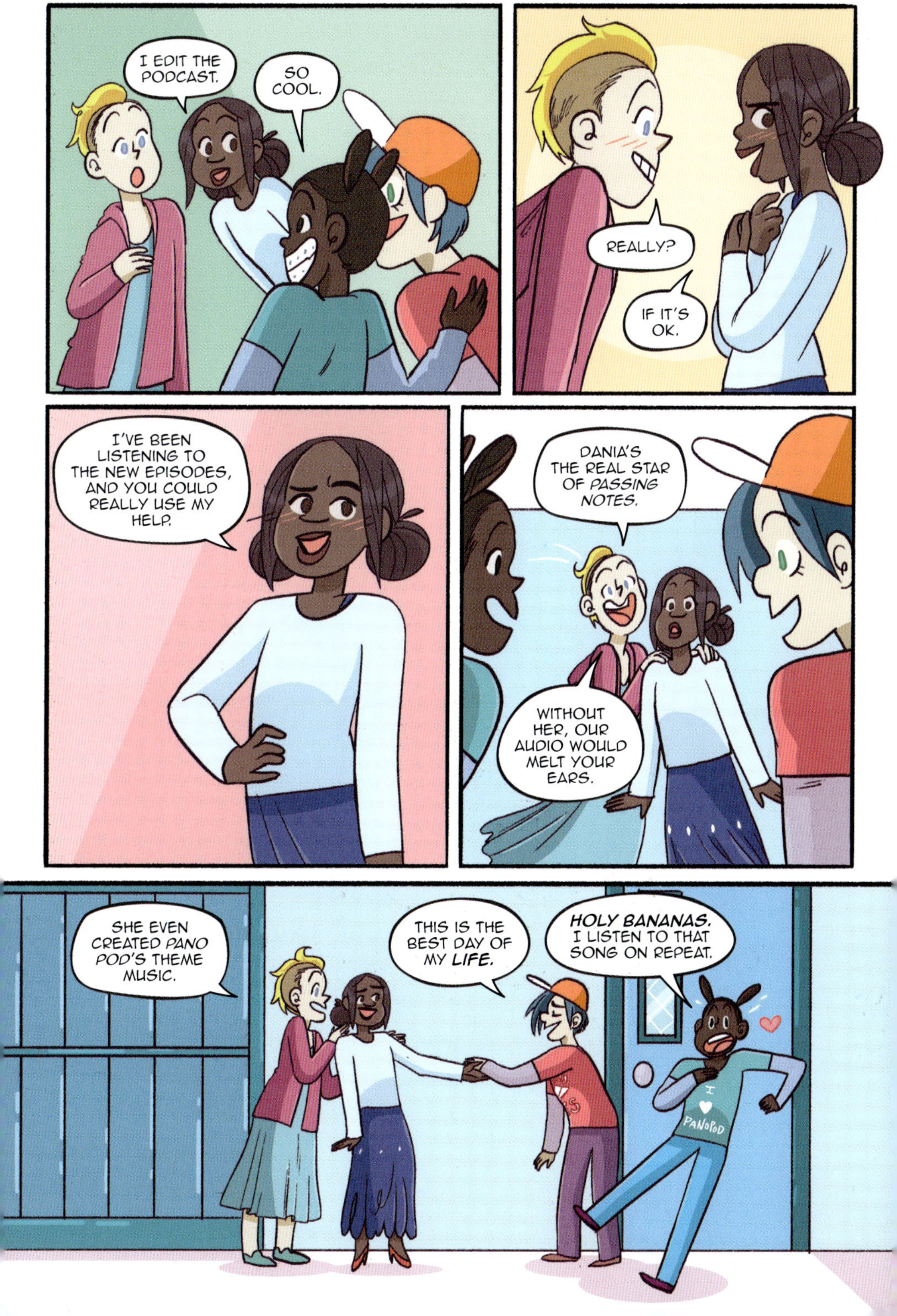

I EDIT THE PODCAST.
SO COOL.
REALLY?
IF IT'S OK.
I'VE BEEN LISTENING TO THE NEW EPISODES, AND YOU COULD REALLY USE MY HELP.
DANIA'S THE REAL STAR OF *PASSING NOTES.*
WITHOUT HER, OUR AUDIO WOULD MELT YOUR EARS.
SHE EVEN CREATED *PANO POD'S* THEME MUSIC.
THIS IS THE BEST DAY OF MY ***LIFE.***
HOLY BANANAS. I LISTEN TO THAT SONG ON REPEAT.
I ♥ PANOPOD

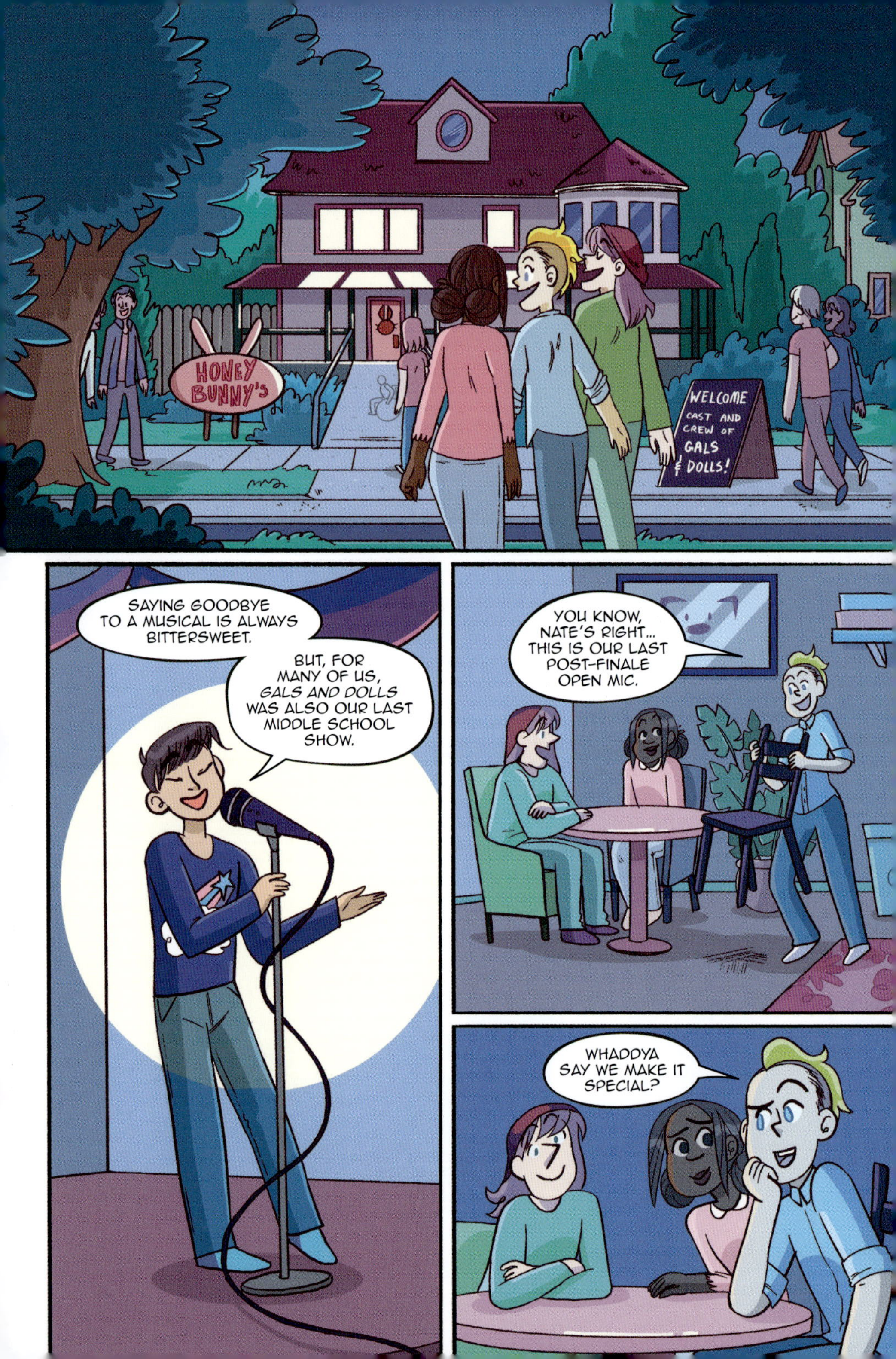
HONEY BUNNY'S
WELCOME CAST AND CREW OF GALS & DOLLS!
SAYING GOODBYE TO A MUSICAL IS ALWAYS BITTERSWEET.
BUT, FOR MANY OF US, GALS AND DOLLS WAS ALSO OUR LAST MIDDLE SCHOOL SHOW.
YOU KNOW, NATE'S RIGHT... THIS IS OUR LAST POST-FINALE OPEN MIC.
WHADDYA SAY WE MAKE IT SPECIAL?

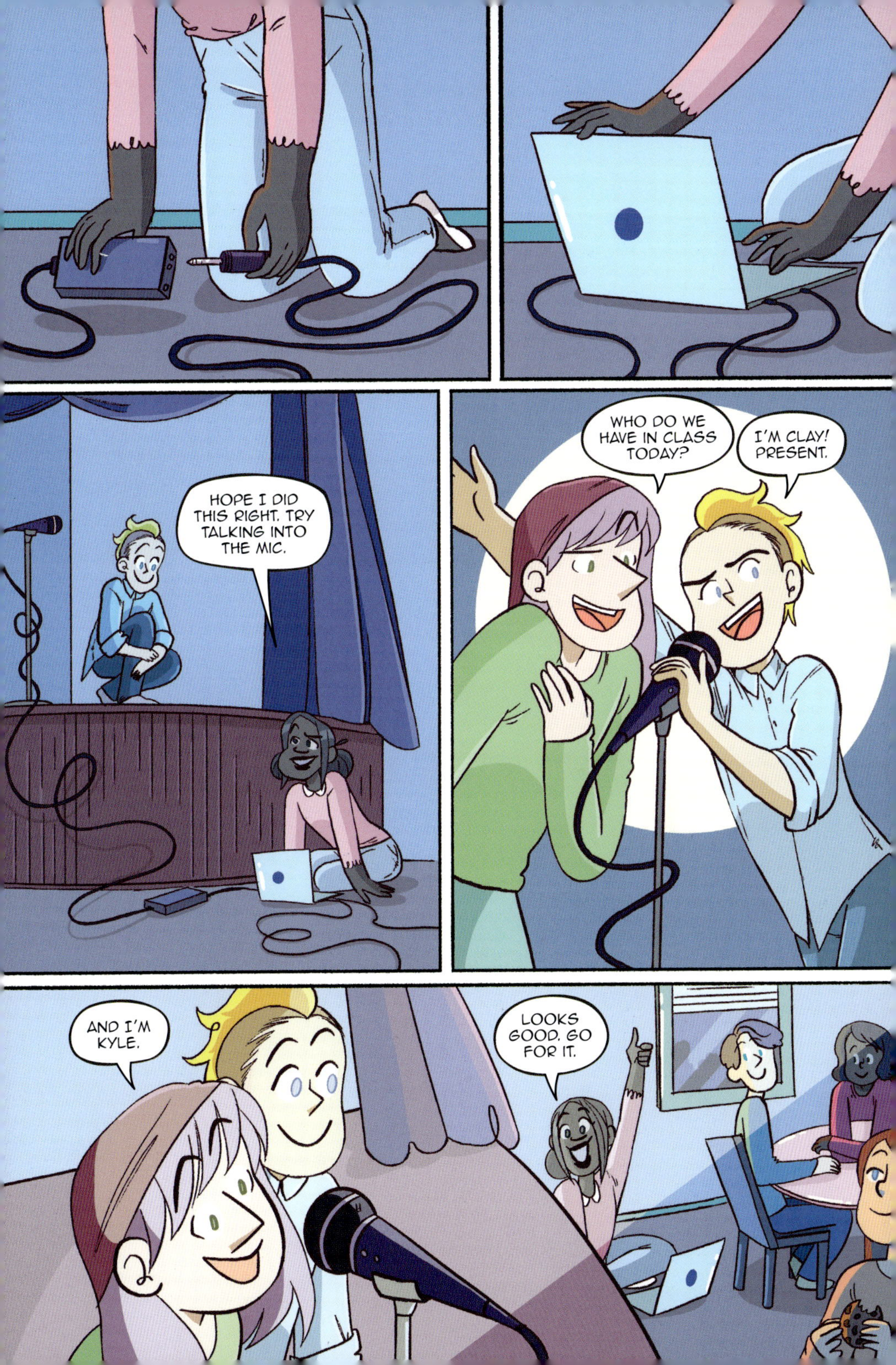
HOPE I DID THIS RIGHT. TRY TALKING INTO THE MIC.
WHO DO WE HAVE IN CLASS TODAY?
I'M CLAY! PRESENT.
AND I'M KYLE.
LOOKS GOOD. GO FOR IT.

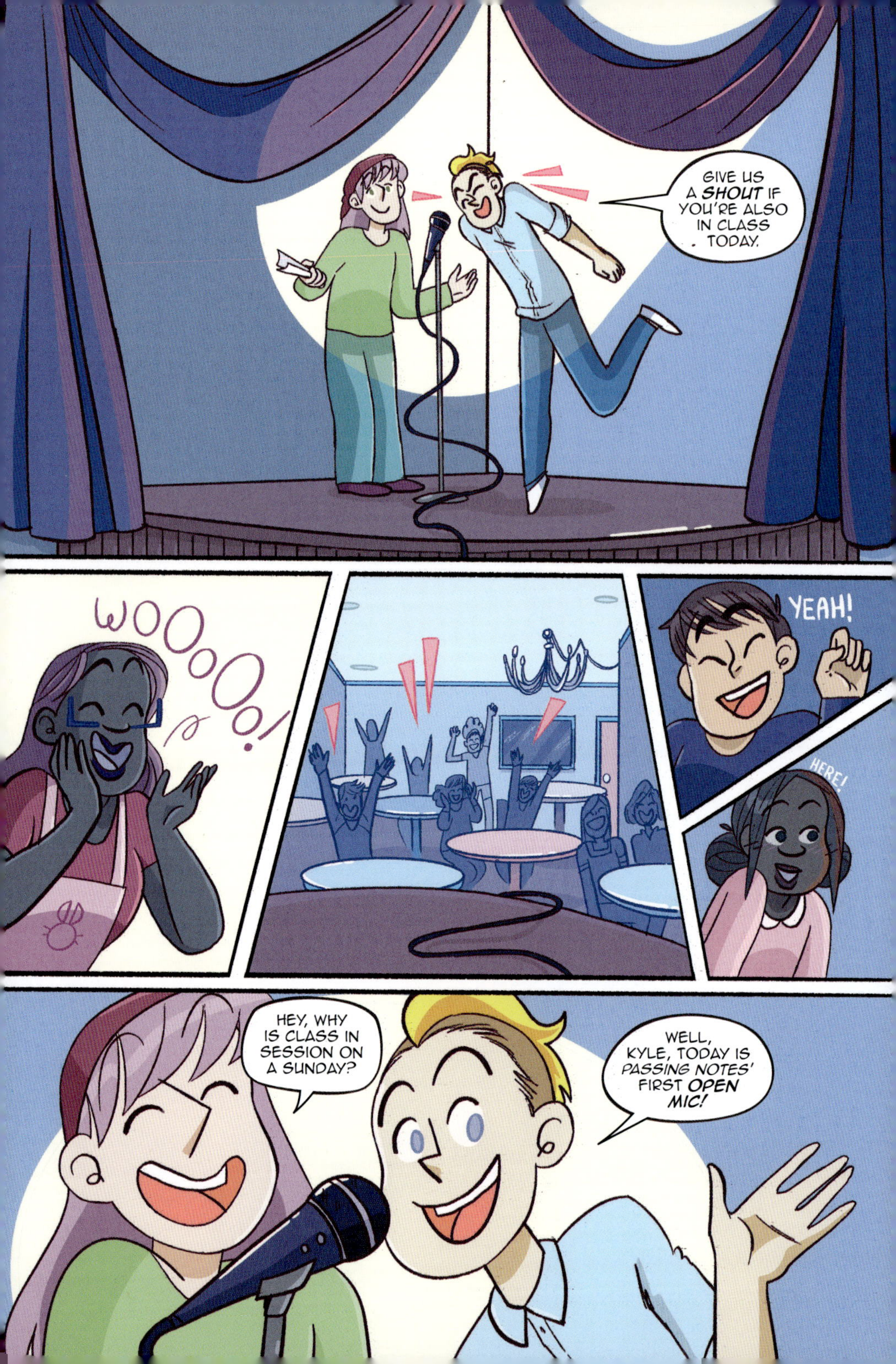
GIVE US A SHOUT IF YOU'RE ALSO IN CLASS TODAY.
WOOoOo!
YEAH!
HERE!
HEY, WHY IS CLASS IN SESSION ON A SUNDAY?
WELL, KYLE, TODAY IS PASSING NOTES' FIRST OPEN MIC!

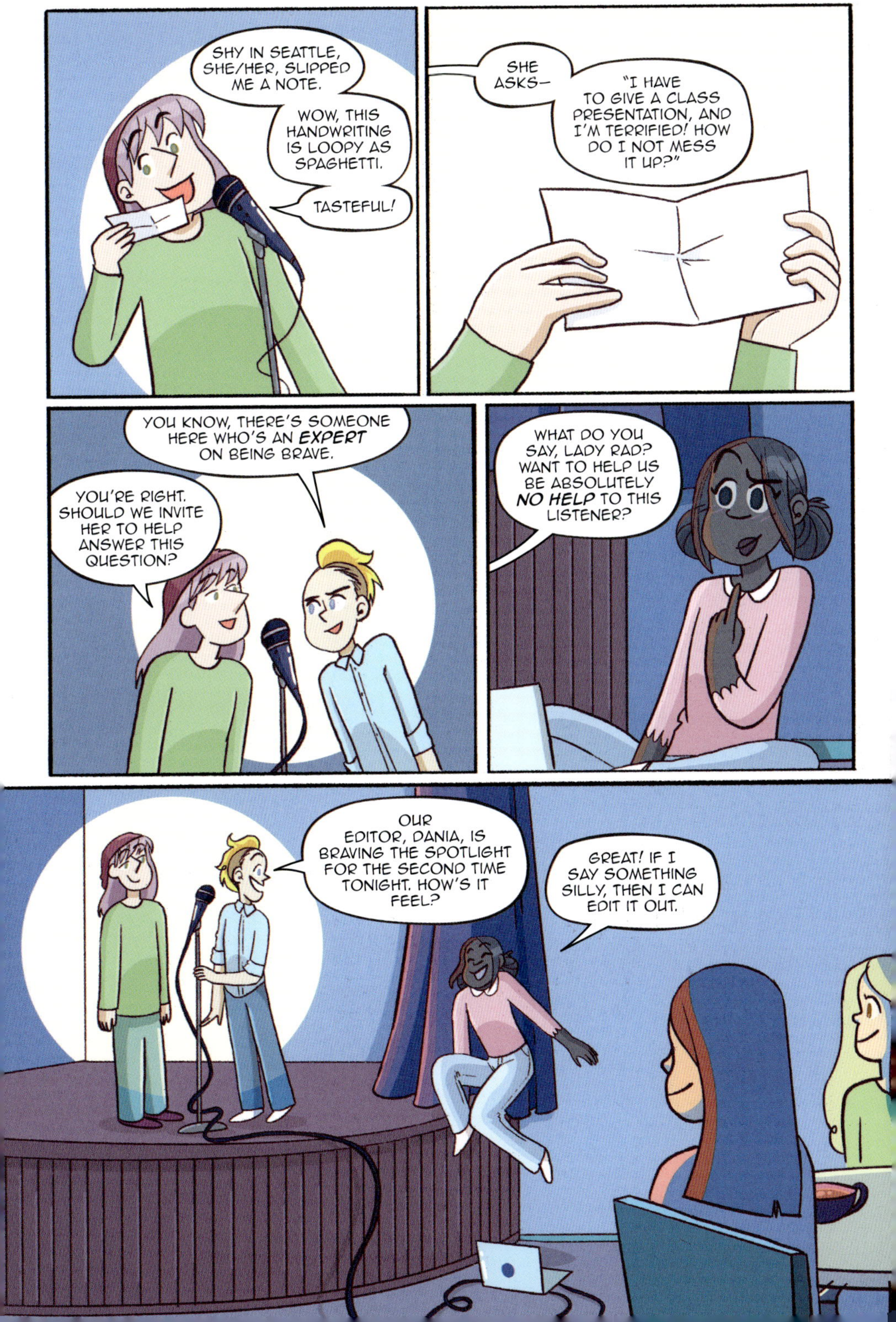
SHY IN SEATTLE, SHE/HER, SLIPPED ME A NOTE.
WOW, THIS HANDWRITING IS LOOPY AS SPAGHETTI.
TASTEFUL!
SHE ASKS—
"I HAVE TO GIVE A CLASS PRESENTATION, AND I'M TERRIFIED! HOW DO I NOT MESS IT UP?"
YOU KNOW, THERE'S SOMEONE HERE WHO'S AN ***EXPERT*** ON BEING BRAVE.
YOU'RE RIGHT. SHOULD WE INVITE HER TO HELP ANSWER THIS QUESTION?
WHAT DO YOU SAY, LADY RAD? WANT TO HELP US BE ABSOLUTELY ***NO HELP*** TO THIS LISTENER?
OUR EDITOR, DANIA, IS BRAVING THE SPOTLIGHT FOR THE SECOND TIME TONIGHT. HOW'S IT FEEL?
GREAT! IF I SAY SOMETHING SILLY, THEN I CAN EDIT IT OUT.

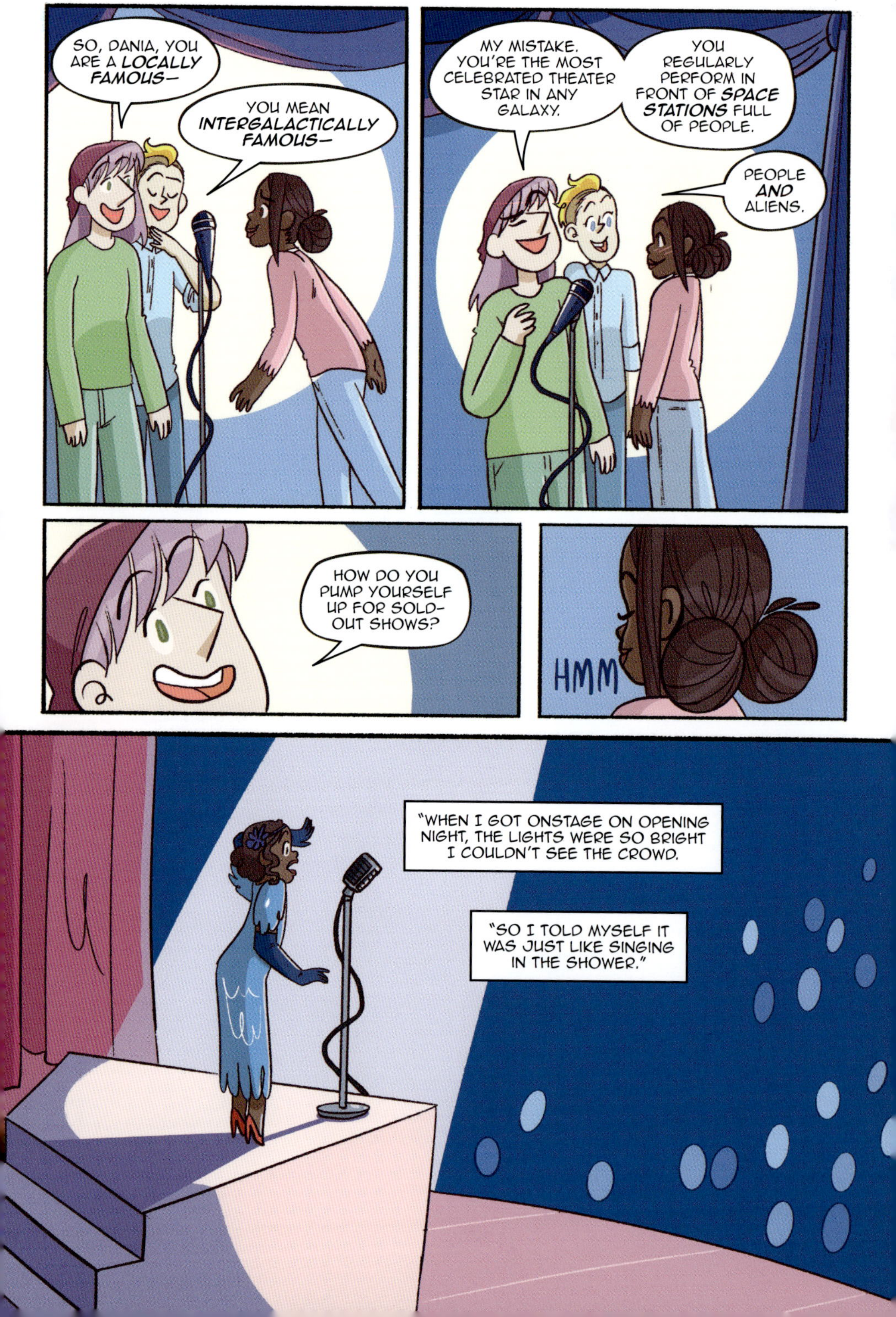
SO, DANIA, YOU ARE A LOCALLY FAMOUS—
YOU MEAN INTERGALACTICALLY FAMOUS—
MY MISTAKE. YOU'RE THE MOST CELEBRATED THEATER STAR IN ANY GALAXY.
YOU REGULARLY PERFORM IN FRONT OF SPACE STATIONS FULL OF PEOPLE.
PEOPLE AND ALIENS.
HOW DO YOU PUMP YOURSELF UP FOR SOLD-OUT SHOWS?
HMM
"WHEN I GOT ONSTAGE ON OPENING NIGHT, THE LIGHTS WERE SO BRIGHT I COULDN'T SEE THE CROWD.
"SO I TOLD MYSELF IT WAS JUST LIKE SINGING IN THE SHOWER."

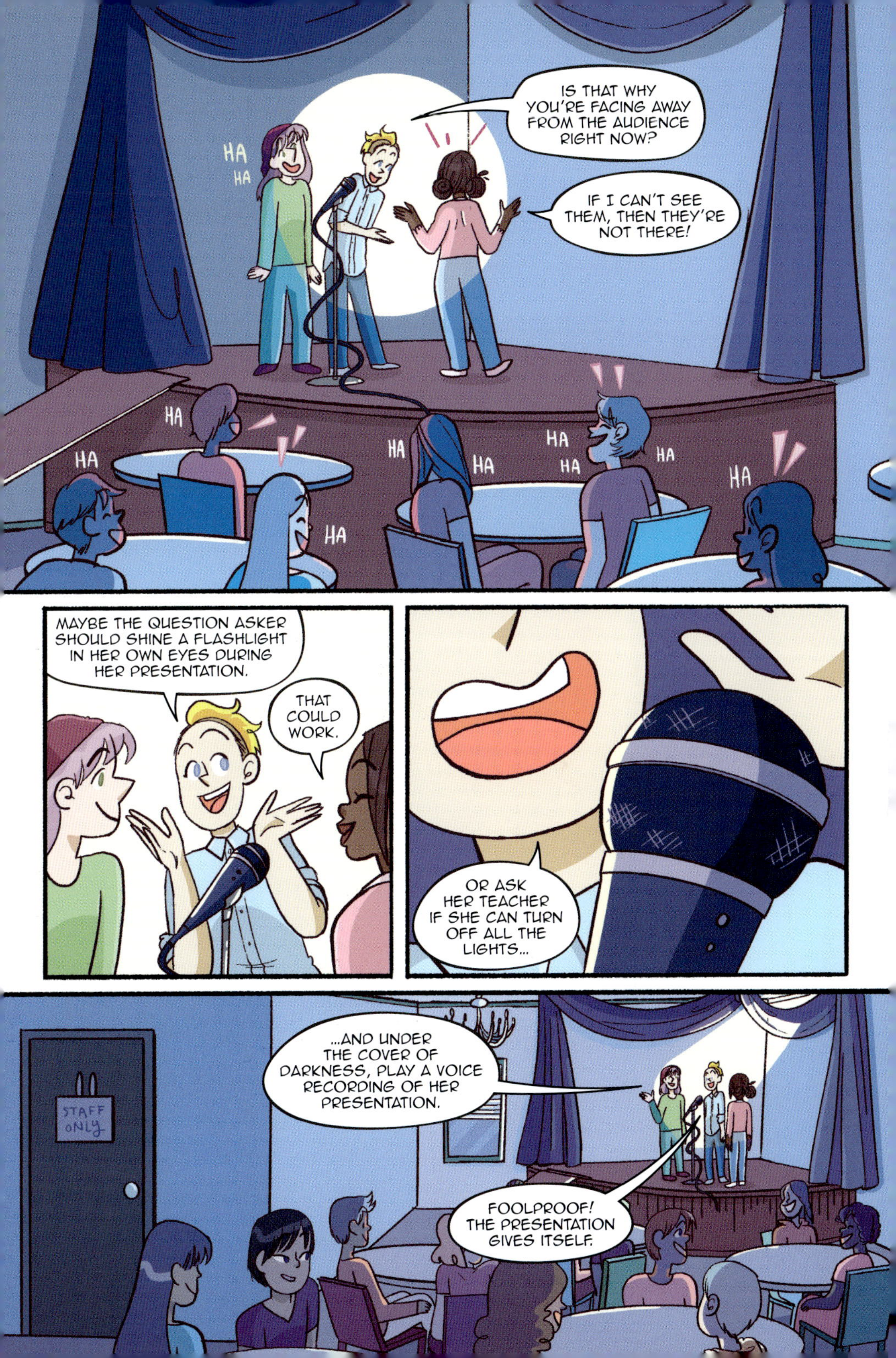
IS THAT WHY YOU'RE FACING AWAY FROM THE AUDIENCE RIGHT NOW?
IF I CAN'T SEE THEM, THEN THEY'RE NOT THERE!
HA HA
HA
HA
HA
HA
HA HA
HA
HA
HA
MAYBE THE QUESTION ASKER SHOULD SHINE A FLASHLIGHT IN HER OWN EYES DURING HER PRESENTATION.
THAT COULD WORK.
OR ASK HER TEACHER IF SHE CAN TURN OFF ALL THE LIGHTS...
...AND UNDER THE COVER OF DARKNESS, PLAY A VOICE RECORDING OF HER PRESENTATION.
STAFF ONLY
FOOLPROOF! THE PRESENTATION GIVES ITSELF.

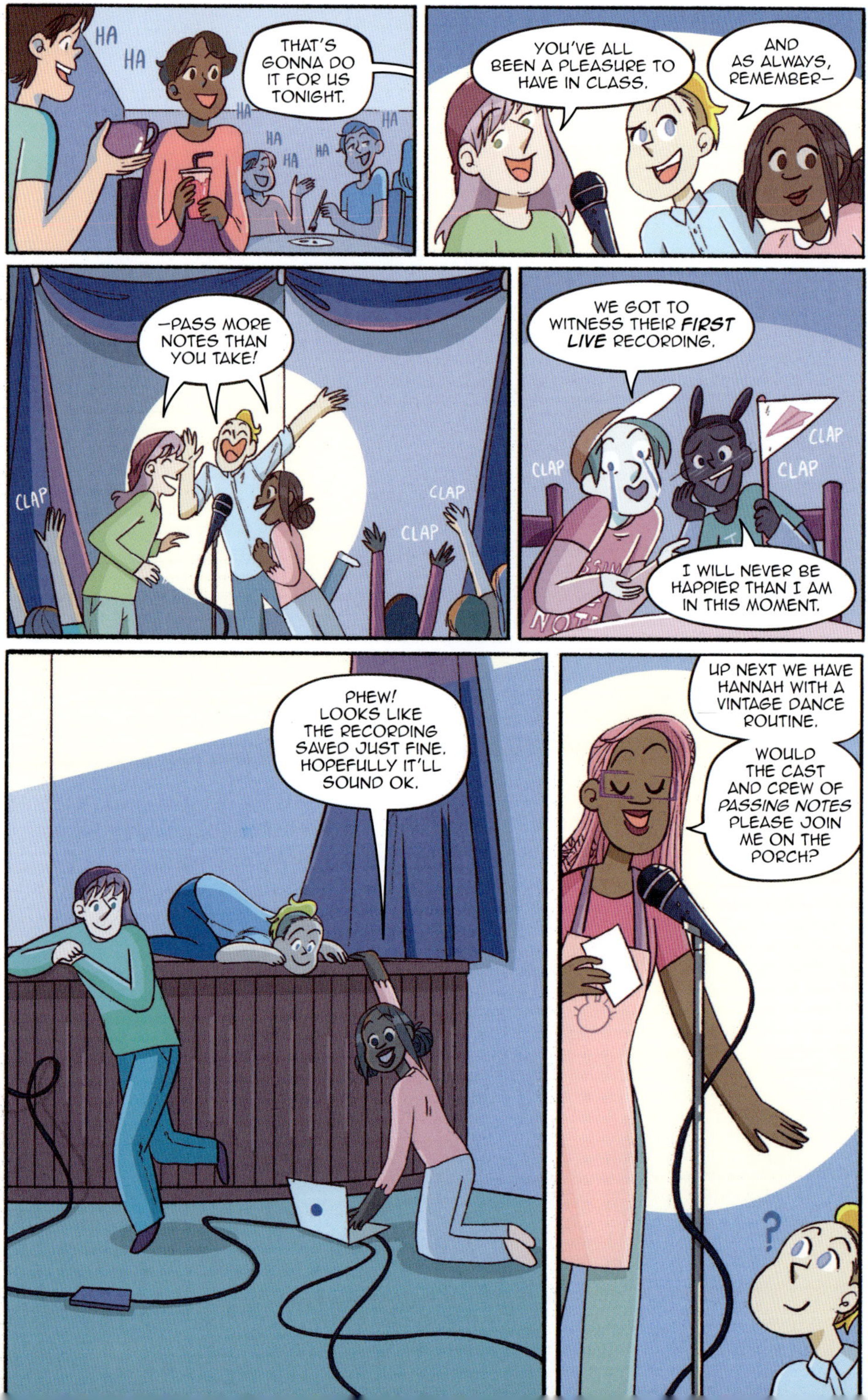
HA
HA
THAT'S GONNA DO IT FOR US TONIGHT.
HA
HA
HA
HA
HA
YOU'VE ALL BEEN A PLEASURE TO HAVE IN CLASS.
AND AS ALWAYS, REMEMBER—
—PASS MORE NOTES THAN YOU TAKE!
CLAP
CLAP
CLAP
WE GOT TO WITNESS THEIR *FIRST LIVE* RECORDING.
CLAP
CLAP
CLAP
I WILL NEVER BE HAPPIER THAN I AM IN THIS MOMENT.
PHEW! LOOKS LIKE THE RECORDING SAVED JUST FINE. HOPEFULLY IT'LL SOUND OK.
UP NEXT WE HAVE HANNAH WITH A VINTAGE DANCE ROUTINE.
WOULD THE CAST AND CREW OF *PASSING NOTES* PLEASE JOIN ME ON THE PORCH?
?

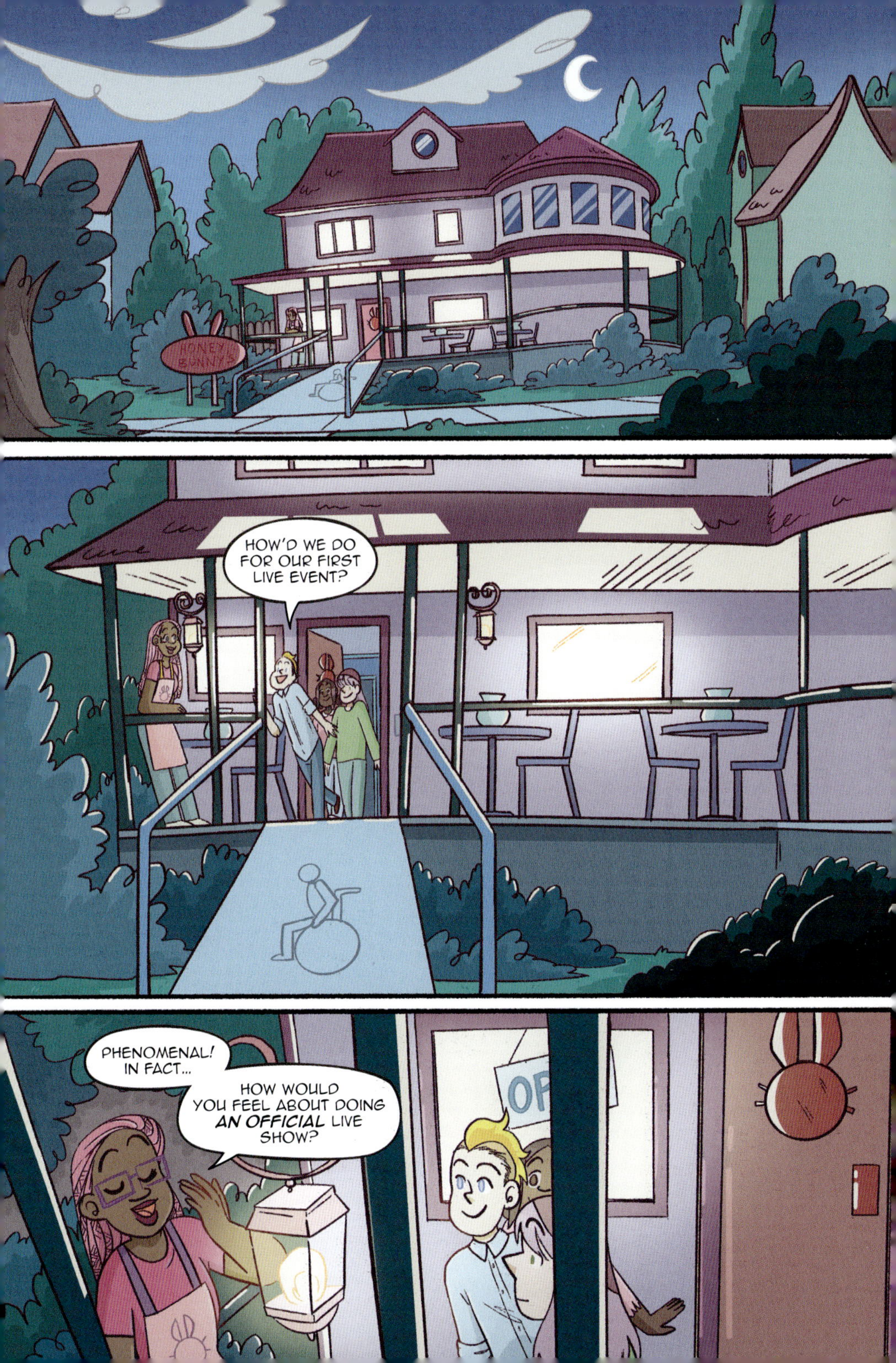
HONEY BUNNY'S
HOW'D WE DO FOR OUR FIRST LIVE EVENT?
PHENOMENAL! IN FACT...
HOW WOULD YOU FEEL ABOUT DOING *AN OFFICIAL* LIVE SHOW?

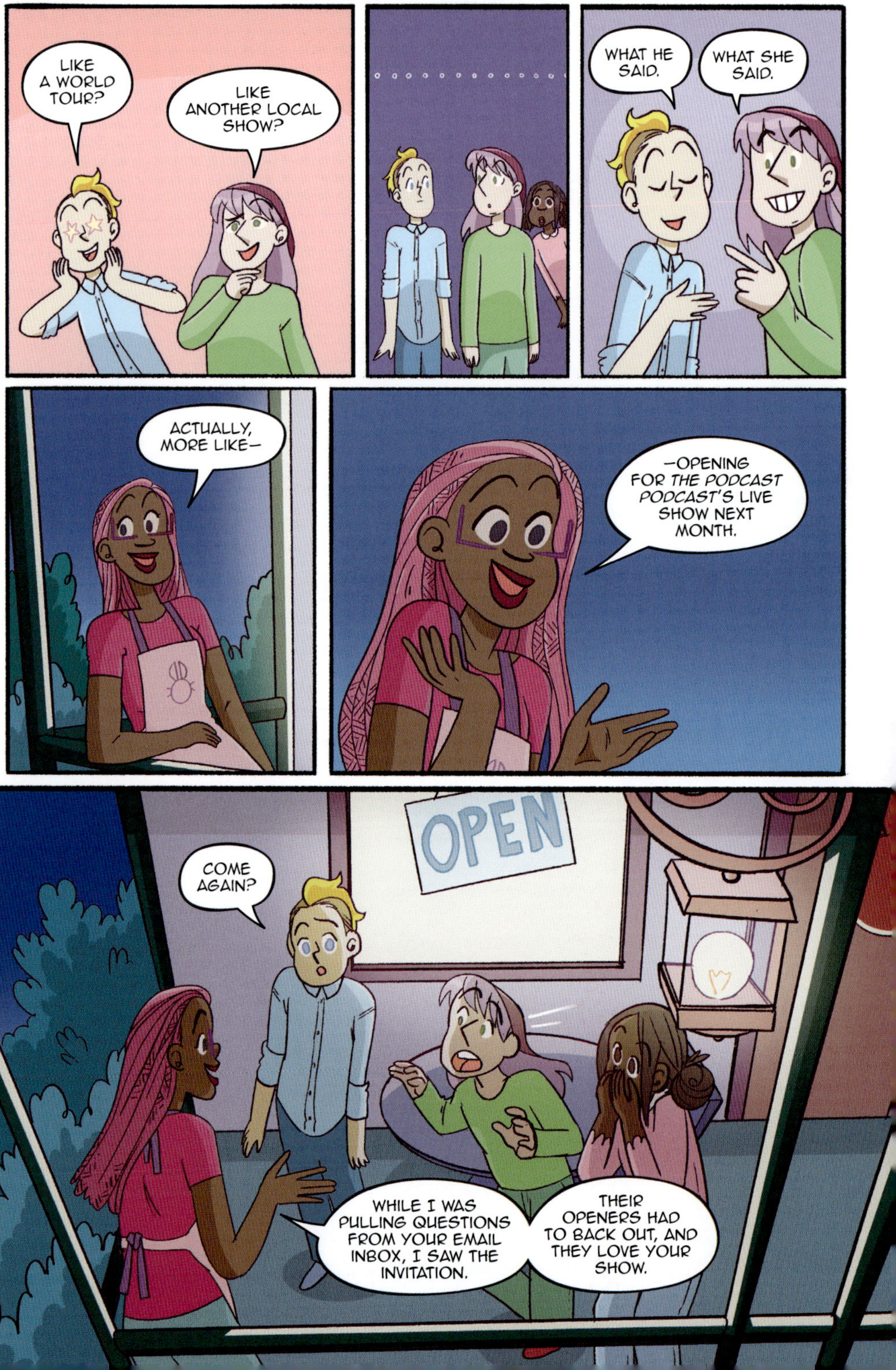
LIKE A WORLD TOUR?
LIKE ANOTHER LOCAL SHOW?
WHAT HE SAID.
WHAT SHE SAID.
ACTUALLY, MORE LIKE—
—OPENING FOR THE PODCAST PODCAST'S LIVE SHOW NEXT MONTH.
OPEN
COME AGAIN?
WHILE I WAS PULLING QUESTIONS FROM YOUR EMAIL INBOX, I SAW THE INVITATION.
THEIR OPENERS HAD TO BACK OUT, AND THEY LOVE YOUR SHOW.

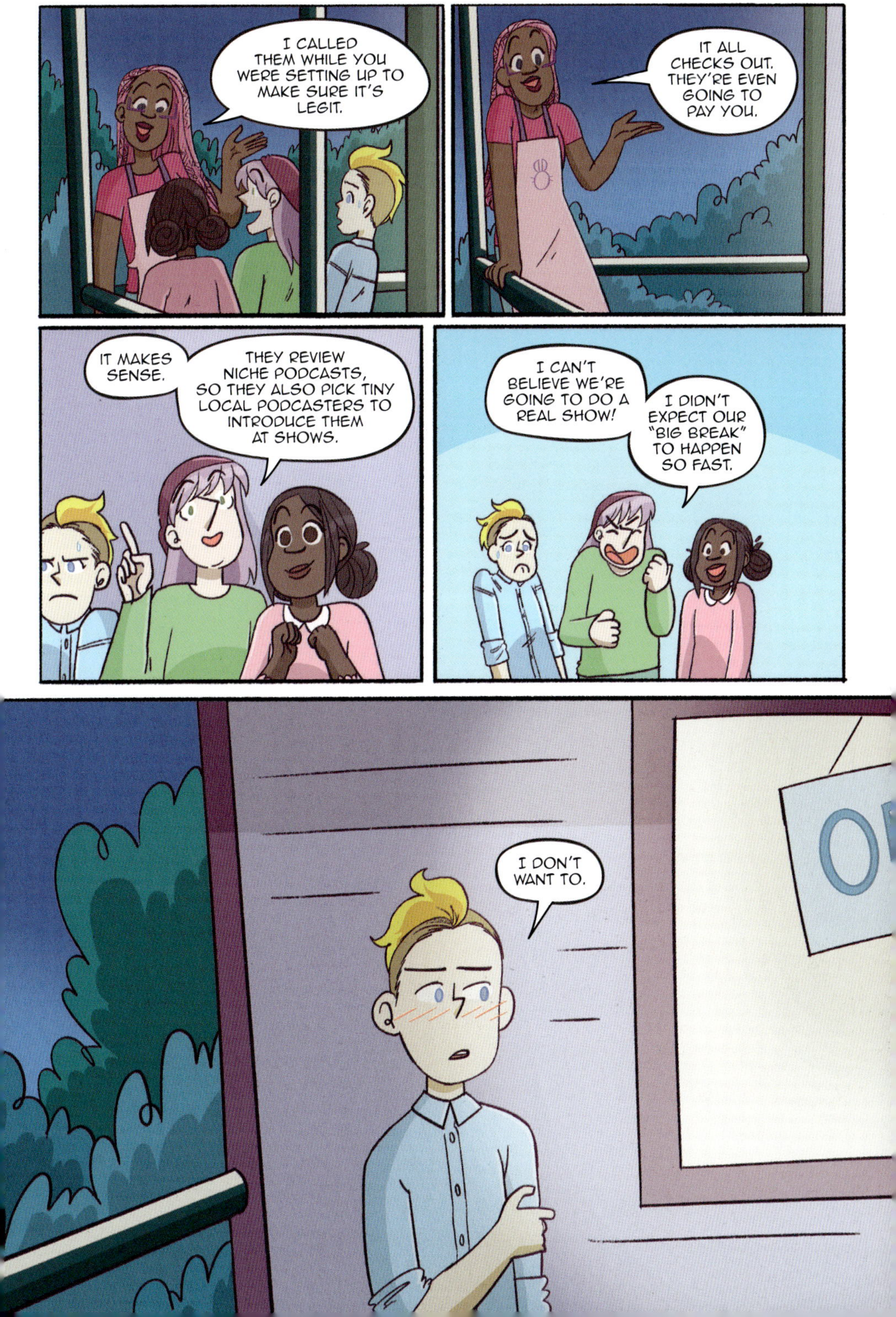
I CALLED THEM WHILE YOU WERE SETTING UP TO MAKE SURE IT'S LEGIT.
IT ALL CHECKS OUT. THEY'RE EVEN GOING TO PAY YOU.
IT MAKES SENSE.
THEY REVIEW NICHE PODCASTS, SO THEY ALSO PICK TINY LOCAL PODCASTERS TO INTRODUCE THEM AT SHOWS.
I CAN'T BELIEVE WE'RE GOING TO DO A REAL SHOW!
I DIDN'T EXPECT OUR "BIG BREAK" TO HAPPEN SO FAST.
I DON'T WANT TO.

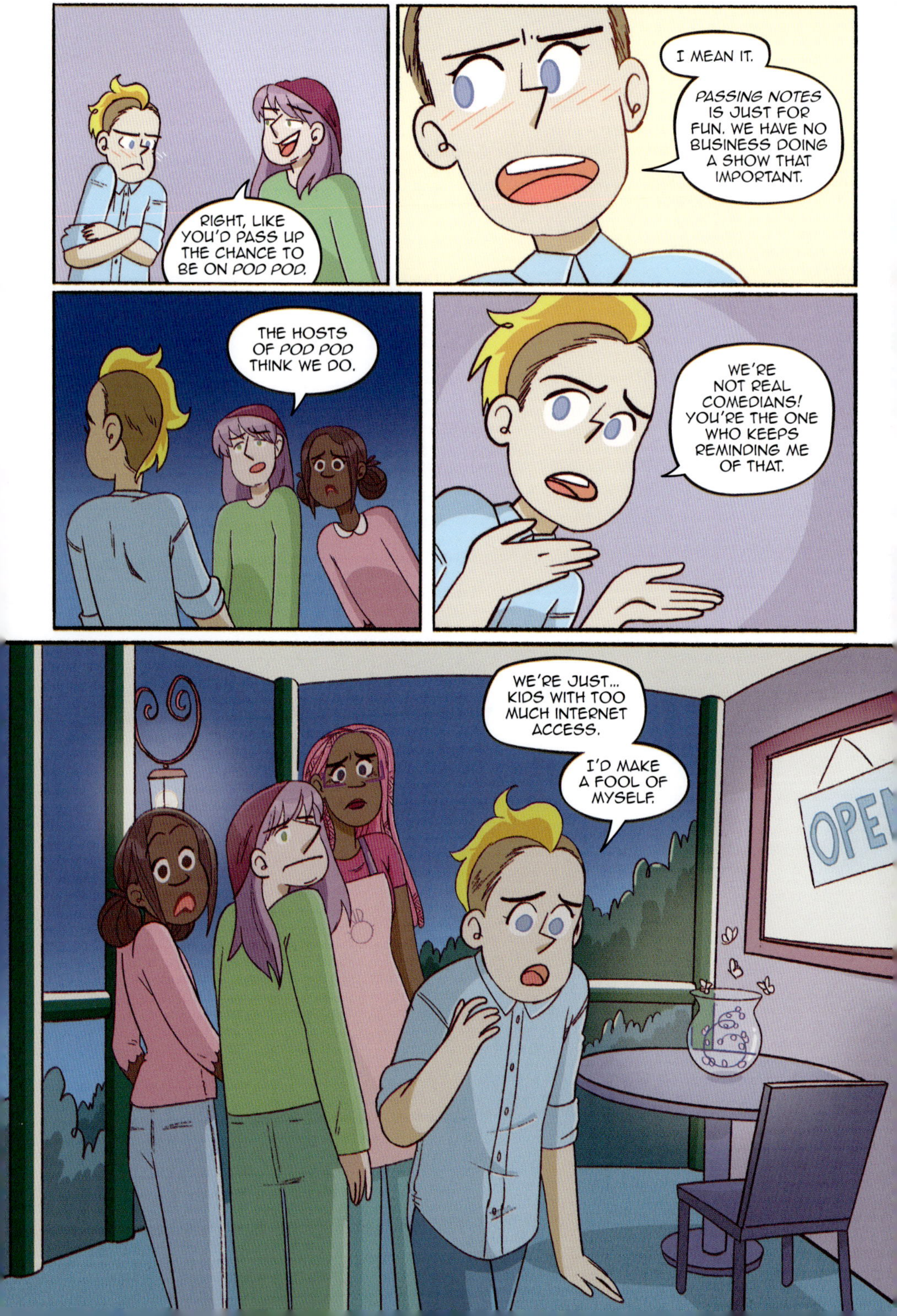
RIGHT, LIKE YOU'D PASS UP THE CHANCE TO BE ON *POD POD.*
I MEAN IT.
PASSING NOTES IS JUST FOR FUN. WE HAVE NO BUSINESS DOING A SHOW THAT IMPORTANT.
THE HOSTS OF *POD POD* THINK WE DO.
WE'RE NOT REAL COMEDIANS! YOU'RE THE ONE WHO KEEPS REMINDING ME OF THAT.
WE'RE JUST... KIDS WITH TOO MUCH INTERNET ACCESS.
I'D MAKE A FOOL OF MYSELF.
OPEN

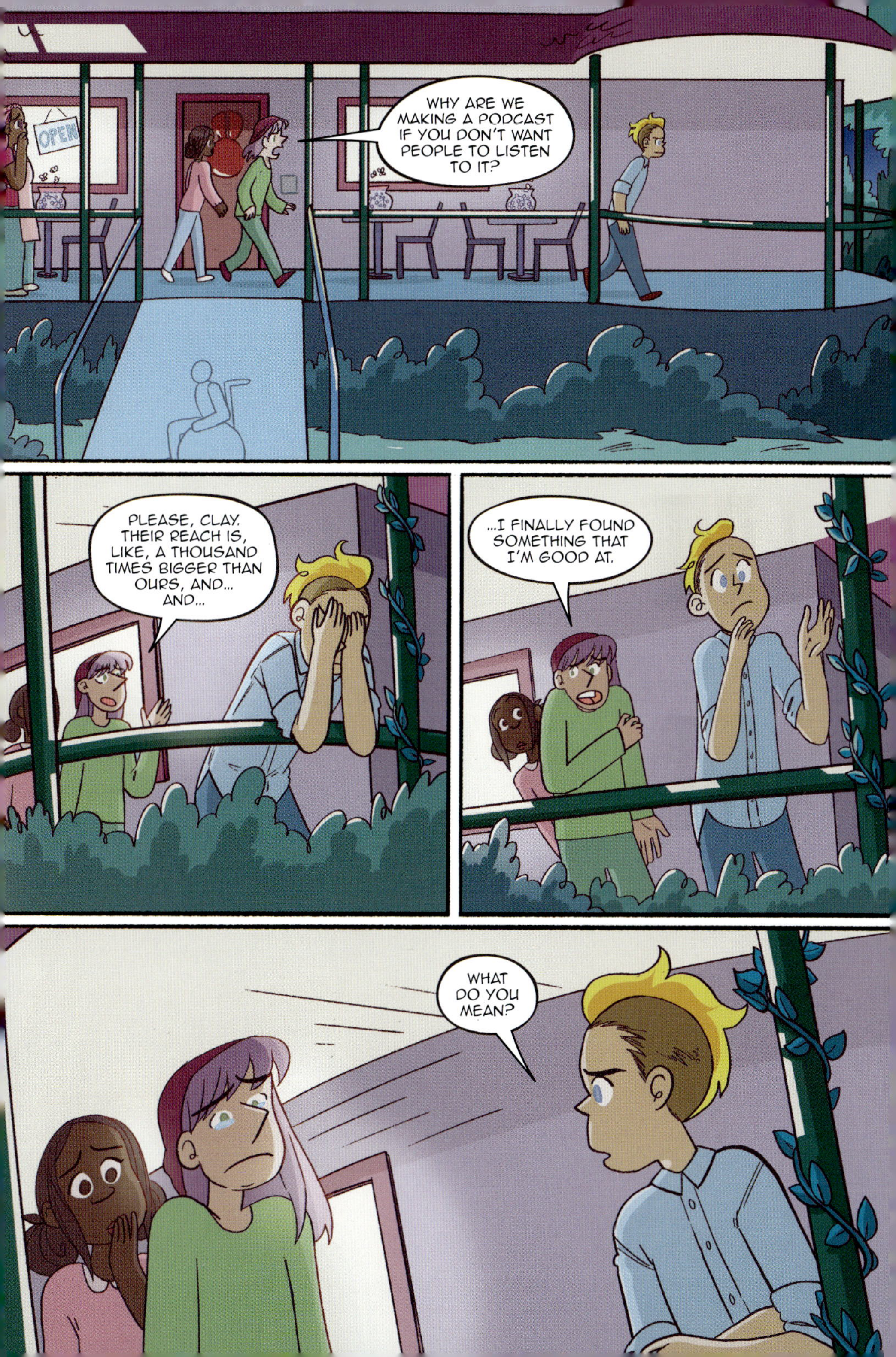
OPEN
WHY ARE WE MAKING A PODCAST IF YOU DON'T WANT PEOPLE TO LISTEN TO IT?
PLEASE, CLAY. THEIR REACH IS, LIKE, A THOUSAND TIMES BIGGER THAN OURS, AND... AND...
...I FINALLY FOUND SOMETHING THAT I'M GOOD AT.
WHAT DO YOU MEAN?

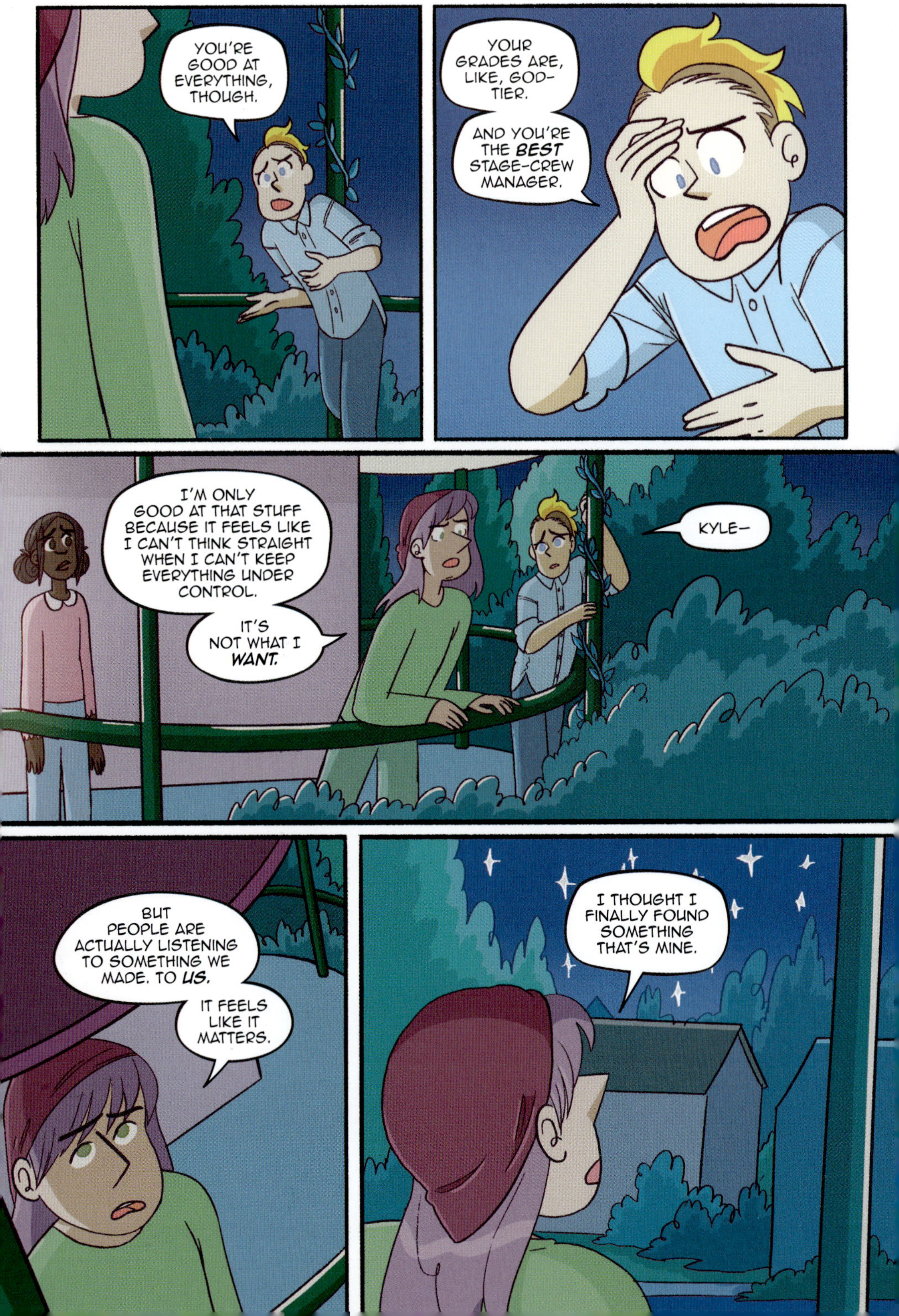
YOU'RE GOOD AT EVERYTHING, THOUGH.
YOUR GRADES ARE, LIKE, GOD-TIER.
AND YOU'RE THE **BEST** STAGE-CREW MANAGER.
I'M ONLY GOOD AT THAT STUFF BECAUSE IT FEELS LIKE I CAN'T THINK STRAIGHT WHEN I CAN'T KEEP EVERYTHING UNDER CONTROL.
IT'S NOT WHAT I ***WANT.***
KYLE—
BUT PEOPLE ARE ACTUALLY LISTENING TO SOMETHING WE MADE. TO ***US.***
IT FEELS LIKE IT MATTERS.
I THOUGHT I FINALLY FOUND SOMETHING THAT'S MINE.

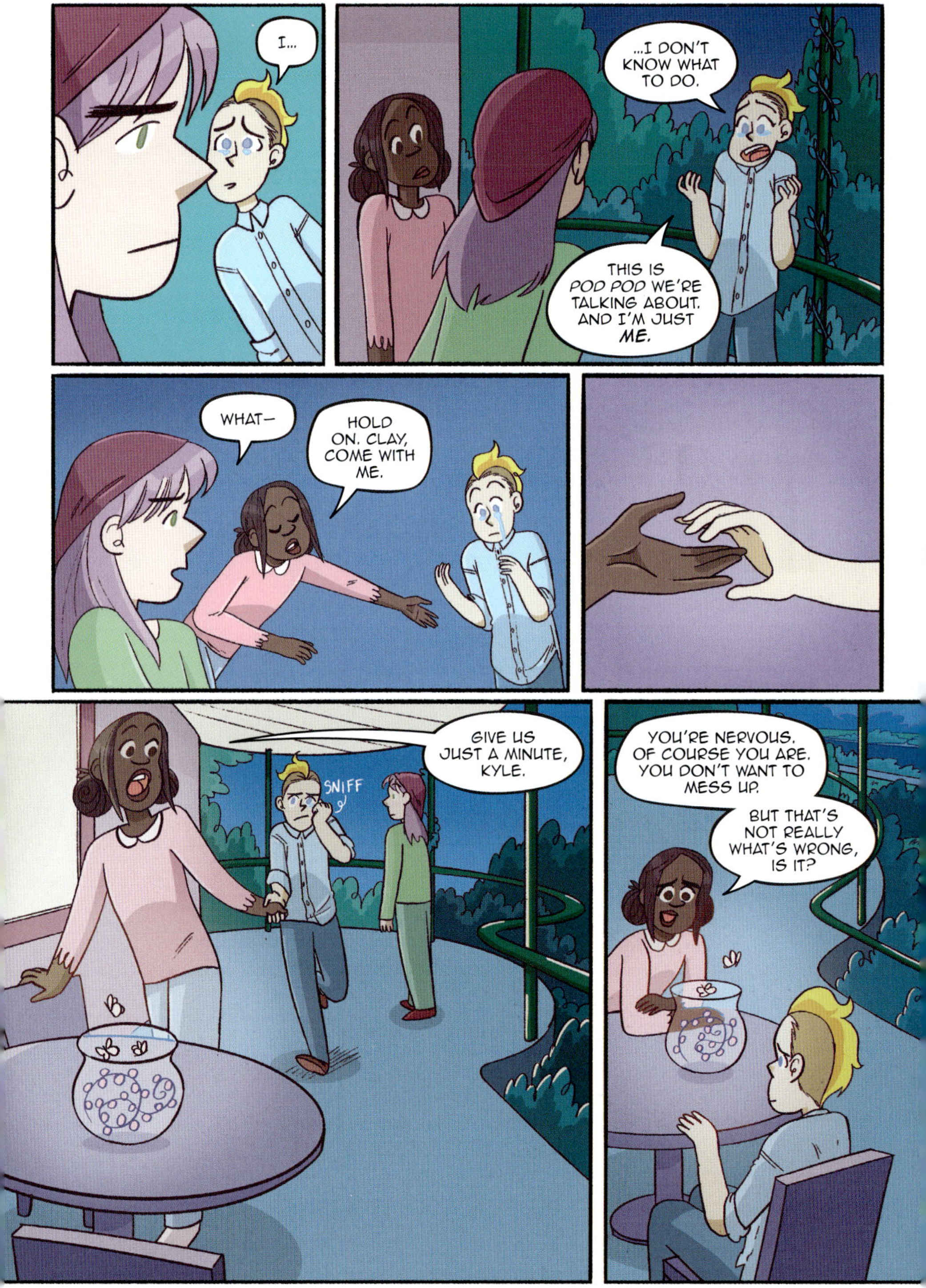
I...
...I DON'T KNOW WHAT TO DO.
THIS IS POD POD WE'RE TALKING ABOUT. AND I'M JUST ME.
WHAT—
HOLD ON. CLAY, COME WITH ME.
GIVE US JUST A MINUTE, KYLE.
SNIFF
YOU'RE NERVOUS. OF COURSE YOU ARE. YOU DON'T WANT TO MESS UP.
BUT THAT'S NOT REALLY WHAT'S WRONG, IS IT?

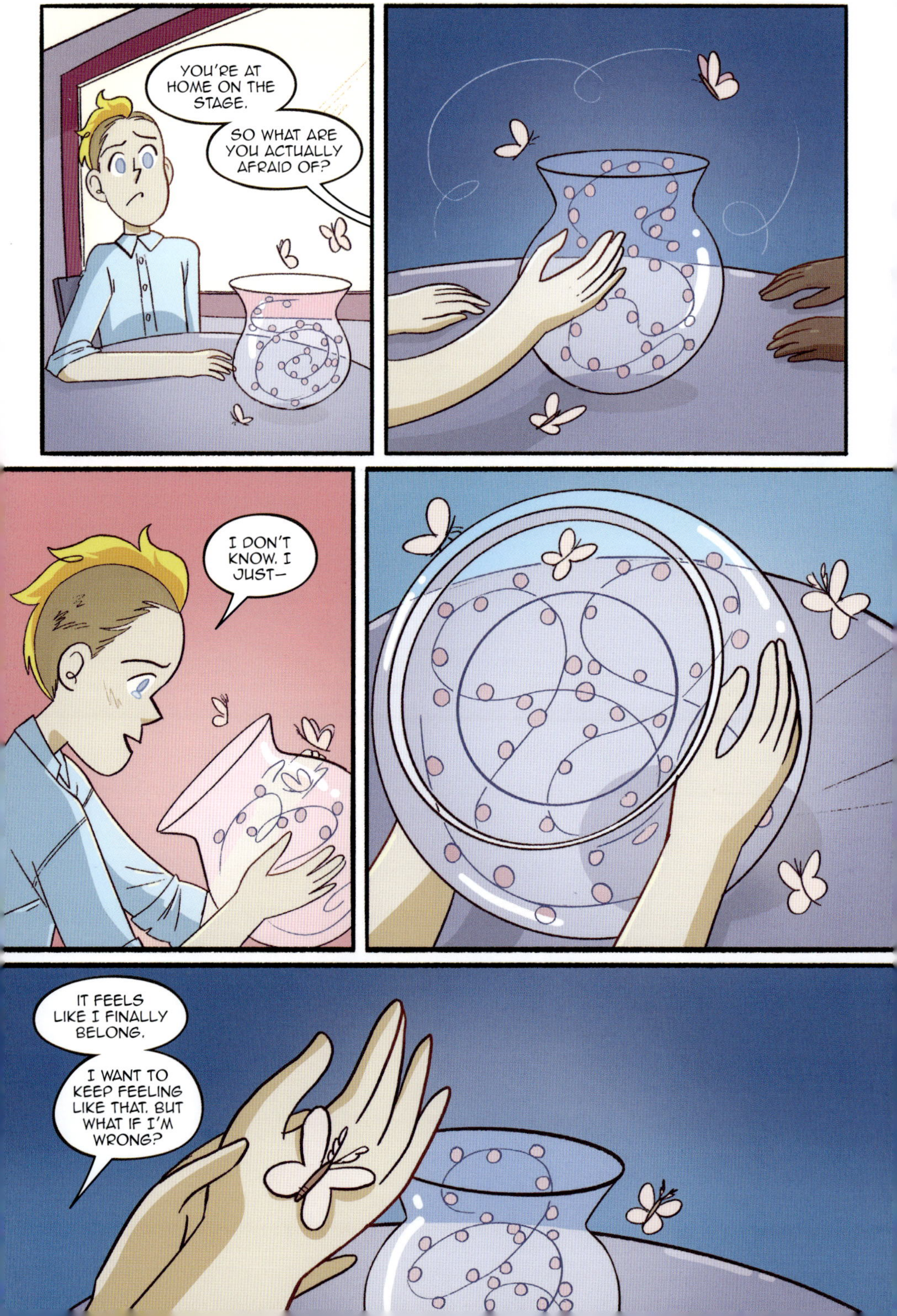
YOU'RE AT HOME ON THE STAGE.
SO WHAT ARE YOU ACTUALLY AFRAID OF?
I DON'T KNOW. I JUST—
IT FEELS LIKE I FINALLY BELONG.
I WANT TO KEEP FEELING LIKE THAT. BUT WHAT IF I'M WRONG?

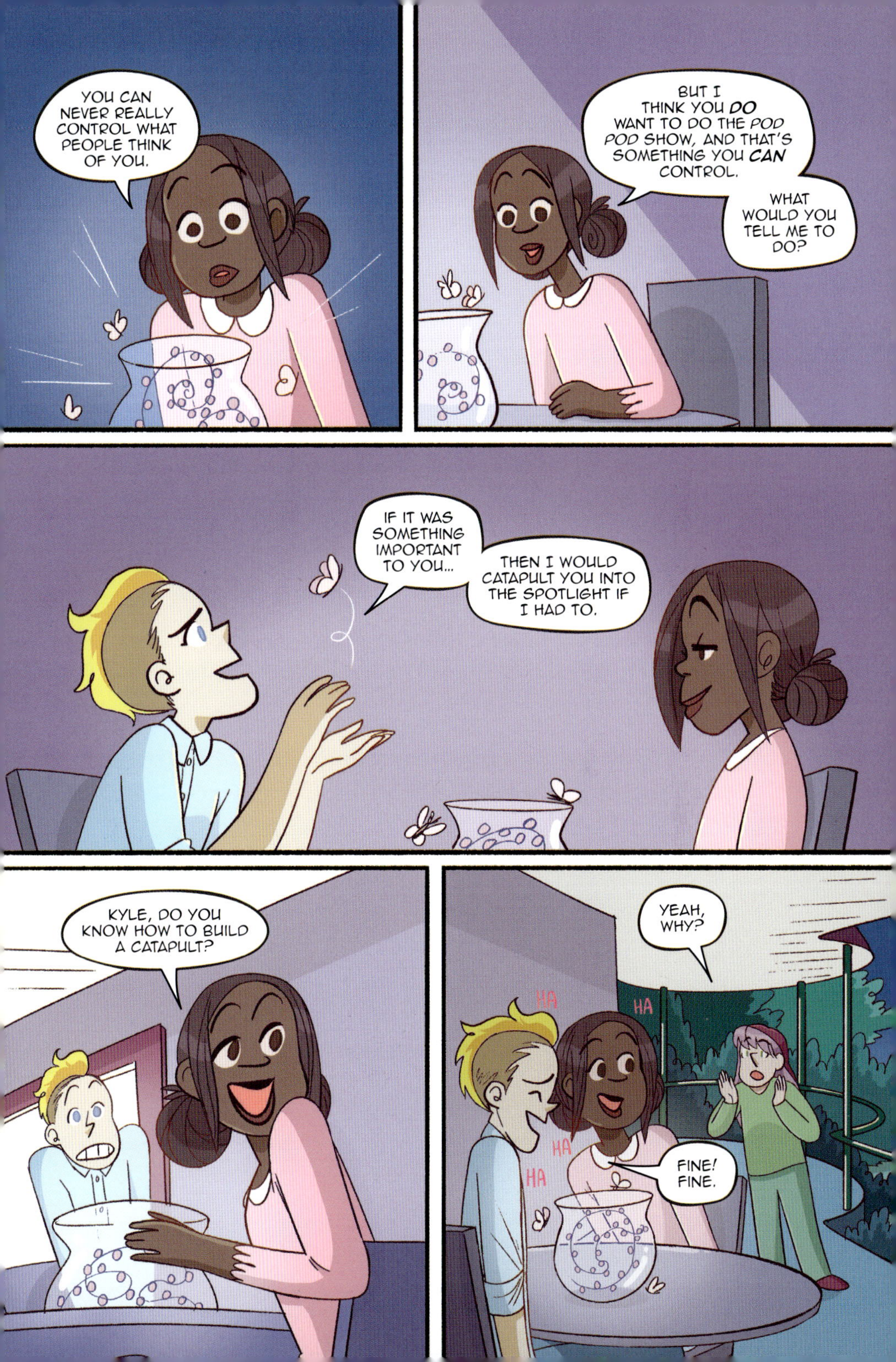
YOU CAN NEVER REALLY CONTROL WHAT PEOPLE THINK OF YOU.
BUT I THINK YOU *DO* WANT TO DO THE *POD POD* SHOW, AND THAT'S SOMETHING YOU **CAN** CONTROL.
WHAT WOULD YOU TELL ME TO DO?
IF IT WAS SOMETHING IMPORTANT TO YOU...
THEN I WOULD CATAPULT YOU INTO THE SPOTLIGHT IF I HAD TO.
KYLE, DO YOU KNOW HOW TO BUILD A CATAPULT?
YEAH, WHY?
HA
HA
HA
HA
FINE! FINE.

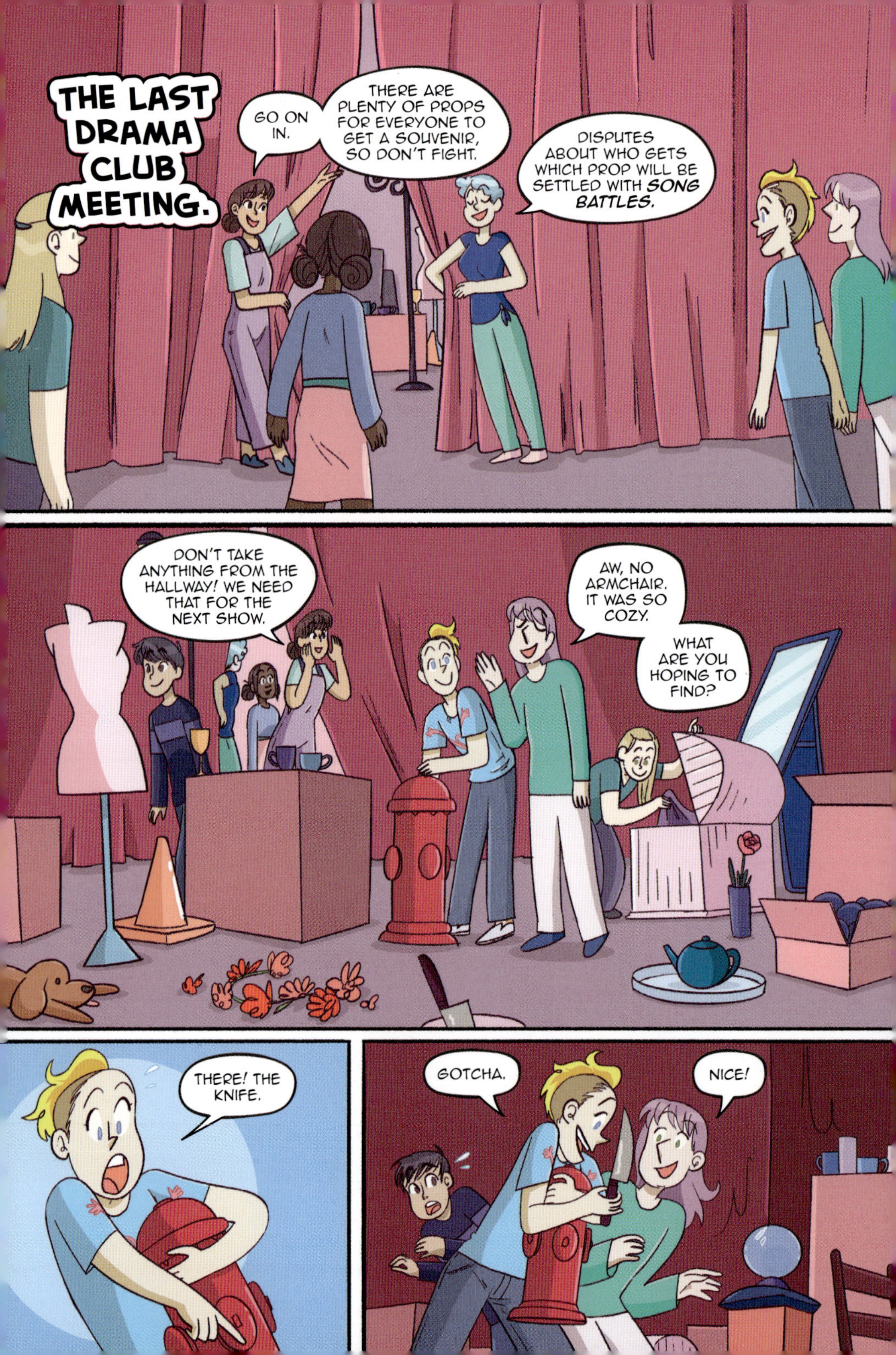
THE LAST DRAMA CLUB MEETING.
GO ON IN.
THERE ARE PLENTY OF PROPS FOR EVERYONE TO GET A SOUVENIR, SO DON'T FIGHT.
DISPUTES ABOUT WHO GETS WHICH PROP WILL BE SETTLED WITH SONG BATTLES.
DON'T TAKE ANYTHING FROM THE HALLWAY! WE NEED THAT FOR THE NEXT SHOW.
AW, NO ARMCHAIR. IT WAS SO COZY.
WHAT ARE YOU HOPING TO FIND?
THERE! THE KNIFE.
GOTCHA.
NICE!

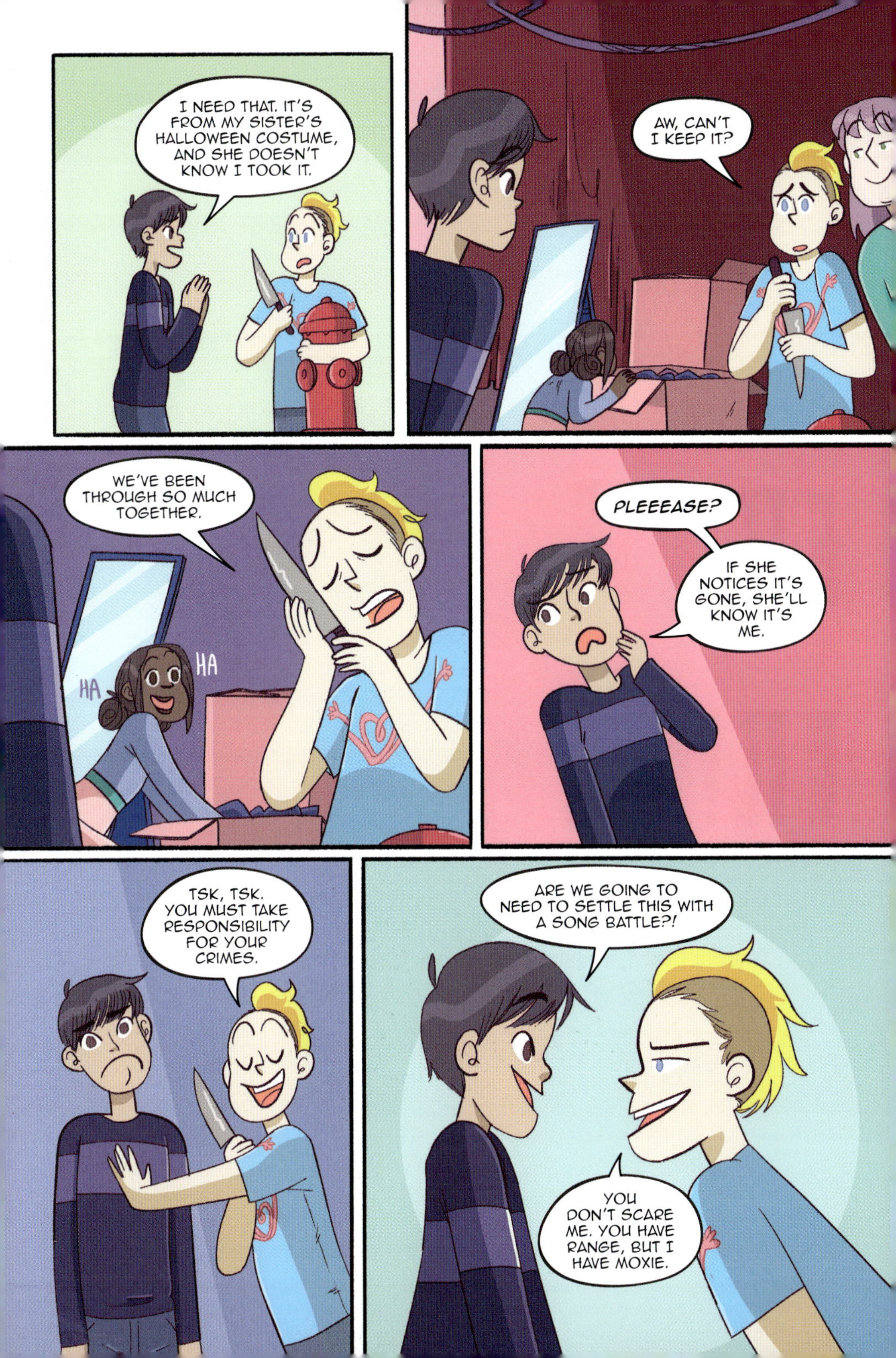
I NEED THAT. IT'S FROM MY SISTER'S HALLOWEEN COSTUME, AND SHE DOESN'T KNOW I TOOK IT.
AW, CAN'T I KEEP IT?
WE'VE BEEN THROUGH SO MUCH TOGETHER.
HA
HA
PLEEEASE?
IF SHE NOTICES IT'S GONE, SHE'LL KNOW IT'S ME.
TSK, TSK. YOU MUST TAKE RESPONSIBILITY FOR YOUR CRIMES.
ARE WE GOING TO NEED TO SETTLE THIS WITH A SONG BATTLE?!
YOU DON'T SCARE ME. YOU HAVE RANGE, BUT I HAVE MOXIE.

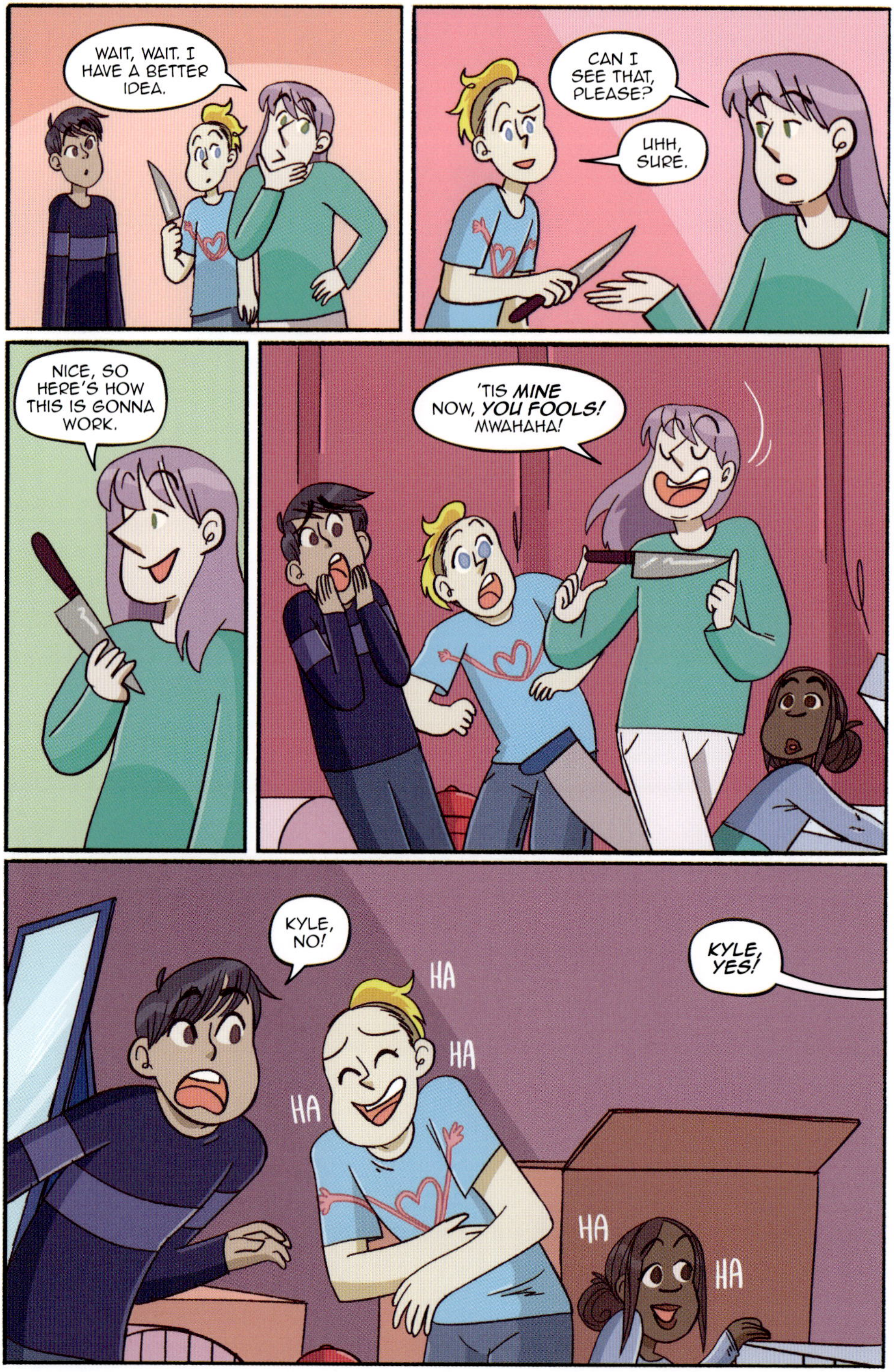
WAIT, WAIT. I HAVE A BETTER IDEA.
CAN I SEE THAT, PLEASE?
UHH, SURE.
NICE, SO HERE'S HOW THIS IS GONNA WORK.
'TIS *MINE* NOW, ***YOU FOOLS!*** MWAHAHA!
KYLE, NO!
HA
HA
HA
KYLE, YES!
HA
HA

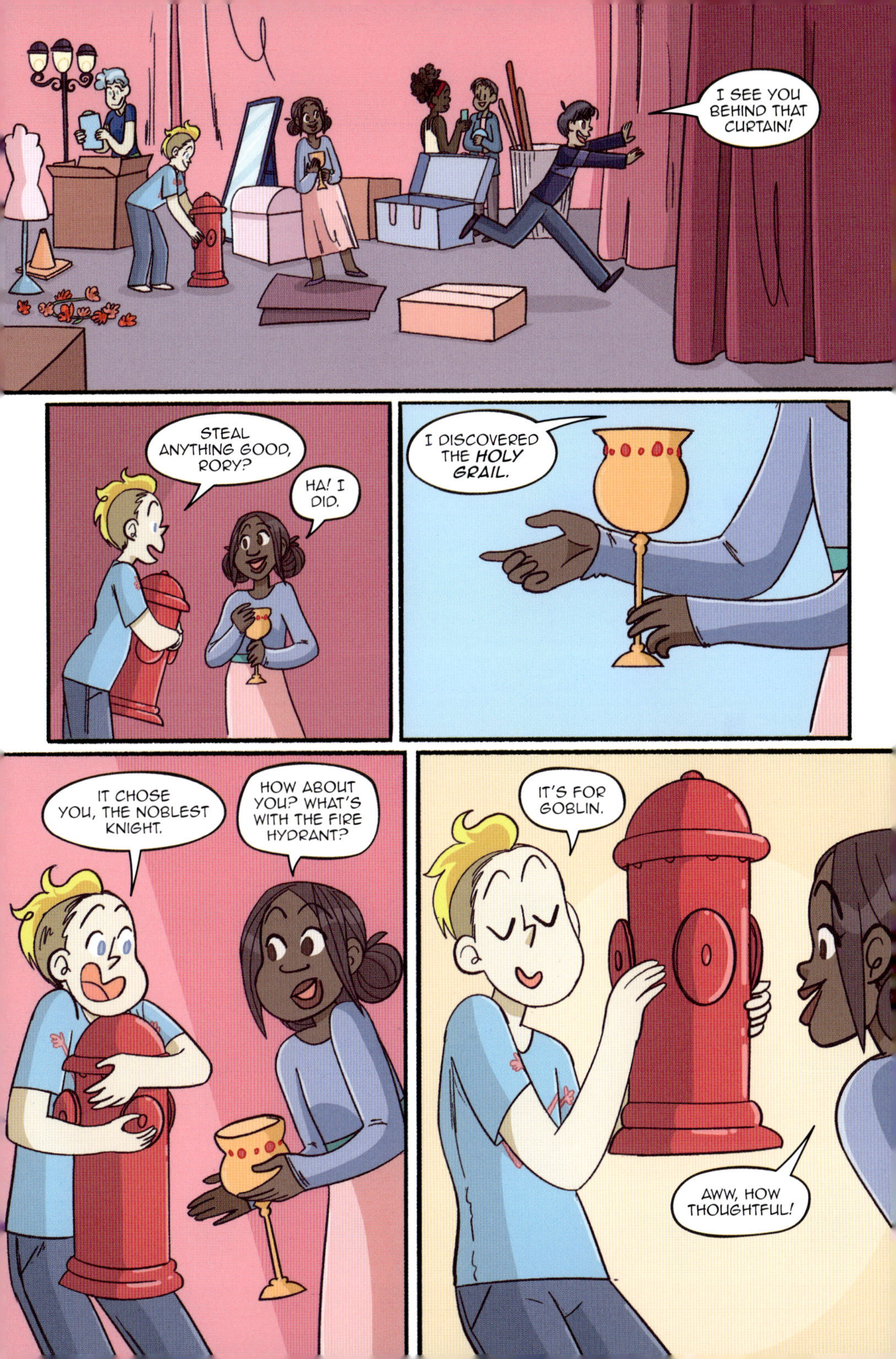
I SEE YOU BEHIND THAT CURTAIN!
STEAL ANYTHING GOOD, RORY?
HA! I DID.
I DISCOVERED THE **HOLY GRAIL.**
IT CHOSE YOU, THE NOBLEST KNIGHT.
HOW ABOUT YOU? WHAT'S WITH THE FIRE HYDRANT?
IT'S FOR GOBLIN.
AWW, HOW THOUGHTFUL!

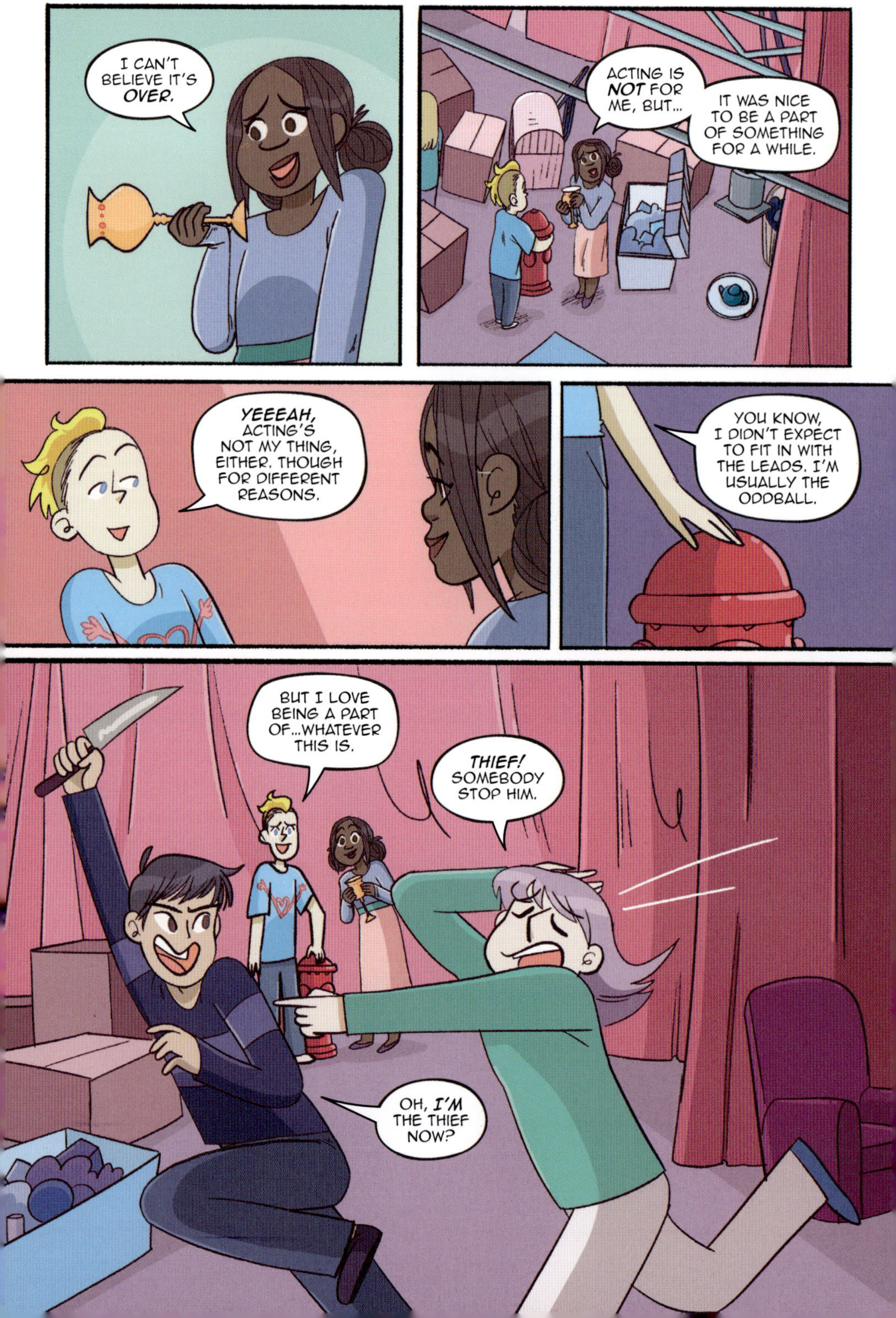
I CAN'T BELIEVE IT'S *OVER.*
ACTING IS *NOT* FOR ME, BUT...
IT WAS NICE TO BE A PART OF SOMETHING FOR A WHILE.
YEEEAH, ACTING'S NOT MY THING, EITHER. THOUGH FOR DIFFERENT REASONS.
YOU KNOW, I DIDN'T EXPECT TO FIT IN WITH THE LEADS. I'M USUALLY THE ODDBALL.
BUT I LOVE BEING A PART OF...WHATEVER THIS IS.
THIEF! SOMEBODY STOP HIM.
OH, *I'M* THE THIEF NOW?

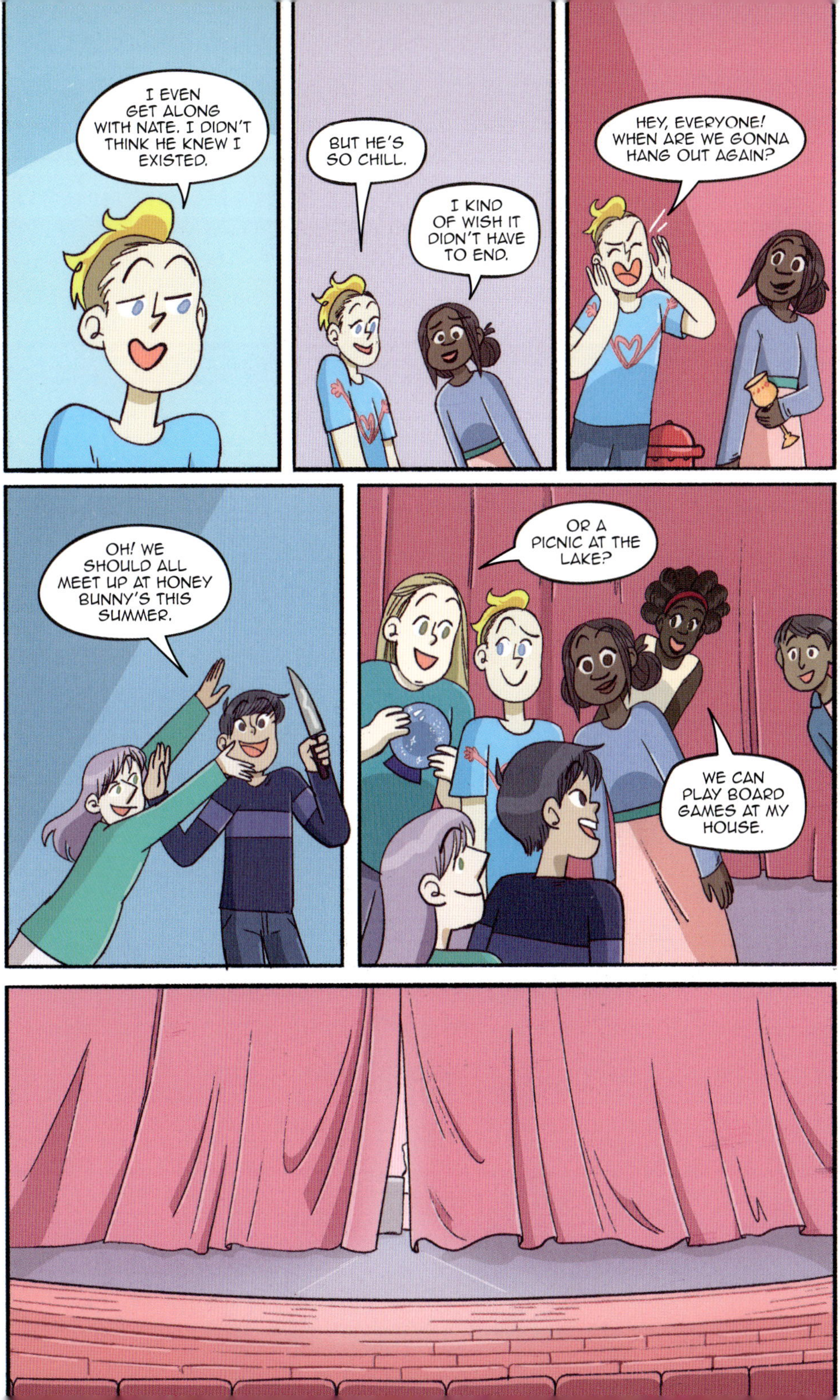
I EVEN GET ALONG WITH NATE. I DIDN'T THINK HE KNEW I EXISTED.
BUT HE'S SO CHILL.
I KIND OF WISH IT DIDN'T HAVE TO END.
HEY, EVERYONE! WHEN ARE WE GONNA HANG OUT AGAIN?
OH! WE SHOULD ALL MEET UP AT HONEY BUNNY'S THIS SUMMER.
OR A PICNIC AT THE LAKE?
WE CAN PLAY BOARD GAMES AT MY HOUSE.

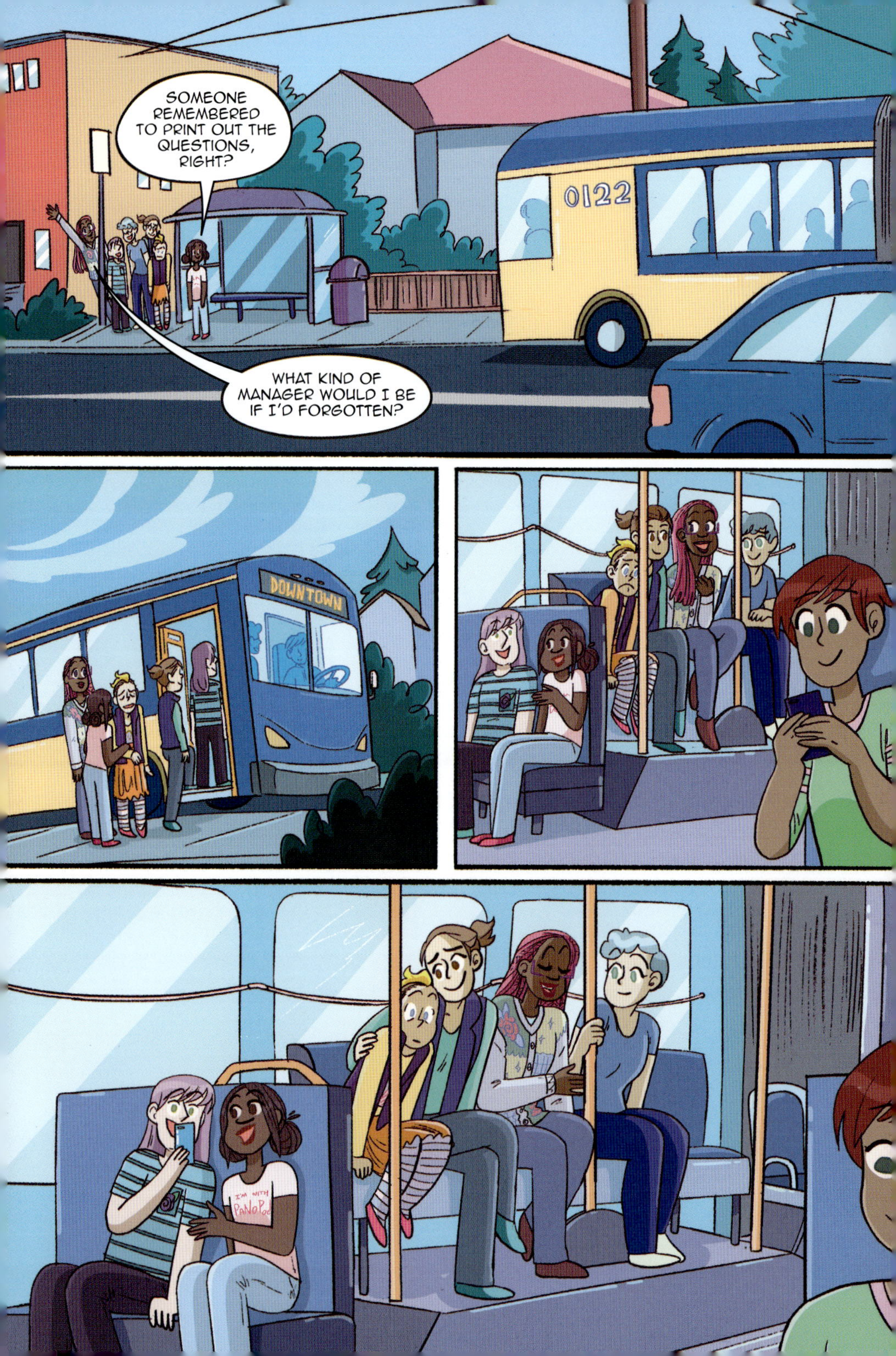
SOMEONE REMEMBERED TO PRINT OUT THE QUESTIONS, RIGHT?
WHAT KIND OF MANAGER WOULD I BE IF I'D FORGOTTEN?
0122
DOWNTOWN
I'M WITH PaNoPo

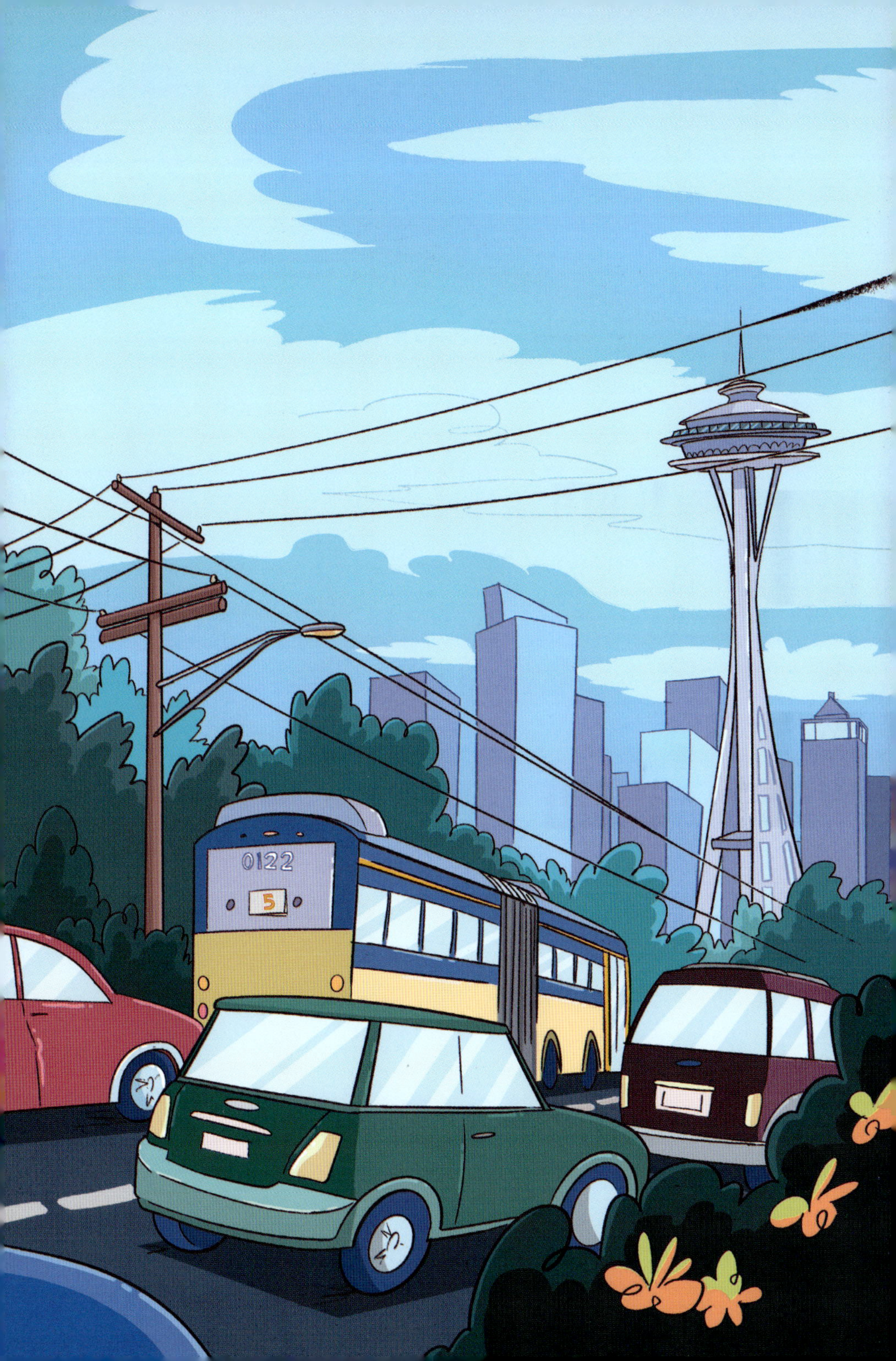
0122
5

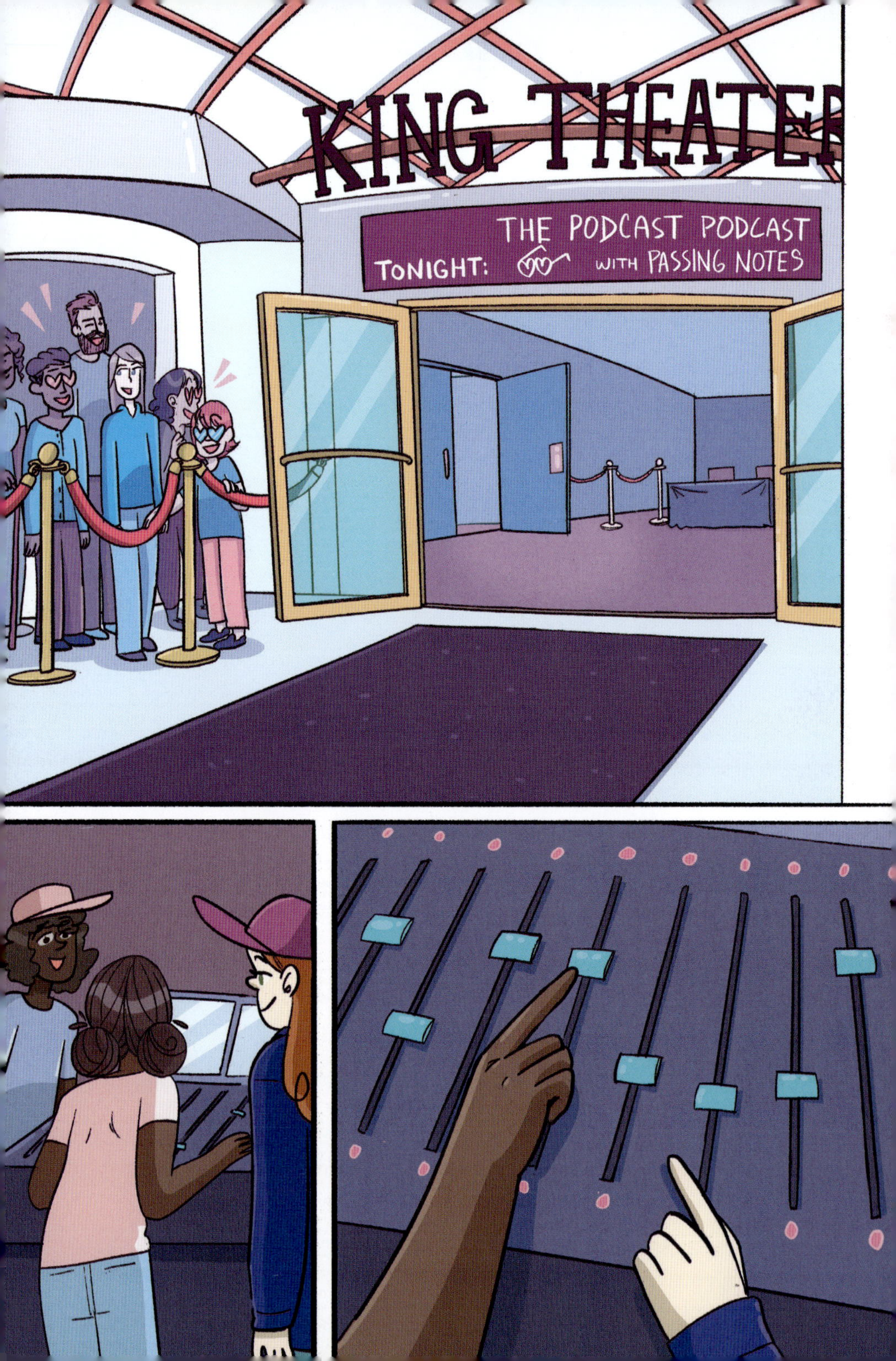
KING THEATER
THE PODCAST PODCAST
TONIGHT: WITH PASSING NOTES

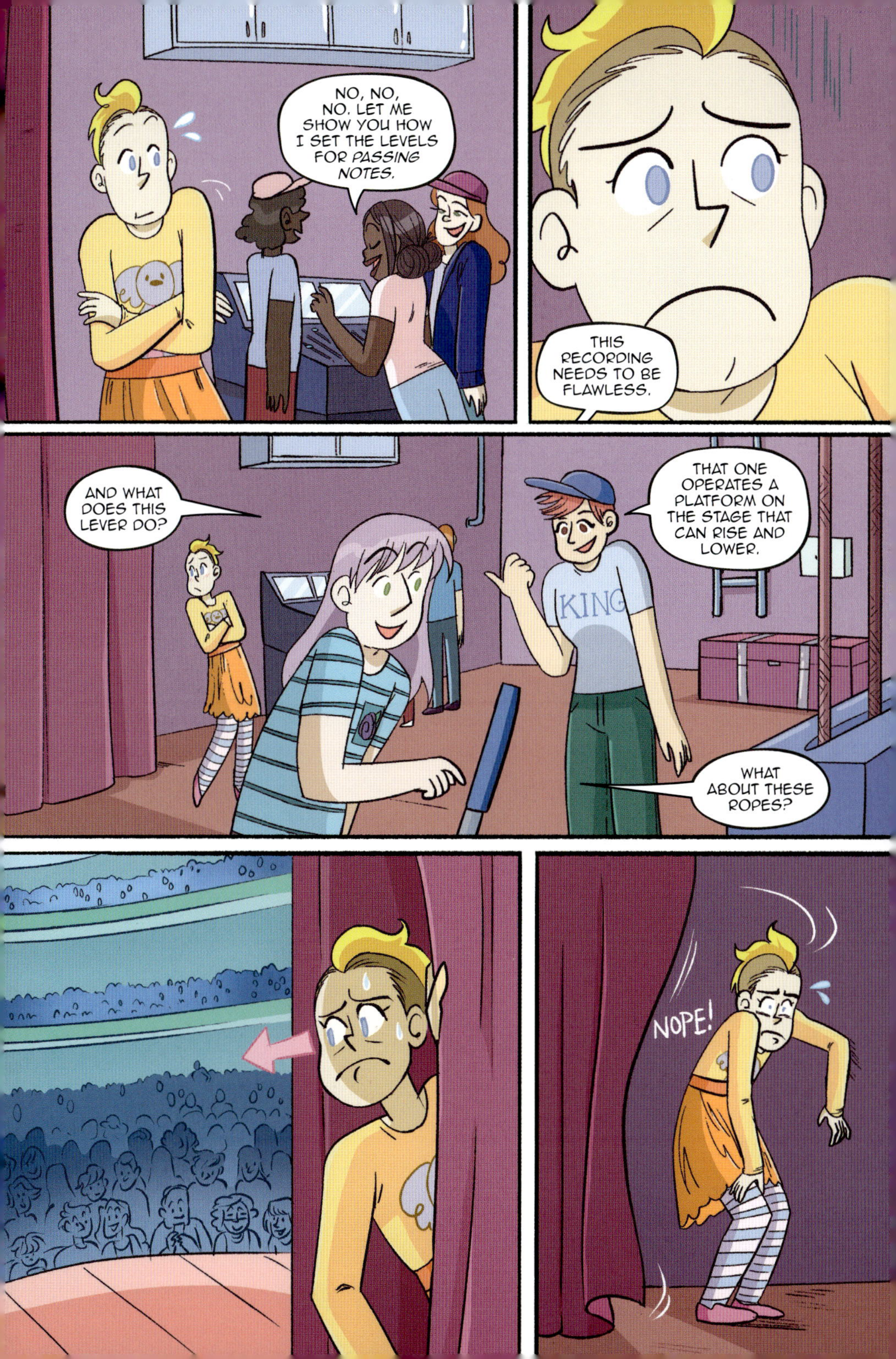
NO, NO, NO. LET ME SHOW YOU HOW I SET THE LEVELS FOR *PASSING NOTES.*
THIS RECORDING NEEDS TO BE FLAWLESS.
AND WHAT DOES THIS LEVER DO?
THAT ONE OPERATES A PLATFORM ON THE STAGE THAT CAN RISE AND LOWER.
KING
WHAT ABOUT THESE ROPES?
NOPE!

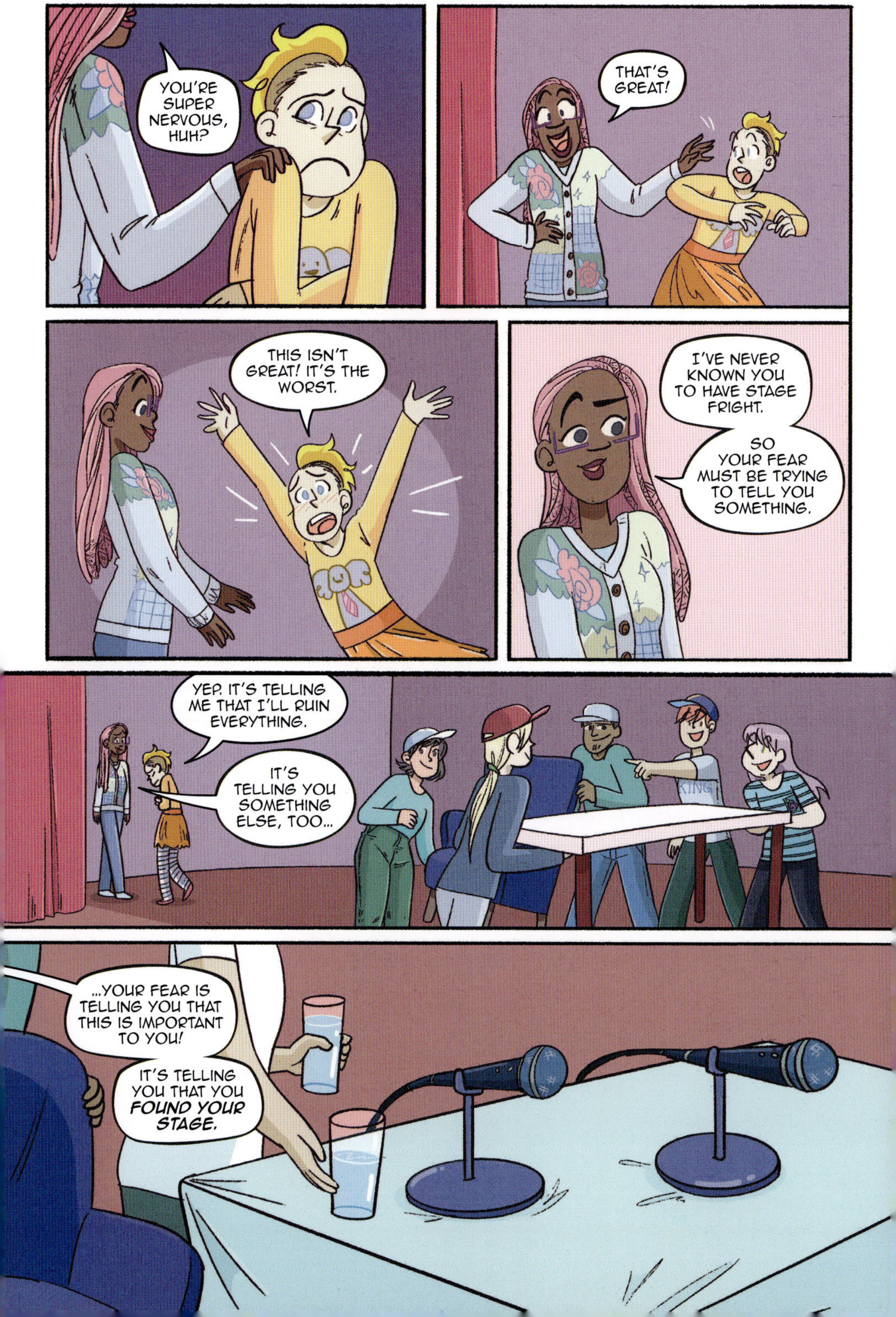
YOU'RE SUPER NERVOUS, HUH?
THAT'S GREAT!
THIS ISN'T GREAT! IT'S THE WORST.
I'VE NEVER KNOWN YOU TO HAVE STAGE FRIGHT.
SO YOUR FEAR MUST BE TRYING TO TELL YOU SOMETHING.
YEP. IT'S TELLING ME THAT I'LL RUIN EVERYTHING.
IT'S TELLING YOU SOMETHING ELSE, TOO...
...YOUR FEAR IS TELLING YOU THAT THIS IS IMPORTANT TO YOU!
IT'S TELLING YOU THAT YOU ***FOUND YOUR STAGE.***

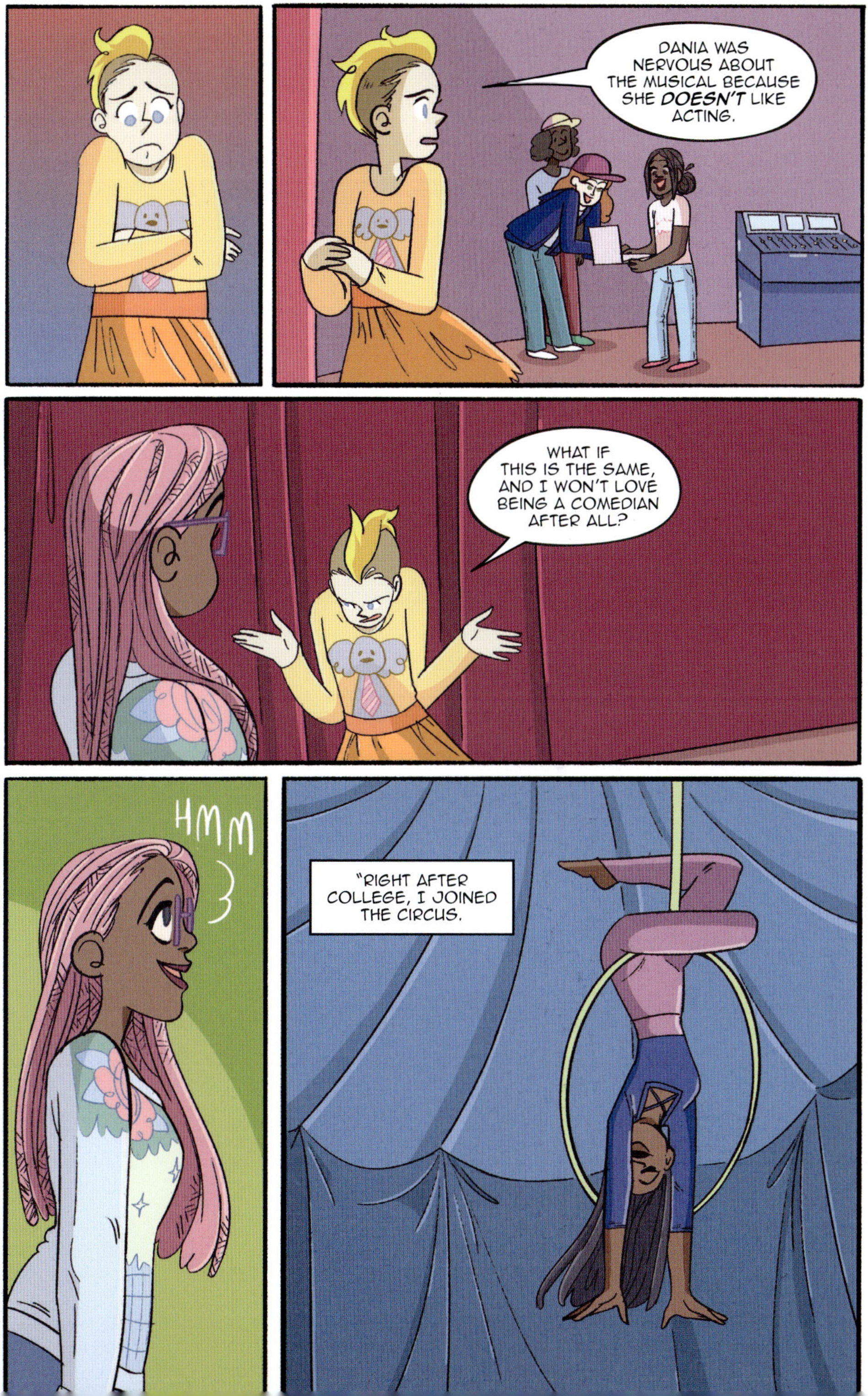
DANIA WAS NERVOUS ABOUT THE MUSICAL BECAUSE SHE *DOESN'T* LIKE ACTING.
WHAT IF THIS IS THE SAME, AND I WON'T LOVE BEING A COMEDIAN AFTER ALL?
HMM
"RIGHT AFTER COLLEGE, I JOINED THE CIRCUS.

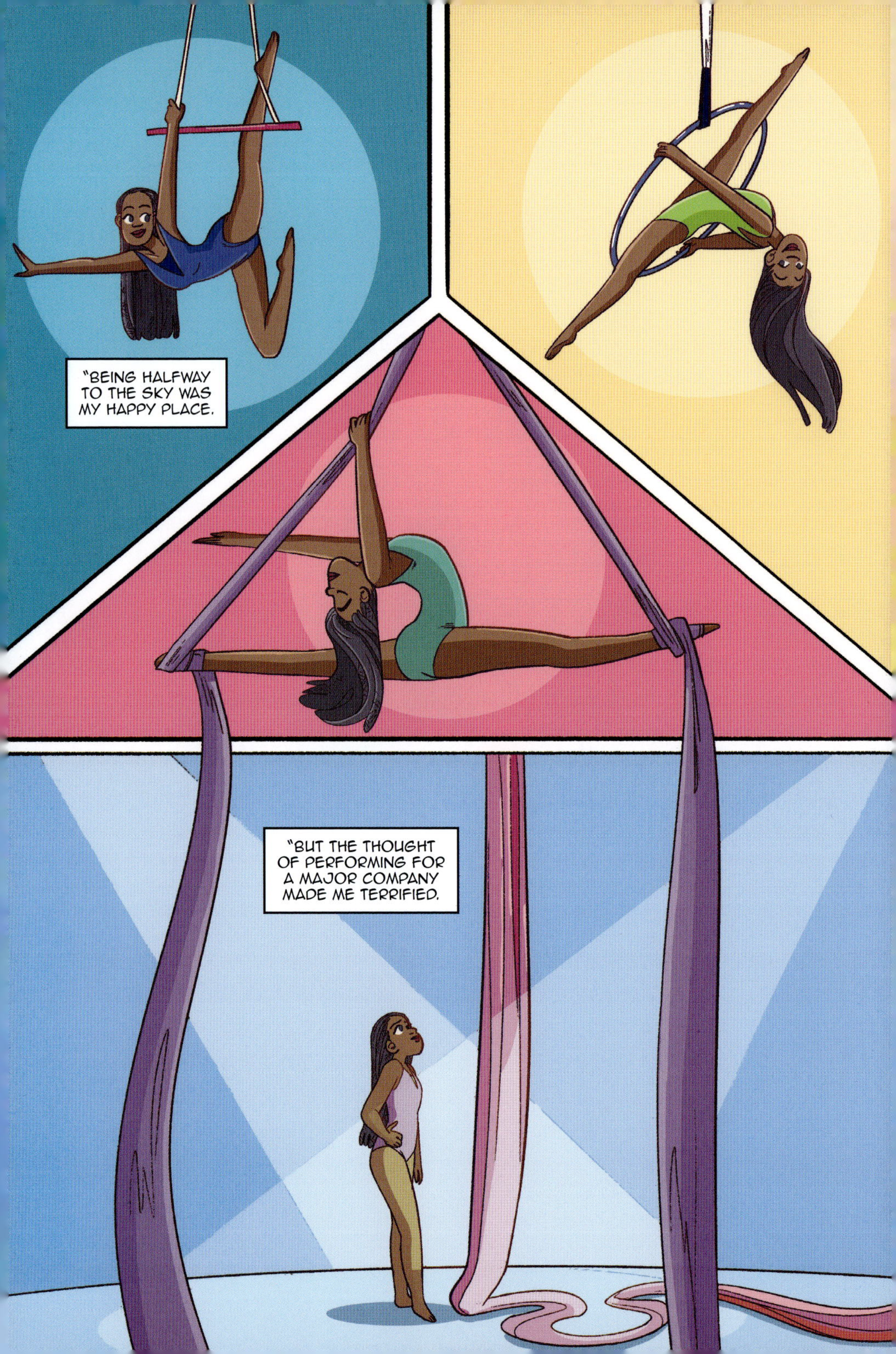
"BEING HALFWAY TO THE SKY WAS MY HAPPY PLACE.
"BUT THE THOUGHT OF PERFORMING FOR A MAJOR COMPANY MADE ME TERRIFIED.

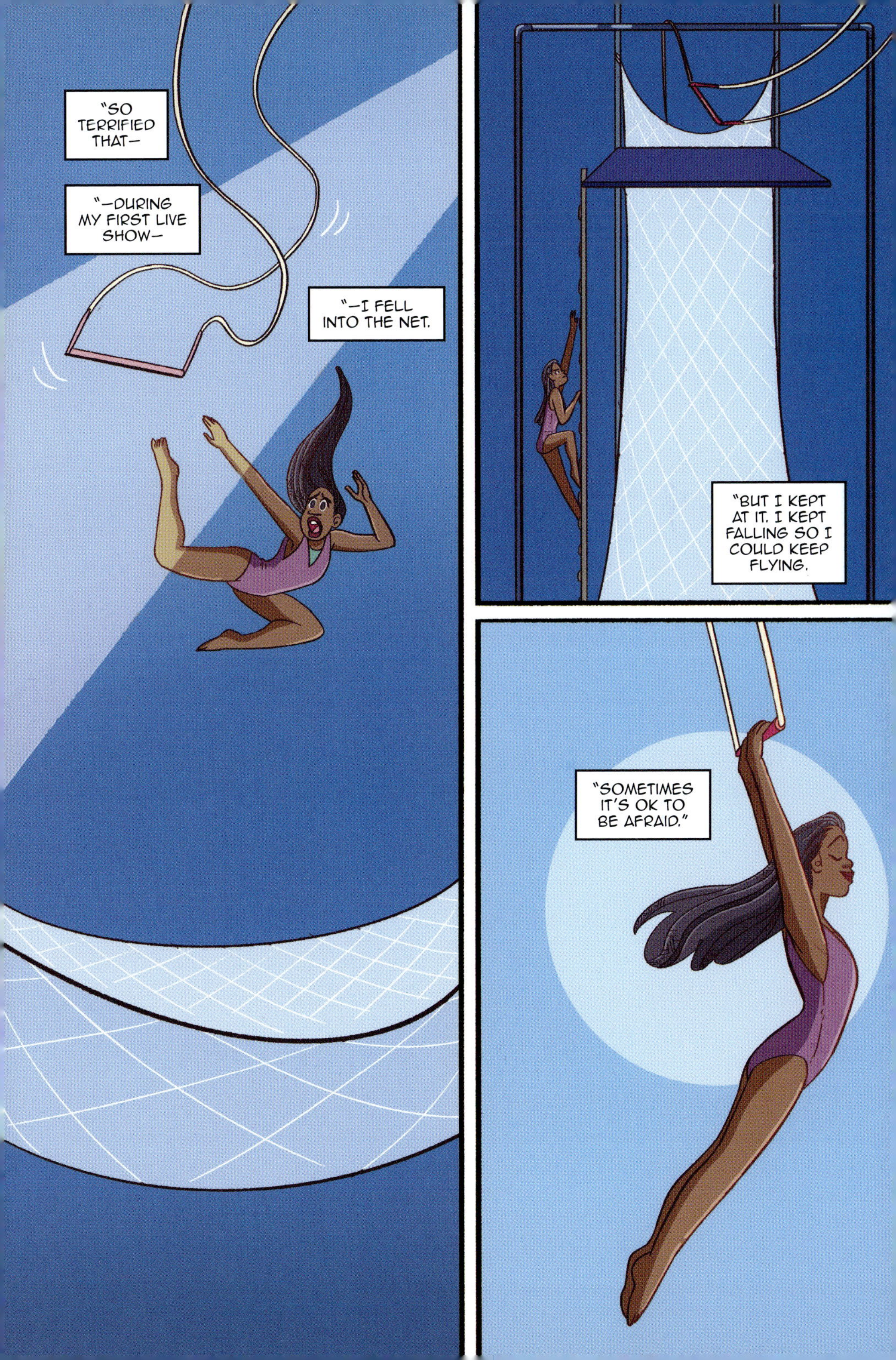
"SO TERRIFIED THAT—
"—DURING MY FIRST LIVE SHOW—
"—I FELL INTO THE NET.
"BUT I KEPT AT IT. I KEPT FALLING SO I COULD KEEP FLYING.
"SOMETIMES IT'S OK TO BE AFRAID."

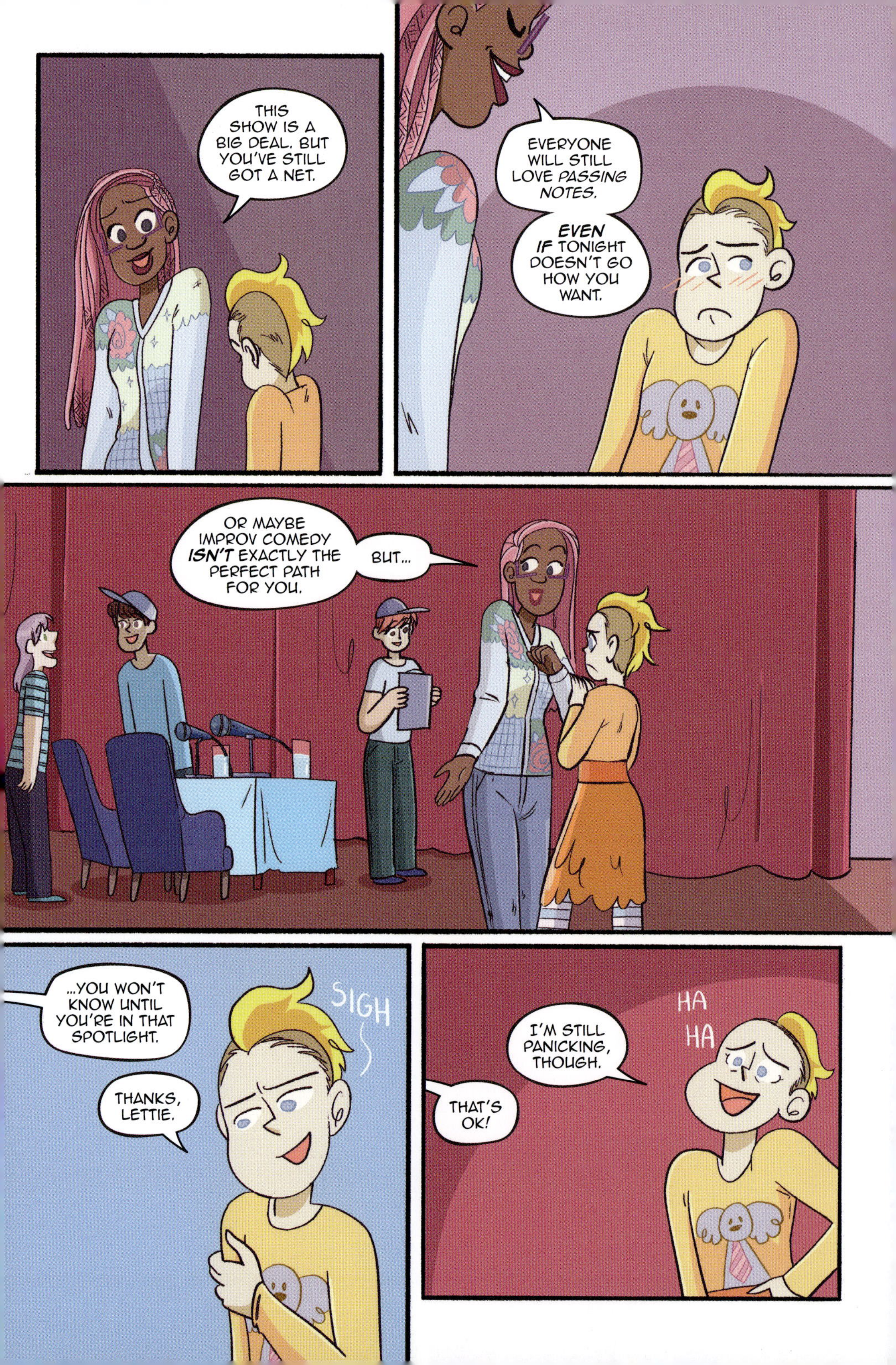
THIS SHOW IS A BIG DEAL. BUT YOU'VE STILL GOT A NET.
EVERYONE WILL STILL LOVE *PASSING NOTES.*
EVEN IF TONIGHT DOESN'T GO HOW YOU WANT.
OR MAYBE IMPROV COMEDY ***ISN'T*** EXACTLY THE PERFECT PATH FOR YOU.
BUT...
...YOU WON'T KNOW UNTIL YOU'RE IN THAT SPOTLIGHT.
SIGH
THANKS, LETTIE.
HA HA
I'M STILL PANICKING, THOUGH.
THAT'S OK!

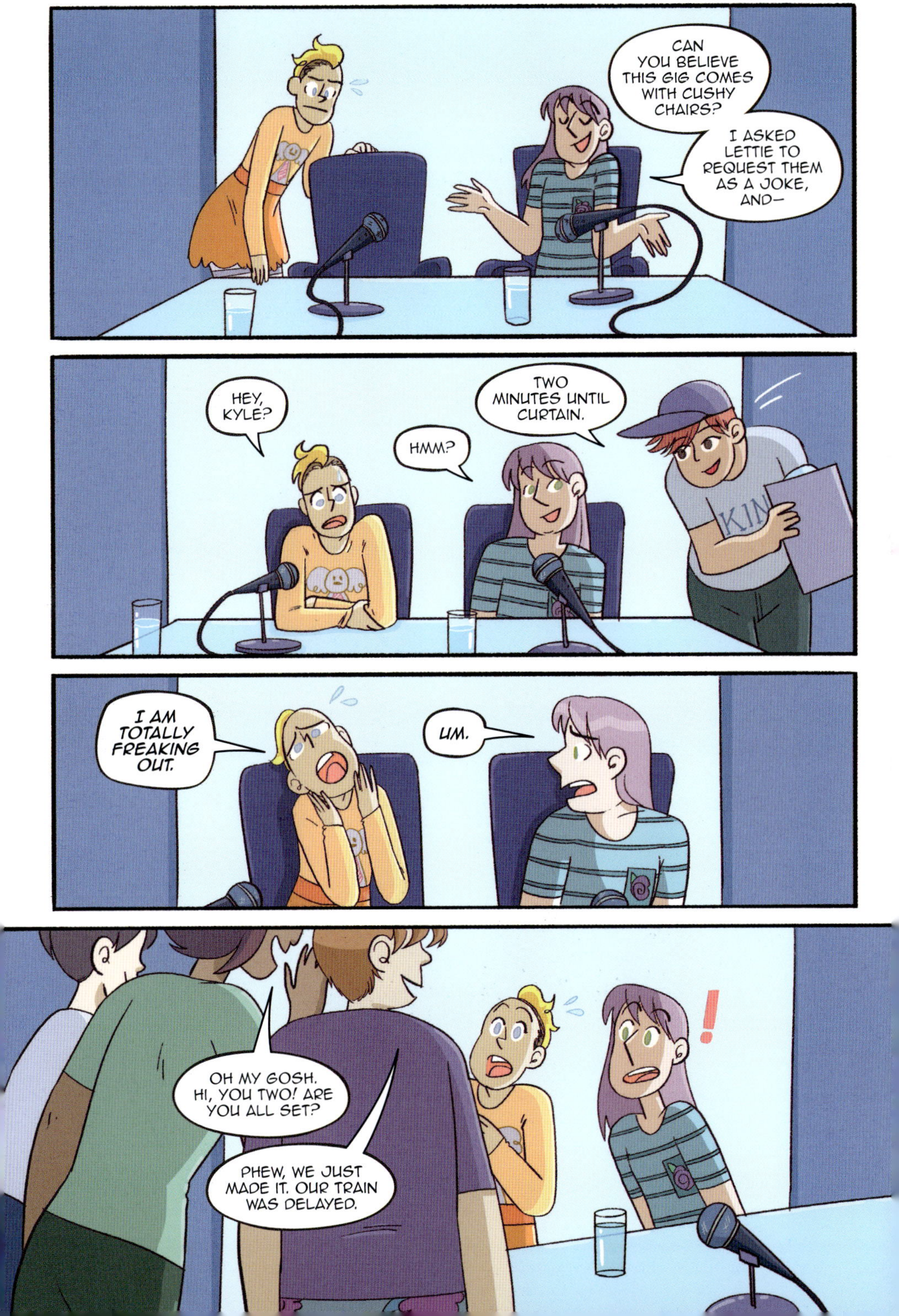
CAN YOU BELIEVE THIS GIG COMES WITH CUSHY CHAIRS?
I ASKED LETTIE TO REQUEST THEM AS A JOKE, AND—
HEY, KYLE?
HMM?
TWO MINUTES UNTIL CURTAIN.
KIN
I AM TOTALLY FREAKING OUT.
UM.
!
OH MY GOSH. HI, YOU TWO! ARE YOU ALL SET?
PHEW, WE JUST MADE IT. OUR TRAIN WAS DELAYED.

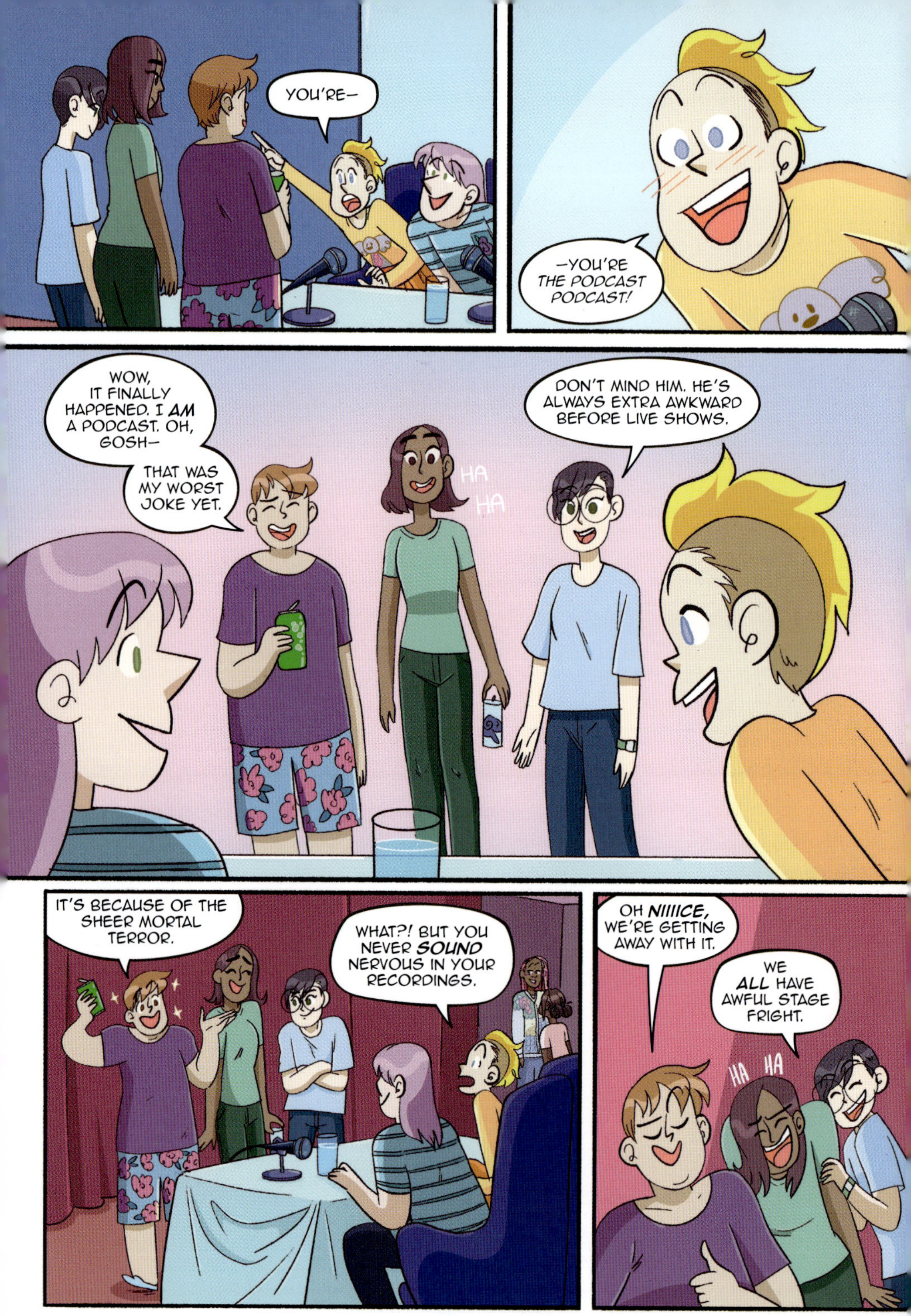
YOU'RE—
—YOU'RE THE PODCAST PODCAST!
WOW, IT FINALLY HAPPENED. I *AM* A PODCAST. OH, GOSH—
THAT WAS MY WORST JOKE YET.
HA HA
DON'T MIND HIM. HE'S ALWAYS EXTRA AWKWARD BEFORE LIVE SHOWS.
IT'S BECAUSE OF THE SHEER MORTAL TERROR.
WHAT?! BUT YOU NEVER *SOUND* NERVOUS IN YOUR RECORDINGS.
OH *NIIIICE,* WE'RE GETTING AWAY WITH IT.
WE *ALL* HAVE AWFUL STAGE FRIGHT.
HA HA

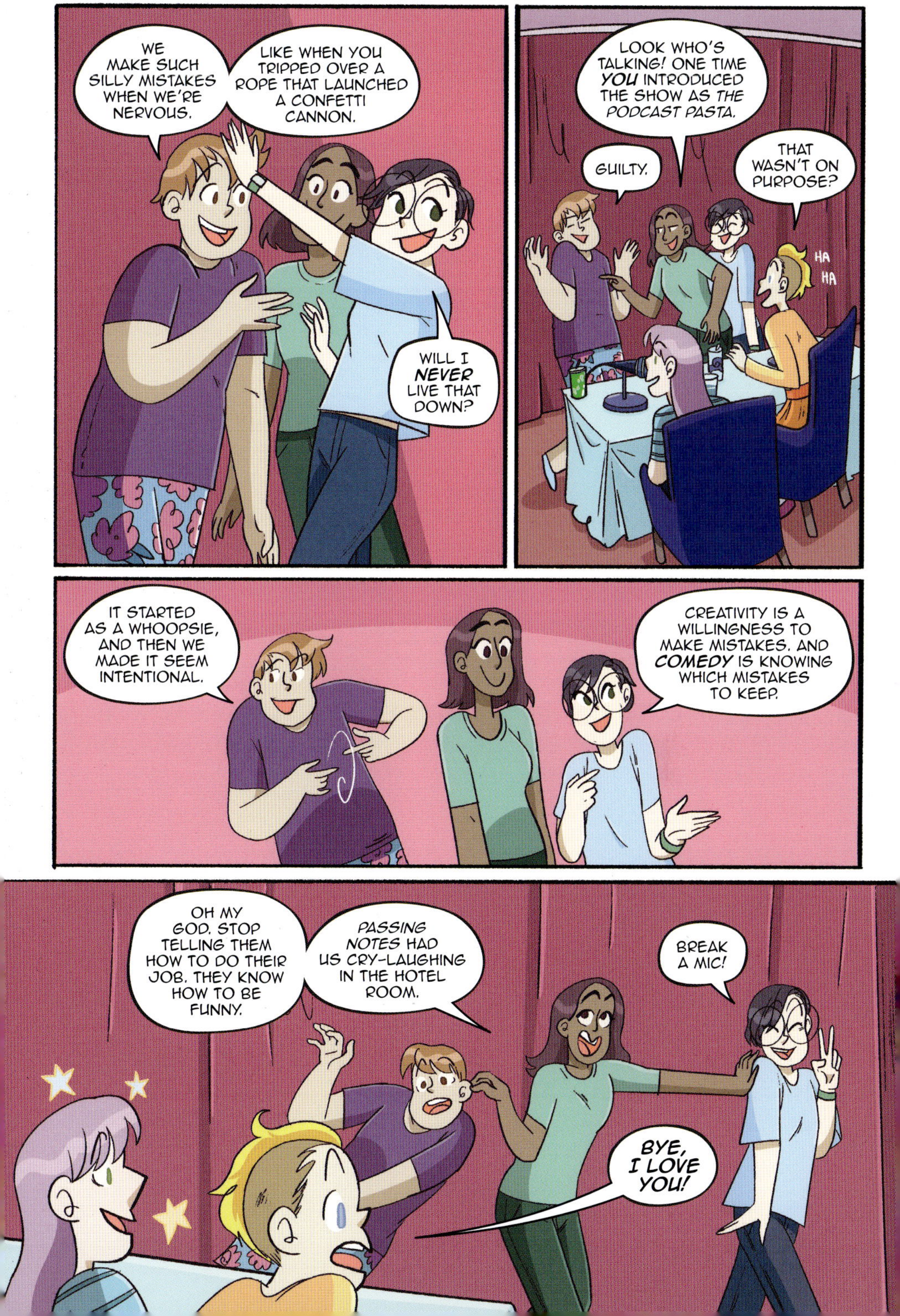
WE MAKE SUCH SILLY MISTAKES WHEN WE'RE NERVOUS.
LIKE WHEN YOU TRIPPED OVER A ROPE THAT LAUNCHED A CONFETTI CANNON.
WILL I *NEVER* LIVE THAT DOWN?
LOOK WHO'S TALKING! ONE TIME *YOU* INTRODUCED THE SHOW AS *THE PODCAST PASTA.*
GUILTY.
THAT WASN'T ON PURPOSE?
HA HA
IT STARTED AS A WHOOPSIE, AND THEN WE MADE IT SEEM INTENTIONAL.
CREATIVITY IS A WILLINGNESS TO MAKE MISTAKES. AND *COMEDY* IS KNOWING WHICH MISTAKES TO KEEP.
OH MY GOD. STOP TELLING THEM HOW TO DO THEIR JOB. THEY KNOW HOW TO BE FUNNY.
PASSING NOTES HAD US CRY-LAUGHING IN THE HOTEL ROOM.
BREAK A MIC!
BYE, I LOVE YOU!

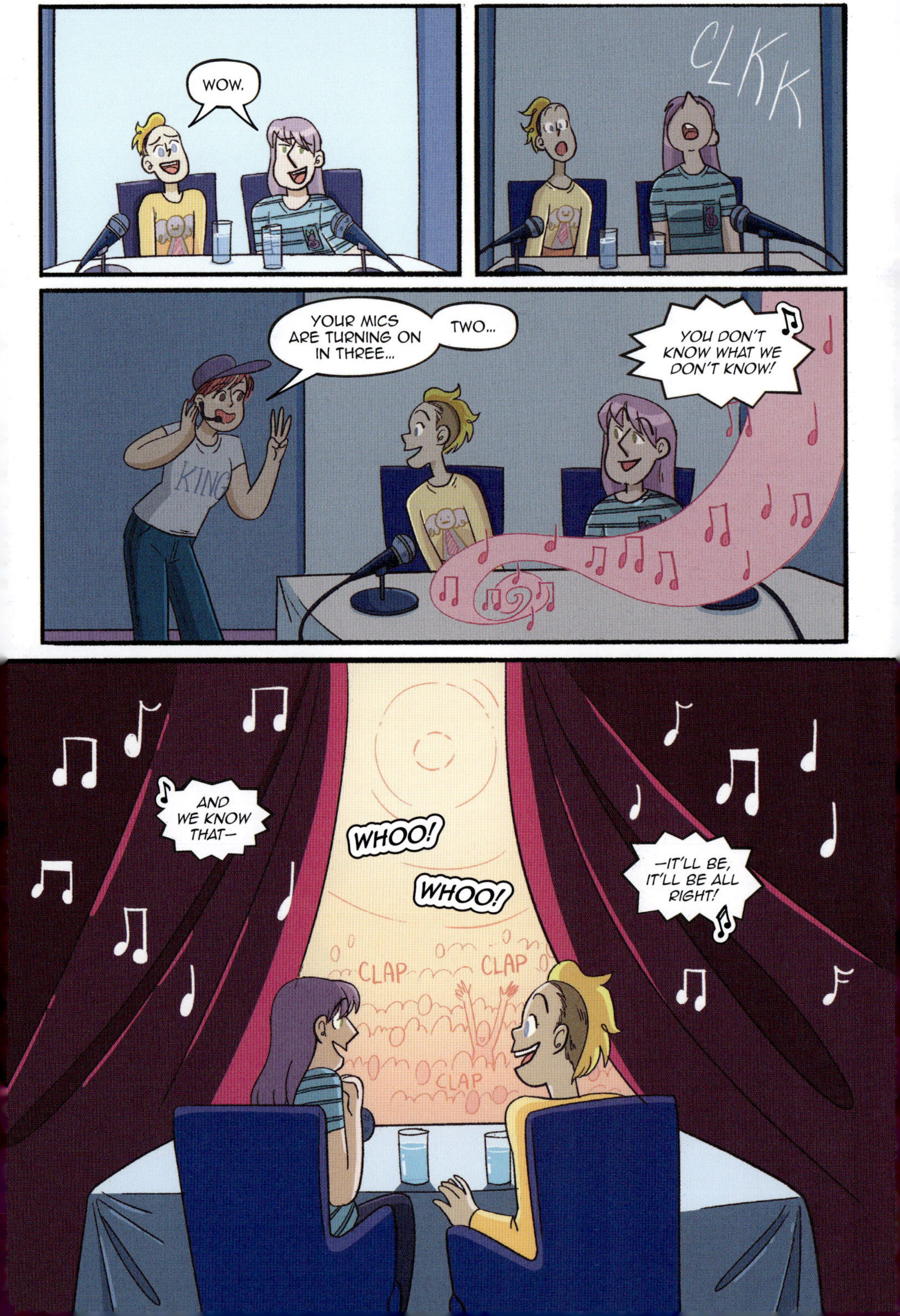
WOW.
CLKK
YOUR MICS ARE TURNING ON IN THREE...
TWO...
YOU DON'T KNOW WHAT WE DON'T KNOW!
AND WE KNOW THAT—
WHOO!
WHOO!
—IT'LL BE, IT'LL BE ALL RIGHT!
CLAP
CLAP
CLAP
KING

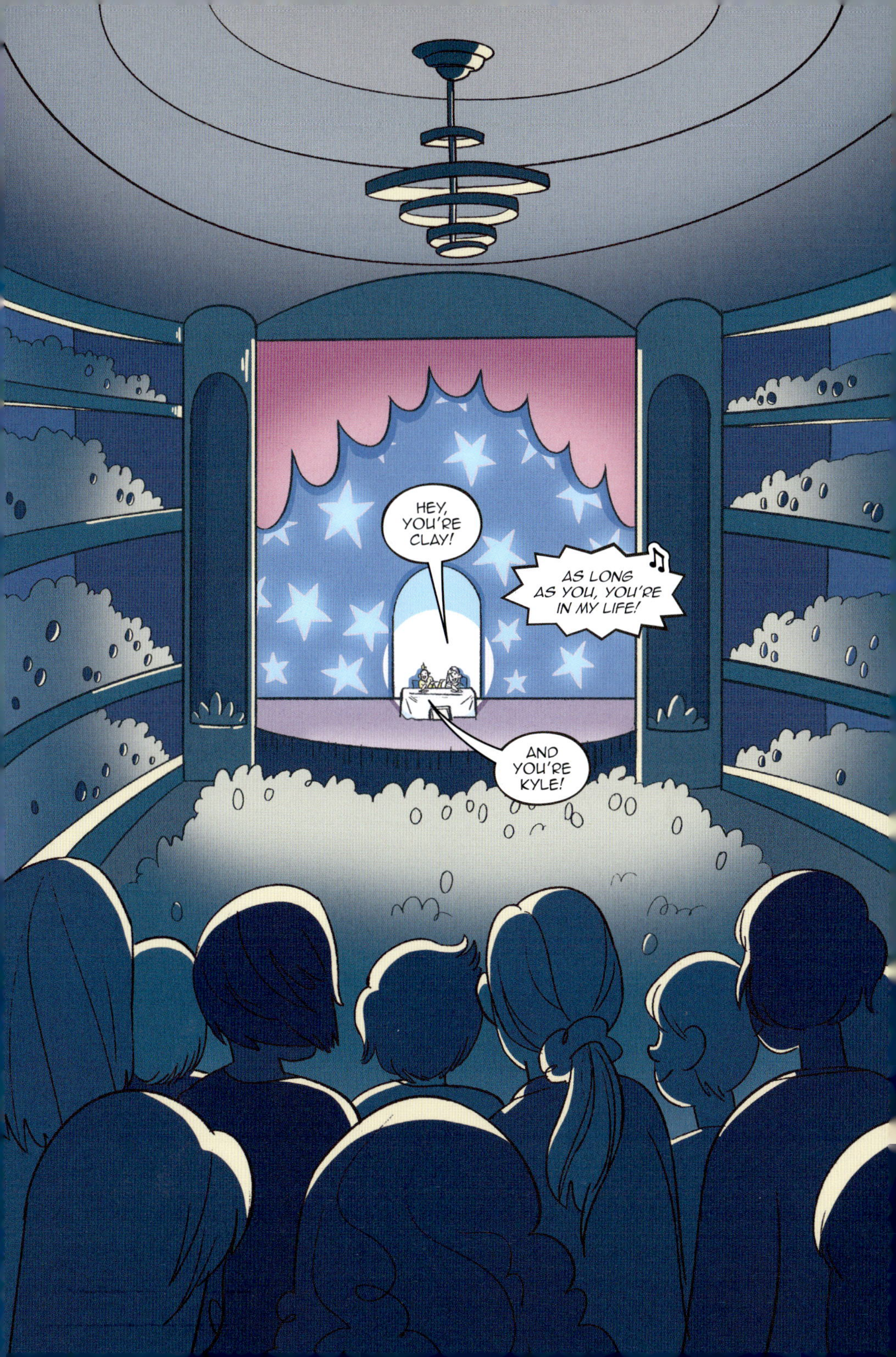
HEY, YOU'RE CLAY!
AS LONG AS YOU, YOU'RE IN MY LIFE!
AND YOU'RE KYLE!

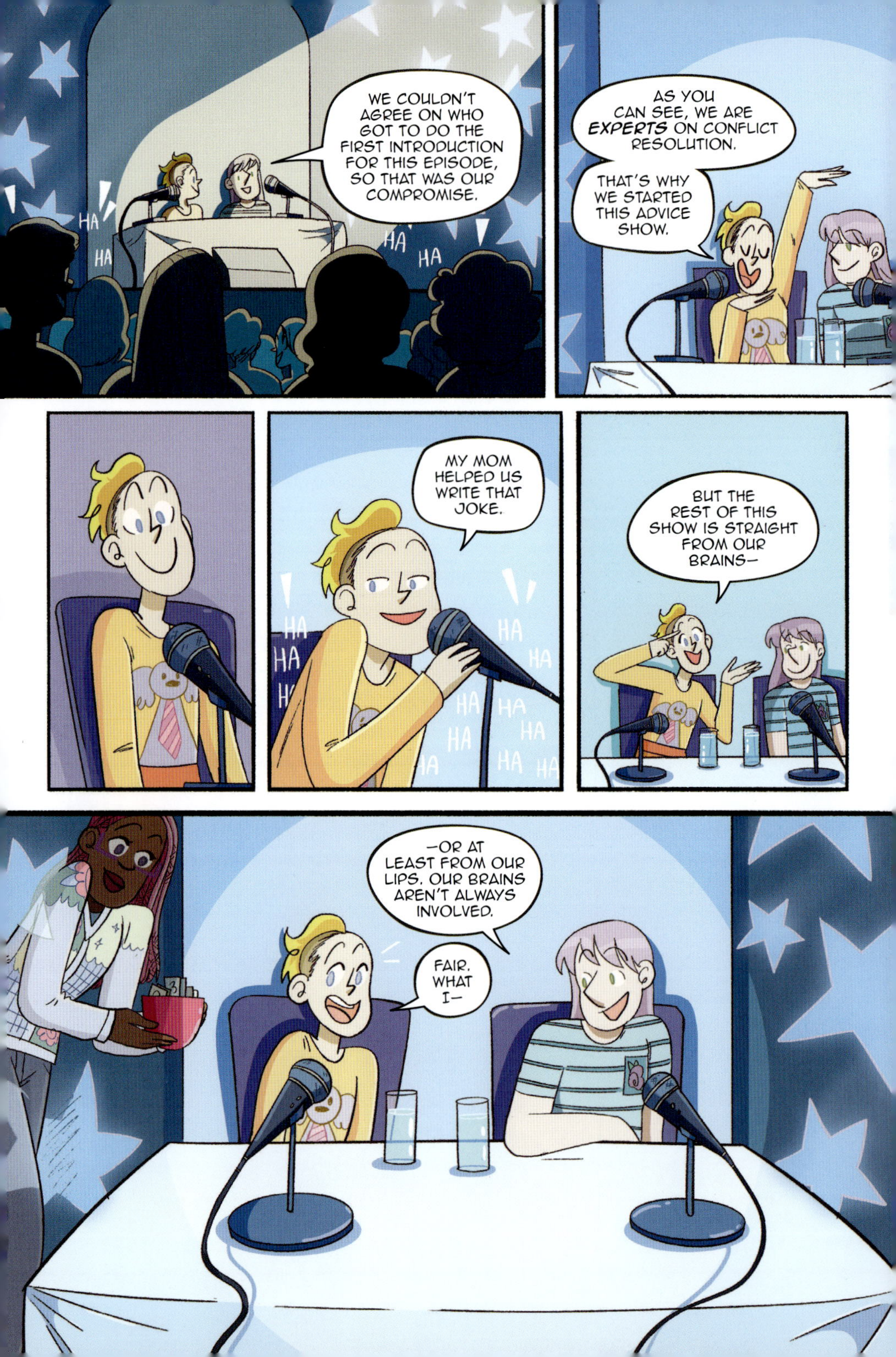

HA
HA
WE COULDN'T AGREE ON WHO GOT TO DO THE FIRST INTRODUCTION FOR THIS EPISODE, SO THAT WAS OUR COMPROMISE.
HA
HA
AS YOU CAN SEE, WE ARE EXPERTS ON CONFLICT RESOLUTION.
THAT'S WHY WE STARTED THIS ADVICE SHOW.
MY MOM HELPED US WRITE THAT JOKE.
HA HA HA HA HA HA HA HA HA HA
BUT THE REST OF THIS SHOW IS STRAIGHT FROM OUR BRAINS—
—OR AT LEAST FROM OUR LIPS. OUR BRAINS AREN'T ALWAYS INVOLVED.
FAIR. WHAT I—

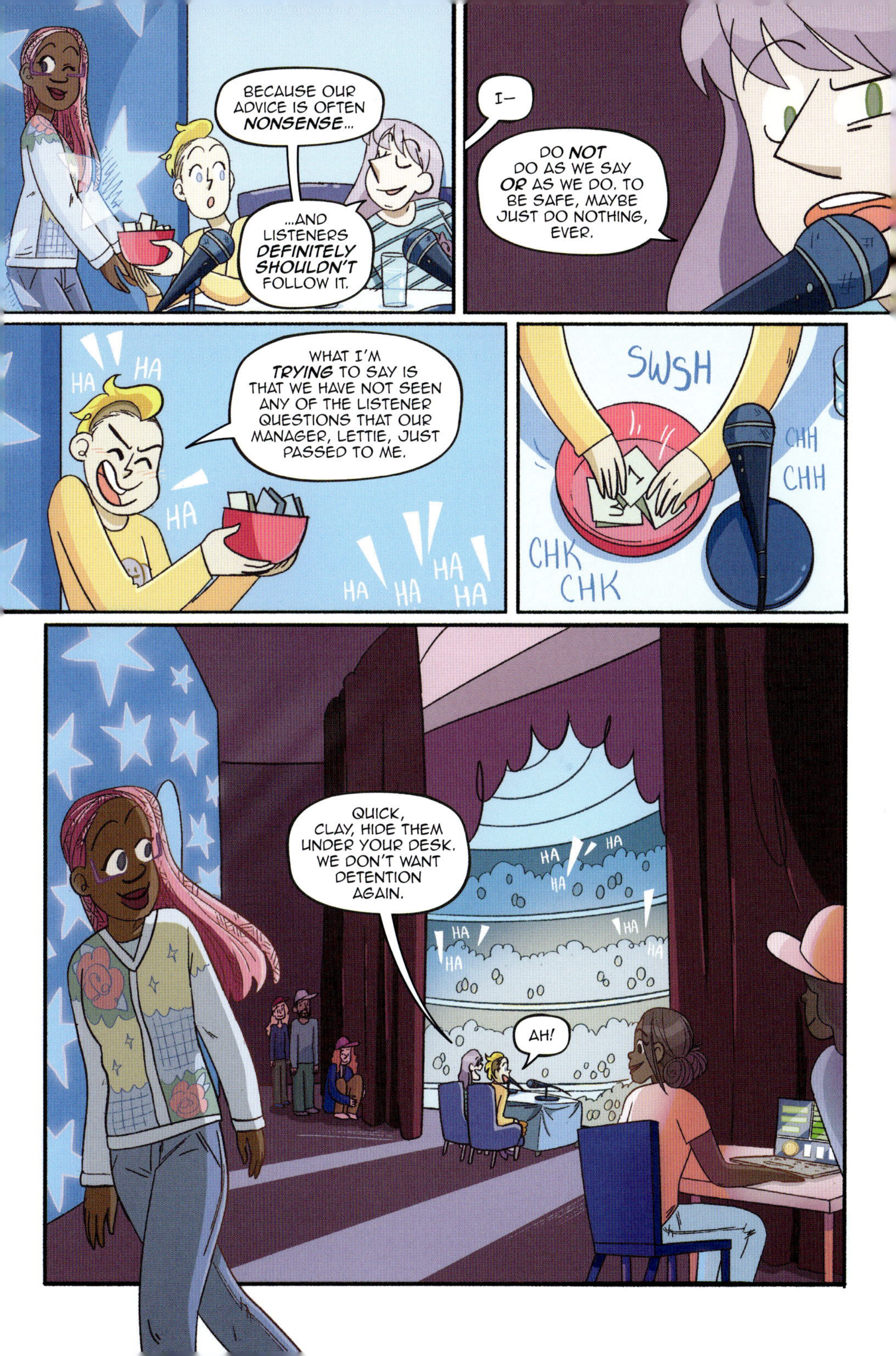
BECAUSE OUR ADVICE IS OFTEN NONSENSE...
...AND LISTENERS DEFINITELY SHOULDN'T FOLLOW IT.
I—
DO NOT DO AS WE SAY OR AS WE DO. TO BE SAFE, MAYBE JUST DO NOTHING, EVER.
HA HA
WHAT I'M TRYING TO SAY IS THAT WE HAVE NOT SEEN ANY OF THE LISTENER QUESTIONS THAT OUR MANAGER, LETTIE, JUST PASSED TO ME.
HA
HA HA HA HA
SWSH
CHH CHH
CHK CHK
QUICK, CLAY, HIDE THEM UNDER YOUR DESK. WE DON'T WANT DETENTION AGAIN.
HA HA HA
HA HA
HA HA
AH!

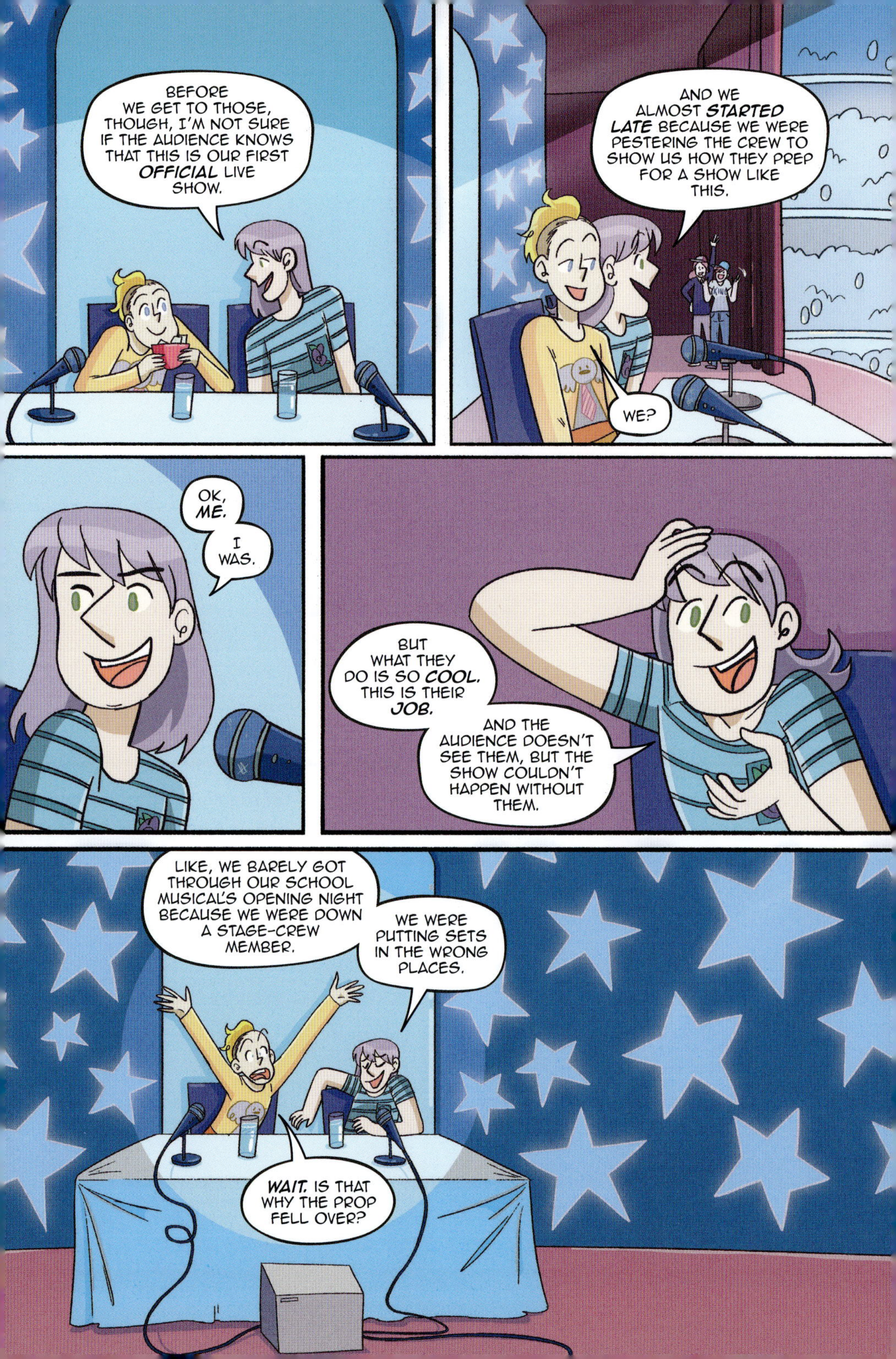
BEFORE WE GET TO THOSE, THOUGH, I'M NOT SURE IF THE AUDIENCE KNOWS THAT THIS IS OUR FIRST OFFICIAL LIVE SHOW.
AND WE ALMOST STARTED LATE BECAUSE WE WERE PESTERING THE CREW TO SHOW US HOW THEY PREP FOR A SHOW LIKE THIS.
WE?
OK, ME.
I WAS.
BUT WHAT THEY DO IS SO COOL. THIS IS THEIR JOB.
AND THE AUDIENCE DOESN'T SEE THEM, BUT THE SHOW COULDN'T HAPPEN WITHOUT THEM.
LIKE, WE BARELY GOT THROUGH OUR SCHOOL MUSICAL'S OPENING NIGHT BECAUSE WE WERE DOWN A STAGE-CREW MEMBER.
WE WERE PUTTING SETS IN THE WRONG PLACES.
WAIT. IS THAT WHY THE PROP FELL OVER?

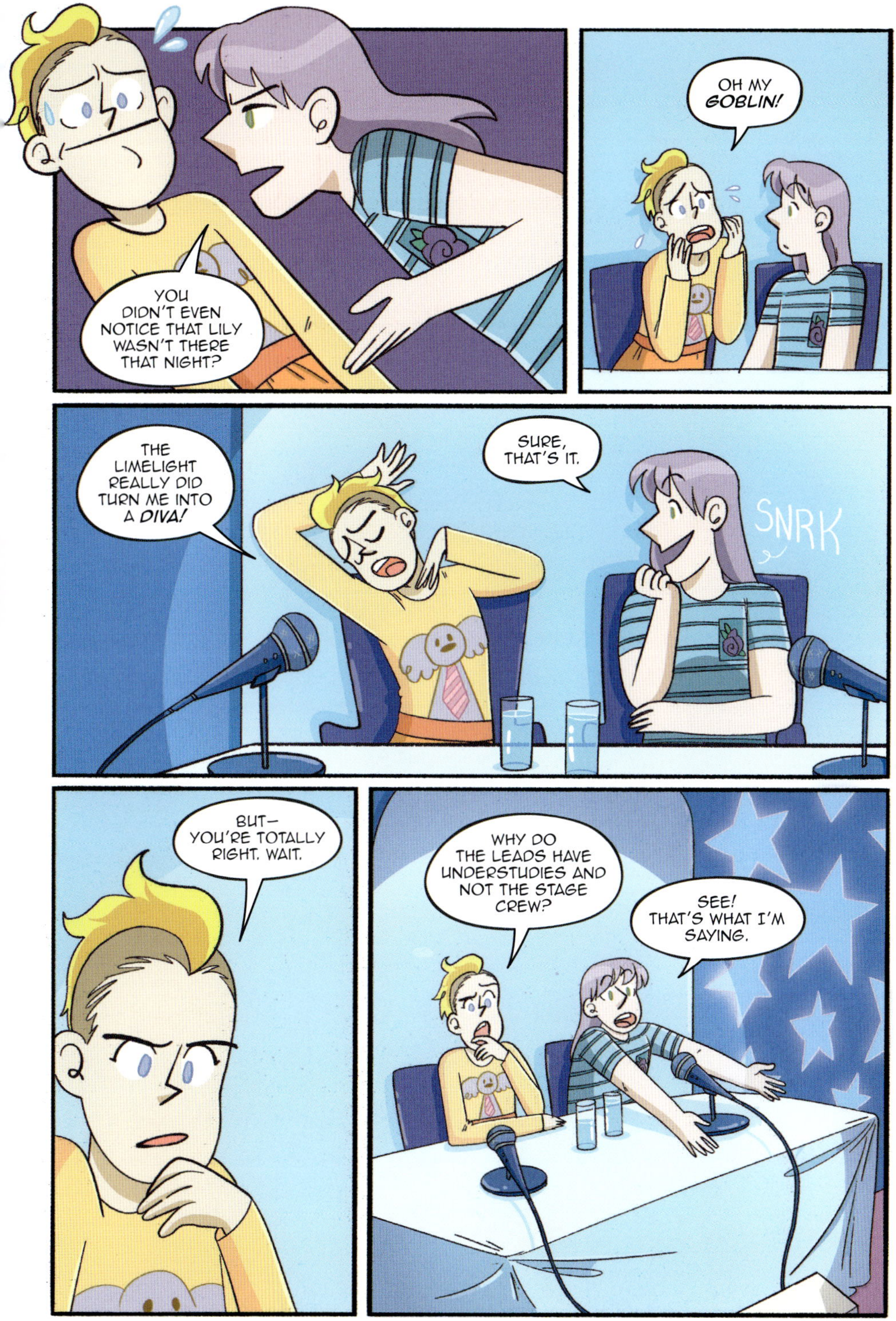
YOU DIDN'T EVEN NOTICE THAT LILY WASN'T THERE THAT NIGHT?
OH MY GOBLIN!
THE LIMELIGHT REALLY DID TURN ME INTO A DIVA!
SURE, THAT'S IT.
SNRK
BUT— YOU'RE TOTALLY RIGHT. WAIT.
WHY DO THE LEADS HAVE UNDERSTUDIES AND NOT THE STAGE CREW?
SEE! THAT'S WHAT I'M SAYING.

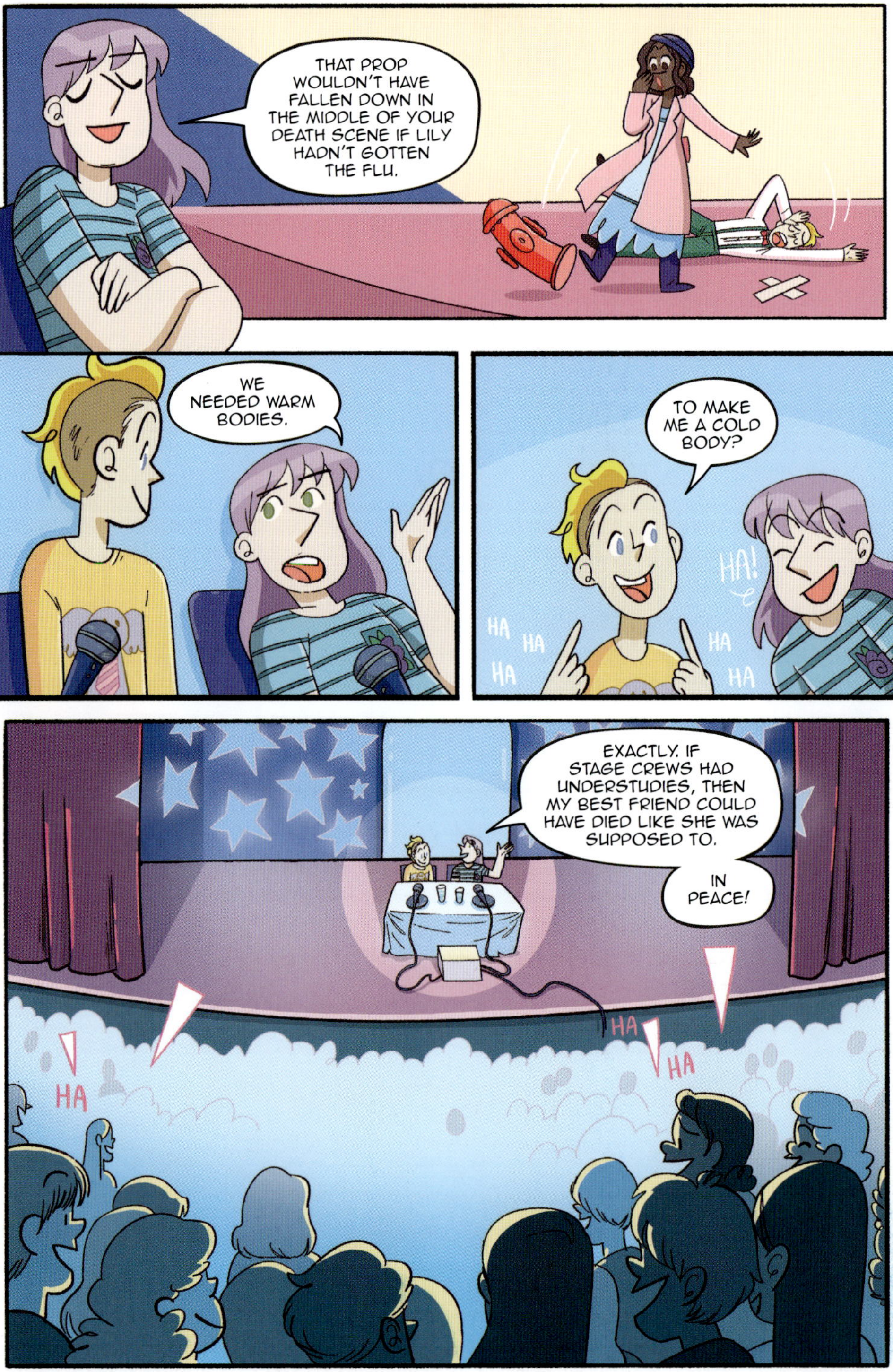
THAT PROP WOULDN'T HAVE FALLEN DOWN IN THE MIDDLE OF YOUR DEATH SCENE IF LILY HADN'T GOTTEN THE FLU.
WE NEEDED WARM BODIES.
TO MAKE ME A COLD BODY?
HA!
HA HA HA
HA HA
EXACTLY. IF STAGE CREWS HAD UNDERSTUDIES, THEN MY BEST FRIEND COULD HAVE DIED LIKE SHE WAS SUPPOSED TO.
IN PEACE!
HA
HA
HA

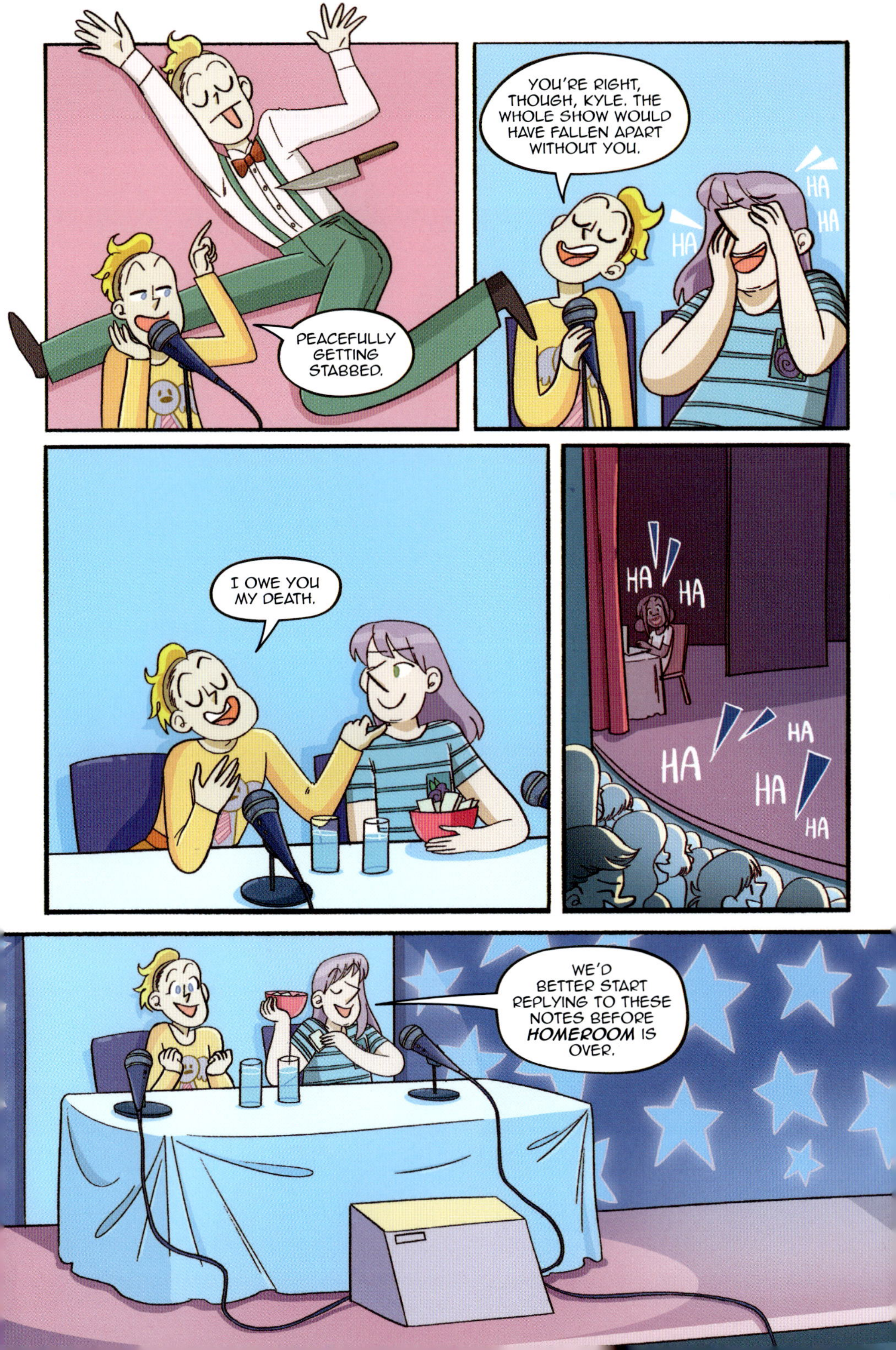

PEACEFULLY GETTING STABBED.
YOU'RE RIGHT, THOUGH, KYLE. THE WHOLE SHOW WOULD HAVE FALLEN APART WITHOUT YOU.
HA HA HA
I OWE YOU MY DEATH.
HA HA
HA HA HA HA
WE'D BETTER START REPLYING TO THESE NOTES BEFORE ***HOMEROOM*** IS OVER.

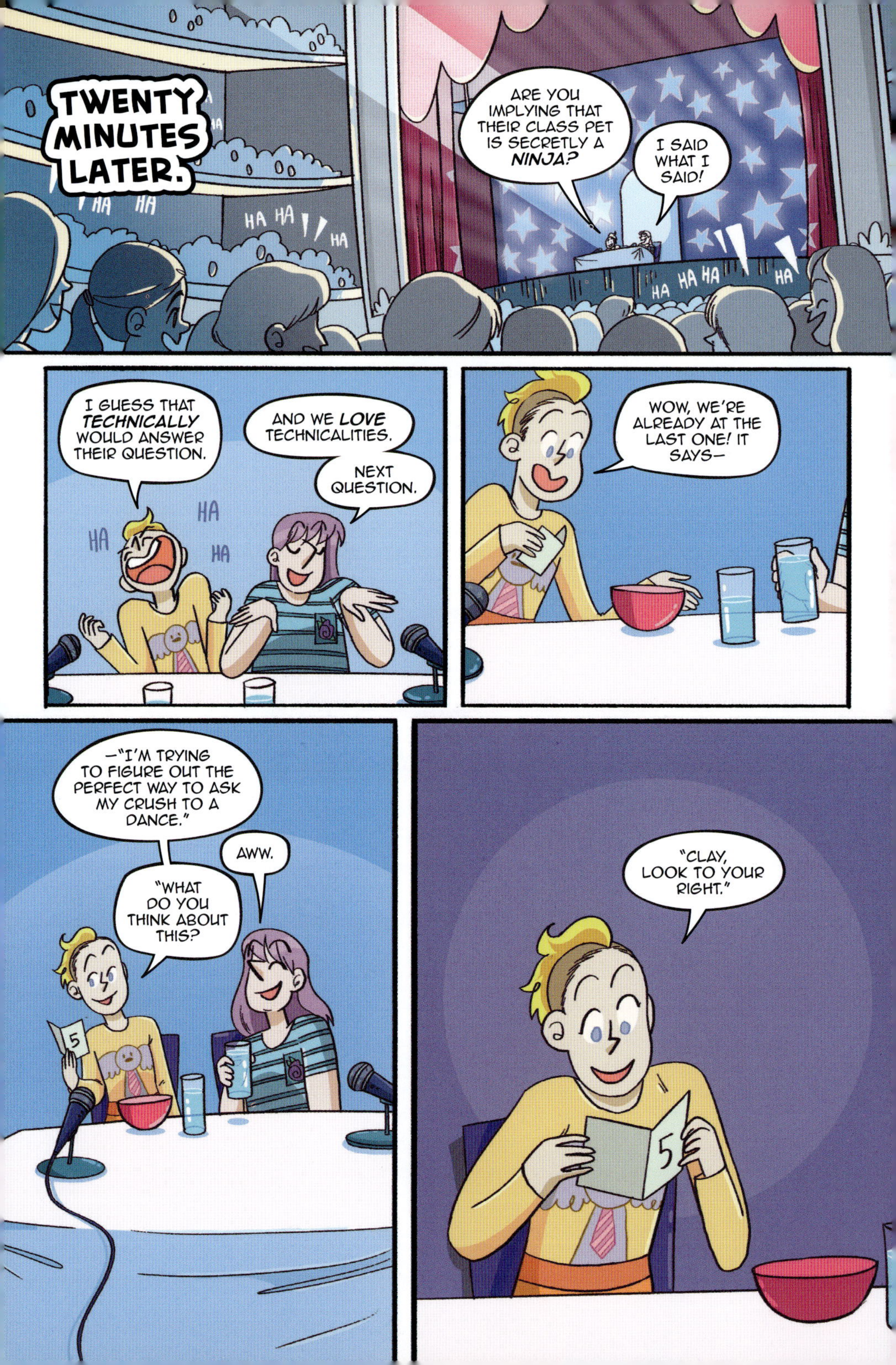
TWENTY MINUTES LATER.
HA HA
HA HA HA
ARE YOU IMPLYING THAT THEIR CLASS PET IS SECRETLY A NINJA?
I SAID WHAT I SAID!
HA HA HA HA
I GUESS THAT TECHNICALLY WOULD ANSWER THEIR QUESTION.
AND WE LOVE TECHNICALITIES.
NEXT QUESTION.
HA HA HA
WOW, WE'RE ALREADY AT THE LAST ONE! IT SAYS—
—"I'M TRYING TO FIGURE OUT THE PERFECT WAY TO ASK MY CRUSH TO A DANCE."
AWW.
"WHAT DO YOU THINK ABOUT THIS?
5
"CLAY, LOOK TO YOUR RIGHT."
5

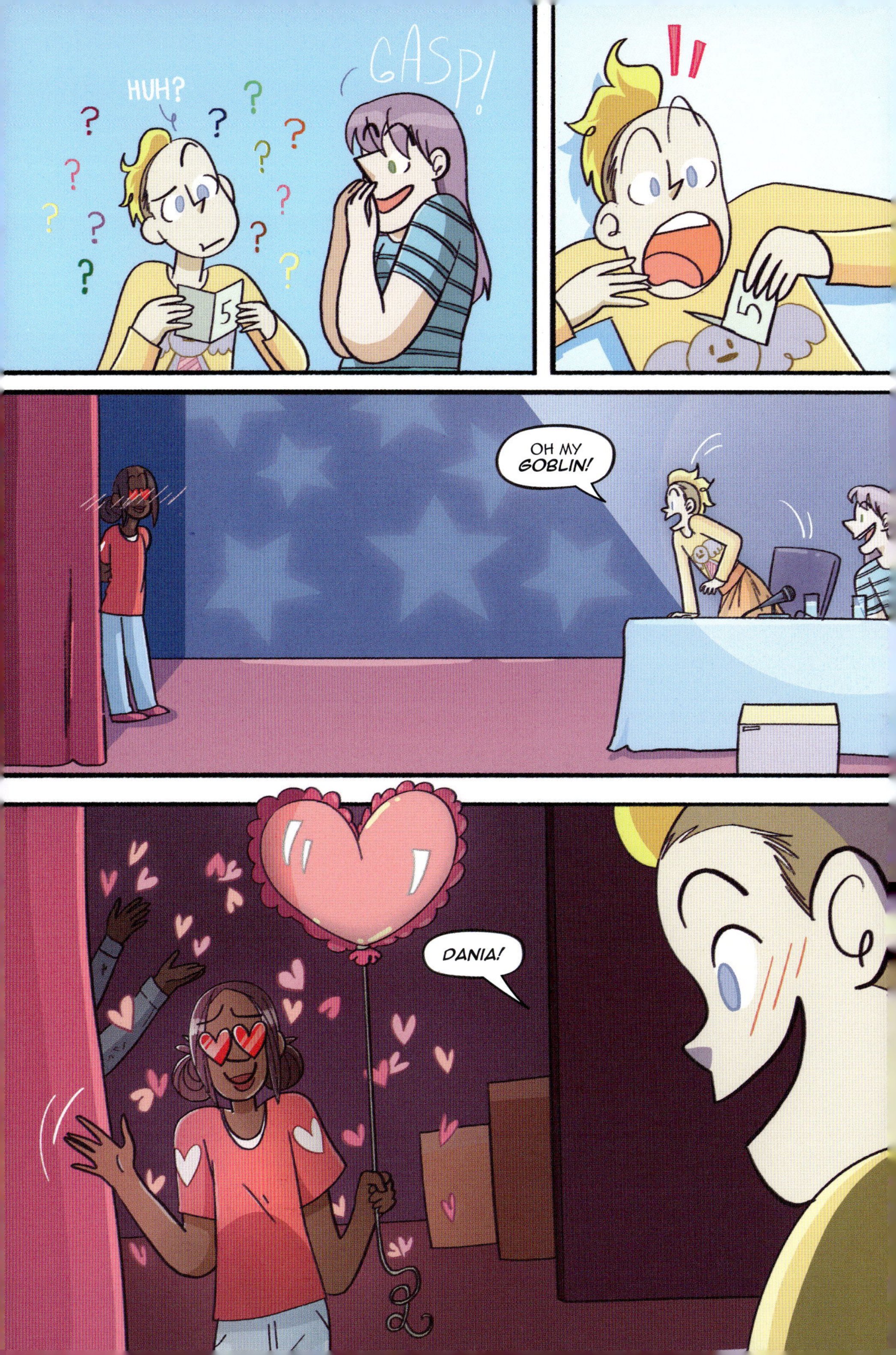
HUH?
GASP!
OH MY GOBLIN!
DANIA!

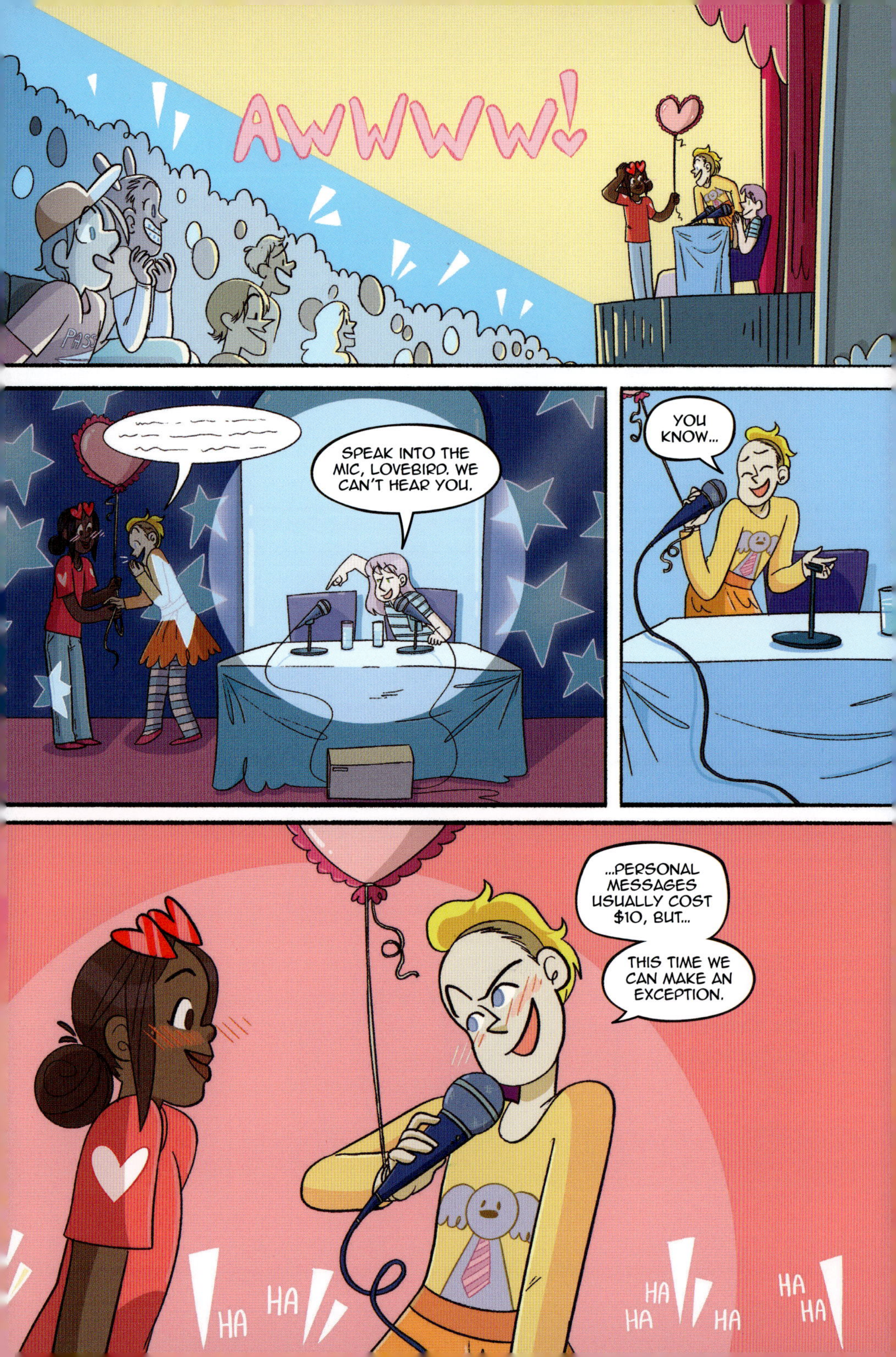
AWWWW!
SPEAK INTO THE MIC, LOVEBIRD. WE CAN'T HEAR YOU.
YOU KNOW...
...PERSONAL MESSAGES USUALLY COST $10, BUT...
THIS TIME WE CAN MAKE AN EXCEPTION.
HA HA
HA HA HA
HA HA

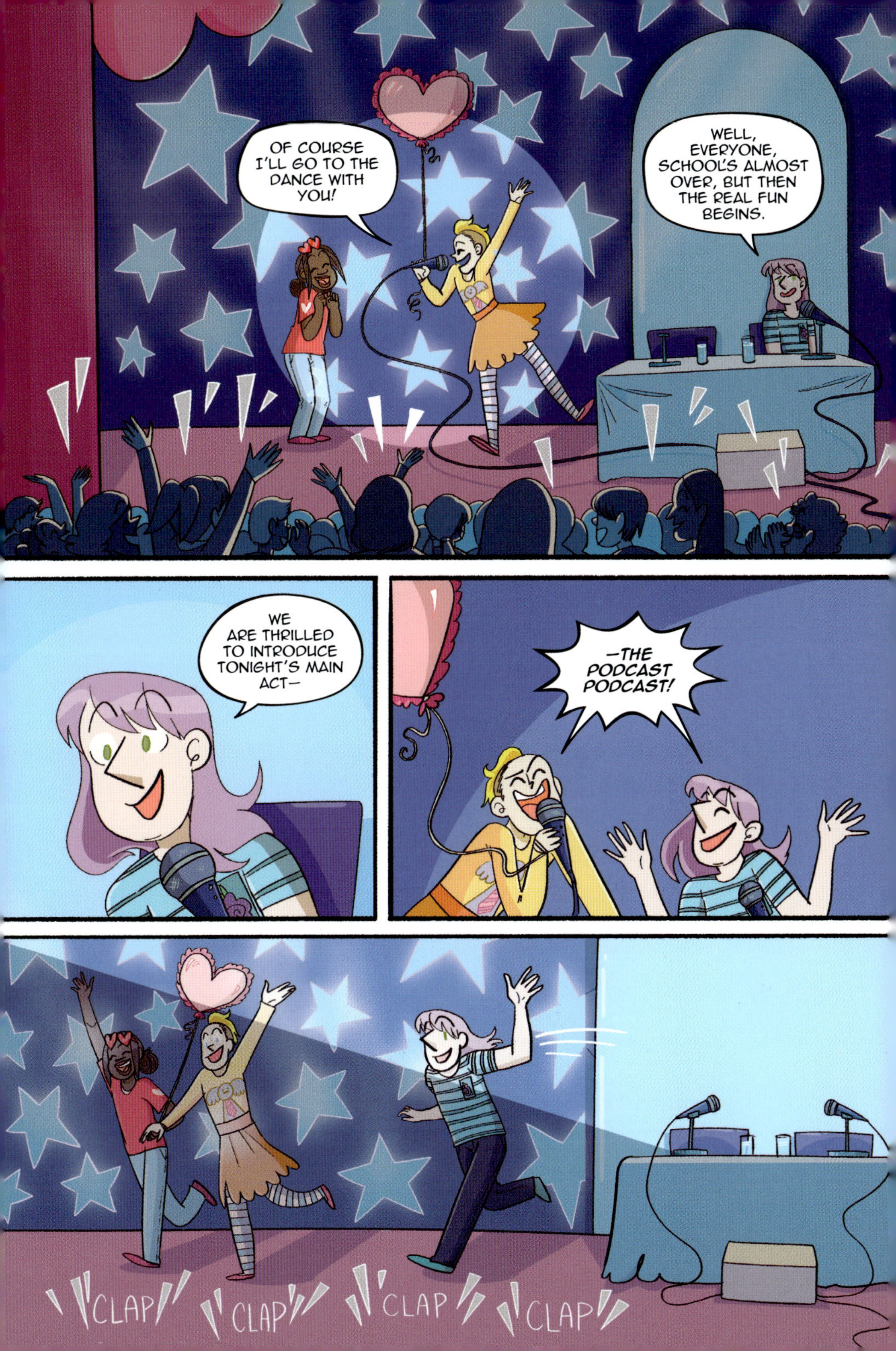
OF COURSE I'LL GO TO THE DANCE WITH YOU!
WELL, EVERYONE, SCHOOL'S ALMOST OVER, BUT THEN THE REAL FUN BEGINS.
WE ARE THRILLED TO INTRODUCE TONIGHT'S MAIN ACT—
—THE PODCAST PODCAST!
CLAP CLAP CLAP CLAP

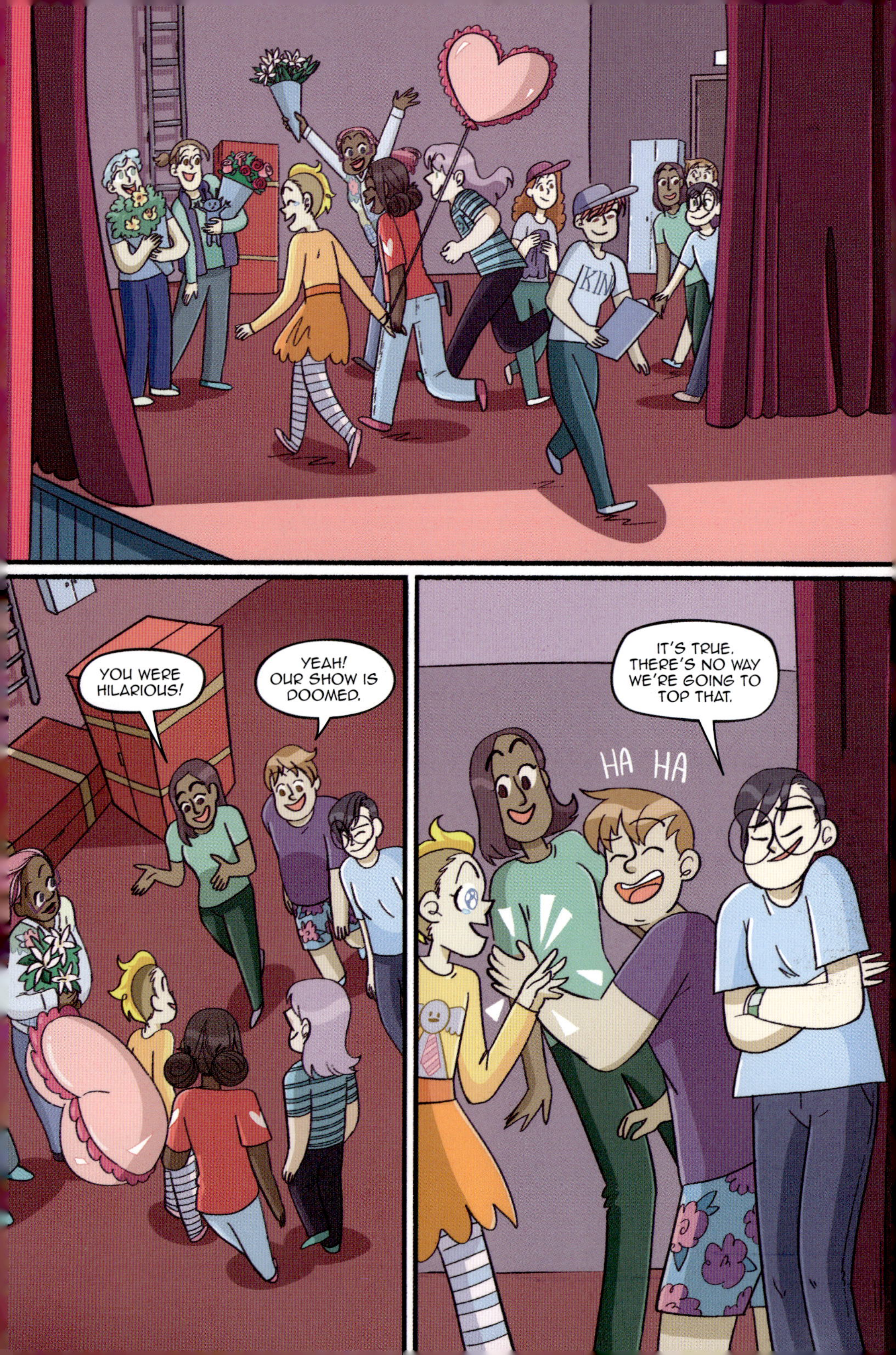
KIM
YOU WERE HILARIOUS!
YEAH! OUR SHOW IS DOOMED.
IT'S TRUE. THERE'S NO WAY WE'RE GOING TO TOP THAT.
HA HA

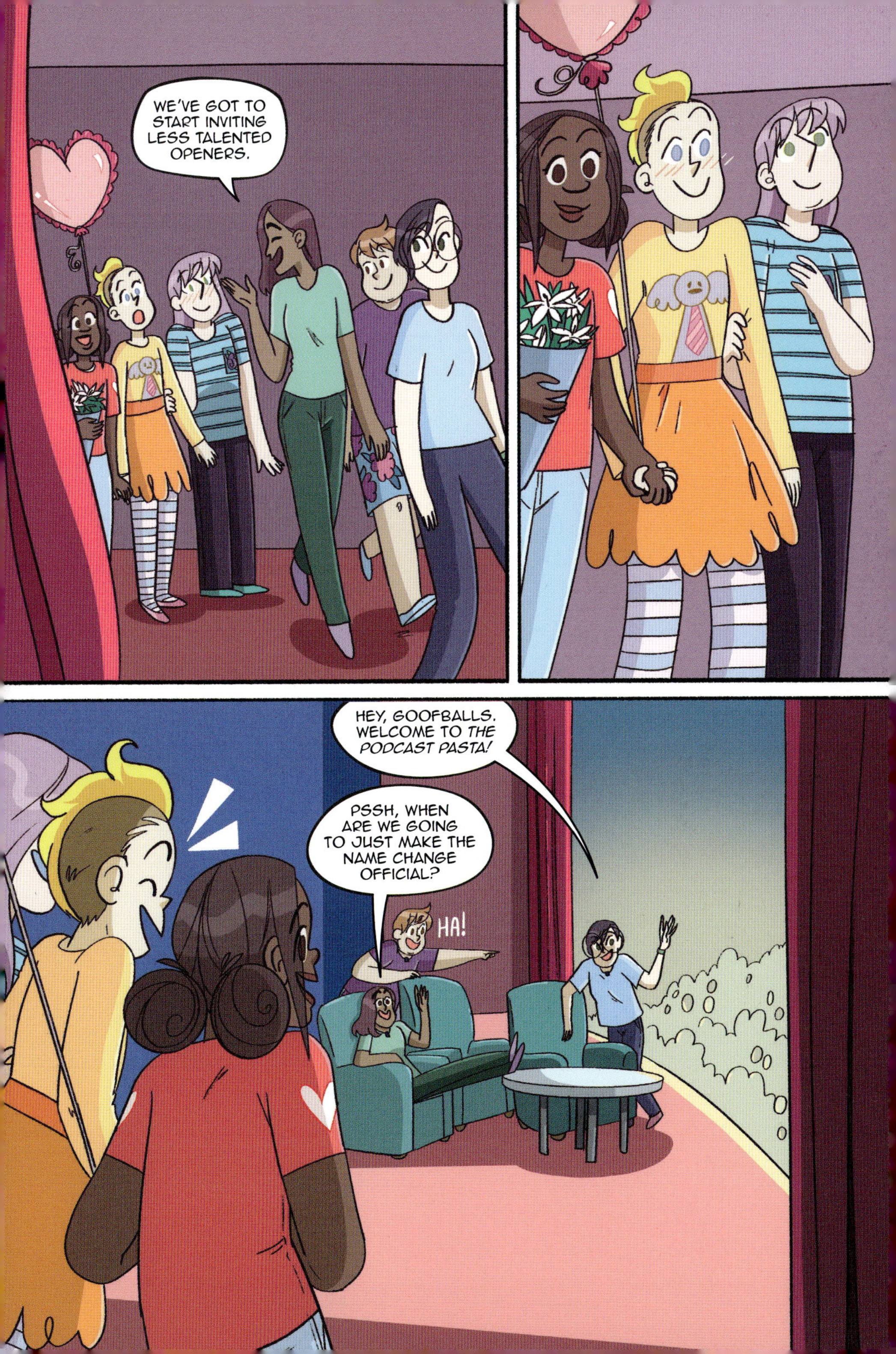
WE'VE GOT TO START INVITING LESS TALENTED OPENERS.
HEY, GOOFBALLS. WELCOME TO THE *PODCAST PASTA!*
PSSH, WHEN ARE WE GOING TO JUST MAKE THE NAME CHANGE OFFICIAL?
HA!

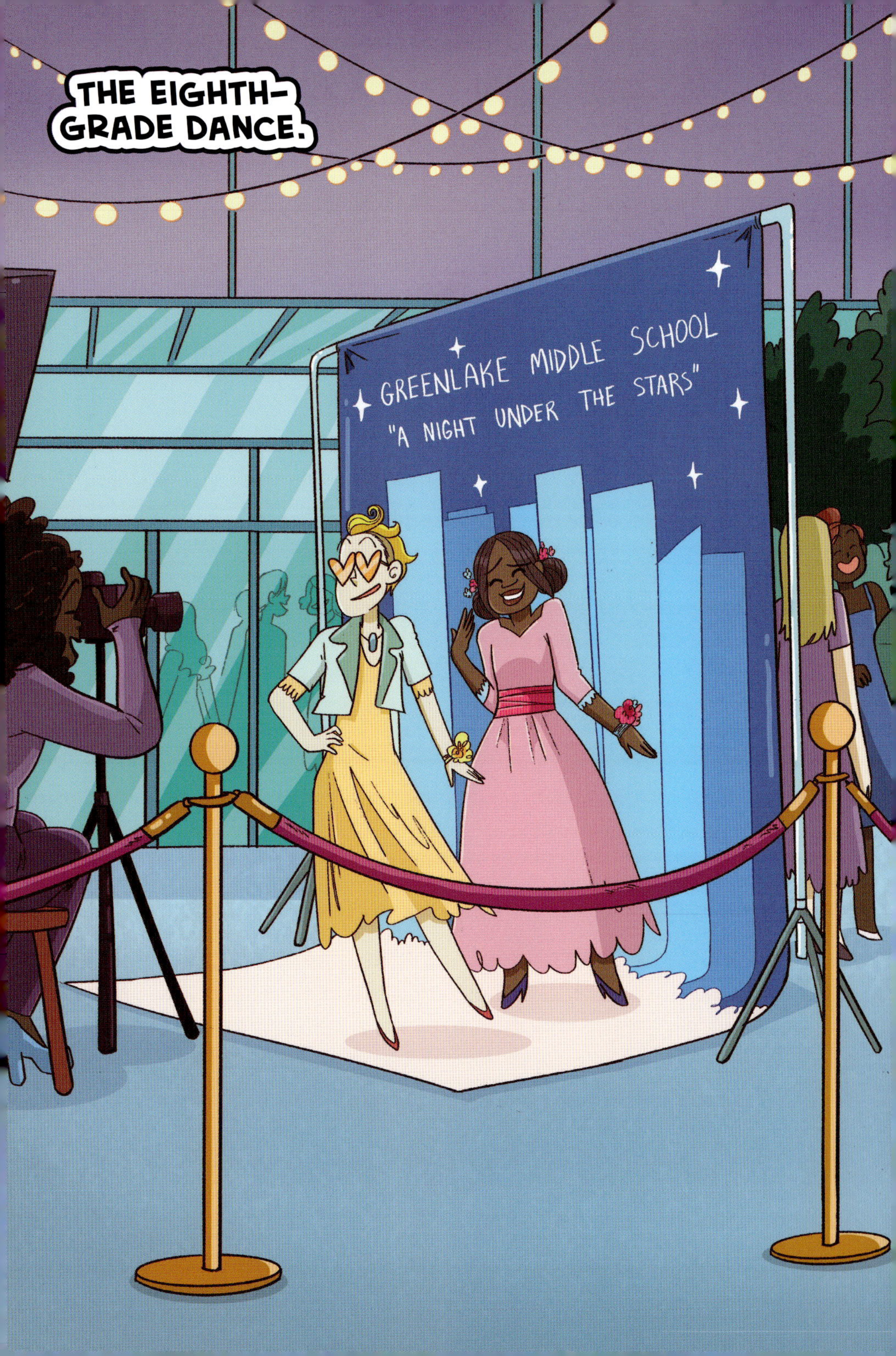
THE EIGHTH-GRADE DANCE.
GREENLAKE MIDDLE SCHOOL
"A NIGHT UNDER THE STARS"

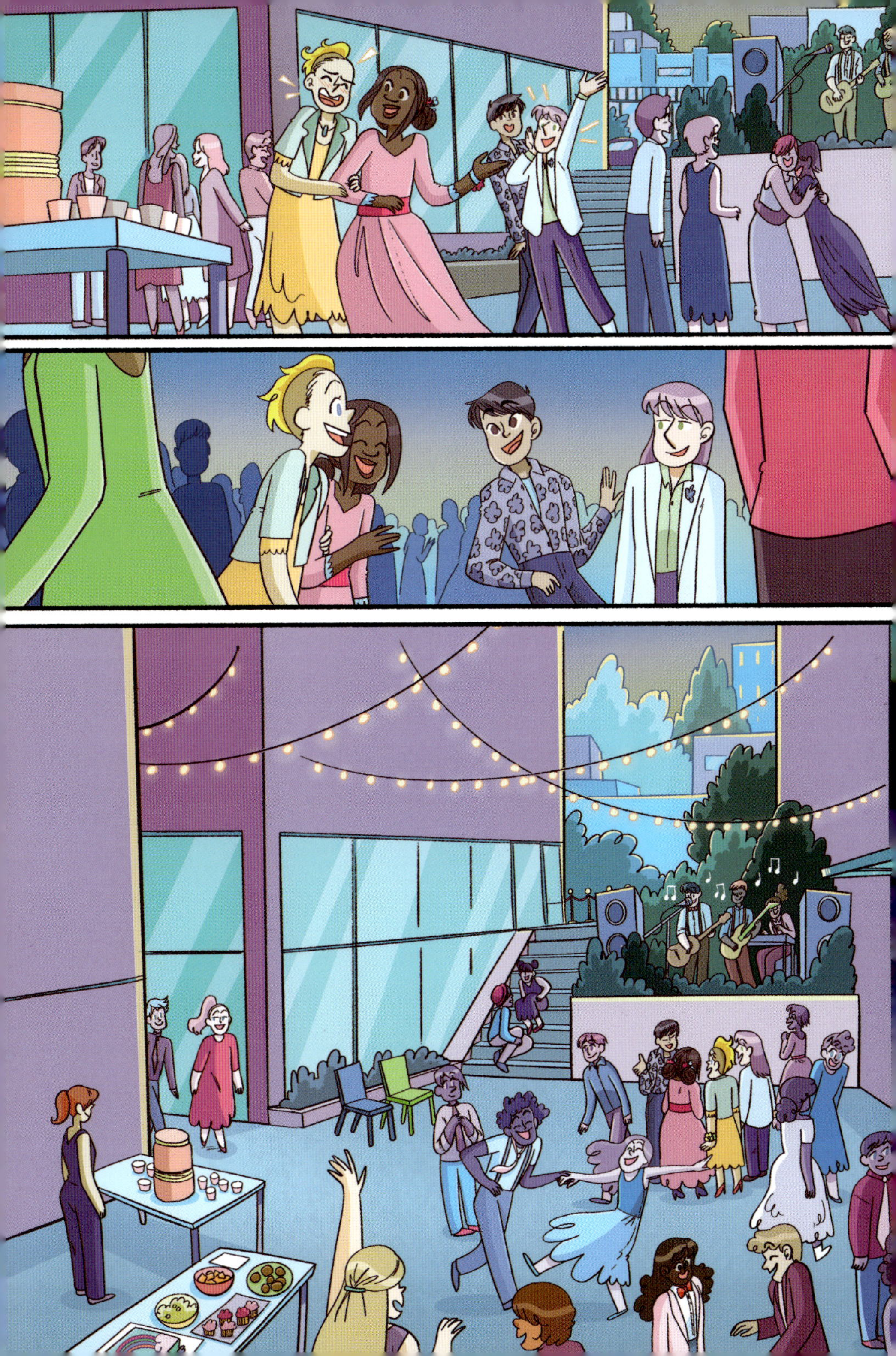

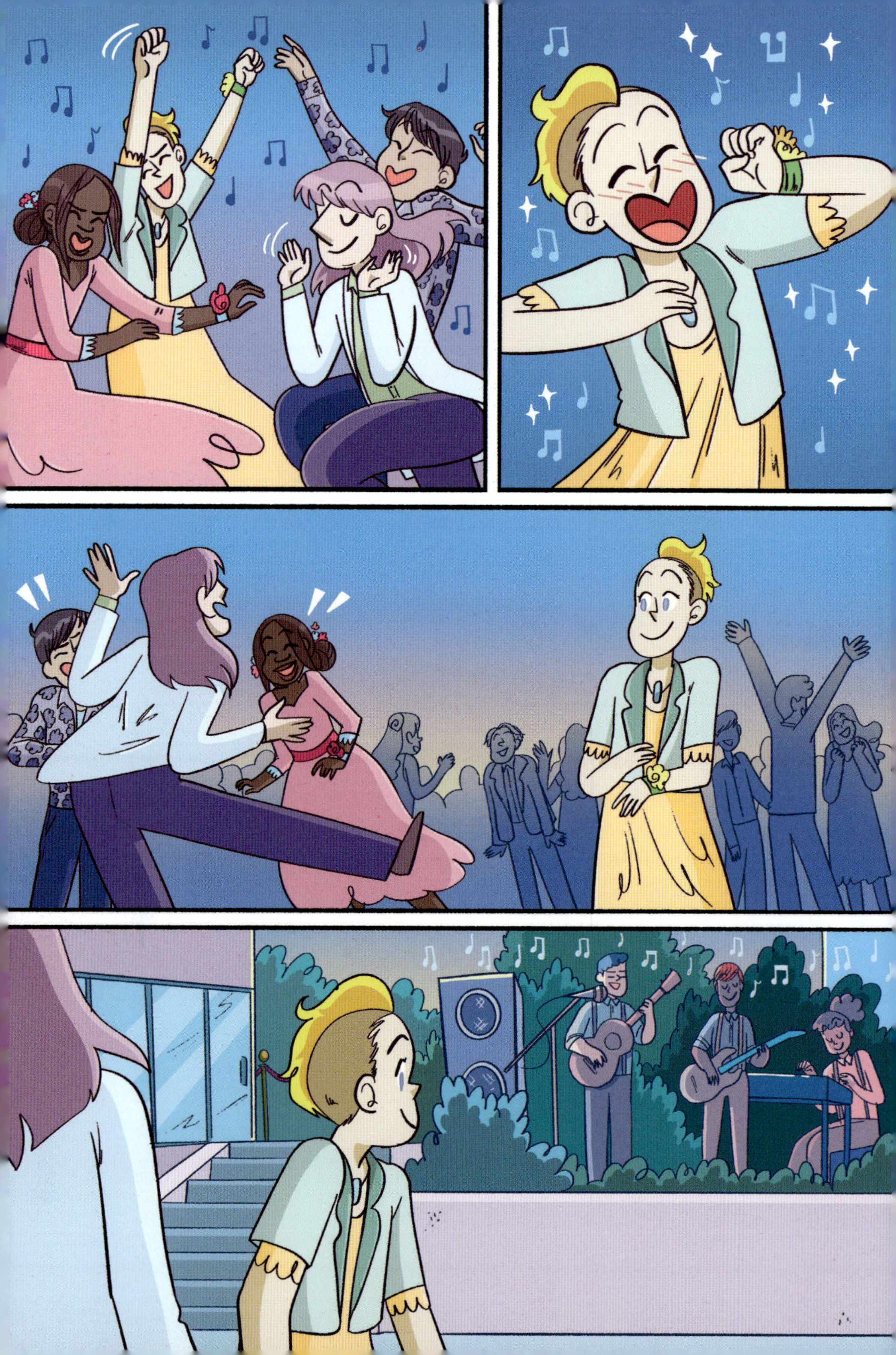

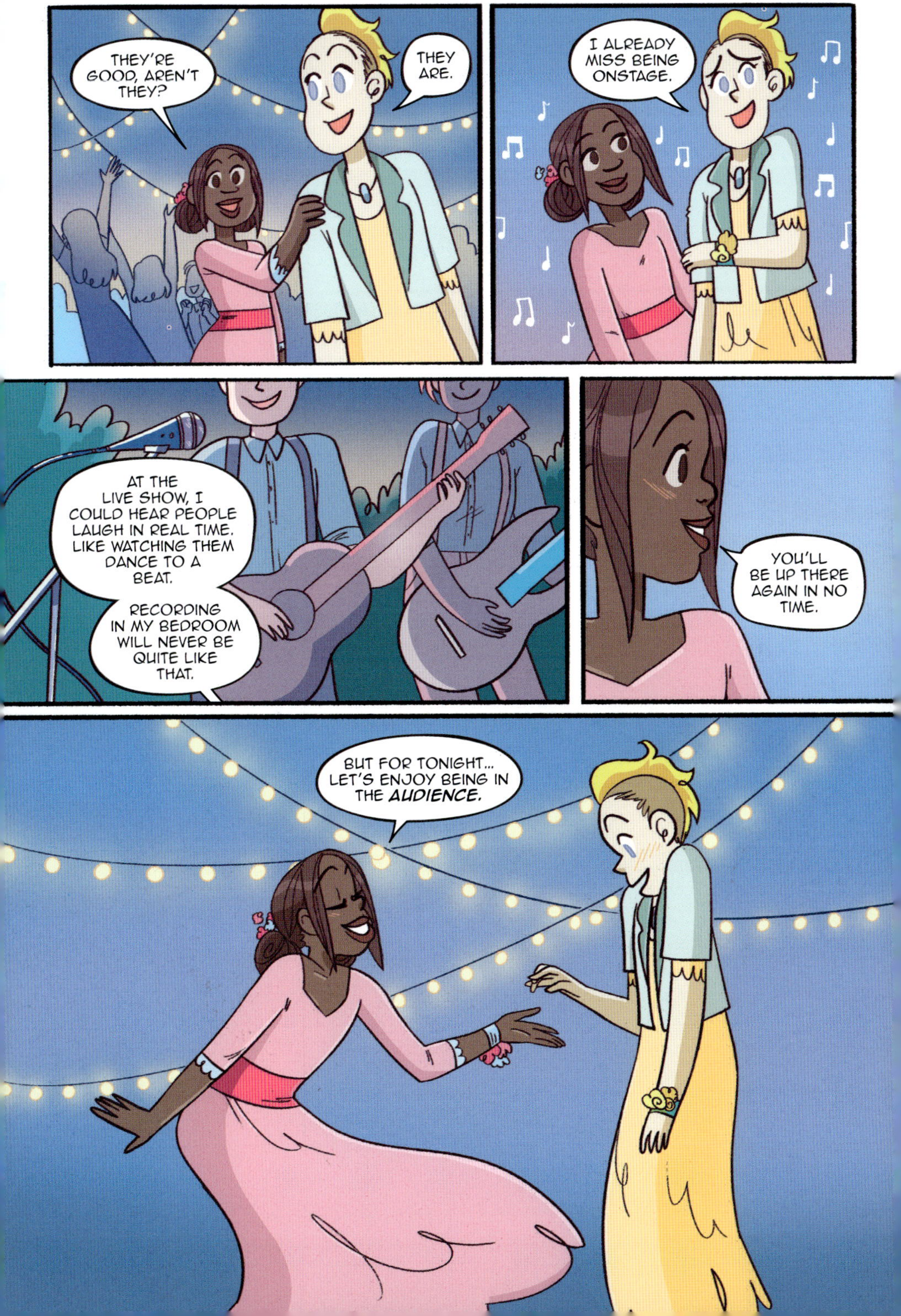
THEY'RE GOOD, AREN'T THEY?
THEY ARE.
I ALREADY MISS BEING ONSTAGE.
AT THE LIVE SHOW, I COULD HEAR PEOPLE LAUGH IN REAL TIME. LIKE WATCHING THEM DANCE TO A BEAT.
RECORDING IN MY BEDROOM WILL NEVER BE QUITE LIKE THAT.
YOU'LL BE UP THERE AGAIN IN NO TIME.
BUT FOR TONIGHT... LET'S ENJOY BEING IN THE *AUDIENCE.*

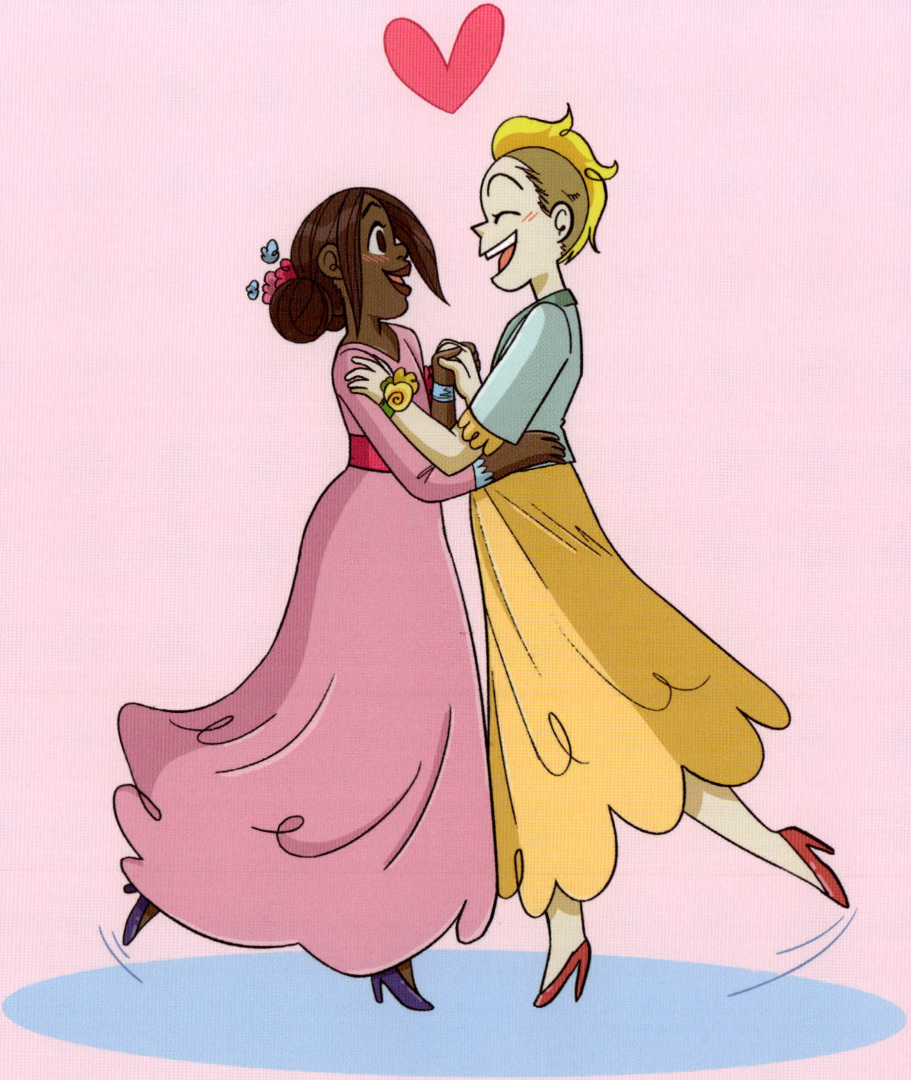

THE END

AUTHOR'S NOTE

I've always known, for my whole life, that I'm a spectacular oddball. You can see it in my silly clothes and bouncy walk. You can hear it in the words I speak and how I laugh about nothing at all. What I didn't figure out until I became a grown-up is that I am also completely normal.

The way people talk about autism and ADHD has changed beautifully over the course of my life. In middle school, I wasn't given any clear words for how I am. I didn't understand what *autistic* or *ADHD* meant, and at the time, those words carried a lot of misconceptions. I just knew that I sang to myself and played with my hair to calm down, I would weep if someone showed the slightest disappointment, I was unable to lie, I *always* left my homework in my locker, I could tune my flute by ear, I couldn't stand fireworks or bright lights but loved glittery things and familiar smells, I couldn't wear turtlenecks or tights without shrieking, I couldn't use conditioner or brush my hair, I walked on my toes in elaborate patterns of steps, and I watched my favorite movie every day.

Growing up, I didn't know many people like this, so I felt as if I belonged in a totally different universe. (It's no wonder my first book, *Just Pretend*, was a memoir all about escaping into stories.) Now I see there are people all around me who, just like Clay and Kyle, wouldn't find anything about me strange.

I'm autistic, and I have ADHD. In *Stand Up!*, I wrote about people with these conditions who (for the most part) are very happy kids. The ways they are affected by their disabilities are written between the lines rather than set center stage. Because of Clay's ADHD, she's often distracted, she has to put extra effort into schoolwork, and sometimes she hurts her friends' feelings because she worries how they'll react if she speaks her mind. Meanwhile, Kyle has intense focus, and he gets stressed when he can't control his routine. He is quite clumsy and sleepy (traits of many autistic people), he is blunt, and he finds his friends' social drama puzzling. Fortunately, Clay and Kyle support each other and help each other see when they've made a mistake.

Even if Clay and Kyle hadn't grown up in the same house, I think they would have been fast friends. They both love podcasts and video games, have zany senses of humor, and know which table in Honey Bunny's is the best: the one tucked against the coziest, quietest corner, adorned with the comfiest chairs.

There are many good, important stories about the *difficulties* of being different. This is not one of them. As more neurodivergent kids and adults discover the words to describe themselves, it becomes easier to find other people like us, and to wonder whether we're so "different" after all. Though we may need additional support, we can lead marvelous lives. (Many of us become authors, artists, and comedians!) There are hundreds of millions of neurodivergent people in the world; we are a minority, and yet we're everywhere. It is possible to be both special and blissfully ordinary.

Likewise, the world is full of girls who get crushes on girls. (It's another thing I have in common with Clay!) Although Greenlake Middle School is a fictional place, Green Lake, Washington, is a real neighborhood where love of all kinds is celebrated. There are many places just like that. However, some communities are not as accepting; people can be wary or unkind about things they don't understand. If you live in a place where you don't feel comfortable being yourself, then please know it's not your fault! A day when you can make your own choices is not as far off as it may feel, and someday you will be able to stand up tall. A secret I didn't understand until I grew up is that you get to be a grown-up for most of your life. In the meantime, I hope you know that you are wonderful just as you are.

Thank you for spending time with this story, my first published work of fiction. It's been a joy to make a book in which characters who are like me can have a happy beginning, middle, and end.

TORI SHARP is a Seattle-based author-illustrator and swing and blues dancer with a BFA in sequential art from SCAD. Her first book, *Just Pretend*, is an energetic, affecting graphic memoir about using her imagination to navigate the fallout from her parents' divorce. It's full of magic, fairies, witches, and lost and found friendships. She invites you to visit her online at torisharp.com.